LINCOLN

A NOVEL

GORE VIDAL

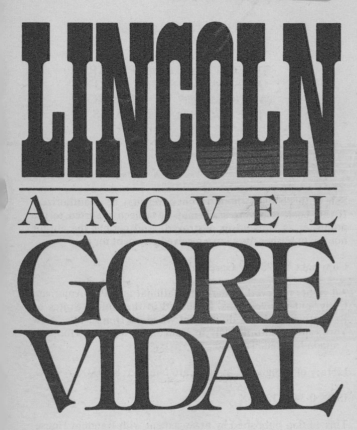

BALLANTINE BOOKS • NEW YORK

Copyright © 1984 by Gore Vidal

All rights reserved under International and Pan-American Copyright Conventions. Published in the United States by Ballantine Books, a division of Random House, Inc., New York, and simultaneously in Canada by Random House of Canada Limited, Toronto.

Library of Congress Catalog Card Number: 83-43185

ISBN 0-345-31221-X

This edition published by arrangement with Random House, Inc.

A signed first edition of this book has been privately printed by The Franklin Library

Manufactured in the United States of America

First Ballantine Books Edition: June 1985

30 29 28 27 26 25 24 23 22

"LINCOLN WAS AN ASTONISHING ACHIEVEMENT, THE GREATEST HISTORICAL NOVEL OF OUR TIME."

Allan Massie
The Scotsman

"*Lincoln* reaches for sublimity, as in the moving account of the president's visit to the Confederate wounded, or the telling of Willie's death and Mary Todd's encroaching madness. There are passages that make one weep. This novel will, I suspect, maintain a permanent place in American letters. There has been no better prose in the last 50 years than that with which Vidal narrates the streaming of the panicked people down Pennsylvania Avenue to the 'soft thud of cannons' from the debacle of the first Bull Run. The portrait of Winfield Scott, in whose face the 'worms [were] at work' as he absorbs the meaning of the disaster, is one of many small masterpieces within the masterful whole."

Andrew Delbanco
The New Republic

"The portrait is reasoned, judicious, straightforward and utterly convincing...even more compelling than *Burr*. In his ongoing chronicle of American history...Mr. Vidal is concerned with dissecting, obsessively and often brilliantly, the roots of personal ambition as they give rise to history itself....There are dramatic ironies which Mr. Vidal handles with exquisite tact and skill. His Lincoln is not a debunked port≥rait by any means...and, as the novel runs its course, he emerges as a truly outstanding man."

Joyce Carol Oates
The New York Times Book Review

"The most vivid personage in the book is Mary Todd Lincoln. The author has taken her rages, her erratic behavior, her extravagance, her pretensions, and out of these, he has made her a startling counterpart to Lincoln himself. His Mary Lincoln is another citizen consumed by the Civil War: loathing slavery—her denunciation of it is a brilliantly moving passage—loving her Southern connections, understanding her husband more profoundly than anyone else, all the while tormenting him more wretchedly than anyone else."

Richard Eder
Los Angeles Times

"There are some wonderful things in *Lincoln*...by far the most important is the presented character of Lincoln himself....He is in Vidal's version at once more complex, mysterious and enigmatic, more implacably courageous and, finally, more tragic than the conventional public images, the marble man of the memorial. He is honored in his book.

George Garrett
Chicago Tribune

"Richly entertaining...In his skeptical panorama of Civil War Washington, awash with fear, greed, ambition, and even nobility, Vidal obviously means to redress Sandburg's several-million-word saint's life. As he did in *Burr* and *1876*, Vidal has used the newspapers, diaries and letters of the time to make a solid historical base; then, maintaining the third-person viewpoint, he lets us pry into the peculiar minds of his true-life characters. The result works like a talisman....For the general reader the elegant explication of the issues of the day gives hearty satisfaction: history lessons with the blood still hot."

Shelby Coffey III
The Washington Post

"Vidal is the best all-round American man of letters since Edmund Wilson....This is his most moving book."

Walter Clemons
Newsweek

Part One

Part One

1

ELIHU B. WASHBURNE OPENED HIS GOLD WATCH. THE SPIDERY hands showed five minutes to six.

"Wait here," he said to the driver, who said, "How do I know you're coming back, sir?"

At the best of times Congressman Washburne's temper was a most unstable affair, and his sudden outbursts of rage—he could roar like a preacher anticipating hell—were much admired in his adopted state of Illinois, where constituents proudly claimed that he was the only militant teetotaller who behaved exactly like a normal person at five minutes to six, say, in the early morning of an icy winter day—of the twenty-third of February, 1861, to be exact.

"Why, you black—!" As the cry in Washburne's throat began to go to its terrible maximum, caution, the politician's ever-present angel, cut short the statesman's breath. A puff of unresonated cold steam filled the space between the congressman and the Negro driver on his high seat.

Heart beating rapidly with unslaked fury, Washburne gave the driver some coins. "You are to stay here until I return, you hear me?"

"I hear you, sir." White teeth were quickly bared and unbared in the black, cold-puckered face.

Washburne buttoned up his overcoat and stepped carefully onto the frozen mud that was supposed to be the pavement of a stately avenue leading to the squalid train depot of Washington City, capital of thirty-four United States that were now in the process of disuniting. He fluffed up his beard, hoping to better warm his face.

Washburne entered the depot as the cars from Baltimore were rattling to a halt. Negro porters were slouched along the sidings. Huge carts stood ready to be filled with Northern merchandise to be exchanged for Southern tobacco, raw cotton, food. Currently, the Southerners were saying that Washington City was the natural capital of the South. But they did not say it, if they were wise, in Washburne's irritable Western presence.

Just past the locomotive, the representative of Illinois's first district stationed himself in front of an empty gilded wagon whose

3

sides were emblazoned with the name of Gautier, the town's leading caterer, a Frenchman who was, some claimed but never he, the lost Dauphin of France.

As Washburne watched the sleepy travellers disembark, he wished that he had brought with him at least a half-dozen Federal guards. Since the guards were just coming off night duty, no one would think it odd if they should converge, in a casual sort of way, upon the depot. But the other half of the semi-official Joint Congressional Committee of Two, Senator William H. Seward of New York, had said, "No, we don't want to draw *any* attention to our visitor. You and I will be enough." Since the always-mysterious Seward had then chosen not to come to the depot, only the House of Representatives was represented in the stout person of Elihu B. Washburne, who was, suddenly, attracted to a plainly criminal threesome. To the left, a small sharp-eyed man with one hand plunged deep in his overcoat pocket where the outline of a derringer was visible. To the right, a large thickset young man with both hands in his pockets—two pistols? In the center, a tall thin man, wearing a soft slouch hat pulled over his eyes like a burglar, and a short overcoat whose collar was turned up, so that nothing was visible between cap and collar but a prominent nose and high checkbones covered with yellow skin, taut as a drum. In his left hand he clutched a leather grip-sack containing, no doubt, the tools of his sinister trade.

As the three men came abreast of Washburne, the congressman said, "Well, you can't fool me, Abe."

The small man turned fiercely on Washburne, hand half out of his overcoat pocket, revealing the derringer's barrel. But the tall man said, "It's all right, Mr. Pinkerton. This is Congressman Washburne. He's our welcoming committee."

Warmly, Washburne shook the hand of his old friend the President-elect of the United States, Abraham Lincoln, a fellow politician from Illinois, who was supposed to be murdered later on in the day at Baltimore.

"This is Ward Hill Lamon." Lincoln indicated the thickset man, who withdrew his right hand from his pocket to shake the hand of Washburne, who stared dumbly at Lamon's hand, ablaze with what looked to be barbarous jewellery.

Lincoln laughed. "Hill, when you're in the big city you take your brass knuckles off."

"It's in *this* city that I better keep them on." And Washburne noticed that Lamon—who spoke with a Southern accent—did exactly that. Meanwhile, Pinkerton had moved on ahead, studying the passers-by with such suspicion that he himself began to attract attention. Lincoln said what Washburne was thinking. "Mr. Pink-

4

erton is what they call a detective, and detectives always make quite a fuss, trying not to be noticed."

To Washburne's relief, no one recognized Lincoln. But then he himself had been in a moment's doubt when Lincoln had pushed down his collar, to reveal a short, glossy black beard that entirely changed the shape—and expression—of his face.

"Is it false?" Washburne stared hard. They were now standing beneath a huge poster of "Abraham Lincoln, the President-elect. Welcome to Washington City." The cleanshaven face of the poster was hard, even harsh-looking, while the bearded face looked weary, but amiable. To Washburne, the President-elect resembled a prosperous, down-state Illinois farmer come to market.

"No, it's real. What you might call an adornment. I had to do something useful on the train from Springfield." Lincoln leapt to one side as two huge black women carrying a tub of pork sausage meat hurried toward the cars. Then Pinkerton motioned that they were to follow him outside.

As they moved toward the door of the depot, Washburne said, "I've hired a carriage. Governor Seward was supposed to meet us here. But he must've overslept. We've put you up at Willard's Hotel. General Scott thinks you'll be safer there than in that house we found for you."

Lincoln did not answer. Washburne wondered if he was listening. Outside the depot, the shrunken wintry sun resembled a small, pale, yellow seal affixed to the parchment-gray sky to the left of where the Capitol's dome should be but was not. Instead, from the round marble base, reminiscent of one of Gautier's white wedding cakes, a large crane was silhouetted against the sky like a gallows.

"They took the old lid off, I see." Lincoln ignored Pinkerton's efforts to get him into the waiting barouche.

"God knows when they'll get the new one on," said Washburne. "There's talk in Congress that we should just leave it the way it is."

"No." Lincoln shivered suddenly. "I always forget," he said, "how cold the South gets in winter."

The four men climbed into the carriage. Pinkerton sat next to the driver. Lamon sat with his back to the driver's seat while Lincoln and Washburne shared the back seat. Washburne noticed that Lincoln never let go of the grip-sack. Even while seated, he clutched it so hard that the huge knuckles of his hand were white.

"The crown jewels?" Washburne indicated the case. Lincoln laughed, but did not release his hold on the handle. "My certificate of good character. It's the inaugural address. I gave it to my son Bob to look after and he mislaid it in Harrisburg. The only copy there is!" Lincoln visibly winced at the memory. "We had to go through two tons of luggage to find it. I could've killed that boy. Anyway, I've carried it ever since."

"We're all sort of curious to hear what you'll say..." began Washburne.

But Lincoln was not to be drawn out. "I see there's been some new building going on." He looked out the window at the north side of Pennsylvania Avenue where the great hotels were lined up, like so many brick barracks interspersed with saloons and shops. Near the corner of Sixth Street was Brown's Hotel.

"Brown's was here when you were here in the forties."

Lincoln nodded. "Mrs. Lincoln and I spent our first night in Washington there. Then we moved to a boardinghouse with the two boys, who were not as popular as they ought to have been. The Widow Spriggs, our landlady was called."

On Twelfth Street there was the Kirkwood House and, finally, on the corner of Fourteenth Street and Pennsylvania Avenue stood the center of the city's political and social life, Willard's Hotel, nicely situated opposite the Treasury Building, which was placed, most symbolically everyone thought, in a line with the hotel and the President's House.

At six-thirty in the morning the city was not yet properly awake. The hacks that were usually lined up in front of each hotel were not to be seen. Only Negroes—slave and free—were on the move, bringing food to the hotels, cleaning the stairs of the houses and taverns, moving briskly in the cold.

"I see they've made a stab at paving the avenue," said Lincoln, as the carriage skittered over cobbles so ill-set that they made the avenue look even more like a vast, wild field than plain frozen mud might have done. "Not a very serious stab," he added.

At the end of Pennsylvania Avenue, the original city planners had intended that the President's House should face, in constitutional harmony, the Capitol. But the Treasury building now blocked most of the view of the Executive Mansion, while the rest was hidden by a large windowless red-brick building, which intrigued Lincoln. "That's new. What is it? A prison?"

"No. That's President Buchanan's barn. He's very proud of it. In fact, it's about the only thing he's done in four years."

A horsecar rattled into view, only half full at this early hour; the stove at the back of the car smoked badly.

"The trolleys are since your time," said Washburne. "They now go all the way from the Navy Yard to Georgetown. That's six miles," Washburne added, aware that he had once again lost his old friend's attention. The curiously lidded left eye—like a

6

frog's—was half shut, always a sign that its owner was either deep in thought or mortally tired.

The main entrance to Willard's Hotel was at the corner where Fourteenth Street and Pennsylvania Avenue met. Bare trees sprouted from the brick sidewalk to either side of the door; farther down the avenue a small Greek temple had been completely enveloped by the huge hotel.

"You remember the old Presbyterian church?" Washburne was beginning to feel like a city guide. "Well, now it's a part of Willard's. It's a concert hall. The Peace Conference is meeting there." He examined Lincoln's face to see what his reaction might be, but there was none.

The carriage stopped at the main door. A uniformed Negro helped the men out of the carriage. "Baggage, gentlemen?"

"By the next train," said Lincoln.

"But, gentlemen—" Pinkerton spun the man to one side. "This way," Pinkerton said, darting into the hotel.

"A very forceful individual," Lincoln observed, with a smile.

Inside the lobby, a half-dozen black porters dozed on their feet while an assistant manager of uncommon whiteness—as if in deliberate hierarchical contrast to the staff—examined a heap of letters at his marble counter. The lobby was high-ceilinged and smelled of coal smoke. Huge dark armchairs were set haphazardly about the room, each with its shining spittoon to hand. Benches of horsehair lined the walls. A few forlorn guests stood surrounded by luggage, waiting to be taken away.

Pinkerton caught the assistant manager's attention by slamming his fist on the marble counter. What had been the whitest of faces turned pink with irritation; then even whiter than before when Pinkerton whispered in his ear. The assistant manager hurried from behind his reception counter; shook Washburne's hand and said in a voice that broke with tension, "Welcome to Willard's Hotel, Mr. President."

"This is the President," said Washburne, indicating Lincoln.

"President-*elect*," said Lincoln. "Let's not tempt fate. There's still ten days to go yet."

"Your rooms, sir, aren't ready." The assistant manager addressed Lamon, who had taken Washburne's place as Lincoln in his mind. "You see, we didn't expect you until this afternoon and Mr. William Dodge, of New York—he's the merchant prince, a valued customer—is in Parlor Suite Number Six and as it's only six-thirty-four, he's not even up yet, I'm fairly certain . . ."

Lincoln turned to Lamon, "You work this one out." At that moment an aged white porter approached Washburne and, in a

7

pronounced brogue, said, "Well, Mr. Washburne, sir, I see you've brought us a president."

"This is Mike," said Washburne to Lincoln, "the most cunning man in the city."

"So cunning, sir, that he'll take you straight to Governor Seward." With that, Lincoln and Washburne were led into the main dining room, where Seward sat alone at the end of a long table, puffing a cigar, eyes half-closed. Back of him, waiters were placing chafing dishes on a huge buffet; otherwise, the vast room was empty.

At the sight of Lincoln, Seward sprang to his feet; he was not, Washburne noted, much taller standing than seated. Once red-haired, now white-haired, large-nosed, pale-eyed, long-time master of the state of New York, not to mention of the youthful Republican Party, as well as President-that-might-have-been had Lincoln's managers not outmaneuvered his managers at the Chicago Convention, William H. Seward was seven years older than his rival, the new President, whose hand he now shook, saying in a husky voice, richly seasoned by a lifetime's addiction to cigar smoke and snuff, "You're every bit as tall as I'd thought you'd be, Mr. Lincoln." Seward looked up at Lincoln, who was exactly a foot taller than he. "I never really got a good look at you when we met for those two minutes during the campaign."

"And you're as handsome, Governor, as your portraits." Lincoln bowed like a jackknife—a droll, swift effect, thought Washburne, delighted to be present at the first real meeting of the great rivals who had threatened to divide the six-year-old Republican Party between the free-the-slaves-at-any-cost abolitionists occasionally represented, if not exactly led, by Seward, and the more moderate no-extension-of-slavery Westerners represented by Lincoln, a successful railroad lawyer and political failure: one term in the House of Representatives twelve years ago; one lost race for the Senate two years ago; and now the Presidency. Even Lincoln's old friend Washburne still found it hard to believe that such an incredible political miracle had indeed taken place. But then Washburne was not alone in being unable to figure out just how it was that Lincoln had managed to seize the nomination from Governor Seward; and then go on to defeat the Northern Democratic candidate, the famous Stephen A. Douglas—who had so decisively defeated *him* for the Senate—as well as two other candidates, the Southern Democratic candidate, John C. Breckinridge, and the Whig John Bell. With not quite forty percent of the total vote, Lincoln was very much a minority president; but he was president.

Seward motioned for Lincoln to sit at the head of the table

with himself to the right and Washburne to the left. When Seward called for a waiter, he was greeted with a hoot of laughter. "We don't serve nothin' till eight."

"Mike!" shouted Washburne. The old porter moved amongst the waiters; in a matter of minutes, they were breakfasting on the first Potomac shad of the year.

"I guess this will be about the last time you'll ever be able to eat in here." Seward helped himself liberally to the shad's roe.

"I'm sure that there will be worse privations in store for me." Lincoln munched an apple. A teetotaller like Washburne, Lincoln was also, unlike his friend, averse to food in general. For several years Washburne, stout and rosy, had been urging Lincoln to eat more, if only to cure himself of a constipation so severe that he seldom moved his bowels more than once a week; and was obliged to drink by the gallon a terrifying laxative called blue mass. But Lincoln looked healthy enough, thought Washburne, if too lean; and he was strong as the proverbial ox; could lift from the floor, with arm outstretched, a heavy ax at the shaft's end.

When the fascinated waiters had moved out of earshot—and Mike had moved to stand guard at the door—Lincoln said to Seward, in a low voice, "I will never live this down, sneaking like a thief into the capital."

"Sir, the plot was real." Seward sneezed; then blew his nose loudly in a yellow silk handkerchief.

Washburne substituted for the momentarily incapacitated leader. He turned to Lincoln: "As your car was passing through Baltimore—they pull it by horses, you know, between the two depots—a gang of plug-uglies were planning to waylay you then and there."

"But with sufficient guards—"

Seward interrupted Lincoln with a wave of an unlit cigar. "There wasn't time between when we got news of the plot and your arrival in Baltimore. So General Scott insisted you come, as you did, with both houses of Congress informally concurring." Seward looked at Washburne, who nodded gravely, as sole representative of the lower house.

Lincoln stretched his arms until his back made a creaking sound. "I can't say I'd have objected too much to getting shot. I tell you I thought that trip would never end. There is nothing more like eternity than a train ride of twelve days, unless," he added, "it's two people and a ham, as my father-in-law used to say." Seward chuckled and lit his cigar.

"The trip sounded like a triumph, from what we read in the press," said Washburne.

"Well, I've never given so many speeches and said so little. So I suppose it was remarkable in that."

Seward blew cigar smoke at the ceiling. "I *was* troubled to read, sir, that you had said somewhere along the line that no great harm had been done, even though six states have already left the Union and even more are threatening to go, while rebels are busy seizing Federal property all the way from Florida to North Carolina."

"I said no harm to *anyone* has been done." Lincoln's voice was even. "As yet."

The last monosyllable had its effect on both Seward and Washburne.

"You know," said Seward, trying a different tack, "that I am supposed to be the war-to-the-knife fellow—"

"The conflict is 'irrepressible' is what you said." Lincoln smiled. "That's how you got me the nomination."

"Damnedest stupidest speech I ever gave!" Seward paused. "I know you don't drink or smoke. Do you draw the line at profanity, too?"

"Why, no! Fact, once when I was out on the circuit in Illinois, a stranger offered me whiskey and I said, no, I don't drink and then he gave me a chew of tobacco and I said, no, I don't chew and then he said, 'Well, I've found that those with damned few vices have damned few virtues.'"

Over the years, Washburne had heard Lincoln tell this particular story a dozen times; and the wording never varied. Lincoln's little stories tended to come at regular intervals, as a form of punctuation—or evasion. But Lincoln was also a master of the long, cumulative, funny story; and many times Washburne had sat at the stove of some backwoods Illinois tavern when the lawyers on circuit would compete in story-telling and it was always Lincoln who won. Once he had got a group to laugh at the first detail, he would then add, relentlessly, more and more wilder and wilder details until men choked with laughter as the easy tenor voice continued, with all due gravity, to make them positively drunk with laughter. He was equally impressive as a speaker on those occasions when he was carefully prepared. But then, except as a humorist, he had no naturally easy way with an audience. He needed a well-prepared brief. Washburne hoped that the grip-sack on the chair next to Lincoln contained such a brief.

Seward suggested that Lincoln visit his new home later in the day and meet the outgoing president, Mr. James Buchanan. "A harmless old thing," said Seward.

Washburne could not let that go so easily. "Harmless? He let the rebels in Florida seize Federal property at Pensacola and Key

West. He let the rebels in South Carolina occupy Fort Moultrie, a *Federal* fort..."

"I don't think Mr. Buchanan can be held entirely responsible." Seward was mild. "After all, they gave us plenty of warning. They said that if our friend here was elected president, they'd leave the Union. And he was. And they did."

"Along with Mississippi, Alabama, Georgia, Louisiana and... and Virginia, too, I'll bet!"

"What about Virginia?" Lincoln was suddenly alert. "Virginia is the key to this particular tough lock."

Seward shrugged. "The so-called Peace Conference has been in session for two weeks now with old President Tyler—the last of the Virginians—presiding."

"What is the mood?"

"Like that of most peace congresses—very warlike."

"If Virginia goes..." Lincoln stopped.

"There will be war," said Washburne.

Seward said nothing; but he studied Lincoln closely for some sign of intent. The face gave nothing away. Then, almost casually, Seward said, "You know, in a way, we are well rid of those cotton republics—and their problem of slavery."

"Where is your 'irrepressible conflict'?" Lincoln smiled, somewhat weakly, thought Washburne; then Washburne attacked a plate of fried oysters, a delicacy unknown in his early days, and all the more to be savored at Washington City.

"Highly *repressible* if we let our erring sisters—poor foolish ladies—go in peace. Then we can turn our attention to Canada, to Mexico, to the Indies—"

"Mr. Seward, you dream of empire for a government which has just lost half its military stations to home-grown rebels."

Seward made a gracious arabesque with his cigar. "Let the mosquitoes occupy those infernal forts. Have you ever *seen* the South?"

"I was in New Orleans once," said Lincoln, "and," he added with a certain grimness, "I am Kentucky-born, as the world knows."

"A *border*-state," said Washburne.

"A *slave* border-state," said Lincoln.

"When I was governor of New York"—Seward was dreamy—"I used to go over to Canada every chance I could get. And you know those Canadians, the ones who speak English—the best of the lot—are eager to join our Union."

"I seem to recall," said Lincoln, putting down his second apple core and pushing his chair away from the table, "that on the two occasions that we invaded Canada—in the Revolution and then again in 1812—they put up quite a fight to stay *out* of our Union."

11

"Misunderstandings of the day." Seward was airy. "That's all. They're different now."

Lincoln got to his feet. "We've got a few misunderstandings of our own now to deal with before we go traipsing off into Canada. We've also got—you and I—some Cabinet-making to do."

"Will you take dinner with me tonight?" asked Seward.

"With pleasure. Now I'm going to get some sleep. There was a drunk in my car last night who kept on singing 'Dixie' over and over again."

"Not our favorite song," said Washburne.

"No, sir, it is not." Lincoln started toward the door where the aged Mike stood guard; then he paused. "'Look away, look away, Dixie Land!'" Lincoln quoted the song's chorus; he frowned. "Look away to *what*?"

"Or *from* what?" said Seward.

"Plainly, from me. But we shall change that." He turned to Seward, "You don't remember, Mr. Seward, but years ago, you and I once spoke together at Tremont Temple in Boston..."

"In September of 1848. You were canvassing New England for Zachary Taylor, and you wore a long linen duster in the street. I thought *you'd* forgotten."

"And you were wearing yellow pantaloons like the ones you're wearing now. I guess politicians like us never forget anything. Good morning, gentlemen." With that, Lincoln was gone.

Washburne turned to Seward. "What do you think, Mr. Seward?"

Seward frowned. "I don't know. I'm not used to prairie statesmen, if you'll forgive me, Mr. Washburne."

"Forgiven. After all, you and I are used to each other. But Abe isn't really Western, you know. In fact, he isn't really like other people."

"In what way? I thought he was very much your typical Western politician, man of the people, a splitter of rails, that kind of thing."

Washburne laughed. "That was all made up for the campaign."

"You mean Honest Abe the Rail-Splitter is a fraud?"

"Yes and no. I'm sure he split a rail or two in his youth, but he's always been a politician and a lawyer. The honest part is true, of course. But all the rest was just to get out the vote at home."

"And here I thought we had another 'Tippecanoe' Harrison on our hands."

"No, Mr. Seward, what we've got on our hands is a very complicated secretive sort of man. Don't understimate him."

Seward stared at Washburne to see if this might be some kind of obscure Western joke. When he saw that Washburne was serious, he smiled what journalists referred to as "Seward's sly, Jesuit smile." "Well, I don't think I'm ever apt to do that, considering this peculiar line of work we're in."

"You'll be his secretary of state, won't you?"

Seward nodded. "That's the plan. *If* we see eye to eye."

"What's your condition?"

"That we agree on the rest of the Cabinet. I would like to see a Cabinet of like-minded men. I'm a Whig. I'm a moderate. So's Mr. Lincoln. So are most of our party's leaders. But I'm afraid he'll insist on including out-and-out abolitionists like Chase, and Whigs like Bates, and Democrats like Welles."

"What's wrong with that?" Washburne played the innocent. Actually, he knew Seward's game—the so-called Albany Plan had been secretly formulated during the fall by Seward and his chief henchman, Thurlow Weed, the proprietor of *The Albany Evening Journal*. They wanted to exclude from the Cabinet such presidential contenders as Chase. They wanted, most ambitiously— not to mention unConstitutionally—to turn Lincoln into a figurehead; the actual administration of the country would be taken over by Seward, the party's national leader and most famous man. Seward would be premier to Lincoln's powerless monarch.

"I think it most statesmanlike," said Washburne cautiously, "to bring together all the pro-Union elements—Democrats and abolitionists as well as Whigs and moderates. Even"—he smiled at Seward—"if some of them are rivals like Chase. After all, he's picked *you*, his principal rival."

"I was." Seward struck the elegiac note. "But no longer. I'm now too old ever to be the President." Seward smiled to show that he was serious; thereby convincing Washburne that he was not. "But to have Chase and the others on the premises may be too much for him to handle. Well, we'll see, won't we?"

Seward slid his arm companionably through Washburne's. As the two men left the dining room, the doors were thrown open for the first breakfasters of the day—a horde of pale children, who shouted and wept as their grim-faced mothers herded them with pleas and cuffs to the buffet table.

2

DAVID HEROLD STARED AT THE FRONT PAGE OF THE *EVENING Star*; then he did something that he had never done before: he actually bought a copy of the paper from the ancient Negro who had been selling newspapers at the corner of H and Sixth streets for all of David's nineteen years.

"He here!" said the old man, giggling. "He snuck in like a chicken thief."

As David walked down H Street, he read the *Star*'s special story of the President-elect's secret arrival in the city. There were not many facts. Apparently, Mrs. Lincoln and their three sons and the rest of the President-elect's party would arrive in the afternoon, as originally planned. But for reasons not yet known, Mr. Lincoln and two detectives had arrived on the overnight cars; and they had been observed in the lobby of Willard's Hotel at about seven in the morning.

David stopped in front of Number 541, H Street, a narrow, lead-colored, four-story brick house with a yard to one side, containing a wooden shack and a number of dispirited chickens. An outside staircase connected the second floor with the street, permanently shadowing the ground floor. From the second floor a pair of firm hands were pounding music out of a piano not entirely in tune.

"Hey, Annie!" David shouted; then shouted again. The head of an eighteen-year-old girl appeared at the upstairs window.

"I'm practising."

"Lincoln's here! He snuck in this morning. Just like a"—David sought for novelty but not hard enough—"some old chicken thief! It's in the *Star*."

"Come on up."

David hurried up the brick steps, opened the door, found himself face to face with Annie's mother, who was carrying a tray of food. "Oh, Mrs. Surratt, it's me..."

"I heard you, David. And I've already heard that Mr. Lincoln's here." Mrs. Surratt was a handsome auburn-haired woman with a body that David, who read romantic stories in yellow covers, knew was Junoesque. In some ways, he found Mrs. Surratt more to his taste than her daughter; and this curious preference con-

14

vinced him that he was probably the monster of depravity that his seven sisters liked to claim he was.

"How's Mr. Surratt?" Thought of the seven sisters reminded him of his manners.

"We hope for the best. I try to get him to eat. But he just— fades away." Mrs. Surratt motioned for David to precede her into the front parlor.

David crossed the flowered Brussels carpet, uncomfortably aware of the terminal state of his huge cracked leather shoes.

In the parlor Annie sat at the piano, with one hand raised over the keyboard; pretty as a picture, thought David, who had seen the actual picture that she was imitating in the window of Jarman's music store on O Street, from an advertisement for Chickering's pianoforte.

"Here's the paper," he said, putting it in her poised and posed hand. "I bought it," he added. Usually David borrowed newspapers; or stole them. Despite the gentility of David's mother— widow of a government employee who had left her with eight children and a house near the Navy Yard—David had grown up with a pack of wild Washington boys, all of them Southern—or Southron, as they called themselves, and devoted to mischief of every sort. They were only a cut above the Baltimore plug-uglies, those real street toughs who were now threatening to invade the city and disrupt the President's inaugural.

"It was the plug-uglies, I guess, that made him sneak through Baltimore."

Annie read the paper as if it were a sheet of difficult music. In the back parlor, Mrs. Surratt's low voice could be heard, pleading with her husband to eat. He merely coughed. He coughed so much that hardly anyone noticed the cough anymore; or Mr. Surratt for that matter. No longer visible to the world, he was no longer part of it.

The Surratt family owned a prosperous truck farm in Maryland, close by Surrattsville, a village named after them. Now that Mr. Surratt was ill—dying, to give it the right word—Mrs. Surratt herself presided over the great wagon that brought the farm's produce to the Center Market, while Annie attended a Catholic seminary. The Protestant David never knew why Mr. and Mrs. Surratt were converts; but both had converted years ago, and now their youngest son, John, aged sixteen, was at St. Charles, over in Maryland, studying to be a priest. The oldest son, Isaac, was an engineer.

The Surratts and the Herolds had been acquaintances for close to a generation; they thought of Washington as a Southern city, which it was—and a Maryland city at that, which meant a population somewhat more volatile than that of staid neighboring Virginia, whose claim to the city was nearly as substantial as Maryland's. The District of Columbia was an anomalous ten-mile-square parallelogram carved out of Maryland and bounded by the Potomac River and Virginia.

Annie put down the newspaper, and turned toward David, who was slumped on his spine in a rocking chair; the black cloth of his trousers, he noticed glumly, was so shiny that the dull February light was reflected in its dark folds. David looked without pleasure at his own short legs; he was too thin, he knew, and he had recently stopped growing; just one inch short of a proper height. Even so, girls liked him. But then why shouldn't they? He had seven sisters. There was nothing on earth that he did not know about the other sex. If only he had had a brother...

"You've got to fix those shoes, David." Annie made a face. Plainly, the broken shoes were smelly to others.

David hid his feet under the rocker; he seldom bathed between Christmas and Easter. In fact, if it hadn't been for certain young ladies in Marble Alley, he would never bathe; would smell like the rest of the wild boys—a not unpleasant odor of moist earth mixed with tobacco smoke. "I guess I'll have to take that job at Thompson's."

"Prescription clerk?"

David nodded. He was related to the owner of Thompson's Drug Store, near the corner of Fifteenth and Pennsylvania Avenue, close by the White House. Over the years, David had done odd jobs for Mr. Thompson. Now, at Mrs. Herold's insistence, he would be prescription clerk and make what she liked to call "a living wage," which is what she, and those of the sisters who were not married, each did in order to keep up the Navy Yard house. Mrs. Herold herself presided over a furniture shop.

"It's about time," said Annie; and smiled at him. He liked her best of the nice girls he knew; he liked to listen to her play piano; he liked the notion of liking her the best of all. "He's crazy, to come here." Annie folded the newspaper as if it were indeed sheet music and placed it behind "Listen to the Mocking Bird," a Song Especially Written for President Buchanan's Niece.

"Who?"

"Lincoln. They'll kill him."

"Who'll kill him?" asked Mrs. Surratt, coming in from the back parlor; the tray untouched.

"Everybody, Mother. You know how the wild boys around here go on."

Mrs. Surratt put down the tray on a round table covered with green velvet where, in frames, the family pictures were ranged around a crucifix and a rosary.

"I've heard," she said, "that there was a plot to kill him in Baltimore. I mean I heard it *before* today. You know how they talk at the bar in Surrattsville."

"And drink!" Annie was ungracious. "But Maryland's going to secede any minute now and so will Virginia and then what on earth will Mr. Lincoln want to be in Washington for? I mean, this is a Southern city and with those two states out of the Union, this is a Southern city spang in the middle of the Confederacy."

"Over in Richmond they're saying that *our* president, Mr. David, wants Washington for *his* capital." Mrs. Surratt picked up the rosary; idly, she fingered beads. "Isaac says that Mr. Lincoln won't be inaugurated here..."

"What'll drive him out?" asked David.

"... or anywhere else on this earth," Mrs. Surratt finished. Then she whispered a prayer to herself and David looked away, embarrassed as always by any outward sign of strange religion.

Raptly, David stared at the Bleeding Heart of Jesus that hung over the fireplace; and thought of dinner. "I saw some Northern soldier-boys at the depot." David made his contribution. "They had piled up so many saddles, you couldn't get to the cars, through the mess."

"I wish they'd just go and leave us in peace." Mrs. Surratt looked sad and, to David's eyes, beautiful. He was, he liked to think, something of a connoisseur of feminine beauty. Ever since he was fourteen, he had had the run of Sal Austin's parlors, where the most attractive girls in the city could be found. Sal, christened Sarah, was an old friend of his mother's and though Mrs. Herold was horrified at the extent and nature of Sal's fall in the world, she was most respectful of her old friend's great wealth, and when Sal offered to give David work as a handyman at her mansion in Marble Alley midway between Pennsylvania and Missouri avenues, Mrs. Herold saw no harm in it. "Because David is too young to be corrupted." The sisters thought this very funny; so did David. For a year and a half he had known pleasure of a sort unknown to the wild boys—doubly unknown because he was not foolish enough, even at fourteen, to go out of his way to excite envy. He never said where he worked; made no response whenever a wild boy would talk knowingly of Sal or her rival Julia's establishment across the Alley.

The girls enjoyed him nearly as much as he enjoyed them; they also made him wash, an unnatural activity that he accepted as a small price to pay for so many carnal privileges. When Sal, finally, got a full-time man to maintain her gilded premises, she

17

said, "Any time you want to pay a call, Davie, you come right along." And he still did, from time to time. "I think the world of that mother of yours, Davie, I really do! Eight children! I tell you she is a Christian martyr. Because she could have had the life, too. But didn't. Such a waste!"

Mrs. Surratt would have been mortified, thought David, if she could have known what wickedness was unfolding in his adolescent mind. But Mrs. Surratt was a good woman; and thought only of murder. "I'm certain they will attempt something between now and next week..."

"Who's 'they,' Mother?"

"The seceshers."

"Like us?" Annie played a bar of "Dixie."

"Heaven forbid, *not* like us! But Isaac tells me that every day there are people coming across the Long Bridge, coming from as far away as Richmond, with guns and ammunition."

"There's a bunch of the wild boys who drill every day," said David. "They call themselves the National Volunteers."

"You think they'd really try to stop the inaugural?" Annie shut the piano; no more "Dixie."

Mrs. Surratt nodded. "Yes. I think they will try and I think they will succeed."

"I think so, too," said David, who had never before seen the wild boys so fired up with hatred of Yankees in general and of Mr. Lincoln in particular.

The three sat a moment in silence, no sound but the dry regular cough of the dying man in the back parlor. Then Mrs. Surratt said, "Isaac's gone to Richmond, Annie. And I think he's gone for good."

"You mean he won't *ever* come back?"

"Not until this is a Southern city, if it ever is."

"But Virginia's still in the Union, Mother."

"By April Isaac says Virginia will have gone, too. Along with Maryland."

"Then there will be war, won't there, Mother?"

"That depends on Mr. Lincoln," said Mrs. Surratt. "Or whoever takes his place as the Yankee president."

"And all because of those crazy preachers in the North who want to free our darkies, who wouldn't know what to do with themselves if they were free!" Annie jumped to her feet. "Come on, David. Let's go to Willard's. I want to get a good look at the devil—before they shoot him."

Mrs. Surratt made a warning gesture. "Don't talk like that in front of strangers."

"Don't be silly, Mother. I'm not an idiot."

"We're an occupied city, for now," said Mrs. Surratt, crossing herself as she returned the rosary to its place on the crucifix.

3

AT ELEVEN O'CLOCK IN THE MORNING, SEWARD AND LINCOLN—the latter still unrecognized—crossed from Willard's to the Executive Mansion, known to those few Americans who were not addicted to the prevailing Latinate English of the nation's orators as the President's House or just plain White House. The single guard at the gate did not even look at the two soberly dressed statesmen, who proceeded up the iced-over, deep-rutted driveway to the main portico, from whose columns the paint was peeling; the glass of the front windows was streaked with dust.

"Last time I was here it was 1848." Lincoln looked about with some curiosity.

"Your friend Mr. Polk was in residence then."

Lincoln nodded. "But never friendly to me, particularly after I attacked his Mexican War."

"Ah, the irrepressible speeches of one's youth!" Seward made a comical face. "You'll be hearing a lot about that speech of yours before you're done."

Lincoln grimaced. "I know. I know. Words are hostages to fortune, they say. The only problem is we never know in advance just what the fortune is."

At the front door, a short elderly Irish usher stopped them. "State your business, gentlemen. The President is *not* available. He's in Cabinet."

"Tell the President," said Seward, "that Mr. Abraham Lincoln has come to pay a call."

The usher turned very red in the face. "By heaven, if it isn't old Abe himself! Oh, forgive me, Your Excellency..."

"It's heaven I can't forgive, for making me old."

"Well, sir, they call *me* old Edward, sir. Edward McManus. I've been doorkeeper since President Taylor."

"Then I shall leave the door just as it is, in your good hands."

Old Edward smiled, revealing few teeth, dark gums. He led them across the musty entrance hall and into the Red Room, just off the foot of the great staircase. "If you'll wait here, sir, I'll go fetch the President."

As the usher hurried upstairs, Lincoln and Seward looked about the Red Room, which was true to its name but shabby withal. Lincoln touched a red damask curtain from which pieces had been hacked.

"Visitors like their souvenirs," said Seward. "When I was governor of New York, at every reception, I'd have a guard with a gun next to every curtain."

"Did you get reelected?"

Seward laughed. "I did. In fact—"

But at that moment, President James Buchanan hurried—or flurried, thought Seward—into the room. He was a tall man, with white hair and a twisted neck, which meant that his left cheek seemed always about to rest on his left shoulder. One eye had a squint, which made the old man look as if he were winking slyly at you, as if his words were not to be taken seriously.

"Mr. Lincoln! I didn't expect you until tomorrow! Mr. Seward, too. What an honor for us. Where is my niece?" This was addressed directly to Lincoln, who said, very gravely, "On my honor, I have not misplaced your niece, Mr. President."

"Of course not. You've never met her. Nor have I. That is, nor do I *know* where she is at the moment. She is looking forward so much to showing Mrs. Lincoln around the Mansion." A lifelong bachelor, Buchanan was sustained by his niece Harriet Lane, of whom a Washington wit had been heard to say, "There is no power *behind* the throne, either."

"We just wanted to pay our respects, sir . . ." Lincoln began to move toward the door. But Buchanan took his arm, firmly.

"You must meet the Cabinet. We're having a special meeting. Texas left the Union this morning. We just got the official word . . ."

They were now in the main hall. Servants—black and white—had begun to appear, to get a glimpse of the new President.

"What answer do you make to the . . . seceders?" Although Lincoln's usual word was "rebels," he used the softer word, because the Democrat Buchanan was close to the Southern wing of his party, as represented by his own Vice-President, John C. Breckinridge.

"*You* will give us inspiration, let's hope." Buchanan bowed to Seward, who could not help but think that this run-of-the-mill Pennsylvania politician had found his true niche not as President but during the time that he was America's minister to England.

As the three men moved up the main staircase, Buchanan said,

"The house is a good deal smaller than it looks. Actually, we're quite crowded up here. Our private rooms are at this end while the offices are at the other end and this corridor that connects the two is for me like the river Styx. Each day I pass like a doomed soul through crowds of people, all waiting to be given something for nothing."

They were now at the top of the stairs, the ominous dark corridor before them. "I was never up here before," said Lincoln.

"You had no private business with Mr. Polk?" Seward lit a cigar; then, to the President, "Have I your leave?"

"By all means, sir." Buchanan indicated four large doors to the left and two doors to the right. "Those are the bedrooms. And there is the bathroom. The taps do not work, of course. Nothing really does here." Buchanan led them down the dusty hall, whose only illumination came from a single large window at the living-quarters end. Midway to the offices, the President showed them a sitting room, which followed the shape of the oval Blue Room below. The room was bleakly furnished, with horsehair sofas and empty bookcases. A number of paintings hung on the walls; but they were so darkened by time and dirt that it was hard to tell who or what they were of. "This is our only *private* parlor. Even so, the people barge in on you."

The President then led them down the corridor to a wooden railing with a gate. "This is where Hades begins," he said, unlatching the gate. Back of the railing was an empty desk and behind the desk, there was a waiting room lined with benches that always put Seward in mind of a small-town railway depot. "This is where the other Edward sits, only he's not here. I can't think why. He's a colored man; and most respectable. He decides who goes into the waiting room. Then here on the left is the secretary's office, which is quite as large as mine, with a small room just off it, which is where Harriet, my niece, keeps the linen. Would you like to see these offices?"

"No, sir." Seward could tell that Lincoln was prepared for flight. But Old Buck, as the President was popularly and unpopularly known, was inexorable. "Then the Cabinet meets right here, just off the clerk's office, as you can see, and inside it connects with the President's office, which is in the corner there, and slightly larger, thank Heaven."

Buchanan had now thrown open the door to the Cabinet Room. The half-dozen men who were seated at the green-baize-covered table got to their feet as the President ushered Lincoln and Seward into the room. "Gentlemen, the President-elect."

Briskly, Lincoln shook hands with each man. Seward noticed that he paused for a moment as he shook the hand of the Attorney-

General, Edwin M. Stanton, a large, bald-headed asthmatic man with steel-rimmed spectacles and an unpleasant sneer, aimed now at Lincoln, who said, somewhat quizzically, "Well, Mr. Stanton, we meet again."

"Yes, we do . . . *sir.*"

Lincoln turned to the others. "Five years ago we were a pair of lawyers trying to determine whether Mr. McCormick's reaper was his reaper or someone else's."

"I remember . . . *sir.*" Stanton stood very straight, his large paunch quivering slightly.

"Yes, Mr. Stanton. So do I."

Buchanan had now drawn Lincoln over to the window with its view of the southern part of the President's estate, bounded at the far end by the old canal, now an open sewer, and the Potomac River beyond. "In the summer, sir, the smell from that canal is absolutely unbearable," said Buchanan. "Drain the canal, I tell them. Or fill it in. Naturally, Congress does nothing. But they do let me use a little stone cottage out at the Soldiers' Home. I spend the summers there and I suggest that you use it, too, if you don't want the fever."

Lincoln was staring at a pile of white marble blocks, at whose center the base of an obelisk rose. "They've still not finished that monument to Washington?"

"No, sir. In fact, nothing is ever finished here! No dome on the Capitol. No street pavings. No street lamps. Nothing's ever done to completion here except, sir, one thing." The old man's head now rested on his shoulder and the bad eye was entirely shut as, with a quiet joy, he pointed out the window. "There," he said. "Look!"

Lincoln stared at a huge red-brick wall. "The one thing that the Executive Mansion has dearly needed since Mr. Jefferson's time was a proper barn. But not a *wooden* barn, sir. No, sir. Not a barn that will catch fire or get the rot. No, sir. But a *brick* barn, sir. A barn built to outlast time itself. You don't know the pleasure it has given me these last four years to see this beautiful barn slowly rise from that swamp they call the President's Park."

"And watch the Union fall apart," said Lincoln to Seward as the two men crossed the President's Park on the way to the War Department.

"He's well-meaning, Old Buck," said Seward, pronouncing the ultimate political epitaph. "What was that between you and Stanton?"

Lincoln chuckled. "Well, Mr. Stanton was this big important lawyer on a patent case . . . sort of *your* territory, come to think of it. And I was the backwoods lawyer that was called in to help him

22

out because I had political connections in Chicago, where the trial was supposed to be. Anyway, when the trial got moved to Cincinnati, I wasn't really needed, as he made absolutely clear. Fact, he cut me dead."

"He's a disagreeable man," said Seward. "But he's the best lawyer in the country. And he's one of us."

Lincoln gave Seward a sidelong glance. "In what sense? He's a Democrat. He was for Douglas, or so people say. He never says, I'm told."

"Last week he told the President that if he lets Fort Sumter go without a fight, he would deserve impeachment."

"Well, well," said Lincoln; and no more. The small brick War Department was surrounded by thirty loud geese which a farmer was doing his best to make move on, to the delight of the two soldiers more or less on guard.

"I shall make no references to Rome and the Capitoline geese." Seward was fond of classical allusions. He knew his Tacitus; loved his Cicero.

"Please don't." Lincoln stared with some distaste at the unexpectedly rustic scene.

"Actually, General Scott has got himself a brand-new War Department across the way there, on Seventeenth Street. This building will only be for the army, just as that one over there"— Seward pointed to a second small brick building—"is for the navy. But the whole thing will be run from Seventeenth Street." Together the two men crossed the frozen mud field that was Seventeenth Street, where stood a large building with no guards at all, not even geese. This was the War Department. As they approached the main door, Seward asked Lincoln who ought to be Secretary of War.

Lincoln's response was sharp. "Certainly, *not* the man best qualified. I think that is already understood, isn't it?" For all Lincoln's serene amiability, Seward detected a sudden edge of true bitterness. As a minority president, Lincoln could only reign by placating certain great powers and dominations. As for ruling . . . It was Seward's view, on the morning of Saturday, February 23, 1861, that Lincoln would be fortunate if he could last out his term as the figurehead president of a mere rump of the dis-United States. Since the wealth and talent of this remaining fragment of the original Union was almost entirely in the north—specifically, in New York and New England—the inexperienced outlander from the west would need a knowledgeable prime minister, a man from the wealthy part—himself, the party's leader. But Seward was in no hurry to impose himself and the so-called Albany Plan upon Lincoln. He was convinced that in the next nine days tu-

23

multuous events would make him so necessary to the new president that he would then be able to assert his dominance in order to avoid the war with the South that Lincoln might blunder into, exclude Chase and the Democrats from the Cabinet, and begin the creation of the new North American—South American and West Indian, too; why not?—empire that Seward felt would more than compensate them for the loss of the slave states.

Seward was no longer the abolitionist he had once been. He was now both more and less ambitious than when, in the very year that Lincoln was attacking Polk for making war on Mexico, he was telling an audience in Cleveland that, "slavery must be abolished and you and I must do it." Now Seward was conciliatory on the matter in general; and beautifully vague in particular. On the other hand, Lincoln was still struggling with the words that he had so proudly hurled in the face of President Polk: "Any people anywhere," Representative Lincoln had proclaimed to the Congress, "being inclined and having the power, have the right to rise up and shake off the existing government..." Seward knew this so-called right of revolution speech by heart, as did every Southerner; and not a day passed that these words were not used to taunt the tall, awkward-moving man who was entering the War Department for the first time.

At seventy-four, Winfield Scott was general-in-chief of the Union armies and at six feet four and a quarter inches, he was a quarter-inch taller than the new president. Estimates of his legendary weight seldom dropped below the three-hundred-pound mark.

General Scott received the Commander-in-Chief-elect in his ground-floor office—he was too large and too old to climb stairs with any ease. Although he suffered from gout, he still loved food and wine; loved glory and himself. The bejowled, red face was huge and mottled; a spider's web of tiny purple lines had netted the nose. Scott wore an elaborate uniform of his own design, gleaming with gold braid and massive epaulets. Like a glittering mountain he stood now before a painting of himself as the hero of the War of 1812. As Lincoln entered the room, the general waddled forward; they shook hands beneath a painting of Scott conquering Mexico in 1847.

"You have come, sir, when, as a nation, we are at the razor's edge." The old man's voice was still deep; but there was a tendency to quaver whenever he summoned up emotion, either real or simulated.

"It's a great privilege to meet you, General." Lincoln glanced at the painting of Scott storming Chapultepec—and looked away.
24

Not an auspicious beginning, thought Seward. Lincoln had detested the Mexican War.

"Sit down, sir." Scott eased himself into a throne that had been designed for a very fat man to get in and out of with relative ease. "I must confess, sir, I did not vote for you—"

"Because you are a Virginian?"

"No, sir. I am a loyal Union man, which is why I am so relieved that you are here to prevent more dis-Union. I did not vote for you because I never vote."

"Well, General, I voted for you in 1852, when you were the last Whig candidate for president, and I was just about the last good Whig in Springfield." Seward wondered whether or not this was true. In the course of the morning, he had duly noted that Lincoln had the gift of flattery, a form of insincerity that Seward tended to think of as being peculiarly his own most delicate art. In any case, Seward regarded Scott as his own handiwork. After all, it had been Seward's idea to run the man for President; and Seward had written every single speech that Scott had delivered in the course of a disastrous campaign.

"I received," said the general, the voice of military command taking on a politician's tone, "one million three hundred eighty-six thousand five hundred and seventy-eight votes. Franklin Pierce"—as the old man said the name, the red face darkened—"got two hundred twenty thousand more votes than I. And now we are faced with a civil war. Because, sir, had I been elected, I would have strengthened the Federal forts in the south. There would have been no trouble at Fort Sumter because I would have made nearby Fort Moultrie impregnable, and Charleston would still be what it is meant to be—a harbor of the United States."

"What is to be done?" Lincoln's voice was soft.

Scott motioned to an aide, who set up a map of the Union on an easel. Scott then picked up a ferule that lay beside his throne and pointed to the various military establishments throughout the South. He presented the bad news directly. With the exception of Forts Sumter and Pickens, the rest of the Federal forts either were in rebel hands—or would soon be. Seward then expected Scott to follow their agreed-upon line: Lincoln should say to the South, "Wayward sisters, go in peace." Although Scott said no such thing, he was hardly sanguine. "We have no fleet to speak of. This Administration has deliberately weakened our military forces. But then Mr. Floyd, the late Secretary of War, is a secessionist and a traitor. You do not object to my candor, sir?"

"No, General. I had come to the same conclusion myself. Now if war *were* to come..." Lincoln paused. Seward sat on the edge of his chair. It had never occurred to him that Lincoln might

25

actually have a plan and that that plan might involve a military action against the rebel states. Like most intelligent men, Seward thought that all intelligent men, given the same set of facts, would react as he did. During the last few hours, he had come to appreciate Lincoln's intelligence if not the rustic western style; now this sallow-faced man, sprawled in an armchair, knees working their way to his chin, was saying, "If war were to come, how long would it take us to raise an army, build a fleet, make all necessary preparations?"

"Six months, sir. What we lack now are good officers. The best of our West Pointers are Southerners. From Jefferson Davis himself, the President of the Confederacy, to—"

Lincoln cut the old man short. "General, that is a title that I do not use nor acknowledge, while the Confederacy is a place that does not exist. Is that clear?"

Seward sat bolt upright. This man Lincoln was hard, all right; or so he sounded. Intelligent men were pliant; or so Seward chose to believe.

"Yes, sir. You are right, sir. Anyway, from Mr. Davis to Colonel Lee, all our best officers are Southern."

"Maybe you should've promoted a few more Northerners—and Westerners."

"Well, sir . . ." Vaguely, Scott gestured with his ferule, which in turn reminded him of the map. "Sir, I have already devised a plan, should it be necessary to restore the Union by force." Scott paused for some response from Lincoln but there was none beyond attentiveness.

Scott continued without, as it were, the looked-for sign. "If Virginia and Maryland go out of the Union, we shall then be obliged to move the capital to Harrisburg or to Philadelphia . . ." Scott paused. Lincoln made no response; the face was impassive. Seward was growing definitely uneasy. What was this man's game? Seward, who enjoyed poker, rather thought that Lincoln was simply indulging himself in the card-player's bluff. Certainly, he hoped that that was what it was.

Scott, signless again, proceeded to divide the South with his stick. "I do not think that a straight assault on Maryland and Virginia will succeed. Virginia is the most populous of the Southern states, the wealthiest, the most ready for war. We should inflict what damage we can upon Virginia but I would say, sir, that our hope is in the west. The Mississippi River is the key. Seize the river. Knock Mississippi out of the war and whatever sections of Tennessee and Kentucky may stand against us. Split the South into two parts, and each part will die for lack of the other."

Scott paused. Lincoln slowly straightened up. "Well, I guess we'd better persuade Virginia and Maryland to stay in the Union a while longer." Seward gave an audible sigh of relief. This was the Lincoln that he had been inventing for himself ever since the election: the cautious vacillator—a Western Jesuit, in fact.

As Lincoln rose, an aide pulled Scott to his feet. "By the way, General, what would you do about Fort Sumter?"

"I would hold out as long as possible."

"And then?"

"I would evacuate the fort. Otherwise, Major Anderson and all his men will be killed or seized. We have not the sea power to dominate Charleston harbor."

"An honor to meet you, General." Lincoln turned to Seward. "My wife and family should be arriving any minute now."

"Well, the mayor will be at the depot, even if you won't be."

Lincoln frowned. "I should have stayed with the rest of the party."

"It was at my advice, sir," said Scott, "that you took the night-cars. I trust our people in Baltimore. They swore to me that you would never have got through alive."

"Well, even if you were right, General, I'm still not sure that you've done me a good turn."

"We could take no chances," said Seward.

General Scott nodded. "That's why I agreed with Mr. Seward when he said you would be safer at Willard's Hotel than in a private house."

"Was that *your* idea?" Lincoln looked at Seward, with some amusement. "I thought it was General Scott's."

Seward was amazed to find himself blushing, as he stammered about safety. Actually, the Albany Plan had dictated Lincoln's removal from a private house to a hotel where Seward and the others would have access to him and his party. The general saluted as they departed.

The weak sun had now vanished behind what looked to be snow clouds. Lincoln and Seward walked in silence down Seventeenth Street to the corner of Pennsylvania Avenue, as usual crowded at this time of day. Carriages and cabs clattered by while the horse carriages rattled on their tracks, bells sounding.

"No soldiers," said Lincoln, watching the traffic.

"No war—so far."

"What a fix we're in," said the President-elect, stepping up on the brick sidewalk that led past the iron fence of the White House, where he would soon be quartered—caged, was more like it, thought Seward. For a brief moment—very brief, actually—he was glad that Lincoln and not he had been elected sixteenth president of what was left of the United States of America.

4

THE SIDEWALK IN FRONT OF WILLARD'S HOTEL SEEMED TO HUM
and throb, and John Hay felt as if he were still on the cars as he
made his way through the crowd of people—mostly colored, he
noticed—who were on hand to get a look at Mr. Lincoln, who
was not visible; unlike Mrs. Lincoln, who was, as well as the three
Lincoln sons, the six lady relations of Mrs. Lincoln's, the two
Lincoln secretaries John George Nicolay (born twenty-nine years
ago in Bavaria; moved to Illinois as a child; grew up to edit a
Pittsfield newspaper) and John Hay himself, aged twenty-two, a
graduate of Brown who had been admitted to the Illinois bar
exactly two weeks ago, thanks, in part, to the fact that his uncle
was Springfield's leading lawyer and an old associate of Lincoln;
thanks, again in part, to the fact that Hay had gone to school with
Nicolay, Lincoln's secretary during the campaign for the presidency. Hay had been able to make himself so useful to Nicolay
in the campaign that Nico had said to the President-elect, "Can't
we take Johnny to Washington with us?" and although Lincoln
had groaned and said, "We can't take all Illinois down with us to
Washington," John Hay had been duly employed as a presidential
secretary. Small, wiry, handsome, John Hay intended to enjoy as
much as possible his sudden elevation in the world.

At Brown, Hay had wanted to be a poet; in fact, he was a poet
who wrote verse that got published. But that was not exactly a
career or a living. For a time, the pulpit had appealed to him—
except for the business about God. Although the law had no great
appeal to him, for a young man named Hay there was not much
choice. He worked in his uncle's office, where he got to know his
uncle's friend, Mr. Lincoln, a man whose ups-and-downs were
much talked of in Springfield, particularly the downs. Mr. Lincoln
was supposed to have gone mad for two weeks just before what
was to have been his wedding day, which had to be postponed.
He had gone into a decline after losing his seat in Congress and
despite the campaigning that he had done for the new Whig
President, Zachary Taylor, he was offered no government appointment other than the secretaryship of the Oregon territory,
which Mrs. Lincoln had turned down for him. Home in Springfield, Lincoln practised law with the brilliant, hard-drinking Wil-

liam Herndon and let himself, many said, sink into apathy, while making a good deal of money as a railroad lawyer. When the great debate on slavery began, Mr. Lincoln found his voice, and after his challenge to Stephen Douglas, he had come to personify the new Republican Party and the new politics—whatever they were. Hay was never quite certain just where Mr. Lincoln meant to take the nation but he did know that wherever that was, he was going to go, too.

At the center of the lobby, the manager of Willard's was greeting Mrs. Lincoln, who was tired and not, Hay could see, in the best of moods. Nicolay and Hay had their code words for the great folk. Mary Todd Lincoln was known, depending on her mood, as either Madam or the Hellcat. Mr. Lincoln was either the Ancient or, in honor of the previous year's visit to Washington by the first ambassadors from that awesome Japanese official known as the Tycoon, the Tycoon.

The slender Nicolay was at the Hellcat's side, smiling grimly through his long, pointed, youthful beard. Although Hay could not hear what the Hellcat was saying, he suspected that a complaint was being duly registered. Suddenly, Hay found himself next to the oldest Lincoln son, Robert, a seventeen-year-old Harvard freshman who said, with pleasure, "Johnny!" as if they had not spent the last twelve days and nights cooped up together on the cars from Springfield, playing cards in the baggage car and, occasionally, taking a swig from a bottle that Lamon always carried, "just in case," he'd say, shoving it into the great side pocket that contained a slingshot, a pair of brass knuckles, a hunting knife and a derringer.

"I think Nicolay needs some help," said Hay, maneuvering himself through the crowd to Mrs. Lincoln's side just as her normal high color was beginning to take on that dusky glow which was the first sign of a Hellcat storm.

"Mrs. Lincoln!" Hay beamed, boyishly; but then with his youthful face he had no other way of looking, to his chagrin. Strange men often addressed him as Sonny; his cheek was often patted; he knew that he must, very soon, grow a moustache, if he could. "Your trunks are already in your rooms." This was a lie. But he knew Mrs. Lincoln's passionate attachment to her baggage and its integrity.

"Oh, Johnny! You do relieve my mind!" Mary Todd Lincoln's smile was, suddenly, winning and so Hay was won; she took his arm and they swept through the hotel lobby to the main staircase, as the manager and his outriders cleared a path for their considerable party.

Outside, the crowd dispersed. David and Annie were disappointed not to have seen the archfiend himself. "They say he's got whiskers now, so as no one will know him," said David, as they walked up Thirteenth Street.

"But once people get used to the whiskers, they'll know him after a while." Annie stopped in front of a raw-wood picket fence. Through the gap between two slats they could see a vacant lot where a number of young men were drilling with old rifles.

"Who are they?" asked David.

"The National Volunteers," Annie whispered, her breath white between them. "One of them is a friend of Brother Isaac."

"What are they drilling for?"

"Inauguration Day. Come on. Let's go. I don't want them to see me."

David and Annie hurried down the street. "They're crazy," he said, "to take on the whole U.S. Army."

In Parlor Suite Six at Willard's Hotel, it was agreed that the National Volunteers were indeed crazy but, potentially, dangerous: such was the intelligence already received by the suite's principal resident, the bewhiskered Abraham Lincoln, who now sat in a huge armchair in the parlor as his two youngest sons, Willie and Tad, climbed over him, and Hay smiled sweetly at this domestic scene. He had never hated two children more than these. Tad, at seven, could not be understood due to some sort of malformation of his palate, while the ruthlessly eloquent and intelligent Willie, at ten, could be understood all too well. Willie was a tendentious explainer, who regarded Johnny Hay as a somewhat dull-witted playmate.

While the children shouted and pummelled their father, Seward and Lamon discussed with Lincoln, as best they could, arrangements for his security. Mary had withdrawn to the bedroom to greet her—Hay prayed—not-mythical luggage.

Nicolay was at the door to the parlor, looking somewhat alarmed. Then Hay saw why. Behind Nicolay towered the unmistakable figure of Charles Sumner, senator from Massachusetts, heir to Daniel Webster, greatest of the Senate's scholars, an orator of such power that audiences had been known, after three hours of his burning-bush language, to beg for more of that incandescent flame, fuelled by a single passion—the conviction that there was no greater task on earth than to liberate the slaves, and punish their masters.

Lincoln positively jackknifed to his feet at the sight of Sumner, scattering his sons upon the flowered carpet. As the boys started to yell with indignation, Lincoln said, "John, you deliver the boys to their mother."

Hay grabbed Tad's hand and pulled him, squeaking, to his

feet, while Willie ran into his mother's bedroom, shouting, "Mamma!"

Gracefully, Seward introduced Senator Sumner to the President-elect. Charles Sumner was not only remarkably handsome but, unlike most modern statesmen, he was cleanshaven. Hay had already sent out a curiously uninteresting story on he wire-service to the effect that Lincoln would be the first bearded president in American history. Face-hair was now respectable or *de rigueur*, as Hay's French-speaking Providence, Rhode Island, muse, Mrs. Sarah Helen Whitman, would say. Since a brief engagement to Edgar Allan Poe, Mrs. Whitman had worn only white, like a shroud; she had also sprinkled herself with ether in order to suggest a terminal illness of the sort that had once ravished Poe; and entirely overwhelmed poetry-loving Brown undergraduates.

"I would've known you anywhere," said Lincoln. "From your pictures."

"I might *not* have known you, sir, with the beard of Abraham, you might say, so newly acquired." To Hay's ear Sumner sounded like so many of his fellow Boston Brahmins, more English than American. Even so, the voice was singularly beautiful in its way, thought Hay, the Westerner, as he slipped into the bedroom, where, to his delight, he found Madam and a colored maid opening a row of trunks. As Willie entered the adjoining bedroom, she said, "Take Tad with you."

"No," said Tad.

"Yes!" said the Hellcat with a sudden change of expression that everyone, including the remarkably spoiled Tad, understood and feared. Whimpering with self-pity, the child obeyed. "Oh, God, will this never end?" Madam appealed to Hay. "I feel seasick from the cars. I hate these trunks."

"Well, you'll soon be settled in the White House. Can I help?"

Madam was holding up a dress of blue velvet; she examined it carefully for signs of damage. "I am a martyr to moths," she said to herself, but spoke aloud, a curious habit to which Hay had got used during their days of confinement aboard the cars. When Mrs. Lincoln wanted to—or was able to (he could never tell whether her erratic behavior was calculated or simply uncontrolled)—she could charm anyone on earth, as she must have charmed the most ambitious young lawyer in Springfield, not that Lincoln would have needed much charming, for she was a Todd and lived with her sister whose house on the hill was the center of the town's social life and it was there that she had been courted by all the other ambitious lawyers, not to mention Judge Stephen Douglas; as a child in Lexington, Kentucky, she had known Henry

31

Clay, the only American statesman, except for Parson Weems's Washington, that Lincoln had ever openly praised.

Madam gave the dress to the maid to hang up; turned to Hay with a sudden, almost girlish smile. "Between you and me, Mr. Hay, there is more to jest about in all of this than I might have suspected, for all the weariness as well."

"I've noticed that, too, Mrs. Lincoln."

But then the smile was gone. She had heard the sonorous voice in the next room. "Who is that with Mr. Lincoln?"

"Senator Sumner."

"Oh." Hay could see that she was torn between timidity and curiosity, which she resolved by going to the half-open door and looking into the parlor. "He's every bit as handsome as they say," she said in a low voice; this time to Hay and not to herself.

"He hasn't stopped talking since he arrived."

"At least he seems to have driven away Mr. Seward, that abolitionist sneak." Mary turned back into the room.

"Surely, Mr. Seward's no sneak—"

"Well, he was a rabid abolitionist once upon a time. Now, of course, he's gone and changed a few of his spots, but right or wrong, Mr. Sumner never changes. I do hope all these abolitionists never forget that Mr. Lincoln is *not* in favor of abolishing slavery. He simply does not want to extend it to the new territories. That is all; all!" In the last twelve days Hay had heard her say this so many times that he had ceased to hear the words. But then Mrs. Lincoln was in a difficult position. The Todds were a great slave-holding Kentucky family; worse, they were, many of them, secessionists, a source of much embarrassment to her, not to mention to the new president. "Find me Mrs. Ann Spriggs." This was unexpected.

"Who is that, Mrs. Lincoln?"

"She is a widow who has—or had—a boardinghouse on Capitol Hill. That's where we lived when Mr. Lincoln was in Congress. She's still alive, they say, and I'd dearly love to see her again and"—the girlish smile returned—"*and show off!*"

"For that," said Hay, again charmed by Madam, who had just taken over from the Hellcat, "I'll find her, Mrs. Lincoln."

With a wave, Madam dismissed him. She is going to be a very royal First Lady, he thought, as he returned to the parlor, hoping to escape the senatorial presence unremarked. But Hay's appearance stopped Sumner in midsentence. "Sir?"

"This is my secretary's secretary, Mr. Sumner. John Hay."

"Oh, yes." They shook hands. Hay felt a certain awe, seeing so famous a man up close. "I heard you speak, sir," he said. "Two years ago. In Providence. I was at Brown."

"I remember the speech." Sumner had lost interest. Hay looked at Lincoln: should he stay? The Tycoon raised his chin, which meant, no. "I'm curious to see which is taller, Mr. Sumner or myself, but when I suggested that we measure backs..."

"I said"—Sumner was not about to allow anyone to say his lines for him—"the time has come to unite our fronts and not our backs before the enemies of our country."

"Yes, that's *just* what you said." Lincoln turned to Hay, "Word for word," he added. With a low bow, Hay left the two statesmen to what, he suspected, was going to be a most disagreeable session. Sumner had supported Lincoln in the election; but now Sumner feared Seward's ascendancy over the new President. Sumner wanted Lincoln to abolish slavery in the seceded states. But Lincoln was not about to do that, not with Virginia and Maryland on the verge of secession, and half a dozen border-states, including Kentucky, ready to follow. On the train from Springfield, as Hay observed the large crowds that cheered the President-elect (everywhere except in New York City, where there was a powerful pro-secessionist movement), he had come to think of Lincoln as a beleaguered fortress, with cannons firing at him from every direction; a fortress waiting to be relieved by... But Hay did not know by what. No one knew what was in Lincoln's mind. Particularly not the boisterous young men crowded at the far end of Willard's bar, drinking cocktails at ten cents a glass.

Hay pushed through the swinging doors of the long bar just off the main parlor of the hotel, where ladies sat beneath a gilded dome, drinking tea and casting disapproving—when not envious—looks at the men as they entered and left the bibulous good fellowship of the smoky, long bar.

Hay found the smooth-faced—the boy could but would not grow whiskers—Robert Lincoln, talking to a short, bright-eyed young man who was already beginning to go bald. Robert introduced Hay to the young man, saying, "He graduated from Harvard the same year you graduated from Brown."

"Well, that's a bond, I guess," said Hay, ordering a brandy-smash.

The Harvard graduate was examining Hay curiously. "You're one of Mr. Lincoln's secretaries, aren't you?"

"Yes, sir."

"Everyone says Johnny's too young." Robert smiled shyly; but then he was shy; and a bit solemn. Two years earlier he had been uprooted by his father and sent east to enroll at Harvard. But since he had not been scholastically ready for that great university he had been obliged to spend a year in preparation at the Phillips Exeter Academy in New Hampshire. It was said that Mr. Lincoln wanted the best possible education for his oldest son just as he himself had had the very worst, which is to say practically none at all. After the debate with Douglas and the lost election, Lincoln decided to travel east to see how his son was getting on at Exeter. It was on this trip—coincidentally, hardly any claimed—that Mr. Lincoln was prevailed upon to speak third in a series at New York's Cooper Institute. He did so on February 27, 1860. The liberal editor of the New York *Evening Post*, William Cullen Bryant, chaired the meeting, while the city's most powerful editor, Horace Greeley, sat in the audience. The next day Lincoln was known to the entire nation. With characteristic eloquence, he had accepted the slavery in the South, but he had opposed its extension elsewhere. This pleased a majority of the Republicans, while arousing great suspicion among Douglas's Northern Democrats, not to mention the Democrats of the South. After Lincoln's triumph at the Cooper Institute, he spoke elsewhere in the northeast, and in the course of this triumphal passage, he took the Republican nomination away from the powerful Seward as well as from that passionate anti-slavery man Salmon P. Chase of Ohio. "So if it hadn't been for you, Bob," Lincoln liked to say, "being up there at Exeter, I'd never have been nominated or elected." Robert appeared to believe this. Hay did not. From the beginning of his close association with Lincoln—less than a year but it seemed like a lifetime—he had been delightedly conscious of the Tycoon's endless cunning. There was nothing that Lincoln ever left to chance if he could help it. He was a master of guiding public opinion either directly through a set speech to a living audience or, indirectly, through an uncanny sense of how to use the press to his own ends. He was also the first politician to understand the importance and the influence of photography; no photographer was ever sent away unsatisfied. He had even grown a beard in order to soften his somewhat harsh features; and to make himself, at least in appearance, the nation's true Father Abraham. It was thus with characteristic forethought he had sent his son to New England to school so that with no other apparent end than ordinary paternal care, he might, when the time came, go east—and seize the crown.

"Hey, Johnny! Hasheesh Johnny Hay!" Hay turned and recognized the face but not the name of a fraternity brother from Brown. They made the fraternal handclasp of Theta Delta Chi. Since the young man was drunk, Hay pulled him to one side, out of range of Robert Lincoln, who was very much enjoying his anonymity, soon to end when the newspapers got through illustrating, one by one, the entire Lincoln family. Hay also did not want anyone to learn his college nickname.

"What're you doing in town?"

Hay recalled that the brother was Southern; was glad that the brother did not know of his appointment. "Oh, I'm just here for the inaugural." Hay was casual.

"If there is one!" The drunken youth scowled as darkly as such a foolish face could. "Me, I'm going home to Charleston to fight, if we have to. I guess you're for the Yankees, aren't you?"

"I guess so," said Hay.

"Well . . ." Words did not come easily to the soon-to-be-rebel. But a sheet of paper did materialize in his hand. "I take the boat in the morning. But as we're brothers, I leave you this. My richest legacy."

Hay looked at a neatly printed list of names and addresses; some were curiously cryptic, like The Haystack—his eye caught that at once—or The Blue Goose, The Devil's Own . . . After each name or title there was a number. "They've been numbered from one—which is the best—to five, which is pretty bad. Three of the brothers put this list together. Took more than a month to do. Now they've all gone South. Anyway, you can give copies of it to anybody you like, I guess. But they did say they'd prefer that only the Delts got the real good of it. 'Bye, Johnny."

It took Hay several days to figure out that he had been given what turned out to be a meticulously graded list of Washington's whorehouses. He was eternally grateful to the brother: at twenty-two, there was no finer gift one Theta Delt could have given another. A similar list had existed in the fraternity house at Providence and Hay had used it, from time to time, to while away what he liked to call "idle hours." One of the fraternity's most legendary idle hours occurred when Hay decided to imitate his idol Edgar Allan Poe. Although he could find no opium to eat, he did come across some hasheesh, which he and the brothers had smoked, with results still recalled in Providence as an idle hour that had expanded to what seemed to the smokers to be an idle eternity. Ever after, he was Hasheesh Johnny Hay.

Hay rejoined Robert and the bald young man, who turned out to be Henry, the son of Charles Francis Adams of Massachusetts, a Lincoln supporter. "I saw our senator on his way upstairs," said Henry. "I assumed he was on his way to Mr. Lincoln."

Hay nodded. "I left them together. I think Mr. Sumner was about to make a speech."

Henry sighed. "He is like a madman nowadays . . ."

"Well, he was knocked on the head with a stick, wasn't he? By that crazy Southerner?" Robert started to order another drink but Hay made a warning gesture; and Robert desisted. There were times when Hay had the sense that he had been hired not as a secretary to the President but as an elder brother to the boys.

"Oh, Mr. Sumner's recovered. Pretty much, anyway. But he seems to have conversed with God altogether too much during those three years that he was an invalid. When he came back to the Senate, he announced, 'I am in morals, not politics.'"

"That *is* chilling," said Hay.

"Much my own view," said Henry; and smiled for the first time. "I should think that the two are probably antithetical. My father disagrees, of course. I'm *his* secretary, by the way. He's in the Congress, you know."

"I know. I know. Mr. Lincoln thinks very highly of Mr. Adams."

"That's right," said Robert. "Fact, he said, maybe he was going to—"

"Robert!" Hay spoke warningly.

"All right, Johnny."

"Mr. Robert Lincoln . . ." Hay began.

"The Prince of Rails, as the press calls him. Oh, they'll enjoy *that* at Harvard," said Henry, whose smile, at best, was thin indeed.

"I'll never hear the end of it." Robert was glum. "At least they couldn't get me to make a speech on the back of the cars. I don't know how Father does it."

Henry turned to Robert. "I know my father's being considered for minister to England. Personally, I'd rather he stayed here."

"And miss out on London?" Hay betrayed his own youthful interest. For Hay, London was literature—Dickens, Thackeray and whoever wrote *Adam Bede*, and history. Washington was just old-shoe politics.

"I'd rather miss out on London than on Lincoln," said Henry.

"Why?" Hay was truly curious.

"Well, if he should fail, there will no longer be a country. And since my family believes that we invented the whole thing, I'd certainly like to see what becomes of the remains."

"I don't think he'll fail," said Hay, who thought that he would; as much as he prayed that somehow Lincoln might yet hold together what was now falling apart with such awful speed.

"In that case, if he succeeds, it will be even more interesting."

"How? It will be just as it was before."

"No, it won't. It can't be."

"What *will* it be?"

"No one knows. That's the excitement."

5

AT EXACTLY NINE O'CLOCK THAT SAME EVENING, SALMON P. Chase, late governor of Ohio and senator-elect, stood outside Parlor Suite Six with the delegation from the Peace Conference. Chase had not seen Lincoln since shortly after the election, when the President-elect summoned him to Springfield. Lincoln then beat a number of times about the bush before he offered Chase— or, perhaps did *not* offer Chase—a post in the Cabinet.

They were walking down the street that passed in front of Lincoln's comfortable mansion—so unlike, thought Chase sourly, the legendary log cabin of Lincoln's birth, which had been advertised from one end of the union to the other. Lincoln was courteous but tentative; and Chase, who had never thought him strong, came away convinced that the President-to-be was dangerously weak. "I look for a balanced Cabinet, naturally," he said, automatically raising his tall hat to a passing lady. It was then that Chase noticed that Lincoln kept an elaborate file of papers *inside* the hat. At least the man was every bit as common as he presented himself; the mediocrity was honest. On the other hand, Chase was less certain about Lincoln's views. Essentially, he had thought him an opportunist. Yet it was Lincoln who had prevailed at the convention and it was the governor of Ohio who was meekly following the tall man down the street. "Mr. Seward, who got the second most votes at the convention, is plainly the party's own choice for Secretary of State."

"Has he accepted?"

"Yes." Lincoln did not elaborate. "You, sir, got the third most votes."

Chase had stopped breathing with excitement: the offer of the Treasury was near at hand. But Lincoln veered off. "Then there was Bates of Missouri and Cameron of Pennsylvania."

"Sir, Mr. Simon Cameron is corrupt."

"I have been told that." Lincoln sounded grim.

"Of course, he controls Pennsylvania." Chase had needled Lincoln.

"But *I* am Honest Abe," Lincoln replied, with what Chase took to be a weak smile. Then he changed the subject. "I want a

37

Southerner in the Cabinet. A real Southerner. Preferably a Virginian. Seward is canvassing for me now."

"Any luck?"

Lincoln stopped then. He had looked down at Chase—a stout, clean-shaven man with a nearly bald Roman bust of a head. "Sir, let me make you a curious proposal. I would like you to be Secretary of the Treasury but I cannot offer you the post just yet."

Chase contained his indignation. He had had, thus far, a splendid career and had he been more expedient and less moral, he, not Lincoln, would have been the Republican candidate. But if you cannot get cream, settle for milk, had always been his practical wisdom. But now Lincoln was suggesting that even the despised saucer of milk might not come his way. Since Chase did not betray his chagrin, the two men had parted on friendly terms. Fortunately, the complaisant Ohio legislature was more than willing to appoint Salmon P. Chase to the United States Senate, so at least he would hold some office in this distintegrating republic.

Now Chase stood at Lincoln's door as the delegates from the Peace Conference fell into place behind him. The Southerners were particularly keen to see the demon. As the clock in the lobby below struck nine, Nicolay opened the door, bowed to Chase, and motioned for the delegation to file into the parlor where Lincoln, quite alone, stood in front of the fireplace.

"Mr. Chase!" Lincoln's handclasp was warmer than his voice, thought Chase, unable to interpret the auguries in question. He had already heard that Cameron was to have not the Treasury but the War Department; and Lincoln was supposed to be having second thoughts about that. The Treasury—after the presidency—was what Chase most wanted. Bates of Missouri was not suitable; and no Southerner would serve. The Maryland Blairs, mad father and two mad sons, were also at work trying to capture Lincoln, but though Chase was convinced that Lincoln was weak, he was equally convinced that he was extremely wily. Chase had not yet heard any particulars of the Albany Plan. If he had, he would have been in despair. Chase truly feared Seward and his mentor Thurlow Weed.

Chase handed Lincoln a letter from the head of the Peace Conference, former President Tyler. "He sends his compliments, sir. He hopes to call on you at another time."

"I shall call on *him*, of course." Lincoln's courtesy was perfunctory. He turned to the semicircle of delegates, who stared at him as if he were some sort of rare beast. "Gentlemen, I know some of you personally from the past. I know all of you by name and repute. I am glad that this conference continues, and I will do what I can to give assurance and reassurance to the Southern states that we mean them no harm. It is true that I was elected to prevent the extension of slavery to the new territories of the Union. But what is now the status quo in the Southern states is beyond my power—or desire—ever to alter."

Although it had been plain to Chase that Lincoln was not the man to lead any sort of crusade against slavery, Lincoln, aided by a powerful Cabinet ... As Seward dreamed that he would be Lincoln's prime minister, Chase saw himself as chancellor, on the order, say, of the Austrian Metternich.

A Southern congressman challenged Lincoln. "Will *you* uphold the laws, where previous presidents did not? Will you suppress the likes of Mr. John Brown and the Reverend Garrison, who preach war against us and our property?"

"Well, we hanged Mr. Brown, and we put Garrison in prison." Lincoln was mild. "That strikes me as a reasonable amount of suppression."

"But the laws of property," the voice continued.

Chase shut his eyes; he could not wait for his daughter Kate to arrive tomorrow evening. Thrice a widower at fifty-three, Salmon P. Chase's whole life was now his twenty-year-old daughter; a thirteen-year-old daughter, Nettie, had not yet had the time to lay any great claim to his powerful paternal affections. But the beautiful and gifted Kate had acted as his hostess when he was governor of Ohio, and she would do the same in Washington. To please Kate, he had just rented a large, expensive town house even though he was, as always, in debt. Like his friend Sumner, Chase dealt not in politics but morals. But morals paid poorly. Chase could not remember a time when he had not been as anxious about money as he had been serene about moral issues.

Lincoln's voice suddenly recalled Chase from his reverie. The President-elect was answering one of the Southerners. "Look, there is only one difference between us. You think slavery is right and ought to be extended. We think it is wrong and ought to be restricted. For this, neither has any just cause to be angry with the other."

If that was not sufficient honey for the bearish South, what was? wondered Chase.

"Then explain, sir," ordered another Southern voice, "why is it that since your election, six states—"

"Seven!" from a dozen voices.

"—seven states, counting Texas, officially, today, have left the Union?"

"That's more for them to explain to me than for me to explain to them." Lincoln was surprisingly cool under the circumstances. But then he was supposed to be a practised lawyer. Curious,

39

thought Chase, how little anyone really knew about this new President.

"But I should like to remind you that *before* my election to the Presidency, the governor of South Carolina announced that that state would secede if I were elected. And so they did. And others have followed, as you remind me. Currently, those elements in rebellion against the Federal government"—Chase liked the use of the word "elements" instead of states; the distinction was sufficiently nice to make it possible for second thoughts all round, not that there would be any—"have seized—stolen, to use the precise word . . ." Lincoln looked in Chase's direction. For an eerie instant, Chase wondered if his mind was being looked into and read. But the look was casual. Whenever Lincoln spoke, he was always careful to look at every part of his audience. First the dreamy gray eyes would glance to one side; and then, as if he had discovered someone of interest to him, the whole head would slowly turn and follow his gaze. ". . . stolen, I repeat, three revenue cutters, four custom's houses, three mints, six arsenals and their contents, and one entire naval yard. All of these are the property of the whole people of the United States and not of any single element of the population."

Voices were raised. Would the Federal government consider selling the "stolen" property? Lincoln thought it a better idea to return what had been stolen; and to forget about the whole thing. He is leaving them every possible escape route, thought Chase, who inclined to the divine view that evil must be punished. An eye for an eye was his religion.

When asked about Fort Sumter at the entrance of Charleston Harbor, Lincoln commended the courage of its commander, Major Anderson. No, he had prepared no instructions for the major because "I have not yet taken the oath of office. I will say how . . . impressed I was last month, as was everyone, when General Scott sent a merchant steamer with reinforcements for Fort Sumter and the governor of South Carolina was able to turn back that ship."

Would Lincoln try to reinforce Fort Sumter? He would not answer. Meanwhile, he took seriously Virginia's effort to make peace between the regions of the country. He was in communication with the pro-Union elements in both Virginia and Maryland, whose governor was a Union man. No, he had not read the speech that Jefferson Davis had delivered when he became President of the Confederate States of America five days ago. "But I just read a newspaper account of my old friend and colleague in Congress Mr. Alexander Stephens of Georgia."

"You mean *Vice-President* Stephens?" asked a challenging voice.

Lincoln affected not to hear. "Mr. Stephens admitted that Thomas Jefferson, a founder of the Union, thought that the principle of slavery was wrong. But Mr. Stephens said that the elements that he adheres to have come to the conclusion that the exact opposite is true, that the correct principle is that since the black man is inferior to the white man, he must be the white man's slave. I mean no disrespect to my old friend when I say that between his brand-new and to me highly peculiar principle and the old-fashioned principle of Thomas Jefferson of Virginia, I must support my predecessor in the office of President of the *United States*."

Which way will he go? wondered Chase, as the delegates filed past the tall man, who had a word for each. To Chase, he said, "I look forward to a continuation of our Springfield conversation."

Several imprudent answers occurred, as always, to Chase and, as always, were replaced with that habitual prudence for which he was never entirely not admired. "So do I, sir. The Virginians—" Chase lowered his voice, as several were nearby, and Lincoln lowered his head, the better to hear him. Chase noticed that Lincoln's thick, coarse hair was as black as an Indian's, with no sign of gray. "They will stay in the Union if you let Fort Sumter alone."

"One state for one fort?" Lincoln smiled. "I think that's a pretty good deal for the fort-owner."

"Yes, sir." Chase moved on. He had got the answer that he had feared, but expected. Lincoln would give in to the South, after a certain amount of calculated bluster.

Mary was awake in bed when Lincoln joined her. The last of the peace delegation had gone, as he put it to her, "in a state of belligerency."

"Come to bed. You look so tired."

"*You* must be tired, Molly." Lincoln began to undress.

"I thought I was. Then I got into bed, and tried to sleep, and couldn't. Too tired to sleep. Too excited, I guess."

Lincoln turned off the gaslight overhead. The lamp beside the four-poster bed cast a blue-and-white glare across Mary's face.

"What did you think of the Old Club House?" asked Lincoln, pulling on a nightshirt that was too short for him; but then all store-bought nightshirts were too short for him. Mary wanted to have some made to order; or she herself would make them to order. But Lincoln was perfectly content to wander about with long legs bare—just like a stork, she'd say, in disapproval.

"The Old Club House? Oh, Governor Seward's Old Club House. An appropriate name."

"Well. It *was* a real clubhouse till recently." Lincoln stared at his beard in the glass; idly, he parted it.

41

"I know. That's where they brought poor Mr. Key to die, after he was shot. I could never trust that man. Never!"

"The late Mr. Key? Or his murderer Mr. Sickles?" Lincoln removed the part from his beard.

"Governor Seward, Father. You know what I think of him."

"Well, I noticed you did quite well by his dinner."

"Oh, the food was splendid! I do have a sufficiency of flesh, don't I." Glumly, Mary squeezed her right upper arm and watched, with sorrow, as the resulting bulge stretched taut the white lace of her nightdress.

"Well, you look in your sufficiency sufficiently beautiful to me."

"Oh, Father, you'd say that if I looked like . . . like General Scott."

"Of course, I would *say* that. But I would not mean it." Lincoln stepped into the adjoining bathroom, where the commode was. Mary had remarked on Willard's comfort and modernity. No chamber pot was necessary in any of the parlor suites. Would the White House be the same?

"Father," she called, "do I nag you about appointments?"

"Yes," came the voice from the bathroom.

"Oh, I don't! It's the vampire press that says I do because I'm Southern and supposed to believe in slavery when *I'm* the only abolitionist in the family and you are just—mild and meek."

Lincoln returned, drying his face with a towel decorated with the W of Willard's. "I suppose any man named Watson or Wilcox would feel justified in stealing one of these towels," he said.

"Or Washington. Did you give Governor Seward your speech to read?"

Lincoln nodded. "He said he'd make notes."

"Don't listen to him."

"I *listen* to everyone. I like him, all in all."

"He thinks he's so clever."

"Well, he has every right to think that. He *is* clever. Though not clever enough to get rid of Simon Cameron for me."

"I thought you'd decided to keep Cameron out of the Cabinet."

"I did. Then I was un-decided. Anyway, I kept him out of the Treasury." Lincoln got under the covers. "He'll be at the War Department."

"Then I suggest you avoid fighting a war."

"I mean to, Molly."

"Who'll be at the Treasury?"

"Salmon P. Chase."

"That crazed abolitionist! He wants to be president."

"They all do. That's why I'm putting the whole lot where I can see them. In the Cabinet," Lincoln sighed.

"I suppose you're right, Father. You usually are. Eventually, anyway. Oh, Cousin Lizzie is going to stay on for the first few weeks we're in the President's House. She's wonderful with upholsterers and all that sort of thing. They say the mansion has been let go to rack and ruin. Just like this country, I said, which I hope the vampire press does *not* pick up, true though it is. Mr. Buchanan has been a disaster and, thank God, it's you who'll take his place and not Judge Douglas, brilliant as he is. Strange how I might have married him! You know, everyone thought I should. Even *I* thought I *should* but then I met you at the dance at our house, and you came up to me and you said, by way of introduction, that you wanted to dance with me, 'in the worst way,' you said, your very words, and so you did dance with me, and I told everyone, it was truly in the worst way! Oh, Father!" Mary smiled at the memory, and turned to her husband only to find him sound asleep on his back. From force of habit she touched his brow—she touched all the brows of those close to her, to detect signs of the fever that had killed her three-year-old Eddie; but Lincoln's face was cool to the touch. Suddenly, he took a deep breath and then, as he exhaled, he moaned.

"Poor man," she said to her sleeping husband; and wondered if his dreams were now as terrifying as hers had been, unknown to him, for so many years.

6

THE NEXT MORNING, GRIP-SACK IN HAND, GOVERNOR SEWARD arrived at Willard's Hotel, fought his way through the crowded lobby and up crowded stairs and then down the crowded corridor to Parlor Six, where Lamon admitted him to a room crowded with two small boys playing tag while Lincoln sat beside the window, glasses on his nose, reading the newspapers.

"I see your admirers are filling up the hotel." Seward gave Lincoln the grip-sack.

"I had never realized how many men are eager to serve their country in high-paid positions that are within my gift." Lincoln took the grip-sack, plainly relieved to have it once more in his hand.

"How do you deal with them?"

"My two secretaries, poor boys, are interviewing the lot. Everyone who wants an appointment from me goes to them in Parlor One and leaves his credentials. Speaking of credentials, what do you think of mine?" Lincoln tapped the grip-sack. Willie tapped Tad on the head. Tad screamed. Lincoln turned to Lamon. "Take the boys to their mother." Despite loud cries of defiance, the huge Lamon carried both boys from the room.

"Well, sir, it is a finely argued case." Seward took his time lighting a cigar. He was still not certain that he understood either the speech or its author.

"It is no more than a legal case?" Lincoln showed an author's dejection, which amused Seward.

"Of course it is more. You have made the point, once and for all, that you were not elected president in order to abolish slavery in the South..."

"I cannot say that enough, can I? But the more I do say it, the more violent the Southerners become."

"They think, in time, we intend to do away with slavery and so they mean to do away with us first—by leaving the Union."

"Which they cannot do. I am clear on that, am I not?" Seward nodded; and removed from his tailcoat pocket the notes he had made on the inaugural address. "I take this passage to be the centerpiece of your... brief." Seward smiled; Lincoln did not.

Seward read, "'I hold, that in contemplation of universal law, and of the Constitution, the Union of these States is perpetual. Perpetuity is implied, if not expressed, in the fundamental law of all national governments. It is safe to assert that no government proper, ever had a provision in its organic law for its own termination.'"

"Yes, that is at the heart of my 'brief.'"

"But the Southern states regard the organization of the Union as a more casual affair. As they entered it of their own free will, so they can leave it."

"But no provision was ever made in the Constitution for their leaving it."

"They say that this right is implicit."

"Nothing so astounding and fundamental would *not* be spelled out in the Constitution." Lincoln's voice grew slightly higher. Seward had read somewhere that when Lincoln made a speech his voice was like a tenor trumpet—a tenor trumpet of war, Seward thought, suddenly aware, for the first time, that war had now become a possibility and that the traditional uses to which his sort of man was put—in particular, the task of conciliation and accommodation—would be of no avail. So many people had spoken

44

for so long of the irrepressibility of conflict, to use his own phrase, that the fact that conflict might now be at hand made the cigar clenched between his teeth lose its savor. Worse, the whole matter might well be decided by the tall, thin figure sitting opposite him, profile silhouetted by winter light. At all costs, the Albany Plan must succeed.

Seward was beginning to get Lincoln's gauge; and he was afraid. He looked back down at his notes. "Your reasoning is good." Then he read, "'If a minority . . . will secede rather than submit, they make a precedent which, in turn, will divide and ruin them; for a minority of their own number will secede from them whenever a majority refuses to be controlled by such minority.' That is plain."

"It is *all* so plain, Mr. Seward. That is the hard part. But I do my best to spell it out when I say, physically speaking, we cannot separate. It's not like a husband and wife getting a divorce and dividing up the property."

Seward nodded; and read, "'Suppose you go to war, you cannot fight always; and when, after much loss on both sides, and no gain on either, you cease fighting, the identical old questions as to terms of intercourse are again upon you.' That says it all, I guess."

"But to say is not to do."

"To say what is true is to do a lot in politics." Seward laughed; for some reason, the mood of panic had gone. "Not that I've had much experience along those lines."

Lincoln, to his relief, laughed too. "Who has?"

"I am afraid of your ending," said Seward, coming to the point. "Too harsh?"

Seward nodded, and read, "'In your hands, my dissatisfied fellow-countrymen, and not in mine, is the momentous issue of civil war. The government will not assail you.'" Seward looked up. "Let them fire the first shot, if shots are to be fired, which I pray not." Seward continued to read. "'You can have no conflict, without being yourselves the aggressors. *You* have no oath registered in heaven to destroy the government, while *I* shall have the most solemn one to "preserve, protect and defend" it. With *you* and not with *me*, is the solemn question of "Shall it be peace, or a sword?"'"

"That is the case. That is *my* case."

Seward inhaled the cigar smoke deeply, comfortably. "Never end a speech with a question."

Lincoln smiled. "For fear you'll get the wrong answer?"

Seward nodded. "People are perverse. I would cut all that I

have just read. It is too menacing. I've written a paragraph to take its place. It's inside the case."

Lincoln opened the case, withdrew the speech which he had had, in greatest secrecy, set up in type by a printer so that there would be exact copies for the wire-services as opposed to the usual garbled reporters' or recorders' shorthand notes; or confusion over his own not-always-clear calligraphy. Lincoln read to himself Seward's flowery coda. He nodded. "I can use some of this. If you don't mind my turning it into my own words."

"It's yours, sir. You'll cut the other?"

"I can't cut the part about the oath that I have sworn to uphold the Constitution. That is what gives me—and the Union—our legitimacy in the eyes of heaven."

"I did not think of you as a religious man, Mr. Lincoln."

"I am not, in any usual sense. But I believe in fate—and necessity. I believe in this Union. That is *my* fate, I suppose. And my necessity."

"You are a man of sentiment," said Seward. "I had not known that." Seward rose. "Since there has always been a rumor that you were not a proper Christian and churchgoer—"

"Founded, I'm afraid, on my *im*propriety and chronic absence from church."

"I, as an important layman of the Episcopal church, am going to take you over to St. John's, where the minister and congregation will be able to see that you are at peace with Our Lord Jesus Christ, and they will then spread the good news."

Lincoln laughed, and got to his feet. Then he noticed the pile of newspapers beside his chair. He frowned. "Did you see the *New York Times?*"

On principle, Seward said that he had not, while doing his best to anticipate Lincoln's response. "Sir," Seward began, "there was no doubt about the plot in Baltimore..."

"If there had been a plot, why was no attempt made on the cars that I was supposed to be in?"

"Because everyone in Baltimore knew by then that you had already gone through the city."

"No, I've made an error that I'll never live down. According to the *Times* I arrived in the city wearing a Scotsman's plaid hat and a cloak. What sort of idle malice invents such a thing?"

"It is the nature of newspapers. I suppose the writer wanted to make the cartoonist's job easier."

"He has. I'll be shown with that hat and cloak from one end of the country to the other. Such lies go out all the time," said Lincoln darkly, "on the telegraph."

"It is a hazard of our estate, sir. Will Mrs. Lincoln join us?"

"No, she's going off with her cousins to see the sights, which is ironic, since she is the churchgoer of the family."

"Then she need *not* go to St. John's, as her soul is saved."

So, together, Seward and Lincoln, guarded by the watchful Lamon, made their way across Lafayette Square, where David Herold stood in the crowd that had gathered—the minister had already spread the word that the President-elect would attend the morning service. David watched the tall man as he walked slowly by, lifting his hat to the people who greeted him. David thought that the old man looked surprisingly pleasant and friendly. In a way, it was a shame that he was going to be shot just before he took his oath of office, by two of the wild boys who, even now, were at target practice across the river in Alexandria, Virginia.

7

At the corner of Sixth and E streets, senator-elect and would-be president Salmon P. Chase had rented an elegant three-story brick mansion for fifteen hundred dollars a year. In addition to this high, even for Washington, rent, he was obliged to pay for servants, Kate's wardrobe, his younger daughter Nettie's school . . . Chase still owed money to Miss Haines's expensive school in New York City, where Kate had been so superbly finished five years earlier.

Like Marius in the ruins of Carthage, Chase thought, without any precise historical analogy in mind, as he stood in front of the marble fireplace and looked up at the spot where the painting of Kate's mother would hang, once the boxes, trunks and crates had been opened and unpacked. Everything that he had owned in Ohio had been shipped to Washington. One way or another, he thought, he would be here to the end.

The newly hired mulatto manservant appeared in the doorway. "Mr. Cooke and Mr. Cooke to see you, Senator."

"Send them in." Chase pushed two chairs apart. Pulled at the huge horsehair sofa that had looked small in the governor's house in Columbus but tended to overpower "Sixth and E," as he now thought of his new house. Kate was not yet down; she had arrived late Sunday night. She deserved her rest, he thought. She worked hard; and for him.

The Cooke brothers entered the room. Henry D. Cooke had

been editor of the *Ohio State Journal*, a paper Chase had been much involved with. Henry's brother Jay was known to Chase only by reputation; and the reputation was nothing more than that he was a wealthy man, who lived in Philadelphia. Jay Cooke was also said to be a sturdy pillar of the Episcopal church, which made him attractive to Chase, who had been educated in the Ohio school of his uncle, one Philander Chase, an Episcopal bishop of noted piety.

"As you see, we are still in the throes of settling in." Chase wondered why, on a first meeting with someone as eminent as Jay Cooke, he had, so stupidly, used a sentence filled with "s"'s. Chase's lisp—his martyrdom—was only noticeable when he said a word with an "s" in it. Over the years, he had learned to select in advance the words that he planned to use and so was able to avoid the dreaded lisp. He now compensated for his error by suddenly and fiercely narrowing his eyes at the brothers Cooke, as though he were still governor of Ohio and they were suppliants.

Henry seemed not to notice either the lisp, to which he was used, or the eyes, to which he was also used; but then everyone knew that Chase was myopic in the extreme; he could never find a pair of glasses to suit him. Hence, the glare, as he tried to decipher through an aqueous haze faces that came in and out of focus in a most disturbing way. But Chase was now able—and pleased—to note Jay Cooke's respectful look. "Take a chair," said Chase, careful not to add the dangerous word "please."

Henry was in town for the Inauguration. Jay was just passing through, and wanted to pay his respects to the senator-elect. They wanted to know about Lincoln. What sort of man was he? Chase was cautious. "I saw him last night. A delegation from the Peace Conference called on him. I would not say he was the strong—" But Chase quickly canceled, as it were, the word "strong," having just managed to get away with the "s" in "say," and substituted for "the strong," "—the *formidable* leader that we need. But then who is?"

"Well, there's you for one, Governor," said Henry D., idly picking dried mud off his shoe. Chase was glad that Kate was not in the room. She was never afraid to express herself precisely in few but well-chosen words. Miss Haines had indeed finished her to a T. With others, Kate was now very like what Chase thought an English duchess might be like. But with him, she was the perfect daughter, councillor and, yes, mate in a way that the three wives had never been. Always have daughters, never have wives; he had once shocked a Columbus drawing room with this heresy. But he had meant it.

Jay Cooke offered Chase a cigar of such quality that he could not refuse it. "There is talk in the financial community that you, sir, are to be Secretary of the Treasury."

"I have heard the same talk," said Chase; and no more.

"I can think of no one better suited than yourself." Jay Cooke lit a cigar. "And I am very close to Mr. Cameron—we're neighbors, in fact. But when he said how disappointed he was that he was getting the War Department and not the Treasury, I said, 'Count your blessings, Simon; you're a natural organizer but the man with the proven talent for finance is Mr. Chase.' He agreed."

"Did he?" Chase did not believe any of this story. But he realized that Jay Cooke wanted him to know of his friendship with Cameron, a disreputable figure, perhaps, but a great power in Pennsylvania. Chase nodded, wisely. From the dining room, there was the sound of a plate smashing to the floor. Chase winced, not only at the loss of a plate but at the reminder that he must buy an entire new dinner service. That would cost at least four hundred dollars, which he could delay paying, of course: newly arrived senators were treated with lenience by the Washington stores, but when four hundred dollars was added to the cost of a new carriage . . . Suddenly, he was aware that he had been asked a question, which he had not heard. "I'm sorry." He narrowed his eyes, to show that although he was politely attentive, as always, to his guests, matters of state could never be entirely excluded from his mind.

"I asked"—the bland Henry D. had now arranged a small neat pile of dried mud beside the chair leg—"if Mr. Lincoln had said anything about the Treasury to you yesterday."

"Oh, he brings up the subject. But that's all." Chase hummed an old hymn to himself; he was aware of the habit, though not always aware when he was humming. According to Kate, he was never, even accidentally, in the right key.

"There is no one else, is there?" For a moment Jay Cooke looked as if he might have paid a call on the wrong person.

"There are the Blairs," said Chase, without fondness. Francis Preston Blair was a rich and famous old man who had been close to Andrew Jackson; he lived in state at Silver Spring, Maryland; he also had two grown sons as ambitious as he. The young Blairs were set on capturing the second western president just as their father had captured, more or less, Jackson, the first western president. Although the Old Gentleman, as Blair was known, did not have the power that he once had when he edited the *Congressional Globe*, he was nevertheless a founder of the Republican Party and together with his son Frank, a congressman from Missouri, and his son Montgomery, a powerful lawyer in Maryland, they had got the border-states to swing their votes to Lincoln on the third ballot at the Republican convention in Chicago. Consequently, candidate Chase had no love for the family that had nominated Lincoln over him. Chase also took the high moral line that no man from a slave-holding state (which included Maryland and Missouri) should serve in a Republican cabinet. But Lincoln wanted balance; wanted, also, to please the Old Gentleman, one of the few friends that he had in Washington; or anywhere, for that matter. Although Chase tended to think of Lincoln as the gregarious story-telling westerner, surrounded by hard-drinking tobacco-chewing cronies, he had already observed, with some surprise, that Lincoln had no cronies at all. The Lamons and the Washburnes, who knew him best, treated him not only with deference but with awe. Chase had noted this at Springfield. Of course Lincoln told his funny stories ad nauseam, but they were calculated, Chase had decided, to hold people's attention whilst keeping them at a distance. Salmon P. Chase, himself so often accused of coldness, found the President-elect, for all his folksy charm, as cold and dense as the Ohio River in February.

"I'm told it's Montgomery Blair who'll be appointed," said Jay Cooke. "But not to the Treasury."

"Attorney-General?" asked Henry.

"Maybe." Jay Cooke was looking at Chase so speculatively that the statesman was almost on the verge of saying what he had already begun to say to his allies: "I prefer my place in the Senate to any Cabinet office," when Kate's entrance put an end to what, considering Jay Cooke's wealth, might have been a tactical error.

"Gentlemen!" The three men rose, in admiration as well as in duty. Kate's hair was dark gold—the color of comb-honey, Chase had once said, in a poetical mood, to which she had replied, "Now I feel sticky!" The eyes were glittering hazel with long fair lashes; the nose upturned; the figure perfect. In one hand she carried a chess set. Kate shook hands with each Cooke; kissed her father. "I found the chess set in my trunk. I thought it was lost. Now we can play."

"You play chess, Miss Chase?" Jay Cooke was highly impressed—or chose to give that impression.

"Why, yes. I've tried to learn to crochet. But that's really man's work, so I gave it up. I'm happier with chess. And gambling, too."

"A young lady after my own heart." Yes, thought Chase, both jealously and delightedly, Jay Cooke was impressed with Kate. Chase dearly wanted her to make a great marriage; and then never leave him. How this was to be done was a challenge to even his ingenious mind.

Kate motioned at the furniture, set haphazardly about the room. "I've only just arrived. There's been no time to unpack. We're camping out."

"Well, I hope that when you come through Philadelphia next,

you'll visit us—my wife and I," added Jay Cooke. "We have a pleasant house outside the town. It's called The Cedars..."

"House!" said Henry. "My brother lives like the Czar!"

"No, there's only one Czar in Pennsylvania and that's Simon Cameron. I'm just a two-bit baron."

"I *will* be visiting New York in the next few weeks and I'd very much enjoy seeing Mrs. Cooke and the... baronial Cedars. I've a week of shopping to do for this house, where nothing from Ohio seems to fit. Look at that sofa!" They looked; and collectively mourned its enormity. "I'll also have to get a proper carriage..."

"Enclosed, yes," said Chase, adding the cost of the carriage onto everything else. Desperately, he began to breathe rather than hum "Bringing in the Sheaves."

"Poor Father!" Kate kissed him on top of his bald head. "We'll pay, somehow. I'll try to find a rich man to marry while I'm in New York..."

"Or Philadelphia. We have a very nice selection," said Jay Cooke, slightly red in the face. "Mrs. Cooke will send you lists with pedigrees."

"Then all our problems will be solved."

"I'd rather live in a hut," said Chase, entirely leaving the last of the sheaves.

The brothers Cooke rose to go. Hopes were high all round. The appointment to the Treasury seemed inevitable. "When you are at the Treasury, sir, call on me at any time," said Jay Cooke. "The government will need money from the financial community; and men to help out. I'll gladly—"

"Give us lists?" asked Kate. "Pedigrees?"

"What else, Miss Chase?"

Chase led the brothers to the front door while Kate remained in the drawing room, rearranging furniture.

"I'll let you out myself," said Chase, in a low voice. Since Kate's finishing school, he had been forbidden ever to show anyone to the door—a servant's function, she had warned him. Chase opened the door: a cold wind filled the vestibule.

Jay Cooke shook Chase's hand with every sign of warmth. "You know, if you're in the market for a carriage, I've got one that you might like."

"Ah, I'm afraid that what you would have and what I could afford would never coincide."

"Take it, sir. As a gift."

"Oh, no. No. Thank you, no." Chase was too experienced a politician not to recognize what was being offered. Without probity, he was nothing. With probity, he was poor, true; but he was also a president-to-be. The brothers departed. Chase returned to

51

the drawing room. Kate was propping a portrait of her mother against a console.

"What a pity that she is not here, to see you grown and to see me..."

But Kate would not let him indulge in any regret, no matter how stylized. "She would only have come between us, Father. You know that."

Chase was not prepared for Kate's sharpness, much less candor. "Oh, Kate! She was not like that at all."

"She was a woman," said Kate flatly. "And I do not like or trust the sex."

"There are exceptions, always." Chase kissed Kate's hand; was rewarded with a smile.

"I suppose I'm not fair," she said, making up for her assault. "I don't really remember her. I do remember how she'd sit with knitting needles in her hand; but would never knit."

"Her health was bad." How often, thought Chase, had he been obliged to say that phrase. For twenty years he had lived with ill health and death. He had attended the funerals of three of his wives and four of his children. Now all he wanted was Kate; and all that she wanted was to be with her father as they made their way to the great tree's top. "The Cookes think that I'll be appointed. But I don't."

"Oh, he has to appoint you!" Kate put down her mother's portrait with a bang. "Everyone else—all the other rivals—are in. Why not you?"

"The Senate is not the worst of places—"

"But the Treasury is the center. You will have hundreds of appointments to make, more than any other Cabinet minister. There are Treasury men in every city, town and village and every last one of them will be for Chase for President in 1864."

"You do look ahead!" Chase was startled that Kate knew so much about the powers of patronage that went with the Treasury. Of course, he himself could think of nothing else. It would be his privilege to build a national organization for himself while administering with perfect honesty the country's finances.

"I've also looked ahead to *my* job, when you're at the Treasury..."

"If..."

"When! Since Mrs. Seward's an invalid, the wife or hostess of the next in line after the Secretary of State, which is you, will be First Lady of the Cabinet, and that's me!"

"Suppose Mr. Seward unearths an aged sister, and brings her to town?"

"Mr. Seward is like a contented bachelor, living in that old Club House of his. He wants cigars, brandy and cronies."

"You've been in the town one day, and you know more than I."

"One of us must keep up with all the trivia, and I am the one. Now I'm off to Woodward's Hardware Store in Pennsylvania Avenue, then to Gautier's, then to Harper and Mitchell—but I'll only *look* at clothes as we're too poor for the moment—and then on to Jardin's to see about a regular supply of flowers..."

"*You* take the Treasury. It is plain that you can run it. And it's also plain that you'll need its entire contents."

Kate laughed. "I'm not that bad a manager. We'll scrape by. You'll be getting eight thousand dollars a year..."

"*If* appointed."

"I've worked out a budget. Don't worry." Kate frowned. "You know, you could get Mr. Cooke to *lend* you that carriage."

"A loan is equal to a gift."

"No, it is not. The property is not yours."

"But there would be the *appearance* of impropriety."

"Only if you do favors for him. And since he is one of the richest men in Philadelphia—"

"How do you know that?"

"In Columbus, I used to talk to Henry Cooke about *non*political matters, too. I also heard about Mr. Cooke when I was at Miss Haines's. We had quite a few girls from Philadelphia there. Anyway, I shall stop off at The Cedars on my way back from New York City. No matter what, we'll need him for the next election."

Chase had dreamed, always, of having a son in whom he might confide, to whom he might transmit what knowledge of the world he had acquired. Now he realized that in this remarkable daughter he also had a son but with none of the problems that two masculine wills are apt to produce.

"Have you seen Mrs. Lincoln yet?" The son was now a daughter again; curious to know about a woman she already regarded as a political and social rival.

Chase shook his head. "She was not visible last night."

"I'm told she's brought along one of her Southern half-sisters and a half-dozen cousins, all ladies from Springfield." Kate went for her coat which was hanging in a wardrobe, marooned in the dining room. "I've also been told that the ladies of Washington have refused to call on her."

"She is the wife of the President. Or soon to be. How can they not?"

"They are rebels, that's why."

Chase frowned. "I sometimes think that this is the most rabidly secessionist city in the country, and why we don't turn it over to the South, I don't know."

"And move the Capitol to Columbus?" Kate smiled at him by way of the dusty mirror as she put on her hat.

"Harrisburg, Philadelphia, Trenton, any place but this wilderness."

"I quite like what I've seen of it. Nothing's finished but the landscape is beautiful and, most beautiful of all, is that lovely old house where you and I are going to live one day."

"Do you really think so?" Chase was wistful.

"Yes, I do, Father. That's why I live."

"For the President's House?"

"For President Chase." Then Kate was gone.

Chase crossed to the study, where case after case of books were strewn across the floor. Now that he was alone, he could attack, full voice, "Rock of Ages," which was bound, he was now certain as he unpacked Blackstone's *Commentaries*, to cleave wide for him.

8

THE DAY OF THE INAUGURAL, MARCH 4, DAVID HEROLD WAS awake at dawn. Since this was not a day to be missed, he had slept in all his clothes, including the disintegrating shoes. As he slept on a bunk in a sort of larder off the kitchen, there were no creaking stairs to worry about. He could hear throughout the house the heavy breathing and restive movements of eight women, all flesh of his flesh. Unlike Chase, who was content to have a daughter who was like a son as well, the nineteen-year-old David still longed for a brother to do things with, like ... well, go to the Capitol and watch Old Abe get shot.

The morning was misty; and not cold. The frozen mud had melted, yielding the first crocuses and snowdrops of the season. At the Capitol, a few streets from David's house, there was no crowd as yet; nor any sign of one. But there were troops everywhere. Some were in regulation blue; others were in dark green, with sharpshooter's rifles. They appeared to be searching for ... wild boys? wondered David, happy to be a mere onlooker.

No one tried to stop David as he walked right up to the small wooden platform that had been built on the Capitol's east steps.

The platform had a roof to it; presumably in order to keep anyone from shooting Lincoln from high up. Then David wandered over to the Capitol's north side, where, to his surprise, a pair of long wooden walls had been built between the plaza and the entrance to the Senate chamber. This meant that when Lincoln got out of his carriage, he would be shielded by two walls of planking as he made his way into the Capitol.

David still remembered the last inaugural vividly. He and the wild boys had had a marvelous time, whooping it up, cheering the President, Old Buck, and the beautiful lady got up as the Goddess of Liberty, as she stood on a moving float just in front of Old Buck's carriage while, back of him, there was a second float on which had been placed an entire warship filled with sailors. But today there were no signs of splendor. There were few flags in evidence and none of the red, white and blue bunting that was traditionally used to decorate the speaker's stand on Inaugural Day. On the other hand, he had never seen so many soldiers.

As David made his way up Pennsylvania Avenue to Fifteenth Street, the town was coming awake. The usual Negro population was being added to by the thousands of out-of-towners who had filled up the hotels. Early as it was, a crowd had gathered in front of Brown's Hotel, and as always, Willard's was the center of much activity. David stared up at the windows of Lincoln's suite. The presidential parlor was right over the main door, and an American flag had been attached to the window.

"Hello, David!" David turned and saw the round, cherubic face of Scipione Grillo, a professional musician, who had just opened a restaurant next to one of the town's most popular theaters.

"Hey, Skippy!" This was Mr. Grillo's universal nickname. "What're you doing up so early?"

"I go to the Center Market. I go buy food. We have a full house for every meal today."

"What's at the theater?"

"I don't notice. But whatever's there, we got good audiences." Skippy maintained that he could always tell what a play was like by what its audience drank at his bar. For instance, they drank wine or champagne before and after a good comedy, while good tragedy required champagne before and whiskey after. But if it was an opera, there was little or no drinking because Americans know nothing of music, said Skippy; and that was why he was abandoning music for the food-and-drink business.

David knew every theater manager in the town. As a result, he could almost always get a seat in the gallery for nothing. If he brought Annie Surratt or some other girl, he was expected to pay for the one ticket. If he should have no money left after a performance at Ford's, Skippy would give him a free beer. In payment, David would do odd jobs for Skippy. He also worked for the various theater managements whenever an extra hand was needed to help load or unload scenery. He was besotted with the theater. In fact, had he been taller and his teeth less bucked, he would have been an actor; or, perhaps, a theater manager.

"You going to watch the inaugural parade, Skippy?"

"How can I? I make dinner. Anyway, there's only the two bands. If there was the three, I'd be there. But I play violin tonight at the Union Ball. Mr. Scala needs me, he said. Marine Band's weak in the string section, he says."

"So you'll get to see the whole lot."

"All I look at is the sheet music. Oh, these new dances . . . !"

As Grillo crossed Lafayette Square, David presented himself at Thompson's Drug Store in Pennsylvania Avenue, close to Fifteenth Street. Although the store was not yet open for business, David knew that "William S. Thompson, Proprietor" was already busy at work, filling prescriptions and supervising the black woman who cleaned up.

David opened the door and took a deep breath. If nothing else, he had always liked the smell of drugstores. In the last three years, he had worked first as a delivery boy and then as a prescription clerk for Mr. Thompson. Now he was about to enter, seriously, Mr. Thompson's employ. He was wretched at the thought; but he had no choice.

"'Morning, Mr. Thompson. It's me, Davie." David blinked his eyes in the dim room, where one entire wall was occupied by a sort of wooden wardrobe containing a thousand small drawers while, parallel to the back wall, a highly polished wood counter supported two sets of scales and six huge china vases on whose sides gold Gothic script testified, in Latin, to their contents. David had picked up enough Latin in his last year at school to read a doctor's prescription; it was about the only thing that he had ever learned that had proved of the slightest use to him. Mrs. Herold had wept bitterly when he left school. But since there was no money in the family, there was no choice. He lived at home; worked when he needed money; enjoyed himself in ways that would have caused his mother distress, but then she was, as Sal always said, a saint; and saints suffer.

Mr. Thompson emerged from the back room. He was a cheery man who wore thick glasses with tiny metal frames. He had been related, somehow, to David's father. But then David was related to half the town: the lower half, Annie liked to say, as she thought of the Surratts of Surrattsville as being gentry, which they were not: just farm folk with a bit of money, in Mrs. Herold's phrase.

"Well, David, are you prepared to enter man's estate?" Mr. Thompson's concern in the past had been with David's entirely undisguised lack of seriousness about work of any kind.

"Yes, sir. I'm ready to go to work now, and settle down and everything." Even as David said this with perfect insincerity, he felt as if a prison door was swinging shut on him. He was only eighteen; he had never been anywhere, or done anything exciting; now he was to go to work as prescription clerk for the rest of his life in a shop just across Pennsylvania Avenue from the Treasury building and just around the corner from Willard's, where the grandees made love to their beautiful women and drank at the long bar and made fortunes at cards and dice and politics, unaware that just up the street David Herold, slave, was at work, filling prescriptions for them, nine hours a day, five-and-a-half days a week, with Sunday off to catch up on all that he had missed during the rest of the week. David felt the tears come to his eyes. Surely, something or someone would save him at the last minute. No young man in any play that he had ever seen had ended up like this.

"All right, Davie. We'll start you in today. You're to be here at seven o'clock every morning. I'll give you a key. Then you let Elvira in at seven-fifteen . . ." Elvira appeared from the back room. She grunted when she saw David; who grunted back. Elvira was not given to human speech.

"I wondered, sir, if I could start tomorrow? You see, I'm supposed to help out at the Union Ball tonight, as a waiter." David was a quick and adroit liar. He had learned how to lie partly from the actors whose work he had studied so carefully but mostly from his sisters on the subject of their beaux. Between what they said of the young men behind their backs and to their faces, there was a stunning gap. When David would taunt them, they would laugh at him; and tell him to mind his own business, which he was perfectly glad to do.

"Well, it is a *half* holiday today." Mr. Thompson was agreeable. "So you can work through the morning and then help me close up at noon, and still get to listen to Mr. Lincoln."

"I can't say that I care to all that much."

"Now, now, Davie. He's the President, after all."

"Jefferson Davis is *our* President."

Mr. Thompson frowned and smiled. "Now let's have no secesh talk in this shop. It does damage to my digestion—and business."

"But you ain't Union, Mr. Thompson. You're from Virginia, like us."

"What I may be in my heart of hearts, Davie"—Mr. Thompson

was now solemn—"I keep to myself, and I suggest you do the same because of our numerous distinguished customers."

"Mr. Davis was one of your customers?"

"One of my *best* customers, poor man. I've never known anyone to suffer so much from that eye condition of his. He'll be blind by the summer, I said to Dr. Hardinge, if you don't change the prescription. But you can't tell Doctor Hardinge anything. On my own, I gave Mr. Davis belladonna to stop the pain—"

"So then he *is* your President."

"If I were in business in Montgomery, Alabama, yes, he would be. But I am here—with my loved ones—in a shop at Fifteenth and Pennsylvania Avenue, and I am the official unofficial pharmacist for the presidents of the United States and as I looked after Mr. Buchanan and Miss Lane—she'll never make old bones, I fear—I intend to look after the Lincoln family, a large one, for a change, and sickly, I should think, wonderfully sickly, from the glimpse I had of them yesterday." Mr. Thompson was smiling, without knowing it, thought David, who was aware that actors' tricks were not exclusive to actors, only the knowledge of them was.

"Well, you may not get your chance. There's talk he'll be shot today."

"Oh, the wild boys." David found disappointing Mr. Thompson's contemptuous dismissal of the dedicated young men of the National Volunteers. "General Scott will shoot the whole lot full of holes before the day's over. Which reminds me, fix a draft for his dropsy and take it straight across the road to the War Department, the new one up the street. The prescription's in the back."

As David entered the familiar back room, he felt as if he had left all life behind. But what else could he do? As he mixed General Scott's prescription, he toyed with the idea of going south, to Montgomery, to join the army that Mr. Davis was supposed to be raising. But wasn't the army just another form of imprisonment? David wanted a world to conquer, any world, no matter how small. Idly, he wondered if he could seduce Annie; he decided that he could, but if he did, the greatest of all prison doors would then swing shut upon him: marriage, children and years of making up prescriptions for the likes of General Scott. It was too late to be General Scott when he grew up; you had to go to West Point for that, or serve a long time in the ranks. Were he better-looking, he might be an actor. After all, he could learn lines; and was a lot better at making believe than most of the touring-company players who came to town. But how was he ever to begin? A single warm tear was inadvertently added to General Scott's prescription.

While David Herold was enjoying a bearable amount of self-pity, John Hay was already at work in Parlor Suite One with Nicolay. Two large crates lay open on the floor and Hay was transferring folders filled with applications, affidavits, supplications, yellowed newspaper cuttings and fervent prayers from the room's wardrobe to the cases. "We have received, personally, nine hundred and twelve applications for jobs," said Hay, studying the last of the folders.

"It seems more like nine thousand," Nicolay still retained a slight German accent which Hay enjoyed imitating. Nicolay sat at a table, making a report to the President on which applications seemed promising.

"How much longer does this go on?"

"Until we leave office."

"I had no idea," said Hay, who had indeed had none. "I thought a few people might show up and he'd give them a postmaster's job and that was that. But we're going to have to deal with all thirty million Americans before we're through."

"Less the twelve million or so Mr. Davis has to find jobs for." In the distance, there was a premonitory roll of drums.

"Did you know Mr. Seward was thick as thieves with Mr. Davis, right up to a few weeks ago, when he left town and the Union?"

Nicolay nodded. "The Tycoon wanted the two of them to talk as much as possible."

Hay frowned. "Do you think Mr. Seward's really serious about taking himself out of the Cabinet?" Hay had been present in Lincoln's parlor when the Albany Plan had been revealed. The New York delegation, echoing Seward, had insisted that Lincoln exclude Chase from the Cabinet, which should be made up entirely of Whigs, instead of the four Democrats and three Whigs that Lincoln had in mind. When Lincoln had reminded the New Yorkers that he, too, was a Whig, which evened things, they had still been intransigent. They warned the Tycoon that Seward would not serve with Chase, to which Lincoln replied that he would be sorry to give up his first Cabinet slate in favor of a second list which he had prepared; but if that was the case, then he would appoint that good Whig Mr. Dayton as Secretary of State, while Mr. Seward could go as minister to London, a city that he had so recently taken by storm.

Alarmed, the New Yorkers withdrew; their Albany Plan a temporary failure.

Seward's rage when Lincoln's words were repeated to him resulted in a letter of withdrawal from the Cabinet. Lincoln had chosen not to accept Seward's defection; and had responded with a polite note, asking Seward to remain where he was. As Lincoln signed the letter, he said, half to himself, half to Hay, "I can't afford to let Seward take the first trick."

"Personally," said Nicolay, "I'd rather Seward stayed out. But . . ."

The door to the parlor opened, and the vast Lamon filled the doorway. "He wants to see you boys." Lamon lumbered out of view.

"What's Lamon going to be in the government?" asked Hay.

"Marshal of the District of Columbia, which means he can go on being a bodyguard."

"One of many, let's hope."

The city was filled with alarming reports. The President would be shot on his way to the Capitol. The President would be shot at the Capitol. The President would be kidnapped at the Inaugural Ball and taken across the Long Bridge to Virginia and held hostage. Of all the rumors this one struck Hay as a possibility. It had also enlivened General Scott, who had placed two sharpshooters in every window that looked upon the eastern portico of the Capitol, as well as sharpshooters all up and down Pennsylvania Avenue, not to mention plainclothesmen everywhere.

Lincoln himself seemed indifferent. For the last few days he had been preoccupied with the Virginians, who were holding a convention at Richmond to determine whether or not to secede. More than once, Hay had heard Lincoln pleading with one Virginian after another. Currently, the remaining Southerners in the Congress were particularly exercised by something called the Force Bill, which would give the President the right to call out the militia and accept volunteers into the armed forces. Lincoln had agreed, privately— and, Hay thought, cravenly—to reject the bill if that would satisfy Virginia. On Friday, acting on Lincoln's instructions, just before the Force Bill was to be voted on, Washburne had asked for an adjournment of the House. With this adjournment, the Thirty-sixth Congress expired. But not before, as a further gesture to the Southerners, Lincoln's party supported a measure, never, ever, to interfere with the institution of slavery in those states where slavery was legal. On that note of conciliation, the House of Representatives shut up shop on Monday, March 4, the day of Lincoln's inauguration. The Senate remained in session.

Nicolay and Hay proceeded down the police-lined corridor to Parlor Suite Six. Lincoln sat in his usual place beside the window, the light behind him, his glasses on his nose. Mrs. Lincoln, the three sons, the half-dozen female relations of Mrs. Lincoln quite filled the room.

Hay had never seen Mr. Lincoln so well turned out. He wore a new black suit that still fit him. But Hay knew that by the time that restless, angular body had finished pushing and prodding with knees and elbows, the suit would resemble all his others. For the present, the white of the shirtfront shone like snow, while beside his chair, next to the all-important grip-sack, was a new cane with a large gold knob. Hay could see that Mrs. Lincoln's expensive taste had prevailed.

"Gentlemen," Lincoln greeted his secretaries formally. "We are about to be joined by the Marshal-in-chief, who will put us in our carriages, show us our seats, give us our orders..." There was a sound of cheering outside the window. Then a fanfare of trumpets. Lincoln got to his feet; and peered out. "Well, if it's not the President himself, I'd say it's very good likeness."

Mary had rushed to the window. "It's Mr. Buchanan! He's come to fetch you."

"In a sense." Lincoln smiled. "Now I shall want a lot of Illinois and"—he nodded to certain of Mrs. Todd's relatives—"Kentucky dignity."

With that, the Marshal-in-chief appeared in the doorway. For a moment, Hay feared that Lamon would not let him through. "Mr. Lincoln, the President," proclaimed the Marshal.

The aged Buchanan, as white of face as of hair, came forward to the center of the room. Lincoln crossed to him. They shook hands warmly. "I am here, sir," said the President, "to escort you to the Capitol."

"I am grateful, Mr. President, for your courtesy."

The two men left the room together. At the door Buchanan gestured for Lincoln to go first; but Lincoln stepped to one side, and the still-reigning President went through the door.

The Marshal-in-chief explained who was to go in what carriage. There would be individual marshals—each with a blue scarf and white rosette—assigned to Mrs. Lincoln, to the sons and to the ladies. Fortunately, Hay and Nicolay were allowed to follow Buchanan and Lincoln down the stairs to the lobby, where the police were holding back a considerable crowd. There was cheering at the sight of Lincoln. "Our applicants!" said Hay to Nicolay.

"Wait till we get outside," said Nicolay ominously.

Buchanan and Lincoln, now arm-in-arm, stood in Willard's doorway. A sudden storm of cheering—and of booing—was promptly drowned out by Major Scala's Marine Band, which struck up "Hail to the Chief" as President and President-elect proceeded to get into their open carriage. A nervous marshal then hustled Hay and Nicolay into a barouche, already filled with Washburne and Lamon.

Hay found Washburne edgy; and Lamon uncharacteristically relaxed. But then Lamon had turned his friend and charge over to the United States Army and if they could not protect him today, no one could. Washburne stared out of the window at the thin crowd along the brick sidewalk on the north side of Pennsylvania Avenue. There was no sidewalk or much of anything else on the south side, which, after a few blocks of houses and the Gothic red-brick Smithsonian Institution, turned into a marshland, the result of overflow from the canal that ended in the muddy waters of the Potomac River on whose banks poison ivy and oak grew in wreaths like sinister laurel.

"That is a dangerous crowd." Washburne stared out the window. They were now abreast the Kirkwood House. Thus far, there had been neither cheers nor boos for the two presidents up ahead.

"They're all secesh in this town," said Lamon, whose pronounced Virginia accent sounded somewhat incongruous to Hay.

"And spoiling for a fight," said Washburne.

"Watch the cavalry up ahead." Lamon pointed to the two rows of horsemen that flanked the presidential carriage. The men rode in such close order that anyone standing on the sidewalk would be unable to get more than a glimpse of the occupants of the carriage.

"Notice how the horses are sort of skittish?" Lamon gave a satisfied smile. "That was my idea. When you get horses pulling this way and that, it's going to be mighty hard for anyone with a gun to get himself a proper sight."

David Herold had exactly the same thought. With Annie on his arm, he stood in front of Woodward's and watched the strangely silent parade. "You can't see either of them," he complained.

"Well, we'll get to see them both pretty clear when they come out on the Capitol steps."

"And when they do," David began; but Annie pinched his arm, for silence.

There was only one float, drawn by four white horses; it represented the Republican Association. On top of the float, girls dressed in white represented each of the states in the Union that was no longer. The girls themselves were roundly cheered from the sidewalk; the Union was not.

David and Annie walked beside the float until they came to the plaza in front of the Capitol. Since noon, close to ten thousand people had been gathering. Boys sat in trees. A photographer had built himself a wooden platform where he was busily trying to get his camera in place while fighting off the boys and men who wanted to share the view with him.

Shoving and pushing, David and Annie were soon within a few yards of the speakers' platform, where a single row of troops held back the crowd. Above the platform, on the steps, the great folk of Washington were being led to their seats by ushers. David stared with awe at the foreign diplomats in uniforms that seemed made of pure gold or silver, while the ladies were resplendent in furs and velvet cloaks. The day had started to turn cold.

"My God," whispered Annie, "have you ever seen so many soldiers!" Soldiers were indeed everywhere; and under the eye of the commanding general himself, who sat in huge solitary splendor in his carriage on a nearby eminence. Winfield Scott had sworn a mighty oath that this president would take office, no matter what.

There was cheering from the north portico, which they could not see from where they were standing. "They're going inside the Senate now."

"I know," said Annie. "I read the same paper. Did you take the job with Mr. Thompson?"

"Yes."

"I'm glad."

"Why?"

"Everyone should work."

"You don't."

"I'm still at the seminary. But I'm going to be a music teacher when I graduate and then . . . oh, look! The Zouaves!"

In fire-red uniforms, a company of soldiers under the command of their uncommonly beautiful drillmaster, the curly-haired, twenty-three-year-old Elmer E. Ellsworth, a pet of the Lincoln family, began to divert the crowd with an intricate and somewhat eccentric close-order drill. David was ravished at the sight; and filled with a profound envy. Why wasn't he wearing that extraordinary uniform? And doing those extraordinary tricks? And making Annie and every girl in the crowd gasp with admiration while impressing even the wild boys who were scattered throughout the crowd, ready, as always, for violence, preferably impromptu.

Inside the Senate Chamber, John Hay had not the slightest envy of Hannibal Hamlin, the newly sworn-in Vice-President of the United States. On the other hand, from his seat in the crowded gallery, he quite liked the look of the Senate Chamber. They might never get a proper dome on the Capitol, but Congress had seen to it that the Senate and the House of Representatives were splendidly housed in chambers of marble, decorated in red and gold and bronze, to set off the solemn statesmen in their rusty black, each with his own armchair and desk, snuffbox and shining spittoon.

Hannibal Hamlin spoke well and to the point, and, for a moment, Hay actually looked and listened to the new Vice-President, who was so dark-complexioned that his predecessor sitting beside him on the high dais, John C. Breckinridge of Kentucky, had been quoted as having said that it was highly suitable that a radical government such as that of Mr. Lincoln should have for its Vice-President a mulatto. But mulatto or not, Hamlin was a former Democratic senator from Maine, who had helped found the Republican Party. Before the election, Lincoln and his running-mate Hamlin had never met. Hay was constantly surprised to learn how little these Northern men of state knew one another, as opposed to the Southerners, who seemed all to be brought up in the same crib.

After the election, Lincoln had invited his Vice-President-to-be in Chicago. They got on well, confounding the old Washington saw: there goes the Vice-President, with nothing on his mind but the President's health. Hamlin had introduced Lincoln to raw oysters; and Lincoln had said: "Well, I suppose I must deal with these, too." The two men had got on so well that Lincoln had told Hamlin that as he intended to place only one New Englander in the Cabinet, Hamlin could make the choice, which turned out to be a Connecticut newspaper editor named Gideon Welles. Somewhat reluctantly, Lincoln made him Secretary of the Navy.

Hay looked up at the presidential party. Buchanan and Lincoln were seated side by side in the center of the gallery. Lincoln was as dark as Buchanan was white. For all the talk of *Old* Abe, most people who met Lincoln were startled to find that, at fifty-two, he had not a gray hair in his black shock, which was, for the moment, contained by the barber's art and Mary Todd's firm brushwork. But once out of public view, the long fingers would start to stray through that haystack and, in no time at all, three cowlicks in opposition would make his head look like an Indian warbonnet.

Lincoln seemed distracted, thinking no doubt of his speech— which had been sent, secretly, to the Old Gentleman at Silver Spring, read and admired, and sent back. How close was Lincoln to old Mr. Blair? How close was he to anyone? Hay was still as new to Lincoln's relations with others as, presumably, they were. But Hay did wonder how on earth Lincoln would meet the present crisis, living in a Southern city, with a government that was more than half Southern, and a Cabinet filled with rivals. Plainly, Lincoln was equally bemused. There were times when he would simply drift off in the middle of a conversation, while the curiously heavy lidded left eye, always the indicator of his mood, would half shut, and he would no longer be present. But the eye was alert today, as far as Hay could tell from his end of the chamber, where the smell of men's cologne and ladies' perfume could not quite mask the stale odors of bodies imperfectly bathed. Hay's nose was sharp; his standards of hygiene high.

Hamlin was finished at last. He shook hands with the somber Breckinridge. Then the two Presidents rose, as the Marshal-in-chief came to escort them to the east portico.

Hay followed the black-robed justices of the Supreme Court onto the Capitol steps; he breathed the fresh air, gratefully. A sharp wind had started up, and Hay was suddenly terrified that Lincoln's speech would be blown from his hands. If it were, could the Tycoon remember it? No. The speech was so closely argued that if one word should be misplaced, a half-dozen more states would secede.

A justice's robe flapping in his face, Hay walked down the steps of the Capitol. Half the notables were already seated. The other half had packed the Senate Chamber. Members of the Congress, Supreme Court, Cabinet-to-be, as well as chiefs of foreign missions and high-ranking army and naval officers, each with family, assembled to participate in history. Hay took his seat next to Nicolay, just above the platform.

Nicolay pointed to the crowd. "Mr. Lincoln drew twice as many people as this just in Albany."

"Well, New York State voted for him," said Hay, "and these people didn't. There must be . . . what? ten thousand out there?"

"See the rifles?" Nicolay pointed to a boardinghouse across the Capitol plaza. Each window contained a man with a rifle.

"All trained on us," said Hay. He had always found the idea of assassination more exciting than not. But now he realized with a chill that had nothing to do with the March wind that he was seated just a row above the speakers' platform, with a thousand military rifles all aimed in his direction, not to mention who knew how many plug-uglies with hidden pistols and derringers and knives, ready to commit slaughter. He pulled his hat over his eyes, as if for protection.

The appearance of Lincoln and Buchanan had been greeted with unenthusiastic applause. Neither David nor Annie had so much as clapped a hand when the tall, dark-haired man took his seat behind a low table. David did notice how awkwardly Lincoln handled himself. He was no actor, David thought, scornfully, as he watched Lincoln take off his hat, and then hold it in the same hand as the cane to which he was plainly unused while, with the other hand, he removed his speech from an inside pocket and then was obliged to transfer the speech to the hand that held both hat and cane. Crazy and old as Edwin Forrest was, he could certainly give Lincoln lessons in how to move, thought David; and how to die.

David looked at the men in the trees but could not find a familiar face. Surely the National Volunteers had not given up.

He would have bet his last penny, which was in his pocket, that they would make their attempt. At the moment he felt the same excitement that he did in the theater when the musical overture, dominated by drums, began.

When all the dignitaries were in place, a distinguished-looking old man rose and came down to the front of the platform; and in a voice that David approved of, full of baritone drama, and even better, with arms outstretched like Edwin Forrest's when between the acts of whatever play he did nowadays, he would come out and, to the audience's delight, with wondrous fury attack his wife, the old man proclaimed, "Fellow citizens, I introduce to you Abraham Lincoln, the President-elect of the United States!" Even David felt like applauding the old man, whoever he was. Meanwhile, Lincoln was having trouble with hat, cane, speech. He stood a moment, trying to manipulate the three, until a short, stocky man David recognized as Stephen Douglas, the defeated Democratic candidate, leaned forward and took the hat from Lincoln, who gave him a grateful smile. Lincoln then placed the cane on the table, put on his spectacles, moved to stage right of the table, which looked like a milking stool next to such a tall man, and began to read.

"Look," whispered Annie, "his hands are shaking."

"Wouldn't yours?"

Annie elbowed David in the ribs.

Hay was suffering stage fright for the Tycoon, who had never before sounded so tentative, even quavery of voice. Nevertheless, Hay knew that the high voice could be heard from one end of the plaza to the other. Lincoln was used to vast crowds in the open air. "Fellow citizens of the United States." The high voice was tremulous. "In compliance with a custom as old as the government itself, I appear before you to address you briefly, and to take, in your presence, the oath prescribed by the Constitution of the United States . . ." Hay was relieved that at the mention of the Constitution Lincoln's voice lost its quaver. He was now moving onto his own formidable high ground, as he made the case for the Union.

Back among the senators, Salmon P. Chase could not help but contrast how different his own speech on this day might have been. For one thing, he would *never* have read out that provision in the Constitution that slaves be returned to their lawful masters. Chase shuddered as Lincoln elaborated. "It is scarcely questioned that this provision was intended by those who wrote it, for the reclaiming of what we call fugitive slaves; and the intention of the law-giver is the law."

"Shameful," Chase muttered to Sumner, who sat very straight behind him. Sumner nodded, listening closely.

"All members of Congress swear their support to the whole Constitution—to this provision as much as to any other."

Sumner turned to Chase, "What he is doing is giving up the slaves in order to restore the Union."

"That is immoral."

"It is worse," said Sumner. "It is *impossible.*"

For Mary the speech was the finest that she had ever heard; and she had heard Henry Clay and Judge Douglas; had heard her own husband proclaim that a house divided against itself cannot stand, losing thereby a Senate seat to Douglas while gaining the presidency for himself. She was also pleased that the new suit fitted him so well; and she was looking forward to showing off her own new wardrobe to the ladies of Washington, who had, thus far, refused to call on her because, she had read in the press, they disdained her as some uncouth westerner, unused to Washington's aristocratic ways. She, Mary Todd of the great Kentucky Todd family, First Lady of Springfield even before she was married, an invitation to whose mansion was the dream of every Illinois lady, if only to observe Mary preside over her witty and elegant court, known, far and wide, as the Coterie. Uncouth!

There was the sharp cracking sound of a gun being fired. Mary gasped. Lincoln stopped in his speech. All Mary could think was—has he been hit? But Lincoln was still standing, if mute. There was a murmur through the crowd. Hay craned forward to see if Lincoln was all right. Apparently, he was; but his face had gone chalk white.

David stood on tiptoe and looked off to the left, where the shot had come from. "Who did it?" whispered Annie. "Can you see?"

"Soldiers, I think." David watched as six soldiers converged on a tree. Then a soldier held up a thick branch. A dazed-looking man was brushing himself off. There was laughter.

"A branch broke off," said David sadly, "under some fellow's weight."

Annie was equally disappointed.

Lincoln resumed his speech. As he came to the coda, Seward leaned forward, eager to hear what Lincoln had cut from his own speech and what of Seward's paragraph he had used.

"You can have no conflict without being yourselves the aggressors. *You* have no oath registered in heaven to destroy the government..." Seward frowned: this was hard, too hard. "... while *I* shall have the most solemn one to 'preserve, protect and defend it.'"

Seward waited for the challenge "With *you*, and not with *me*, is the solemn question, 'Shall it be peace, or a sword?'" To his great relief, Lincoln had cut this most dangerous question, and in its place came Seward's text, ruthlessly pruned of its richer blossoms. "I am loth to close. We are not enemies, but friends. We must not be enemies. Though passion may have strained, it must not break our bonds of affection. The mystic chords..."

Seward, eyes shut, chanted softly his own original phrase: "The majestic chords which, proceeding from so many battlefields and so many patriotic graves, pass through all the hearts and all the hearths..." Tears came to Seward's eyes whenever he declaimed this particular passage, first tried out many years ago at Utica. But Lincoln had changed the language. With some irritability, Seward heard the trumpet-voice intone the new "mystic chords of memory, stretching from every battlefield, and patriot grave, to every living heart and hearthstone, all over this broad land, will yet swell the chorus of the Union, when again touched, as surely they *will* be, by the better angels of our nature."

Lincoln stopped; took off his glasses; put the speech into his pocket. As Seward applauded politely, he could not help but think how odd it was that some men have a natural gift for elevated language while others have none at all. Lincoln had made a perfect hash of Seward's most splendid peroration. Since any one of Seward's speeches was apt to sell nearly one million copies, he had, suddenly, the sense of being jilted—worse, of being a great beauty abandoned at the altar by a plain and unworthy man. But Seward would prevail in time. The Albany Plan may have misfired but since the principle of it was still very much in his mind, he had taken back his letter of withdrawal. He would be Secretary of State; and prime minister yet.

Chase turned to Sumner. "What does he mean?"

Sumner was bemused. "He will take the South back—slaves and all. Anything, to preserve the Union."

"Thank God, they will not come."

"Thank God, they will not come, without a bloody war."

The speech was well enough received by the crowd in the plaza. Lincoln had now recovered his color, Hay noticed. The new President stood beside the small table waiting for the ancient Chief Justice to give him the oath of office.

At the age of eighty-three, Roger B. Taney was several years older than the Constitution, whose interpreter he had been for a quarter century, as the fifth Chief Justice of the United States. Seward was peculiarly aware of the irony of the present situation. Had the fragile, withered Chief Justice not said, in the course of a decision to return a slave to his master, that Congress had no right to ban slavery from any territory, Abraham Lincoln would not now be President. Lincoln looked down, gravely, at the little man who did not look up at him but looked only at the Bible in his right hand. In an inaudible voice, Taney administered the oath. Then Lincoln, hand on the Bible, turned from the Chief Justice to the crowd assembled and ignoring the slip of paper on which his response had been printed, declared in a voice that made even Chase's cold blood turn warm, "I, Abraham Lincoln, do solemnly swear that I will faithfully execute the office of President of the United States, and I will, to the best of my ability..."

Lincoln turned full-face to the crowd in the windswept plaza; and the famous war-trumpet of a voice, until now muted, sounded its declaration and what was meant to be its justification for all time, "... preserve, protect and ... *defend* the Constitution of the United States!"

On the word "defend," as if by prearrangement, the first battery of artillery began to fire; then the second; then all guns fired their salute to the new President, who remained at attention throughout the bombardment.

"My God," said Hay to Nicolay, "it is going to be war!"

"I have known that for some time," said Nicolay. "The real question is how will it go for us?"

9

HAY STOOD AT THE FRONT DOOR OF THE EXECUTIVE MANSION, waiting for the President to arrive. Mary and the children and the relations were already exploring the house, and Nicolay had gone to the bedroom which he was to share with Hay, just across from the President's office. Hay had already moved in earlier that morning. Old Edward had helped him up with his baggage, and then asked for a tip, which Hay had given him. It was the first time that the White House had appeared to him as what it really was, a run-down hostelry for politicians. But the bedroom he was to share with Nicolay had a fine view of Lafayette Square; and their double bed looked comfortable. At least they were only two to one bed. Lincoln used to speak, not unfondly, of his early days out on circuit in Illinois when five lawyers would share the same bed and it took all of his celebrated wiliness to secure the outside corner, where, by the light of a single candle, he could read as the others snored.

There was a crowd outside the White House gate; guards staggered the arrival of carriages. General Scott himself stood on the top step of the portico, proud of his handiwork. There was cheering as the carriage containing Buchanan and Lincoln rattled through the gate. Both men raised their top hats. As the carriage stopped, Old Edward helped down, first, Lincoln, and then his predecessor.

As the two men, accompanied by Hay, went up the steps, Buchanan said to Lincoln, "If you are as happy, my dear sir, on entering this house as I am in leaving it and returning home, you are the happiest man in this country."

Lincoln smiled. "Well, second happiest, maybe."

General Scott saluted the new President. "Welcome, sir, to the Executive Mansion."

"Thank you, General. And my congratulations."

"I said we would have us a President today, no matter what. And we have. My mission, sir, is accomplished." Then General Scott saluted; and departed, in a jingle of metal and a whispering of gold braid.

During this, Buchanan stared, head cocked to one side, at the brick barn off to his left. When Scott had gone, he turned to Lincoln.

"You will find, sir, that my niece has prepared some dinner for your party."

"I wish that you and your niece would join us."

"Sir," said Buchanan, with some warmth, "I never want to set foot in that house again."

"Is it really so bad?"

"Oh, the house is all right. It needs some repairs, of course. No, sir. My objection is to the office itself that I filled and that you must now fill. Mr. Lincoln"—Buchanan's voice dropped to a whisper—"the office of President of the United States is not fit for a gentleman to hold."

"Well, that's lucky for me, I guess." Lincoln tried to make a joke; but the old man was serious.

"You will see what I mean, sir. And now, farewell; and may God bless you and yours." As the fifteenth President got into his carriage and drove away, the sixteenth waved to him until he was gone. Then Lincoln went into the house.

Dinner was a haphazard affair. Seventeen sat down for dinner in the so-called family dining room on the ground floor. Miss Lane's taste was for plain cooking, which suited Lincoln but not Mary or the ladies, who had dreamed of lobsters and canvasback duck and soft-shelled crabs and Potomac shad with roe instead of sturdy roast beef.

Mary held forth on the horrors of the mansion. "The upstairs is abominable. It's like the worst boardinghouse you ever saw."

"Now, that's plain impossible, Mother," said Lincoln mildly, helping himself to a single boiled potato. "Why, the boarding-houses that I've seen..."

"You know what I mean, Father."

"Oh, it's true, Cousin Lincoln!" Cousin Lizzie always came to Mary's rescue. "There's only one good piece of furniture in the President's bedroom and that's a mahogany French bedstead, only the headboard's split right in half."

"Just the thing for me to sleep in," said Lincoln; but only Hay got the allusion. The ladies were too busy with their account of what they had found and not found in the course of their tour.

"There's no proper gaslight, either!" Mary spoke now with a sense of drama. "None! Only candles for now! And though the water taps turn, mud and rust come out."

"How's your room?" asked Lincoln of Hay.

"Like Versailles, sir."

"Which you've never seen?"

"No, sir."

"Nor I. Well, since we've never seen it, we can always say we live in royal splendor."

Mary rose to her feet before the last plates were taken away. "We must dress for the ball, everyone. There's not much time." As the ladies hurried from the room, their great hoops struck one against another like ships in a narrow slip, thought Hay, who had taken enormously to boats when he was at Providence.

Lincoln motioned for Hay and Nicolay to come with him. "Let's take a look at Mr. Buchanan's hell," he said, leading the way upstairs.

The three men walked down the long gloomy hall to the bal-ustrade that marked the beginning of the presidential offices. There was no one in sight, not even the Negro Edward, whose task it was to keep an eye on those visitors who had been passed upstairs by Old Edward at the main door. On the first clerk's desk, a kerosene lamp cast long shadows. The waiting room beyond was dark and forbidding.

Lincoln entered the reception room, where Buchanan's Cab-inet had met. In the center of the table, a single lamp made ghostly the room in which, Hay thought, dramatically, so many administrations had made so many wrong decisions in recent years. He wondered where Jefferson had worked; but then re-membered that since the British had burnt down the house in 1814, Jefferson's ghost had probably burned up, too.

Lincoln picked up the lamp from the table, then he opened

the connecting door into the President's office. The first thing that they saw clearly in the gloom was a painting of Andrew Jackson over the white marble fireplace. "Well," said Lincoln, neutrally, "I guess we'll leave old Andy where he is."

"What about a painting of Jefferson?" asked Nicolay.

"If Virginia stays in the Union, I will have only portraits of Virginians in this place. Madison, Monroe, Mason, every last one of them. Otherwise..." Lincoln had seated himself in the President's chair, a battered armchair of maplewood. The President's desk proved to be a tall affair with numerous pigeonholes, and a fine view from one of the room's two windows of the Potomac, and the blue hills of Virginia beyond, now fading as the sun set.

"What about a painting of General Washington, sir?" Hay ran his finger round the frame of Jackson's picture, and collected an inch of dust. "Or is he too Virginian?"

"No, the father of our country is just right. Only I might look too ambitious, moving him there." Unconsciously, Lincoln ruffled the hair that Mrs. Lincoln and the barber had so carefully arranged for the day; then he leaned back in the chair and put his feet up on the desk and stretched his arms. "This is not the worst of rooms," he said, judiciously.

In the glare of the kerosene lamp, Hay noticed how tired Lincoln looked; and he had been President for only a few hours. Nicolay must have noticed the same thing because he said, "Don't you think you should rest, sir? Before the ball?"

"Well, there's no business left to transact, that I can see." Lincoln was now going through the drawers and cubbyholes of the desk. "Mr. Buchanan has cleared up nicely."

"He was at the Capitol till noon today," said Nicolay, "making last-minute appointments."

"I suppose that comes of being a gentleman." Lincoln grinned suddenly at Hay, who noticed, as he always did, that in a world of men who smoked or chewed tobacco, Lincoln, who did neither, had white teeth, unlike Madam, whose smile was always slightly compressed in order not to reveal the dinginess of her own teeth.

Lincoln rose and went to the door that led to the narrow waiting room. Then he crossed the waiting room to the secretaries' bedroom. "You've got almost as much space as I do," he said to Nicolay.

"But no view of Lafayette Square..."

"Or that peculiar statue of Mr. Jefferson." Lincoln was now in the small room just off the bedroom. "Miss Lane has taken her linen home, Johnny, so you'll have a place to work." Hay had already commandeered a desk from the basement, where quan-

72

tities of shabby furniture were stored, as though for some bankrupt's terminal auction. Lincoln turned, suddenly, to Nicolay. "I want you, first thing tomorrow morning, to send Mr. Chase's name down to the Senate, for confirmation as Secretary of the Treasury."

"Have you told him, sir?" Nicolay was surprised.

"Well, no, not exactly. I've hinted, of course. But I had to wait until I got the Cameron business sorted out—and then there was the New England mess... Now, with Mr. Chase, I've got just about one of everything. He'll be my radical abolitionist while Mr. Seward is my radical trimmer..."

"Suppose Mr. Chase refuses?" Nicolay was concerned. "He's most outraged, he tells everyone."

"Oh, he won't refuse. But"—Lincoln turned to Hay—"you go pay him a call tomorrow, in my name, and soothe the terrible beast of ambition that resides in that Roman bust—or breast, I suppose, it's called. Do you know why God gave men teats?"

This was a new one to Hay; also to Nicolay. They said the ritual "no's" that must always precede a Lincoln story. "Well, there's nothing more pointless, of course, than a man's teats, but a preacher, when challenged as to the point, said that it was possible, in God's good time and mysterious way, that a man might one day give birth to a baby and if he did, why, he'd be all set up to feed it." On that note, the sixteenth President led the way back to the private apartments, where the noise of the Springfield ladies sounded to Hay just like an afternoon of the Coterie at the Edwards mansion.

Hay arrived alone at the Union Ball because he intended to leave alone. Tonight he would indulge the flesh, exactly like Mr. Poe, he thought in justification. Poets were intended to live to the full the life of the senses. In his pocket was the list of names that his fraternity brother had given him.

The ball was being held in a temporary structure of wood and white muslin that had been built back of the unprepossessing City Hall. Troops stood guard at every entrance, as well as in the City Hall itself, where the men's coats, cloaks and hats were piled up in the courtroom while the extra garments of the ladies were stacked in the council chamber.

Hay pushed his way through a crowd of well-dressed Northerners and Westerners. Hay's ear was always sensitive to accents; he duly noted that there were none from the South. As predicted, old Washington was boycotting the ball, while most of the Southern congressionals had either gone home to their seceded states or declined to attend the Inaugural Ball as they had declined to attend the inauguration itself. The newspaper-dubbed Palace of

73

Aladdin was ablaze with gaslit chandeliers. In the first room there was a monster buffet, courtesy of the ubiquitous Gautier; every sort of delicacy had been arranged on long trestle tables at whose center was a confection dedicated to the Goddess of Peace, depicted half life-size and all marzipan, with a cloak of spun sugar. But before the grandees could descend, locustlike, upon the food, they were obliged to file past the President and Mrs. Lincoln, who stood at the pavilion's center.

Hay noticed that Lincoln still wore the white kid gloves that he had arrived in, while Madam was splendid in a blue gown with a blue feather in her elaborately arranged hair; she also wore pearls, gold. Back of Madam stood the relatives, the heart of the Springfield Coterie, consisting of one sister, two nieces, cousin Lizzie and two half-sisters from Kentucky, of whom one was said to be a secessionist.

"He had better take those gloves off."

Hay turned to find Henry Adams at his side. "He hates gloves," said Hay, "but the State Department insists he wear them."

"But he must take them off when he shakes hands. That is our Republican way."

Lincoln, as if he had heard this most Adams-like criticism, stopped his handshaking and pulled off the right glove, which he let, absently, drop to the floor.

Lincoln was now shaking hands rather as if he was pumping water from a well. Hay noticed that the Tycoon's eyes seldom looked at the men and women passing in front of him. This was most unlike him. Usually, he tried to say something of a personal nature to each citizen; but not tonight.

Madam had solved the business of handshaking by holding, firmly, in both hands, a large bouquet of flowers. Whenever anyone was presented to her, she nodded and smiled graciously; and that was that. Hay had to admit that, side by side, the Lincolns were a somewhat comical couple—he so tall; she so short. For this reason, she had never allowed a photograph to be taken of the two of them standing side by side. "Because we are," Lincoln would say in explanation, "the Long and the Short of it."

"This morning at Willard's," said Hay, "the State Department read us five pages of do's and don'ts. There is a lot of protocol, isn't there?"

"Democracy requires a good deal of ceremonial. Will he learn it, do you think?"

"Plainly, *you* don't think so." Hay had got Adams's somewhat saturnine drift.

"For someone from outside, all this . . ." Adams gestured at the

74

crowded room, filled now to overflowing with General Scott in full golden uniform.

"He's not that far outside. Anyway, he's quick to learn; and never forgets. He also does what he says he will do if you can get him to say what he means to do."

"As in the case of Mr. Hamlin?" Adams was mischievous.

"He kept his word; and let Mr. Hamlin pick the New England Cabinet officer. Was your father . . . displeased?"

"My father is never displeased. He is, also, never pleased."

"I hope he gets the London post."

Adams shrugged. "As I said at Willard's, this is the place to be. London is simply our hereditary post."

"Like the presidency?" Hay was mischievous, too. It was hard to realize that this small young man was grandson and great-grandson of two presidents.

"Oh, don't get me on that subject! If my father does not go to London, I think I'll stay here as . . ." He paused.

"As what?"

Adams sighed. "I suppose a . . . journalist. That's all I'm suited for, really. I simply want to observe the world's grandest zoo." Adams drifted off.

In due course, the shaking of hands came to an end, while M. Gautier's feast came to an end in a matter of minutes, as did the Goddess of Peace herself. Hay overheard two journalists comparing notes. "What did old Abe say to you that made everybody laugh?" asked one.

"When I asked him if he had any message for Mr. Bennett of the *New York Herald*, he said, 'Tell him that Mr. Weed now knows that Seward was not nominated at Chicago.'" They laughed; moved on.

Hay stationed himself at the entrance to the ballroom as Scala's Marine Band struck up "Hail to the Chief" and Lincoln entered the ballroom on the arm not of his wife but of the mayor of Washington. Despite the fatigue of the day, Hay thought that Lincoln looked moderately tickled by this incongruity. Behind Lincoln, Mary made her entrance on the arm of Senator Stephen Douglas, whose large face was dulled by an unhealthy pallor. There was applause as the political symbolism of this pairing was duly noted: the chief of the northern Democratic Party was now as one with his ancient rival the new Republican President.

As Madam swept by Hay, he saw in her bright, round face a rare and perfect happiness. She was on the arm of the man she might have married; and she was the wife of the President whom she did marry. There will never be such a night, thought Hay, yielding to that melodrama he had learned from Mr. Poe—and melancholy, too.

Lincoln stationed himself at one end of the room and watched the dancing with benevolence—at least, with *one* benevolent eye, for the lid of the left was beginning to fall. Hay danced waltzes, a quadrille, a polka, even a square dance; and worked up a good sweat. But when he saw the President slip away just before twelve-thirty, Hay also left. In the courtroom, he joined several dozen furious men in the search for coats and hats. After half an hour, he found only his hat, and abandoned the search.

Hay walked from City Hall to Pennsylvania Avenue, which he crossed. On the south side, Marble Alley ran a short distance between Pennsylvania and Missouri avenues, not far from the odiferous canal. The night was chilly and he regretted the loss of his coat as the sweat on his body turned icy; but the thought of earthly pleasures to come made bearable the chill. The avenue was filled with carriages and hacks waiting to take home the revellers. There were also ominous sounds of "Dixie" being sung in dark barrooms; while in the side streets gangs of fierce-looking young men staggered about drunkenly—how drunkenly, he could not help but wonder. In future, he decided, he would carry a gun. Luckily, tonight, the Federal police—some fifty strong—were all in the area between the City Hall and the White House, while good General Scott had every soldier within a hundred miles of the city stationed in Washington this night. From the Long Bridge to the Capitol to the White House, the troops stood guard.

The previous night, Hay had gone to the Wolf's Den, an agreeable house kept by the eponymous Mrs. Wolf; she had been most agreeable, but far too talkative. "Everyone of distinction comes to me," she said. She named senators by name until Hay began to grow uneasy; and once he had had his passage-at-arms, as he liked to think of these venereal encounters, he had left, with no intention of returning. He did not want his name added to her glittering list. Meanwhile, he had made casual inquiries in the bar at Willard's and, of the lot, Sal Austin had been most highly praised for discretion as well as for the richness of her waiting rooms, for the comfort of her bedrooms, for the variety of her food and drink, and, finally, for the marvelous choice of girls. "There is even," said a knowledgeable youth, "a doctor who comes twice a week to see if they are free from pox." Brandy-snifters were raised to Sal Austin.

Now Hay stood in front of a dark building in a dark alley where a number of restless pigs slept in a cluster near a pile of garbage, like applicants for political office. After a single deep breath, Hay rapped on the door. A mulatto butler opened the door a crack, took in Hay's evening clothes with practised eye, smiled and bowed and said, "This way, sir."

There was a small vestibule with a narrow staircase, covered in red velvet held in place by golden rods, making ascent and descent agreeably silent. To the left and the right of the vestibule were parlors, elaborately furnished with mahogany and walnut; red plush predominated in the left parlor and royal purple at the right. Voices could be heard from both rooms, decorous men's voices, carefully modulated female voices. The butler motioned for Hay to remain at the foot of the stairs while he went into the red parlor, returning a moment later with a tall, grave woman in her forties. She was dressed in black, like a widow. Although she wore no makeup, her most elaborately arranged hair was as glossy as a chestnut. She came forward, graciously, and extended her right arm, almost as if she expected the hand or the huge diamond ring on her second finger to be kissed. Hay shook the hand, grinning stupidly, as she said in a low gentle voice, "I am Mrs. Austin."

"Yes, I know," he said; stupidity had plainly gone to his head. "I mean, I was told of you. By friends."

"Of course. Do come in and let us have a talk." She was about to lead Hay into the red parlor when he pulled back. She looked surprised; then, to his relief and delight, she got the point. "Come to my office." She led him to the back of the vestibule, where a small door led into a large study with a second door to the outside.

In a businesslike way, Sal sat at a rolltop desk and indicated that he sit beside her. "The advantage of this office—for certain visitors, that is—is the door to the backyard, which is over there. Then," she pointed to a third door, "you can go through that door into what I call the alcove. It is at the back of the purple parlor. There, through a charming lattice in the Persian style, you can see what goes on in the parlor, and not be seen yourself. Then when you have observed someone who intrigues you, Chester, the butler, will arrange for you to meet her in one of the bedrooms on the second floor, which can be reached by the back stairs."

"I was told that you were the best." Hay was filled with admiration.

"I am," said Sal. "But accidents have been known to happen even here. So, I would appreciate it if you'd give me a day's notice as to the exact hour of your arrival. That way I can see to it that the alcove will be empty. There is nothing more embarrassing than to have two ... friends meet on such a private occasion. Sherry?" she asked, picking up a crystal decanter on her desk. He nodded; she poured each a glass. As they raised the glasses to each

77

other, Sal said, "In order for me to be entirely on the safe side, I should know *which* you are—Mr. Nicolay or Mr. Hay?"

Hay nearly inhaled the sherry. "What makes you think...?" he stammered.

Sal was motherly. "We all know that Mr. Lincoln—I am Union, by the way, but many of the girls are not, I must warn you—brought two young men with him. Three, counting his son. But you're too old to be the son and too young to be anyone else except—Mr. Hay?"

Hay nodded. "You see, Mr. Nicolay is engaged to be married," he said, with bright stupidity.

"I accept this intelligence in the spirit with which it is proffered but I do not actually seize, as it were, your point."

Hay was now convinced that he was not made for the world of the demimonde. "Oh, I was just commenting on the fact that Mr. Nicolay's bride-to-be was supposed to come to Washington for the inaugural, but she could not get away. That is why, ordinarily, he would be not here but with her tonight."

"That is very modern," said Sal. "I am not entirely sure that I approve. In my day, a young man and woman were chaste until their wedding night. I continue to think that this is a worthy custom of our race."

Hay gulped down the rest of the sherry, conscious that he was making a fool of himself. But Sal rose to the occasion. "I misunderstood." Sal got to her feet. "Now I shall show you to the alcove. But you will have only thirty minutes to choose because someone else—not actually engaged, I fear, but securely married—will be arriving."

"You're very kind," said Hay, feeling as if he were reliving that first time in Providence all over again.

Sal opened the door to the alcove, which was done in the same royal purple plush as the rest of the parlor. Divans were placed on two sides, while the third was filled by a carved teakwood buffet, covered with food both cold and hot, and numerous bottles. Through the "Persian latticework" he could indeed see everything that was going on in the parlor.

"When you espy what you want," said Sal, "tug this cord." She indicated a purple velvet bellpull against the wall. "Chester will come and act as Cupid."

"I could not have found a more amiable Venus," said Hay, rallying.

"I think," said Sal, "that, mythically, I am closer to Minerva." With a smile, she was gone.

Hay poured himself a goblet of brandy; tore off the leg of a guinea hen; squatted on a chair and peered through the lattice.

The parlor was divided by potted plants into four separate sitting areas, each providing a degree of privacy. He recognized a face or two of men who had been at the Union Ball, but could attach no names to any of them. Elegantly dressed waiter-girls, as they were euphemistically called, poured wine, carried trays of cocktails or, simply, bottles of bourbon to the customers, who sat about, for the most part, like club members, well acquainted with the rules of the house and the inmates. Chester and two elderly black women presided over the inevitable buffet. People ate quite a lot at Washington, thought Hay, suddenly very hungry himself. Over the last few days, the succession of mammoth meals at Willard's had gradually taken away an appetite that was only now coming back.

Hay had started in on the boned turkey when he saw his destiny, as he liked to think of whatever girl caught his fancy. She was tall, slender of waist, high of bosom; she wore yellow watered silk that set off her black hair and eyes and café-au-lait skin. She was a mulatto; and Hay had never before crossed even this less-than-precisely drawn color line. Hay rang for Chester, who arrived, smiling. "Marie-Jeanne is a delightful creature, young master." Either Chester or Sal had decided that it might enhance the magic of these parlors in this most Southern of cities to act as if the entire provenance had been changed to New Orleans in an earlier part of the century. As Hay ran three steps at a time up the back stairs, he was glad that he was not an out-and-out abolitionist and so able, in good faith, to enjoy the play-acting.

Marie-Jeanne received him in the bedroom assigned. She was filling two glasses with champagne. "Good evening," she said; and smiled; she had good teeth. "Have some Widow."

"Hello . . . , Marie-Jeanne?" Hay was not certain of the etiquette. But she took charge; gave him Veuve Clicquot—known familiarly as the Widow to Sal's clients and employees.

"You're French?" Hay made conversation rather more awkwardly than he might have done with even the fiercest governor's fierce wife.

"Well, somewhere in the past, in Port-au-Prince, to be exact, there was very definitely a Frenchman. You're new to town?"

Hay nodded, pleased that Sal had kept his secret. If the girl knew who he was she would not have asked. "I'm going to be at the Treasury. As a clerk," Hay enjoyed lying to strangers, inventing a new personality, complete with such eccentric details as: "My mother came to live here while I was up north at school. She was an opera singer until she broke her hip in Paris. Now she's in a wheelchair, in O Street in Georgetown. She gives singing lessons." During this inspired, Hay thought, aria, he had slipped his arm around Marie-Jeanne, and pulled her back onto the divan. With a smile, she undressed him, to his pleased surprise; usually, he fell upon such girls with a lion's roar and tore their garments, but now, out of respect for his invalid mother—should he give "Mother" a glass eye? No, that was too much—he was passive as she stripped away his clothes. Then, lowering the gas lamp to a mysterious harvest moon glow, she, too, undressed. The body was as marvelous as he had ever experienced, even in Chicago during the recent convention, much less Providence, Rhode Island.

As they lay, side by side, on the bed, he now pleasantly exhausted and she smiling and attentive, he thought that this was just what a poet should do, preferably several times a day. Hay caressed her pale-brown skin, and wondered if anything so beautiful had ever come Poe's way. Actually, if what his poetess friend who had known Poe said was true, Marie-Jeanne was a bit old for the lover of Annabel Lee.

To Hay's astonishment, Marie-Jeanne was thinking along the same lines. As she ran her hand across his smooth chest, she said, "You're younger than I am."

"Oh?" Hay looked down at himself. For some time, he had thought of himself as a nicely finished mature male in excellent working order. Now he wondered if, perhaps, he still looked too boyish. Should he be covered with more hair? or grow a moustache?

Marie-Jeanne quickly soothed him; and dark limbs entwined with white. "That's what I like," she whispered in his ear. She smelled faintly of sandalwood. He wondered whether or not that was her own natural smell. Certainly, she looked as if she ought to smell of some exotic wood or jungle flower or... Hay stopped thinking, as again she took control of him. He could not know that what she had said she had really meant; had, in fact, two years earlier, whispered something very like it into the ear of the seventeen-year-old David Herold.

10

THE DAY AFTER THE INAUGURAL BALL SPIRITS WERE LOW AT
Sixth and E. Chase had not gone to the Senate that morning.
Instead he had continued to arrange and rearrange the books in
his study while Kate worked with an upholsterer in the front parlor.
Servants came and went. Out of such confusion, Chase had said,
darkly, at breakfast, there can come no order.

The arrival of Charles Sumner did not improve Chase's mood.
The two men were so much as one on so many of the great issues
that they never had much of any interest to talk about; or, rather,
the eloquent Sumner never ceased to declaim, while Chase, from
time to time, would add a choric note to the great actor's surging
threnodies.

Sumner's blue frock coat was ablaze with gilt buttons, which
made him look slightly absurd to Chase, who preferred sober black.
Sumner gave his outer coat to the manservant; kissed Kate's hand
without affectation—to Chase's mild envy. But then he had not
come to know Europe even better than he knew the United States;
nor had he mingled with the most famous men and elegant ladies
on both sides of the Atlantic. The famous men most intrigued
Chase, whose hobby it was to collect the autographs of celebrated
people. When Sumner once, casually, read him a note from
Longfellow, Chase could not help but ask, humbly, if he might
have, if not the letter, plainly no business of his, the signature at
the bottom? Sumner had been amused; and generous. Chase got
the entire letter. He was delighted; yet filled with self-disdain, the
inevitable result, he told himself, echoing Bishop Philander Chase,
of an unbridled passion: in this case, for the calligraphy of the
great. "Remind me," Sumner had said—this was two years earlier—"and I'll give you a Tennyson letter." Twice, Chase had
discreetly reminded Sumner of his promise, but no autograph was
forthcoming.

After ten years in the Senate, Sumner was now that body's
most brilliant figure; yet three of those ten years had been spent
away from Washington, as an invalid. A Southern congressman
had attacked Sumner with a stick while he was seated at his Senate
desk. A powerful man, Sumner had been able to rise to his full
height, wrenching the desk from the floor to which it was nailed.

Then he collapsed, with a concussion. After years of painful cures, Sumner had returned to the Senate.

As Sumner entered Chase's study, he looked at the newly installed books, and took down a volume of John Bright's speeches. "The most eloquent man in the British parliament."

"Did you—do you know him?"

Sumner nodded; dusted off a chair from which a stack of books had just been moved; arranged his frock coat with some fastidiousness, as he sat, very straight, and intoned, "'The angel of death has been abroad throughout the land.'"

Chase nodded; and recited the next line of the famed speech against the Crimean War, "'You may almost hear the beating of his wings.' But you couldn't have *heard* that speech. He gave it only six years ago."

"No. But I read and learn his speeches, as do you, I see. I met Mr. Bright at the time of the repeal of the Corn Laws. He always dressed as a Quaker. I suppose he still does. We correspond occasionally."

Chase's heart beat more swiftly. "You would not happen to have . . . Oh, perhaps, a *tiny* scrap of paper with his name on it? A card is all, really." Chase, who would not ask Lincoln for a post in the Cabinet, was on his knees to Sumner for an autograph.

"Of course. I'll find you one." Sumner looked vaguely at the portraits of two ladies. They hung side by side over the small fireplace.

"My first wife," said Chase. "And my third. The second, Kate's mother, hangs in the front parlor. Three times a widower," Chase added, more with wonder than self-pity.

"As I am thricefold a bachelor," said Sumner, which struck Chase as a somewhat heartless response to his own tragic fate.

"Have you never been tempted?" asked Chase.

"I don't think so. I don't know. I don't think I really notice women, unless we have a subject in common. I'll tell you what a Boston lady once said to me." Sumner almost smiled; since he had no sense of humor at all, no one ever knew just what his smile might mean. "She asked me some gossipy question about an acquaintance, and I said, 'I fear that I no longer have any interest in people, as such,' and she said, 'Why, Senator, not even God has gone as far as that.'"

Chase laughed; and Sumner laughed with him, but more out of politeness, Chase thought, than from any true purchase on the lady's wit.

"You must let me take you to your new home," said Sumner after a pause, during which he had been checking the title and author of nearly every book in the study.

"Oh, I think I had better stay here today—like Achilles in my tent." Chase attempted lightness; and failed.

"The thing is still not decided."

"I'm afraid it is. But why do I say afraid? To be senator from Ohio, the way that you are senator from Massachusetts, is a far greater thing than to be in any president's Cabinet."

"True," said Sumner: then he added with exquisite lack of tact, "but since you dearly want to be President and I don't, the Treasury is the better place for you to be. And"—Sumner may have lacked tact but he did not lack manners—"that is where *I* want you to be for the good of the country."

Kate entered with a tray containing all the necessaries for tea. Sumner was on his feet, to help. If Chase had not known Sumner's misogyny, he would have thought that that noble figure found Kate interesting. Although Chase had no idea what would ever happen to him if Kate were to marry—the thought of a *fourth* Mrs. Chase made him feel like Bluebeard—he could think of no husband finer than Charles Sumner, who, he noticed, was, like himself, cleanshaven. Since Lincoln had grown his beard, all sorts of odd excrescences had begun to blossom on political faces.

Kate poured tea; Sumner assisted. "I did not see you at the ball last night. I looked, Miss Kate, truly I did."

"You looked in vain. I was not there. Father?" she offered Chase tea, which he took, filling the cup with sugar.

"Surely you are not a secret secessionist?"

"No, Mr. Sumner. Quite the opposite. I am a *true* abolitionist." Kate's smile was mischievous. "Unlike so many of our men of state."

"Oh," said Sumner, frowning. "Oh, I say, that *is* a hard blow to the head."

Considering Sumner's recent history, Chase thought that references to blows to the head might not be in order; but Sumner was so entirely conscious of himself as to be, in no usual way, self-conscious. "You have a point, Miss Kate. Yesterday when Mr. Lincoln quoted the Constitution's word and not its spirit, my heart sank. But as he is weak, why, all the more reason that we rally round him."

"To support him in his support of slavery?" Kate was sharp. She would have made an extraordinary lawyer, Chase thought. Certainly, she had a better legal mind than he but then Chase had seen to it that her education had been finer than his. It thrilled him to hear her speak as intellectually the equal to Sumner, who was not known to suffer gladly even the brilliant if they were less brilliant than he.

"To guide him. To counterbalance Mr. Seward, the prime minister..."

Chase nodded agreement. "Seward *is* the administration of this country now."

"There is no one to counterbalance him in the Cabinet," Sumner began.

"Except Mr. Chase," Kate concluded.

"But I am not there," said Chase.

"But Seward is," said Kate.

Sumner looked bemused. "I have been told that Mr. Seward dreams of some sort of war between us and all of Europe to distract our attention from the matter of slavery. He spoke to me in the most alarming way of Spain's influence in South America and of France's in Mexico." Sumner groaned. "He thinks we should invoke the Monroe Doctrine and drive them out of the Western hemisphere, *with* the support of the Southern states, who would then, presumably, extend slavery over the entire southern half of our hemisphere."

"Thank Heaven," said Chase, "that you are the chairman of the Foreign Affairs Committee."

"Curious how Seward has changed." Sumner was thoughtful. "He gave the greatest speech, as a lawyer, in defense of a black man..."

"The Freeman Case." Chase nodded.

"William Gladstone wrote me that that speech was the finest forensic effort in the English language."

"Gladstone *writes* you often?" Inadvertently, Chase shivered with pleasure.

The manservant entered the study; he murmured something to Kate. "Who?" she asked.

"Mr. John Hay, he says his name is..."

"Oh, Father!" Kate sprang to her feet. "I'll bring him in. You stay right there. Both of you." She hurried from the room.

Sumner nodded gravely. "It is the call, Mr. Chase."

"I do not count on it."

In the vestibule, Kate was astonished to see a handsome young man only a year or two older than herself. "Miss Chase?"

"Yes, sir. And you're Mr. Hay? The President's secretary?"

Hay nodded. "One of two, Miss Chase." Hay had been prepared for Kate's youth but not for her beauty—or level gaze. There was nothing at all feminine in the way that she looked at him, as if she wanted to open up his forehead and discover what he knew. For all Kate's dark-golden hair, slender waist, luminous skin, she was just another shrewd politician—as opposite to last night's Marie-Jeanne as dawn to dusk, he thought, in an ecstasy of what might have been poetry. Oh, he was smack-dab in the middle of life at last!

"Might I see Senator Chase?"

"Of course." But Kate did not move. She looked up at him: hazel eyes met hazel eyes. Hay was still energized by Marie-Jeanne—or electricized, to use the word made popular by the electric-shock machines that had recently become fashionable for sluggish men and neurasthenic ladies. Hay saw no reason not to turn upon this enchanting-looking if not entirely enchanting girl his newly electricized charm. As he looked straight into her eyes, he let himself revert to the mood of the night before. Suddenly, as if an electrical shock had been transmitted, Kate gave a little cry, and turned pale. "Oh, come in. Come in." She was a virgin, Hay decided, with the sharp intuitiveness of a man who knows, at a glance, all that there is to know about women.

Hay was not entirely surprised to see Senator Sumner in Senator Chase's study. Both statesmen rose, very slowly, at the young man's entrance. Kate stayed in the doorway, not part of the meeting but not apart from it either.

"Gentlemen." Hay shook hands all round.

"You were at . . . Brown," said Sumner, to Hay's surprise. He had not thought the great man would remember.

"Yes, sir. I heard you speak there."

Chase cleared his throat. He was now at the crucial moment of his career. He was aware that the tremor that sometimes appeared in his left hand had begun. He shoved the hand into his coat, like the first Napoleon. "Mr. Hay . . ." he began.

"Mr. Chase," the young man broke in. "I have come from the President, who wishes me to inform you that he has, this morning, sent your name to the Senate for confirmation in the office of Secretary of the Treasury."

"Bravo!" Sumner clapped his hands. Hay heard a sigh from Kate behind him; he was an expert now at women's sighs.

Chase was very pale. "You must tell the President that it is customary to inquire *in advance* if the one nominated to an office chooses to accept that nomination."

"But, sir"—Hay had been prepared for this—"the President assumed in the light of his conversation with you at Springfield that you would be pleased to accept the office."

"That was some months ago." Chase was furious; and he could not think why. He wanted very much the office. But he did not want to accept it from Lincoln. The fact that he was the man's superior morally and intellectually did not matter so much. After all, he fully expected to succeed him at the next election. But to be so *used*—that was the word!—by an inferior, to be kept dangling like this until the last possible moment; all this was unbearable. "I have now," Chase heard himself say, as if from a far distance, "taken my oath as a United States senator, and I look forward to serving with men of the utmost morality and honor like Senator Sumner..."

"Now, Mr. Chase." Sumner gave his colleague a warning look. "Mr. Lincoln has been torn this way and that since he arrived from Springfield. But I do know that he told me that he knew of no one more suited for the Treasury..."

Kate intervened. "Mr. Hay, I think the President should give my father a day or two to decide where his highest loyalty lies. To the people of Ohio, or to the people of the entire Union."

Hay bowed to Chase and Sumner; then Kate led him to the vestibule, where the manservant waited to let him out. "Tell the President that this is all a bit abrupt."

"I will tell him that." Again Hay felt the electrical impulse between them. But this time he realized that it was all on his side. Although he was still a young male, she had ceased to be a desirable young female and had become a hard political manager, with a long-range presidential campaign to administer.

"Thank you, Mr. Hay. Good-day, sir."

When Hay was gone, Kate hurried back to the study and while Hay took the horsecars back to the White House, contemplating in an ecstatic blur the dark and the light of feminine bodies, Kate joined Sumner not so much in changing Chase's mind as in finding a way for this proud, stubborn man to accept the office that he wanted so desperately from the hands of a man he so deeply despised.

"He'll accept in a day or two," said Hay to Nicolay. "My God, she's a looker, that daughter of his."

"So they say. Congratulations, by the way. You are now a clerk in the Pension Office of the Department of the Interior."

"I'm *what*?" Hay was stunned.

Nicolay laughed. "Congress won't let the President have two secretaries, so we've got you on the payroll at Interior. Sixteen hundred a year."

"A fortune," said Hay; and meant it.

They were in Nicolay's office with its view of Lafayette Square and the rampant statue of Andrew Jackson atop his horse, the worst piece of equestrian sculpture in the world, according to Senator Sumner, who always made newcomers to Washington swear to him, solemnly, that they would never actually look at the statue no matter how close they might be to it.

Hay's office was no more than a cubbyhole off Nicolay's spacious room but with the adjoining door open, Hay felt less confined; also, since their duties overlapped, each was constantly in and out of the other's office. The center of their activity was a huge secretaire brought up from the basement. Here, in dozens of drawers, they did their best to file some eighteen thousand applications for government jobs. On a large table in front of the window, the nation's press was arranged each day, including newspapers from the South. It was Hay's task to make a daily précis for the President of what might interest him, which was surprisingly little.

Outside Nicolay's office the waiting room was full from nine in the morning until six at night. The clerk behind the railing took down each name before allowing the supplicants into the waiting room, while, downstairs, the doorman Old Edward screened everyone at the main door. Old Edward was adept, usually, at separating the plain mad from those simply crazed for office. The would-be appointees would then make their way up the stairs to the waiting room and, in the process, they would fill up the dark corridor that led from the President's quarters to the offices. Mary had already made one scene that morning when a half-dozen would-be postmasters burst into the oval sitting room of the living quarters where she and her lady relatives were sitting about in their morning robes.

"McManus, I will not endure this, do you hear me!" She had shouted at Old Edward, as he led the shaken postmasters-that-might-have-been from her presence. Old Edward had then returned with a full-time guard, "Who'll shoot to kill, ma'am, should anyone try to break in on you."

By then Mary's humor was somewhat recovered. "Ladies do not like to be seen by strangers in the morning," she said. Old Edward said that he understood.

Mary laughed when the door closed behind him. The relatives laughed, too. None of the women was properly assembled for the day. The crinolines and the vast hoopskirts had been put away, and although each enjoyed showing off her morning robe to the other ladies, strange men were forbidden to gaze on these feminine mysteries.

Mary wore a rose-colored cashmere wrapper, with quilting down the front; and her hair was done up in a red turban like Dolley Madison—or, said Cousin Lizzie, "Like a Zouave."

Since breakfast, the ladies had been analyzing the previous night's ball. Mary's full sister, Mrs. Edwards, taller than Mary but not quite as plump, took a hard line against the ladies of Washington. "They are so ill-mannered," she said, pouring coffee from a dented silver urn that Cousin Lizzie swore had been thrown out by Martha Washington.

"The few that were there," said Mary, frowning; all morning she had felt as if she might, at any moment, be struck by The Headache, which she feared more than death. When the clamp of fire went round her head, she could not see for the pain and, often, she would end up flat on the floor, vomiting from the pain. The Headache, as she always thought of it, to differentiate it from ordinary headaches, had begun some years earlier. She knew that many thought that she was shamming but her husband was not one of them. Whenever he could, he would stay with her, no matter how terrible her behavior and it could be, she knew, or, rather, had been told, like that of a mad woman. But if The Headache was near, it was not yet ready to srike her down; if it did, she was surrounded by relatives and friends, women who understood the problem.

Meanwhile, the behavior of the Washington ladies was meticulously discussed by the Springfield-Lexington contingent. "They seem to think," said one of the nieces, "that we are log-cabin women, never before out of the woods."

"Well," said Lizzie, "Cousin Lincoln can take full credit for that. All that nonsense about being born in a log cabin when that's all there was to be born in in those days in that part of Kentucky. But during the campaign was there ever a picture of Cousin Lincoln's Springfield mansion in the press?"

"Well, I don't think Mr. Lincoln would have thought that appropriate," said Mary. She had had that argument with her husband; and lost. "Anyway, the local ladies hereabouts strike me as provincial in a way that Springfield and certainly Lexington ladies are not. If nothing else, we have better manners. Did you see the story in the paper, criticizing the way that I address gentlemen always as 'Sir'? That is hardly provincial."

"But, maybe, a bit old-fashioned," said Lizzie.

"Well, it's definitely Southern and sounds right to me," said the half-sister from Alabama. "Anyway, Sister Mary, we're kin to the only two high-and-mighty families hereabouts, the Blairs and the Breckinridges, and that's more than these tacky shopkeepers' wives can ever claim!"

The ladies applauded this celebration of their family. "It is strange," said Mary, "that *everyone* was at Lexington when I was a child, except Mr. Lincoln, who was nearby in Indiana. We had Mr. Clay at his estate, Ashland." She smiled in memory. "Harry of the West; everyone in the world called him that. As if he was our country's king, which he was, or should've been. Then there was this little boy with the pale eyes, who is now...who *was* until now, Vice-President Breckinridge. And I can remember a handsome young man at Transylvania University, very pale and very elegant he was, who gave an address on graduation day called 'Friendship,' just before he went off to West Point."

"Who on earth was that?" asked Lizzie, who knew but the younger women did not.

"Jefferson Davis," said Mary, just as one of the housemaids opened the door from the bedroom adjacent to the oval sitting room, and said, "Mrs. Lincoln, the mantua-maker is here."

Mary excused herself and went into the bedroom, where she found a well-dressed mulatto woman, who gave a little curtsey. "I am Elizabeth Keckley, Mrs. Lincoln. I heard that you needed someone to make you a dress, and so I offer myself. I am well recommended." She opened her reticule and gave Mary a number of letters. Mary took them; but she did not glance at them. She studied the woman's face carefully; and liked what she saw. The face was strong and not at all negroid. The nose was large and aquiline; the mouth straight. She appeared to be in early middle life.

"Now I cannot afford to be extravagant," said Mary. "As you know—and as everyone says—we are from the outlandish West, and very, very poor. You know that, don't you?"

"Yes, Mrs. Lincoln." Keckley smiled.

"Good. We begin to understand each other. Now every Friday we are obliged to give a reception in the evening. That is expected of us." Without thinking, Mary began to make the bed; and Keckley helped her. The room was currently inhabited by two of the Springfield ladies; and their previous evening's finery was everywhere; and in disorder. "I shall need a dress . . ."

"That's only three days from now," said Keckley, taking over entirely the making of the bed.

"I know it is short notice. But I was told that you were not only good but quick." Mary was at the window. She glanced at the letters in her hand.

"You have the material?"

"Yes, and the pattern. The stuff is rose-colored moiré-antique and . . ." Mary had found a familiar hand. "You worked for Mrs. Jefferson Davis. How strange! I was just speaking of Mr. Davis."

"Yes, I worked for Mrs. Davis." The bed was now made. "I was very fond of Mrs. Davis."

"Then why didn't you go South with her?"

"Well . . . Look at me." Keckley gestured.

"I *am* looking at you."

"I am colored."

"But free."

"Even so, I could never live in a slave state. I am an abolitionist. In fact, I must warn you, Mrs. Lincoln, I am very political."

"Oh, so am I!" Mary was delighted. "But, of course, I must be careful in what I say. The vampire press is always ready to spring at me." Mary had begun to pace the floor in front of the window, with its view of the incomplete monument to Washington. "It is so comical. They say that I am pro-Southern and pro-slavery and that I try to influence Mr. Lincoln, who is really, they say, a secret abolitionist. Well, it is nearly the reverse. Mr. Lincoln knows nothing of slavery, except what he has heard from me and my family in Lexington. Yes, we had . . . and we have slaves. But we did not traffic in them, and they governed our lives and not the other way around. Nelson was the butler. He made the finest mint juleps in Kentucky, so everyone said, while Mammy Sally brought us all up and gave us the most thorough spankings you could ever imagine! I see her yet . . ." Mary paused; then frowned. "We lived on Main Street. One of my first memories is that of the slaves, chained together, being marched to the auction block, which was in a corner of the main square of Lexington, the courthouse square, while in the other corner there was the whipping-post, some ten feet high, black locust wood, made even blacker because of the blood. Oh, I can hear the screams yet." Mary shut her eyes; and remembered. "We had a mark on our house, a secret mark that meant that runaway slaves would be fed by Mammy Sally. She tried to keep me from seeing them but, of course, I had to. And I talked to them. Saw their scars. Heard how families had been broken up. Oh, and then there was Judge Turner!"

Mary swung away from the window; the Potomac shone silver in the distance. "They were neighbors. Mrs. Turner came from Boston. She was a large, showy, violent woman. She beat to death seven slaves that we know of. She threw out the window a six-year-old boy, and broke his back. My father was furious—he was a considerable political force in Kentucky. So he was able to insist that a jury inquire into Mrs. Turner's sanity. But while the jury was being impanelled, Judge Turner sent his wife to the lunatic asylum. So by the time the jury was ready to act, the asylum had let her go, saying she was perfectly sane. Which, no doubt, she was, as monsters so often are. When Judge Turner died, he left his slaves to his children. But he put it in his will that none should go to his wife—Caroline her name was—because if they did, she would torture them to death. But she overturned the will and got the slaves, including a handsome, bright-yellow boy, brighter than you, named Richard, who was her coachman. Richard could read and write and would, no doubt, be free by now. This was seventeen years ago. But one morning she chained him up and started to beat him—to beat him to death. He was in such pain that he pulled out of the wall the hook to which his chains were attached, and then he seized the monster by the throat, and choked her to death, then and there."

"A happy ending," said Keckley, grimly.

"A *righteous* ending for her but not for Richard. He was arrested by the sheriff, one of Mr. Lincoln's cousins, curiously enough, and tried for murder, and hanged."

"There is no justice on earth."

"There will be some, when Mr. Lincoln is finished with his work on earth."

Keckley smiled, "You make him sound like the Lord."

"Do I?" Mary laughed. "Well, if he is the Lord, he is not a Christian one. When Mr. Lincoln was elected to Congress, his opponent was a Methodist preacher who kept accusing Mr. Lincoln of being an infidel. One night during the campaign the preacher was giving one of his hellfire sermons in a church when Mr. Lincoln walked in, and sat in the back. The preacher decided to trap Mr. Lincoln. So he shouted, 'Those of you who expect to go to Heaven, rise!' Well, Mr. Lincoln did not stir. The preacher then pointed his finger at Mr. Lincoln so that everybody would know that he was there. 'Those of you who expect to go to hell, rise!' Mr. Lincoln did not stir. So the preacher said to the congregation, 'All those who think they are going to Heaven and all those who think they are going to hell have risen to their feet but Mr. Lincoln has not moved. So where, Mr. Lincoln, do you think that *you* are going?' At that, Mr. Lincoln got up and said, 'Well, I *expect* to go to Congress,' and left the church."

The two women laughed together. Then Mary said, "Ask the housekeeper for the material. And remember, no matter what you hear, that I am the one who wants slavery destroyed once and for all, and it is Mr. Lincoln who thinks it's a bad thing but nothing to make any fuss about if a fuss can be avoided."

"They do not depict you as you are," said Keckley with a certain wonder.

"When do they ever? But this earth is only a passing show, Mrs. Keckley."

"Call me Lizzie, ma'am."

"Lizzie."

11

THE SECRETARY OF THE TREASURY STOOD IN FRONT OF THE
fireplace in his front parlor, and stared raptly at the smouldering
coals while in a soft but displeasing voice, he urged Jesus to carry
him home. Just as the sotto voce was about to become voce itself,
two arms reached around him. "You're ready at last!" he said.

"At last!" said Kate. Proud father turned, and was prouder yet
when he beheld her in a dress of white and gold. "Well?" She
spun around.

"Superb, you look like..."

"The Empress Eugénie. I heard you admiring that painting of
her, and I was so jealous that I had this made, to outdo her."

"She is outdone!"

The manservant opened the front door for them and the groom
opened the door of a roomy, new, closed carriage from Brewster's
in New York. Reluctantly, Jay Cooke had told him that the carriage had cost $900. Sternly, Chase had insisted that it be duly
noted as a loan. For an instant he had been tempted to accept
the carriage as a gift, but probity never deserted him for very long,
not to mention an unrelenting awareness of the importance of the
appearance of things.

"*La belle des belles,*" intoned Chase in his bad French, quoting
what *Frank Leslie's Illustrated Newspaper* had written of Kate's
first appearance at the White House in February, when, on meeting Mrs. Lincoln for the first time, Kate had responded to the
older woman's polite, "Pray call upon us whenever you like, Miss
Chase," with "*You* may call upon *me* any time, Mrs. Lincoln."
Kate had sworn to her father that no offense to Mrs. Lincoln had
been intended; nevertheless, the First Lady never tired of repeating
the story of Kate's rudeness.

"Why is the meeting so secret?" Kate looked at Chase, who
stared out the window at the ugly but imposing marble facade of
Brown's Hotel, all lights ablaze at this hour.

"I'll know after it's over." Chase had told Kate that after tonight's
dinner for the Cabinet, the Cabinet would go into secret session.
He ought not to have told her but he knew that she was the very
soul of discretion, unlike her father.

"I suppose it is to do with Fort Sumter."

"Or Virginia. They keep making new demands. And Lincoln keeps giving in to them."

"I'd drive them out of the Union," said Kate, fiercely.

"You may not be obliged to," said Chase, as the carriage drove up to the portico of the White House, where Old Edward stood, waiting at the door.

Father and daughter were shown into the Red Room, where the dinner guests were gathered. Chase was delighted at the effect Kate made. The men hurried to greet her; the ladies stared hard at the new dress, and murmured behind their fans. Brand-new gas lamps, improperly installed, hissed in much the same way that the ladies did as they discussed Kate's appearance.

Chase stationed himself beneath the painting of Washington that dominated the room, and talked to Mrs. Grimsley, the agreeable cousin of Mrs. Lincoln, who told him, "The other ladies have gone home. I think we all of us stayed much too long. I know Cousin Lincoln was looking more and more grim every morning when he'd get up to find all seven of us in our wrappers, taking up every chair in the upstairs sitting room."

"I've never seen the living quarters," said Chase, his eye on Kate, who was now enchanting all three Blairs. The fierce Old Gentleman was either grimacing with agony or smiling; the latter an expression so rare that no one could positively identify it. The Postmaster-General, Montgomery Blair, was beaming as he told Kate a story in Negro dialect, while his brother, Representative Francis Blair, Junior, snapped his fingers. Kate gave every appearance of being enchanted by the three lean, wiry, ambitious men, who were plainly enchanted by her.

One who had *not* yielded to Kate's enchantment now stood in front of a pier glass in the southwest bedroom, and adjusted Lizzie's handiwork so that slightly more of her dimpled shoulders would be revealed. As she did, Lincoln crept up behind her and pulled the dress up. "Father!" she slapped his hand, not entirely playfully. "What do you know of fashion?"

"You look like a fancy woman, Molly."

"A *beautiful* fancy woman?" Lincoln kissed the top of her head for answer.

"It is curious," said Mary, studying her features in the glass, "that when I was young I had no vanity at all, and now I can think of nothing but my appearance, and wish so much that I looked young."

"You do to me. You don't change."

"But you never look at me. So how would you know?" She turned; stood on tiptoe and straightened her husband's tie.

"Who am I to sit next to?" he asked.

"Well, not that dreadful Miss Chase. I suppose you think she's pretty."

"I can't say I've ever noticed." Lincoln grinned, and started to ruffle his hair; then thought better of it.

"Nor Mrs. Douglas, who is far too handsome. Nor any of the Blair ladies. Nor..."

"I'll have to sit next to somebody."

"There's always Cousin Lizzie," said Mary, with a sweet smile; and took his arm. Together, they paraded down the corridor, hissing with the blue-white gaslight flames. Together, they descended the staircase, he with mock hauteur and she as erect as Queen Victoria, with whom she had recently been, flatteringly, compared in the *New York Herald*. As they got to the bottom of the staircase, Old Edward preceded them to the door to the Red Room and shouted, "The President and Mrs. Lincoln!"

Women as well as men rose as they made their entrance. Mary was now quite used to this phenomenon. Lincoln affected to find it embarrassing, even though he had always taken it for granted that whether or not anyone rose at his approach, he would be the center of attention.

At table, protocol required that Kate, as the highest-ranking lady present, sit on the President's right, and Mrs. Douglas on his left. Senator Douglas was at home, ill. Mary was flanked by Seward and Chase, her two least-favorite politicians. Although she favored the abolition of slavery, she was not an abolitionist, a distinction that her husband claimed to find more mysterious than the Trinity. But Mary had long since determined to her own satisfaction exactly what should be done. Had she not grown up a neighbor of Henry Clay, the idol of the Whigs and the only politician that she had ever heard her husband, with any sincerity, praise both as a speaker and as a moralist? All those who were now slaves would remain slaves but their children, when of age, would be free. In a single generation, the terrible institution would be at an end, and the slave-holders could hardly complain that they were being robbed of their property.

As the waiter served Chase terrapin, Mary saw a look of true greed cross his face. "That is something, sir, that we never had in our part of the world," she said.

"No, nor in Ohio. But surely there is terrapin in Lexington, Kentucky?"

"I was thinking of Springfield. Oh, yes. We had all sorts of game, too. Do you know the town, sir?"

Chase nodded. "In fact, I met your father once, years ago. That was in my abolitionist phase."

"Surely not yet at an end?"

Chase was serene. "The Cabinet is as one behind the President, in every way." What, he wondered, would the votes be tonight? "I was involved in the so-called Fairbank Scandal, which nearly started a civil war in Lexington. That was close to twenty years ago."

Mary was suddenly alert. "Calvin Fairbank, sir? the minister?"

"That's right. A group of us in Ohio would raise money so that we could buy slaves and then free them. Mr. Fairbank was a sort of agent of ours."

"*Eliza!*" Mary exclaimed. "I was there that day, at the slave auction, in the courthouse square."

"I am told that no one who was there has ever forgotten what happened."

"So you, sir, were behind Mr. Fairbank?"

"I was indeed. When I heard of Eliza's case, I gave him the money to buy her."

"I never knew that, sir." For the first time, Mary looked at Chase with something close to admiration. The girl Eliza had belonged to a well-to-do family; she had been gently treated and well educated. When the family died out, she was put up for sale by their distant heirs. Ordinarily, this would have been a familiar if depressing story, but the case of Eliza was much discussed in the press because she was a lovely white girl of eighteen who happened to be one sixty-fourth Negro. At the auction, the Reverend Fairbank had bid against a Frenchman from New Orleans who, it was rumored, kept a brothel. The courthouse square was crowded. People had come from miles around. Abolitionists had threatened violence. With some horror, Mary had watched the bidding. She herself was only a few years older than the girl who stood, shuddering, on the block, the tall auctioneer beside her. When the Frenchman's bids began to flag—the price had gone to a thousand dollars—the auctioneer had shouted, "Come on, you mean-hearted gentlemen! Look at what I've got!" With that he pulled down the girl's blouse. Mary could still remember the horrified gasp from the crowd. Many ladies hurried away. Yet when a black woman was stripped, no one had ever noticed. The bidding resumed; then flagged again. This time the auctioneer pulled up the girl's skirt to show her naked thighs. There were now shouts of anger from a part of the crowd; and raucous shouts and whistles from the other. Finally, the girl was sold to the Reverend Fairbank for one thousand four hundred eighty-five dollars—Mary could still hear the auctioneer's voice intone, "Fourteen eight-five, going, going, gone! And sold damned cheap."

When Fairbank came to take the weeping girl down from the

block, a loud voice shouted, "What're you gonna do with her now?"

"I'm going to set her free!" shouted Fairbank. There was almost, as Chase had noted, a civil war right there and then in Lexington's courthouse square.

When it came Mary's turn to speak to Seward at table, she smiled the slight smile that she had been practising ever since Cousin Lizzie had told her that if she objected to being depicted as a moon-faced little old woman, she must diminish her smile, which tended to make round her cheeks, "Just like a chipmunk's, Cousin Mary."

"What news, sir, of your wife?"

"She still enjoys to the full her ill-health, Mrs. Lincoln. She is home at Auburn, New York."

"I do wish she were here, to help me." Inadvertently, Mary looked at Kate, who had somehow got the President to laugh out loud, something women, by and large, seldom did, either because he was in awe of them or because he never took them as seriously as he did his lifelong audience, men.

"You do quite well enough, Mrs. Lincoln. I like the new gas lamps."

"They still make that awful noise." Mary frowned. "You don't think they could be leaking, do you?"

"How long since they were installed?"

"Ten days."

"If they had been leaking, Mr. and Mrs. Hannibal Hamlin would now be at the head of this table."

"Really, Mr. Seward!" Mary disliked Seward's total lack of gravity. "Sir, are you still opposed to the provisioning of Fort Sumter?"

Seward gave a sidelong glance over the canvasback duck. Did she know about tonight's Cabinet meeting? One of the new President's numerous faults was an inability to keep a secret, unlike Seward, whose capacity to maintain his own counsel had won him the title, in his gubernatorial days, the Sphinx of Albany.

It was the Sphinx who now answered. "Well, at our first Cabinet meeting, three weeks ago, the President asked each of us to write a memorandum on whether or not we should provision the garrison at Fort Sumter, and it was my advice, as you know, not to do anything of a provocative nature."

"Do you feel the same now?" Mary did know that there was to be a secret meeting of the Cabinet after dinner; but since Lincoln had told her no more than that, she had asked no questions. She knew that he had been greatly disturbed by whatever it was that Lamon had told him that morning: Lamon had only just returned from Charleston, where Lincoln had sent him on a private mission to South Carolina's governor. Plainly, tonight's meeting would have to do with Fort Sumter, the last Federally controlled property in the state, and its garrison.

"Well, it depends on the circumstances, I suppose." Seward was vague. "Actually, the entire Cabinet, except for Mr. Blair, voted for giving up Fort Sumter."

"I believe Mr. Chase was in favor of giving it up if it meant peace, and against if it meant war."

"You *do* follow these matters, don't you, Mrs. Lincoln." Seward was now confident that she knew about tonight's meeting. "I suppose Mr. Lamon's report will be interesting." He tried to draw her out. All day he had been trying to discover what Lamon had told the President, but if anyone knew, they would not tell him; even young Johnny Hay had been evasive.

"I've not talked to Mr. Lamon. And the President tells me nothing." With that, Mary changed the subject.

When the last course was taken away, Mary rose to her feet, as did Lincoln. Neither had taken to the European custom of allowing the ladies to withdraw while the gentlemen remained at table. "For a man who doesn't drink, it's perfect torture," Lincoln had remarked after a recent dinner at the British legation. But Lincoln did enjoy a story the minister, Lord Lyons, had told of the exotic Chancellor of the Exchequer, Benjamin Disraeli, who also hated to sit with the gentlemen after dinner and, whenever he could, he would insist that everyone depart with the hostess. After one particularly inedible dinner, Disraeli, thinking that the hostess had made a move to rise, leapt to his feet, only to hear her say, "Not yet, Chancellor. There is champagne."

"At last," Disraeli was heard to murmur, as he slumped in his chair, "something warm."

The twenty-eight ladies and gentlemen withdrew to the oval Blue Room, where Hay and Nicolay and Lamon were waiting. The plan was for the Cabinet officers, one by one, to say good-night to Mrs. Lincoln; and then go upstairs to the President's office and wait for him, as he would be, contrary for once to protocol, the last to leave the guests.

Neither Hay nor Nicolay had the slightest idea what Lamon had reported to the President; nor was Lamon about to tell them other than to say, "They did try to lynch me in the street until an old friend happened along and told them that they'd have to contend with him." Lamon chuckled. "He took me to a bar and we overcelebrated my escape."

As the company spread out across the room, Hay bowed to Kate Chase, who bowed back, with a brilliant smile; then she turned to Senator Sumner, who seemed on the verge of losing his reputation for misogyny.

Hay and Nicolay were to go to the Cabinet Room as soon as the last member had made his farewell. Meanwhile, Hay found himself seated in a stiff chair against the rounded wall, while in front of him and, presumably, unaware of his presence, stood the President with old Francis Blair. Hay tried not to listen; but not too hard.

"Strange how the more this room is changed around the more it seems always the same," observed the Old Gentleman. Due to the absence of certain crucial teeth, he tended to salivate as he spoke, a fact of which, unlike so many old people, he was very much aware; he kept a handkerchief in one hand, ever ready to dry his withered chin. "I still expect to see General Jackson come through that door, after one of his dinners of rice. He had trouble with his teeth like me; and trouble with his appetite, unlike me."

"Well, I wouldn't in the least mind if he did come through that door and I could turn this whole damned thing over to him and go back to Springfield." Although Lincoln's delivery was droll, Hay had detected in the last week a growing anxiety and, worse, indecision.

"Well, sir, the first thing he'd tell you would be—stick to your guns." Old Blair mopped his lips; and the smoky eyes gazed up at the President, who looked away, distractedly. "*Which* guns should I stick to is the problem."

"You must hold Fort Sumter to the end."

"How do you see the end?"

"I assume you will try to provision the garrison?"

Lincoln looked at him a moment; then, in answer, he did not answer.

Old Blair nodded. "I take the point, sir. Let me put it another way. Should you try to provision or, better yet in my view, increase the garrison, the rebels will open fire and then you will have the right to restore the Union by force."

"Who then will have started this war? I who provoked an attack upon Federal property or those who responded to my provocation?"

"Mr. President, the winner need never explain why or how he won, or if he was the aggressor or not." Hay felt a premonitory chill. As he listened to the thin old southern voice, he felt as if the ghost of Andrew Jackson was indeed in the Blue Room, counselling his successors; an ancestral voice, prophesying war.

"Mr. Blair, I am a minority president. I am not the first, of course, and I am still the only rightful President between the Canadian and the Mexican borders. But I must think now of the minority that chose me. Seward and Chase were rejected because, rightly or wrongly, the public saw them as abolitionists, spoiling for war. So the party—and later the nation—turned to me, a man from slave-holding Kentucky, a man of the border-states, a so-called disciple of Henry Clay of Lexington, Kentucky, where my wife comes from, a man who said that although he would not countenance the extension of slavery, he had not the power to abolish slavery in any state where it now flourishes. Mr. Blair, what do I say to those men who voted for me in the hope that I would do what I said I would do, and keep the peace?"

Old Blair swung slightly away from Lincoln, so that he faced the portrait of the beturbanned Dolley Madison. "You might say to them what you said to them three years ago when you accepted the nomination for Senate. 'I believe this government cannot endure permanently, half slave and half free.'"

Lincoln looked suddenly irritated. Hay had noticed that Lincoln truly disliked it when others quoted him, which was odd since he had very much the politician's habit of self-quotation. "The emphasis, Mr. Blair, was on the adverb 'permanently.' Of course it cannot; and in the normal course, it will not."

"What *is* the normal course then?"

"I have not yet had a vision." Lincoln half smiled. "I did say 'I do not expect the house to fall.'"

"Sir, you also said, 'I do not expect the Union to be dissolved.' But the Union is dissolved."

"I do not recognize any dissolution." Lincoln's voice was cold and deliberate. Hay had never heard him strike this note before. "It is true that certain elements have rebelled against the Federal authority. Since that rebellion must cease, I must bring those elements around to my way of thinking. All we need now is patience." Lincoln's voice lightened. "Anyway, those cotton republics will never amount to a hill of beans."

"They will if Virginia and my Maryland and your Kentucky and the other border-states join them. A confederation of those states will make up quite a sizable mountain of beans."

"That is why, every day, I talk to the Virginians."

"Any progress?"

"Why, yes. Fact, they are now developing a new kind of logic. It goes like this: If I let Fort Sumter alone, and if I let South Carolina and the other states remain *out* of the Union, why, then Virginia will stay *in* the Union. Isn't that brilliant?"

"They have a way with them." The Old Gentleman dried his lips. "There will be war, of course. All through the South, the men are arming. Right here in Washington, they are drilling to beat the band." Blair turned to face Lincoln head-on. "Sir, when you destroyed the Democratic Party, you took upon yourself the responsibility of the whole political system of the country. You are now all that remains of the original republic. If you don't assert yourself"—Blair gestured to include the Blue Room, the house, the city, the idea that contained it all—"all this is done for."

Lincoln stepped back, as if from a stove that had become too hot. Hay wondered what he would reply; what he could reply under the circumstances. The inaugural oath still sounded in Hay's ears: the high voice that positively shouted the word "defend."

"What?" asked Lincoln mildly, "do you mean when you say that I destroyed the Democratic Party?"

"You destroyed Judge Douglas in those debates."

"I was under the impression that he defeated me in the election that followed."

"Mr. Lincoln, you are the subtlest man I have ever come across in politics. Oh, I'm not saying you aren't green in many ways, particularly with your appointments . . ."

"No one ever likes *any* president's appointments, including those appointed. But how did I destroy Judge Douglas?"

"You admit that two years ago he was the natural leader of the Democrats, and that he would be their presidential candidate?"

"I said as much at the time." Lincoln nodded; and frowned, as if he knew and did not like what was coming next.

"You admit that you were already thinking about getting the Republican nomination for yourself?"

"The taste was in my mouth, I suppose."

"Judge Douglas, who was very popular in the South, would, ordinarily, have kept the Democratic Party united, and gone on to win the South and the election if you hadn't asked him that question at Freeport during your debates."

Lincoln raised both his eyebrows. "Are you one of those who think that the question I put to the judge at Freeport was a deliberate trap that he fell into?"

"Yes, sir. I do. When you asked Douglas if the people of a territory could lawfully exclude slavery *before* the territory became a state, you knew that he would answer, yes, because that was the popular answer in Illinois that season and it would help him to defeat you. But you also knew that the moment he said, yes, he would lose the South two years later, which he did when the Democratic Party cracked in half, thereby making it possible for you to become President, a minority President."

"Do you think I plan so far ahead?" Lincoln's voice was distant. It was his turn now to stare at Dolley Madison.

100

"Yes, sir, I do."

"Well, I have no plan now, Mr. Blair."

Blair laughed, a shrill high sound. "Then *that* is your plan! And all success to you."

Lincoln turned to Hay. "Come on, Johnny, with those big ears flapping. You have some work to do upstairs."

Hay blushed; bowed to the Old Gentleman; and hurried from the room while the President and Mrs. Lincoln said good-night to their guests. Hay found Nicolay already in his office.

"What's your guess?" asked Hay.

"We give up Fort Sumter," said Nicolay.

"You should have heard old Blair just now. He's lit some kind of fire under the Ancient."

In the Cabinet Room, beneath the globe of a gas lamp, Lincoln's face was filled with shadows. He looked saturnine, thought Hay; even simian, he thought disloyally: the opposition press had taken to calling the President Honest Ape.

Of the seven Cabinet officers only six men were present. The Secretary of War, Mr. Cameron, was absent, as Hay duly noted in the ledger which would be the President's own version of the meeting. Nicolay sat across from Hay. He, too, made notes; he was also in charge of the various documents that the President might need.

Lincoln sat at the head of the table with Seward to his right and Chase to his left. Next to Chase was the Secretary of the Interior, Caleb B. Smith of Indiana—another border-state; he had been forced on Lincoln by the party managers. Smith was, as usual, frowning, and out of his depth. Opposite him sat the impressive Gideon Welles, whose vast gray beard was beautifully complemented by the most elaborate wig in all Washington, a masterpiece of curls and unexpected maritimelike waves. Next to him was the bearded Attorney-General, Edward Bates of Missouri; he, too, had been a border-state candidate at the convention; he, too, had been bitter at Lincoln's elevation; he now wore a beard exactly like Lincoln's, only much longer and fuller and more presidential; he was the oldest member of the Cabinet. Opposite Bates was Montgomery Blair; although the Blairs were originally from Kentucky, the Old Gentleman had staked out Maryland for his kingdom, while the two sons, Montgomery and Francis, Junior, or Frank as everyone called him, chose to make their way in Missouri. Montgomery had been mayor of St. Louis. Frank was a congressman from the state. "The compound Cabinet" filled Hay with awe—for Lincoln. If the President had known what he had let himself in for when he put all his rivals together, he had, if nothing else, a lion's courage.

"Gentlemen, Mr. Lamon has just returned from Charleston. I think we should listen to him. Ward!" Lincoln raised his voice and Lamon entered from the President's office. "Take a seat." Lamon pulled up a chair beside Lincoln and proceeded to tell them, first, of his interview with the United States postmaster at Charleston, who had gone over to the rebels; second, his interview with Major Anderson at Fort Sumter, which had been arranged by the rebels. "The major waits for his orders. He has enough food for two weeks. After that, he will have to surrender. Or fight." Lamon looked at Lincoln, who simply ruffled his hair until it stood up in clumps like turkey feathers. Lamon continued. "The governor of South Carolina gave me a message for the President, of which the gist—it was very flowery—the gist—"

"The thorn," supplied Lincoln, to Chase's indignation: was the man ever serious?

"—was that if we try to reinforce Fort Sumter, there will be war."

"Thank you, Ward."

Lamon left the room. Lincoln put on his spectacles; picked up a sheet of paper. "The reason for this meeting is that General Scott has sent me the following advice: We would do well to give up both Fort Sumter and Fort Pickens in Florida."

"Good God!" Montgomery Blair's voice was almost as shrill as his father's, thought Hay. "Whose side is General Scott on?"

"Well, he's on our side. But he doesn't think much of it. He's given all his reasons, of which the principal one is that we don't have enough ships to relieve Fort Sumter, or the twenty thousand men he thinks will be needed to subdue Charleston. But we still have the problem of whether or not to provision the garrison that's already there. I have been in communication with a naval officer—Mr. Welles and I both have." Lincoln nodded to his Secretary of the Navy. "I have told this officer, a Captain Fox, that I want an expedition ready to sail no later than April 6. He has already submitted to me his plans. I find them plausible. Also, Captain Fox was recently in Charleston, and he spoke with Major Anderson. He is confident that we can provision the fort. But we must move quickly. Now I would like each of you gentlemen, between now and tomorrow's Cabinet meeting, to write out your views of what ought to be done. But since we are all here and since you now know General Scott's military advice, I am curious to know how it strikes you. Mr. Seward."

Seward chewed a moment on his unlit, out of deference to the President, cigar. He had already conferred privately with General Scott. He knew what ought to be done but there, in his path, was this political novice. He liked Lincoln well enough, but he

102

had yet to see in the man's character the slightest sign of anything but timidity and vacillation. "Well, sir, I take seriously General Scott. If we don't have the means to make a winning fight at Charleston, then I'm for giving up the fort..."

There was a bark from Blair, which Hay could find no way of translating. So he wrote the words, "Blair: bark." They could always be erased. Seward ignored the sound.

"This does not mean that I am in favor of allowing the Confederacy to get off scot-free. I believe that we should prepare for war, but with an eye to extending our domain southward into Mexico. So I would concentrate on Florida and Texas. Those states can easily be regained, and that will then put us in a position to keep the French out of Mexico and drive the Spanish from Cuba and other points south."

"But what," asked Blair, the family sneer in place, "will those states between here and Texas and Florida be doing while we are fighting France and Spain?"

"I think, sir, that a war, in the name of the Monroe Doctrine, will unite them to us."

Blair's response was a strangled sound. Hay wrote, "strangled sound."

Chase was appalled by Seward. "I voted yes and no last time we met on this issue. I am now in favor of provisioning Fort Sumter, no matter what the risk."

When the others had spoken, Lincoln took the vote: Seward, Smith and Bates favored the evacuation of the fort, while Chase, Blair and Welles were in favor of provisioning it.

Lincoln's knees were now under his chin, the shins pressed against the table's edge. "You see, gentlemen, the division among you is pretty much like the one inside of my own head."

Seward listened with despair to this presidential Hamlet. There must be some way, he fretted, of removing Lincoln from the active execution—or, in this case, nonexecution of the office. Perhaps he and Chase could form some sort of regency...

Chase was thinking along the same line. Plainly, the President was inadequate for the task ahead. He lacked entirely that moral foundation without which no great work may be accomplished in the world. He was nothing more than a run-of-the-mill politician of the western sort. He would have made a splendid governor of Illinois; and no more. But here in this room where Jackson and Polk had sat, he seemed—unlikely was the kindest word that Chase could think of. He wondered what Kate and the President had been laughing about at dinner. Mrs. Lincoln had not been pleased; on the other hand, he felt that he himself had made some headway with her. Strange that she should have been in Lexington the day of Eliza's auction. The South must be destroyed. There was no real alternative anymore. What was the President saying?

"Mr. Welles, I have prepared the following order for you." Lincoln handed a sheet of paper to Welles, who read it and smiled and nodded until the huge false mane of hair resembled a tidal wave ready to overwhelm the Cabinet table.

"What is the order, sir?" asked Seward, suddenly uneasy. Better a president who did not act at all to one who did the wrong thing in a perilous time.

"I have just ordered Captain Fox to prepare to set sail from New York Harbor any time before April 6, with the means to provision Fort Sumter, and perhaps more."

Seward bit in half his cigar, and threw both halves in the spittoon at his feet. "But, Mr. President, I thought the Cabinet was evenly divided on the matter, and that you wanted our considered opinions written and that Captain Fox's departure should be delayed and that..."

Chase answered for Lincoln. "Mr. Seward, if *preparations* are not made *now*, they can never be made. Isn't that correct, Mr. President?"

Lincoln nodded, somewhat absently, thought Hay. "Many things can happen between now and the time that Captain Fox's fleet is at Charleston. But it is better for us to have a range of choice than none at all."

"I know Captain Fox," said Blair. "He is a splendid officer. He was at the Naval Academy at Annapolis not so long after I was at West Point."

To the extent that Seward's essentially Jesuitical nature allowed him to dislike or like anyone in the practise of his trade, he disliked all the Blairs. But the time was drawing near, Seward knew, when he must drop his mask with Lincoln and speak openly of the dangers of a presidency that was still without direction. He had already fathomed what Blair, plainly, had not: the departure of Captain Fox meant nothing in itself. Fort Sumter would be evacuated, peacefully, long before Captain Fox arrived; or reduced to rubble; or, best of all, forgotten.

"Captain Fox may have some trouble raising money for the ships." Lincoln turned to Chase. "You may have to go searching in the larder."

"It is not exactly a full larder that we were left." Chase understated the case, so pleased was he at the President's sudden semblance of activity. The Treasury was in a state of total confusion. Should war come, Chase had, as yet, no idea how to finance a military establishment. Through the Cookes, he was becoming acquainted with the magnates of the banking world: he

104

found that their ways were as strange to him as his were to them. One did not even try to sound moral in their presence.

Lincoln rose, undid his tie, yawned. "Gentlemen, I bid you good-night." The others rose; and remained standing in place until the President was gone. Then Seward turned to Chase. "Will you stroll home with me?"

"Of course. Kate has taken our carriage..."

Seward now occupied all of the Old Club House that looked upon Lafayette Square. The nearby spire of Saint John's Church was like a dark iron nail against the night sky. "I am able to pray," said Seward, indicating the church, "at a moment's notice."

"Did you ever get the President to go to St. John's again?"

"No, but I'm working on it. I believe that he goes now to the Presbyterian church." As they crossed the damp, wooded park, the lights were going off in the Executive Mansion, while a single street lamp served the entire street that edged the park.

As the two men entered the house, they were greeted by Seward's large, enthusiastic dog, Midge, heiress to many canine bloodlines. Midge led them into the downstairs study where Seward's son, Frederick, sat by the smoldering fire; at work in his shirt-sleeves. The young man greeted Chase; and excused himself. While Chase sat in a sofa beside the fire, Seward poured himself a goblet of brandy. "I am as thirsty as the great Sahara," he said.

"I have not the habit," said Chase. "Nor the thirst," he added, precisely.

Seward sat opposite Chase, twisting the goblet between his hands. "You and I disagree on Fort Sumter, but only as to means, and timing."

"We disagree, perhaps, about the urgent need to abolish slavery," said Chase mildly.

"You would go to war for that?"

"If it was necessary, yes."

"Wouldn't you rather go to war against Spain, and acquire Cuba? Against the French, and acquire Mexico?"

"I would rather acquire Charleston."

"But we would have outflanked the cotton states." Seward was persuasive; and elaborate. Chase listened, carefully. The concept was ingenious. The famed two birds that it was always his dream with one stone to kill might, at last, be snared.

"Let us say," said Chase, when Seward had finished with his design for empire, "that I am open to the idea in general. But in particular..."

"There is a log in our way, Mr. Chase. Or should I say a rail?"

Chase nodded. "It is plain to me that Mr. Lincoln is a well-meaning but inadequate man."

"And it is plain to me that you and I, together, could administer the country better than he, and if war comes, we could prosecute it better than he."

"I agree." Chase had never liked Seward or his morals—or lack of them. But Seward was the consummate politician of the age. Between Seward's wiliness and his own high moral purpose, they could indeed conduct a successful administration and prosecute, if necessary, a winning war. Chase said as much. "But"— he added the obvious—"*he* was elected President."

"Because he was elected, we have lost—or will lose—close to a third of our population. Seven states are gone. Others will go. The minority that elected him disunited the country. Should war come, then such a high emergency would dictate that some combination—with his agreement, of course—would be called upon to direct the government."

"He has us, the *compound* Cabinet." Chase came as close to irony as his temperament would allow.

"He has you and he has me. Do we have him?" Seward squinted through cigar smoke.

"In what sense?" Chase began to feel not unlike Cassius listening to Brutus. Or was it the other way around?

"Mr. Chase, I am going to propose to him, openly, that either you or I or both be allowed to direct the Administration. No more votes of three to three. No more funny stories. No more procrastination—"

"*You* will ask him to abdicate?"

"Of course not. He will continue to be what he is, the President. But the engine of this Administration will be us." Seward was surprised at his own magnanimity in allowing Chase to share with him, as it were (each now tended to think in Roman terms), the consulate. But he knew Chase to be a formidable figure; and not easily put aside.

"I shall be curious to see what he has to say to your proposal." Chase was always slow to take to new ideas. But once absorbed, they became a part of his very flesh. On this noncommittal note, Chase lifted his considerable flesh from the sofa, and asked that a hack be summoned. In politics, as in love, opposites attract, and the misunderstandings that ensue tend to be as bitter and, as in love, as equally terminal.

12

THOMPSON'S DRUG STORE SHUT AT NOON ON SUNDAY, APRIL 14. Ordinarily, the pharmacy would not have been open at all on a Sunday but there was so much excitement in the city that Mr. Thompson could not bear to shut up shop when, after the bar at Willard's, Thompson's Drug Store was one of the city's finest rumor centers. Already that morning the doorkeeper to the Executive Mansion, Mr. McManus, had come with a prescription to be filled for Mrs. Lincoln, whose nerves craved laudanum, and an extra supply of blue mass to move yet more urgently the presidential bowels.

While David made up the prescription in the back room, Mr. Thompson and a half-dozen of the shop's regulars questioned Mr. McManus closely.

"What will the President do, do you think, sir?" Mr. Thompson treated with deference anyone connected with the great house across the avenue.

"A stern retaliation, you may be sure. But I must not say, of course, what form it will be taking." McManus always affected to know the inner councils of the Presidency; and Mr. Thompson thought him an oracle, though in David's few encounters with the old Irishman he had never heard him say anything that he could not have read in a newspaper.

"What will happen to Major Anderson and the garrison?" asked a customer.

"There is talk of the rebels holding them for ransom like common bandits." David doubted this; whatever the faults of his countrymen, and so he regarded the South Carolinans, they were not bandits but men of honor.

"It was heroic," said Mr. Thompson, arranging the patent medicines on their special shelf, each according to size. He was devoted to symmetry. "Thirty-four hours of bombardment from the rebels. The flag in flames. The fort in flames . . ."

"It would've been a whole lot more heroic if they'd fought to the death," said a distinctly Southern voice.

"To what point?" asked McManus. "General Beauregard has thousands of men in Charleston Harbor. Why, I've seen the map

107

in the President's office. He keeps it on an easel, like it was a picture."

"Why," asked Thompson, a copy of the *Star* in front of him, "didn't the ships arrive in time to provision the garrison?"

"They did arrive, Mr. Thompson, they got there just when the bombardment started."

"So why didn't they go and fire back at the... rebels?" said the mocking Southern voice.

David entered the front part of the store, two packages in hand. McManus was getting more red in the face than usual. "Because they was stopped by the tide. There is this sandbar at the harbor entrance. Until the tide comes in, you can't enter the port." This was *not* in any of the papers that David had read. Perhaps McManus did know something after all, and if he did... David gave Mr. McManus the packages. "Thank you. Good-day, Mr. Thompson, gentlemen."

Mr. McManus left the shop. "I've never seen so many people at the White House, on a Sunday," said one of the regular customers. "Every big frog in the town has come to call."

"I reckon there's a lot of croaking going on across the street," said the Southerner, with quiet malice. Mr. Thompson made a soothing noise. He made it a point never to take sides politically; he sold his pills and powders and tonics to all.

As Mr. Thompson and David proceeded to shut up shop, David received the unpleasant news that he was to go across the river to Alexandria that afternoon. "I got this urgent message from old Mrs. Alexander herself; the town's named for their family, you know, and I'm the only one who can make up the exact prescription she needs so as to lose the water she must lose for the dropsy. It's right here." Mr. Thompson indicated a package next to the porcelain jar that contained essence of pure mint. "The address is written on it."

"But this is Sunday, Mr. Thompson..." David began; and shortly thereafter ended. He was to go by foot to Alexandria, across the Long Bridge. No, he could not have the money for a hack. He was young; while the exercise was worth all Mr. Thompson's wares rolled into one vast pill, said the proprietor, whose hatred of walking was so great that he had been known to wait an hour for the horsecars to take him from Tenth to Fifteenth streets.

The day was mild; the air warm. The first white lilacs had opened in the President's Park. David paused in front of the White House gate. Open and closed carriages were depositing stout, solemn figures at the portico, where Mr. McManus stood, bowing them inside. The war had started at last. Although David knew which side he would be on, the notion of serving in an army,
108

anyone's army, did not delight him. Nor did he want to join the wild boys, who had so signally failed to assassinate Mr. Lincoln on March 4: "There was these guards at the Long Bridge, and they wouldn't let us back in the city till it was too late," one of them had whined. In any case, most of the wild boys had already gone South to join the new Confederate army. Perhaps he could be some sort of spy. He was well placed at Thompson's Drug Store. When Annie got back from Surrattsville, he would ask her advice. He knew that Isaac had vanished—into Virginia, people said. But neither Mrs. Surratt nor Annie ever mentioned Isaac. They were a close-mouthed family, unlike his own. David groaned aloud at the thought of the house of women—nice women—to which he had been, by fate and his father's thoughtless death, consigned and condemned.

As the carriage containing a small, thick-chested, large-headed man clattered past David and through the gate, he turned and made his way, slowly, toward the Long Bridge.

Mr. McManus bowed very low to the short man. "Senator Douglas, the President is waiting for you, sir. In the Red Room."

"Good to see you, Old Edward." The resonant bass voice was as firm as ever but the face was colorless. And the hand that its owner gave Lincoln to shake was cold and weak. "Well, Mr. President," he said, "here you are."

"Here *we* are, Judge," said Lincoln, leading Douglas to a chair beneath Washington's portrait. "Just the two of us, like old times."

"All in all, Mr. Lincoln, I'm sort of glad that it's me calling on you and not the other way around."

Lincoln smiled a weary smile. "You know, Judge, I have a peculiar hunch that you might mean exactly what you say."

"What can I do?" Douglas sat very straight in his chair, and looked taller than he was.

"I want you to listen to something. Then we'll talk." Lincoln removed a document from his pocket. "It's a proclamation. I'll read you the salient points. I start by condemning those elements in the states of South Carolina, Georgia, Alabama, Florida, Mississippi and Louisiana for obstructing the execution of the law . . ."

Ever the sharp lawyer, Douglas picked up on the word "execution." "You are deliberately invoking your oath, to execute the laws. Am I right?"

"Yes, Judge. That oath is my bulwark and my shield and my . . . sword." Lincoln pronounced the "w" in sword; and smiled. "Remember how that was the way we always pronounced the word as boys? Because we'd only *seen* the word in books . . ." Lincoln looked down at the text. "Therefore, I, Abraham Lincoln, President of the United States . . ."

Douglas blinked his eyes rapidly, as if he had just awakened from a dream, to find that his rival was in his place; and that he was now nowhere. ". . . in virtue of the power in me vested by the Constitution and the laws . . ."

"The oath," murmured Douglas, nodding. He was beginning now to understand what Lincoln was doing; he also understood the perils implicit in such a high royal progress to an end that no one on this earth could anticipate or even imagine.

". . . have thought fit to call forth, and hereby do call forth, the militia of the several States of the Union to the aggregate number of seventy-five thousand, in order to repress said combinations and to cause the laws to be duly executed." Lincoln looked up. "Well?"

"*Executed* again." Douglas nodded; and in the round sick face he managed a smile. "But it's like Hotspur, isn't it? You may summon all you like. But will they come?"

"They have no choice when I call upon them to preserve, protect and defend the Union." Lincoln spelled it out, as if he were carving his own epitaph in marble.

"Yes, they will come." Douglas nodded. "But it won't be easy. I think seventy-five thousand is too few. Ask for two hundred thousand men."

"I must demonstrate the need first." Lincoln glanced at the paper. "I go on to say that these troops will be needed to repossess our forts and so on, peacefully, of course." Lincoln sighed. "And then I address the so-called governments of the rebellion and I say, 'I hereby command the persons composing the combinations aforesaid to disperse and retire peaceably to their respective abodes within twenty days from this date,' which is as of tomorrow April 15, 1861. I then call Congress into session on the Fourth of July. Well?"

"Well, you've given yourself until July 4 to play the dictator, and I suggest that you do *all* that you think must be done to crush the rebellion *before* Congress comes back."

"I had not thought of it in quite those terms, Judge." Lincoln smiled; and began to tug his hair into wild and characteristic disarray. "It's true that I don't want Congress here until I know who's going to be in it and I won't know that until I see what other states decide to leave the Union. I reckon by the Fourth of July we'll know the worst."

Douglas nodded. "Certainly, Virginia will go. Maryland?"

"I am prepared to hold Maryland by force."

"Can you?"

"If I don't, we lose this city. The governor of Maryland is with us, unlike the governor of Kentucky, who is working for secession.
110

Fortunately, our friend old Doctor Breckinridge—you know, John C.'s uncle—is holding fast to the Union, and he carries great weight. It is also helpful that our first—and only—hero so far, Major Anderson, is a Kentuckian."

"What did happen yesterday? Was he captured?"

"No. That was just our friends in the press. The major turned the fort over to Mister Beauregard, formerly of the United States Army, who then put him and his men aboard one of our ships. He's on his way here now."

"Why did Mister Beauregard fire on Fort Sumter when all you were going to do was provision it?"

"You will have to find some way to enter the mind of Mr. Jefferson Davis, who gave the order to Mr. Beauregard. A week ago, I sent a clerk from the War Department down to Charleston to read to Governor Pickens a note from me to the effect that if they did not try to stop us from provisioning our fort, we would in no way add to its manpower or fire power. The clerk left my note with the governor, who sent it on to Mr. Davis, who then gave orders for Anderson to evacuate the fort, which he refused to do. I have always been told that Mr. Davis, when you really get to know him, is one of the damnedest fools that ever lived, and now I believe it." Lincoln folded the proclamation; and put it in his pocket.

"Well, you said that *you* would never be the aggressor, and I guess you're not." There was a faint smile on Douglas's lips.

"What does that smile mean, Judge?" With left eyebrow raised, Lincoln gave Douglas a look of comical suspicion.

"After that deep grave you dug for me at Freeport—and unlike Mr. Davis I am no damned fool—I suspect you of . . . maneuvering."

"Oh, not like that, Judge. Not like that." Lincoln was on his feet, pacing the room, pulling at his hair. "It is true that I could have let the thing go. What difference does it make who holds a fort that is worthless to us and probably not much use to them if war comes?"

"War has come, Mr. President."

Lincoln stopped at the window; turned back into the room. "Yes, it has come."

"So now you have your chance to re-create the republic."

Lincoln was startled. "What do you mean by that?"

"Well, when I was getting ready for our last set of debates, I rummaged around and found a copy of an old speech you gave to the Young Men's Lyceum in Springfield."

"My God, Judge, I was a boy when I gave that talk."

"You were twenty-eight, at which age Alexander the Great had

111

been remarkably active. You mentioned him, too. And Julius Caesar. And Napoleon, I believe."

"As tyrants, yes, but..."

"As tyrants, yes." Douglas was inexorable. In a sense, this was his revenge on the man who had put him forever to one side. "You said that the founders of the republic had got all the glory that there was and that those who come after can never be anything except mere holders of office, and that this was not enough to satisfy 'the family of the lion, or the tribe of the eagle.'"

Lincoln stared down at Douglas. There was no expression on his face; he had frozen in an attitude of attention; and nothing more.

"Your lion and your eagle cannot endure the notion of following in the footsteps of any predecessor, or of anyone at all. Your great man 'thirsts and burns for distinction; and, if possible, he will have it, whether at the expense of emancipating slaves, or enslaving free men.' I learned a lot of that speech, just in case."

Lincoln continued to stare down at Douglas, who gave a half salute to the figure between him and the room's far window. "Well, you are the eagle, you are the lion. You have it in your power, thanks to that marvelous oath the Constitution unwittingly gave you, to free the slaves or to enslave us all. Which will it be?"

Lincoln shook his head as if he had been dreaming; and said, "I have already given the proclamation to the Associated Press." The manner was matter-of-fact. "It will be in every newspaper tomorrow."

"You won't answer me?"

"There is nothing to answer, Judge. But I seem to remember that I ended that speech with the hope that we would return to George Washington, and never violate his principles."

"But you also said that those principles had quite faded away. And that there must now be something else." Douglas waited for an answer; but there was none. "Well, whatever else there is, you have it now."

"Yes." Lincoln nodded; and looked away; and spoke as if to himself. "I have it now."

Hay was at the door. "Mr. Seward is here, sir."

"Tell him to wait in the Cabinet Room."

"What can I do to help?" Douglas repeated.

"Make a statement to the effect that you support the proclamation and the Union."

"And the eagle and the lion?"

"I would refrain from zoological metaphors." Lincoln smiled.

"I will say that we are all Republicans, that we are all Democrats. *I* don't mind imitating the founders."

112

"And you think that I mind?"

"I have never heard you praise any president or any political leader—except that one time when you were called on to give an obituary of Henry Clay."

"Well, there is one that I always praise—when I remember." Lincoln pointed to the portrait of Washington.

"The first of them all. Well, let us pray that you will not be the last."

"Let us pray that I am the last of what we have been enduring for half a century."

"It is not enough to be James Buchanan?"

"Oh, Judge! Go on like that and you will really hear the lion's roar!"

Laughing, the two men left the Red Room. As they crossed the entrance hall, Mary and Lizzie came toward them from the East Room.

"Mary Todd!" Douglas threw wide his arms.

"Judge Douglas!" Impulsively, Mary embraced the man the world thought that she might have married. Then she pulled back. "Oh, what have I done, Father?" She turned to Lincoln.

"Well, I won't tell the State Department about your unseemly display if you won't tell them how many pairs of white kid gloves I've lost."

"You grace this house, Mary Todd." Douglas looked at her intently. She noticed, as she always did when they were face-to-face, that each was the same height and so they could look each other, levelly, in the eye. Then Douglas turned to Lincoln. "If she had consented to marry me, I'd be here instead of you."

"But, Judge, suppose she'd gone and married John C. Breckinridge? Then *he'd* be here."

Mary laughed, amused and proud. "I don't think any other woman was ever in such a position, with three of her beaux all running for president in the same year."

"Or," said Douglas, "if she'd been a bit older, she might have got off with Jefferson Davis when he was at Transylvania College; and been queen of the South."

Lincoln chuckled. "Or a bit younger and she could've married Montgomery Blair. He was at Transylvania, too."

"Now you go too far, Father. I was never searching for a politician to marry, only a brilliant man. Having been courted by the two of you, that's more than enough honor for me."

"That was joy for me," said Douglas, swaying slightly.

"Are you all right?" Mary took his arm. Lincoln came forward and took the other arm.

"You should go back to your bed, Judge," said Lincoln. "Save

113

up your energy and get well. There's work for us to do." Lincoln shook Douglas's hand with both of his own.

"I know." Douglas started toward the door. Lincoln motioned for Old Edward to help him. "I'll write my message straight away, and give it to the wire-service. I'll see that it appears alongside your proclamation."

"Thank you, Judge."

When Douglas was gone, Mary turned to Lincoln. "Father, he's dying."

Lincoln nodded. "That is my impression, too."

"Our past is leaving us, isn't it?"

"Well, I reckon we're sort of in motion ourselves."

"Father!"

"I didn't say *today*, Molly. Now I've work to do."

Seward was staring out the window of the Cabinet Room at the shaggy south lawn, strewn now with daffodils and narcissus and truly gorgeous weeds. Across the river, the hills of Virginia were a smoky blue—like good cigar smoke, he thought, removing the unlighted stump from his mouth just as Hay opened the door and said, "Sir, the President."

Lincoln entered, hair on end. As Lincoln took his place next to Seward at the Cabinet table, Seward noticed that he had not shaved for at least two days. He also noticed several gray hairs in the coarse black whiskers at the corner of the President's beard.

"Judge Douglas was just here. He thinks I should've asked for two hundred thousand men. But I'm afraid we'll have trouble enough getting the ones I've called for."

"Will he support you publicly?"

Lincoln nodded. "He'll make a statement tomorrow."

"He carries great weight, particularly in New York, where we will have our problems."

"But I thought that your mayor of New York..."

"Sir, he is not *my* mayor."

"Mr. Seward, I think of the whole state of New York as being your personal farm. Anyway, the mayor has just sent me a message saying that he would like New York City to secede from the Union, and become what he calls 'a free city.'"

Seward sighed. "He is a great fool. But he is sly; and a lot of New Yorkers feel as he does. It's all those immigrants, particularly the Irish, the Papists. I must say they have always loved me. Probably too much for my own good." Seward suddenly smiled. "They ended my political career, you know. I thought we should give state money to their schools. The bishop thought me a splendid fellow. The West did not. What did you say to the mayor?"

"I said I was not about to let the front door set up housekeeping on its own."

Seward laughed, genuinely amused; he was also genuinely uneasy. On April 1, he had written Lincoln a long memorandum, outlining the problems that faced the Administration and, in the process, he had delivered himself of certain "home truths," as he described them to Chase, which he feared that Lincoln might take offense at. Nearly two weeks had passed and Lincoln had made no mention of the memorandum. Seward presumed that the reason he had now been sent for, on this day of all days, was to discuss those truths. Seward was right.

Lincoln put his hands behind his head and the long splayed brown fingers intertwined. "I have taken some time to answer your thoughts for my consideration, dated April the first."

Seward wondered if this might be a pointed reference to All Fools Day; but if it were, Lincoln gave no particular sign. "I wrote you a letter the same day, but thought we should talk before you read it. In your . . . bill of indictment, you tell me that at the end of the Administration's first month in office we have no foreign policy and no domestic policy even though we had met, President and Cabinet, seven or eight times and together made many decisions, of which you were a part. Today, for instance, I have called upon the states for troops. I believe you think that I did the right thing?"

"Yes, sir. Naturally, what I wrote you was before you decided to provision Fort Sumter, and of course their attack—"

Lincoln interrupted him, somewhat abruptly. "I take two essential points from your memorandum. The first is that we should begin a continental war with the European powers as a huge diversion, including a declaration of war on Spain. Precisely *how* we are to overthrow the Spanish garrisons in Santo Domingo and Cuba when we cannot, properly, support one of our own forts in South Carolina, you do not say."

"In the event of war, there would be, naturally, armies raised, ships built, as you are doing now. What I would count on, sir, is the unifying principle that would have its effect on all Americans if we were to go to war with France and Spain."

"I respect your opinion, Mr. Seward, as always." Lincoln was bland as he withdrew the—fatal, Seward was beginning to think—memorandum from his inside pocket. "You make the point that we should shift the issue between us and the rebels from that of slavery to that of union or disunion. I was under the impression that that was exactly what I did in my inaugural address." Lincoln looked Seward straight in the eyes. Although the gray eyes were as dreamy as ever, the left lid was drawn higher than usual.

115

These are the eyes of a hunter, thought Seward; and he shifted his ground. "I have, perhaps, felt that you pay too much attention to the abolitionists, and that this is causing distress in the border-states."

"Your opinion is valuable to me, Mr. Seward." The eyes continued to stare into Seward's until the Secretary of State affected a cigar-smoker's cough in order to pull out his handkerchief and escape that curiously equable yet entirely disconcerting gaze. "I think Mr. Chase and Mr. Sumner and every so-called abolitionist in the country would tell you that I have favored too much the sensibilities of the slave-owners. But it is your last point, Mr. Seward, which most concerns me." Lincoln looked at the paper in his hand. "You say that whatever policy we do adopt must be prosecuted energetically."

"I think, sir, we are all agreed as to that. The drift must stop..."

"The drift..." Lincoln looked out the window. "How strange that you should use that word! I dreamt last night that I was on a raft on a river so wide that I could not see either shore, and I had no pole, and I was drifting." Lincoln turned back to Seward. "Plainly, Mr. Seward, you were visiting me in my dreams. Now this is what I find most curious." Lincoln put on his glasses and read. "'Either the President must do it himself, and be all the while active in it or devolve it on some member of his Cabinet.'" For a moment, Lincoln looked over the top rims of his glasses at Seward, who maintained his Jesuitical smile. Lincoln continued to read. "'Once adopted, debate on it must end, and all agree and abide. It is not my especial province. But I neither seek nor assume responsibility.' This is a most unusual document, Mr. Seward. Most unusual." Lincoln half crumpled the paper and, idly, stuffed it in his side pocket. "You are saying that we need a strong leader from within the Cabinet, and that we must all obey him when he raises a navy to attack, let's say, the French coast."

"Sir, I see no alternative to this sort of leadership."

"Would you rather that I did *not* consult the Cabinet? That I did not open myself to the views of all?"

"I think there can be too much discussion and too little action."

"That is possible. But it is not my way to rush into any great event, particularly if it looks as if war is a more than likely result at a time when we have no army to speak of, no navy to speak of, and a Treasury that is close to empty."

"Nevertheless, firm, decisive action..."

Lincoln tapped the table with one long finger; and Seward stopped as if he had heard the cracking of a whip. "There is nothing firmer nor more decisive—nor, I fear, more irrevocable—than my summoning of the troops. Now I realize that it is your view
116

that our party made a significant error in nominating me instead of you..."

"Sir, I have never said such a thing."

Lincoln smiled. "I am sure that you are far too loyal a member of my Administration ever to *say* such a thing. But you have just gone and written it, confidentially, to me." Lincoln paused.

Seward had a sense of having, somehow, lost control of a situation which he had assumed had been very much in hand. "Sir, I have in good—and open, to you, that is—faith made known my deep opinion—"

"For which I thank you. We shall now act as if this exchange never took place."

Seward rose. "Under the circumstance, sir, I think it best for me to resign."

"Well, I don't. So you just stay where you are. We have more than enough work for two men to do." Lincoln led Seward to the door to the Cabinet Room, which Seward opened; then he stood back so that the President could precede him through the door. Lincoln looked down a moment at Seward. "I think we better keep this to ourselves. Who else knows about your memorandum?"

"Only my son, Frederick."

Lincoln nodded. "Nicolay and Hay have seen it. But they will be silent as the tomb. We don't," said Lincoln with a half smile, "want Mr. Chase hearing about any of this, do we?"

"Why, no. No, we don't." Seward smiled his conspiratorial smile, as Nicolay came forward to lead him through the unusual-for-Sunday crowd that had gathered in the waiting room to hear the latest news from Charleston.

Lincoln motioned for Hay to join him in the President's office. It was Hay's self-appointed task to keep Lincoln moving when he tarried too long with visitors. Hay could never understand Lincoln's endless patience with even the most audacious of bores or boors. "They get so little, most of them," Lincoln would say, as if in explanation of the time wasted.

Once inside the President's office, Lincoln sank into his maplewood chair. "The seat of office," he would say of the shabby chair when showing visitors around. "Tell General Scott that I would like him to put a telegraph machine in the small room there." Lincoln pointed to the sliver of a room which was Nicolay's office.

Then Lincoln handed Hay the Seward memorandum. "Lock this away in the strongbox. I don't think Mr. Seward will ever want anybody to look at it." Lincoln chuckled. "He thinks he runs me. Well, I don't suppose there's anything wrong with his *thinking* that."

"Sir, that friend of Senator Hale is waiting to see you. He wanted the consulship at Liverpool, and we gave him the consulship at Vera Cruz. He's not happy."

"Send him in."

The would-be consul was a well-dressed young New Englander, with chains of gold across a youthful paunch. "Mr. Lincoln, sir. This is an honor, sir."

Lincoln shook his hand. "Sit down, friend. What can I do for you?"

"Well, sir. I'd hoped for Liverpool, and Senator Hale said it was all arranged with Mr. Seward. But then, I got the official letter which says I got to go to Vera Cruz, where I hear the bugs there eat you alive . . ."

"Well, in that unhappy event, sir, I can only say that they'll leave behind a mighty fine suit of clothes and a watch chain . . ."

Suddenly a disembodied, treble voice sounded in the room. "Pa, don't you ever get tired of folks?"

The consul-to-be leapt in his chair. "We have a ghost in the White House," said Lincoln, gently prodding Tad with his foot; lately, the boy had taken to hiding under his desk. "But we think it is benign."

13

HALFWAY ACROSS THE LONG BRIDGE, THE SWEATY DAVID paused to undo his tie, and stare down at the swift, yellow Potomac, swollen and muddy with the spring rains. All in all, he could not imagine a less agreeable way of wasting a Sunday afternoon than walking to Alexandria and back. He was also unpleasantly aware of the hard-eyed Union soldiers who were stationed along the bridge, studying the passers-by; particularly the few who were approaching the city from the Virginia side. Occasionally, a wagon from the South was stopped and searched as if it might contain the mysterious elements of secession. From the city, there was a great exodus of carriages, accompanied by wagons piled high with household goods—not to mention crates of chickens. The Union soldiers made no move to stop any of this traffic. They knew that there were secessionists, fleeing what had once been home but was now the capital of an enemy nation.

As David stared down at the river and thought of the pleasures of fishing, he heard a familiar sound, a staccato, dry coughing that seemed, somehow, all wrong in this setting. He looked up and saw what he took to be some sort of farmhand or tramp—a thin old man in tattered clothes, who moved slowly, as if in pain. It was not until they were face-to-face that David recognized old Mr. Surratt, who was supposed to be wasting away in the back parlor of H Street.

At first, Mr. Surratt looked away; but then David said, "Mr. Surratt, sir. I thought you was sick, sir."

"You thought right, Davie." Mr. Surratt rested a moment, back to the bridge's railing. The cough was not constant but came at intervals. There were respites when he could speak normally.

"I thought you never stirred from the back parlor."

"Well, now you see that I do. Fact, lately, I've been dressing up in these old clothes and going off to visit my friends on the Virginia side."

"Mr. Surratt, I want to help."

"Help?"

"Yes, sir. I think I know what you're doing. I think I know what Isaac is doing, too. You're passing information along to the Confederates. I want to help, any way I can."

Mr. Surratt gave David a sharp look. The face was pale with illness but the eyes were bright. The old man gestured. "You walk a bit ahead of me, like we don't know each other. We'll talk on the other side."

Although there were no guards on the Virginia side, a Confederate flag flew over a tavern door while, just opposite, a neighbor displayed the Union flag.

The carriages and wagons from the city did not pause; they continued their southerly journey toward Richmond and beyond. Mr. Surratt entered the tavern, followed by David. In the dim light of the main barroom, farmers sat about drinking whiskey, and talking what David assumed was either treason or the price of tobacco, each a subject calculated to excite these dour men, his own kin, his true confederates, he thought, suddenly sentimental. Mr. Surratt gave an envelope to a stout man, who motioned for him to go into a back room. David followed.

Mr. Surratt and David sat at a long wooden table, a bottle of whiskey and a number of dusty glasses between them.

"You're a good boy, Davie," said Mr. Surratt. "You're with us, I know. I hear that from my wife. I hear that from Annie. You can help us, too. There's work for you. But there's work for all of us who feel like we do. Now the best thing for you to do is go on down to Montgomery and sign up. President Davis has just got himself twenty thousand men, already under arms, they say."

119

"Don't you think, sir, I'm more use where I am? In the city, working at Thompson's."

"Working at Thompson's?" Mr. Surratt poured himself a whiskey. "Right across from the White House?"

"Yes, sir. The Lincolns and the Sewards and the Blairs and the Welleses all get their medicine from us. Fact, Mr. Seward lives almost next door to us, and Mr. Welles is a few doors from him, while the Blairs . . ."

They were joined by the stout man, the tavern's owner. "Who's this?" he asked, indicating David.

"Davie Herold. He's all right. He's with us. I've known him all his life."

The stout man poured whiskey for the three of them. "Well, I think after what you just now gave me, we drink a toast." He held up his glass. "To the Confederate States of America."

David drank his whiskey in a single gulp, just the way the wild boys did.

"When that message of yours gets to Richmond, which, I reckon, will be about ten minutes from now, Virginia will secede."

"It's about time." With an effort, Mr. Surratt held back a new series of coughs. David knew of a mixture that would reduce the coughing if not cure the disease, whatever it was. Had there ever been any money in the Herold family, he could have become a doctor, he thought, reaching for the whiskey bottle; or a lawyer, maybe. Mr. Surratt turned to David, "Who comes in?"

"Who comes in where?"

"Thompson's." Mr. Surratt turned to the stout man. "Davie is a prescription clerk at Thompson's Drug Store on Fifteenth Street, right near the White House. The Lincolns use the store, and so do a lot of members of the Cabinet." He turned to David. "So, just who comes in?"

"Well, there's Mr. McManus. He's been the White House doorkeeper for twenty years. He acts like he knows a lot. This morning, for instance, he said there's a map of Charleston Harbor on an easel like a picture in the President's office. Then there's Mr. Hay, the President's secretary. He's a young fellow, very snappy looking. He doesn't talk much. Then there's this high-yellow woman, Lizzie Keckley. She's a dressmaker to Mrs. Lincoln, and she spends quite a while every single day at the Mansion, or so old McManus says. He don't like her 'cause she's thick as thieves with Mrs. Lincoln, who suffers bad from the headache . . ."

"What does Mr. Lincoln suffer from?" asked the stout man.

"He has trouble sleeping. So we mix him the Thompson's special, which is mostly laudanum. And his bowels don't ever move properly, so we fill him up with blue mass. Otherwise, he's
120

all right. The two little boys just had the measles, a light case. Then there's Mr. Seward, practically next door. He suffers from the headache, too, but different from Mrs. Lincoln. His come from all the brandy he drinks. So we have to settle his stomach for him, too. Mrs. Gideon Welles..." As David described Thompson's distinguished customers and their various ailments, Mr. Surratt and the stout man exchanged a glance; and the stout man looked well pleased.

When David ran out of data, Mr. Surratt said, "The boy was asking me how he could help the cause. I said stay right where you are, and listen."

"I concur. Young man, you can be of real value to us just by keeping your ears open, and getting to know better the folks at the Mansion—and at Mr. Seward's house. He's the real boss of the government. Sometimes, we may have something specific we'll need to find out, and we'll get the word to you through Mr. Surratt here."

"Or through Annie in case I am no longer here." The withheld series of coughs now erupted; and the old man buried his face in his hands, shoulders heaving with pain. Whatever was wrong, David decided, it was not the consumption.

David turned to the stout man. "I could be useful as a courier, couldn't I?"

"We have enough of those. Besides, you don't want to lose your job at Thompson's."

"I guess not." David was disappointed. He had seen himself riding hard through the enemy's line, with coded messages in the heel of his boot.

When Mr. Surratt was done with his coughing, he rose, shakily; and took leave of the stout man. "I might, on a Sunday, say, send you Davie here."

"Take good care of yourself, John." The stout man did not accompany them to the front door. Outside the tavern, David said, "I got to go deliver medicine now."

"That's good, Davie." Mr. Surratt nodded. "When Virginia secedes, which could be as soon as tomorrow, thanks to what I just had my friend put on the telegraph, you'll probably need a pass to go back and forth across the Long Bridge, and they'll hand out one, easy as can be, to the boy from Thompson's."

"Then I might be a courier yet?"

"Why not? But as our friend said, keep your job. That's where you can help, really help our country!"

David could no longer contain his curiosity. "What was it that you gave him, that he's put on the telegraph? Or is it a real secret?"

"Well, it's a secret now but it won't be tomorrow. We got our hands on a proclamation that Old Abe is issuing tomorrow, calling on all states, including Virginia, to send him troops. They'll send him troops all right." Mr. Surratt laughed and coughed simultaneously. "They've just been waiting for something like this so as to leave the Union. Maryland, too."

David was excited to be almost a part of the secret service of the Confederacy; and, again, he saw himself riding through a dark and moonless night on some crucial mission. Exhausted and near collapse, he would give Jefferson Davis himself the vital, heretofore inaccessible information that the South needed to win the war. Head high, he walked toward Alexandria; and sang "Dixie" almost aloud.

Chase sat at his huge black-walnut desk and contemplated on the wall opposite him the portrait of the first Secretary of the Treasury, Alexander Hamilton, whose problems were negligible compared to his own. Chase was a meticulous man who enjoyed hard work. This was fortunate, as the President had said, with considerable sympathy, when Chase had told him what a nightmare it was, trying to make order out of the finances of the United States in the vast Treasury Building, where only three hundred eighty-three clerks presided over the finances of each of seven governmental departments, as well as the Customs Department, the Lighthouse Board, the Marine Hospitals, the Coast Survey and a dozen other miscellaneous activities that had accrued to his department.

"Where," Chase asked Jay Cooke, who stood now at the window, smoking a cigar and staring at Willard's Hotel across the avenue, "are we to get the money?"

"Borrow it, like any other business would." Cooke turned. With dismay, Chase watched as the ash from Cooke's cigar fell onto the pearl-gray velvet rug that his predecessor had only recently laid down; at the same time, the room's six black-walnut chairs had been upholstered in what was, to Chase's eye, a most tasteful blue. The office was far more luxurious and beautiful than that of the President or any of the other Cabinet officers. Particularly satisfying to Chase were the gilded window cornices that displayed the Treasury's ornate seal, surmounted by Justice's scales.

"I cannot say that I very much like the idea of the American government being placed in the hands of bankers, if you'll forgive me, Mr. Cooke."

"Don't look at me, Mr. Secretary. I hate the breed. That's why I've just started a bank of my own."

"I would rather raise the money through a direct tax on income."

"No Congress has ever allowed such a tax."

"No Congress has ever been faced with a crisis like this. Here we are, totally cut off from the rest of the world. The telegraph lines are down. The railroads..." Chase paused; he found it hard to believe what he was about to say; but he said it: "If the rebels should attack, we shall have to abandon the city." Chase looked wistfully around the beautiful office. "But no matter *where* the government is, we must prepare to finance a most costly war."

"How long do you think it'll take us to beat 'em?"

Chase frowned. "A few months ago, a few months. But Mr. Buchanan would not move against his Southern friends. Now that Virginia has seceded, we've lost the Norfolk naval yard. Worse, we've lost the arsenal at Harper's Ferry. So it is my guess that it will take us close to a year to defeat the rebels, at a cost of one hundred million dollars."

"You're quite the pessimist, Mr. Chase. But if you're right, then all the more reason that you issue Federal bonds right away. Twenty-year bonds that you can't cash in for, let's say, five years, paying a premium of eight percent..."

"Six percent," said Chase, automatically.

"Make it seven and a half..."

"I am not an auctioneer. Whatever the percent, the lower the better for the country."

"But the higher the better for the bankers, who are the ones who'll buy your bonds."

Chase sat back in his chair; and looked at Alexander Hamilton for inspiration. "I wonder," he said, somewhat inspired, "if we could entice the people at large to buy their government's bonds. In that event, each owner of a bond would certainly feel himself involved in the war, and our successes would make his bonds more valuable..."

"But our defeats, God forbid we have any, would make those bonds less valuable and unsalable."

"*You* are the pessimist, Mr. Cooke. But I must say, so far, under our war leader"—Chase had vowed to himself that he would never criticize Lincoln, outside the Cabinet; but there were times when he could not hold back—"we do nothing. Last night at dinner, the British minister complimented the United States on its originality in war. Most nations at war, he said, try to do harm to the enemy. But you only do harm to yourselves. Everyone laughed. And I felt ashamed. Because, of course, he's right. Since the proclamation on Monday, all that we have done is blow up our own arsenal at Harper's Ferry and set fire to our own Navy Yard at Norfolk."

"Well, it did keep them out of the hands of the rebels. Kate's staying with my wife, by the way; at The Cedars."

Chase contracted his left eye to adjust to the new subject. "I had no idea she was going to stop off in Philadelphia after her positively Roman orgy of buying in New York." Chase sighed. "You know I'll be happy to lend you any amount."

"No, no, Mr. Cooke. That would not look right. By the way, we must have some sort of *written* agreement on the carriage. I can only borrow it, you know."

"I know."

Chase got to his feet and looked out the window. A horsecar rattled by. The sidewalk in front of Willard's was empty. "Last week there were a thousand guests at Willard's. Now there are forty." But then, as Chase watched, several hundred men with rifles and fur hats came into view from the direction of Lafayette Square. "That must be the Clay Battalion." Cooke joined Chase at the window. A number of the men stood guard in front of Willard's, while the rest went inside.

"Who on earth are they?" asked Cooke.

"Mostly Kentuckians. Border men. One group is camping out at the President's Mansion. *In* the Mansion. They sleep in the East Room. Imagine! The Pennsylvania boys are camping out in the House of Representatives. I don't know where they've put the regiment from Massachusetts."

"How badly mauled were they in Baltimore?"

"Four soldiers killed. Thirty wounded by a mob of plug-uglies. They were lucky to get through at all."

"If Maryland secedes . . ."

"We abandon the city." Chase turned to his desk. He picked up a document. "Then there is the business of the spies." He squinted at the paper. "Of the four thousand four hundred and seventy civil and military officers, two thousand one hundred and fifty-four come from the rebel states."

"Looks like the South is a bit overrepresented."

"Particularly in the military. According to General Scott, our best army officer is a Virginian named Lee."

"The man who caught John Brown?"

"The same. Old Mr. Blair is a great friend of his. On Thursday, when Mr. Blair offered Colonel Lee the command of our army, Lee said that although he believes secession is wrong, and slavery worse, he can be no party to an invasion of his native state. I don't understand Southerners, do you, Mr. Cooke?"

"I can't say I ever tried."

Chase's mind reverted now to business. "I shall attempt to place a tax on personal incomes."

"I don't think you'll be exactly popular anywhere, if you do."

"Oh, a two- or three-percent tax will hardly be noticed. Naturally, anything higher will be out of the question."

"I hope you're right. But don't forget, we've got to get you elected in 'sixty-four."

"If it's not too late," said Chase grimly. He was certain Maryland would secede within the next few days; nevertheless, he was careful to sound more cheerful and confident than indeed he was, on the ground that the financial community was a delicate and skittish animal in constant need of reassurance. Privately, Chase was in a state of panic. Once Maryland was gone, the city would be abandoned by the government. Once the capital had been lost to the rebels, there would be a movement, probably successful, to impeach Lincoln. Once Lincoln was gone, Seward would seize power; particularly if the capital should be moved anywhere north of Harrisburg. Once Seward was in power, an election in 1864 would be a moot affair. Chase could think of no way to stop the chaos that had begun to envelop the never-entirely-stable North American republic, which had been so arranged in its very Constitution that everyone ruled so that no one could rule, save the unexpected tyrant—a small, smiling, gray New Yorker who smoked cigars.

But the small, smiling, gray New Yorker who smoked cigars was not at all in a tyrannical mood when, the next morning, he and his son left the nearly empty church of Saint John's, and together walked in silence over to the White House gate, where smart-looking soldiers of the Sixth Massachusetts Regiment now stood guard. As father and son tried to enter, they were stopped. "Who goes there?" asked a sergeant. From the portico Old Edward shouted, "Mr. Seward."

The soldiers saluted as the Sewards walked up the driveway not to the Mansion but off to the right, where dingy glass conservatories made curiously ugly the prospect. In the woods of the President's Park just off the Mansion's west wing with its glass attachment stood, side by side, the old War and Naval Department buildings, while opposite the east wing of the Mansion a small red-brick building housed the State Department, literally in the shadow of the Treasury's palace.

Two sailors stood guard at the Naval Department. Here father and son separated; son to go to the State Department; father to go to a meeting which was so secret that it was being held not at the Mansion, where spies reported everything that went on, but at Gideon Welles's establishment.

Seward was recognized by the sailors; and he took their salute

125

with a wave of his cigar. In the small office of the Secretary of the Navy, the President was already at the head of the table, the hair on his head already in a state of alarm. Except for Chase, the entire Cabinet was now present. Overflowing a special armchair to the President's right was General Scott, his huge gouty leg resting on a stool. Hay and Nicolay sat beneath a watery painting of John Paul Jones.

As Seward took his seat beside the President, he murmured, "There's a rumor that all the telegraph offices in the North were raided yesterday."

"Well," said Lincoln, "that's the first rumor I've heard this week that's founded on fact. Yesterday, at three in the afternoon, I ordered every U.S. marshal in the country to seize the original of every telegram that has been sent and a copy of every telegram that has been received in the last twelve months."

Seward whistled softly. "The *legal* basis for this seizure...?" He cocked an eye, comically.

"The *broader* powers inherent in the Constitution." Lincoln appeared to savor the word "broader." "Anyway, now we'll have a better notion of just who and where our enemies are, particularly in this part of the world."

Chase made his entrance; bowed to the company; took his place at the table. Then Lincoln began. "Gentlemen, Mr. Seward and I have just been discussing rumors, which is about the only productive thing we have at present. I have heard a brand-new one. General Scott." Lincoln turned to the huge old figure which came, more or less, to attention in the outsize armchair. "The newspapers at Richmond have announced that you were offered a high command in the rebel army and that you have accepted it."

General Scott raised high the many chins attached to his massive head. "The first part is true. I was asked to transfer my allegiance to Virginia. The second part is untrue. I declined. I also told them that, henceforth, the soil of my native Virginia is enemy territory."

Lincoln nodded. "I thought as much. Have you made any headway with Colonel Lee?"

"None, sir. I spoke to him. Then Mr. Blair spoke to him. Colonel Lee was the soul of courtesy—and of honor. This morning I received a dispatch from Richmond. Colonel Lee is now a commander of the rebel army."

"It will be interesting," said Lincoln, "to see what sort of commander he will make, since he claims to abominate slavery and to regard secession as treason."
126

"He will fight very well, sir," said General Scott, gloomily. "It is a matter of honor."

"I see," said Lincoln, who plainly did not, thought Hay, as he made his notes. "Now I've called what will, I hope, prove to be a secret meeting in order for us to begin the financing of the war." Lincoln unfolded a piece of paper and put it before him; then he turned to Chase. "As there exists a state of armed insurrection against the Federal government, I shall now ask you to withdraw from the Treasury two millions of dollars, which will be sent in the form of money orders to..." Lincoln put on his glasses and read off the names of three men. "They are all located in New York City. The addresses I will give you."

Chase could not believe that he had heard the President correctly. "I am to make out these money orders without any security from three gentlemen who are unknown to me?"

"That's right, Mr. Chase. They are also, personally, unknown to me, too. Anyway, I have authorized these gentlemen to buy whatever is needed to supply the troops that have arrived and are arriving. They will submit their accounts to you at regular intervals, and they themselves will receive no compensation."

"But this is highly irregular, Mr. President..." Chase began.

"That's why this suits so eminently the times, Mr. Chase."

"But only Congress can authorize this sort of expenditure."

"Congress won't be back for nearly three months. Would you have me do nothing until then to defend the city?"

"No, sir. But..."

"Gentlemen." Lincoln interrupted Chase with a wave of his long-fingered hand. "I would like a unanimous vote as to this emergency appropriation."

"You will have it, I am sure," said Seward, finding this sudden bold assault on the Treasury singularly unlike Lincoln's usual tentative and vacillating style. Plainly, the thought of losing the city of Washington to the rebels had concentrated marvelously that curious mind.

Lincoln asked each Cabinet member, in turn, if he favored the appropriation, and each said that he did, including Chase, who was not happy but saw no alternative. Once the vote was taken, Lincoln sat back in his chair. "I have arranged to get these orders to New York City in a somewhat roundabout way, since neither trains nor ships are to be trusted for the moment. As for our military situation here, it has its perilous side."

Hay was impressed by Lincoln's air of serenity, in such marked contrast to the previous night when Hay, at midnight, had passed by the door to the President's room, where Lamon always sat on guard, and heard the most terrible sighs and moaning. When Hay had asked Lamon if the President was ill, Lamon had said, "No, he is only dreaming. God knows what."

But now the President was awake. "General Scott, what did you tell me it would take for the rebels to seize Fort Washington downriver?"

"I said, sir, that it would take no more than a bottle of whiskey."

Lincoln smiled. "I was struck by the image. Let us hope we will not be struck by the enemy's bottle just yet. We have the Sixth Massachusetts Regiment quartered in the Senate. We have the Pennsylvanians in the House. General Scott feels that we have enough men to defend the Capitol and the public buildings in case of a major assault. Is that true, General?"

Hay noted, as always, the lawyerlike way that Lincoln deliberately committed others to specific courses. On the great issues, he insisted that each Cabinet minister write out his views or speak openly to the record or cast a yes or no vote. He was not about to let anyone off his singularly sharp and precise hook, or as he had remarked to his secretaries, "When things go wrong, people like to say they told me so. Well, I like to have the proof—in their own words—that they didn't."

General Scott rumbled a moment; then spoke. "This is what we know for certain about the enemy. Four miles below Mount Vernon, some two thousand troops are building a battery on the Potomac, in order to control the river at this narrow point. About the same number of men are on both sides of the river, ready to attack Fort Washington. This morning, special cars went up to Harper's Ferry to bring down another two thousand men for a general attack on the city. They could put as many as ten thousand of their men in the field. For now, we can hold them off with the troops we have. For later, we can take Richmond with the troops that are supposed to be on their way."

"Through Baltimore." Lincoln shut his eyes. "What shall we do about Baltimore? What shall we do about Maryland?"

As the ranking Cabinet officer, Seward felt obliged to express his outrage at the mob's attack on the Sixth Massachusetts Regiment as they marched across the city from one depot to another. "I would put a Federal garrison in the city," said Seward firmly. "And keep order."

"Well, so would I, Mr. Seward." Lincoln was mild. "But, at the moment, we don't have much of anybody to put there. Meanwhile, the mob has taken over and Governor Hicks, who's usually well disposed toward us, shows signs of succumbing to the local fever."

"Mr. President, we must, at all costs, keep Maryland from seceding." Chase was as stern as Seward.

128

"Well, if I had an army and a navy, I would certainly do it. But I don't. I *will* have those things. But I don't have them now."

Montgomery Blair spoke up. "I am a Marylander. And I know there's enough good sense in the state to keep the secessionists at bay..."

While Blair was speaking, a naval officer entered the room and gave Lincoln a note; then he gave Gideon Welles a second note; then he withdrew. Lincoln glanced at his note; and motioned for Blair to continue. "The main problem is the Baltimore mob, the plug-uglies, as they're so nicely called. They are able to tie up the city, which is the only direct railway link we have to the North, and they are also able to tie up the mayor, Mr. Brown, who is, I gather, in town, ready to explain just how he happened to let our troops be attacked the day before yesterday. I echo the idea of a garrison in Baltimore as soon as possible. I would also do everything to keep Governor Hicks from summoning the state legislature, which now has a majority in favor of secession."

"Well, we all agree, more or less, on the what. It's the how that's a puzzle." Lincoln looked down the table at the Secretary of the Navy. "All right, Father Welles, if you tell me what was in that note to you, I'll tell you what was in the note to me."

Gideon Welles adjusted his splendid wig to a martial angle. "Sir, the commandant of the Navy Yard here in Washington has sent me his resignation. He has been kind enough to inform me that he and most of his staff will be going South, as will the commanding officer of the battery of artillery, which is our chief defense on the Potomac side."

Lincoln winced. The appearance of serenity was beginning to fray. "Three days ago, that artillery commander came to me and swore his loyalty to the Union. And I believed him; and left him in command. Well, good as your news was, Father Neptune, my news is far and away the best of all. Gentlemen, our friends in Baltimore have torn down the iron bridge on the Northern Central Railway. There will be no more trains from the North. We are completely cut off by land."

The silence in the room was broken only by the heavy irregular breathing of General Scott. Lincoln rubbed the back of his hand across his face; as though, thought Hay, to blot out this world once and for all. Then the President was on his feet.

"We are to keep all this to ourselves—as best we can," added Lincoln wryly. "One of our principal problems at this exact moment is the matter of trust. The bureaus of the government are filled with rebels, who are now beginning to leave for home, for which we give thanks. But there are all sorts of sympathizers that mean to stay on. We must be on our guard against them. They will do everything possible to bring the enemy within the gates."

Lincoln motioned for Nicolay and Hay to accompany him back to the Mansion. As the three men passed in front of the glass conservatories, a crowd of geese blocked their way. "I think these geese are some sort of omen," said Lincoln.

"Perhaps..." Nicolay began, but Lincoln silenced him with a gesture.

"Perhaps it's better that we do no interpreting. We're in enough of a fix."

Old Edward greeted the President with the news that Mayor Brown of Baltimore, with a delegation of the city's leading citizens, was waiting for him in the Blue Room. Meanwhile, in the East Room, the Kentucky volunteers were cooking their dinner in the fireplaces, and singing sad songs.

Without a word, Lincoln crossed to the Blue Room, followed by Hay and his notebook. Nicolay returned to the second floor. At Lincoln's approach Mayor Brown, a small, deep-voiced man, rose and came forward, hand solemnly outstretched. Hay was astonished to see that of the seven or eight Baltimore worthies, three remained seated. As Lincoln and Brown shook hands, Hay said, in a loud voice, the ceremonial phrase: "Gentlemen, the President."

Reluctantly, the three got to their feet; and each shook, some more reluctantly than others, the President's hand. Lincoln then indicated that they be seated, while he remained standing, hands behind his back, a gentle smile on his lips, always a sign that he was angry, as Hay now knew; and the rest of the world did not.

"I'm glad you could accept my invitation, Mr. Brown. And that your friends, also, could come. Naturally, I was much distressed by Friday's attack on our troops. I had hoped that this would not happen..."

"Sir, as you know," Brown's voice boomed in the room, "I have warned you repeatedly that feeling is very high among our people and that they regard your proclamation of April 15 as a declaration of war on the whole South, which naturally includes Maryland."

"Mr. Brown, Mr. Brown," Lincoln was placating, "I am not a learned man. When I write in haste, as I did that proclamation, I may not always express my exact meaning." Hay almost burst out laughing. If ever a man understood the nuance of every written or spoken word and phrase, it was Lincoln. But, for his own reasons, the President was now playing the bumpkin that these men had all read about in the newspapers.

130

"In any case, Mr. Lincoln, whatever the *exact* intention of your call for seventy-five thousand troops, you can imagine what our high-spirited citizens felt when they first heard that northern troops were only fourteen miles from the city, at Cockeysville."

"I appreciate that, Mr. Brown, and if I could have recalled them then, I would have done so. But they were on their way here not to make war on the South but to defend this city from an attack, which could come any day."

Hay noticed that a number of the men looked very pleased at this information. But Lincoln pretended not to notice. Instead, he apologized, almost humbly, for the trouble to which the mayor had been put and he promised that, in future, troops would go around Baltimore on their way to the capital.

"Could you put that in writing, sir?" asked Brown.

"Why, yes." Lincoln motioned to Hay who gave him pen and paper. Then Lincoln sat at a round table and began to write. Smiling, he said, "Now if I grant you this concession, that no troops shall pass through the city, you will probably be back here tomorrow saying that none shall be marched around it."

"The Maryland legislature will determine that in good time, sir."

Lincoln signed his name; and gave the letter to the mayor. "By the way, I understand that the railroad bridge is down..."

"Yes, sir. Governor Hicks and I both agreed that it should be so disabled that no trains with troops can ever again come through Baltimore to Washington. After what happened Friday, I cannot hope to protect northern troops from our people's—"

"High spirits," supplied Lincoln, with an attempt at lightness.

"Fury is more like it, sir. We are a slave-holding state, much connected with our neighbors in Virginia."

"You are a border-state, yes." Thus Lincoln continued to do his best to ease the mood until, in due course, the delegation departed.

After a brief visit to the Kentuckians in the East Room, Lincoln went to his office. Hay had never seen the Tycoon quite so absorbed in whatever it was that he was thinking. Thanks to the war scare, the waiting room was empty; and only the other Edward was to be seen at his desk behind the balustrade. As Lincoln entered his office, he said, "Johnny, get me a map of Maryland."

Hay went into Nicolay's office, where the maps were kept. Nicolay was busy writing letters for the President to sign. In the first days of the Administration, Lincoln had insisted on reading, carefully, everything that he signed. Now he read very little of what he signed. He was satisfied that if Nicolay or Hay had written the document in question, it would conform with government

131

policy. Needless to say, Seward had already tried to take advantage of Lincoln; but caught once in the act, he had not tried again.

Map in hand, Hay entered the President's office. Lincoln was standing at the window, peering through a telescope at the Virginia side of the Potomac where a Confederate flag could be seen flying over Alexandria. "You know, John, if I were Mr. Beauregard or Mr. Lee or whoever's over there, I'd attack right now."

"Don't you believe General Scott, sir? That he could protect the city?"

"No, I don't." Lincoln put down the telescope. "But lucky for us, they aren't any readier to attack than we are to defend. Put the map on the easel." Lincoln's finger touched a point to the south and west of Baltimore, to the north and west of Annapolis. "We can always bring the troops by water to Annapolis Junction. That way we can avoid Baltimore altogether. It will take longer but . . ." Lincoln stared at the map.

"What happens if Maryland secedes?"

"Well, we just won't let them. That's all."

"If Governor Hicks calls the legislature into session, they'll vote to secede."

"Governor Hicks has held the fort for us so far." Lincoln frowned. "But I must say, it was a sort of shock to hear that he went along with tearing up those railroad bridges. *If* he did, of course. I don't trust Mr. Brown. Let's send the governor a telegram. Say: The President would like to know . . ."

"Sir, there is no telegraph. Remember?"

Lincoln sat at his desk; and rubbed his face with the back of his hand. Hay noticed that the lid of the left eye was now almost shut. "Well," he said, turning once more to the window and the irresistible to him pale blue-green hills of Virginia, "those rebels did swear that they'd have this city by the first of May. Nine days to go."

"If they should come, what is your plan, sir?"

"My plan, Johnny, is to have no plan. Particularly, when I don't have much of anything to plan with." Lincoln paused. "How quiet it is," he said.

Both were still a moment. Except for the stirrings of the militia camped out in the East Room, all the usual sounds of the city had stopped. There was no sound of traffic. If the horsecars were running, their bells were silenced. Hay found it hard to believe that he was in the office of a bona-fide president of the United States at the capital of the country, and they were entirely cut off from the outside world. Worse, on every side of the ten-square-mile rectangle known as the District of Columbia, enemy states were preparing for an attack.

132

Nicolay entered to announce: "General Scott's outside, sir. He can't walk up the steps but he wonders if you'd come down."

General Scott was seated in the back of his barouche, gold epaulets gleaming in the sun, face gleaming, too—like an eggplant, thought Hay.

"Sir, forgive me for not rising. But I am in some pain."

"That's all right." Lincoln leaned against the carriage door, rather the way a farmer would lean on a fence to chat with a neighbor on a Sunday evening. "What's the bad news now?"

"One of our couriers just got through from Maryland, from Annapolis. I came straight here to tell you. The Eighth Massachusetts Regiment under General Benjamin Butler is aboard the ferryboat *Maryland*. They are anchored in the city's harbor."

Lincoln whistled. "How did he get to be aboard a ferryboat? Butler was to come by train, or on foot."

"When General Butler heard what happened Friday in Baltimore, he figured that the rebels would cut the railroad line, so he commandeered a ferryboat at Havre de Grace and came down the Chesapeake. He has now told Governor Hicks that he means to disembark in Annapolis."

"I must say I like General Butler's enterprise." Lincoln's cocked eyebrow revealed his sense of the oddness of the situation. "Butler of all people! A rabid Democrat, who supported Mr. Breckinridge in the election."

"I do not keep track of those things, sir," said General Scott, austerely. "Thus far, our intelligence suggests that he is a highly resourceful commander. Thanks to his example, the New York Seventh and the Rhode Island First regiments are also approaching Annapolis, by way of the Chesapeake."

"I was beginning to think that I had dreamed the North. That Rhode Island and New York were just names." With a creaking sound, Lincoln stretched his long arms until he looked like a scarecrow. "What's the condition of the railway out of Annapolis?"

"Twenty miles of track have been torn up."

"Do you think the rails have been destroyed?"

"I would be very surprised, sir, if they had been. I think once General Butler is ashore he'll be able to persuade the rebels to restore the track to what it was. But that will take time. Meanwhile, I've sent him word that the main body of his men are to march overland from Annapolis to Washington. The rest will remain in Annapolis and regain the Naval Academy, which is now in enemy hands."

"If General Butler can land his troops without incident, there is still a militia in Maryland that is hostile to us."

"I don't think, sir, they will be a match for him. He is very

133

much in charge. I am told that he was elected brigadier-general by his own men. Then the Republican governor of Massachusetts was obliged to confirm him in that rank."

Lincoln nodded, more in bemusement than agreement. "You say the Naval Academy has been occupied?"

"Yes, sir. But their troops are few; and their governor fears us even more than he does his own rebel elements."

"There is still no telegraph?"

"None to the north, sir. We have some communications, for what it's worth, with the south. Anyway, in the absence of the telegraph or of any postal service to or from the city, our only connections with the rest of the world are my outriders."

"I guess you are all the eyes and ears I've got left, General. When do you think Butler's men will arrive?"

"No later than Tuesday, sir."

The General-in-Chief then saluted the Commander-in-Chief, and the carriage pulled, slowly, away from the portico, as if the horses were having trouble with Scott's deadweight. Lincoln stood a moment, staring at the back of General Scott's neck. As usual, Hay wondered what the President was thinking; as usual, he did not have the slightest clue. They turned back to the Mansion. Willie and Tad intercepted them at the portico; each was riding, piggyback, a Kentucky volunteer. At the sight of the President, the two tall young men put down the two small boys.

"Howdy, sir, Mr. President Lincoln," said one.

The other just touched his cap; and blushed.

"Boys," said Lincoln to the volunteers, "carry on, as you were. And you pair of codgers," he said to his sons, "stop pestering our defenders."

"They enjoy our company very much. Don't you, sir?" said Willie, looking up at the tonguetied youth. Hay was struck by the child's vocal resemblance to his mother; even to the way that he used the word "sir" more as punctuation than politeness.

"Sure, Willie," said the Kentuckian. With that, Willie was again hoisted on the volunteer's back as was Tad, whose contribution to the scene had been noisy but incomprehensible. There were times, to Hay's ear, when the beloved son of his beloved President sounded exactly like a goose *in extremis*. The volunteers galloped off. At the door, Old Edward said to Lincoln, "They're at it cooking again. In the East Room, sir."

"Well, as long as they don't use the furniture for kindling..." Lincoln paused in the entrance hall and looked toward the open door to the East Room, where a hundred Kentuckians were billeted. Smoke filled a fireplace where something large and quad-
134

ruped was being roasted. The volunteers were in a fine mood; one played a banjo, while the others sang.

"Smells good," said Lincoln, motioning for Hay to follow him into the Blue Room, empty now of Baltimoreans and filled with Mary's Coterie, as Cousin Lizzie called those few who still came to pay court to the beleaguered First Lady of the divided land.

Mary sat in an armchair, back to a window, while Senator Sumner and Cousin Lizzie shared a loveseat without any great outward sign of amorousness or even amiability. On another loveseat, sat two men; one was known to Hay by sight and repute. This was the handsome, dashing—the press tended to run together the two adjectives when referring to New York's forty-two-year-old former congressman and now brigadier-general—Dan Sickles, who was pleasant-enough looking to Hay's cold, youthful eye. But then, for Hay, anyone older than thirty was already a palpable dinner for worms and not to be regarded seriously in a fleshly way. Nevertheless, this small officer with the narrow waist, deep-circled eyes and full moustaches, was not only a notorious lady-killer but also a gentleman-killer—literally, a gentleman-killer. Two years earlier, Washington's district attorney, the equally handsome and dashing Philip Barton Key, son of Francis Scott, who had written Hay's least favorite patriotic song, had shown the sort of attention to Congressman Sickels's wife that Sickles found intolerable. One day, as Mr. Key was signaling Mrs. Sickles from the sidewalk, Mr. Sickles shot him. Mr. Key was taken to the Old Club House, where he expired in what was now Governor Seward's dining room, a source of endless fascination to the premier, who liked, especially at table, to enact Key's hideous death agonies.

The ensuing trial delighted the entire nation. Sickles was defended by the soon-to-be attorney-general, Edwin M. Stanton, who made the jury weep as he recounted the sufferings of his client when first he learned that the horns had been placed upon his unsuspecting and altogether innocent brow. So overwhelmed was the jury that Stanton was able to get them to accept a plea of something that Stanton had invented called "temporary insanity"—extremely temporary insanity, as it proved, because had it lasted longer than a day or two Mr. Sickles might have been obliged to resign from Congress. As Seward had said to Lincoln in Hay's presence, "Any lawyer who can do what Mr. Stanton did in that case can probably do anything." Lincoln had agreed that he himself had never pulled off such a miracle in court.

As introductions were made, Sickles shook Hay's hand, very man-to-man. Sickles was having his problems with the governor of New York over the brigade that he had raised. The President

135

was supposed to intercede, thanks to Madam's latest favorite and chief courtier, one Henry Wikoff, an old friend of Sickles who was known as the Chevalier. While Lincoln and Sumner conferred, Hay sat a moment with the Chevalier, a stout, honest-faced man with gray eyes and hair, and brown moustaches that looked as if they might have been gray, too, given a chance.

"I knew Mr. Sickles—I should say General, now—in London." Wikoff smiled charmingly. He spoke with what Hay thought of as the Sumner Boston Brahmin—or whatever it was—accent. "When Mr. Sickles was with our legation, we saw a good deal of each other back in the fifties. Then, of course, when he was in Congress, he was close to my old friend President Buchanan."

Hay noticed that Wikoff was holding a book, partly concealed by his frock coat. "What is the book, sir?"

Wikoff flushed. "A present for Madam President. Do you think it presumptuous? To give her one's own book?"

Wikoff showed Hay the slender volume entitled *The Adventures of a Roving Diplomatist* by Henry Wikoff. Hay opened the book; turned the pages; said, politely, "You have roved in many countries, sir. Your title . . . ?"

"Oh, good Americans cannot have titles, sir. But it used to amuse Mr. Buchanan to call me Chevalier because I was so honored by Queen Isabella of Spain, for a small service I did her Most Catholic Majesty."

For Hay, any news of the great world across the Atlantic was spellbinding. He envied Henry Adams, who would soon go to England with his father, once the Ancient got around to making the appointment. "You know the Emperor Napoleon?" Hay's eye had seen this name more than once as he turned the pages.

"Oh, yes. I've always been a Bonapartist. I first knew the emperor's uncle, Joseph Bonaparte. You see, I was at the American legation in London. This was around 1836, years before Mr. Sickles served there, of course. I was an attaché, which means that I was a spoiled young man with more money than was good for him and a liking for adventure. Since then, what I have managed to lose in money I have gained in adventure, beginning with my mission for Joseph, which was to smuggle out of France some of the first empress's jewels. I was rewarded with a silver cup and the family's friendship. During the six years that Napoleon III was in prison at the fortress of Ham, I often brought him messages from the outside world. As a reward, when he became emperor, he made me a chevalier of the Legion of Honor."

"Twice a chevalier!" said Hay, enormously impressed. "So what brings you here to . . ." For Hay the word "prosaic" or something like it was floating about in his head, but then he remembered
136

that as dim and unexciting and republican as the United States was, they were still in the presence of its homely and most puissant Chief of State. So "this dull place" became "Washington?"

"My love of adventure, I suppose. And Mr. Sickle's kind invitation. I saw him, by chance, at Mr. Bennett's..."

"Of the New York *Herald*?"

"The same. We are old friends, Mr. Bennett and I. Anyway, Mr. Sickles said, Come back to Washington and get a front seat to watch the war. So I did. I'm at the Kirkwood, looking out the window with my spyglass for signs of *la réforme* and Lamartine. Not," he added quickly, "that Mr. Lincoln is another Louis Philippe. Quite the contrary."

"You were in Paris during 1848?" Hay was awed.

"Oh, yes. I was a secret agent for the British, engaged by Lord Palmerston himself. You will find a chapter devoted to me in Charles Schermerhorn Schuyler's *The Barricades of 1848*. A superb history, as you know. Mr. Schuyler, who lives in Paris... But all that is yesterday. This"—Wikoff gestured toward Lincoln's back, which was turned their way—"is the adventure now."

"I suppose it is." But Hay was unable to find any trace of high romance in the grim events that had overtaken the American republic. Madam joined them.

"As I keep warning you, Chevalier, this is not the court of France." Mary smiled up at Wikoff, who bowed low.

"I would not trade our Republican queen," he said, "for two empresses of the French."

"*Vous êtes tellement charmant, Chevalier. Mais, l'on dit, l'Impératrice Eugénie est si belle que tous les hommes...*"

Hay was surprised that Madam's French was both fluent and reasonably unaccented. He himself had learned German as a boy from the Germans in Warsaw, Illinois, and French at school. He was as enchanted as Madam by the Chevalier's tales of the French and Spanish courts, as well as by the long and curious account of the fifteen months that Wikoff had spent in a Genoese prison; put there, the Chevalier was convinced, by British duplicity. Like Madam, Hay only knew of the European world from books, while Wikoff had managed to live at least one book's contents in Europe, which he proceeded to present to the Republican Queen, who was rapidly developing a taste for flattery on the grand scale, now ecstatically fulfilled by Senator Sumner, whose French was the most elegant of all and who knew even more of Europe's great figures than did the Chevalier himself. But Hay was quick to note that Sumner did not quite approve of so much traffic with royalty and so little with the world of the mind. Where the Chevalier would deal, as it were, with the Empress Eugénie, Sumner would

137

deal with Victor Hugo and Lamartine. Mary was now aflame with delight; she quoted Victor Hugo at incorrect length, allowing Sumner to win the exchange.

Hay was almost relieved to be taken away from the French corner by plain Cousin Lizzie, who said, "I wish you'd talk to Cousin Lincoln about sending the family North."

"The family won't go, Mrs. Grimsley. You've heard Madam ... I mean Mrs. Lincoln." Hay stammered; the nicknames were only for Nicolay and himself. Fortunately, Cousin Lizzie thought he was referring to the firework's display of French beneath the portrait of Mrs. Monroe. "Oh, Cousin Mary can jabber for hours in French. She went to this French academy in Lexington, run by two marvelous old things called Mentelle. Then she was given these special lessons by this old retired Episcopal bishop, who thought her smart as paint, which she is." An usher served them fashionable French cakes—to go, Hay thought, with the conversation as well as the tea. A large woman, who liked her food, Mrs. Grimsley had become noticeably larger during her extended stay in the Mansion. "Cousin Mary has the courage of a lion, I must say, and won't leave if there is any danger. But I tell her, you have the two small boys! What happens to them when the rebels attack the city?"

"We hope that won't happen," said Hay, who was reasonably certain that if the rebels did not attack before the arrival of the northern regiments in the next few days, the city was safe. But he tended to agree with the President that if he were the rebel general, he would attack as soon as possible—immediately, in fact; because, despite General Scott's official optimism, the only part of the city that could be held for any length of time was the White House and its neighbor the massive stone Treasury Building, where howitzers had been placed in the corridors and grain stored in the cellars. Preparations for a siege had begun.

"Well, I would appreciate it if you were to put a word in Cousin Lincoln's ear. At least send the children North."

"How?" Hay rather enjoyed alarming Mrs. Grimsley.

"Well, by the cars, I suppose."

"There are no trains to the North. There are no ships available because of our blockade."

Mrs. Grimsley's mouth twitched involuntarily. Then she laughed. "The roads South are open, aren't they?"

"Oh, yes. There are even boats still, in spite of the blockade."

"Then the boys can be sent to Lexington. Kentucky's certain to stay in the Union."

"Mr. Lincoln got only two votes in Lexington. The rest voted for Breckinridge."

"Cousin Mary and I are still trying to guess who the two were. We *think* one was her oldest half-brother... Oh, Ben Helm has agreed to come pay a call." Hay's blank look inspired Cousin Lizzie to a genealogical flight. "He's the husband of Little Sister, that's Cousin Mary's half-sister Emilie, whom she adores. Anyway, Emilie married Ben Hardin Helm, who graduated from West Point, and Cousin Mary has been doing her best to get them to come here and accept a commission in the Union army. Anyway, we just got word from a Kentucky friend, who arrived at Willard's Thursday, that the Helmses are on their way!"

"To accept a commission?" Hay had heard a great deal about Madam's secessionist family, particularly her three half-brothers and her three half-sisters who still lived at the South, many of them in Lexington, under the vigilant matriarchy of Mrs. Lincoln's stepmother.

Mrs. Grimsley helped herself to another of Gautier's confections. "Yes, I believe so. For Cousin Mary, I pray so. It's embarrassing for the President, for one thing." She looked at Hay, as if she wanted him to say that it was not; but he did not. She went on, jaws grinding evenly. "And it is heartbreaking for her to have all those brothers and sisters so much younger than she, the ones that she looked on as if they were her own babies, at war with her."

"I can think of nothing more tragic," said Hay, honestly.

"Once Little Sister and Ben are here, I'm sure that things will be better. Anyway, I can't stay forever. Cousin Mary's threatening to go to New York some time next month, to do some shopping for this"—Mrs. Grimsley looked around the shabby but unmistakably, despite the marks of greasy hands and tobacco spit, Blue Room—"depressing old house." She lowered her voice. "I wouldn't live here if I was paid a fortune! We've better places, let me tell you, in Kentucky, let alone Virginia. Anyway, once we're in New York, I'll try to take the cars for Springfield." Mrs. Grimsley looked across the room at the glowing Mary, still talking French. "I fear for her in this place."

"Because of the rebels?"

"Oh, no. She's a Todd. She can handle an invading army just fine. No, it's these terrible Washington ladies, who have no manners. But then, as her stepmother Mrs. Todd says, it takes seven generations to make a lady. Most of the *women* here are at the first jump."

"Ready to be thrown?" Hay could not resist elaborating on this dangerous hunting metaphor.

Mrs. Grimsley chose, after seven generations, to let Hay's rhetorical question go unanswered. "She also suffers from the vicious

139

press that has no mercy—not to mention an endless talent for invention."

"Mr. Lincoln has pretty much stopped reading Northern newspapers. He says that since they are filled with nothing but speculations about him, he'd be no wiser."

"I wish she'd be as wise. But she reads the worst things about herself and the President and takes them so to heart. She needs friends in this place. You're too young to remember the Coterie..."

"But I know all of you now."

"But we're all of us old now. While then we were young, and Cousin Mary was the center of everything, the wittiest and most charming of the lot and, tell this to no one except Mr. Nicolay, she is a devastating mimic. Last night she had us in stitches, imitating a certain proud young lady."

"Miss Chase?" Hay let the name slip.

"I never said the name, Mr. Hay."

The Blue Room was suddenly made clamorous by the entrance of Willie and Tad, accompanied by Elizabeth Keckley, who spent most of every day at the Mansion, helping Mrs. Lincoln with the renovation of the house, with the children, with the entrenched bureaucracy that ruled the White House inside and out. Both Hay and Nicolay suspected vast corruption on the part of the head groundsman, whose bills were astonishing; and minor corruption on the part of Old Edward, of the housekeeper and of the chief cook. Madam had also asked for her own secretary, to be paid for by the Commissioner of Public Buildings, a dignitary whom she had personally selected even though he was a friend of Mr. Seward.

While the delighted parents watched as Willie and Tad annoyed everyone with their antics, Hay asked the President if he might withdraw.

"Yes, Mr. Hay. Yes." When Lincoln was distracted, he always called him Mr. Hay; in normal temper, he called him John. What, Hay wondered, had Sumner been telling him?

Later that night, as Hay sat at the desk in his bedroom, and Nicolay snored in their common bed, Lincoln appeared in the doorway, wearing an overcoat, slippers, and no trousers. Hay got to his feet. But Lincoln gestured for him to sit down. Then the President sat on the edge of the bed, and crossed his long, thin legs; and asked, "Are you keeping a journal?"

Hay nodded; and blushed, as if caught in some shameful act.

"Well, there should be a lot to write about, worse luck for me. Anyway, tomorrow I want you to go over to the Library of Congress and see what you can find on the President's wartime powers."

"Yes, sir."

"Because," the Ancient sighed, "Mr. Sumner thinks that in the event of civil war, which this certainly is, I can free the slaves as 'a military necessity.'"

"Would you, sir?"

"Well, Mr. Sumner would," said the President.

14

FOR HAY, THE NEXT FEW DAYS WERE CURIOUSLY TRANQUIL. The city was empty. The horsecars ran at whim. The troops were silent as they stood guard at the public buildings, waiting for the enemy and a battle that the Union would surely lose; or for the reinforcements that did not come even though thousands of Union troops were only forty miles to the north in Maryland.

The day that General Scott had promised Lincoln the Eighth Massachusetts Regiment, Tuesday, came and went much like troopless Monday. Tuesday afternoon when Hay entered the President's office to tell him that Mr. Seward wanted to see him, he found Lincoln standing once again at the open window; he was looking out across the odiferous marshes to the jumbled blocks that surrounded the unfinished shaft of Washington's monument, which he was now addressing, urgently, "Why don't they come? Why don't they come?"

Hay coughed. Lincoln turned; lips still moving but, now, soundlessly. "Mr. Seward, sir. He has a message from the governor of Maryland."

As Seward entered, Hay withdrew; and Lincoln sat back in his chair. "I only hope, Mr. Seward, the message came by telegraph."

"No, sir." Seward sat in the chair to the President's left, the light in his face. "The telegraph is still down. But General Scott's couriers are almost as good."

"Where are the troops?"

"Apparently they landed at the Naval Academy, which they retook as well as that old frigate, the *Constitution*."

"This is all very good to know," said Lincoln, impatiently. "But *where* is General Butler now?"

"I can only read between the lines of this message from Governor Hicks." Seward consulted the much-creased sheet of paper in his hand. "First, he replies to my answer to his proposal that we ask the British minister to mediate between Maryland and the United States in this matter."

Seward looked up. Lincoln was shaking his head. Gradually, Seward was beginning to read the moods if not the mind of this curious figure. The present mood was one of intense anger. "It passes all belief!" Lincoln now addressed the portrait of Andrew Jackson over the mantelpiece.

"At least, I think the governor was properly stung when I wrote, declining on your behalf his ingenious suggestion that whatever disagreement any American has with any other American, the agent of a foreign monarchy is hardly a proper mediator."

"Good. What about General Butler?"

"Apparently, both General Butler's regiment and New York's Seventh Regiment landed without incident."

Lincoln brightened. "That's two thousand men. And Rhode Island's just behind. But," he turned from the Jackson portrait to Seward, "exactly *where* are they now?"

"As of this morning, still in Annapolis. Naturally, the governor objects to the presence of Northern troops . . ."

"Northern!"

Seward interrupted the President; something that he had, only lately, got out of the habit of doing. "General Butler anticipated you, sir. He, very respectfully, I gather, told the governor that he was never again to refer to Union troops as Northern troops. The governor alludes, somewhat petulantly, to this."

Lincoln smiled for the first time. "They say he is a great actor, Ben Butler. Do you know him?"

"I do. Butler's easily the best trial lawyer I've ever seen in action."

Lincoln nodded. "Full of dramatic tricks, they say. With a liking for low criminals, the guiltier the better." Lincoln chuckled. "Just think, here's a trial lawyer, commanding troops in a state that's trying to secede, on his way to save the capital of a country whose president was, until recently, an attorney for the Illinois Central Railroad."

"While, at the risk of boasting, sir, the Secretary of State is still considered the finest patent lawyer in New York State . . ."

Lincoln laughed. "Here we are, practically the whole legal profession, running the Administration and now the army, trying to hold together with our fine legal minds a Union that is being torn apart by men who have spent their lives killing animals and one another in duels of honor. If you'll forgive me, General Jackson," Lincoln nodded to the picture on the wall, "a renowned duellist . . ."

142

"...*and* lawyer," added Seward. "Anyway, Governor Hicks, whose field appears to be divorce..."

By now, Lincoln was laughing helplessly at the growing absurdity of the situation. When, finally, the laughter ceased, Seward thought that Lincoln looked like a man who had just taken a tonic or received the beneficial shocks of the latest patented electrical machine. But then Seward had already come to understand Lincoln's almost physical need for laughter. "So Governor Hicks has been reprimanded. We occupy Annapolis. Now what?"

"Part of General Butler's troops remain. That's what the governor is objecting to. They are repairing the railroad to the city. He wishes that they would not because of what he calls his excitable people. He also says that because of our restoration of the railroad, the legislature cannot come to Annapolis. Apparently General Butler, always one to have the last word, has said that until the railroad is repaired, our troops cannot leave the city any more than the legislature can enter it. The logic is nice."

"When is the legislature to convene?" Lincoln sat up in his chair, suddenly alert.

"The twenty-sixth."

"This is the twenty-third. We have not much time."

"To do... what, sir?"

Lincoln rose. "I'm not ready to say. So when are we to expect these mythical troops?"

"Tomorrow or the day after."

It was the day after, Thursday, April 25, that the troops arrived in Washington. Although the railroad had been restored, there were sufficient cars only for the sick, the baggage and one howitzer battery. The main body of the troops departed Annapolis Wednesday morning on foot; and arrived, without incident, at the capital the next afternoon.

The Massachusetts, New York and Rhode Island regiments then proceeded down Pennsylvania Avenue, bands playing and banners unfurled, to the White House, proving to the President that there was indeed a patriotic Northern part of the Union, ready to fight for the preservation of the whole.

Hay watched the glittering display from the front gate of the Mansion, standing just behind the President and Mrs. Lincoln and the two loud boys. The city seemed, mysteriously, to have filled up again. All sorts of people, until now invisible, lined Pennsylvania Avenue in order to cheer the troops.

But David Herold was not one of them. He stood beside Mr. Thompson, who held a small Union flag in one hand but, out of deference to the volatile mixture of his clientele, he did not actually wave the flag. He had shut the drugstore for the day: in celebration or in mourning, depending on his customer's predilections.

"There sure are a lot of them New Yorkers!" Disloyally, David thought that the dark-blue uniforms of the Yankees were smarter looking than the gray Confederate uniforms that had begun to appear in Alexandria, now a foreign city, to be entered only with a military pass, which he possessed, signed by the Adjutant-General of the U.S. Army, confirming David's status as "delivery boy for Thompson's Drug Store."

Mr. Thompson tapped his foot in unison with the marchers' tread. "I think, Davie," he said, absently, "that we should order more sticking plaster, for feet. I think there will be a run on sticking plaster. A real run!" He chuckled at his own small joke.

"There must be three thousand of them," said David, glumly. "Maybe more." He knew that the Confederate garrison at Alexandria numbered no more than five hundred men. At a distance, the Yankee soldiers looked impressive; well outfitted and sharp drilled. But when one of the companies moved in too close to the sidewalk where David was standing, he could see and smell the sweat that trickled down necks, note the imperfectly shaved cheeks, the look of strain and fatigue in every face.

Suddenly, there was a cheer from farther down the avenue. A cavalry company was approaching, led by a splendid youthful figure wearing a yellow-plumed hat turned up at one side.

"Who's that?" asked David.

"I don't rightly know," said Mr. Thompson. "But those are beautiful horses, which means that's a rich man's company."

"Who's that?" asked Kate, standing between her father and Sumner at the window of Chase's office.

"He looks familiar." Chase hummed these words, allowing them to replace for a moment, the gnarled verses of that old rugged cross, a favorite hymn which, in his joy at seeing the capital city succored, he had been humming as he watched the armies, plainly, of the Lord of Hosts.

It was Sumner who identified the young man just as he came abreast the Treasury, causing the crowd in front of Willard's to cheer excitedly. "It's Governor William Sprague. Of Rhode Island. He raised that regiment himself. And paid for it himself."

"They say he is one of the wealthiest men in the country," said Kate.

"I am glad," intoned Sumner, "to see that he is also one of the most patriotic."

Sprague raised his plumed hat and waved it in their direction. Kate waved back. "Do you think he saw me?"

Chase laughed; and that old rugged cross was, for the moment, put aside. "Not without his spectacles." He turned to Kate. "Remember?"

"Oh, yes."

"Then you both know him?"

"Yes, Mr. Sumner." Kate stared with some fascination at the trim figure, whose golden epaulets glittered just beneath their window. "I should've recognized him, too, because he was in uniform when we saw him in Cleveland. But he's added the plume to his cap; and he's taken off his spectacles, which could be dangerous because he's as blind as a bat, or so he says."

"I cannot say that I *know* him at all," said Sumner. "The family own textile mills in Providence. Since they depend on Southern cotton, I shouldn't think that they are too happy about our blockade."

"All the more to his credit that he comes now to the Union's aid." Chase had not been particularly impressed by the young man when he had come to Cleveland to take part in a patriotic display the previous October, the last of a number of such occasions over which Chase had presided as governor of Ohio. But Kate had found Sprague intriguing, if only because of his youth; he had become governor at twenty-nine, a year younger than the law required and had been obliged to wait some months before he could take office. It was said that Sprague had bought his governorship, which Chase found absolutely enviable. But then anyone who did not have to worry about money was, for Chase, singularly blessed.

"Who is that back of him?" asked Kate, pointing to the colonel in actual command of Sprague's regiment, a tall, slender fellow, not yet forty, with huge whiskers.

"I have met him," said Chase, frowning. "He is a West Pointer, who left the army. Presumably, he was not Southern enough for General Scott. He is—or was—with one of the railroads. He lives—or lived—in Chicago."

For a moment, the three stared, with varying sensations of relief, as Rhode Island's artillery battery passed beneath them, bright and shining in the warm April sun. Then Sumner turned to Chase. "I have a request, sir, from General Butler, who is still at Annapolis. Would you allow our Massachusetts men to board here at the Treasury?"

"With pleasure, Mr. Sumner. Unless Kate would rather we take on Rhode Island?"

"Oh, no, Father. I am devoted to General Butler."

"Plainly, you don't know him." Sumner sighed. "He is all that is despicable. He is a Democrat who voted for Breckinridge. He is an anti-abolitionist. He is a sly lawyer. He is..."

"He is here in Washington!" exclaimed Kate. "Or at least his troops are, for which we should all be thankful."

"All be thankful," were also the words that the President used, as the various commanders filled the Blue Room. Lincoln stood at the center of the room, flanked by General Scott and Gideon Welles. Hay and Nicolay stood against the wall, enjoying the scene. The entrance hall was crowded with people, mostly ladies led by Mrs. Lincoln, waiting to welcome the warriors once the President was done with them.

Hay was one of the few spectators who had been able to identify the beplumed William Sprague. "In Rhode Island, they call him the boy governor," he whispered to Nicolay, as the small, imperious figure entered the Blue Room, accompanied by his tall colonel.

"Did you know him when you were at Brown?"

Hay nodded. "I met him. That's all. But everyone knows of the Spragues. A. & W. Sprague & Company. That's the family firm. They own nine cotton mills. I used to see him and his sisters at dances in Providence. In civilian clothes, he looked like a mouse."

"The mouse has gone to war," said Nicolay. As Sprague put on his pince-nez in order to see the President, Nicolay added, "Now I begin to see something slightly rodentine in the face."

"This," said Sprague in a loud voice, introducing his chief of staff to the President, "is Colonel Ambrose Burnside, West Point class of 'forty-seven, now commander of the First Rhode Island regiment, *under me*."

"It's not often I get to meet a *Yankee* West Pointer," said the President amiably, shaking hands.

"Well, sir," said Burnside, "I'm actually from Indiana, originally..."

"That makes two of us," said Lincoln, beaming.

"The Ancient has more states of origin than there are stars in the flag." Nicolay was amused.

"At least, Nico, he's *lived* in Indiana, unlike Virginia, which he used to claim."

Lincoln was now staring quizzically at the tall, bewhiskered officer. "I know you, don't I, Colonel?"

"Yes, sir. We've met, sir. I was with the Illinois Central, when you were our legal counsel."

"Another railroad man!" exclaimed Lincoln. "I feel better already."

Once the introductions had been made and patriotic sentiments
146

exchanged, the ladies filled the room. Sprague proved to be magnet-in-chief. Amused, Hay watched the nearsighted young man try to keep in place his pince-nez while maintaining the Napoleonic manner. Mrs. Lincoln and Mrs. Grimsley never left his side, while Tad tried on his cap and Willie fingered his sabre.

Hay turned to a young Massachusetts officer, who was wearily mopping his face with a dirty handkerchief. "You've had a long day, I guess."

"Oh, it's been that, all right." The voice was purest Yankee. "We thought for a while they'd fire on us. That was back in Annapolis. But old Ben, he went and put the fear of God in those rebels." The officer chuckled. "They were also pretty flabbergasted at how fast our boys put their railroad back together for them. I expect old Ben will keep order pretty good now."

"He's settled in?"

The man nodded. "He's at the Naval Academy, with two pistols beside his bed. When the governor told him to go, old Ben said someone has to stay on to welcome the next shipload of troops—and the next, and the next. He's scared the governor half to death."

"Was there much secession talk?"

"Mmm, yes. They talk a lot, those people, don't they? But when we're around, they don't do much except talk. Even so, I reckon soon as we leave Annapolis, they leave the Union."

"So we should stay?"

"Yes, sir, we should stay."

In the general melee of the entrance hall—to which had now been added the Kentucky volunteers from their quarters in the East Room—Hay found himself at the main entrance, face to face with the boy-governor himself, who offered his hand to be shaken as if in blessing. Hay held the soft hand for a moment in his own; and received, as it were, the benediction of the god of war. Then he let go the hand. "I'm John Hay," he said. "We met in Providence, when I was at Brown." Hay noted that Sprague was shorter than himself; and looked even younger than he was, with an unlined, pale face, clear gray eyes and a widow's peak as perfect as a girl's.

"Never saw you before in my life," was the hero's abrupt answer.

Hay felt his cheeks grow warm. "No reason why you should remember me," he said. "I'm only the President's private secretary," he added, in an attempt to achieve a degree of parity. But Sprague paid no attention to him. The gray eyes looked at the door. "I want," said the boy-governor, "a cocktail. Where can I get one?"

"At the bar, at Willard's."

"Come on," said Sprague, and started out the door, not looking to see if Hay had obeyed him.

More awed than not, Hay accompanied Sprague across Pennsylvania Avenue to Willard's. As they passed the Treasury Building, Sprague said, "Where's Chase?"

"Home, I suppose."

"I met him once. He's bald."

"I have noticed that, too." Hay found amusing Sprague's somewhat disjointed conversational style.

"*You* went to Brown," said Sprague, in an accusing tone. "*I* quit school at fifteen. I went into the family business. I was a bookkeeper. I liked that."

They were now in the lobby of Willard's, which had filled up as if by magic since the arrival of the troops. The boy-governor was duly recognized; and hailed by all. He paused at the cigar stand. Absently, he shook hands with everyone in sight, his eyes on Hay, who knew the way to the bar.

At last, Hay maneuvered Sprague through the bar's swinging doors. But not before a dozen ladies in the domed reception room had had a chance to celebrate him. Like an hereditary prince, which he was, Sprague accepted adulation as entirely his due. There was more handshaking at the bar. Senator Zach. Chandler of Michigan, tall and jovial, and Senator Hale of New Hampshire, tall and sour, each shook the hand of the small, glittering figure, who had now removed the yellow-plumed cap.

Hay found them a table in the corner, farthest from the long, crowded, smoky bar. A waiter brought a brandy-smash for Hay and a gin-sling for Sprague. With one practised gulp, Sprague emptied half the frosted glass; dried his drooping moustaches with the back of his hand; and then, eyes considerably brighter than before, he smiled. Sprague looked, Hay thought, like a twelve-year-old boy with a moustache. "That regiment's cost me a hundred thousand dollars so far," said the youthful hero. "Of my own money."

"I know. The President is grateful . . ."

"He damn well should be. Did you know I'm the first volunteer of the war? I saw to that. Got my name in first. Well, which is it going to be? Ben Butler or me?" Hay was beginning to wonder if the brandy-smash he had been carefully sipping might be having a premature effect.

Sprague finished his gin-sling; and motioned for another. "Ben Butler's got all the attention so far. But *I* paid for this regiment. I drilled 'em. I've been with the Rhode Island artillery volunteers since I was fifteen. I'm also a governor. Ben Butler's just a lawyer; and a Democrat—a *Southern* Democrat. I was elected on what

148

we called the Unionist ticket. Cooked up the name myself. So—Butler or me?"

"For what, sir?" Hay found it odd addressing as "sir" a twelve-year-old with a false moustache, an illusion sustained by the blue cigar smoke that now softened the glare from the gaslit globes which illuminated the long bar. Hay kept reminding himself that Sprague was not only eight years his senior but the governor of Rhode Island—the smallest of the states, true; but then Sprague was the richest of governors—a multimillionaire, a rare breed, in Hay's experience, which was mostly of Springfield, where a hundred thousand dollars was regarded as a sizable fortune.

"Major-general of volunteers," said Sprague, smoothing his silky moustaches, glossy now from gin. "There's to be one commission for New England. I know. I heard. So who's to get it? Butler or me?"

"I have no idea, sir."

"What does the President say?"

"Nothing that I know of. Promotions are decided at the War Department, by General Scott."

"Major-generals are decided by the President, Mr. Hay. They have to be. They're political. Where do you find girls?"

Hay finished his brandy-smash in a long swallow. He now felt more competent to deal with Sprague, whose conversational style was reminiscent of that of Tad Lincoln. "There are some excellent houses, sir."

Sprague looked eager. "Where?"

Hay described for him Sal Austin's establishment. The hidden alcove appealed to Sprague. "Funny," he said, solemnly. "You can't be seen at those places. But," he added with inexorable logic, "you've got to go to them. Cotton," he continued, "was ten cents a pound when you announced that blockade of the Southern ports last week."

"We announced the blockade, sir. You are Union, too."

"That's right. When you people started that blockade, cotton was ten cents a pound. Now even though there's no real shortage yet, cotton's gone to twenty cents a pound. That's ruinous for my business. Do you know Kate Chase?"

"Yes, sir."

"Met her in Columbus. Ever notice the way *he* suddenly squints his eyes at you?" Sprague imitated the way that Chase first widened his eyes; and then slowly narrowed them. The effect was so comical that Hay burst out laughing. "What's so funny?" asked Sprague.

"The way that you looked just like Chase."

"Funny the way *he* looks just like Chase. Secretary of the Treasury has all sorts of powers in these matters."

"What matters?"

"Can we get something to eat at Sal's?"

"Yes, sir."

"Let's go. Only, first, I've got to check out my regiment. They've put us in the Patent Office. Don't know why. We've got tents. Brand-new. Twenty-seven dollars apiece, wholesale." The boy-governor was on his feet, arranging the yellow-plumed cap at a jaunty angle. Hay felt as if he himself were an entire regiment as he followed, meekly, the first volunteer of the war out of the long bar.

15

LINCOLN STARED AT THE PAINTING OF GENERAL SCOTT CON-quering Mexico while Seward stared at the painting of General Scott winning the War of 1812. General Scott stared at the bust of General Scott, executed in white marble by a student of Canova who had, in Seward's view, failed to matriculate.

General Scott's office was filled with all the usual sounds of the city, particularly the horsecars rattling up and down the Avenue, to which was added the thudding sound of troops marching, of drums beating the tattoo, of cavalry . . . In four days the empty, doleful city had filled up with troops; and the office-seekers were once more in evidence. Each train from the North brought more troops to the depot, while the telegraph in the War Department had been restored and, at frequent intervals, the President was told of the success of his call for troops. To date, more than seventy-five thousand men had offered to fight, while the various state legislatures had contributed, thus far, millions of dollars to the Treasury for the defense of Washington; and for a successful prosecution of a war that everyone agreed would be brief but bloody.

Finally, Lincoln spoke to the youthful General Scott storming Chapultepec rather than to the ancient, mottled man who was propped up opposite him, one huge cylinder of a leg resting on a low table. "If the Maryland legislature meets as planned today, they are certain to vote an ordinance of secession."

"In the presence of General Butler?" Seward shook his head. "If they do such a thing, he has threatened to arrest the whole lot of them."

150

"To what end?" Lincoln shifted his eyes from the heights of Chapultepec; and looked at Seward. "The legislature of any state has the right to meet whenever they choose."

"Even if they plan to withdraw from the Union, which we hold to be not possible?" Seward was now lawyer for the prosecution.

Lincoln took the defense. "Until they actually meet and pass such an ordinance, we cannot presume to know what they will do."

"But, sir, if they do meet and they do secede?"

"We shall be in a worse fix, certainly. But put it this way, Mr. Seward. If we forbid the legislature to meet, which we have no right to do..."

"But we could stop them, sir." General Scott had not, as Seward thought, gone to sleep. The eyes were now so ringed with fat that it was hard to tell whether or not they were open, while the old man's breathing was that of a heavy sleeper.

"Oh, we can disperse them, General," said Lincoln. "We can lock them all up. But if we do, another legislature will convene somewhere else, and we'll be exactly where we are now. We can't keep shutting down legislatures from one end of the state to the other." Lincoln was now studying General Scott's winning of the War of 1812. "This morning we created the Military Department of Annapolis, with General Butler as its commander. I think Governor Hicks understands what I have done by making the capital of his state a *Federal* city, with a formidable garrison and a highly dramatic and bad-tempered commander."

"Governor Hicks may understand," said Seward, "but I don't. What is your intention?"

Lincoln slumped in his chair; and grabbed his knees in such a way that his chin could now rest comfortably upon them. The hair as usual resembled a stack of black hay after a wind. "I think the governor will take the hint, and guide the legislature in such a way that it will do nothing provocative for fear of our garrison."

"My informants," said General Scott, "tell me that he is planning to move the legislature out of the Department of Annapolis altogether."

Lincoln frowned. "That could be good for us. That could be bad for us."

"It would *look* good," said Seward. "We would not appear to be coercing them. But those fire-eating Baltimore secessionists are in the majority and once free of us..." Seward contemplated General Scott as if he were already a monument—to food if not to victory.

"I think we must run a certain risk in the eyes of the world."

Lincoln's beard now resembled a bird's nest once the young had flown. "I've already instructed General Butler to let the legislature meet. But I have also given him orders to arrest anyone who takes up arms—or incites others to take up arms—against the Federal government."

"I assume that this comes under your 'inherent' powers?" Seward was always amused by Lincoln's solemn attempts to rationalize such illegalities as the removal of two million dollars from the Treasury or the confiscation of all of Western Union's files.

"An *inherent* power, Mr. Seward, is just as much a power as one that has been spelled out. But I realize now that I am going to have to stray a mite beyond our usual highly cautious interpretation of those peculiar powers." Lincoln gave Seward a look of such dreamy candor that Seward was immediately on guard.

"I thought, sir, that you'd strayed about as far from the usual as is possible."

"Well, there's always another stretch of field up ahead, as the farmer said." Lincoln turned to General Scott, who came to massive attention in his chair. "You are to instruct General Butler, in your capacity as general-in-chief, that he is to wait upon the legislature and if an ordinance of secession is passed, he is to interpret this as an incitement to take up arms against the United States, and those legislators—who would incite the people to take up arms against us, or attempt to seize Federal property, as they did when they occupied the Naval Academy—shall be promptly arrested and held in prison at the government's pleasure."

"I shall transmit this order gladly, sir. But what are the legal consequences? I mean, sir, with what are they to be charged?"

"I don't think we should be too specific. After all, if we were to put too fine a point on it, the charge would have to be treason, and such trials are endless, and very hard on the innocent, who might easily be rounded up along with the guilty."

Seward was too stunned to say anything. As for General Scott, although his legal training was a half-century in the past, he did understand treason trials. "You are right, sir, about the difficulty of proving treason. I myself testified at Richmond in the course of the trial of Colonel Aaron Burr, who was no more guilty—"

Seward interrupted the old man without even a show of courtesy. "Mr. Lincoln, you are willing to arrest and to hold men indefinitely without ever charging them with any offense?"

"That's about it, Mr. Seward." Lincoln's face was uncommonly serene.

"But on what authority?" Seward felt as if two millennia of law had been casually erased by this peculiar lazy-limbed figure, now twisted in his chair like an ebony German pretzel.

"On my authority, as Commander-in-Chief."

"But you have no authority to allow the military to arrest anyone they like and to hold them without due process of law."

"Plainly, I think that I do have that right because that is what I am about to do." Slowly, the coiled figure straightened out. Then Lincoln addressed General Scott. "Telegraph the order to General Butler."

"Yes, sir." Scott rang a bell. An orderly entered, received his instructions from Scott; and then departed with the order to overthrow the first rule of law—*habeas corpus*.

"The most ancient of all our liberties," said Seward, with some awe, "is the right of a man who has been detained to know what he is charged with and then to be brought, in due course, to trial . . ."

"Mr. Seward, the most ancient of all our human characteristics is survival. In order that this Union survive, I have found it necessary to suspend the privilege of the writ of *habeas corpus*, but only in the military zone."

Seward whistled, very loudly; something that he had not done in years. "No president has ever done this."

"No president has ever been in my situation."

"President Madison was driven from this city by the British, who then set fire to the Capitol and the Mansion. Yet Madison never dreamed of suspending *habeas corpus*."

"The times are not comparable." Lincoln got to his feet. "Madison was faced with a foreign invasion that did not affect any but a small part of the country. I am faced with a war in which a third of the population has turned against the other two-thirds."

As Seward got to his feet, General Scott said, "You will forgive me, sir, if I do not rise."

"You are forgiven, General." Absently Lincoln patted the old man's epauleted shoulder.

Seward now stood next to the heroic bust of Scott; he looked up at Lincoln. "Will *you* be forgiven, sir, when the people learn of this?"

"Well, I don't plan to make a public announcement just yet—"

"But the word will spread."

"Mr. Seward, for the moment all that matters is to keep Maryland in the Union, and there is nothing that I will not do to accomplish that."

"Well, you have convinced me of that!" Although Seward chuckled, he was more alarmed than amused. "What happens when those hotheads in Baltimore find out?"

"Well, as we have a list of the worst of the lot, I reckon Ben Butler will lock them all up in Fort McHenry."

"What happens if the people of the city resist our troops?"

"We burn Baltimore to the ground. We are at war, Mr. Seward."

"Yes, sir." Seward wondered what precedents there were for the disposal of a mad president. Like so many other interesting matters, the Constitution had left the question unduly vague.

"Before you go, Mr. President," said General Scott, "what am I to do about the commissioning of General Butler and Governor Sprague? Each expects to be made major-general of volunteers. Each has made the point that he is a Democrat loyal to the Union and that you favor such men."

"That's true, of course. I must woo the Northern Democrats. Commission Butler. As for Governor Sprague . . ." Lincoln sighed. He turned to Seward. "Rhode Island is such a small state."

"And the governor is really such a small sort of Democrat."

Lincoln turned to General Scott. "If Governor Sprague pesters you, as he's been trying to pester me, offer him a brigadier-generalship. If he takes it, which I doubt, he can command his Rhode Islanders. But he'll have to resign as governor."

"Yes, sir."

As Lincoln and Seward stepped into Seventeenth Street, they were suddenly deafened by a military band playing "Columbia, the Gem of the Ocean."

"That's not the Marine Band," said Seward, whose ear for music was sharp, or so he liked to think—and always said.

"You're right. It's the New York Seventh's band. They're on the south lawn, giving a concert. Willie persuaded me that it was a good idea."

As they crossed the street, hats were raised to the President, who responded by raising his own hat and smiling, gravely.

"What was Willie's advice on *habeas corpus*?"

"Why, in those matters, I always turn to Tad, whose approach is singularly direct—like mine." An office-seeker stopped Lincoln at the White House gates.

"Mr. President, sir, I am a lifelong Republican from Dutchess County, New York . . ."

"But, sir, our party's only seven years old." Lincoln was amused.

"Exactly, sir, lifelong," the man repeated; and thrust a sheaf of documents at Lincoln. "The postmastership of Poughkeepsie is open . . ."

Politely, Lincoln stepped aside. "I'm not about to set up shop here in the street. You come during office hours." Lincoln strode through the White House gates; Seward behind him. At the gates, soldiers saluted smartly. When Seward's short legs had caught up with Lincoln's long ones, he asked, "What will Tad have to say when Congress impeaches you?"

154

"I reckon Tad will say, 'At least Paw saved the Capitol of the country, just so they'd have a nice place to impeach him in.'"

Seward was not prepared for so much blitheness; there was no other word. But Seward had also noticed that whenever Lincoln appeared to be vague and disturbed it was invariably before an important decision was made; after the decision was made, he acted as if he had not a care in the world, until the next crisis got him to brooding again.

At the portico, Lincoln paused. "I have high hopes for that railroad colonel, Burnside. He's a first-rate engineer who's invented something to do with the loading of guns. He's a trained military man, not like . . ." Lincoln paused and watched as a company from the New Jersey regiment marched past the gates of the Mansion. As the officer in charge shouted, "Eyes right!" and saluted the President, Lincoln lifted his hat.

"Not like Ben Butler," Seward supplied a name; then another, "or Governor Sprague."

"The governor has a plan to win the war quickly. I told him to put it in writing."

"That should take some time," said Seward wryly.

"That was the idea." Lincoln entered the Mansion, while Seward strolled across the shaggy lawn to the State Department building, which he had more than once compared to a brick privy in its close proximity to the vast stone palace of the Treasury.

Seward was having some difficulty in comprehending what he had just witnessed. Two lawyers and a professional general, who had been called in his day to the bar, had sat in a room and removed from an entire people their one inviolable right which had proved, upon test, to be as easily violable as a man transmitting a dozen or so words from a slip of paper to the telegraph wire. In six weeks, Congress would return. In six weeks, Seward was certain that an act of impeachment would be drawn up against the President. He wondered what his own line should be. After all, *he* was the advocate of the strong line; and certainly there was nothing stronger than what Lincoln had just done. Yet no Congress would ever allow the basic law of the land to be overthrown. Lincoln would be called to account. But could the country endure an impeachment and a trial of the President during a war? Perhaps Lincoln could be persuaded to resign.

Seward was smiling as he entered the office of the Secretary of State, where his son Frederick—the Assistant Secretary—sat in his shirt-sleeves at a table beneath a portrait of John Jay. The office was barely big enough for the two of them; yet, across the way, Chase sat alone in vast teakwood splendor, amidst crystal chandeliers, gilded cornices, velvet rugs.

If Lincoln were to go of his own free will, or otherwise, Hannibal Hamlin would be president; and Hamlin, Seward knew, was a modest man who would understand the need for a strong man from within the Cabinet to direct the war, a man who not only knew intimately how the nation functioned but had a vision, which all the others lacked. Seward's vision was simple: he wanted the entire western hemisphere to belong to the United States. Yet while Seward dreamed, splendidly and practically, of empire, the railroad lawyer in the White House wanted only to bring back into the Union a half-dozen or so rebellious mosquito-states—as Seward thought, contemptuously, of the Gulf states, so many irrelevant parcels of third-rate territory that would promptly revert to the Union once Mexico had come to accept American rule, much as Cisalpine Gaul had come to accept that of Rome. There were times when Seward felt that Chase shared his imperial vision. But those times were few. Essentially, Chase was a man in thrall to a single cause—the abolition of slavery. It was a cause that tended, in Seward's view, to drive men quite mad, assuming that they were not already mad to begin with and so turned to the cause of abolition as a means of legitimizing the furies that drove them.

"Don't forget this evening, sir," said Frederick, putting down a month's worth of dispatches from London and Paris and Saint Petersburg.

"This evening?" Seward sat at his desk, where a file labelled "Charles Francis Adams" had been set in front of him. Seward found Mr. Adams difficult; but able. Seward was also very much aware that he was seated at the desk of Mr. Adams's father, who had been eight years Secretary of State; and then President. Seward was also, glumly, aware that in eight years he himself would be either close to seventy years of age or dead; on the other hand, if President Lincoln did not seek reelection . . .

Frederick reminded his father that he had accepted an invitation to attend a reception at the Chases, in honor of Governor William Sprague IV. Seward sighed.

William Sprague sat on a sofa, explaining the "IV" to the attentive Kate while all about them uniformed men and frock-coated men swirled with behooped and bejewelled women to the music of four violins, led by David's friend Scipione, who had an evening free. "Then my uncle became William III, after William II died." Sprague looked Kate directly in the eye; she smiled back at him.

"Then," said Kate, rising to the conversational challenge, "when your father died you became William IV."

"No," said Sprague sharply. "My father didn't die. He also wasn't William III. That was my uncle."
156

"But if he's not dead . . . if *they're* not dead, how can you be William IV?" Kate's brilliant smile never varied; but her spirit was sorely tried. The boy-governor was, conversationally, hard going.

"Oh, my father's dead all right. But not like other people are dead. He was murdered. Shot one night, in the dark, on his way home. Shot in the arm. Then the assassin clubbed him to death with the gunstock and ran away."

"Who do you think did it?" Kate was at last intrigued.

"They hanged a man named Gordon. But I don't think he did it. I think someone else did it. My father died by the assassin's blow."

"That must have been such a . . . such a terrible thing for a child."

"Yes. Someday I'll find who did it. Remember when we met in Cleveland?" Sprague removed the pince-nez; and looked, as always, wonderfully handsome and youthful. When word had spread at Sal Austin's that the boy-governor they had all watched lead the parade down the avenue was in Marble Alley, the girls had flocked about him and he had abandoned his anonymity in order to be fussed over until Sal and Chester had got him to bed, rigid with drink.

It was astonishing, thought Hay, crossing the crowded parlor, how much Sprague could drink and how little of it showed in the face. Hay was still not feeling himself since their nocturnal excursion, to which Sprague had not once alluded, as Hay escorted him to the Patent Office the next morning.

Later that morning, Nico had dealt with the boy-governor when he had appeared at the Mansion with a design for victory that would take no more than an hour of the President's time. The Ancient had been benign; and before the governor knew it, he was in and out of the office, with no promise of the major-generalship that he had insisted was his by right as the war's first volunteer, not to mention newspaper hero. But before Sprague left the White House, he had presented Nico with a number of press-cuttings from the Northern newspapers, all in praise of the youthful statesman and commander. "I am ready, no matter what," he had said, as he put on his plumed hat and strode through the mass of office-seekers in the waiting room.

Hay paid his respects to Mr. Chase, whose manner was, as always, a nice balance of cordiality and aloofness. Chase was stationed before the fire-place in the back parlor, flanked by Senator Hale of New Hampshire and the British minister, Lord Lyons, a small plump subtle bachelor who seemed to be giving an absentminded imitation of a British minister.

Hay was saluted respectfully by his three elders, each aware that, young as he was, he was at power's center in a way that even the Secretary of the Treasury was not. They spoke of the situation in Maryland, and Hay was able to tell them the latest news. Governor Hicks had called for the legislature to meet the next day not at Annapolis but at Frederick City. "That's outside General Butler's military zone."

Senator Hale scowled. "That means they'll feel free to pass their damned ordinance of secession."

"The President thinks the opposite, sir." Hay was respectful. "He thinks Governor Hicks is with us but that he must appear to mollify the rebel element."

"Mollify? Hang them!" was Hale's fierce response. Although he was the blackest of black Republicans, he was chairman of the Senate Committee on Naval Affairs, and of great importance to the Administration.

Hay was exquisitely diplomatic. "But, sir, *you* who abolished flogging in our navy would not now go in for hanging statesmen?"

"Traitors, yes. Always!"

"Was it really you," asked Lord Lyons, with some curiosity, "who did away with flogging in the American navy?"

"Yes, sir. In 1847, sir."

"And you people wonder why you don't have a proper navy!" Lord Lyons laughed, a barking sound. "Flogging is the backbone of the British navy . . ."

"Backside," said Hale, who was known to dislike the British.

Chase intervened. "Each nation has its curious customs and crotchets." He was soothing. "You have flogging, Lord Lyons . . ."

"And you have slavery, Mr. Chase." Lord Lyons was known for the bricks that he artfully dropped, and Hay found the man's self-confidence irresistible.

"*We* don't have slavery, sir," said Chase. "*Others* do. But we are willing to go to war to free those slaves, something that no other nation has ever done."

Before Lord Lyons could drop another fragment of masonry, the only representative of the presidential family, Mrs. Grimsley, swept into view, arm in arm with a huge young woman, who proved to be Bessie Hale, the daughter of the senator, who beamed happily at this remarkable issue, in size at least, of his New England loins.

"I've so wanted to meet Mr. Hay, who's as handsome as I've heard tell!" Bessie was not shy, thought Hay, blushing girlishly himself, as he bowed low over her thick, damp hand.

"Mr. Hay is the only eligible bachelor at the Mansion now that Mr. Nicolay is engaged." Mrs. Grimsley match-made with practised skill. Although Chase looked benignant he did not feel particularly benignant. The Lincolns should have attended Kate's first reception since Sixth and E had been made presentable. Of course Mrs. Lincoln was jealous of Kate's youth, beauty, charm (it would be unnatural if she were not); even so, the President and his wife ought
158

to have been able to transcend personal feelings in order to create harmony within a notoriously divided Administration.

Chase looked across the room at one of the divisions—Simon Cameron, the Secretary of War. Cameron was tall; white-haired; slender. The face was noble; the character was not. Worse, Cameron was proving to be hopeless when it came to administering the crucial War Department. He left all military management to General Scott, who was senile; and to Gideon Welles, a newspaper publisher who knew little of naval affairs. Meanwhile, Cameron's promiscuous letting of contracts was a cause of much concern to Chase, who did his best to control the War Department's spending; but Chase's best could never be good enough without the President's help and that help was not forthcoming, even though Lincoln had no illusions about his Minister of War. In fact, before the appointment, Lincoln had appealed, somewhat plaintively, to the dour Thaddeus Stevens, a Pennsylvania congressman and sometime ally of Cameron. "You don't mean to say," asked Lincoln, "you think Cameron would steal?"

Stevens's answer had been much quoted in the town: "No, I don't think he would steal a red-hot stove." When Cameron had heard what his fellow-Pennsylvanian had said, he demanded an apology, which Stevens promptly gave: "All right, then. I do not think that you would not steal a red-hot stove." For political reasons, Lincoln was forced to make this dubious appointment.

Kate approached Chase, with the boy-governor in tow. They made a handsome couple, Chase thought; and he could not help but ponder for a moment the Sprague fortune, which the *Evening Star* had put at a hundred million dollars. Although a younger brother and a cousin shared with Sprague in the management of A. & W. Sprague & Company, Sprague, as the oldest and most experienced of the three, dominated the company. In fact, according to the ever-informative if not always accurate *Evening Star*, Sprague was a financial genius, entirely lacking in any of those colorful hobbies that make American magnates so interesting to read about if not to meet. Before his metamorphosis as a warrior, he had often been mistaken at social gatherings for an accountant or divinity student. Now he had captured the imagination of every American who could read newspapers. He was a governor, a hero—*above all, he was a bachelor*. In every story that Chase had read, this one sentence blazed before his eyes, dazzling them to the point of genuine tears. Chase could not lose Kate, ever; and yet this weedy—there was no other word, thought Chase, smiling sweetly down at Sprague—young man was all that he had ever dreamed of for Kate, rolled into a single most dashing, if nearsighted, package.

"Cotton," Chase heard, as from afar, "was ten cents a pound a week ago."

"I beg your pardon." Chase continued to smile.

Kate interrupted, "Governor Sprague is concerned with the blockade."

"So are we," said Chase, missing the point. "We have not the ships to seal off the rebel ports. They do constant business with the Europeans. But we are increasing the navy, aren't we, Senator Hale?"

"Oh, yes. We'll starve them out in six months. But until then, there won't be any rebel cotton for those mills of yours, Governor." Hale looked delighted.

Sprague was sharp. "Twenty thousand people out of work in Rhode Island won't look so good for us at election time."

"Oh, it will never come to that." Chase was soothing. All in all, Sprague was not a bad-looking little fellow. Certainly, his brown hair and mud-colored eyes set off Kate's blond-gold beauty as a dark foil does a clear rare gem, thought Chase, poetically. "By the time your current supplies of raw cotton are used up," he said prosaically, "our army will be at Richmond with you, sir, I hope in the vanguard." This worked nicely, as Chase knew it would.

"I've applied to Mr. Lincoln. I said I have to be a major-general. Rhode Island won't like it if I'm offered less than Ben Butler. You see, we don't think all that much of lawyers from Massachusetts."

"What about lawyers from New Hampshire?" asked Senator Hale.

Sprague's answer was to turn his back on the senator, just as Hay and Bessie approached.

"Here's a *daughter* of New Hampshire," said Hay, "Miss Bessie Hale."

"Oh, I am trembling like a leaf!" Bessie was indeed flushed, Hay noticed, as she stared down at Sprague, who stared up at her great *poitrine*, like New Hampshire's own White Mountains.

"How do you do?" Sprague started to step backward but Bessie, who still held his hand, drew him toward her. Since Bessie had much to say about heroes and heroism, Hay took the occasion to slip away with Kate to the dining room, where creamed oysters were the centerpiece of the buffet.

"Well, Miss Chase, what do you think of Governor Sprague?" Hay was mischievous.

"Oh, I *think*! And then I think some more." Kate smiled at him. Even her teeth were perfect, Hay noticed, aware that he must not allow himself to daydream of her. "Did you know his father was murdered?"

"I haven't been able to read every single newspaper story about him." Hay realized that he sounded as if he were envious; and he
160

was not. It is hard to be envious of a man you have been obliged to dress, with the help of Sal Austin.

"He told me just now. It happened when he was a child. It made a tremendous impression on him."

"So have you." Hay was bold; why not?

Kate looked him directly—and disconcertingly—in the eye. "Have you been studying us?" This was blunt; and was meant to be.

"It is hard not to notice such a . . . fabulous couple in these rooms."

"Fabulous? So we resemble characters in a fable, do we? But *which* characters? And *what* fable?"

Hay thought rapidly—classical pairs from Pyramus and Thisbe to Zeus and Ganymede (most inappropriate, the last) filled his brain. He settled, lamely, for: "Venus and Mars. Who else?"

Before Kate could counter, Congressman Washburne paid his respects; then he greeted Hay with: "I'm just back from Illinois. We raised twenty thousand dollars in Chicago, contributions for the war."

"In Cincinnati," said Kate, "they have raised more than two hundred thousand dollars."

"But that's to be expected in your father's state." Washburne was polite. "It's a personal tribute to him." Washburne addressed Hay. "I hope the President will have a moment for me tomorrow."

"Whenever you like, sir." Washburne bowed to Kate; then he laid siege to a massive silver chafing dish in which simmered terrapin.

"As of last week, Father's raised close to twenty million dollars, in contributions alone." Kate was proud.

Hay was teasing. "You must admit that it was uncommonly wise of the President to make Mr. Chase Secretary of the Treasury."

"Oh, I've never denied that! Who is the large man over there, by the fireplace, against the wall? I see him everywhere, including my own house. But he never speaks to anyone. He just stands, as if he were furniture."

Hay recognized the powerfully built young man who, indeed, looked to be a piece of furniture placed next to the fireplace. "If he has a name, Mr. Sumner is the only one who knows it. He's Mr. Sumner's bodyguard. He goes with him everywhere. He's paid for by one of the senator's Boston admirers, who doesn't like the idea of anyone as vague as Mr. Sumner wandering alone around a city filled with secessionists."

"Well, at last I know who my guests are." Kate turned to Hay; she smelled of lilac. "Is it true that Mrs. Lincoln's half-sister and her husband are staying at the Mansion?"

"Where did you hear that?"

"My spies can resemble wallpaper, if need be."

"Well, it is true. Your wallpaper is presently looking down upon Mr. and Mrs. Ben Hardin Helm of Lexington, Kentucky."

"Two secessionists."

"Neither Mr. nor Mrs. Helm has seceded as yet; and Kentucky remains loyal to the Union."

"Barely loyal. I hear—not from my wallpaper but from the newspapers—that Mrs. Lincoln's full brother, her three half-brothers and her three half-brothers-in-law are all secessionists, and that they have all enlisted—the men, that is—in the Confederate army."

"If Mr. Helm has turned rebel, it will be news to Mr. Lincoln. Actually," said Hay, realizing that he was saying far too much but he wanted, most sincerely, to impress Kate—because . . . of Sprague? "Mr. Helm is a West Point graduate, who is about to be appointed U.S. Army Paymaster, with the rank of major."

"Oh?" Then Kate took Hay's arm and together they made a triumphal tour of the dining room and back parlor. As they greeted the French minister Mercier and the Prussian minister Gerold, Kate was able, between the compliments and flurries of French and German, to ask, with sweet malice, "What are Mrs. Lincoln's true politics?"

Hay responded with what he took to be near truth. "She is the true abolitionist of the family, and embarrassed by her family."

"A Southerner?" Kate put on a thick Southern accent: "Embarrassed by kin? Oh, never!"

"Oh, yes!" said Hay.

"Oh, yes!" said Emilie Helm, eighteen years her half-sister Mary's junior. They stood facing each other across a row of gardenia plants in the White House conservatory.

Mary had not expected such vehemence. "You would even go with him to Richmond?" Mary asked.

"I'm his wife, Sister Mary."

"Oh, Little Sister, and I had thought that of all of you . . . that of all of us, you would stay loyal."

Emilie took the scissors that she held in one hand and began to harvest the gardenias which were in full-forced, white-fleshed bloom. Mary found the scent both ravishing and overpowering. Neatly, Emilie arranged the gardenias in the straw basket that the head groundsman had given her. "I must go where my husband goes," said Emilie, eyes on the flowers. "After all, that's what *you* have done, and no one in Lexington criticizes you for it."

"Then that must be the only thing that they do not criticize me for." Mary still resented the response of the Todds to her marriage to a scrub, as they called a man not of their class. "Mr. Lincoln is going to offer Ben a commission in the army. Will he take it?"
162

"You will have to ask Ben." Emilie turned from Mary, who had always looked upon the girl less as a half-sister than as the daughter that she had never borne. "The Hardins are so political. Ben's father, the governor . . ."

"Oh, Emilie, we are all political! But Kentucky isn't South Carolina. We are people of the border."

"We are really Southern, Sister Mary. You know that."

"Well, *your* mother was a Virginian, that's true." Any mention of Mary's stepmother was apt as not to bring on if not the dreaded Headache an ordinary headache that was quite bad enough. "Let's get out of here, Little Sister, I'm sweltering."

Together they made their way through the heated, sweet-smelling air of the long, glassed-in conservatory where row after row of exotic flowers grew in earth-filled stone troughs. This was Mary's refuge when life grew too hectic in the Mansion or when the wind was southerly and the foul air from the canal filled every room while mosquitoes and gnats and flies were wafted into the Mansion through the tall screenless windows. Because of the crisis, the President had decided not to move out to the relative coolness of the stone cottage at the Soldiers' Home. Because of the crisis, Mary had refused to go North. But now that the city was secure from attack, she had decided that a visit to New York City might soon be in order, to shop for the Mansion.

At the door of the conservatory, Mr. Watt, the head groundsman, respectfully bowed to the ladies. He was a courtly man; and Mary liked him. He had worked at the White House for years; he understood the ins-and-outs of hiring and firing the army of servants, gardeners and just plain hangers-on that had attached themselves over the years to the Mansion.

"Mrs. Lincoln, I talked to Mr. Wood about . . . our project. He thinks it will be all right."

"Good, sir." Mary had seen to it that one William S. Wood whom the government had assigned to them as escort on the trip to Washington from Springfield would be Commissioner of Public Buildings, and so in charge of the President's House. Although Mr. Wood was a friend of Mr. Seward—never a recommendation—Mary thought that she could trust him to help put into effect her secret plan to make the President's House the most magnificent residence in the nation if not the world. Mary herself had not seen much of the world, but her teachers, the Mentelles, had been at the court of Louis XVI and Marie Antoinette, and Mary had grown up with tales of Versailles and the Tuileries that were now as much a part of her childhood memories as Harry of the West himself. Mary also delighted in the company of the Chevalier Wikoff, a man of perfect

163

taste who had been presented at most of the courts of Europe; and remembered, in detail, every drapery, every ornament.

Although it was not yet five o'clock, Lincoln was in the upstairs sitting room, playing with Tad and Willie. As the children rushed to greet mother and aunt, Lincoln sat up in his chair. "I'm taking a holiday from that grinding mill down the corridor."

"I wish you'd take more." Mary indicated the basket of fresh-cut flowers. "Little Sister's making us a floral arrangement."

"I better begin before they wilt." Emilie left the room, escorted by two nephews, with news of an attractive pet goat named Nanda. Mary sat in a sofa; she felt odd, unsteady, disoriented.

"What does she say?" asked Lincoln.

Mary let the back of her head rest on the cool horsehair. "She will go where he goes. What does *he* say?"

"Nothing. I gave him the commission this morning."

"And Ben said nothing?"

Lincoln shook his head.

"I'd better speak to that boy . . ."

"Better not. Let him make up his own mind." Lincoln smiled. "Anyway, we have good news."

"Mr. Davis is dead!"

"Not that good—or bad, as the case may be. No, Ben Butler's occupied the city of Baltimore, and the legislature doesn't think that, all in all, secession is such a good idea, and so the governor now says he'll send us the four regiments I asked him for."

"Father!" Mary looked with delight at her husband; then with less delight at the frayed green curtain just back of him. "I would've sworn an oath, were it ladylike to swear—"

"*First* Lady-like," he proposed.

"First Lady-like, that we would lose Maryland. Now you've held the state to us. You and you alone. Mr. Seward must be gnashing his teeth." Mary frowned. "What about Kentucky?"

"We'll hold the state, by a whisker."

"That means that all those crazy brothers and brothers-in-law of mine will have to go South." A group of gnats gathered about Mary's head; she dismissed them, vigorously, with her fan. "I cannot think what demon possesses those men."

"The same as possesses us, I suppose." Lincoln slumped farther down on his spine. "They have convinced themselves that I will free all their slaves and make them poor, when all I want is . . ." He stopped; as if weary of the repetition of a theme that no one chose ever to hear. "North Carolina will go next week. It is now certain."

"That makes . . . ten states?"

Lincoln nodded. "And Tennessee will go as well, if I don't do something, though what I can do is not much."

164

"You can strike at Richmond!" Mary sat up very straight. "If you can take Richmond, Virginia is ours again and that will be the end of the rebellion, once and for all."

Lincoln laughed. "I agree, Mother. Only I'm not ready for such a large undertaking. But I do have something smaller in view."

"What?"

"If I tell you, you'll repeat it."

"If you tell me, *you've* repeated it."

"That's true. So, if I can't keep a secret, why should you? Anyway, we've hung on to Missouri, thanks to Frank Blair and a few others, though the fighting in St. Louis was fierce . . ."

Emilie returned with her husband, Ben Helm, a tall, lanky young man whose resemblance to Henry Clay had been remarked upon all his life. Emilie's vase of flowers was duly admired by Mary, while Lincoln turned to Helm and said, "Did you talk to General Scott?"

"Well, no. I didn't. I just went looking at the sights instead." The soft Southern voice did not go at all with the cold, gray hunter's eyes that seemed a Kentucky characteristic, shared by Lincoln, too, though his hunter's eyes were often masked—smoky-looking was how Mary thought of them on those occasions when he was present in the flesh but, in spirit, withdrawn from the company.

Mary rose to help Emilie place the flowers on a console of the Oval Room, at whose center, in a straight chair, Ben Helm sat just opposite Lincoln, who said, "Well, I'm sure that once you've seen all the sights, you'll go and look at Winfield Scott, who's just about the largest sight we have in the town."

"He actually knew Thomas Jefferson," said Mary, returning to her sofa, "but did not think him sound. He preferred Mr. Madison, and then Mr. Jackson and now—Mr. Lincoln!"

"I suspect, Mother, he's just being polite in my case. But it's true he has a partiality for war presidents. Fortunately, I'm not really one, just yet." The gray eyes that now searched out Helm's eyes were those of a hunter, too. Mary gave an involuntary shudder: When two hunters stare at each other, it is the women who will weep at the end.

"I have thought about this, Brother Lincoln." Helm's voice was soft. "I thought and thought about it before we came. But I must tell you that I only really came up here for Emilie's sake because she wanted me to, and because she wanted to see Sister Mary one more time . . ."

"One more time!" Mary's cry sounded in the room. Yet she was not aware that she had even spoken; she was aware only that she had been harshly struck.

Emilie put her arm about Mary's shoulders. "Oh, Sister, I know it is hard."

Mary stared up at Emilie; but saw her not at all through the tears that now filled her eyes.

Lincoln rose and paced the room. "I had hoped, Ben," he said, "that you and I could reason together. Because the matter is now sorting itself out back home, and that Kentucky will stay in the Union is now about as certain as anything on this earth."

"I guess you have seen to that, Brother Lincoln." In the gentle voice there was an edge of menace that made Mary recoil; made Emilie hold her all the tighter.

"I see to nothing. Events see to me. I am acted upon, no more. You have a great career ahead of you. You'll be governor of Kentucky like your grandfather; and maybe more. Who knows? Who would've dreamt that I'd be here, for all my sins, as it is now proving?"

"Oh, Ben!" said Mary. "We are so isolated in this place. Father needs you. I need Little Sister. We are without friends; and we are possessed of altogether too many enemies in this rebel city . . ." Mary stopped; she had said the forbidden word; she could not recall it.

"They are not rebels to us, Sister Mary," said Emilie. "They only want to be let go in peace, like us."

"We cannot let go that which has no place to go because it is where it is and it is what it is, a part forever of this Union." Lincoln appealed directly to Emilie. "As for peace, we only defend what is ours."

"Brother Lincoln, our lives are not your lives and our property is not your property and if we wish to have a new country, who can stop us?"

Lincoln turned up the palms of both hands; to show that he had no more to say. Mary could no longer see the room for the tears that had begun to flow. But she could still feel Emilie's arm about her shoulders. Blindly, she looked up at the girl. "You will not stay here with me?"

"I must go with my husband."

"I have been offered a commission in the Confederate Army, Brother Lincoln." The voice was soft and inexorable as the south wind that always brought the rains to Lexington.

"You will accept that commission." There was now no real question in Lincoln's voice.

"Yes, Brother. That is my intention."

"You will break my heart," said Mary; and so her youth came to an end, once and for all.

16

DAVID WAS HELPING MR. THOMPSON TO SHUT UP SHOP WHEN Annie Surratt appeared at the door. Since this was the first time that she had come to see him at Thompson's, David asked her to come in, but she shook her head. She seemed nervous; and flushed. "It's your mother, Davie. She's been taken ill."

"What's wrong with Mrs. Herold?" asked Mr. Thompson, coming from the back of the shop where the woman-of-all-work was doing no work at all. "Oh, it's you, Miss Surratt. How is your father?" Mr. Thompson knew just about everyone in the town; and most of their illnesses, as well.

"Sick, too. He never leaves his bed. Davie, your mother's had a fall. The doctor's with her now. They're not sure what she's broken. But she's asking for you."

"Which doctor?" asked Mr. Thompson, who sat in constant judgment upon the entire profession.

"I don't know, Mr. Thompson. It was Davie's sister who saw me in the street and said, 'Fetch Davie, Mother's asking for him.' So I came straight away."

David looked at Mr. Thompson, who nodded benignly. "We're finished for the day. You go on now. If she needs special medicine, let me know. I'll make a discount for her." This, David knew, would be five percent off the hundred-and-fifty-percent profit that Mr. Thompson made on each sale. If the life was not so dull and confining, David knew that he could do a lot worse than setting up shop as a druggist. He pulled on his linen hot-weather jacket and hurried after Annie.

At Fifteenth Street they were obliged to wait ten minutes while an artillery battery moved slowly down the middle of the street and guards kept the pedestrians to the sidewalk. As David suspected, there was nothing wrong with his mother. "It's Father wants to see you. Something urgent, he said."

"How is he?"

"Oh, the same. He still goes across the river from time to time but it's wearing him out fast. I think he wants you to go across."

That was exactly what Mr. Surratt wanted. David sat in a flimsy straight chair beside the old man's bed. Mr. Surratt was paler than usual; and, as always, the cough came and went according to its own mysterious series. The room smelled of medicine; and dying flesh. Over Mr. Surratt's bed hung a blue-tinted picture of the Virgin; beneath the picture was a large crucifix. As usual in the Surratt household, David wondered how anyone could change from real religion to Irish mummery. "I should go, Davie; but I can't. It's short notice: too short for me. I'm not strong. So you'll have to move fast as you can. Cross the Long Bridge before nightfall; make contact with our friend at the tavern."

"What do I give him?"

"You don't give him nothing but a spoken message."

"So what do I . . . speak?"

"Lucifer, the son of morning, and Satan."

"That's easy enough. What does it mean?"

"He'll know. It's better that you don't. Now get moving, quick as you can."

"Yes, sir."

Annie was at the piano in the front parlor; but she did not play. She looked up at him, anxiously. "You're going to the other side?"

David nodded; he felt, suddenly, not only entirely grown-up but of supreme importance in the scheme of things. He had, also, recently, begun a moustache. He smoothed its dark silkiness. "What do you think?"

"I think something's about to happen. I think the Yankee troops—"

"I meant about my moustaches."

"Oh, they look nice. You look . . . older."

"That's good?"

"Yes. That's good. I'll walk you as far as the river."

Arm in arm like any young man in a linen jacket, with a moustache, and a pretty girl on his arm, David strolled along the dusty streets. Washington was a city where if you did not choke on the dust you got stuck in the mud. Today the heat had been considerable; but now a cool dusty breeze dried the trickle of sweat at David's temples.

Troops were everywhere. Somewhat nervously, David and Annie tried to look like young lovers, or the way that David thought that young lovers should look on an early evening late in May, with the evening star not yet visible in a violet sky over the Potomac Heights.

In the President's Park, troops were bivouacked. Rows of tents had been pitched; and the stoves for cooking had all been lit. A group of soldiers was singing sad songs. A cow was being milked. An officer shaved himself in a mirror hanging from a tree. As they turned into Ohio Avenue, which led to the nearest bridge across the canal, they could see even more troops encamped among the white stone blocks at the base of what was to be, one day, Washington's monument. Nearby, an aged black man sat fishing for catfish in the stagnant canal. The smell was appalling—like rotted flesh.

"There must be fifty thousand Yankees in the town," said Annie. "I would never have believed it if I hadn't seen them, practically all of them, I'd say, with my own eyes since I got back from Surrattsville. They're in the Capitol, sleeping on the floor. They're in the Patent Office. They're . . ."

"They say *we've* got fifty thousand men across the river, all set to take the city."

"Well, I haven't *seen* any of them. I've only heard tell. But I've seen these." Annie held tight his arm. How many men of eighteen, with practically full moustaches, were embarked on a mission which would spell the doom of the Yankee capital? David was certain that his diabolic message had something to do with the much-predicted and much-longed-for attack on Washington. As formidable as the Yankee boys looked, they were no match for the wild boys, who lived only to fight. "Where is Isaac?" David asked, put in mind of Southern valor.

"I don't rightly know. But I suspect that now Richmond's capital of the whole Confederacy, he'll be there, right next door to us."

"Hope he'll help try and kick the door in!" David was fierce; then he sighed. "Oh, what I'd give to go to Richmond, and work for President Davis, or something." Actually, David had once been to Richmond, which was no more than a hundred of the crow's miles from Washington, and he'd thought it a poor sort of city compared to Washington or even to Baltimore, a town more to his liking, in some ways, than either.

"Father says you're better off where you are, keeping an eye on what's going on in the White House."

"I don't pick up much. But I've noticed that when something's up, they do have a way of just disappearing over there. They disappeared yesterday, come to think of it."

"What do you mean, disappear?"

"Well, things get very quiet. And Mr. Lincoln sneaks across to the War Department, and everyone else acts like nothing's going on and then something happens. I could swear the President's been out of sight for over a day now, so something is about to happen."

"What do you hear at Thompson's?"

"Well, I hear that Mrs. Lincoln went up to New York City to buy things for the Mansion and that the President's told this Mr.

169

Wood who's in charge of public buildings that he didn't keep a good enough eye on her because she spent too much at the stores . . ."

"I saw all that in the papers. What else do you hear?"

"I heard that the President is all riled up because he thinks that Mrs. Lincoln and Mr. Wood was having this love affair together at the Metropolitan Hotel in New York City."

Annie stopped in her tracks. Behind her the dark red Gothic fantasy of the Smithsonian Institution was turning to black in the now silver light. "Mrs. Lincoln? A woman *her* age, carrying on?"

"That's what people are saying."

"I was told that she was crazy." Annie shook her head. "I never heard of a woman of her age—what is she? forty-five?—carrying on like that, unless, of course, she is a professional like your friend Mrs. Austin."

"Well, sometimes they do, Annie." David was not about to tell her that he knew at firsthand that they did. There was a handsome stout widow of more than forty-five, who owned a grocery shop back of the Navy Yard. She had kept one of the wild boys in groceries until he had gone South. She had now made it plain to David that he, too, could become the owner of an occasional ham if he were to dally with her and enliven the sadness of her widowhood. Annie, David decided, did not know much about women. But then she was a nice girl; educated by nuns.

"Anyway, Mrs. Lincoln's back now, and Mr. Wood is still around and as thick as thieves with Mr. Watt, the head groundsman, who makes a fortune every year, stealing from the Mansion, selling jobs, and filling up the Center Market with all the truck he grows on the sly in the park." As David spoke, he was surprised at just how much Mansion gossip he had picked up without particularly meaning to. But, of course, the doings of the permanent staff at the Mansion were of great, even vital, interest to the town's tradespeople, all of whom had to keep on Old Edward's good side, and give him an occasional tip. Then there was Mrs. Cuthbert, the housekeeper—and a power to reckon with; also, the mulatto Elizabeth Keckley, who was close to Mrs. Lincoln but a distant woman to others, and new to the Mansion game, unlike Mr. Watt, who had made his fortune ten times over by simply charming each new Administration.

At the Long Bridge, Annie kissed David on the cheek; and whispered in his ear, "I'm playing like we're sweethearts."

"Ain't we?" David nuzzled her ear; she gave a little cry; giggled; fled.

David approached the small guardhouse that had recently been erected at the Washington end of the bridge. He knew that the sergeant had been watching his performance with Annie; and he felt a lamb's innocence as he presented his pass to the sergeant, who was new to him.

"Thompson's Drug Store," the man read. "Aren't you a bit late to be delivering prescriptions?"

"No, sir. At least not late for Mrs. Alexander, who's sinking fast, they say . . ."

"Go on."

As David crossed the bridge, he found himself walking straight into a splendid sunset. Dazzled though his eyes were, he could see that there was practically no traffic from the Virginia side except for an occasional wagon of farm produce, while from the Washington side there were a few lone walkers like himself but no carriages. Those who had intended to leave the Union for the Confederacy had long since done so. Halfway across the bridge, he stopped and looked downriver to Greenleaf's Point, red as blood in the sunset, as was the Capitol on its hill farther to the east. It was then that David noticed an odd metallic glitter just below the point where Maryland Avenue converges with the Long Bridge.

"Move on," said a voice. He looked up. A patrol of Union infantry was marching from the Virginia side to the Washington side. A corporal had spoken to him.

"Yes, sir," said David; and he moved on, aware that what he had seen in the swamp south of the bridge was, at the very least, a regiment of infantry, and the flashing lights were bright bayonets reflecting the red sun.

On the Virginia side, David was recognized by the Confederate sergeant, a large-limbed fellow a few years older than himself. "Off to the tavern, Davie?" The sergeant winked at him.

"Well, I'm a bit dry in the throat, if the truth were known."

"See you then," said the sergeant. "When I go off duty."

David made his way straight to the tavern. The main barroom was half empty. Before the trouble, the musty, beer-and-sawdust-smelling room would have been crowded with local farmers as well as with thirsty travellers from the South, having one last drink in Dixie before proceeding on to the capital; but now there were only gray-uniformed soldiers, and a few travelling-salesmen types, all standing at the bar, feet on the never-polished brass rail.

David ordered a beer; ate a pickle; asked the bartender, "Is Mr. Mayberry here?"

"No, Davie. He's over to Alexandria."

"When's he due back?"

"Most any time, I guess."

David waited until midnight. He drank and swapped stories with the Confederate sergeant and his friends. From time to time he would go outside to relieve himself beneath a full white moon that made the night like day. All was quiet at the Virginia end of the bridge, where soldiers whispered passwords to one another as they came and went, while, to the south, the lights of nearby Alexandria made a yellow glow in the black sky.

At midnight, David was beginning to feel the effect of all the beer that he had drunk; he took the barman to one side. "Maybe I should go looking for him."

"I don't know where to tell you to look. He should've been back hours ago." The barman was plainly disturbed. "There's rumors," he said in a low voice.

"That's why I got to get my message to him."

"I don't honestly know how you can, Davie."

Despite the beer that he had drunk, David took seriously his mission. He walked the six miles into Alexandria, where he went straight to the Marshall House, a small hotel on whose roof was visible the Confederate flag. In the hotel's barroom, David found the owner, a man named Anderson, whom he knew by sight. Anderson was seated at a table with what looked to be a number of local businessmen. David gestured from the bar that he would like to speak to the owner, who joined him at the bar.

"I know you, don't I?"

"Yes, sir. I'm David Herold. Thompson's Drug Store. I visit with Mr. Mayberry some, when I come over here on errands."

"That's where I know you. Whiskey," said Anderson to the bartender. "You growed a moustache since I saw you last."

"Yes, sir." David downed the whiskey. "I got to find Mr. Mayberry, sir. I got an important message for him."

Anderson frowned. "I saw him earlier. He looked in to say all was well—for now. He was in a hurry, I thought. Can I help you?"

"I don't think so."

"Good boy. Trust nobody. Well, drink all you like. Wait here if you want." Anderson went back to his table. David was now sleepy from drink. He had also been up since five. He asked the bartender if there was a place where he might lie down; and he was shown to a shed back of the hotel where he stretched out on a bare cot; and slept.

David was dreaming that he was caught in a thunderstorm on the river's bank when, suddenly, the thunder was right on top of him. Awakened by the sound of gunfire, David flung himself from the cot to the earthen floor; then got himself out of the shed to find that the moon was down and the sun almost up, and the street crowded with people; some still in their nightshirts; others half dressed. Everyone was hurrying toward the Long Bridge.

172

"What's happening?" David managed to stop an old man who, perversely it looked, was going in the opposite direction.

"Yankees gone and crossed the river. They's attacking Alexandria!"

As the sun rose, David saw again the bayonets that he had seen the previous evening, only now they were silver-bright, not blood-red. The Confederate garrison had been given one hour to evacuate Alexandria, which they had done; they were now on their way to Richmond. As David watched, Alexandria filled up with Union troops, mostly men from New York's Seventh Regiment.

The townspeople simply stared at them, more astonished than angered or frightened. But then no one quite knew how to behave when American troops occupied an American town except the town's pigs, who screamed in terror at all the horses that threatened to trample them to death.

A group of Yankee officers walked past David. They were in high spirits. One of them was the twenty-four-year-old colonel of the Zouaves, Ellsworth, who had been delighting Washington—and David—with his regiment's extraordinary drill, not to mention their recent performance when a fire broke out next to Willard's and a group of them—New York firemen in civilian life—made a human ladder against the side of the burning building and then, passing buckets of water from hand to hand, had put out the fire to the loud applause of a thousand spectators, among them David.

More than ever, David wished that he was Colonel Ellsworth. The young man moved like a tiger, a highly enraged tiger when he saw the Confederate flag atop the Marshall House. Ellsworth was within a yard of David. "I'll take care of that," he said, grimly. "Sergeant!" Ellsworth turned to the soldier next to him. "Fetch me a company of men." The man saluted; and hurried off. "Major!" He turned to a nearby officer. "Occupy the telegraph office."

"Yes, sir."

"Captain!" He turned, smartly, to another officer. "Take a company and occupy the railroad depot."

"Yes, Colonel."

Disastrous though this day was for the Confederacy, David would have given an arm to be this extraordinary young man, so cool, so precise, so—heroic.

Ellsworth, followed by several officers and men, dashed into the hotel. A moment later, Ellsworth was on the roof of the hotel. There was a gasp from the Alexandrians in the street below as he cut down the flag with a Bowie knife. For an instant, in perfect triumph, he waved the flag over his head; and David knew perfect ecstasy as he imagined himself up there. Then Ellsworth vanished

173

through a trapdoor in the roof. A moment later, there was the sound of a shotgun going off inside the hotel; followed by a second blast; and a loud cry. Suddenly, framed in the doorway of the Marshall House, a corporal stood, holding in his arms the plainly dead body of Ellsworth from whose chest the arterial blood made jets, like a miniature fountain, in response to the last spasmodic beatings of the heart, covering the pale face and black curls with a scarlet film. A woman screamed at the sight. David fled toward the Long Bridge.

Mr. Surratt moaned when David told him what had happened. "We could have saved the town if Mayberry had got my message." The old man lay, propped up with pillows, clutching a crucifix in one long, yellow hand.

"Not with all those Yanks, sir. There was thirteen thousand, the papers said. There was only five hundred of our boys in Alexandria." David wondered what had happened to his drinking partner of the night before. If anyone as handsome and heroic as Colonel Ellsworth could be shot to pieces, what chance did a mere Confederate boy or, for that matter, anyone have once a war had started? David had never seen a man shot before. He could not get over the way the spurting blood had seemed to have a life of its own just as its owner ceased to have any life at all.

"They could've been warned. They could've brought in Beauregard's troops. They could've made a show, at the least."

"What did the message mean?"

"Lucifer was Alexandria. That meant it was to be attacked within twenty-four hours. The son of morning was the Hampton Roads. That's just opposite Fortress Monroe, where Ben Butler's holed up, within striking distance of Norfolk and Richmond. I reckon he's already attacked Hampton and Newport News. That was the plan. While Satan is the Potomac Heights just across from Georgetown, which we lost at dawn, which means our railway line is cut. Oh, these God-damned white Northern niggers!" A fit of coughing cut short the old man's fury.

As David made his way through crowded, generally joyous streets to Thompson's, he wondered why the message had not been sent several days earlier. But then he had no way of knowing exactly how it was that Mr. Surratt got his secrets from inside the War Department. The fact that he got them at all and that there were a thousand Davids in the city to take the news across the river was one of the few good things to contemplate on this entirely bad day.

That day and the next were equally bad at the President's House. On the second day Colonel Ellsworth lay in state in the East Room, and a long line of people came to look down at the
174

now-clean marble-white face and dark curls. Keckley stood with Willie and Tad; held them each by a hand, and let them watch for half an hour as the weeping Zouaves filed past their fallen leader. Then Cousin Lizzie appeared and took the boys to the upstairs sitting room, where Mary and the Chevalier Wikoff were seated, drinking tea. From the window, the Union flag was now clearly visible atop the Marshall House. The Confederate flag that Ellsworth had died for lay folded now on a table in the oval sitting room. To Mary's horror, the flag, drenched in Ellsworth's blood, had been presented to her at the funeral service as a memorial of the war's first hero. Once she had left the East Room, she had given Lizzie the flag; and tried not to be ill, as they fled upstairs.

Mary had not been as fond of Ellsworth as her husband, but the fact that someone close to all the family was suddenly dead and lying in the East Room was in itself quite enough to bring on the old panicky feeling that often presaged The Headache. Grimly, she made conversation. Fortunately, the Chevalier was easy to talk to and delightful to listen to.

"Colonel Ellsworth worked in Mr. Lincoln's law office." Mary talked rapidly, in a race with her inner demon. "He had no gift for the law, even Mr. Lincoln saw that, but he was a natural soldier, and marvelous with his hands, with guns, with the training of soldiers."

"Mr. Lincoln has taken this hard, I suppose?" Wilkoff sipped his tea, a look of compassion on his grizzled yet still handsome face.

"God, yes! As hard as I have ever seen him take any such death, excepting that of Eddie, our boy who died. One never grows used to these things. It is odd, isn't it? Particularly in the West, where there is the cholera and all sorts of other sickness that can sweep like the wind through a family or a town, taking the best with it." Mary could feel the dull ache beginning just back of her eyes. She prayed that this was simply an ordinary headache; she had not the time to be ill now. She would fight it, she decided, pouring herself more tea.

Cousin Lizzie entered with Willie and Tad. "They were crying, the soldiers," said Tad, with wonder. "I didn't know they ever did that."

"They do," said Mary, "when they are very sad, as they are now because their colonel's dead."

"But you always say when I cry that soldiers don't cry like I do." Tad's mind was already of the legal sort.

"You don't cry because something important has happened," said Willie, severely, "like your friend being shot in a war. You cry because you don't get what you want."

175

"I cry when I fall down." Tad began to enumerate the numerous fair instances of his weeping.

But Willie cut him short. "What happens, Ma, to Ellsworth, now?"

"Why, they'll send him home and bury him in the churchyard." The ache was beginning to spread from the back of the eyes to a place deeper inside her head.

"And that's all?" Willie looked sad; he was growing into an uncommonly handsome boy, she thought; the large, blue-violet eyes were those of her own mother, born again.

"That's all there is for anybody at the end," said Cousin Lizzie, a bit too complacently, thought Mary. Lizzie loved funerals; and *memento mori* of any kind.

"How could he be playing with us this time day before yesterday in the backyard there"—Willie pointed to the Park—"and now he's all cold and white-looking and lying in a box?"

"It's God's will," said Cousin Lizzie.

"Yes," said Mary, beginning to feel faint. "'There is a time to be born...'" She could not finish the familiar passage because the pain in her head was setting the room afire. Chairs and tables were developing lurid nimbuses. But she would not give way; not this time. She stared at Willie; he seemed to be standing, pale and serene, at the center of a mandala of flame. "You don't remember Eddie," she began with difficulty.

"Everyone dies," said Tad, cheerfully, rushing from the room.

"That's true, isn't it." As Willie turned away, the fiery envelope turned with him. "We never know," he said, "when we'll die, which is really unfair, isn't it, Ma? Because you can't plan or anything. He was going to get married..."

The pain forced Mary to shut her eyes; forced her to scream; forced her onto the floor. But when she was able to open her eyes again, the pain had grown tolerable; and she was in her bed. Lincoln sat beside her, holding her hand. Keckley sat on the other side of the bed, keeping watch.

"Oh, Father," she said. "Of all times..."

"Don't talk, Mother. You've had a bad bout. But it looks to be over."

"How long have I been here?"

"Two days, Mrs. Lincoln," said Keckley, when Lincoln would not answer her.

"God, no! Of all times," she repeated. "Are the boys all right? I was talking to Willie when..."

Lincoln smiled. "Willie has now taken to writing poetry. He wrote a very pretty ode to Ellsworth. I'll give it to you later."

Suddenly, Mary heard the sound of a loud high voice singing

nearby: "Old Abe Lincoln, a rail-splitter was he, and that's the way he'll split the Confederac-ceee!"

Lincoln chuckled. "Tad's in excellent voice today. He doesn't bother you, does he?"

"Oh, no!"

Mary succeeded in smiling, too. "I think that's a bit discourteous, calling you a rail-splitter."

"Well, Mother, they can hardly sing 'Old Abe Lincoln, Counsel for the Illinois Central Railroad was he.' It just don't scan. Anyway, I can still split a rail if I have to." Tad began, with unusual insistence, to sing the same verses again. "I'll go quiet him down." Lincoln left the room. Fearfully, Mary turned to Keckley, "What did I do? What did I say?"

"You were mostly unconscious. When you were not, you were delirious." Keckley put a powder in a glass of water.

"I hope the doors were shut, and no one heard."

Keckley gave her the potion to drink. "Don't you worry. No one heard a thing. I got you to bed straight away, and no one's set foot in this room except Mr. Lincoln and me."

"I sometimes think," said Mary, beginning already to feel drowsy, "that there really is such a thing as hell, but that we must live in it *before* we die, not after."

Mary suddenly recalled a jingle that she had not thought of in years. "Mammy Sally, who brought us all up, used to tell us that every Friday night the jaybirds all go down to hell and report to the Devil on who was bad during the week. So every time we saw a jaybird, we used to sing, 'Howdy, Mr. Jay, you are a tell-tale-tell. You play the spy each day, then carry tales to...hell...!'" On the word "hell," Mary drifted off into a dreamless sleep.

17

SALMON P. CHASE STOOD BEHIND THE MASSIVE BLACK-WALNUT desk. In a semicircle before him sat a dozen of the country's leading bankers. Jay Cooke had summoned them to Washington for a consultation with the Secretary of the Treasury, whose report to Congress on the state of the nation's finances was now being composed. The president and cashier of New York's Bank of Commerce, Messrs. Stevens and Vail, sat side by side, polite, attentive, inscrutable; as well as the officers of the Albany Exchange Bank and the American Exchange Bank; as well as assorted independent bankers like Morris Ketchum and William Henry Aspinwall.

At first, Chase had struck the confident note that all was well with the nation's finances. But these men knew better and, ultimately, they would have to help him finance a military establishment that was threatening to cost the government a million dollars a day even though no battle had yet been fought anywhere. The capture of Alexandria had cost only one life, that of Colonel Ellsworth, while the seizure of the Hampton Roads and Newport News had been bloodless, but expensive. Chase did his best to emphasize the cost of simply keeping an army and a navy.

"We have received," said Chase, aware that the bankers already knew the sum, "twenty-three million dollars in voluntary contributions from various state legislatures, municipalities and private persons. Since the President's second proclamation on the third of May, calling for forty-two thousand volunteers to serve three years, the costs of our military efforts have sensibly increased." Chase stared with some pleasure at the gilded window cornices surmounted by the Treasury's seal, *his* seal. "As you know, gentlemen, when this Administration took office, we found an empty larder. The panic of 1857 turned what had been a Treasury surplus into a deficit, while our Southern friends who were still in the Congress managed to keep us from imposing excise taxes. The few loans that were floated in the general market were done so at exorbitant rates of interest." Chase studied their faces on the phrase "exorbitant rates of interest," the reason why those money-men were now seated so demurely in his office. They would be more than happy to buy up the government's bonds if they were short-term and paid twenty-percent interest. Chase had made up his mind not to go above seven percent. Plainly, there was going to be a good deal of haggling; he thought of St. Paul's letter to the Ephesians, as he always did in times of trial.

"It will be necessary to finance three fourths of our next budget through borrowing." The demure faces began, ever so slightly, to turn wolfish, while the president of the Bank of Commerce developed fangs; with fascination, Chase watched the magnate's grooved upper lip withdraw in a predatory snarl. "I shall want to increase the tariff. I shall also wish to put some sort of small nominal tax on individual incomes." The wolves leaned forward when they heard this. Chase heard, distinctly, a low growling. "I know that the American has always resisted such a tax, but I can think of a no more direct method of raising revenue."

"Mr. Chase," said Mr. Aspinwall, the mildest of the wolves,

178

"you can put a tax on an American's income any time you like, but will he pay it?"

"Surely patriotic duty would induce any citizen . . ."

Mr. Ketchum laughed. "You'll have to hire so many agents to make sure that these taxes are collected that all your new revenue will be used up just paying for them."

"I am not so pessimistic," said Chase, struck by the notion of a thousand new Treasury agents at work in every state; and each beholden to him. He knew that it was ignoble to think of his political career at such a time, but if the national welfare should coincide with his own legitimate political interests he would have no choice but to serve both with the same zeal. As always, St. Paul consoled him.

When the bankers began to question him about the necessity of minting more currency, preferably through their own bank notes, Chase recalled his own inaugural address as governor of Ohio. "As I said then, the best practical currency would be a currency of coin, admitting the use of large notes only for the convenience of commerce. I stand by that, in principle. But in practice . . ." Chase was now very much at sea; the bankers were also at sea, but unlike Chase they had in mind a specific golden landfall. Reluctantly, Chase gave in to them. Yet he was consistent in this. He had always been against a central banking system. He had worshipped General Jackson, who had broken the Bank of the United States, and he had regarded a plurality of banks as the very emblem and essence of democracy. But now that he sat in this altogether satisfactory office—except for the pearl-gray velvet carpet, which, despite the conspicuous placement of a shining spittoon at every chair, had started to darken from tobacco juice— Chase was by no means as certain as he once was that the financing of the Federal government by these . . . wolves (he could think of no better word) was in the best interest of the people. No alternative had yet suggested itself. Grimly, he hammered out a treaty with them. After first stating, as eloquently as he knew how, that the idea of a perpetual debt is not of American nativity, and should not be naturalized, war is war. But the bankers were after high profits on short-term loans, and Chase agreed to what he and Jay Cooke had come to think of as the "5–20's": twenty-year bonds that could be redeemed after only five years. Although he was able to keep the rate of interest below eight percent, the bankers were able to drive him to the wall in other ways, obliging him to sell certain government issues considerably below par. Chase had the sense of being outwitted; had no sense of how to gain control of the situation. But before he was finished, he thought grimly, as the bright-toothed, well-fed wolves, one by one, shook his hand

179

and said good-bye, he would reinvent the banking system of the United States; or be devoured in the process.

After the last of the bankers had departed, the chief secretary announced that Governor Sprague was in the anteroom. Chase's mood immediately lightened; and he greeted the young man cordially; led him to a sofa where they could sit at opposite ends, and be both intimate and formal.

"Where," said Sprague, "can I get a new pair of spectacles?"

Since Chase's callers usually spoke in terms of millions of dollars and of complex tariff matters, he was, for an instant, speechless; but then he rallied. "I go to Franklin's," he said. "Just down the street. My secretary has the address. I'm delighted that you have the time to visit me so... spontaneously."

"Oh, I've got Burnside looking after the regiment. You couldn't put in a word with the President, could you?"

"About your commission as...?"

"As major-general, yes. Butler's got his already."

"Well, I'm not exactly certain that this is within my province..."

"What is *habeas corpus*?" asked the governor of Rhode Island.

Chase had not found conversation with the young man altogether easy at the reception. Now he found himself constantly jolted by the shifts in subject. Chase liked to begin a conversation by making clear-cut the subject; then after an examination of the pros and cons, he would move, in a stately fashion, to a reasoned conclusion. This was not possible with Sprague, who jumped about from subject to subject. It was now quite plain to Chase that the problem was not that Sprague was ill-educated; he had, simply, not been educated at all. Yet the mind was quick; very much a businessman's mind, thought Chase, whose own mind was, he knew, more suitable to that of a bishop than to a man of finance.

"*Habeas corpus*," Chase began, wondering if he would be allowed to finish what promised to be a satisfactory aria, "is a Latin phrase meaning 'thou shalt have the body.' Although the concept dates back to the thirteenth century, it was not until 1679 that the English Habeas Corpus Act became the law of their land—and ours." Chase had had to take this particular examination twice. "According to the act, anyone who has been arrested *must*, in response to a writ, be produced in a court for a trial. Neither in England nor in the United States, can anyone be held without due process of law." Chase watched, somewhat anxiously, as Sprague shifted a half-filled spittoon from the side of the sofa to the front of the sofa where the nacreous glory of the carpet was still virginal. "This act is the foundation of all free societies in general
180

and of ours in particular." Chase was finished; he had not been interrupted; he felt a warm glow. The boy *was* educable.

"Not any more," said Sprague, twirling his glasses by their cord. "There's all hell to pay. I was at the President's House. I couldn't see him. Nobody could. The Chief Justice is after him. Mr. Lincoln went and arrested a friend—or something—of the old fellow's."

Chase nodded. "A Mr. Merryman of Baltimore."

"That's right. They got him locked up in Fort McHenry and when the Chief Justice told the general in charge of the fort to produce the body, the general told the Chief Justice to go to hell, on Mr. Lincoln's orders.

"I'm certain, sir, that that was not General Cadwalder's *exact* message to the Chief Justice," Chase began.

"Whatever it was, the old fellow's gone and thrown the Constitution at Mr. Lincoln's head. They say Mr. Lincoln should be put in jail for breaking the law. May I ask Miss Chase to go riding with me Sunday, before I head back to Providence?"

"May you . . . ?" Chase had followed one hare almost to its form: now Sprague had flushed a second.

"Invite your daughter to go riding on Sunday. On horseback." Sprague spelled it out as if Chase was uncommonly slow to understand. "Monday, I have to take the cars to Providence. But I'll be back in time for the war."

"By all means, sir. If that should be her pleasure, why, I would be pleased, too. You said the Chief Justice means to *arrest* Mr. Lincoln?"

"Something on that order. Now let's talk about cotton."

There was no talk of cotton at the White House. But there was a good deal of talk of *habeas corpus*. Lincoln sat at the head of the Cabinet table with Attorney-General Bates at his elbow. The waiting room was, as always, filled with people. In fact, a few moments earlier, when Lincoln and Bates had made their way down the crowded corridor, a dozen letters and petitions were handed the President, who was obliged to respond graciously to assorted cries of, "One minute, sir, please! Only one minute!" Lincoln had murmured to Bates, "I feel sometimes like I'm the proprietor of a boardinghouse that's caught on fire. While the back rooms are burning up, I'm busy renting out the front rooms."

But now, in the relative tranquility of the Cabinet room, there was a bit of a fire burning, too, thought Hay, in the form of a letter that had just arrived from Chief Justice Taney, written in the old man's shaky hand. "It was a bit of bad luck," said Bates, "that old Taney lives in Baltimore and so they could produce him fast."

"It's a bit of hard luck that Mr. Taney is a Marylander to begin with," said Lincoln. "It's even worse luck," he added, "that Jackson made him Chief Justice. But there he is. So what is this kindly message to me?" Lincoln pushed the letter, unread, back to Bates.

"He says"—Bates glanced at the message—"that his order to General Cadwalder to produce Mr. Merryman was disobeyed. He now reminds you that you are under oath—sworn to him at your inaugural—to uphold the Constitution, and that you must see to it that the laws, and the Chief Justice, are obeyed."

"So what am I supposed to do now?"

"Bring Mr. Merryman to trial immediately."

"If I don't?"

"You will be in contempt of the Supreme Court of the United States, and in violation of the law, and . . . so on."

"Well, he doesn't want to arrest me, does he?"

"I'd say, sir, that he does, very much, but he says that he has not the might though he has the right."

"I think we should, first, persuade Mr. Taney that though it might've *looked* like I was swearing an oath to him because he happened to be holding the Bible that morning, I was really swearing an oath to the whole country to defend the whole Constitution. Have you got that, Johnny?"

"I'm getting it, sir." Hay was writing very fast.

"I think," said Blair, "that you should invoke your inherent powers and tell him . . ."

"No, no." Lincoln now angled his chair so that it teetered dangerously on its back legs. One day, thought Hay, the remarkably long First Magistrate was going to go crashing to the floor. For some reason, he could never allow a chair to remain foursquare once he had taken it on. "We'll handle Mr. Taney by not mentioning him."

Bates showed his surprise by shaking his bearded Old Testament head to denote the negative. "How can you *ignore* the Chief Justice?"

"Oh, easy enough. What I'll do is make my case to Congress, when they get back in July. Nicolay, where's the Constitution?"

"I don't know, sir. I think they keep it down at the Capitol, somewhere. I'll ask . . ."

"No, I meant where's a copy of it?"

"I don't know." Nicolay looked at Hay, who shook his head. Lincoln turned, comically, to Bates. "Tell no one that there's not a copy of the Constitution in the President's House."

"People have already guessed that." Bates was dour.

"Well, Nicolay, you come up with a copy from somewhere. Now here's the line I'll take." Lincoln shut his eyes. Hay was always fascinated whenever the Tycoon began to think aloud. He would circle and circle a subject and then, like an eagle, strike at its heart. "After I called forth the militia, I told the commanding general—that is, I felt it my duty to tell him—that he could arrest or detain any individual he suspected of being a danger to us—to the public safety, that is. At my *spoken* request." Lincoln gave Bates a sidelong look. "There's no written order."

"That was wise, sir."

Lincoln again shut his eyes. "The general has used this power sparingly. Nicolay, how many arrests have been made to date?"

"Around forty, sir, including the police-marshal of Baltimore."

"If a police-marshal does not set an example, he will be the example. That is my maxim for the day. Now someone in a high position—we won't mention his name—reminds me that I have sworn faithfully to execute the laws. Well, when I took that oath"—automatically, Hay wrote "registered in Heaven," even though Lincoln did not, for once, invoke this usual formula—"*all* of the laws which I'd sworn to uphold were being resisted and broken in one-third of the states. So then, are all the laws except this one to go unexecuted? More to the point, in my view, I would have totally betrayed my oath if I should have allowed—should even now allow—the government to be overthrown, all because I have chosen not to disregard this one law." Hay was enjoying the clarity of Lincoln's subtle negative. "I have violated no law..."

"Sir," Bates interrupted. "You have not only violated the law but you have chosen to ignore an order of the Supreme Court."

Lincoln opened his eyes; and gazed thoughtfully for a moment at Bates, then he turned to Hay, "Make that: '*in my opinion*, I have violated no law.' Is that better, Mr. Bates?"

"Probably not. After all, I'm a lifelong old-fogey Whig. But your language is less categorical."

Lincoln nodded; and shut his eyes again. Hay decided that there must be some sort of huge tablet in the President's mind on which appeared, in words of fire, the sentences that he, in turn, read off to the nation. "The Constitution provides that... We'll put in the exact wording later. I paraphrase: that *habeas corpus* can only be suspended in cases of rebellion or invasion. I have decided that we have a rebellion, and I have suspended, in certain particular cases, the writ of *habeas corpus*. It is insisted that the power to do this is invested not in me but in the Congress. But the Constitution is silent as to which of us is to exercise... to *execute* this power. As the Congress was not in session when the rebellion endangered the city of Washington, I acted as swiftly as I could to preserve the city." Lincoln brought down his chair with a crash. He turned to Bates. "Then I'll ask Congress to approve what I've done, which they'll do, as we have a good majority, and let us hope that the Chief Justice will be satisfied that this is wartime."

"Well done, sir," said Bates.

"Let's hope so," said Lincoln. "I am improvising from minute to minute. Have you any news from Missouri?"

"Nothing that you probably don't know, Mr. Lincoln. I had a letter from Frank Blair, who says there is still trouble in St. Louis. But he, personally, will keep it under control. He likes playing soldier, he says."

"Will he come back to Congress?"

"Only if you need him. He'll try to keep both his seat in Congress and his army commission. Frank loves to fight, you know."

Lincoln smiled. "I know. All the Blairs do." Lincoln turned to Hay and Nicolay. "There's an old saying back in Kentucky that when the Blairs go in for a fight, they go in for a funeral." Lincoln rose. "All right, Johnny, you can write that up to be added to my message to Congress. Nico, you can turn the folks loose on me."

Lincoln towered over the other three. "I often think," he said, "that if ever this country is destroyed, it will be because of people wanting jobs with the government, people wanting to live without work, a terrible fault..."

Lincoln looked out the window at the company of New Jersey infantry that was drilling beneath the stern gaze of Tad and of Willie, who was mounted on Nanda the goat. "...A terrible fault," he repeated, "from which I am not entirely free myself. It was once my dream, twenty years ago, to be American consul in Bogotá. Thank God, I failed to get appointed."

"I guess we're all in God's debt," said Bates.

"Don't speak too soon." Lincoln put his finger to his lips. Then he went into his office, followed by Nicolay.

Hay walked Bates down the long corridor, filled today with moustached men seeking army commissions. At the beginning of the private quarters, they encountered Madam and Mrs. Grimsley.

"Mr. Bates, sir!" Mrs. Lincoln exclaimed, with pleasure. To Hay's cold eye, she looked somewhat pasty of face. But she was, at least, no longer insane. Hay and Nicolay often debated whether or not she was really sick when seized by The Headache, or simply shamming in order to get her way with the Tycoon. Lately, she had begun to meddle once again in appointments, to the dismay of the President's two secretaries. What the President himself thought of her political activities neither secretary knew.

Hay left the Attorney-General in Madam's care and went back to his own office to begin the search for a copy of the Constitution.

18

ON THE MORNING OF JUNE 29, CHASE RECEIVED IN HIS OFFICE the man whom he regarded as the perfect modern warrior: Irvin McDowell, brigadier-general of volunteers, and commander of the Army of the Potomac. At forty-two, McDowell was civilized so far beyond the military norm that the fact that he was not a bachelor caused Chase an occasional moment of regret when he saw the sturdy figure seated beside Kate on the piano bench at Sixth and E, teaching her a Mozart sonata, or holding forth on Roman architecture, or the landscapes of Capability Brown, or simply withdrawing into French, which he spoke even better than Kate's highly finished French because he had been educated in Paris, that most civilized of communities whose elegant *Revue des deux mondes* was faithfully read, albeit with difficulty, by Chase himself.

McDowell was one of the few non-Southern graduates of West Point never to have left the army. For gallantry in the Mexican War, he had been breveted a captain in the field. But over the years, as Scott tended to promote only Southern officers, McDowell had vanished into the office of the Adjutant-General. Now he had come into his own. He had established headquarters across the Potomac at Arlington House, the home of the rebel commander Robert E. Lee.

It had been agreed the evening before that Chase and McDowell would go together to the White House, where McDowell would present, for the first time, his plans for the immediate invasion and conquest of Virginia.

"Is General Scott now in agreement?" Chase sat at his desk, its gleaming black surface covered with a blizzard of white paper representing a thousand applications for jobs as Treasury agents.

"Oh, General Scott is seldom in agreement. He still resents my appointment." McDowell seemed not in the least disturbed. Chase admired enormously the man's cool ease with everything and everyone. Chase also knew what a difficult time McDowell had had since his promotion over General Scott's favorite, General Mansfield, the conqueror of Alexandria and the Potomac Heights; also, because McDowell did not wish to incur the jealousy of his fellow commanders, he had rejected a major-generalship. It was

185

as a brigadier that he now set about the task of preparing the army for a response to the cry that was, if not shouted each day, read each day in the press, particularly in Horace Greeley's New York *Tribune*: "Forward to Richmond!"

"I should think that we have them pretty well encircled on three sides." Chase had always felt that he had a military capacity as yet untapped in a career that had been nothing if not pacific. Nevertheless, he dearly loved a map. "We have General Butler at Fortress Monroe. That takes care of the coast. We have General Banks in Maryland—which is, in effect, under martial law. I never thought," Chase drifted from his subject, "that Mr. Lincoln would have so much audacity as to suspend *habeas corpus* and arrest all those chiefs of police."

"When he decides to do something, he does it. Or so," said McDowell, cautiously, "it seems to me."

"The problem is always to get him to move; and in the right direction. What do you know of General McClellan in the West?"

"I knew him in Mexico, of course. He's eight years younger than I. He graduated from the Military Academy in 'forty-six; and went straight to Mexico with General Scott. We both came out of that war captains."

Chase admired the serenity with which McDowell noted that McClellan was a captain at twenty while he was a captain at twenty-eight. "For a while, he taught engineering at the Academy. I seldom saw him. Then he quit the army..."

"To become," Chase spelled it out sonorously, "the chief engineer of the Illinois Central Railroad." Chase pushed all the applications on his desk into an orderly military pile at the center. "I believe Mr. Lincoln knows him."

McDowell smiled. "And I believe that McClellan was a Douglas man."

"Such a loss, such a loss!" Chase hummed softly. The death in Chicago, three weeks earlier, of Stephen Douglas had saddened the capital. All flags had been at half-mast. Chase had not entirely approved; but even he appreciated the fact that the Little Giant had died in the service of the Union. Douglas had literally driven himself to death, speaking in the border-states, commanding fellow-Democrats to rally round his one-time rival Lincoln. "I hardly know McClellan," said Chase. "It was my successor as governor of Ohio who made him a major-general, despite his youth..."

"Thirty-five is old for a general, as Julius Caesar would have been delighted to explain to us. Certainly, at forty-two, I am very old..."

"And General Scott at *seventy-five?*"

"Oh, he is simply a memorial to other times. Anyway,

McClellan is an excellent officer. He has managed to separate western Virginia from the rest of the Confederacy."

"With a good deal of assistance from the inhabitants. You know that they wish to organize themselves as a separate state. I have advised their leaders to do the sensible thing and attach themselves to Ohio. But they are stubborn." Chase rose. "Shall we walk?"

"By all means, Mr. Chase. My aides are already at the Mansion. So I am unencumbered."

As they crossed the long anteroom where six clerks sat at desks, each communicating with a particular department of the government, McDowell unexpectedly asked, "What is Mr. Seward's military policy?"

"I pray," said Chase, "that it is like mine. None at all. We are in your hands, sir."

But Mr. Seward had all sorts of cloudy military plans; and today they were more than ever cloudy since each involved a war with a foreign power. But now, as he sat at his desk, unread dispatches piled high, he was uncomfortably aware that he might very well have a war with England on his hands, a war which was by no means part of his master plan. The latest dispatch from Charles Francis Adams at London was ominous. Mr. Adams had been Seward's own choice for minister to Great Britain. Although Lincoln had been curiously unenthusiastic about Adams, he had indulged Seward "as you ask me for so little." Apparently, Her Majesty's Government was under heavy pressure from a combination of textile manufacturers and old-fashioned imperialists to recognize the Confederate states. The London *Times* was already commenting, more in joy than in sorrow, on how short-lived the union of the American states had been, remarking that there were still men alive who had actually witnessed the birth of what was now so palpably dying.

Frederick came in to say that Mr. John Bigelow was waiting upon the Secretary. Seward stumped out his cigar. "You take over, son!" he said; and left the office.

John Bigelow was a bright, youthful-looking man in his middle forties. He was a part-owner, with William Cullen Bryant, of the New York *Evening Post*, whose managing editorship he had just resigned in order to become the American consul-general at Paris. Seward and Bigelow were old friends and political allies. As they walked down the dusty gravel path to the President's house, Bigelow admitted to some nervousness. "I've never met Mr. Lincoln before," he said.

"Well, he don't bite." Seward was airy. "He also has no interest at all in foreign affairs. So you're not going to be exactly overinstructed. How is Mr. Bryant?"

"Lately, he seems somewhat aged."

"I'd say that he has seemed somewhat aged for the better part of this century. I should tell you that the President likes his poetry more than his politics. So skip the editorials, and quote 'Thanatopsis.'"

"I don't know it!" Bigelow moaned in mock despair.

"Well, Mr. Lincoln's bound to. He can quote poetry by the yard."

But there was no time for either poetry or France in the President's office. Lincoln sat on the edge of his desk, studying a sheaf of heavily marked maps, as Hay and Nicolay came and went on mysterious errands that usually involved taking a document from or inserting a document into one or another of the pigeonholes of Lincoln's desk. "You sit right there, Mr. Bigelow," said Lincoln, absently indicating a chair. Thus far, the President had yet to look at his visitor.

Seward tried to attract the President's interest. "Mr. Bigelow just resigned from the *Evening Post* . . ."

"A fine paper as fine papers go." At last, Lincoln looked up; and smiled the full, white-toothed smile which meant, Seward now knew, that the President had not the slightest interest in the smile's recipient. "Mr. Bigelow, I am sure that Mr. Seward has told you, as he tells everyone, that I know nothing of foreign affairs."

"Oh, no, sir . . ." began Bigelow, nervously.

"Well, if he hasn't told you, you're the first fellow I've appointed to a foreign post that he hasn't. Anyway, I *don't* know much about these matters; and so I leave your mission to you—and to Mr. Seward. I *will* say that the Emperor Napoleon should never be allowed to forget that we don't look favorably on any French military excursions in Mexico. But as long as he demonstrates no sympathy with our rebels, we are not inclined to do much of anything for the present. Emphasize for the present. Quote Mr. Monroe and Mr. Adams. Keep him neutral. Is that understood?"

"Yes, Mr. President."

Hay entered to announce, "The Cabinet is waiting, sir."

Lincoln gave Bigelow a firm handclasp. "Good luck to you, sir." Before Bigelow knew what had happened, Lincoln and Seward had entered the Cabinet Room. As Bigelow stepped into the waiting room, he saw General McDowell standing at the outer door to the President's Office, talking to a military aide. When the general saw his old friend Bigelow, he said, "There's still a place for you on my staff."

"Only if your command extends as far as Paris." Once each

had congratulated the other on his appointment, McDowell entered the President's Office, followed by his aide.

Everyone was seated, except General Scott, who was enthroned near the President. The Secretary of War, Mr. Cameron, was answering a question that the President had just asked. "We have, altogether, in the military, in various stages of training, three hundred and ten thousand men, which makes our military establishment about the largest in the world."

"As well as the least trained," grumbled General Scott. "They are mostly volunteers, Mr. President, with no discipline and no training, and too few qualified officers to make them into a proper army at this time."

"Is that your view, General McDowell?" Lincoln turned to McDowell.

"Of course, General Scott is right," said McDowell. Chase was glad that his protégé was so straightforward. "The actual number of trained men available is barely a third of the number that Mr. Cameron mentioned. And of that one hundred thousand, only fifty thousand are available at this city, and as this city must be guarded, not more than thirty to thirty-five thousand of those men can be used for an invasion of Virginia."

Lincoln turned to McDowell. "Is that enough, do you think?"

Seward thought that the President seemed ill-at-ease, placed, as it were, between Scott and McDowell. On the other hand, Chase thought that Lincoln was entirely at ease with McDowell, who was plainly, the man of the hour. "Yes, sir. In the next two weeks, I can put thirty to thirty-five thousand men in the field. This will be, by the way, sir, the largest military force ever assembled on this continent."

"How many men will the rebels be able to field?" Lincoln was staring at the large map of Virginia on the wall opposite.

"We're not certain, sir. But fewer than ours." McDowell was now at the map. General Scott's eyes had shut. "General Beauregard is here at Manassas. He is known to be drilling some twenty-five thousand. While over here, along this line from Winchester to Harper's Ferry, General Johnston is guarding the Shenandoah Valley, with ten thousand men."

"So their army is just about the same size as ours." Lincoln frowned.

McDowell nodded. "But their army is in two parts that will not have time to come together *if* we are fast enough. After all, Manassas is only thirty miles from here."

"General Scott." Lincoln turned to the old man, who opened his eyes.

"You know my views, Mr. President. I would make no move until the autumn. The men are not ready, sir."

"Some of them are too ready . . . to go home." Lincoln sighed. "A lot of the three-month enlistments are coming to an end. If we don't use the men we've got by the end of July, there won't be an army, and we'll have to start all over again."

"Sir, those men are too green to fight."

"Well, the rebels are just as green. So we are all green alike."

"They are on their home ground, sir," said Scott. "I have already submitted my own plan, which requires the splitting of the Confederacy in half by seizing the Mississippi River from Memphis to New Orleans. Each half will then wither on its own, as we squeeze them, like the great anaconda snake."

"Ultimately, I think you are right, General." Lincoln was conciliatory. "But we have a rare chance now to strike a blow at the head of the other . . . snake. Thanks to General Horace Greeley, 'Forward to Richmond' is now on every lip, up North. At least, it is daily on *his* lips, and everyone, they say, reads the *Tribune*." Lincoln glanced at Hay, who smiled. Hay was often obliged to placate the fiery foolish New York editor who never ceased in public and private to bombard the President with eerily bad advice. At the time of the Lincoln-Douglas debate, the Republican Greeley had favored Lincoln but plainly preferred the Democrat Douglas, to Lincoln's despair. Yet it was Greeley who had given such coverage to the Cooper Institute speech that, overnight, Lincoln was famous. Yet again, at Chicago, as a delegate, Greeley, having fallen out with Seward, voted for Bates. But then, for a time, Greeley had wanted to let the Southern states go. Meanwhile, so extensive was his published and private advice to Lincoln that one entire pigeonhole of the presidential desk was devoted to Greeley. After all, half a million people read the weekly edition of the *Tribune*, particularly in the midwest.

Ordinarily, the very fact that Greeley favored a prompt advance on Richmond would almost certainly have impelled Lincoln west to the Mississippi River. But Hay knew what hardly anyone else knew: that Lincoln had been struck by one line in Greeley's latest outburst. The Confederate Congress was to meet for the first time at Richmond on July 20. If Lincoln could prevent such a meeting, the rebellion would be considerably shortened; and Chase's war bonds would sell at par; and Seward's disagreeable relations with those European powers that were threatening to recognize the South would grow more agreeable.

McDowell spread out his own map of Virginia on the Cabinet table. Everyone—except General Scott—rose and leaned over the map as McDowell explained his strategy. "Beauregard is here
190

at Manassas with over twenty thousand men. He protects this railroad line, which is the northern link of the entire Southern railway system. He is now placed between two depots. The one closest to us is here at Fairfax Courthouse. The one farthest from us is at Manassas, which is also a point of junction between two lines, the Manassas Gap Railroad and The Orange & Alexandria line. I propose to move on Fairfax from three directions, with some thirty thousand troops. At Fairfax, our forces will converge. Then we move on to Germantown and Centerville, where we engage the enemy."

Chase nodded appreciatively. This was the sort of terse bareboned briefing that he would have given had he been the commanding general. In a sense, there was no great difference between what he was obliged daily to do at the Treasury and what McDowell was doing now. Each commanded men; each added and subtracted numerous sets of figures that represented resources. Finally, Butler and Banks and Frémont were all politicians, and though he himself had no particular liking for any of the three, he took some collegial pride in the fact that they were, at the moment, the most illustrious of the Union generals.

On the other hand, Chase felt truly secure with McDowell. Here was a perfectly trained soldier in the French style. Chase looked at Seward. The constant schemer seemed to be scheming— or, perhaps, only daydreaming. Seward chewed, idly, an unlit cigar; nodded at all the wrong moments during McDowell's discourse; pulled at one of his huge ears as if to reassure himself that the all-important-to-a-politician organ was in place, not to mention in good working order.

Chase was aware that the relationship between Lincoln and Seward had somehow altered. The prime minister was less offhand with the sovereign than before. He tended to interrupt Lincoln less in Cabinet; unfortunately, as if in compensation, he interrupted his colleagues more. Gideon Welles and Blair both openly despised Seward, while Chase was quite aware of the unscrupulous way that Seward and his familiar Thurlow Weed influenced the politics of the North. Although Chase could never be an admirer of Seward, he was perfectly wiling to be an ally. In politics, the years move more rapidly than in ordinary life. Soon it would be 1864. Since Chase was reasonably certain that Seward would not put himself forward as a presidential candidate, the party was left with only one viable candidate, Salmon P. Chase. Thus, like it or not, Chase and Seward were potential allies; also, Chase had made it clear to Seward that he was perfectly willing to share in a sort of consulate with him. But Seward had never again adverted to the matter. Had he given up the idea? Or had he worked out

191

some new *modus operandi* with the symbolic—Chase had yet to find a more descriptive word—president? What, he wondered, was in Seward's mind?

At that moment, there was nothing of any great moment in Seward's mind. He was hoping that McDowell knew what he was doing. Although Seward had more than once used Winfield Scott for his own political ends, he respected the old man as a soldier, if only because Seward knew nothing of warfare and, unlike Chase, he did not see himself as a Bonaparte-in-waiting. Seward assumed that Scott's knowledge of warfare equalled his demonstrable ignorance of politics. In any case, Seward's use of the old man had ended with the rejection of Scott's advice to abandon Fort Sumter, prompted entirely by Seward, who had believed then and still believed that, given a foreign war, the seceded states would return to the fold. But Lincoln had undone this policy. Seward was still not certain just how it was that Lincoln had taken the initiative from him but he had. Now Seward must wait for the New Congress to assemble next week. Since a third of the membership belonged to states that had seceded, there would be a Northern Congress, with a large Republican majority. Unfortunately, the firm of Seward and Weed would control not much more than the New York delegation. Worse, powerful committees of the House and Senate were dominated by hard-core abolitionists like Sumner. Although these powerful chairmen had little respect for the cautious Lincoln, they positively hated Seward. To a man, they favored Chase. Seward looked across the table and found that Chase was looking at him with the curious myopic intensity which usually meant that Chase was undertaking a new move in their game of political chess. Seward smiled benignly. Chase dropped his eyes to the map; plainly, in some distress at being observed observing.

McDowell had finished his explanation; and his aide folded up the map. Lincoln looked about the room. "Are we all . . . satisfied?" he asked. Everyone looked grave and martial, except General Scott, who seemed to be asleep. No one spoke. "Very well, General McDowell." Lincoln shook the general's hand. "It rests with you now."

Lincoln then disappeared into his own office while Hay joined Nicolay in the secretary's office, where Lincoln's first message to Congress was strewn across Nicolay's desk. The Tycoon had already written and rewritten it a number of times. Certain sections had been shown to the Cabinet officers involved. Bates had helped with the section on *habeas corpus*, while Chase had justified not only the raid on the Treasury but the various bond issues that they hoped would finance the war. Seward had contributed some
192

flowery passages on foreign affairs and, to Seward's disgust, Lincoln had carefully pruned the loveliest of those blossoms.

"All in all a noble document," said Nicolay, assembling the pages as if they were his own.

"How is it delivered?" Hay was curious.

"How is what delivered?"

"Well, does the Ancient go down to the Capitol and knock on the door, and then read it to Congress, or what?"

Nicolay frowned. "I don't know. Ask Edward."

As always, Edward was instructive. A somewhat prim colored man, he regarded the inner workings of the Executive Mansion as comparable to those of Heaven; and as immutable. "Mr. Jefferson was such a bad public speaker that he used to write out his messages and send them over to Congress, where one of the clerks would read them. All of the later presidents have done the same."

"But how, exactly, do we get the message to them?"

Hay was inspired. "We give it to the Postmaster-General, Mr. Blair..."

"You," said Edward, who did not much like levity in these high matters, "Mr. Nicolay, will present yourself at the door to the House of Representatives. The Sergeant-at-arms will then approach you, and you will say, 'I have a communication from the President of the United States.' The Sergeant-at-arms will take the message, while the Speaker interrupts the business of the House, so that the Senate can be summoned, and the message read to all of Congress by Mr. Forney, the Clerk to the Senate."

"That is very satisfying," said Hay.

"Thank you, Mr. Hay," said Edward, returning to his post as the waiting room's helmsman.

"I wonder who they'll elect Speaker?" Nicolay was now assembling the pages of the message inside a vellum cover.

"The Tycoon thinks Frank Blair can be elected, but he'll have to give up being a colonel, which he probably won't." The previous year Hay had worked for Frank Blair's Missouri *Democrat*, acting as its Springfield correspondent. Although Blair had been a Bates man at the Chicago convention, the family had quickly shifted to Lincoln; and Hay had done his part to make sure that Missouri was kept informed of Lincoln's candidacy. Of all the Blairs, Frank was the most appealing to Hay—even romantic. When Frank fell in love with the same Maryland girl that one of his brothers wanted to marry, Frank's solution was typical; he promptly moved west to the Missouri Territory, where he more or less invented the state, with some assistance from a third brother, Montgomery. In imitation of Frank, the other brother went off to sea; and the now-entirely Blair-less girl dropped from history.

Hay retired to his own small office, uncomfortably shared with William O. Stoddard, known, familiarly, as Stodd, a recent acquisition whose difficult task was the management of Madam, who now regarded Nicolay and Hay as, collectively, the enemy. At twenty-five Stodd was an amiable youth with a sensibly worried expression. He had written a Lincoln-for-president editorial in 1859 for the *Central Illinois Gazette*; he had then sent this rousing document to hundreds of newspapers; and many had used it. Hay had always thought that the Tycoon had put Stodd up to writing the editorial at a low moment in Lincoln's political career, but Nicolay was inclined to the view that it was the Tycoon's law partner, Billy Herndon, who had arranged the matter. Herndon was a newspaper-reading addict who thought in headlines. Years before Lincoln was spoken of as a serious candidate, Herndon was busy proposing his candidacy to the newspapers.

"Is Madam in good spirit?" Hay enjoyed teasing Stodd.

"We're going to Long Branch in August."

"Where's that?"

"New Jersey, I think. By the sea."

"Will the precious children go?"

"Yes."

"How quiet the White House will seem, with only us and the war."

"That depends on whether or not the President has seen all the bills from the New York stores." Stodd was grim. The New York press had enjoyed describing "Mrs. President's spring spending spree." Although Stodd gave no details to his rivals Hay and Nicolay, it was plain that he was worried; also, the as-yet-unconfirmed Commissioner of Public Buildings had told Hay that he found alarming the grandeur of Madam's vision of what the White House must be. Thus far, the Tycoon seemed to be unaware of the gathering storm of unpaid bills, both private and public. But then there were other storms. Congress was in the city...

19

ONWARD TO RICHMOND!

"I wish," said Mary, from behind her silver tea service, "Mr. Greeley would leave the war to Mr. Lincoln."

"So do I, Cousin Mary," said John C. Breckinridge, late Vice-President of rather more United States than his successor was Vice-

Presiding over. Breckinridge was now the newly elected senator from Kentucky. "With Mr. Lincoln in absolute charge, Mrs. Davis will be pouring tea in this room by the end of the month." Although Breckinridge's blue eyes were bright with what was meant to be good humor, they did not quite negate his thin-lipped smile.

"Oh, Cousin John!" Mary maintained what she thought of as her own small correct Queen Victoria smile. She must, at all costs, charm her turbulent cousin. "How you tease me, sir! Sugar?"

Breckinridge indicated two lumps. They were seated in the Blue Room. As usual, the Chevalier Wikoff acted as lord-in-waiting. As usual, there were more men than women at Mary's levee. The Washington ladies who had been so eager to snub the Lincolns were now themselves snubbed; and denied the glitter of her social gatherings, where Sumner was almost always to be seen, as well as such statesmen as Fessenden and Trumbull from the Senate, and Thaddeus Stevens and Frank Blair and Elihu B. Washburne from the House of Representatives.

The return of Breckinridge to the Senate had caused a sensation. Although Kentucky was being held in the Union by Lincoln—with both hands, as he had observed somewhat grimly— the new Senator Breckinridge was suspected of favoring secession. "I've already had several pleasurable meetings with President Davis, Cousin Mary."

Breckinridge's large round face against the dark blue of the room's wall resembled, Mary decided, the full moon at midnight. She responded with exquisite sweetness, "I don't know of any president called Davis, Cousin John."

"Oh, there's such a president, all right." Appreciatively, Breckinridge looked about the newly papered and gilded Oval Room. "He'll be much in your debt for going to all this expense. Or at least Mrs. Davis will. You know what they're saying all over the South now? 'Onward to Washington.'"

"If one rebel gets as far as this room, Cousin John, he'll have me to contend with! With a rifle, sir."

"What if the soldier's Ben Helm? Or one of your own brothers?"

"I would," said Mary coldly, "shoot him dead for a traitor."

"Well, you are a Todd, after all."

"When, sir, will *you* be joining Mr. Davis?" Mary allowed the Queen Victoria smile to fade entirely.

"Why, I'm a Union man. You know that. In my way, that is. I'm also curious to see how this session of Congress goes."

"They will support the President, entirely."

At the other end of the room Elihu B. Washburne was not so certain. "The President will only get about half of the four hundre~'
million dollars that he wants."

"But," asked the English journalist, "will he get the four hundred thousand men that he's asked for?"

Washburne had been prepared to dislike William Howard Russell, the stout, florid, London *Times* correspondent, but in life, if not in print, this somewhat prickly chronicler of wars from the Crimea to India proved to be a most engaging if hard-drinking and plain-speaking man. Washburne nodded. "We're doing well with new volunteers..."

"But not so well with your three-month enlistment lads. Just now, as I was coming out of Willard's, one of them came up to me and begged me for some pennies to buy whiskey."

"Did you give them?" asked the slender young army captain who had gravitated to England's greatest observer of warfare.

"Certainly not!" Russell laughed until his face turned the color of Washington's indigenous brick. "I do want you people to win. But you've got to train your men better. They are rabble. Not like the Southerners. I was impressed with *them*, let me tell you."

"You've been at the South—lately?" Washburne was surprised.

"I've only just got back. I went everywhere. Saw everybody. Pleasant chap, Mr. Davis. But looks sickly. No wonder. That climate! Those mosquitoes! Even so, they're spoiling for a fight. I've never seen any people like them."

"We are the same, sir," said the young captain, whom Washburne now recognized as General McDowell's aide, a rich New Yorker named William Sanford.

"No, Captain, you're not. That's the problem. Every single one of those Southerners is fighting for his own country against invaders, which is what you are to him. Of course, the North is more populous, more rich. But where are your soldiers to be found? Mostly immigrants from Europe. Mostly German and Irish, who've only just arrived. They are truly alien, sir; and have nothing to fight for except the pennies that you pay them."

Since this was exactly Washburne's private view, he was obliged to object strenuously, as befitted an American statesman.

Russell was genial, but unconvinced. "Farmers and hunters will fight for their own land in a way no factory worker will, much less a new arrival who doesn't even know the language. You know what I heard in Charleston?" Russell chuckled at the memory. "A group of quite serious people told me that if we'd send them a ~~royal~~ prince or princess as sovereign, they would rejoin our

~~ver~~ thought the rebels had that much sense of humor."
~~was~~ something new, and Washburne wondered if some
~~ht~~ not be made out of the South's treason not only to
~~tates~~ but to the great republican principle itself.

"They have no sense of humor, as far as I can tell. They are serious, like you."

There was a stir as the President entered the Blue Room. Absently, Lincoln held a folder in his right hand, which he then moved to the left hand, as he greeted Mrs. Lincoln's guests. Finally, he put the folder on a console. "He looks somewhat..." Russell paused.

"Tired," said Washburne, not about to allow the Englishman a characterizing adjective that might look disagreeable in the hostile columns of the London *Times*.

"That, too," said Russell, with a smile.

"My father," said young Captain Sanford, suddenly, "told me that Mr. Lincoln was the best railroad lawyer in the country."

"Did he mean that as a compliment?" Russell positively grinned.

"Of course he did." Washburne was emphatic. "And your father's right. Is he a railroad man?"

"No, sir. We have mills. In Lowell, Massachusetts. Encaustic tiles. And jean and cotton. But when this is over"—the young man gestured vaguely at a painting of classical ruins which, presumably, represented to him a land at peace—"we shall go into railroads."

"With Mr. Lincoln as your counsel?" asked Russell, eyes on the President, who was being harangued by Sumner.

"I'm sure Mr. Lincoln is beyond all that now," said the young man sadly.

Mrs. Lincoln had begun making a circuit of the room, on the arm of Chevalier Wikoff. When she saw Russell, she stopped; and smiled with what Washburne took to be real pleasure. "Mr. Russell, sir! You are back. Did you get the flowers?"

Russell kissed her hand in a graceful gesture which involved, Washburne noted, the actual presentation of his lips not to the back of her hand, as Washburne had always imagined this abominable European transaction required, but to his own thumb. "I've already written you a long letter. Your flowers were the first thing that I saw when I entered the two furnished clothes chests that my landlord tells me is an apartment."

"You've left Willard's?" Mrs. Lincoln gave her hand to Washburne, who did not kiss it, old friend that he was, and to Captain Sanford, who bowed low and looked nervous.

Washburne had heard that Mrs. Lincoln had taken to sending flowers from the White House conservatories to various esteemed personages. He was somewhat surprised that Mr. Russell of the *Times* should be so favored. For one thing, he was a great friend of Seward. For another, the *Times* was, editorially, more and more pro-rebel. But the President had gone out of his way to be amiable to the famous correspondent; and Washburne knew that there were times when seemingly ill-matched husband and wife worked smoothly as a political team.

"A powerful newspaper, the *Times*," Lincoln had said when he first met Russell; and he had affected wonder. "I can't think of anything on earth anywhere so powerful, unless maybe the Mississippi River."

"Is it true," asked the Chevalier Wikoff, "that the rebels would like to re-join the British crown?"

"That is what many of them told me," said Russell.

"Poor Queen Victoria." Mary was serene. "I would not wish them on her."

"Why," Russell boomed, "we would handle them just the way we do the Irish!" As all laughed, Mrs. Lincoln continued her circuit, pausing, finally, at a console where Senator Trumbull of Illinois stood. As always, Mary was glad to see him; but she often wondered if he was ever glad to see her. Despite so much idle speculation about her and Judge Douglas, the only man that she had ever loved in youth was the handsome elegant Lyman Trumbull, whose wife, Julia, she could not help but hate, even though they had once been close. Mary spoke to Trumbull of the Coterie days, when they had all been friends. "In another age," she heard herself say, as she smiled up at him.

Washburne joined the President and Sumner at the window through which could be seen the President's Park. The area around the unfinished obelisk had recently been made into an abattoir for the army. Here, in plain view of the White House, cattle and hogs were daily slaughtered; then hung on hooks. As a result, the blocks of white marble were now all splattered with blood and when the wind was from the south the stench of blood combined with the odor of the stagnant canal was overpowering.

Sumner was trying to draw out the President on the timing of the attack on Richmond. "The *New York Herald* says that the rebels expect an attack before their so-called Congress meets, but our own *Daily Morning Chronicle* predicts a Fourth of July attack."

"Do they?" Lincoln gazed absently out the window. Since at least one congressional committee had been shown McDowell's plan, Washburne wondered just why Sumner was so pressing. Of course, no date had been given. But there were rumors that McDowell would not be ready in time to stop the Confederate Congress from meeting. Certainly, a Fourth of July attack was out of the question.

"I realize," said Sumner, "that the press is hardly reliable."

Lincoln turned from the window; suddenly, he grinned. "Oh,

yes, they are. They lie. And then they re-lie. So they are nothing if not re-lie-able."

As Washburne laughed, he was pleased to note that the humorless Sumner had remembered to smile. Then Breckinridge joined them. Lincoln was amiable: "Well, sir. I'm always glad to see a brand-new senator from my native state."

"I'm always happy to see you, sir—as Cousin Mary's husband, naturally."

"Naturally. Anyway, your presence in this session of Congress is bound to . . . elevate the tone of the discourse." Lincoln was courtly. "Don't you think so, Mr. Sumner?"

"Tea," said the most eloquent man of his time, "does wonders for the dyspeptic." Sumner stalked away, in the general direction of the silver urn.

"I shall do my best to represent . . . our state, sir." Breckinridge made the "our" sound very dramatic indeed.

But Lincoln chose to ignore the drama. "I'm sure you will. And I'll be curious to see how you react to my Message to the Congress, which is . . ." Lincoln held up both hands, as if one of them might contain the document; then, anxiously, he felt his coat pocket. "What did I do with it?"

Washburne motioned to the console where Mrs. Lincoln had been standing; but stood no longer. "You put it down there. On that table. I saw you."

"But where is it?"

Suddenly, Chevalier Wikoff was at the President's side. He presented the folder to Lincoln. "I thought it wise, Your Excellency, to hold this for you."

"Well, that was good of you, Mr. Wikoff. And careless of me." Lincoln put the folder under his arm. He turned to Wikoff. "What news of our friend Mr. Bennett?"

Washburne knew that for over a year Lincoln had been doing his best to woo James Gordon Bennett, the publisher of the *New York Herald*, the most powerful of the country's newspapers and the most read in the European capitals. Everyone was agreed that Bennett was a singularly coarse and repellent man. To the extent that he was at all political, he was a pro-Southern Democrat. The previous summer, when Lincoln had begun his wooing of Bennett, Washburne had advised him to write Bennett off. But Lincoln was stubborn. "I must bell that cat, somehow," he said. The first attempt was a complete failure. Bennett had supported the Democratic party in the election. Lately, Thurlow Weed had been conducting secret negotiations with the publisher, who had everything on earth a man could want in the way of power and money

199

but lacked the one thing that he ought not to have cared about but did, a position in the world of the brightest society.

To Washburne's disgust, Lincoln was now ready to offer Bennett the ambassadorship to France. "That is a small price to pay, Brother Washburne, for a good account of the Union in Europe." So far, the bait had not been taken by His Satanic Majesty, as Bennett was known to even the few who liked him. Since Chevalier Wikoff was Bennett's personal ambassador to the White House—and as the Chevalier was equally enamored of both Satanic majesty and Republican excellencies—he was often able to mediate between the warring powers. He did so now. "Mr. Bennett would like to give his yacht to the revenue service."

"That is a fine gesture." At this point Breckinridge saw fit to withdraw as temporal power and ephemeral press met in not-atypical *agon*. "Mr. Chase will be gratified, I know."

"Mr. Bennett is more and more Your Excellency's admirer..." Wikoff began.

"Then I admire the tactful way that he keeps this admiration out of his paper."

"I think that will change. You know he has a son, James Gordon Bennett, Junior, a young man dedicated to you and to the Union. He would like to fight."

"I shall not stop him, Mr. Wikoff. That is a promise."

"He would like to fight as a lieutenant in the navy, Mr. Lincoln."

Although Washburne had spent his entire career as a politician in making trades of this sort, he was somewhat taken aback by the boldness of His Satanic Majesty's ambassador. One yacht for one commission as a naval lieutenant was hardly exorbitant. But that was not the point. Yacht and commission cancelled each other out, and Bennett would still be in no way committed to support the Administration. Plainly, Lincoln was going to lose this round, too.

The President nodded. "Tell him to send the young man to me. And to send the yacht to Mr. Chase. But *not* the other way round. Now I must return to my labors." Lincoln patted Washburne's arm and crossed the room to the door, followed by Wikoff.

As Lincoln shook hands with Breckinridge, Washburne stared idly at the folder under Lincoln's arm. Then Washburne, as idly, looked at Wikoff, who was again in attendance upon Mrs. Lincoln. Then, not so idly, Washburne wondered why Wikoff should have taken from the console Lincoln's only copy of the Message to Congress, whose contents no one but Lincoln and his secretaries knew.

20

FOR ONCE DAVID HEROLD PREFERRED THE DARK BACK ROOM of the drugstore to the lively and gregarious front room. Today the heat was peculiarly unbearable—more like August than July. Although David sweated quite as much in the windowless room, he was at least spared the sight of the bronze-bright sun that made Lafayette Square's greenery shimmer like the surface of a pond after a frog's sudden leap. All morning, in his shirt-sleeves, he'd been thinking of cool ponds, frogs, swift rivers, fish, dark woods, as he prepared prescriptions, his tie loosened and collar opened and shirt stuck with sweat to his back.

Mr. Thompson's call: "David!" was not welcome. But he mopped his face with a towel, and joined his employer in the shop. The fierce light from the windows brought tears to his eyes. He wondered if there was any water left in him. He wanted, desperately, a glass of beer. Mysteriously, Mr. Thompson did not sweat, ever. He held in his waters. On the hottest of days—and this was one—the pale face slightly pinkened; and that was it. Mr. Thompson wore his linen coat, coolly. "David, take this"— he gave David a package—"to Mrs. Greenhow's."

"Just down the road?" David was annoyed at being called from his dark lair in order to make a delivery a block away on Sixteenth Street. "Where's her girl?"

"I don't know where her girl is, and I don't care where her girl is." Thus did the heat get to the usually equable and always dry Mr. Thompson. "But I got the message for you to deliver this quinine right away. She's got the ague."

Without a word, still in shirt-sleeves, David took the package; and stepped out into the blaze of noon. The street was empty of people; the horsecars seemed not to be running at all. Later, of course, troops would be on the move again. Every day they came down the avenue from the depot. Thousands and thousands of young men in ill-fitting blue uniforms that looked to be uncommonly hot for Southern weather; and any day now the long-awaited "March on Richmond" would begin. Mr. Surratt did not think that the Yankees would get very far; not that he himself got very far anymore. In fact, it was now plain to everyone that the only trip that he would ever take again would be to leave the

201

world altogether. He no longer crossed the Long Bridge. Occasionally, he would send David on errands. But none had been of any great interest; to David at least.

Mrs. Greenhow lived across from St. John's Church; and close to the house of the Secretary of State, who had been seen, on occasion, entering or leaving her chaste widow's house.

Rose Greenhow was a dark, good-looking Southern woman in her forties; well-connected in the highest circles of old Washington. She was a great-niece of Dolley Madison; she was the aunt of Mrs. Stephen Douglas. Although Mrs. Greenhow was supposed to be in a state of mourning for a daughter who had recently died, she still received occasional visitors, among them Governor Seward, who was suspected, by those who gathered at Thompson's, of conducting an affair with her. She had also been close to President Buchanan and his niece, as well as to the Jefferson Davises. Of Washington's numerous secessionist ladies, she was the only one to make an effort to get on with the Lincoln Administration and to receive, in her house, Republican potentates.

To David's surprise, Mrs. Greenhow's maid opened the door. Suddenly angry, he shoved the parcel into the black woman's hands. "Here," he said. "From Thompson's. I've got to go."

"Come in," said a soft but clear voice from the front parlor. "Please."

David entered the parlor where Mrs. Greenhow lay on a sofa. The high-ceilinged room was cool because the sunlight was diffused by shutters, while red gauze hung between the front and back parlors, making rosy the room's light; not to mention its occupant—Rose. A large rose-wood piano stood against one wall, and a smell of roses was in the air, making David more than ever aware of his own sweatiness in the presence of this slender dark cool woman, who motioned for him to sit in a chair beside her sofa: like a doctor with a patient, he thought.

"You'll want some lemonade," she said, plainly aware of all the water that he had lost—and was losing. "Theresa! Lemonade." She raised her voice slightly; then lowered it.

"I have to go, ma'am," he said, not moving.

"Stay a moment. I'm sorry to get you out on such a day. But I wanted to meet you."

David could not believe his ears. Why would this grand lady want to meet a prescription clerk with, admittedly, a fine new moustache but nothing else to recommend him? Visions of the Navy Yard widow came and, somewhat guiltily, went. If Mrs. Greenhow wanted youthful masculine company, there were thousands of well-born Federal officers in the city, eager to oblige. David was so engrossed in the contemplation of his hostess's motives that he neglected to respond, verbally, to her surprising statement. He simply stared at her, noticing the fullness of her bosom beneath the white lace, a material so delicate that he thought that he could glimpse... David was aware that he was both staring and blushing at the same time, while the silence in the room made a roar in his ears.

But Mrs. Greenhow took no notice of his embarrassment. "I wanted to meet you," she repeated, "because Mr. Surratt spoke so highly of you and as you work practically next door to me, why, I thought to myself, we must be friends, you and I, in these difficult times." Mrs. Greenhow smiled at him. Forty years old if she were a day, she still had a youthful air. There were no lines in that camellia-white skin. He would not, he decided, even want a ham.

With an effort, David controlled himself. "I never knew you knew Mr. Surratt," David's voice broke like a young boy's midway through the sentence. He felt a fool. Noisily, he cleared his throat; sat up straight. "But I've always heard that you were one of us, even though you see all those Yankees."

Mrs. Greenhow laughed. "Oh, I see everyone nowadays. After all, most of my friends have gone South. So if I didn't see my Yankee... friends... I'd see no one at all. Of course, I'm still in part-mourning for my daughter. So I don't really see much of anyone except old friends like Mr. Seward..."

David nodded. "I've seen him come here."

"You *are* sharp-eyed." The black woman brought them lemonade. Mrs. Greenhow discussed the weather until they were again alone.

"Mr. Herold, I think you can help me."

"*You*, Mrs. Greenhow?" David finished the glass of lemonade in one long inelegant swallow.

"Not really me, Mr. Herold. The Confederacy. I supply Richmond with information that I get, from time to time, from my Yankee friends."

David was awed. "They *give* you the information?"

Mrs. Greenhow nodded. "Without knowing it, of course, they will, every now and then, let slip something of use to us. Then, sometimes, cases that have been placed in my cloakroom are... examined while I pour tea. For instance, I have—or had— a map showing General McDowell's line of march. I also know the day and the hour that he will cross over into Virginia."

David was entirely thrilled. "How do you get all this over to the other side?"

"The map is already in the hands of General Beauregard. But

203

that particular courier..." Mrs. Greenhow paused; and sipped her lemonade.

"You want *me* to go to General Beauregard?" This was the moment that David had been dreaming of. He would ride at dead of night through the owl-haunted woods of Virginia. He would... But he would not. Mrs. Greenhow had other uses for him.

"This is too important, I'm afraid, to leave to someone I trust but do not really know."

"I've crossed the Long Bridge, ma'am, a dozen times for Mr. Surratt. I've also got a military pass and..."

"Perhaps another time. I have a courier ready. By the way, you should know that I am constantly watched."

"You? A friend of Mr. Seward and Senator Wilson and..."

"That's *why* I'm watched. Because all those people still come to me. My sympathies are well-known. But my activities are not. I hope. There is a Mr. Pinkerton—from Chicago. He is something called a detective and the War Department has given him a number of agents who keep an eye on dangerous ladies like me. So I must be careful whom I see and where I go. Fortunately, the prescription clerk from Thompson's can always come here to make a delivery. He can always serve our country, unsuspected."

"That's just what Mr. Surratt said when I told him I was fixing to go South and join up with the Confederate Army." There were times when David enjoyed an out-and-out lie.

"Obviously, that's what any brave young man would want to do. But what you can do for us now is far more valuable. Believe me." Mrs. Greenhow plunged her long white hand into her décolletage, and withdrew a scrap of paper no larger than a sugar cube. She gave the paper to David, who did not know whether or not he should read it; and so read it. There were six meaningless words.

"It is code," said Mrs. Greenhow. "My late husband enjoyed inventing codes. In fact, he was a translator for the State Department. I learned from him. You are to give this to a certain young lady in Georgetown." Mrs. Greenhow got up from her sofa and crossed to a secretaire, where she wrote a few words on a slip of paper. "Say that you come from me. She'll be expecting you. She'll know what to do." Mrs. Greenhow was now standing so close to David that he could smell her rose-water scent; he hoped that she could not smell him. "This is her name and address. She is staying in a house not far from Chain Bridge. She'll expect you at six-thirty this evening."

As David took the paper, he noted that he was the same height as Mrs. Greenhow. Restored by lemonade to his normal component of liquidity, he felt desire. He could tell that Mrs. Green-how felt it, too. She gave him a luminous smile, like that of the Madonna on the wall of the Surratt front parlor; then she took his hand in her silk-smooth cool one; and led him to the front door, where she whispered, "Once the young lady has the message safely, pass by this house at noon tomorrow. I'll be at the window. That way I'll know."

"I can't come in?" David was plaintive.

"We must not see each other too often. Unless," she smiled, "there is a crisis... in my health or that of my daughter, Little Rose, and then we shall need all sorts of medicine." She pressed his hand; but before he could press back, she had, somehow, got him out the front door.

The heat made him gasp. The glare made him shut his eyes. Glowworms writhed behind the lids. Then he opened his eyes; looked about to see if a detective was on duty. But there was no one in sight except the inevitable cavalryman, astride his horse in the shade of St. John's. Because of the constant troop movements, a cavalryman stood guard at every street corner in the city, reg-ulating traffic, forcing carriages to pull to one side if troops were passing by. An armed camp, thought David, as he strolled back to Fifteenth Street. An armed camp secretly filled with an invisible enemy like the fashionable Mrs. Greenhow—like himself. This was a real war, and they were real spies. Oh, this was life, real life.

This was indeed war, thought Chase, as the carriage containing him and Kate pulled up to the main portico of Arlington House, from which General McDowell commanded the Army of the Potomac, an army that could be seen encamped all about them on what once had been the lawns and gardens of General Wash-ington's family and now was—or had been until a few months ago—the manor house of Robert E. Lee.

"It is cool," said Kate, "or cooler, at least." She held her parasol high as she got out of the carriage, assisted by the general's aide.

An old milky-eyed Negro greeted them. "I was here when General Washington used to come to see his kin the Eustises. I was a Eustis boy for sixty years." The thin voice had said these same words so many times to so many visitors that all meaning had gone out of them for him. But he had most of his teeth; and spoke distinctly. "I saw the general many times. He called me Josephus, my name." The old man stopped, abruptly; then he grinned and bowed and held out his hand.

"A coin will do," the aide said. "He's quite deaf," he added. Chase gave the man a coin. Then they climbed the steps of the portico, where they paused and looked southeast toward the Capitol on its hill, the unsightly crane poking skyward from that circular emptiness where a dome was meant to be. The city seemed to dance in the heat waves.

"The general's still at dinner. Will you join him?" He wasn't sure when you'd be here, so he began."

"That's quite all right, Captain . . . ?"

"Sanford, sir."

"My daughter, Miss Chase."

Sanford gazed at Kate with awe; or what Chase took to be awe. The latest set of spectacles from Franklin's had a habit of erasing the center of his vision while making too vivid the periphery. All in all, he preferred his constant myopia, which was not unlike trying to see underwater, where everything was cloudy and imprecise until he was within a few feet of it; then all the details were clear. He knew that much of his reputation for aloofness was because he could not, simply, see.

But Chase could now make out the command-center of the Army of the Potomac, which was four tents pitched next to the Mansion. Aides hurried from tent to tent, carrying dispatches. Troops drilled on lower terraces. Horses were being shod at a nearby smithy. The commanding general was seated alone at a long trestle table, eating an entire watermelon.

As the Chases approached, General McDowell rose. Wiped his lips. Bowed to Kate; and greeted her in French. Bowed to Chase, and said, "You must dine with me. We keep ungodly hours, as you can see . . ."

The Chases had already dined but each agreed to a slice from a second watermelon, which was being held in reserve. Chase had not thought it possible for a man to eat an entire watermelon after, presumably, a large dinner. As they sat at the table in the shade of a huge oak tree, the general ate, received aides, gave orders and entertained his guests.

Chase stared at the green-blue below him where men were drilling; to his eyes the effect was not unlike that of a shoal of minnows in a muddy stream. "Your men look fit," he hazarded.

"Oh, they're fit enough. But, though they are fit enough," McDowell dextrously flicked with right forefinger melon seeds to the grass at his feet, "to be men, they are not fit to be soldiers. I just saw that correspondent from the London *Times*, what's his name? The famous one?"

"Mr. Russell," said Kate. "What do you think of him?"

"It's what he thinks of me that matters." McDowell signed an order that Captain Sanford had placed before him. "He's been present at all the great battles of the last dozen years. He makes
206

me nervous, looking over my shoulder. Do you realize, Miss Chase, that I am the first American officer ever to command, in the field, an army of thirty thousand?"

"But, surely, three thousand or thirty thousand..." Chase began.

"It is *not* the same," said McDowell gloomily. "Our so-called Mexican War was a very small affair. A kind of Indian skirmish. That's why my senior officers have had no experience in the modern field. Nor have I. Your regiments can't even perform a brigade evolution together." McDowell mimicked Russell so expertly that Kate laughed aloud; and Chase smiled, despite his growing panic: *Could the Union army fail?* The thought had never seriously occurred to him. But if the Union army were to fail, he would never be able to sell his five-twenty bonds at par.

"Well, sir, Mr. Russell's right. The men are nowhere near ready. Oh, yes, the President tells me that the rebels are green, too. But they are on their home ground. It is we who must attack them. They can fight us like Indians, and do very well. We must fight them as if this was the Crimea—a *modern* war. Worse," as McDowell lowered his voice, Chase and Kate leaned forward to hear him whisper, "*I have no accurate map of Virginia.*"

Chase said nothing. Kate opened her parasol; then shut it again. There was a long moment as the three studied the remains of McDowell's watermelon. Finally, Chase said, "You seemed confident when you presented your plan to us the other day."

"Oh, Mr. Chase, it was not *my* plan. I looked to the details, of course. I take full responsibility. I am the commanding general. But I've always agreed with General Scott that we should wait until the autumn."

"If it was not your plan, General, whose was it?"

McDowell pushed away the mountain of green melon rinds that had accumulated on his plate. Chase wondered how it was that a man who ate so much could still remain somewhat less than stout. "The plan, sir, was the President's."

Chase was startled. "But, surely, he said that it was yours..."

"No, sir. He's never said that. But he has said all along that we must use the troops before the three-month enlistments are up. Well, a great many are up on July the twentieth. He's also sensitive to the press. All that 'Onward to Richmond' noise of Horace Greeley." McDowell's jaw set. "I'd like to send *him* on to Richmond. That man is always wrong."

"On abolition, he is right." Chase still could not sort out precisely who had done what. "It was Mr. Lincoln who put you up to this?"

"No, sir. That is not the way things are done. The President
207

told General Scott that the country could not wait. So General Scott told me to make a plan for an invasion of Virginia, while training thirty thousand men, so that they could then take the field in eight weeks' time."

"Has he the right?" Kate was sharp.

"Has who the right?" Chase waved his handkerchief at a wasp.

"Mr. Lincoln. After all, he is not a military man, to say the least..."

"He is Commander-in-Chief," said Chase, glumly.

"He has *every* right," said McDowell. "He also has every responsibility. I don't envy him. He will learn, of course. But then, I suspect, that we will all learn many things that we never knew before. At the moment, he is a politician playing soldier—with real men who are also playing soldier but know nothing of this kind of warfare."

"But *you* studied in Paris..." Kate began.

"I studied strategy, Miss Kate. I did not study war."

On that note, the boy-governor of Rhode Island strode toward them, yellow plume shining like a redundant flame in the sunlight, pince-nez on a cord about his neck.

"General McDowell!" Sprague saluted the general, who was now on his feet. "I hear you're moving to Richmond. I want to go with you." Sprague turned to Chase, whom he did not recognize. He is as blind as I, thought Chase. "Sir, I'm Governor Sprague. Of Rhode Island."

"Sir, I am Governor Chase. Late of Ohio. My daughter Kate..."

"Oh," said Sprague, putting the pince-nez on his nose; thus transforming himself from military chieftain to chief accountant. "Oh, it's you. *And* you," he said, turning to Kate.

Kate smiled. "That must mean then that this is, also—*you!*" she exclaimed.

"Yes," said Sprague, turning back to McDowell. "I came straight from Providence to the White House. I don't know what's happened to my commission. But they say I can go with you when you go."

"We'll be honored, Governor. Deeply honored. You can go with your own Rhode Island regiment."

"Who else would I go with? When are you starting?"

Chase intervened. "That is still a secret of state, Governor."

"I usually read *those* in the *New York Herald.*" Sprague sat beside McDowell and ate some strawberries from a wicker basket. The juice stained his lips a most girlish red, thought Chase, wondering what Kate really thought of this potential consort. She had not mentioned Sprague to him after their ride together in the woods, shortly before his return to Providence. Chase was under
208

the impression that letters had been exchanged but it was not his way to ask questions. When she was ready to tell him, she would.

As the wasps and yellowjackets helped the boy-governor eat the remains of the fruit, they discussed how it was that newspapers sometimes knew all sorts of secrets that they ought not to have known—and certainly ought not to publish, when the rest of the time they had no interest in facts at all. "Whatever sounds as if it might suit the prejudices of the reader, that is what will be published," said Chase.

McDowell agreed. "But imagine what we in the military must now face. Thanks to the telegraph, journalists can make our secrets known to all the world, even while a battle is in progress."

"I'm sure the President will put a stop to that," said Chase.

"Do you think that he is strong enough to engage both Mr. Greeley *and* Mr. Bennett in battle?" Kate shook her head. "He's terrified of them."

"I would," said Sprague, eyes on Kate, "shoot them."

"So would I, Mr. Sprague," said Kate. "We are—in this—as one."

Chase smiled benignly. Captain Sanford presented General McDowell with a stack of orders. The general was on his feet. "I must now invent a strategy," he said.

"Can I help?" Sprague looked keenly martial.

"In due course, Governor." McDowell looked sadly at the rinds of the vast watermelon he had eaten. "That was monstrous fine, I must say." Then he saluted his guests and walked down the shaggy lawn to the second of the four small tents. Chase was awed to think that there, at his feet, was the headquarters of the Army of the Potomac, the largest American army ever assembled. But then he was distracted by a company of infantry that marched, ineptly, even to his civilian's eye, past their table. The lieutenant in charge was a huge blond red-faced brute, who shouted his commands to the men in German.

Kate blinked. "Have we a German army, Father?"

"So it would seem."

Sprague replaced his pince-nez and stared at the sweating men. "They're out of step," he said. "They need drilling. And look at those rifles! They need cleaning, the lot of them. This isn't an army."

Chase did not enjoy hearing this sentiment expressed twice in a day so close to the advance on Richmond, which his friend Sumner predicted would promptly fall.

"Well," said Chase, rising, "the Hessians fought very well in the Revolution."

"For the British," said Kate, unfurling her parasol in all its green and yellow splendor, "who lost."

"Are Hessians German?" Sprague stood very erect.

"*Deeply* German," said Kate. "Give me your arm, Governor. And show us to our carriage."

Walking slowly, Chase followed the young couple; he enjoyed the coolness of the Arlington Heights. He was also impressed by the vast military display all about him; or what he could see of it, which was mostly color—white and gray and brown tents against the dull green of grass and the darker green of woods. Troops of every sort at drill. Horses being shod and curried; fed and watered. Artillery being polished to mirrorlike brass-brightness. He took a deep breath. He was growing used now to the acrid smells of an army—sweat, both human and horse, saddle wax, kerosene, burnt gunpowder, all mixed in a not-displeasing, even exciting sort of perfume, dedicated to Mars. But thought of that pagan deity restored Chase to his Christian senses. Guiltily, he thought of Christian love, and murmured to himself the last verse of the First Epistle of John. As he did, he wondered if General McDowell had already decided upon the day that he would begin his advance on Richmond.

Naturally, General McDowell had already determined upon the day; and twice postponed it, due to the unreadiness of the troops. Now the day's date, and the hour, and the line of march were all encoded on David Herold's scrap of paper.

Mr. Thompson had not wanted David to leave early, but talk of heat prostration had excited the Aesculapius who resides in every druggist's bosom. David was obliged to drink several potions; ingest a number of salts; and go straight home. But, instead, David boarded the streetcar at Fifteenth Street for Georgetown.

The sky was violet behind the White House, which looked more leaden than white in the dying light. At the War Department, a crowd of officers was standing on the sidewalk, in deep discussion. Even *they* seemed to know that the war was about to begin at last.

At the end of the line, where the red-brick houses of old Georgetown came to an abrupt end, David got off the cars. The street was now the so-called Upper River Road, which proceeded parallel to the detested-by-all canal. The River Road itself ran between canal and river bank. Fortunately, the canal was not as foul as it was in the center of the city.

Unpainted shacks lined the road. Here darkies lived, their children everywhere, playing in the dust. As this was washday, ropes tied to trees were hung with clothes like banners in the failing light. Just as David recognized the small frame house which was
210

his destination—"Three willow trees in the backyard, of such enormous size and sheer romance," Mrs. Greenhow had said, "you cannot miss them"—a cavalry company clattered from out of nowhere, obliging David to leap out of their path and into a raspberry bush. He swore silently, heart beating fast, as the horsemen vanished around the bend that hid Chain Bridge up ahead. Then when David got to his feet and straightened his clothes, he saw in the half-light berry stains like blood on his linen trousers; and he swore again, this time aloud.

Bettie Duvall was no older than he; and no prettier, either, he thought, sadly, as the thin, wiry girl showed him into the parlor of the frame house where a single lamp illuminated a room that looked to be half furnished or half unfurnished. The last was the case. "This is my aunt's house," said the girl. "She's still here. She's upstairs now. But all the rest—my uncle and everyone— have gone South."

"Will you go, too, Miss?"

"Oh, yes."

"When?"

Bettie Duvall smiled. "In about an hour." She had already received Mrs. Greenhow's message, which was now wound in a coil of her thick dark hair. "Thanks to you. Thanks to Rose Greenhow. Thanks to Mr. Lincoln. I'm to cross Chain Bridge at eight o'clock."

"You going to stay in Virginia?" David wondered whether or not he should ask to go with her. If she had had so much as the sign of a curve anywhere, he would have insisted. Unfortunately, she looked like a highly intelligent, even handsome crow; and crows were not to his taste.

"No, I'll be back. Long as I can be useful, I'll stay in Washington." She pronounced the city's name the way that all its true citizens did—Washnone.

"Like me," said David, feeling somewhat heroic. A warm wind stirred the one window curtain, and he was almost overwhelmed by the smell of honeysuckle.

"Just like you, Mr. Herold. With luck I'll be in Fairfax before midnight."

"General Beauregard?"

But Bettie Duvall only smiled.

"How do you cross over to Virginia?" David was curious. "I mean I got me this military pass because I work at Thompson's, but you . . ."

"An innocent young farm girl never needs a pass. I dress up like . . . like an innocent young farm girl and join some real farmers that I know, two families, who bring food in to Washington from the other side, and I travel with them, among the lettuces and the melons."

"They taking you to Fairfax?"

Bettie Duvall laughed; and started to shake her head. Then, plainly, she thought better of it as she recalled the importance of what was hidden amongst her braids. "I'm given a horse, a post-horse, and I ride all night. Once I rode two days and one night without stopping. They had a fresh horse for me at each junction."

David wondered if anything so exciting could be true. But he was not allowed to brood much longer in that honeysuckle-scented room where a million gnats were now attacking the single lamp's flame; and burning themselves up.

"I must go, Mr. Herold. I thank you. The Confederacy thanks you. Pray for me tonight."

"When do you think the fighting will start?" David paused at the door.

The girl touched her braid. She smiled: "When the great guns go off at Centerville and Manassas, you'll know it's started, and you'll hear the guns all the way to Thompson's, because when a cannon's fired among those hills, the sound is going to carry all round the world, I should think!"

The sound of doors slamming, one after another, awakened Mary Todd Lincoln in her carved wooden bed. For a moment she lay, neither asleep nor awake, and wondered who was slamming doors in the Mansion, and why they were allowed to make so much noise on a Sunday morning. Then Mary was fully awake; and knew that what had been doors slamming in her dream was cannon-fire across the river; and the real war, begun at last.

"Father!" Mary called. But there was no answer from the small bedroom next to hers where Lincoln often slept when he slept at all these days. But Keckley had heard her. She came into the bedroom and drew the curtains. Mary could tell that it was early morning from the light. They were supposed to go to the Presbyterian church at eleven o'clock.

"Has it begun, Lizzie?"

"Yes, ma'am. At six-thirty we heard the first shots fired. Mr. Lincoln's already at the War Department. But he says he'll still be going to church with you."

As Keckley helped Mary into a dressing gown, Lizzie Grimsley peered into the bedroom. Lizzie was also in morning-dress—or undress as the ladies called it among themselves.

"Mary, did you hear all that racket?"

"How could I not? They sound so near."

212

"Let's hope they're not," said Lizzie, large and pale. "I'm hungry."

"Well, I'm sure that even if they should seize the White House they'll let us have our breakfast before they shoot us." Mary was excited; and wished that she was not. The war was serious. Men would die, even as that poor boy Ellsworth had died. But the sense that the familiar world was now dying obscurely delighted her. What was about to be would not be like anything that ever was before. She was certain of that. She was also certain that Mr. Lincoln would prevail, which meant that the new world would be better than the old. When she was young, she had feared change; now she embraced the very idea. Is this age? she wondered.

At the first sound of artillery, Hay tumbled out of bed; washed his face but did not shave; dressed quickly to the sound of distant cannon-fire, almost as loud as Nicolay's snoring in the bed. Hay let the First Secretary sleep on. In these matters, they were often competitive with each other. After all, this was history; and nothing like it was apt to befall either of them again, much less the country, thought Hay, as he entered the President's office, which proved to be empty. The small telegraph room next to the office looked as if someone had stepped, temporarily, away from the transmitter. Hay then went to the waiting room, where he found a young officer, who was reading a Bible at Edward's desk. The young officer came to attention when he saw Hay. "Sir, the President's at the War Department."

"What's the news?"

"General McDowell is advancing on Manassas. From Centerville. That's all we know, sir."

In the cool morning air, Hay ran from the White House to the War Department, where a dozen carriages were already drawn up, and two companies of infantry stood guard. Breathing hard, he returned, casually, the commanding officer's salute, and entered the building. He found the President in General Scott's office. Aides ran from room to room, while down the hall the telegraph transmitter clattered.

Lincoln nodded, absently, at Hay. Scott ignored him. The general stood like a pyramid beside the map of Virginia. Hay noticed that silver stubble glistened like flakes of mica on the dark red cheeks: the commanding general had not shaved either. "General Beauregard's here on this side of a river or creek that is known, thereabouts, as Bull Run. General McDowell has just moved into position here, to his left."

"Has only just moved?" Lincoln was as attentive as a prosecuting attorney in a capital case.

"Yes, sir. He was to have moved at half-past two this morning. But he was delayed and now..."

"This is the second delay." Lincoln began to twist his legs around the rungs of the chair. "He was supposed to have arrived in Centerville Wednesday. Instead he stopped at Fairfax. He's already lost two days. That means there's been time for Johnston's men from Harper's Ferry to join Beauregard at Manassas."

"Time, sir. But not occasion. Remember we have General Patterson at Harper's Ferry. He is a superb commander. He has Johnston penned in. We are now face to face with the enemy here at..." An aide gave General Scott a message. Scott glanced at the message; then gave it to Lincoln, who held it close to his eyes. The Ancient sighed. "That's two thousand men who won't fight?"

"Yes, sir. The Pennsylvania Fourth Regiment and the artillery battery of the New York Eighth... Their three-month enlistments ended at midnight last night, and now these brave citizen-soldiers are going home just as the battle is to begin."

"That is why," murmured Lincoln, "I prayed that McDowell would not lose those two precious days. Well, the fault is mine. I should have said three-year enlistments from the beginning."

"You could not have known, sir."

"It is my task *always* to know, particularly when I don't." Lincoln unwound himself from the chair. As he did, a second message arrived.

Scott read, with a smile that broke his face in two, like a harvest moon neatly halved, thought Hay, feeling lightheaded. He prayed the ague was not about to visit him again, today of all days. "We are successfully crossing Sudley Ford, to the enemy's left flank. The rebels are falling back. We are now in a position to attack. The plan proceeds, sir, as desired."

"If not on the day designated." Lincoln motioned for Hay to accompany him, and they left the old general at his map, explaining to his aides the similarity between today's complex operation and his own strategy at Chapultepec.

As a hundred men saluted, the President raised his hat, eyes on the road, head and neck pushed slightly forward, always a sign of anxiety, Hay now knew. If Hay could not read the Ancient like a book, he had at least committed to memory a number of much-thumbed pages.

They crossed to the White House without interception. Even the most intrepid office-seekers were still abed. As they entered the President's Park, Hay asked, "Is there no way you can hold those men in the army, the ones who decided to go home last night?"

"Of course I can hold them. I can oblige them to fight a thirty-
214

year war if I want. But if I do, I'll never get another volunteer ever again, will I?"

"No, sir."

Lincoln stared at the ground as he walked. "On the other hand, we're going to have our problems should we have to conscript men, which is what we'll be obliged to do if General McDowell doesn't get that army to Richmond pretty fast."

"How many men will we need?"

"Three hundred thousand, says General Scott. That means every American man between eighteen and forty-five will have to have his name registered by his local sheriff. Then all the names will be written out on slips of paper and a blind man—or a man with a blindfold if the real thing's not available—will start drawing the names."

Hay had followed the Cabinet debates on the subject. There had been much speculation on what should be done to those men who refused to go. It was agreed that the local authorities could handle individuals who would prefer a long prison term to military service. But suppose, said Mr. Bates, that large numbers of men refused? There were a number of solutions to this problem, and the Tycoon seemed ready to choose what Hay thought was the worst. "I incline to letting any man who doesn't want to serve pay a certain amount to a substitute who does want to go, or will go, at least..."

"Father!" Madam's voice sounded as if from Heaven, and assisted by the treble voices of cherubim, all hailing, "Paw, Paw, Paw!"

Lincoln and Hay looked up. On the roof of the White House stood Madam, Willie, Tad and Lizzie Grimsley. Tad shouted, "Come on up, Paw, and see the war!" Lincoln waved noncommittally; and entered the White House.

Mary held a telescope in both hands, and she trained it on the distant low green hills behind where the guns still sounded at irregular intervals. Against the pale hazy morning sky, she could make out puffs of smoke like new cotton growing in a pale-blue field. From time to time, flashes of fire lit up the sky, stormless lightning to go with the stormless thunder.

"Let me look!" Tad grabbed for the telescope. Mary cuffed him hard. Tad howled.

"Serves you right." Willie was, as always, a moralist. "Say 'please.'"

"Shut up," said Tad, and kicked his brother.

"Stop that!" Lizzie Grimsley grabbed each by an arm and separated them. "Imagine scuffling up here with no railing or anything. Oh, Mary! I think I have the vertigo."

Mary gave the telescope to Lizzie. "We are certainly high up,"

215

she agreed, looking across the black tar-covered roof, whose numerous fissures were filled with stagnant water from the last rain. "I have no fear of heights," she said, with serene bravado.

"Well, I have no fear of thunderstorms." Lizzie trained the telescope on Virginia.

"I do." Mary shuddered. Since childhood, she had always known that she would one day—or worse, one night—be killed by a bolt of lightning. Even if she were in the basement of a large house, covered with an eiderdown beneath a four-poster bed, the lightning would find her. On the other hand, she had no fear at all of cannons or of gunfire, or of rebels.

The President appeared on the roof. "Mother, come on to breakfast."

"What's the news?" Mary tried to keep Tad from climbing his father like a tree; and failed. The black formal Sunday suit was now developing a set of new creases, as Tad took his place, triumphantly, on his father's shoulders.

"We've begun our attack. That's all I've heard."

Lizzie gave Lincoln the telescope. With a practised gesture, he held it to his eyes and carefully swung it from left to right. "We can't tell anything yet," he said, putting down the telescope. He cocked one ear; and frowned. "We have stopped our covering fire. I wonder why?"

"Do we know any of the soldiers?" asked Willie. "You know, like poor Ellsworth."

Lincoln and Mary exchanged a glance. "I can't say that we do," he said, finally. "Of course, there's General McDowell. We all know him. And..."

"I mean boys," said Willie, who had grasped, at the age of ten, the difference between that race of stout men with beards and gray in their hair and the others with hair all one color and fresh faces, narrow waists, who still liked to play games with ten-year-olds; and laugh.

"No." Mary was stern. "We don't know any of them."

"What about the Southern boys? The ones from Kentucky?" Willie was persistent.

"Come on to breakfast." Mary put her arm around Willie's shoulders; they were now the same height.

"Willie wants to write another poem like the one about Ellsworth, who got killed!" Tad roared with laughter from high atop his father's shoulders.

"Wait till you get down," said Willie.

"Let's all go down," said Lincoln. "And get ourselves ready for church. It's my favorite time of the week, as the convict said when
216

they . . ."

"We know the story, Father." Mary took his arm, aware that Lizzie was close to swooning as they walked in single file along the White House roof to the trapdoor where steep stairs led to the interior. "And speaking of your favorite time of the week, Lizzie and I were just discussing the Reverend Dr. James Smith . . ."

"Oh, no!" Lincoln groaned.

"Oh, yes!" Mary was the first to start down the steps. "He's our favorite minister in Springfield."

"Then we must keep him there."

"But, Father, he's Scotch."

"All the more reason. He will preach against extravagancies, and the vanities of this world, and land speculation." Mary's head was now below the roof. But her voice was clear. "He must go to Dundee in Scotland. As our consul."

"Yes, Brother Lincoln," said the pale Lizzie, clutching at the trapdoor, while her foot searched for the step. "He is a perfect choice."

"On a day like this, Cousin Lizzie, you corner me—your President—for a consulship?"

"It's not the first time." Mary's voice came from far away. "But you always put us off."

Lizzie was now inside. Willie followed. Then Lincoln, with Tad on his shoulders. "Well, first, you ladies must get me a certificate of good behavior for him. For all I know your Reverend Smith drinks, smokes and swears, and is a libertine."

"What's a libertine?" asked Tad, as his father descended the stairs.

"A libertine is a man who loves liberty only a little bit instead of a whole lot like us."

The cannon-fire had ceased. The puffs of smoke had now been dispersed in the general haze of the high summer sky, at whose edge rain clouds had begun to mass.

Hay and Nicolay took advantage of the peace in the executive offices to answer mail, write letters for the President's signature, file newspapers. Hay was aware that the preliminary signs of the ague had begun: heaviness in the eyes, which were unnaturally dry; a heaviness in the region of the liver; a heaviness of the skeleton itself, as if the bones longed to be freed of flesh. Sooner or later, everyone in the city suffered from Potomac fever, save the natives, who seemed inured from birth to their misasmic climate unlike most Southerners, who tended to be lifelong sufferers from the ague, as Madam was—and the Ancient not.

When either Hay or Nicolay came down with the fever, their common bed was left to the healthier one while the valetudinarian

217

was obliged to sleep on a military cot, wrapped in sheets and blankets, shivering and sweating until the thing had run its course.

"It is my gay old delirium come back," said Hay, as he held out an arm that had begun to shake of its own accord.

"The cot for you," said Nicolay, without much sympathy, eyes on a mountain of correspondence. "The boy-governor is back in town."

"The war is won." Hay loosened his collar; and felt better. "What is to be done with him?"

"McDowell has let him go to Virginia, as an observer. Why is it everything of importance around here happens on a Sunday?"

"It is the Lord's will, I suppose." Hay took a long pair of scissors and began to cut from a Richmond newspaper a story about the convening of the Confederate Congress which had taken place, presumably, yesterday. "I also suppose that we will be hearing a lot from the preachers about the blasphemy of fighting a battle on a Sunday."

"If we win, who will listen?"

"If we lose, who will care?"

Although Hay was in the first stage of the fever, he stayed on the job for the rest of the day and night. He accompanied the President to General Scott's office, where the general received them on a bed that had been placed beneath the painting of the War of 1812. He apologized for not rising. Plainly, he had been sleeping off one of his enormous dinners. Lincoln dismissed the apology with a gesture. The soft thud of cannons was plainly audible everywhere in the city, and the bar at Willard's was crowded, as the latest "news" was discussed while a crowd had gathered in front of the Treasury, hoping to coax—if coaxing was ever necessary—some oracular statement from Mr. Chase. There was no crowd at the White House, where irritable troops stood guard in front of the gates, and let no one through without a military pass. Hay had never seen the Mansion quite so tranquil.

"The guns seem close to us, General," said Lincoln; and pointed, oddly, to the window, as though the battle was in the street. Although the battle was not, the noise of the battle was.

Scott listened a moment. Then shook his head. "The wind plays tricks, sir. Anyway, our artillery is in place, as is theirs. I cannot imagine that any artillery will now be moved, or if moved, set up again."

Lincoln removed a number of telegrams from his hat. "This last dispatch from Fairfax Court House says that the rebels have fallen back."

"Better than that, sir. At three o'clock, they were in retreat."

"*But* that it is possible that they may be reinforced." The left eyebrow went up. "How?" Hay was aware of the effort it took Lincoln to maintain his usual air of calm if melancholy authority.

"I don't know what they could mean by that, sir. Where would the reinforcements come from? General Johnston has thirteen regiments near Harper's Ferry. If he had moved, we would know. Never fear, sir. The day is ours." The old man gave a great yawn; and requested a general pardon, which was granted. He was then allowed to go back to sleep.

"Jefferson Davis is on his way to Manassas by rail," said Lincoln, more to himself than to Hay.

"How do you know this, sir?" Hay could now hear the chattering of his own teeth; he hoped the President could not.

"We have our spies, too."

"Did their Congress meet yesterday?"

Lincoln was precise. "There was a *meeting* at Richmond. I guess just about any meeting can call itself a congress—a bringing together of people; in this case, rebels."

At five o'clock, Nicolay insisted that Hay take to his bed but Hay was not about to miss a moment of what might be the decisive—even the terminal—day of the rebellion. Assured that all was well, the President and Madam went for a drive in the cool of the evening. Although there was no decisive word from McDowell, Hay had noticed that the guns were firing at less-frequent intervals. Could they have run out of shells? he wondered, beginning to feel a bit light in the head and unreal. But reality was restored at six o'clock when Seward appeared like a ghost at the door to Nicolay's office. Seward's normally pink face was sallow white, and the plumes of white hair were as dishevelled as Lincoln's. He smelled, even more strongly than usual, of cigar smoke and after-dinner port. Nicolay and Hay sprang to their feet.

"Where is the President?" Seward made a curious gesture: he pressed the backs of his hands against the door frame, as if to keep from falling; but then the premier's short legs in their flapping pantaloons always looked to Hay as if they were about to buckle. Nicolay said that the Lincolns had gone for a drive at five o'clock.

"Had he—have you any late news?"

Nicolay said, "No more than what we have heard since morning. The rebels have fallen back. We are winning . . ."

"Tell no one." Seward's voice was a harsh whisper. "But the battle is lost. It has just come in on the telegraph. McDowell is in full retreat, and he has just urged General Scott to do whatever he can to save the capital."

"My God!" Nicolay stood, mouth working, as though trying to catch his breath. Hay wondered whether or not this might all be part of the delirium which did not set in, usually, until close to midnight.

Hay moved for the next few hours as in a fever dream, which indeed he was; yet he knew what was happening, and did what he had to do. On the authority of the Secretary of State, he sent word to each member of the Cabinet to come immediately to the Mansion. But in the end, one hour later, Cabinet and President met not in the Mansion but in General Scott's quarters.

Lincoln had gone the color of old ashes when he was told of McDowell's dispatch. But he had said nothing; and seemed grateful that Hay had not reported the bad news until Madam had gone into the White House. By now, guards or no guards, a considerable crowd had begun to gather in front of the Mansion. The word was spreading. Also, the long-threatened rain had begun, lightly, to fall.

In full uniform and fully shaved, Scott was enthroned beside the map of Virginia. Generals came and went like boy-messengers, while Mr. Cameron stared at the cracked ceiling, as if wondering to whom the contract should be given for its repair, and how much commission he should ask.

Hay now saw everything in, as it were, lightning flashes. The room filled up with the Cabinet. Pale Chase said, "We will have to evacuate the city." No one listened to him. He repeated himself, more loudly. But all eyes were on Lincoln, who glared at the map as if the map held some secret.

Scott was stunned; and for all his bulk seemed fragile. "I could not believe it. Would not believe it if McDowell himself hadn't sent word. Sir, at three o'clock, the rebels were in flight."

"But then they were reinforced," said Lincoln, almost casually, as if presenting some minor evidence to a jury of no particular consequence. "General Beauregard had twelve regiments in the field this morning. By afternoon, he had twenty-five. How do you think this happened?"

The lightning in Hay's head illuminated for an instant Scott's ancient face; saw the worms at work in it; saw the massive skull that soon earth would know. "The rebel General Johnston," Scott wheezed, "who was at Harper's Ferry, made rendezvous with Beauregard sometime last night."

Lincoln turned to Scott. "Why did our General Patterson not stop him? Or at least tell us that Johnston had moved out?"

There was no answer from Scott. But the militant and military-minded Blair suddenly roared an oath, which caused Chase to shudder with revulsion, which inspired Lincoln to take command, as if Scott was no longer present.

"We shall want every soldier on duty in and around the city

to be on the alert this night. The Long Bridge, Chain Bridge and the Aqueduct are to be heavily guarded at either end."

"Yes, sir," said Scott.

In the course of the meeting, Hay heard the Adjutant-General announce that the brother of the Secretary of War was among those killed. For an instant, Hay felt a certain compassion for this lord of corruption, who ceased his study of the ceiling and looked as if someone had flung snow in his face. Lincoln put his hand on Cameron's shoulder; and said nothing.

Further dispatches were read aloud. At first, McDowell hoped to fall back and make a stand at Centerville; then he hoped to make a stand at Fairfax Court House; then he reported that the troops would not re-form, that they were in full flight to the Potomac. He had no idea whether or not the rebels would follow up their advantage, and seize the city.

As orders were given for the defense of Washington, Hay was experiencing a sense of extraordinary well-being, which was in no way disturbed when he heard Scott say to the Tycoon, "Sir, I am the greatest coward in America. I deserve removal because I did not stand up, when the army was not in condition to fight, and resist this campaign to the last."

Lincoln turned on him, the left eyebrow raised; often, Hay knew, a sign of danger—to others. "Do you imply, General, that I forced you to fight this battle?"

"No president that I have served has ever been more kind to me," said the old man, which was not, Hay knew, an anwer.

There was no sleep for anyone that rainy night. Lincoln lay on a settee in his office and received a stream of visitors. A number of senators had gone out to watch the battle, along with a crowd of sightseers, including diplomats and society ladies, all eager to cheer the army on to Richmond. Picnic lunches had been catered by Gautier's and the mood that morning had been most festive as hundreds of carriages had crossed the bridges to the Virginia side. Now the would-be celebrants were scurrying back in a state of panic.

One member of Congress, whose name Hay could not recall, declared, "I saw it all! We beat them hollow. There's absolutely no doubt of that, Mr. President. They are beaten."

"So," said Lincoln, a harsh edge of mockery in his voice, "after we beat them, our soldiers ran all the way home?"

Senators Wade and Chandler and Grimes and Trumbull and Wilson each came to report. Their clothes were covered with dust; their faces dark with dust and sweat. Lincoln listened; and listened; and listened. "It is damn bad," he said at one point, and Hay

221

realized that this was the first time he had ever heard the Ancient swear.

Meanwhile, Nicolay urged Hay to go to bed, but Hay would not, not yet. He compromised. "I'll go over to Willard's and see if there's something to eat." In the early stages of his ague, he was hungry; and could eat and drink enormous amounts. Later, the sight of food would make him ill.

As Hay crossed Pennsylvania Avenue, he was astonished to see, late and rainy as it was, that the entire avenue was filled with people. At the door to Willard's, a Zouave—one of Ellsworth's so-called blood-tubs—was enthralling a group with his account of the battle, while all up and down the avenue, Union officers rode toward the War Office to report, and the first cavalrymen could be seen, moving toward camp. The infantry would not appear for several hours.

Hay was greeted at the cigar-stand by Thurlow Weed. "What news?"

"Nothing good, sir."

"I just saw Burnside. He went up to his room without a word to anyone."

"And without his troops?" Hay knew that he ought not to betray bitterness to the ever-devious Thurlow Weed; but he was now beyond mere discretion.

"You look a bit green," said the great politician and newspaper editor.

"A touch of the ague, sir. It will pass."

"Most things do." Weed held out his hand to Senator Wade, who had just come from the President. Hay pushed through the crowd to the first dining room, which was shut—not only was this Sunday but all the best provender had been sent on to Manassas for the elegant onlookers. Hay's friend, George Washington, the headwaiter, was nowhere in sight. Finally, Hay was obliged to go into the crowded bar; here he stuffed himself with ham and drank brandy-smashes, all the while staring into the gaunt dirty face of the boy-governor, who was emptying glass after glass of gin. Men pressed against them; and called out for drinks. The smoke of cigars was heavy. Hay wondered what time it was. He had the sense that he had, somehow, mislaid most of the night.

"I took over the artillery battery," was Sprague's constant refrain. "Look," Sprague pulled at the sleeve to his dirt-smeared tunic. There were two bullet holes, one above the other, near the left elbow.

"Were you hurt?"

"I was scratched. There's another hole..." Sprague searched in the dim light for his third martial souvenir but could not find it. "We held the line forty minutes. Just us. Just Rhode Island. I was in front. They cheered me. All twelve hundred men. Then my horse was shot from under me. I changed the saddle in front of them. We held on. But nobody came. We were ordered back. Burnside led them back. That's when I took over the battery. That's when Johnston's army appeared. God knows how they got there. That's when our soldiers—not mine, theirs—started to run. The Zouaves were the first. Yellow to the core. Then they all ran and ran and ran. There is no army now."

Hay listened, as if in a dream; and then, still dreaming, he left Willard's, to find that it was indeed morning; and that he had not slept all night unless, of course, he had been asleep on his feet and had dreamed that he had been talking to Sprague in the bar at Willard's.

In the secretary's office, Nicolay was talking to a group of journalists. When he saw Hay at the door, he excused himself. "Get to bed," he muttered. He touched Hay's hand. "You're burning up."

"I will. I will. What's happening?" At that moment, the door to the office opened and Lincoln appeared, Cameron beside him. The President looked exhausted, thought Hay, himself now barely conscious. From what seemed the other side of the Potomac, Hay heard Lincoln say, "Mr. Cameron, send for General McDowell."

Hay blundered through the usual crowd in the corridor to his bedroom; flung himself on the military cot; and let the fever take charge of him. But before he lost all consciousness, he realized that Lincoln had not said, "Send for General McDowell." Lincoln had said, "Send for General McClellan." They were now back at the beginning.

Part Two

Part Two

1

THE SUN HAD NOT YET RISEN ON CHRISTMAS DAY, 1861, WHEN
the Secretary of the Treasury, Salmon P. Chase, entered the
dining room of the now comfortable but entirely resplendent house
at Sixth and E to be greeted by his daughter Kate, both comfortable
and resplendent in morning robe, as she presided over a vast
breakfast of buttermilk cakes and honey, of two kinds of Virginia
sausage, and hominy grits with red-eye gravy, a rebel dish to which
he was addicted, and Kate not.

Kate sprang from her chair; embraced him. For an instant, he
was enclosed by the scent of lemon verbena that reminded him
of her mother, who had worn no other scent, as perfume was
distilled by Satan, while lemon verbena was a leaf from one of
God's fragrant trees. "Merry Christmas, Father!"

"Merry Christmas, dear Kate! Where's Nettie?"

"Asleep, lazy child." Kate drank her coffee and watched with
sharp eye the way in which the mulatto manservant—a new
acquisition—served.

Chase tried not to gobble his food; and gobbled. He was already
too large for his frock coat, or "toga," as Kate called it. The cakes
were perfectly cooked, neither too light nor too dark. Kate spent
hours each week with the cook patiently trying out new recipes
and improving old ones. She was like a general in the house.
Chase had often wondered what she might have done had she
been a boy. She seemed to him to combine, in the most natural
way, the best qualities of the two sexes. The previous evening
had been typical. As they celebrated Christmas Eve alone together,
the next day's elaborate menu already seen to, Kate had beaten
him four times in a row at chess, a man's game that he fancied
himself a fair master of.

"Why is Mr. Lincoln so irreligious? It's bad enough the way
he holds Cabinet meetings on Sundays. But now there's one on
Christmas Day!" Kate was teasing him, of course; he knew that
she lacked his own deep religious faith. But if she lacked it, that
had been his fault for having her so thoroughly not to mention
expensively "finished" at a distinguished New York school. Nevertheless, he was certain that she would one day come, willingly
and joyfully, to her Savior.

227

"Sunday is one of the few days the White House is not filled with office-seekers. Except for the ones that actually spend the night in the corridor, so that they can get to the President first in the morning."

"I'd throw them out." Kate accepted from the butler a single soft-boiled egg in a porcelain cup, her one excess at the day's first meal.

"So would I, all in all." Chase began on the fried sausage patty into which a great deal of red and black pepper had been kneaded. "But Mr. Lincoln cannot say no . . ."

"Except when he does." Kate was sharp.

"Well, yes. He is often *weakly* firm—or *firmly* weak."

"Will he say no to the English?"

"I'm not certain."

"What would—what *will* you advise?"

"To give the prisoners up, as painful and embarrassing as it will be for us." Ever since early November when an American ship, the *San Jacinto*, had stopped the *Trent*, a British mail packet-boat, off the coast of Cuba and seized two Confederate Officials en route, as commissioners, to England, public opinion had been duly inflamed in both countries. Elements in both Britain and the United States were eager for war.

At the moment, there was an impasse; and Seward was very much in his element. "We shall wrap the world in flames!" he had recently shouted, full of brandy, in the presence of Mr. Russell of the London *Times*. Everyone had been horrified, except Chase, who was now used to Seward's style. The more bloodthirsty he sounded at a time of crisis, the more energetic he tended to be to find a safe way out. As far as Chase could tell, Seward had long since given up his master plan to start a worldwide war in order to restore the Union whilst acquiring new exotic territories for the greater American republic.

Characteristically, the President had been of no particular use in the crisis. He allowed Seward to deal as he saw fit with Lord Lyons, who tended to be surprisingly pacific in this matter. No doubt, Lyons was vividly aware of something that the British ministry at London was not: the United States was now the largest military power on earth. In and around Washington alone, there were close to two hundred thousand well-trained troops—three-year not three-month volunteers, a tribute to the organizing genius of their youthful commander General McClellan. Although the Union navy was as yet of no great consequence, it would grow—and grow—and grow. As Chase started, inadvertently, to think of the expense of this unprecedented military establishment, he

228

inhaled a bit of red pepper, which lodged in his throat, and burned; he coughed, tears came to his eyes. Kate patted his back.

"What's wrong?"

For a moment, the fierce pepper took away his voice; then tea restored it. "I was thinking of money."

"Oh, poor Father!" Kate went back to her egg. "Our bills..."

"Not ours. The government's. The war is costing us one-and-one-half million dollars a day. The bankers... The bankers!" Chase paused, as if frozen. The financing of the war was a nightmare to which he could see no end. In August he had borrowed from the banks one hundred fifty million dollars in gold and silver coins to be paid in three installments against three-year Treasury notes, paying 7.30 percent. After the first installment, the bankers began to complain; Chase had then asked Congress to set up a national banking system so that the government might issue its own paper currency, a proposal which made him almost as nervous as it did the banking establishments. Now the bankers were threatening not to pay the current installment. Jay Cooke was his only comfort in all of this. "Fight the sons of bitches!" he had said, and Chase had excused the profanity as it so closely, if crudely, approximated his own view of the moneychangers in the Temple.

Kate created a diversion. She knew that he would never be able to get his breakfast down if he were to think, even for a moment, of the country's finances, much less his own. Kate spoke of the latest gossip. Although the President's annual message had not gone to Congress until December 3, some days earlier the newspapers had printed sections of it. This had been particularly upsetting to Lincoln and to the Administration because the press was able to report something that no one was supposed to know until the actual day. Lincoln would make no mention of the *Trent* Affair. This was to have been a signal to the British ministry that, despite the war spirit abroad in the land, particularly in the pages of the *New York Herald*, the Administration did not want matters to get out of hand.

"Everyone is now saying that it was Mrs. Lincoln who gave a copy of the speech to the *Herald*."

"Who is everyone?" Chase had not heard this particular rumor.

"Everyone *I* talk to. The town, that is. After all, isn't she really a secessionist? With all those brothers of hers in the Confederate Army."

Chase did not like Mrs. Lincoln any better than he did her husband. But he was, by nature, judicious. He also recalled her conversation about the famous abolitionist purchase of Eliza in Lexington. One must be fair in these matters. "It is my impression," he said, "that of the two, she is the one most opposed to the South."

"But surely that is what she would want everyone to believe."

"Then she is an excellent actress."

"Most women are, Father."

"I would not know that, Kate." Chase noticed, as he often did, how like a boy Kate looked whenever she raised her chin slightly and half smiled. She was son; she was daughter; and he was happy sire to both.

Then Kate was again a pretty girl, laughing at her father. "Married three times and never once did you notice what actresses women are—and all the time!"

"Perhaps my wives were unusual." Chase blinked his eyes. If he looked straight at her left ear, he could not see the left ear, which was to him no more than a pink blur, but he could see the eyes, nose and mouth. He shuddered involuntarily. He feared blindness more than anything; and he was reasonably certain that he was going, gradually, blind.

Kate detected the shudder. "Are you cold? Is there a draught?"

"No. No. But speaking of my wives long since departed, what news of Governor Sprague?"

"Equally departed—from Washington if not this earth. I had a note from him last week. He is still trying to become a general. I must say I admire his persistence. And his bravery. I can't think why his conduct at the battle of Bolivar Heights was overlooked, but it was."

"We lost the battle," said Chase, bleakly. "That's why it is overlooked. We seem always to lose."

"That is whenever we do anything at all. Will General McClellan be at the meeting?"

"I don't know. I still have faith in him. Of course, he is not McDowell. But he has done wonders with the army. They are superbly trained now; and they are devoted to him."

"If not to the Union." Kate finished her egg; had crumbled but did not eat a fragment of cornbread. Almost alone among Washington's ladies, Kate had a horror of growing fat. She was thought eccentric by all but the slender company of the thin.

"I believe that that is a commander's first task, to make an army loyal to him and then..."

"Not use it! He has done nothing for six months."

"He has a plan. A superb plan, I think. He's confided it to me, and to no one else." Chase had rather wondered at McClellan's wisdom in singling out the Secretary of the Treasury as his sole confidant in the Administration. But then who else was

230

there? The President was notoriously indiscreet. Seward was reckless, Cameron hopeless.

"Even so, I still wish General McDowell had been kept on."

"The McDowells are coming to us New Year's Day. With Captain Sanford." Chase smiled; and looked directly at Kate's nose and saw in all its perfect shell-like detail her ear. He must really go back to Franklin's and keep trying on new lenses until he found what he needed. Otherwise, he would be like Oedipus at Colonus, old and blind, with only a loyal daughter to look after him. Although William Sanford was not the most prepossessing of young men, he was enamored of Kate, while his father, a rough-hewn type from Lowell, Massachusetts, was almost as rich as the Spragues.

"Oh, Captain Sanford!" Kate laughed. "Whatever a mooncalf is, that's what he is. He hates business. He hates his father. He loves music and when the war is over, he wants to go to Paris and wear a red velvet jacket and compose music."

"Paris? Music? *Red* velvet?" Chase could not decide which of the three he liked the least—for a young American. But then Nettie ran into the room and threw her arms around him and wished him a Merry Christmas. She did the same to Kate; and asked if she could open her presents.

Breakfast at the Sewards' was a more masculine and less festive affair. Seward sat at one end of the dining-room table while the Assistant Secretary of State, his son, Federick, sat at the other. Seward's head throbbed only mildly. The previous evening had been spent most merrily at his own hearthside, where he had given dinner to eminences who were, due to choice, geography or death, bachelors, among them the sixty-nine-year-old, lifelong Pennsylvania bachelor Thaddeus Stevens, chairman of the Ways and Means Committee of the House of Representatives as well as a member of the new and potentially dangerous Joint Congressional Committee on the Conduct of the War. Stevens was easily the wittiest man in Washington; he was also one of the most learned; he was also a dedicated abolitionist, as was most of the committee, which was chaired by the harshly disagreeable Ben Wade, and included such hard men as Zach Chandler and Lyman Trumbull.

As Seward sipped his morning coffee, he tried to recall exactly how the previous evening had ended. Stevens, of course, was sober; he had given up alcohol years ago, after the death of a drinking crony. But unlike so many who come late to temperance, Stevens was neither disapproving of others nor, ever, the common flaw of the professionally sober, dull.

Seward reviewed the events of Christmas Eve. As the club-footed Stevens limped into Seward's drawing room, he stumbled on a loose rug. When Seward caught his arm, Stevens had thanked him demurely, "I have always so much admired your tact," he murmured, "in never making the slightest allusion to my admittedly eerie resemblance to the late Lord Byron." This so delighted the company that the early part of the evening was spent telling Thaddeus Stevens stories, while the eponymous source smiled his thin-lipped smile, occasionally adding, in a soft voice, some devastating gloss. Stevens had even laughed when someone described how, at the beginning of the session, a woman enthusiast had cornered him in his office at the Capitol and begged for a lock of his hair. With a courtly gesture, he had removed his enormous chestnut wig and said, "Pray, Madam, select any curl that strikes your fancy."

Despite himself, Seward smiled through the mild but persistent pain, located just back of the eyes. "What's that, Father?" Frederick was not only son and assistant but surrogate for his ailing mother back in Auburn, New York. Fortunately, for Frederick, Seward had no need of a daughter, unlike his colleague who was now breaking his fast at Sixth and E.

"I was thinking of Stevens last night. Wondrously droll, he was."

Frederick smiled. "I was in the House last summer when one of the New York congressmen kept walking up and down the aisles as he was declaiming, until Mr. Stevens finally said, 'Do you expect to collect mileage for this speech?'"

Seward laughed; and felt somewhat better. He lit his first cigar to go with the last of the morning's coffee. The best part of the day had now begun. He chose to reminisce. "You know, Horace Greeley once caught Honest Abe cheating on the mileage that congressmen are paid when they go home from Washington."

"Cheating?" Although Seward knew that his son was very much a Seward partisan, he also knew that the young man was also under the spell of Lincoln's pervasive myth. Even Seward had difficulty separating the practical if evasive and timorous politician from the national icon that Lincoln and his friends had so carefully constructed before and during the convention at Chicago: Honest Abe, the Rail-Splitter, born in a manger—or, rather, log cabin... Thanks to the telegraph and the modernization of the daguerreotype, Lincoln's managers had been able to impress an indelible image on the country's consciousness. Even the famous beard that Lincoln had grown on the train from Springfield to Washington had been a deliberate calculation and not, as Lincoln had said so sweetly if disingenuously at the time, the result of a letter from a little girl who liked whiskers. Actually, the letter had come from a number of influential New York Republicans who thought that a beard might give him dignity, something that they had found dangerously wanting in the quaint western teller of funny and not-so-funny stories. So Lincoln had grown the beard.

Seward caressed his own cleanshaven cheeks. *He* would never change; but then he had never lacked dignity. He told his son of Greeley's famous charge. "In 'forty-eight, Greeley was appointed for a few months to the House of Representatives. Naturally, being Greeley, he came there looking for trouble, and the first thing that he found was that most of the congressmen were kiting their travel allowances. So the apostle of virtue then did some investigation, and he published all the particulars of who had been charging how much for travel, and there was Representative Lincoln, charging the government nearly double what he was owed."

"What did Lincoln say to that?"

Seward exhaled blue smoke and, with the smoke, the last of the headache departed. "He said Greeley had figured the mileage by the shortest way—the mail route from Washington to Springfield, which hardly anyone takes, as opposed to the Great Lakes route, which he had taken. He also reminded Greeley that the law only requires that you take 'the usually travelled' road, which is what he took. He's a sharp lawyer, Mr. Lincoln. But not yet Andrew Jackson or even 'Tippecanoe' Harrison, whose log cabin he borrowed in the campaign against me." Seward paused; he could feel the pulses beating rapidly at his temples. He must not relive the campaign, even for a moment. "Greeley is the wisest fool I've ever known."

"Let's hope Mr. Lincoln doesn't jail him, too."

"More likely the other way round. The President's afraid of him. Bennett, too. I can't think why."

"At least," said Frederick, "he's taken care of the New York *Daily News*." In August this inflammatory Democratic newspaper had been forbidden to use the government's postal system. The editor—a brother of the secession-minded mayor of New York City—had then tried to transport the newspaper by railway express, but Mr. Pinkerton's secret service had quickly put a stop to that. As a result, the *Daily News* was obliged to suspend publication. Elsewhere, not only were newspapers being shut down but their editors were being imprisoned. Seward not only supported the President in all of this, but he himself ordered most of the arrests in his capacity as the Secretary of State, whose "inherent powers," he had pointed out to an amused if nervous President, had never been entirely explored.

Seward's strategy was to hold the editors for an indefinite period; then, without ever charging them with any crime, he would let

233

them go—to sin no more. Since Congress had, at presidential request, suspended for all practical purposes the First Amendment as well as *habeas corpus*, there was nothing that the Administration could *not* do, under its wartime powers.

"Now what will he do to the *Herald*?" asked Frederick.

"Nothing," said Seward, looking at the clock. In five minutes he must stroll over to the Mansion, where the emergency Cabinet was due to meet. "Bennett's too big for him; and too clever."

"I should think he was vulnerable. It must be against some law to steal or borrow the President's message to Congress."

"I agree." Seward, wistfully, stumped out the end of the first cigar of the day. Later cigars would be good; but not like the first. "It would be highly embarrassing for a President to admit that he is so careless with secret documents that someone from the *Herald*—or whoever it was—could get a copy of the speech. His Satanic Majesty is safe." Seward rose. Frederick rose, too. "Have you the *Trent* folder?"

Frederick nodded. "How do *you* think the *Herald* got a copy?"

"I think," said Seward, who had indeed thought a great deal about the matter, "that Mrs. Lincoln gave it to her friend the Chevalier Wikoff, who then gave it to his friend Mr. Bennett."

"But why would she do that?"

Seward shrugged. "She is deeply in debt."

Frederick was shocked. "You mean she sold it to Bennett?"

"I *mean* nothing, my boy. But I suspect something like that has happened. We've not heard the end of this."

As the Sewards, father and son, stepped out into Lafayette Square, a smiling Rose Greenhow saluted them from the window of her house, where she and a number of other rebel ladies had been under arrest since August. Rose enjoyed embarrassing Seward from her window, aware that it was he who had ordered Mr. Pinkerton to arrest her.

Seward lifted his hat; and gave the imprisoned lady a courtly bow. "What a fool," he said to his son, "that woman was, to be so open. Personally, I like my spies to be totally clandestine—as well as lovely."

Father and son crossed the avenue to the President's House, which was almost as white as the icy sky, and far whiter than the banks of snow that had suddenly accumulated at the end of November and never since melted.

In a romantic mood, Seward thought of Rose Greenhow, whose late husband he had known in days gone by. He had enjoyed visiting her in those rose-lit, rose-scented parlors where, now, a dozen very angry Southern ladies were quartered along with Rose, under lock and key.

"Do you think Mrs. Greenhow is really a Confederate spy?" Frederick seldom had much difficulty in reading his father's mind.

"Oh, yes. But she fooled me for a long time. You see, she was so open about being a spy that I thought she wasn't one. I broke my own first law, which is that people are always, without exception, exactly what they seem."

Frederick grinned. "Then what is Mr. Lincoln?"

"The President," said Seward promptly. "And somewhat sly." As soldiers saluted at the gates of the Mansion, a carriage containing a thoughtful Chase passed them by.

In the White House living quarters, Mary helped Keckley dress Tad. Ordinarily, one person was enough for this task. But whenever the boy was more than usually excited, two people were needed. For reasons that Mary did not allow herself to think about, the eight-year-old Tad was still unable to dress himself or read or write, despite a series of tutors and a blackboard and schoolbooks that had been assembled for the two boys at one end of the state dining room. Where Willie was unusually advanced for his age, Tad was unusually retrograde. Mary had consulted doctors; but they had been of no use at all. They gave Latin names to his speech defect, and to his excessive energy; but they could not explain why a child so bright should have such trouble with simple tasks like dressing himself or learning to read. She, of course, understood Tad's every word, as did Mr. Lincoln, but to others, as Cousin Lizzie had somewhat cruelly told her, he simply quacked like some sort of bird. "Poppa dear," his phrase for the beloved father—Mary knew that she came second with him. Just as she came first with Willie—sounded like "Pappy-day." Yet for all of Tad's deficiencies, he was endlessly well organized and inventive. He arranged circuses on the White House roof, charging five cents admission, which he kept. He drilled the soldiers. He loved to imitate his father, even to wearing his gold-rimmed spectacles, to the fury of John Hay, who once spent an entire day searching for them only to find Tad on the roof, surrounded by children, wearing the President's spectacles and top hat, and singing war songs.

"Hold still!" Keckley shouted; and Tad who had seldom if ever heard that serene woman raise her voice stopped wriggling, curious to see what other new sounds she was capable of. Mary let go his arm.

"What will we eat today?" asked Tad, sociably, as if he had not been causing both women endless trouble.

"You won't eat anything if you keep on like this." Mary straightened her morning-dress in the dusty mirror that hung over a table strewn with toy soldiers and cannons.

"Like what?" Tad was lamblike.

"Wait and see. Thank you, Lizzie." As Mary left the room, Lincoln came out of the bedroom, his hair disordered, and papers stuffed in every pocket. "You're even worse than Tad." She tugged his lapel, the signal for him to lower his head to her level so that she could flatten the hair.

"What's Tadpole up to now?"

"He wouldn't let us dress him." Mary retied Lincoln's tie; tried but failed to smooth out the black frock coat. Nicolay appeared from the executive end of the corridor.

"The Cabinet's all present, sir."

"All right." Absently, Lincoln bent low and kissed the top of Mary's head. Then he followed Nicolay down the corridor. There were times, Mary noticed, when he walked toward his office like a man approaching the scaffold, with slow, deliberate, flat-footed tread, head pushed forward and face concentrated. At such times, she wished devoutly that they had not come here. The ongoing rumors about her Confederate sympathies had been bad enough; now she was being accused of selling the President's message to the *Herald*. Mary was enough of a politician to realize that this sort of thing was to be expected; also she knew that as Tad had his disability, she had hers—the spending of money. She had exceeded the budget set by Congress for renovating the White House; worse, she had no clear idea exactly how much in debt she was because whenever figures were mentioned to her, she heard only a sort of scream in her head, not unlike The Headache. Although Major French, the Commissioner of Public Buildings, was her ally, even he could not mention dollars to her without causing the panic to set in. Meanwhile, the visits to New York City had grown more and more ecstatic. Great department store magnates like Alexander T. Stewart himself would wait upon her; and she would buy and buy. For a year the credit had seemed endless but now, at year's end, the bills, respectfully addressed to "Mrs. President Lincoln," were beginning to arrive. But just as she could not hear sums, she could not read them either. The figures simply blurred on the page. She gave her personal bills to Stoddard and the White House bills to Major French, with the injunction that they tell no one. She was desperate for money; but did not know how much. She refused to tell her husband, out of shame.

In the oval sitting room, Mary began arranging the Christmas presents. Now that Lizzie Gormley had gone back to Springfield, she had no one to talk to except Keckley, who did not count, good as she was. The sight of the room's new silk curtains cheered her somewhat, as did the thought of the triumphal ball that she was planning for February to celebrate the completion of the

White House. If nothing else, future generations would be grateful for what she had done to what was, after all, the nation's own unique palace. As Mary arranged a wreath of holly above the mantel of the fireplace, she wondered just how the Chevalier Wikoff had managed to steal the President's message to Congress.

At the other end of the Mansion, the subject of Wikoff did not come up during Cabinet, though Seward did make a joke or two about arresting James Gordon Bennett, and Lincoln had laughed, without much enthusiasm, thought Hay, who took notes. Hay was personally convinced that Madam had received money from the *Herald* but Nicolay thought that she had simply let him see the message. In either case, both Hay and Nicolay were agreed that Wikoff was the guilty party. But what could ever be done to him? Thanks to the Chevalier's celebrity as a White House habitué, any move against him would cast upon the throne itself a shadow.

The President teetered back in his chair; and came to the point. "I think the Cabinet should know that I recently set Mr. Seward one task and myself another. He was to write out all the reasons why we should turn over to England those rebels that we seized, and I'd write out all the reasons why we should hold on to them. Well, he completed his task, and I never began mine, because I couldn't think of any urgent reason why we should risk a war with England at a time when, I think, we are all agreed," and he looked toward Seward, whose full lips were arranged in a seraphic half smile, "one war at a time is about all that we can handle. So Mr. Seward has prevailed in this matter."

Hay admired the way that the Tycoon had gradually eased Seward, the advocate of worldwide war, into the role of peacekeeper with England.

Seward himself had been quite aware of what Lincoln was doing but then he knew what Lincoln did not know, that he had never for one moment wanted war with England at a time when he much preferred to reveal himself to the world as the man who had kept the peace despite the rantings not only of the press but of his own considerable Irish Catholic constituency. Seward then proceeded to read aloud a statesmanlike paper, proposing arbitration between the two powers and, meanwhile, *the cheerful*, as he put it with some panache, return of the rebel commissioners.

When Seward had finished, Lincoln motioned for Chase, as the second-ranking Cabinet member, to comment. All in all, Chase had been relieved by Seward's approach. "I give my adhesion," he said at the end of his own thoughtful analysis of the affair, "to the conclusion to which the Secretary of State has arrived." Chase did feel obliged to add that "although it is gall

237

and wormwood to me to give these rebels up, we must demonstrate to the world that for the sake of inflicting just punishment on rebels, we will never commit even a . . . technical wrong against neutrals." That was indeed well said, thought Chase, happy in the knowledge that the "s" in the word "against" had not been lisped, as he had feared when he saw it coming up in his mind.

The Cabinet did not debate the matter for long. No one was happy with the business. Lincoln summed up for them all: "It is a bitter pill for us to back down. It looks like we're afraid of England, which we are—but only at this particular awkward moment. Anyway, I reckon their little triumph will be short-lived, because by the time this war ends we will have a navy superior to theirs, and the world will be a different place. But I can't say this course, which we must follow, has given me the greatest pleasure." Lincoln turned to Cameron, who was staring straight ahead, lost in his usual world of contractors and commissions. "Mr. Cameron, I want you to release the rebels before the New Year and send them on to England."

There was a long silence in the Cabinet Room. To the embarrassment of all, it was plain that the Secretary of War had not heard the President. Then Cameron became aware that all eyes were on him. "I'm sorry," he said, mildly, "I must've missed something there."

Lincoln repeated his order. Cameron nodded. "Well, if that's what you want, that's what you'll get." He sounded as if he were concluding a deal with a Harrisburg legislator. Seward sighed. At the beginning of the Administration, Cameron had been his creature. In fact, if not in title, Seward alternated with Chase as Secretary of War, a state of affairs that did not in the least distress Cameron, whose innumerable other fish were constantly in the fat frying. But this happy state of affairs was now drawing to a close. During the course of a recent meeting in General Scott's office, Lincoln had turned to Cameron. "How many troops," he asked, "do we have in the vicinity of the city of Washington?"

"Well, I'm not all that sure." Cameron had not been in the least taken aback. "There is a list somewhere, I guess."

The President had then turned to the commander of the Army of the Potomac, already known to the nation's press as the Young Napoleon even though he had yet to win a major battle. "General McClellan?"

"I don't have the figures at hand, Your Excellency. I can give you the figures for the Army of the Potomac, of course. But not the rest."

With some wonder, Lincoln had turned to General Scott. "You are general-in-chief . . ."

"Yes, sir. I am general-in-chief." The old man's red-glazed eyes stared at McClellan. "But I am given no information."

At this point, wanting not only to be helpful but to avert a scene, Seward had undone at a single stroke his own power over the War Department. "I have the figures here." He had then produced the small notebook that he always carried with him. Halfway through his reading of the statistics, Seward realized, too late, the immensity of his error. Lincoln's face had set as if cast in bronze, while the low brow of the handsome McClellan was now so creased with thick lines that between thick straight brows and glossy auburn hair there was practically no brow at all to be seen. Cameron alone was unmoved.

When Seward was finished, Winfield Scott got, unassisted, to his feet. "This is a remarkable state of affairs," he rumbled. "I am in command of the armies of the United States, but have been wholly unable to get any reports or any statements of our actual forces. But here is the Secretary of State, a civilian for whom I have great respect." The old man stared hard at Seward, who did his best to appear at ease, yet eminently respectful—had he not invented presidential candidate Scott? written all his speeches? *governed* him? "But he is *not* a military man nor conversant with military affairs, though his abilities are great. Even so, this civilian is possessed of facts which are withheld from me." Like some ancient arcane engine of warfare, Scott swiveled round to face Cameron, whose tricky eyes were now at rest upon a chandelier. Seward found himself sweating. He glanced at Lincoln, and saw that that usually restless body was unusually still in its chair. Meanwhile, the huge engine was now swinging toward the President, who began, slowly, to sit up like an unprepared schoolboy about to be called upon to recite. "Am I, Mr. President, to apply to the Secretary of State for the necessary information to discharge my duties?"

Lincoln turned to Seward, who said, "General, I simply collect this sort of information because it interests me. I like to know which regiments have come, which have gone . . ."

Scott spoke through him. "Your labors are very arduous." The old man's contempt was withering. "But I did not before know the whole of them. If you, *in that way*, can get accurate information, the rebels can also, though I cannot." It was not until then that Seward realized that Scott must have known all along that it was McClellan who had given him the figures, on the not unreasonable ground that of all the officers of state, including the President, Seward alone had been able, not to mention *obliged*, to gather in his hands the reins of power. But those reins now snapped.

Scott's last mischief to the nation was to break up what Seward had been convinced was the winning team of Seward and McClellan. The old man now turned on McClellan, who promptly thrust his hand inside his tunic, like Napoleon—was he not the Young Napoleon? But then, in the face of an actual hero of the republic's wars, McClellan withdrew the hand from his tunic. "You were called here by my advice," said Scott. "The times require vigilance and activity. I am not active and never shall be again. When I proposed that you should come here to aid, not supersede me, you had my friendship and confidence." General Scott paused; then he murmured, "You still have my confidence." On that note, the old man left the room, something that his sense of protocol had never before allowed him to do without the President's leave.

At four-thirty in the morning of November 3, General Winfield Scott left Washington from the Baltimore depot, en route to Europe. McClellan was now general-in-chief as well as commander of the Army of the Potomac. "I can do it all," he had told the President.

But now, thought Seward, as he gazed at his former minion, Cameron, all was changed. McClellan no longer turned to Seward as the natural leader of the government; but then he did not turn to anyone, so great was his youthful vanity. Meanwhile, Cameron had made an unexpected alliance with Chase and the radically minded Republicans in Congress. Cameron had come out for enlisting in the army those former slaves that had been liberated by the Union army. Lincoln had been as furious with Cameron as he had been in September when General Frémont had not only declared martial law in Missouri but had then announced that he would confiscate the property of all secessionists, including their slaves, who were to be freed. This had delighted the abolitionists while causing Lincoln to declare, with anguish, to Seward, "This is a war for a great national idea, the Union, and now Frémont has tried to drag the Negro into it!" Lincoln annulled the proclamation; relieved Frémont of his command; and incurred the enmity of Congress's radical Republicans.

Lincoln rose. Cabinet was over. As Chase said good-bye to the President, he hoped that he could be out of the room before Cameron could buttonhole him. "We'll see you New Year's Day, won't we?" The President was amiable. "With both your handsome daughters?" Lincoln stared down at Chase, a vague smile on his lips. He was never anything but the soul of courtesy and forebearance, thought Chase, full of Christian charity on this the anniversary of Christ's miraculous birth.

"Oh, yes, sir! My young ladies look forward with pleasure to seeing you—and Mrs. Lincoln, as do I." Chase managed to ruin every "s" in the sentence; but did not care. Although he was not exactly at ease with Lincoln, he never felt any constraint when they were together. Chase was also aware of Lincoln's profound regard for him as an educated man, with a lifetime's experience in the higher realm of politics. "By the way, I suspect that the bankers will let us down on the payment *in specie* of the next loan, and I think that we should plan seriously for the issuance of our own government notes..."

"Mr. Chase!" Lincoln winced in a comical way. "Today, of all days, let me brood upon five sad things, not six. Be merciful."

Chase inclined his head. "Our watchword—today—shall be 'All quiet on the Potomac.'" This had been the daily report in every newspaper since McClellan had taken command of the army.

The President sighed. "As we all know, General McClellan is a great engineer, but I sometimes think his special talent is for the *stationary* engine."

Chase smiled; and said good-day. He was first and forever a McDowell man. But after Bull Run, McDowell had been superseded by the thirty-four-year-old McClellan, who had kept a number of Virginian counties, now known as West Virginia, in the Union. McClellan was considered the perfect modern soldier, having been trained in Europe like McDowell but, unlike McDowell, he had seen action in the Crimea. He had then left the army to become chief engineer and vice-president of the Illinois Central Railroad, supporting for Senate the railroad's counsel, Douglas, over Lincoln. McClellan was a Democrat, which Lincoln liked; but Chase did not. Lincoln tended to pamper pro-Union Democrats at the expense of loyal abolitionist Republicans. McClellan had just been made president of the Ohio & Mississippi Railroad, when he was called back to duty—and glory.

McClellan had taken Washington and the country—and even Chase—by storm. He was youthful, handsome if somewhat short and thick in stature, and confident to the point, Chase could not help but think, of hubris. But in a matter of months he had turned a frightened mass of men into a formidable modern army. Even Mr. Russell of the *Times* would now approve of their drilling. Chase had never realized just how awesome it could be to watch a well-drilled army of a hundred thousand men pass in review. But General McClellan loved the army so much and the army loved him so much that there had been, thus far, no military engagement of any kind except for a fracas at Bull's Bluff, in nearby Virginia, which the Union army had lost, leaving dead on the field one of the President's old Illinois friends, former senator Edward D. Baker. It was said that Lincoln had wept uncontrollably when he heard the news. Chase thought this unlikely. Despite all of Lincoln's charm and cunning, Chase found him, at bottom, an unexpectedly hard man, who would never weep for anyone—or anything, saving perhaps power withheld.

As Chase stepped out into the upstairs corridor, Cameron linked arms with him; and propelled him away from the others. "Governor," Cameron's voice was low and whispery and conspiratorial. "We have all the generals with us. There's Frémont, who's bound to get another command, which I'm working on. There's Hunter. There's Ben Butler, who's declaring every nigger we free—I mean Negro—*Federal property*, so that he can confiscate them. He calls 'em contraband..."

"I know. I know." Chase hated being told things that he already knew, which was how most of every day was spent, listening politely while others told him his business.

"I guess you heard what a success my swing through the North last month was. 'Free the slaves!' I said. 'Arm the slaves!' I said. The audiences just ate it up." With an unexpectedly powerful grip, Cameron positioned Chase on the grand staircase; then helped him down, as if he were an elderly lady.

"It is certainly my wish," said Chase. "But I'm alone in the Cabinet except, now, for you." Chase could hardly believe that he and this embodiment of American political corruption were speaking so intimately. It must be a dream, he thought, as Old Edward met them at the bottom of the stairs. Cameron whispered in Chase's ear, "We've got Sumner, the whole Committee on the Conduct of the War, the big generals..."

"Yes, yes," said Chase. "I shall see you here, I suppose, on New Year's Day."

"Growing very cold, sir," said Old Edward, as he led Chase out onto the portico where a line of carriages with smoking horses waited to collect the magnates.

"And the autumn was so beautiful," said Chase, wistfully. It was true. There had never been such beautiful dry weather. There had never been such a perfect time to send an army straight to Richmond. There had never been such a rare opportunity, so peculiarly lost by the Young Napoleon.

As Chase drove away from the White House, the Chevalier Wikoff was being shown into Bettie Duvall's parlor in Seventeenth Street. From time to time, in the most casual way, they had met at those houses where the grand people of every persuasion gathered. They had first been introduced to each other by the Widow Greenhow, whom the Chevalier had already come to know. He
242

had found Miss Duvall plain in appearance but delightful in manner, largely because of her bold secessionist statements. Since the house arrest of Mrs. Greenhow in August, he had got to know Miss Duvall even better; and if she had charmed him he had also charmed her. But then, in a sense, each was in the same business.

Miss Duvall led the Chevalier into her somewhat overfurnished and overheated parlor. Miss Duvall's aunt was not in view. But then she was never in view. Miss Duvall came and went as she pleased. It was said that she had money of her own. It was said that she had a beau, in the Confederate Army.

"This is a pleasure, Chevalier."

"I was on my way to . . . the *other* house," delicately, he indicated that corner of the Mansion which was visible through the iced-over window, "when I thought I'd pay my respects."

Miss Duvall sent for tea. Then they sat in front of the coal fire. "I'm glad you dared to come. Mr. Pinkerton's men watch me morning, noon and night. I expect to end up any day at Fort Greenhow."

Wikoff was grave. "I pray you remain at large, Miss Duvall."

"That is a generous prayer, Chevalier. Does this mean that you are a secret secessionist?"

"*Pas moi.*" But then Wikoff realized that despite Miss Duvall's name, she did not speak French, unlike his patroness the Republican Queen, Wikoff's epithet for Mrs. Lincoln had so caught on throughout the country that now both the unfriendly as well as the friendly Press had taken it up, to the President's dismay and to Mrs. Lincoln's delight. Happily, neither suspected that Wikoff was the author. From the beginning, Bennett had agreed that Wikoff must never sign his dispatches; thus, he could continue to be not only Mrs. Lincoln's devoted *cavalier servente* but Mr. Bennett's man at the Mansion.

"I am," said Wikoff, "simply a friend of the Lincolns. I particularly admire her. I always told Mrs. Greenhow what a pity it was that she did not go to the Mansion when . . . she could. She would have had a lot in common with Mrs. Lincoln."

Miss Duvall was sardonic. "If what the papers write is true about Mrs. Lincoln's loyalty to our native country, why, yes, I'm sure that our hearts all beat as one. But if that's the case, then all the more reason for Rose—and me—to stay away and not compromise her. You realize, sir, that I am notorious for my outspoken sympathies."

Wikoff raised one hand, as if in benediction. "Miss Duvall, you are much admired for your candor and your courage. I shouldn't be surprised if the President himself does not think you a valuable asset at this time, to keep a line, as it were, of communication to the reb—To the Confederates."

Miss Duvall stared into the silver teapot to see at what state the brewing had got. "Well, if he is so eager to use me—and I am happy to be of use—tell him that I'd appreciate it if he would ask Mr. Pinkerton's secret service to stop staring through my windows, and going through my desk when no one's in the house. We spies *never* leave evidence lying about."

"I don't quite know how I shall put *that* to him, but I'll do my best if I have the chance." Wikoff was somewhat uncomfortable. He had not been aware that the house was being watched. But then the ambassador of James Gordon Bennett ought to be above suspicion. "Actually, General McClellan's the person to speak to about the secret service. Apparently, Mr. Pinkerton used to work for the Illinois Central, the General's old employer. Anyway, the secret service now reports directly to our Young Napoleon and not to the Executive Mansion."

"Whoever his men report to, they're watching us now, especially today."

"Why today?"

"Because we've just won a great victory." Miss Duvall added hot water to the teapot. "Mr. Lincoln has given way. He will let our commissioners go on to London. Now, if I were truly brave, I'd give you champagne, to celebrate. But I don't want to go to Fort Greenhow just yet. So we shall have tea instead—and liberty. How, by the way, am I to know whether *you* are not a spy, sent here to trap me?"

Wikoff made a self-abasing gesture. "I am practically a foreigner. I'm hardly apt to be trusted by Mr. Pinkerton. Besides, I did *not* encourage you just now to compromise yourself by pouring champagne."

"That is true." Miss Duvall poured tea; and the Chevalier stated his errand. "I want," he said, "to go to Richmond."

With a sharp click, Miss Duvall put her saucer down on a mother-of-pearl inlaid table. "Why?"

"I want to write a sort of...peace letter for the *New York Herald*."

"What is a peace letter?"

"Just that. As you know, Mr. Bennett is against the war. He also inclines to the South."

"But not too far. After all, he has yet to go to jail for his principles. How many newspapers has Mr. Lincoln shut down?" Miss Duvall's somewhat beaky smile did not waver as her thin lips tightened, and the sharp curved nose more than ever resembled a crow's beak.

244

"A dozen, perhaps. But I think that it is more Mr. Seward—and the generals—who do the shutting down of presses and the arresting of editors. It is my impression, perhaps mistaken, that Mr. Lincoln spends a great deal of his time getting Mr. Seward's political enemies *out* of prison. But then this is war, Miss Duvall."

"A war that your generals don't dare fight."

"Oh, dear lady, not *my* generals. I take no sides. I'm not a Republican or a Democrat or a Confederate or a Unionist. I've lived abroad too long. If anything, I'm a Bonapartist. Anyway, Mr. Bennett and I do not want to see this war grow any bloodier than it has been thus far. That's why we think that if I should, somehow, get to Richmond, I could then send back a peace letter to the *Herald*, showing the Confederacy in a favorable—and formidable—light, and mentioning on what terms the South might be willing to make peace, terms acceptable to President Davis and to . . . Mr. Bennett, if not Mr. Lincoln. I should tell you that last July Mrs. Greenhow had agreed to try to get me through. But then she was arrested."

Bettie Duvall stared a moment into the fire. The Chevalier stared at his own large white soft hands. "Let me . . . talk to friends," said Miss Duvall, finally, as the maid appeared in the doorway. "It's the boy from Thompson's, Miss."

"Oh, give him my prescription, will you? It's upstairs on the . . ." But then Miss Duvall was on her feet. "I better talk to him." Wikoff had risen but she motioned for him to take his seat. "I'll be right back." Bettie Duvall crossed to the vestibule, where David stood, shivering slightly despite a heavy, brand-new, only slightly adapted Union army overcoat, bought on the sly at half price from an army quartermaster.

"You wanted to see me?" Since the arrest of Mrs. Greenhow, Miss Duvall had had two or three occasions to send David on mysterious errands. Since she did not dare to be seen talking to him at Thompson's, they had agreed that whenever she placed a certain vase in the front-parlor window, he would stop at her house when he made his rounds of the neighborhood.

"I did. But I don't now. It's too late."

"For what?"

"Next week Mrs. Greenhow and all the other ladies are being moved to Old Capitol prison."

David whistled; then he smiled. "I reckon she'll give them Feds a mighty hard time."

"I reckon she will," said Bettie Duvall. "But, one thing, we'll have an easier time getting to her there than we've had here, with everybody watching. So you be careful," she added, as she turned back into the hall.

"Don't worry, Miss. Nobody ever pays me any mind." This was true, he thought, bitterly, as he went out into the street. Despite the new overcoat, he found the day arctic. But then for the true Southerner, winter is never not a disagreeable surprise.

David turned left into Pennsylvania Avenue. At Lafayette Square, he stopped and stared at the President and his spiffy-looking young secretary Mr. Hay, whose moustaches were now longer and silkier than his own. Of course, Hay was at least four years older than he. Even so, Hay's new moustaches were far more effective than his own dull dark ones. The two men, one tall and thin, the other short and slight, looked like two black sticks against the snow. They were walking, quickly, toward Mr. Seward's house. As always, they were talking animatedly; and, as always, there were no guards in sight except for the cavalryman at the corner of Sixteenth Street who sharply raised his sabre in salute, causing the President absently to raise his tall silk hat. Then the two men entered the Old Club House.

Miss Duvall and the Chevalier Wikoff had also witnessed this not unfamiliar scene. "How easy," said the girl, thoughtfully, "it would be to kill him."

"He says the same, which is why he won't have guards. Mrs. Lincoln is terrified for him. But he is indifferent, or so he says."

"He's also safe." Miss Duvall turned back into the parlor. "At least from the Confederate government. They would never do such a thing. After all, what would be the point? Mr. Seward's the real power..."

"So shoot Mr. Seward!" The Chevalier was buoyant.

"It is certainly tempting." Miss Duvall was equally buoyant. "Unfortunately, assassination is abhorrent to President Davis, and all that he... that *we* stand for. For now the tyrants are safe. Tell me, was it you who gave the President's message to the *Herald*?"

Wikoff took, smoothly, this sudden assault. "As assassination is abhorrent to President Davis, so theft is abominable to me, dear lady."

"Then how could you *ever* have been suspected, Chevalier?" Miss Duvall held out her hand, which the Chevalier actually kissed, instead of his own thumb.

"At every court, Miss Duvall, there are favorites, and I am thought to be one at this court. Also, at every court, there are gossips. I hope that I am *not* a gossip—except when I praise the brilliance of our Republican Queen. Finally, at every court there are those who envy the favorite, and so... Dear Lady, you know the world."

"Better, I believe, for having known you, Chevalier." Miss Duvall swept him a great mock curtsey. "Come back in a week," he said in a low voice. "I shall have an answer for you from Richmond."

Happily, neither Seward nor Lincoln had the slightest inkling of what was being plotted in nearby Seventeenth Street. The President was stretched out on a settee with his legs dangling over the arm—so long were the legs that the feet rested on the floor—while Seward sat, demurely, at the massive desk which he had used in the days—happy days, he now thought—when he had been governor of New York. John Hay and Frederick Seward had been sent off to the adjacent parlor, as Seward had jovially put it, "To play."

"Governor, tell me, what shall I write to the Queen of England?"

Seward was prepared. He had written a draft of a letter of condolence to Queen Victoria, whose husband, Prince Albert, had died, while making more palatable to the Americans the British government's response to the *Trent* Affair. Seward read the letter in his special high-Episcopal voice. He was pleased that Lincoln seemed pleased. "Send it tomorrow, Governor, and I'll copy it out."

"Prince Albert was the best of the lot over there, and not even a politician. I suppose you've seen the press today on our statesmanlike resolution of the *Trent* Affair?" Seward could never believe that Lincoln was as indifferent to newspapers—other than Messrs. Greeley and Bennett—as he claimed.

"Well, I've looked at some. The boys read them for me. It would appear that the Southern papers are jubilant, while Mr. Bennett and Mr. Greeley are saddened and sickened." The President pulled a cushion into place just back of his head. Seward had often wondered whether or not he should keep a pair of slippers at hand so that Lincoln might enjoy every comfort of home in the Old Club House. Certainly, the President tended to make himself entirely at home both here and at the War Department. Seward wondered if Lincoln put his feet up in Chase's parlor. Although he rather doubted it, one never knew with this curiously unselfconscious man, who often spoke as if he was simply reporting on the thoughts that crossed his mind just as they were crossing it; yet, simultaneously, it was Seward's impression that Lincoln never said anything that he did not very much mean to say.

"I have been studying the art of war," said the President, dreamily, eyes half shut. "Almost every day I send John down to the Library of Congress to take out books that I see referred to in my reading. You know, there are actually times when I think that I may have the knack, since war is not at all that different from politics..."

"'An extension of politics by other means.'" Seward quoted; or paraphrased—he was never certain what the line was. He had come across it a good deal in his own recent reading—of English newspapers.

Lincoln nodded. "Clausewitz," he said, drawing out each syllable deliberately and correctly. "Or however he calls himself. John translates him for me. John's German is first-rate. Anyway, I don't see why *we* shouldn't try our hand at it—in a sort of auxiliary way, of course. I respect McClellan, if only because whatever secret genius I may or may not have for strategy, it stops a mile or two short of training an army and victualing it, the way he does. But, basically, our Young Napoleon is really an engineer, just the way we're lawyers. Now engineers have their uses, but I wonder if fighting a huge and complicated modern war is one of them."

Seward blew smoke rings at the smoky wood fire. "I think he can do it."

"I think he can, too. If I didn't . . ." Lincoln stretched his long legs so that they were now at a hundred-eighty-degree angle above the sofa. As he stretched, there were a number of crackling sounds. Seward was pleased to note that the President shared at least one of his own afflictions—arthritis. "But I do wonder, from time to time, at his reluctance to use this wonderful—and wonderfully expensive—army that we've given him."

"It's possible he has too much to do. After all, he must now do Scott's job as well as his own. That's a lot for any man."

"In a funny way," said Lincoln, "I've always thought that General Scott was right. This war can only be won in the west. Take Richmond, and what have you? A section of Virginia. But split the rebels in two, and they have no country. You've cut Virginia off from its hog and hominy. The Mississippi is the key. That's why I want us to build a railroad from Lexington to Knoxville."

"I don't think Congress will let you."

"Then we must find a way to persuade them. Or just do it ourselves, you know, under our . . ."

"*Your* inherent powers."

Lincoln nodded. "East Tennessee is pro-Union, which means the rebels are holding that territory by force. Senator Johnson swears that with the slightest aid from us, the folks back there will drive every last rebel out of the state."

"But McClellan has most of the army right here, on the Potomac. General Halleck hasn't got the means."

"You know General Scott's last official words to me were, 'Make Halleck general-in-chief.' But McClellan wanted the job, so he got it. And Halleck seemed the man to take Frémont's place in the west."

"Where he does nothing, either."

"At least he's not gone and freed all the slaves in his district." Lincoln shook his head. "I have never known such a subtle, calculating total fool as Mr. Frémont."

"But you must admit he's made himself irresistible to every abolitionist in the country, which means he's popular with the Committee on the Conduct of the War."

"On the other hand, Governor, he's not very popular with me." Lincoln was mild. "Why, if I'd let that order of his stand, we'd have lost Kentucky and East Tennessee and Missouri..." Lincoln drifted off. How, Seward wondered, not for the first time, did this man's mind work? "You know, after I ordered Frémont to cancel the order, he sent his wife to me." Seward knew, of course; everyone knew. But he said nothing, curious to hear Lincoln's side of the story. "Now you may not know this"—Lincoln shut his eyes—"but when I first ran for the Illinois legislature, I came out, more or less, for female suffrage; not exactly the most popular position to take back then, and in that part of the world."

"It is still not the most popular issue *anywhere* in the world, thank God."

"Well, Mrs. Frémont comes to see me late at night—right off the cars from the West—and threatens me to my face with an uprising against the government, led by the Frémonts and their radical friends. So I called her, in the nicest way, I thought, 'Quite a lady politician,' and she was madder than a wet hen and went and told everyone that *I'd* threatened *her!*" Lincoln sighed. "Is it possible that female suffrage may not be the answer to every human problem?"

Both men were silent. From the street came the sound of Negroes singing Christmas hymns. Seward felt in his pocket for coins. It was the custom in Washington, he had been told by his officious secretary in charge of protocol—what the President called white gloves and feathers—to give no more than a dollar to any one of the numerous groups of singers who went from house to house, celebrating the birth of the Lord.

"I gave General McClellan the fruit of my latest reading. I even devised a plan for him to use our army in both a frontal and flank attack on Manassas but..." Lincoln stopped.

"He told you that he had a better plan, which he would execute before the end of this month."

"Exactly!" Lincoln swung his legs to the floor. "Has he told you just what this better plan is?"

Seward shook his head. "No. He hasn't confided in me since

the unfortunate day when I alone seemed to know how many men we had on duty in the army."

"Yes, that was a most unfortunate day. It lost us General Scott."

"I wanted only, as always, to be helpful. It is my impression"— Seward's eyes filled suddenly with tears: an unexpected icy draught had blown his own cigar smoke into his own face—"that he confides in Mr. Chase."

"Perhaps." Lincoln was always noncommittal on the subject of the rivalries within the Cabinet.

"Mr. Cameron has also abandoned me for Mr. Chase."

"Well, Governor, you should be relieved." Lincoln rubbed the back of one hand across the deep-set small gray eyes, as if to erase all thought of Cameron. "I regard Cameron's appointment as the most... disgraceful thing I have ever done, or had to do, in my life."

"But isn't that how you got the nomination?" Seward kept his voice at the most casual level.

"No," said Lincoln, "that is *not* how I got the nomination but that is what people say, which is what matters. Actually, Judge Davis may take full credit for our alliance with Cameron. Just as I must take full blame for honoring an agreement to which I was not a party. Anyway, we must get him out of the War Department fast. What does he want?"

"The key to the Treasury."

"He can have it, once I've changed all the locks. What else?"

"I'll sound him out. I think you should send him some place far away..."

"Make him minister to France?"

"No. He's not got the right sort of keys for that. I was thinking maybe... Russia."

Lincoln roared with sudden laughter. "Why, Governor, that is capital! Cameron in Russia! Oh, that is real inspiration. I can just see that white bent face of his in all that snow they've got up there, trying to sell watered stock to the poor Czar. Well, that's your department. You clear the way for him."

"I've already taken it up with Baron Stoeckl, who doesn't object too strenuously. Now if I can persuade Mr. Chase that it was all *his* idea, the rest should be easy."

Lincoln leaned forward and picked an apple from a large silver bowl, a form of rude sustenance that did not much appeal to Seward but since Lincoln was addicted to every sort of fruit, Seward kept the bowl filled for presidential visits. As usual, Lincoln encircled with thumb and forefinger the apple's equator and then, no doubt in honor of the new envoy to Russia, he took a bite out of the apple's North Pole. As he chewed, slowly, methodically, like a horse, he talked: "Father Bates took me aside after Cabinet this morning and said that I was far too disorganized for my own good. He thought I should have military aides who would take down what I said, and then keep following up to see that what I wanted done was done; and then keep me informed, and so on."

"Well, I don't suppose any man is ever entirely wrong." Of the Cabinet ministers, after Blair and Welles, Seward disliked Bates most. "You know what Mr. Bates called me?" Seward shook his head with wonder. "An *unprincipled* liar. And here I am one of the most heavily principled men in politics."

Lincoln chuckled. In every way, making allowances for regional differences, Seward's humor was not unlike his own. "And since you're a smart man, Governor, you never actually lie. Smart men never have to." Lincoln put down the apple core; locked his fingers behind his head; stretched his back. "Which reminds me of this rich man from Lexington, Kentucky, who used to travel all over the world with his own servant, a white man. Now the rich man was a monstrous liar, and he knew it, and the servant knew it, and everyone in Lexington knew it. So, finally, after they got home from Europe one time, the rich man says to the servant, 'Now I want you to sit next to me tonight at dinner and if I start to spread it too thick, I want you to sort of nudge my foot with yours under the table.' So they go out to dinner and the rich man starts to describe one of the Egyptian pyramids which was, he says, 'made mostly of gold.' So, under the table, the servant kind of taps his shoe. 'So how high is it?' asks somebody. 'Oh, about a mile and a half,' says the rich man. As the servant's foot comes crashing down hard on his foot, someone else asks just how wide is this pyramid, and our man says, 'Oh, about a foot.'"

Laughter plainly invigorated Lincoln. It also acted as a challenge to Seward, himself no mean story-teller of the western New York variety. They swapped tales until, sides aching, lungs gasping for breath, Seward rose and opened the door to the parlor and said, "Come on in, boys!" And the boys did as they were told.

Hay had been pleased to hear Lincoln's laughter. Lately, there had not been much to laugh about. Whatever reservations Hay had about Seward—and they were many—he knew that the bright little man could relieve the President's mind, unlike Chase, who only added to his native gloom.

"Sir, I've written you a sonnet," Hay said to Seward.

"But, John, it is still six weeks to Valentine's Day."

"But it is today that war with England was averted, which is my subject."

Since the Tycoon and Seward insisted that Hay read his sonnet, he did, resonantly, to great applause. "I'll just take that for safekeeping," said Seward, slipping the poem in his pocket. "I shouldn't be surprised if our Johnny was a famous poet one day."

Seward then sent for champagne. "It is Christmas, after all." When Seward offered the President a glass, Lincoln took it, to Hay's surprise; and when Seward proposed a toast to the Union, Lincoln drained the glass. "I believe," he said, putting down the glass, "that that is enough champagne to last me the year..."

"Which ends six days from now. An eternity for me. Did you *never* drink, Mr. President?"

Lincoln straightened first his hair and then his coat. "Governor, I am a product of the Kentucky backwoods of forty years ago. I don't think there has ever been such heavy drinking anywhere in the world as there was back then—the men, the women, even the children." Lincoln looked suddenly somber in the flickering firelight. "Of course, I tried whiskey, like every other boy. But I could not bear the effect that it has on the mind, which is all I had in this world. You see, I never had more than a year of schooling and that was 'in littles,' as we called it—a month here, a week there. Anyway, when I saw what the drink was doing to so many of my friends, I said, no, it is not for me. So except for a glass of champagne kindly offered me once a year, I am usually dry as the African desert. But I am entitled to no great credit for abstinence, since I really hate the stuff."

"Hear that, son?" Seward turned on Frederick with mock ferocity. "If you would only do as your President does!"

"I was taught, sir, to imitate my father in all things," said Frederick, pouring himself and Hay champagne.

"'How sharper than a serpent's tooth...'" Seward began; then stopped and turned to Lincoln, curiously: "You were never temperance, were you?"

Lincoln laughed. "No. I am not given to oaths; and I never prescribe for others in these matters."

"I am relieved." The Premier was in a rare good humor and Hay was pleased that he had managed, for a time, to divert the Ancient from his cares. When Lincoln said, at last, that it was time to go, the Sewards, father and son, led them to the door. As Lincoln and Hay returned to the White House, they passed through a group of Negro singers who, much to Lincoln's amusement, did not recognize him. Solemnly, Lincoln proceeded to give them all of the coins in Hay's pocket. Hay had never known the Tycoon to carry money.

2

IT WAS KATE'S NOTION TO CELEBRATE BOXING DAY, WHICH NO one in Washington had ever thought to do before on the sensible ground that since Christmas was bad enough, it seemed perverse to celebrate yet again the next day. But Kate decided that this holiday, observed with such affection by the British, ought to be equally celebrated by their American cousins, particularly now that the *Trent* Affair had been solved.

Lord Lyons agreed. "Much the nicest of all the holidays," he said. "At home, anyway," he added, peering into the second parlor, where what looked to be most of the Senate was mingling with most of the generals in front of a huge crystal punch bowl that contained stimulants highly displeasing to the host, for whom water had been provided.

"You won't think our giving up the rebels a sign of total surrender to England?" Kate took the minister's arm and guided him away from the French minister, whom he did not much like, and toward General McDowell, whom he did.

For an English diplomat, Lyons could be surprisingly diplomatic. "Both sides surrendered to reason."

"Then you bear no grudge?"

"Oh, we hold no grudges in England. We never do, you know."

"I never knew!"

"Well, *now* you know, Miss Kate. I thought we all behaved marvelously well. Mr. Seward and I were particularly brilliant, if I may say so, controlling public opinion both here and at home." Lyons frowned. "But our greatest ally was Prince Albert." Queen Victoria's husband had died twelve days earlier. The British legation was in mourning. "It is too sad," he said.

"It is sad, *his* death," Kate answered, "but the end is happy, anyway." Then Kate turned and saw John Hay, smiling at her. For Hay, she was, simply, the most attractive girl in the town; of her sort, of course, which meant that she would be easily outshone at Sal Austin's, an unthinkable thought that he liked thinking about. "Oh, Mr. Hay!" Kate's teeth were small but even; and reasonably white. "Will the President be coming?"

"I don't think so. He's still recovering from the *Trent* Affair."

253

"Lord Lyons thinks that it was he—and Mr. Seward—who saved the day."

"As long as the day is saved, let them think it. Do you ever go to the theater?" Hay made his move.

"Naturally, I go. As often as possible. What you mean is, will I go with you?"

"Will you?"

"Will I?" Kate gave a small sigh. Then she was suddenly alert, eyes on the parlor door. "Here comes the Young Napoleon!" The room was suddenly still as General McClellan and his wife made their entrance, accompanied by half-a-dozen brilliantly uniformed aides. Hay noticed that the French princes were not among them. Usually, the princes were in close attendance upon McClellan in order to learn, firsthand from a master, the art of war. There were three of them: the Count of Paris, who was the rightful king of France (and known, locally, as Count Parry), his brother, the Duke of Chartres (known as Captain Chatters) and their uncle, the Prince of Joinville (seldom known to anyone). This evening they were elsewhere, to the relief of the French minister, M. Mercier, who represented the man who had usurped their throne, the Emperor Napoleon III.

McClellan stepped away from wife and aides and, solitary in his glory, he walked to the center of the front parlor, where Chase shook his hand. Kate curtseyed. Hay watched, grimly. Both Nicolay and Hay had come to the conclusion that the Young Napoleon was a fraud. But neither dared breathe a word of this to anyone, particularly to the Tycoon, who seemed, most of the time, under the spell of this small muscular young man, whose flashing eyes now took in the room as though it were the field at Austerlitz.

"I am here," he said, as if he had won some incredible victory.

"So you are, unmistakably," said Kate, with a delicate malice that warmed Hay's heart.

"I am happy that you could tear yourself away from camp," said Chase, to Hay's amusement. McClellan lived in a small house in H Street, not far from Seward's Old Club House. Although Little Mac—the soldiers' affectionate name for their commander—was constantly on the move from encampment to encampment, usually in the company of journalists and Democratic politicians (he was already spoken of as the Democratic candidate for president in '64), he spent no time at all in camp much less in confrontation with the enemy. All quiet on the Potomac, thought Hay, as he returned to the punch bowl.

Proudly, Chase presented to McClellan those grandees that the general did not know. The general's manners were exquisite. But then he was, as everyone including himself said, well-bred, the

254

heir to a well-to-do Philadelphia family. McClellan knew the world. He also knew china. "Unusual Meissen," he said to Kate, lifting a plate from the buffet and turning it over.

"I take pride in it," said Kate, pleased. "I didn't know you were a connoisseur of china, too."

"I know a *soupçon*, Miss Chase." The Young Napoleon gave her a quick smile. "I'd like to know more. One day . . ." McClellan looked sadly historical.

Once the ceremonious insertion of the hero into the party had been accomplished, Chase proceeded to draw McClellan to one side. "I think," he said, in a low voice, "that you should tell the President of your plan."

"And have him tell Tad? And have the rebels read all about it in the *Herald*? No thank you, sir. You, Mr. Chase, are the only member of the government I can trust with a secret, and whose counsel I value." The short general stepped back so that he would not have to look directly up at the tall Chase. Even so, Chase still looked down at him and noticed, with unusual clarity, how white and straight the parting in the general's sleek hair was. By squinting his right eye, Chase was able to make out clearly a set of handsome features through the now-perpetual haze. Chase also noticed that McClellan's face was somewhat tallowy looking in the bright glare of the gas lamps and that the face looked to be strewn with diamond dust, which, upon due reflection, Chase decided must be sweat.

"General, I am honored that you put so much confidence in me. I shall not betray it. But the President has asked you to move against Manassas . . ."

"His Excellency knows nothing . . . *nothing* of strategy. He reads a few out-of-date books and then spouts them at me." Abruptly, McClellan curbed his tongue. "His Excellency is a splendid man in many ways but he should leave fighting to us soldiers."

"That is what he is trying to do." Chase was diffident.

"It is pointless to go overland to Richmond. It is also pointless to go back to Manassas. But my plan, which involves surprise, of course, cannot fail." The voice was now almost a whisper; fortunately, Chase's hearing was uncommonly acute. "We go downriver. We establish ourselves at, say, Urbana, in the peninsula. Then, *from the east*, we move on to Richmond, and Richmond is ours."

"You know that I favor your plan . . ."

"I know. And I shall remember that, Mr. Chase."

"Well, yes. Thank you. That's good of you. Yes." Chase was still unable to deal with McClellan's Napoleonic style.

But Hay was more than capable of dealing with the Young

Napoleon; and was sorely tempted to do so. Later in the evening, he got his opportunity when he heard McClellan proclaim: "If the only way I could save the Union would be to become dictator and then, at the very moment of victory, die, I would do so."

Although a number of ladies applauded this sentiment, Senator Ben Wade looked skeptical, as befitted the chairman of the Joint Committee on the Conduct of the War. "Well, General, so far we haven't offered you the dictatorship."

McClellan mopped his brow with a handkerchief. "Of course you haven't, Senator. I was simply responding, hypothetically, to what the newspapers are writing. *They* have suggested it, not I." Wade of Ohio was a cleanshaven, hard-eyed little man who spoke out of the side of his mouth, and whose usual response to any statement by anyone was smiling disbelief. Wade was the Senate's leading Jacobin, as Nicolay and Hay always referred to the radical Republican element that found Lincoln weak and generally irresolute in the holy war against slavery anywhere and everywhere on earth. "We'll be holding hearings soon, General," said Wade, pursing carplike lips as best such lips can be pursed, thought Hay, currently fascinated by the logic of similes; he had begun to write poetry again. "We look forward to hearing your plans for next year now that this year is over, with no victories."

"No victories?" McClellan turned to the others. "Senator Wade is too modest. At Bull Run, when our highly . . . trained army was in retreat, Senator Wade and Senator Chandler—two civilian observers—drew their pistols and stopped the rout."

"I had no idea you were so brave, Mr. Wade." As always, Sumner was without irony. As always, he was literal. He turned back to McClellan. "But, General, brave as our senators are, they could not stop the rout for long."

Wade smiled with anger. "We did what we could, which wasn't much that day. The troops were not ready."

"Of course not, Senator. That's why I was called in. To make them ready." Hay admired McClellan's coolness at a moment when the Young Napoleon was, literally, sweating. Either he was suffering unduly from nerves, not very likely in the familiar arena of his greatest triumphs thus far—the Washington salon—or he had a touch of Potomac fever. McClellan turned away from Wade, only to find himself face-to-face with Hay, who gave Little Mac his very special backwoods grin. "Good evening, General."

"Mr. . . . uh, Hay." McClellan looked about for reinforcements but there were none at hand.

"We were sorry about the other night, when you were indisposed."

256

"The other night?" McClellan affected not to know what Hay was talking about. "Indisposed?"

"Don't you remember? The President and Mr. Seward and I came to your house in H street, and the porter said you had gone to a wedding. So we waited in your parlor for an hour. Then you came home and went upstairs, passing right by the President. So we waited another half hour, and then the President sent the porter to you to say he was still waiting and you sent down word to us to say that you'd gone to bed." Hay was delighted at his own courage. Although Lincoln had been amiable about the whole affair, Hay had been furious at the insult to the President.

"There was some misunderstanding, I believe." The Young Napoleon glared at Hay. "I had not realized that it was His Excellency. He comes to me so often, without warning." McClellan again mopped his now nacreous face.

"I don't think that he will do so again." Hay bowed as he had seen Lord Lyons bow to the President, endlessly courteous and entirely superior. But the effect was somewhat spoiled by the arrival of the French princes, who came between him and McClellan. Aware that he was now bowing to the ample backside of the Count of Paris, Hay straightened up and turned away. Chase gave him a hesitant vague smile. Since Hay knew that Chase saw less than he pretended, he always identified himself, politely, to what he and Nicolay regarded as the President's only real rival.

"Of course I saw you, Mr. Hay." Chase drew Hay toward him in order to present him to Thaddeus Stevens, whose hard Roman face cracked slightly in order to produce a smile. "I'm sorry that the President and Mrs. Lincoln could not come."

"The President has gone to bed, and Mrs. Lincoln has her relations at the Mansion," said Hay, studying, as always, Stevens's wig, so much more serious in its classical pretensions than Gideon Welles's somewhat too romantic seascape of false hair.

"I suspect," said Chase, "that I made a mistake in renting a house so far from the Mansion. Mr. Lincoln never drops in." Chase was as droll as Chase could be, which was not much. "On the other hand, Messrs. Blair and Welles and Stanton are right across the street . . ."

"General McClellan, too," added Stevens, hard eyes taking in the prizefighter figure of the general, posed now beneath a chandelier at the room's center, right hand in his blouse like Napoleon, face streaked with sweat.

"Yes, the general, too."

At that moment, the pale Cameron was upon them. "Oh, Mr. Stevens," said Cameron, softly to his perennial enemy.

"Oh, Mr. Cameron," repeated Stevens, in exactly the same

whispery tone of voice. Hay thought of the red-hot stove story; and wondered, as always, at how much abuse politicians could so easily take from one another.

"Things are really moving now, aren't they?" Cameron said to Chase, ignoring Hay.

"*Some* things, yes," said Chase, vaguely.

"Which things?" Stevens affected innocence.

"Oh, the war." Cameron looked at Stevens with what Hay took to be calculated neutrality.

"Then you must come before our committee and tell us all about it. You see, because we are so remote from the grand strategy, we never know anything at all, and because we are so patriotic, we'd never think of prying." Stevens's intellectual elegance appealed to Hay, even though the man was so radical that he would gladly destroy the Union to free the slaves. Hay took it as an ominous sign that now two members of the Conduct of the War Committee seemed to be proposing immediate hearings.

Chase also picked up on this. "You must wait, Mr. Stevens, until the grand design has taken shape."

"I am not a young man, Mr. Chase. But I would like to live long enough to see the Negro freed."

"Oh, you're too hard on us, Mr. Stevens." Cameron affected comity. "Mr. Chase and I are exactly the same. You read my report to Congress, on the necessity of freeing and arming the niggers? Slaves, that is."

"A late conversion is better than none at all. Isn't it, Mr. Chase? Or as the Bible says, 'He who believeth in me . . .'"

Cameron was not amused by Stevens's mocking tone. "I did not know you had been converted to Christianity, Mr. Stevens. Is this the work of Mrs. Stevens?"

Chase cleared his throat nervously. Everyone knew that Stevens was a free-thinker, while, behind his back, everyone referred to the mulatto woman with whom he had lived for twenty years as "Mrs. Stevens." Chase was about to change the subject, when Stevens's cool response came: "Since my late mother, to whom you allude, Mr. Cameron, was a dedicated Baptist, and since all that I am or ever hope to be is thanks to her example and to her sacrifice on my behalf, I have read all the Holy Books, and subscribe wholeheartedly to the Ten Commandments, which must make me an oddity, particularly to those who regard as not binding the Eighth Commandment."

Cameron affected not to hear any of this. "General McDowell is signalling to me," he said; and moved away.

"You must be kinder to our latest recruit." Chase had been both alarmed and delighted by Stevens's ornate insult.

"Oh, kindness . . . !" Stevens turned to Hay. "Are you kind, sir?"

"No, sir," said Hay. "I don't think I am."

"But surely," said Chase, the only believing Christian of the three, "you *try* to be."

"Well, no, sir, I don't think I do. At least not very hard." Hay was caught up in the Thaddeus Stevens style, which he admired quite as much as he feared, on political grounds, its possessor.

"You see, Mr. Chase? There is a candid young man. He is like me. What kindness we possess is of a general nature. You will be a statesman one day, Mr. Hay. No doubt of that. Meanwhile, be candid, and tell us, who is the spy in the White House?"

"I don't know. I don't know that there is one." Hay was not prepared for this brutal assault.

"If the *New York Herald* can steal state papers, just think what a good Confederate spy like the delicious Mrs. Greenhow might get her hands on."

"Mrs. Greenhow has never set foot in Mrs. Lincoln's White House." Hay rallied. "But it's true that thousands of people come through every day, and who can stop them?"

"I would," said Chase, "if I were in Mr. Lincoln's place. He sees far too many people. He wastes his time. He tires himself out."

"That," said Stevens, "is what we have a president for. Even so, you should have a strongbox, Mr. Hay. With a padlock and a key."

"We do, sir. But somehow . . ."

"Somehow things vanish. Well, we shall be getting around to all that in due course. Meanwhile, in my capacity as chairman of the Ways and Means Committee, I must warn you that Mrs. Lincoln has gone over her budget for the renovation of the house."

"Oh, has she?" Hay feigned innocence.

"Oh, has she?" Stevens mocked Hay's tone. "Yes, she has. We will have to look into that, too."

All in all, a dark winter, thought Hay, as Chase went to bid farewell to the McClellans and the French princes, and Stevens joined Wade in a corner, where Hay could see them grinning like a pair of alligators. Hay looked at his watch. He was due to meet Robert Lincoln at Harvey's Oyster Bar; then they would drop in on the Eameses; then there was a dance at the house of the Russian minister, Baron Stoeckl, where he would abandon the virginal son of the President for the delights of Marble Alley. He might not be the poet that Poe was, but he could at least live to the full the poet's life of the senses. Could he marry Kate? he wondered, as he said good-night to her. He decided that he probably could;

259

but should he? There was so much he had not done yet. She would have to wait, poor girl. From now until New Year's Day, he could give himself up to pleasure. The President was in a lenient mood, and the current crisis passed.

On the other hand, Mr. Thompson was never lenient with employees. He would not allow David to take so much as an hour off until the beginning of the official holiday, which was the afternoon of New Year's Eve, and all of New Year's Day. "Though if ever there was a time for us to be open, it is on the afternoon of the first day of the New Year, when we can supply the one thing that most men will most desperately need."

"Women, too," said David, who had more than once noticed elegant ladies getting in and out of their carriages in a drunken state. The city was turning into one continuous party, which David quite enjoyed, even though no one had thought to ask him to it.

But David had been asked to have supper with the Surratts on New Year's Eve when, at midnight, Annie would celebrate her nineteenth birthday and become, for the next six months, the same age as David. He had seen little of her since last summer. When she was not at Surrattsville, she was giving music lessons. Also, as the old Surratt weakened, David had less reason to go to their house. He had no reason at all to go to his own house except to sleep. Thanks to the war, those of his several sisters who were unmarried—the majority—were in constant turmoil, like a half-dozen hens surrounded by two hundred thousand roosters. Mrs. Herold was now in a state bordering on madness. She could think of nothing but the endangered virginity of her daughters; even the ones who were neither entirely youthful nor well-favored caused her loudly to despair. The house in the Navy Yard was now like a military encampment. "Who goes there?" was the shrill greeting from upstairs whenever a daughter or the single family rooster came home late, to the sound of warped floorboards groaning.

In the daytime, officers were encouraged to pay calls. Private soldiers were discouraged at all times. The Herold daughters were repeatedly lectured on dangers that they understood far better than their worthy mother, who favored, one day, marriages to men who might soon be killed; then, next day, wept at the thought of young widows left with babies in a harsh world. Just to be out of the house, David had lived for two months with the ham-lady of the Navy Yard. Since she was a successful grocer who let rooms, she was not suspected by Mrs. Herold of powerful appetites; in fact, the deeply innocent Mrs. Herold thought that the ham-lady, whom she knew slightly, might be a good influence on David. But when he finally tired of ham, and returned to what he now thought of as the hive of the queen bees, Mrs. Herold was glad to have a man about the house again, and straight away cooked him a splendid dinner, featuring, to his distress, ham and red-eye gravy.

David wished Mr. Thompson a Happy New Year. Then he set out for the Surratt's house by way of Scipio's bar. The streets were full of soldiers, many already drunk. Nowadays, David seldom saw any of his old cronies, the true Washingtonians. It was not that they had all left the city. Rather, the city had so filled up that the natives were lost amongst the tens of thousands of strangers, not to mention the altogether-too-sturdy-for-David's-taste boys in faded blue uniforms.

As usual, Scipio's was crowded. But then every bar in town was crowded. Attempts to keep soldiers out of the bars and in the camps had, so far, failed.

David found himself a place near the cash register, jammed between two Union corporals who talked across him and spat tobacco juice on the sawdust-covered floor.

"Happy New Year, Davie." Scipio served David a beer. "Like you see, it never lets up now. I get no time to play violin anymore."

David looked sorrowfully about the bar. As recently as a year ago, he would have had half-a-dozen wild boys to talk to, not to mention actors from the theaters and, best of all, actresses. But now the soldiers had crowded everyone else out of the barroom, just as the two corporals now crowded David away from the bar, obliging him to shove his way through the crowd, narrowly avoiding, en route, a sudden jet of vomit from a beardless youth. David looked into the dining room. Here, at least, there were no soldiers. Washington theatergoers were still in the majority at the round marble tables; and there were actors, too. David recognized the famous ingenue, Emily Glendenning. She was eating lobster at a corner table. On stage, she looked no older than he. But like so many actresses, she looked a good deal older up close. At the moment, she was cracking a lobster's claw, and pretending to listen with interest to John T. Ford, the proprietor of the theater next door, a pleasant man of thirty who not only knew David by name but gave him jobs whenever he could.

As David waved good-night to Skippy, who did not see him, he felt like a stranger in his own city. Perhaps he should go south to Richmond, after all, and join the army.

But Mr. Surratt said no. Propped up in his bed, the old man was skeletal; the cords in his neck were like hangman's rope, thought David, always sensible of the fate that could befall anyone the Yanks decided was a traitor.

David sat in the chair beside Mr. Surratt's bed and tried not to breathe too deeply the air in the room, which smelled partly of coal-smoke from the front parlor and partly of dying. In David's professional capacity as Thompson's courier, there was little that he did not know about the ways and the smells and the sounds of the dying. In the front parlor, Annie was playing a very sad Scottish ballad on the piano, while singing voices joined in from time to time, some taking the high road, others the low.

"I'll soon be gone." The old man seemed so pleased at the prospect that David did not bother to contradict him. "But, first, I want you to promise me you won't leave where you are." Since Mr. Surratt was going in any event, David could not see why he was now making it a condition of his departure that David stay at Thompson's. But he told the old man, "Of course, I'll stay there, if that'll help us."

"Oh, it will help us. Don't worry." There was a pause, as Mr. Surratt gasped for breath. He no longer coughed. Any day now, he would, literally, lose his breath, and life. "There is a man coming tonight. He is called Henderson. From the Center Market. Been there for years. Poultry. He'll tell you what to do." The old man reached under the covers and withdrew a rosary, which he proceeded to drape around long yellow knotty fingers. "He'll take my place, Henderson will."

Mr. Surratt shut his eyes. David assumed that he was praying. In the other room, the ballad had ended; and some were in Scotland afore others. There was a good deal of laughter. Mr. Surratt opened his eyes. "Mrs. Greenhow's a real loss to us."

"They're moving her to Old Capitol next week, or so Miss Duvall says."

"*She's* good." Mr. Surratt nodded. "Mr. Pinkerton thinks he knows all about us but we know more about him and General McClellan than they'll ever know about us. Davie..."

"Yes, sir?"

"Right now, we got one thing to do above all others. It's this. Feed 'em wrong figures." Mr. Surratt chuckled. "That's the ticket!"

David was puzzled. "Wrong figures about what?"

"Size of our army. Henderson sees to it that a pack of coded messages from Richmond comes Pinkerton's way. They all tell about troop movements, and they all give the numbers, and every number's wrong. That's how we got Little Mac thinking our army's twice the size of his, when it's nowhere near."

"But we got as many men as the Yanks, don't we?" This is what every newspaper had written.

Mr. Surratt's smile was like that of a skull whose bottom jaw had come unhinged. "We got barely half the men they got and close to no arms at all."

"I didn't know."

"You didn't hear me, neither. But that's our game from now on. That's orders from Richmond. Fool the fool Yankees who want to be fooled anyways, after Bull Run. Kind of hard having to admit you got whipped by a smaller army. So don't forget that now. We double the figures."

"Yes, sir."

"John's home. He'll help. Don't know just how." The beads of the rosary now began to slip more rapidly through the long fingers.

At eighteen, John Surratt, Junior, looked exactly like Jefferson Davis. "Except," said David, "you don't have that little beard."

"I'm doing my best to grow it," said John, whose voice was deep and educated, and belonged to a man twice his age. The two young men sat side by side on Mrs. Surratt's dining-room chairs, watching some thirty relatives and friends of the family, mostly from Surrattsville, celebrate the successful end of 1861. Annie played dance music; and Mrs. Surratt danced a reel with her brother Zadoc Jenkins; and John told David that he would finish up next June at St. Charles, a Catholic school in Howard County, Maryland. "I went there all set to go into the priesthood, but now that we're at war, I think I'll be more use to God fighting on the right side."

"It must be nice to have so much education." Although David knew ten times what this sheltered boy knew of the world, he felt oafish when he was with him, as he never felt, say, with Annie. But then she was a girl.

"Oh, it serves a purpose, I guess. In ordinary times, I'd have been a priest, I think—or thought. I had the vocation—or thought I had. So did the president of the college, Father Jenkins—no relation of ours either."

"Will you fight now?"

John frowned. "It's being useful that matters, isn't it?"

"I think so. I do what I can." David was pleased with himself; he had never sounded so useful or so patriotic before; but then he had not had much chance to show off. He dared not with Mr. Thompson and he could not, really, with Mrs. Greenhow and Miss Duvall, while old Mr. Surratt was the one who gave him orders and Annie was—Annie.

"That's all any of us can do. My father says you're worth a whole regiment of cavalry to us."

"Does he?" David glowed; and drank more punch. As Surrattsville's general store-owners and tavern-keepers—not to mention Roman Catholics—the Surratts were not temperance like Mrs. Herold. There was good rye whiskey in the fruit punch. The

263

Surratts also ran the town's post office. "I expect to take over as postmaster in July."

"I'd like that, to be a postmaster." David had never heard of a postmaster as young as John.

"What's it like, riding through the Yankee lines?" John had lowered his voice. He looked at David with what David took to be piercing eyes. David had read enough novels to know that his own eyes were darkly glowing.

"You just act stupid, that's all. You know, like a dumb ole farm boy. They don't even search you then. Oh, I've had a few scares, let me tell you." David told him of some, pleased to see the piercing eyes become palely glowing.

Then Annie asked him to dance, as her mother played. "It's almost midnight," she whispered. "The New Year."

"And now you're nineteen like me."

"Oh, don't remind me!"

At midnight, everyone related to Annie—half the room as well as David—kissed her. Then Mrs. Surratt raised high her glass of punch and said, "Let's drink to victory."

They drank to victory. Then David kept on drinking to victory for the rest of the night. But before he got drunk, he was able to talk to Mr. Henderson of the Center Market, not an easy task.

Mr. Henderson was small and round and gray, with a beaked nose and shining eyes. Like so many of the farmers at Center Market, he resembled what he sold. David had grown up in terror of the Market's pig-lady, who came in once a week from Virginia with ham and sausage; though toothless, she was, plainly, not harmless; she seemed capable, like any formidable old sow, of eating up a child. Though Mrs. Herold would talk to her for hours at a time about mutual acquaintances in Berryville, David could never understand a word the old woman said. To his ear, it was simply the ominous sound of a pig snuffling.

Mr. Henderson did not speak; he clucked, "I know your mother, Davie. Years back, she used to buy poultry from me. In the southwest corner, that's me. Then we went and disagreed over a pullet's age. That was in 'fifty-one. She buys now from the Mayberrys. In the southeast corner. No hard feelings."

"I hope not, Mr. Henderson."

"No hard feelings," the plump chicken repeated. "I work with Mr. Surratt, too."

"I know. He told me. Just now."

"Old John's about to end, I fear. Hope all this popery"—with a wave, Henderson indicated the painting of Jesus's heart, the crucifix on the table, the rosary—"helps. I'm Baptist. So all this is just," Henderson literally cackled, "Pope's *nose* to me!"

Dutifully, David laughed. Then said, "What'll you want me to do?"

"Stay at Thompson's. Keep your eyes and ears open. Do the McClellans ever stop by, now they're in H Street?"

"I never saw the general. But she came one day. She's bossy but not bad-looking. Usually, they send a soldier. They got a new baby so there's all kinds of things they buy."

"Try to make a delivery yourself. Get to know people at the house. The way you've done with Mr. Seward, who leaves papers lying around." It was not David but Mrs. Greenhow—when at large—who had noticed the previous summer a memorandum on Seward's desk, listing the strength of each regiment attached to the Army of the Potomac. "Pity you can't get inside the Mansion."

"But I can, and I have. I been there two, three times," said David. "But the place is so big you've got to know where to go, which, I guess, is back of that funny wooden fence they got in the upstairs hall where the President and the others all work, and which they guard most of the time."

"But not *all* the time." Chicken Henderson cocked his head to one side, like a hen listening for thunder or the fox. "We have our people there, too. But not enough. Well, keep on. Stay away from Miss Duvall, fine young lady that she is."

"They fixing to arrest her?"

"Yes. I told her to go South. But she says she won't. I hope she will. Well, Happy New Year, Davie. I must go. I hope it's not still raining."

The rain had stopped; and remained stopped through most of the morning of New Year's Day when David, for patriotic reasons, stationed himself in front of the White House, despite a head that hurt him even after a pint of his own variation of Mr. Thompson's famed morning-after painkiller and pick-me-up. The guards were letting everyone through the main gate. In principle, David could have joined the long line of people who wanted to shake the President's hand, but he preferred to stand at the foot of the steps to the portico and watch the invited guests descend from their carriages, take the arm of Mr. McManus or one of the ushers and cross the frozen mud to the steps.

While David was doing his best to act like a spy, an army band appeared in front of the Mansion and began to serenade the President. As the band struck up "Hail Columbia!" the great door of the White House swung open and Father Abraham himself appeared. A round of cheers filled the frosty air with steam. He lifted his hat and smiled. The sentries to the left and the right of the door came to a sharp attention. As Lincoln moved to the edge of the portico, the crowd fell back on either side of him, under the busy direction of Mr. McManus. But David was so positioned that if he were to lean forward as far as he could, he could have touched the President, who looked skinnier than ever, he thought; and somewhat yellow in the face. Nevertheless, all in all, David thought him a pleasant-looking man.

The band had now finished "Hail to the Chief." Lincoln then spoke in a loud high voice that could be heard all the way to St. John's Church on the far side of Lafayette Square. "I am happy to see all of you at the beginning of the New Year, a year that will bring us, I am certain, to the end of this great trouble."

There was cheering from the crowd. Lincoln took off his hat; gave a nod of his head; then started to go inside. At that moment, the band struck up "The Star-Spangled Banner" and the President was obliged to remain standing, hatless, looking toward the band on the muddy lawn. Behind him, a small boy appeared in the White House doorway, clutching a folded flag. David recognized the famous Tad; so did McManus. But before Tad could be intercepted, he had unfurled a large Confederate flag, which he began merrily to wave. The crowd on the lawn started to laugh. Puzzled, the President turned; then he stooped down, gathered child and flag in both arms and, to the cheers of the onlookers, he marched into the White House, holding his struggling burden at arms' length. Mr. McManus shut the door behind them.

As David walked down the White House driveway, the carriage of the Secretary of the Treasury nearly ran him down. Even so, he was able to get a quick glimpse of the famous Kate, who looked very pretty—and wonderfully clean. A younger girl was with her; and a spinster-looking woman. David decided that he should keep a commonplace book. But first he would have to learn how to write in code.

Chase led his daughters, Kate and Nettie, and his old friend Susan Walker of Cincinnati into the crowded East Room, where Lincoln stood, shaking every hand, while Mrs. Lincoln, stationed to one side, shook no hands but smiled and nodded to all—except Kate, to whom she merely nodded, and to Chase, to whom she merely pursed her lips, unaware that her expression was entirely invisible to him as he glided through his usual subaqueous element.

Lincoln shook Chase's hand; then he said, in a low voice, "Have you seen our Young Napoleon?"

"No, sir. I called. But they would not let me in to see him."

"I had the same experience."

"I am told that it is typhoid. He'll be in bed at least a month."

"I heard the same." Lincoln frowned. "Others have seen him."

266

"Who?"

But Lincoln merely shook his head; and turned to the next visitor in line, the minister from the Hansen Republic of Bremen, Baron Schleiden, a drinking crony, Chase knew, of Seward's. The redoing of the East Room was almost complete. Kate pointed out to her father what she took to be the most expensive highlights, beginning with the huge velvet rug. "Sea green, with roses," she said.

"Yes, I see the green. I will take the roses on trust."

"I rather think that's how she got the rug," said Kate, beaming and nodding as the diplomatic corps made the rounds of the room, wishing everyone a Happy New Year. "They say it cost two thousand five hundred dollars."

"Does she mean to compete with the youthful mistress of Sixth and E?"

"Father! I am economical. Mrs. Lincoln is not."

"I know. Mr. Stevens tells me she has gone so far over Congress's budget that the President will have to pay out of his own pocket. He won't like that. He is a frugal man."

"Like you."

"Oh, I am doomed to debt."

"Shall I marry Governor Sprague, and finance the debt?"

"No, let us be poor together."

"In debtors' prison," said Kate, giving her hand to Lord Lyons, who kissed it while Chase beamed and said, "*Pax est perpetua!*"

"Oh, let's hope so, Mr. Chase. Let's hope so. We've done good work, all of us."

"You and Mr. Seward, particularly," said Chase.

"Mr. Seward has heard his name invoked." The small roguish figure was suddenly at Chase's side, shaking Kate's hand with his right and Chase's with his left, while looking at Lord Lyons, who said, "I was discussing the good work we did, you and I, to keep the hotheads from going to war."

"Simply newspaper talk," said Seward airily. "Also it helped my having got to know your government in the summer of 'fifty-nine when I took my grand tour of Europe, and everyone greeted me with such warmth. You see," he said to Kate, "they thought I was going to be the next President."

"Which is exactly what you thought, wasn't it?" said Kate.

"Well, let's say if I *didn't* think it, I never let on. Anyway, I met the lot, from Queen Victoria, who shows slightly more than an inch of upper gum when she laughs—"

"Sir, this is *casus belli.*" Lyons was stern.

"Sir, in western New York a show of gum is considered the outward and visible sign of God's especial favor."

267

"War is averted. We shall not set the world aflame just yet."
Lyons enjoyed quoting Seward to Seward. "But I must remind
you, we are all in mourning for Prince Albert."

Kate turned to Lyons. "The press tells us that she is mad with
grief."

"Your press will tell you anything, Miss Chase." Lyons was
serene, as always. "The Queen is not mad. But she is in deepest
mourning. Curious, isn't it, Mr. Seward, that the Prince should
have died while consulting with the ministry on the *Trent* Affair."

"I suspect we are all in his debt," said Seward, graciously. "But
I have never been able to fathom just how powerful your powerless
sovereigns are."

"We have the same difficulty," said Lyons, "trying to fathom
exactly how powerful the Secretary of State is in a presidential
system."

"*Touché!*" Kate exclaimed. Then she asked Lyons for news of
the journalist Russell. During this, Seward slipped away, having
caught a glimpse of the one person whom he most wanted to see.

The short, thickset Edwin M. Stanton stood alone, royally
framed by the East Room's splendid new damask curtains. Stanton's black frock coat, with fashionable black velvet lapels, was
open to reveal a not-so-fashionable black waistcoat with, again,
black velvet lapels. Stanton always reminded Seward of the Auburn, New York, bank manager who had murdered his mother.
Stanton was gazing about the room through small pebble glasses,
his habitual sneer curiously accentuated by the bristly gray whiskers that appeared to be attached to his plump chin as arbitrarily
as an Egyptian Pharaoh's ornamental beard. It was rumored that
Stanton kept the ashes of his first wife—or was it his daughter?—
on the mantelpiece in his parlor; and that the second wife was
obliged to polish, each day, this somber reliquary.

Warily, the two men greeted each other. Seward knew that,
earlier in the week, Stanton had intended to resign as special legal
counsel to the Secretary of War; and go to New York, where a
rich law partner awaited him. But when the word began to spread
that Cameron would soon be gone, and that Stanton might succeed him, Stanton had delayed his removal to New York. Presently, he was in a state of irritable limbo. The President had not
yet offered him the post that was still unrelinquished by Cameron.
Although Seward knew that Chase was doing everything in his
power to get the War Department for Stanton, Seward took some
pleasure in the fact that Chase did not know that Stanton was also
Seward's own choice. Like Lincoln, Seward wanted pro-Union
Democrats in high places. Unlike Chase, he did not want abolitionists anywhere. On this burning issue, Seward tended to ad-

mire Stanton's wonderfully righteous hypocrisy. With Chase and the radical Republicans, Stanton was an abolitionist, constantly railing at the moderate "original gorilla," Stanton's much-quoted description of Lincoln, in the White House. With Lincoln and Seward, Stanton simply stood for the Union and deplored radical zeal. Seward also knew something that hardly anyone else knew. It was Stanton who had not only written for Cameron the fatal recommendation to Congress that the freed Negroes be armed but it was Stanton who had convinced Cameron that in this way he could maintain his hold on the War Department, by giving pleasure to the Committee on the Conduct of the War. With Iagoesque skill, Stanton had led to destruction his chief. Now Iago stood, somewhat bleakly, in the East Room, uncertain of his own future.

"I must," said Stanton, controlling heroically his asthma, "congratulate you on the *Trent* Affair. I thought your . . . summing-up was masterful."

"I know so little international law." Seward played at modesty. "And I know almost nothing about arbitration."

"But you know everything, sir, about politics."

"Well, I certainly know something." One of the things that Seward knew which Stanton did not know that he knew was Stanton's anger at the Administration for having given way to England. Seward smiled, almost warmly, at the odd but brilliant Ohio lawyer who would soon be joining a Cabinet that, such was his oddness and honesty and irritability—there was no other word— he could never stop attacking in private. "Stanton is two-faced," a disapproving senator had said to Seward, who was rather pleased with his own classical response: "So was Janus, the god of war." But Seward was not above torturing, ever so slightly, his highly anxious soon-to-be colleague. "I saw your old friend Joseph Holt at the White House yesterday."

The look of pain in Stanton's face gave Seward exquisite pleasure; thus, he began to balance out their accounts with each other. The Kentuckian Holt had served with Stanton in Buchanan's Cabinet. Like Stanton, Holt was a pro-Union Democrat; he was also an anti-abolitionist, unlike Stanton, whose second face forever smiled upon the radicals. "The President is more inclined to you than to Holt, of course. But there are great pressures upon him. Great pressures." Seward frowned.

Stanton scowled. "Mr. Holt is very able, of course. And does not hate the black man as much as people say."

Feeble, thought Seward; but prompt. "Mr. Chase, of course, is your sponsor in all of this. You are both from Ohio."

"But I am removed to Pennsylvania."

"Like Mr. Cameron, yes. You are also Mr. Cameron's choice, if he should leave."

"I did not know."

Seward appreciated the honest and open way that Stanton lied; it was the hallmark of the truly great lawyer, and demonstrated a professional mastery not unlike his own. Otherwise, they had little in common. Stanton was mercurial and vain and compulsively duplicitous; nevertheless, he was incorruptible when it came to money—a matter of some importance in the wake of Cameron and his friends who, like so many carrion-birds, had feasted off the Treasury. Stanton was also a passionate worker; again, a perfect contrast to the indolent Cameron.

"Mr. Blair favors Senator Wade," said Seward, accurately.

"In order to get him to leave the Joint Committee?" Stanton was quick to respond.

"Well, sometimes it is better to have your critics and rivals working for you than against you."

"I am sure," said Stanton, upper lip curling, "that Mr. Lincoln has been a beneficiary of this unusual system."

"Oh, he has! He has! But there are times when he knows that when all is said and done, the most able man must be appointed." Seward was aware that he was somewhat overdoing what his critics enjoyed referring to as Seward's Buncombe; but he could not help himself. "How do you get on with General McClellan?"

"We are very close," said Stanton. "In fact, he came to me just the other day for a legal opinion on the *Trent* Affair."

Seward laughed; to disguise his anger. "And here I thought he was busy, twenty-four hours a day, getting the army ready to attack Richmond. Instead, he concerns himself with the laws of nations."

Stanton flushed. "It was simply in the line of what he takes to be his duty as general-in-chief."

Seward let the matter drop. "You think him capable?" he asked.

Stanton nodded. "He is certainly preferable to Halleck. General Scott's . . . legacy."

"Yes." Seward was noncommittal. Then his friend Baron Schleiden approached, and wreathed Seward with compliments for his resolution of the *Trent* Affair. When Seward had accepted the last of a dozen verbal garlands, he turned to Stanton; and found him gone.

"Is that . . . or *was* that," asked Schleiden, "the next Secretary of War?"

"Now, Baron, if I didn't know for certain, I would gladly tell you." Seward linked his arm through Schleiden's. "Come by my house later, and we shall play a rubber of whist, and I will give you news that will inflame the Baltic sea, and turn to ashes your native Bremen, the Venice of the north."

"Actually, we are more the Leghorn of the north," said the amicable Baron, bowing low to Mrs. Lincoln, as they passed.

Mary gave a courteous nod to Baron Schleiden, whom she mistrusted because of his friendship for Seward; and she gave Seward a sweet smile because of the President's mistaken trust in him. Then, to her horror, she saw the Chevalier Wikoff enter the room. He stood in the doorway a moment; bowed at Mary, who did not respond; then he withdrew, to her relief.

"I told him not to come." Resplendent in his uniform as brigadier-general, Dan Sickles had seen the whole mute exchange.

"Would, sir, that he had followed your advice." Mary carefully set a smile on her lips. As they talked to each other in low voices, her eyes were not on Sickles but on the parade of notables who moved past her, bowing and curtseying. "Why does he stay on in Washington?" she asked.

"Mr. Bennett's orders."

"Why does he come *here?*"

"To ingratiate himself, I suppose. He's asked me to be his defense attorney."

"*Defense!*" Mary's smile vanished. She turned to Sickles. "Is there to be a trial?"

Sickles shook his head. "I wish there was. You'd both be safer."

"We . . . *both?* Sir!" Mary was torn between anger and terror.

"I'm sorry, Mrs. Lincoln. I only meant that since your name will be brought into all this in any case, we could control events more easily in a court of law."

"Where, if not a law court, is he . . . are *we*, as you put it, sir, to be tried?"

"Before the Judiciary Committee of the House of Representatives."

"My God!" Mary wrung the stems of the hothouse flowers that she held in both hands.

"Because they are all my old colleagues, the Chevalier wants me to act as his counsel."

"But, sir, what do they have to go on? Simply rumors in the vampire press . . ."

"I'm sorry, Mrs. Lincoln. I thought you knew. Yesterday the committee obtained a copy of the telegram that our friend Wikoff sent to the *Herald*. There were parts of the President's message in it, word for word. The telegram was sent four days before the message went to Congress."

Mary wondered what the effect might be if she were to faint; and to remain unconscious until all of this had passed; or, better

271

yet, to die. Between the Wikoff scandal and the constant turmoil regarding the money that she was spending on the White House, death would be a convenient release. "What," asked Mary, summoning up every reserve of coolness that she possessed, "will your defense be?"

"I don't know." Sickles looked at her, thoughtfully. "What do you think it should be?"

"Whatever," said Mary, "is the truth, I suppose. Does the Chevalier say who it was that gave him the message?" Mary was pleased with her own show of coolness.

"No," said Sickles. Then he added, ominously, "Madam."

"Will he say that it was I?"

"He *must* not." Sickles stared directly into her eyes.

"I agree, sir. He must not, ever, say such a thing. Can you . . . see to that, General?"

"I think so, Madam. We are at war."

"Yes." Mary was grim. "And we must not give comfort to the enemy, or show any division in our ranks."

The President approached them, smiling. "Come on, Mother," he said. "The Marine Band wants to serenade us. Good to see you, General."

"Mr. President." Sickles clicked his heels. He was, Mary decided, loyal; and if anyone could manage a committee of this particular Congress, it would be their popular former colleague.

En route to the door, Lincoln paused to whisper something into the ear of an unprepossessing man. "Who is that?" asked Mary. But Lincoln was now distracted by the French princes, who bowed to him but not too low, as befitted their royal birth, while Mary simply inclined her head, as befitted her Republican Queenhood. Absently, the President patted a princely shoulder. As they proceeded to the door, Lincoln said, "Oh, that was Mr. Stanton, who defended Dan Sickles when he shot his wife's gentleman friend. Hard to say which of the two is best at getting away with murder."

Mary was relieved to hear the cleverness of Dan Sickles endorsed; and somewhat bemused at being reminded by her husband of the famous shooting in Lafayette Square. In effect, the murderer Dan Sickles must now protect the wife of the President from being charged with . . . What would the charge be for having given, in wartime, a state paper to a journalist?

As President and First Lady stepped out onto the gaslit portico, Mary allowed, for an instant, a long-dreaded word to surface in her mind: Treason.

3

SEWARD STARED AT DAN SICKLES, WHO STARED BACK AT HIM. The small office of the Secretary of State was blue with their combined cigar-smoke. Not for the first (and certainly not for the last) time did Seward think with envy of Chase's magnificent airy office. Plainly, the difference between the two offices symbolized the importance of the "almighty dollar," as Washington Irving had called it, over every department of the government, including that of the first magistrate himself. Although the Secretary of State was the first Cabinet officer, the duties were negligible except when a crisis, like the *Trent* Affair, arose. Fortunately, with the President's hearty concurrence, Seward had now been allowed to take over the delicate business of censoring the press as well as the even more delicate task of determining, upon the advice of the various military commanders, who ought not to be at large. Currently, by Seward's order, the mayor of Baltimore and the mayor of Washington were both in prison, where they would remain without trial until such time as he or the President was inspired to let them go. As a lawyer and as an office-holder, sworn to uphold the Constitution and its Bill of Rights, not to mention those inviolable protections of both persons and property so firmly spelled out in the Magna Charta and in the whole subsequent accretion of the common law, Seward found that he quite enjoyed tearing up, one by one, those ancient liberties in the Union's name. Never before had anyone ever exercised such power in the United States as he did now, with Lincoln's tacit blessing. Although, officially, the secret service was under the military, regular reports were made to Seward, in whose name letters were opened, copies of telegrams seized, arrests made.

"If only he had not sent that telegram to the *Herald*." Seward knew, of course, that the "if only's" of the world were the traditional solace of the condemned man and never of his lawyer. Even so, a major scandal involving Mrs. Lincoln would be a blow at the Administration, whose *de facto* chief he liked still to think he was; certainly, the world thought that he was the acting chief of the government.

Sickles made the usual lawyer's response. "Forget the 'if only,'

Governor. Wikoff sent the telegram. And the committee has a copy."

"By what authority?" Seward had a sudden vision of United States marshals arriving at the Capitol and arresting the members of the committee. Then he recalled King Charles the First; and thought better of it.

Sickles ignored the question. "They have it. That's enough. And they are in a foul mood. And they are mostly radicals. And they think Lincoln is too weak. And they think you're too strong. And they think McClellan is too slow, not to mention too sick..."

"He sat up this morning, and had soup for lunch," said Seward, idly; then added, "Well, the committee is not altogether wrong in its view of things."

"So we will let them call Mrs. Lincoln?"

Seward gazed at Sickles, who had always been, in their native state of New York, loyal to the Seward-Weed organization. Now this was Washington; now this was war. "No," said Seward, "we will not let them call Mrs. Lincoln."

"How do we stop them?"

"We tell them that as she is not a government official, she does not come under their surveillance. To the extent that they might want information from her, she will gladly submit a written statement, that you and I will concoct."

Sickles twirled his right moustache until it resembled a corkscrew. Seward thought, longingly, of port. "If that does not satisfy them?" asked Sickles.

Seward spread his hands. "It will have to. That is all."

"I see," said Sickles, without a smile. "You will send Congress home."

"No. No. I pray that we shall never have to come to that. But the President's inherent powers are such..."

"... as you choose to make them." Sickles laughed, without much joy.

"The key to this," said Seward, "is not Madam, but her chevalier. What does Wikoff intend to say?"

"No more than what he told the Speaker of the House, in private: that he is under an obligation of strict secrecy."

"What does he say to you, Dan? This is between us."

Sickles shrugged. "He does not say. But it is pretty clear. It was Mrs. Lincoln who gave him a copy of the message."

"Why?"

Sickles got to his feet and began to pace the small room, whose worn Brussels carpet was as full of holes as the case Sickles had taken on. "Mrs. Lincoln is deeply in debt," he said at last.

"Do you think that Bennett pays her? Through Wikoff?"

274

"I don't know." Sickles turned toward Seward. "I don't want to know. But . . ." Sickles paused to stump out his cigar in a metal tray. "Shall I send for Wikoff? Do *you* want to talk to him?"

"No, no, Dan. I don't want to talk to him, ever, in this vale of tears. Anyway, he was arrested an hour ago. He's in Old Capitol prison."

"My God! How could you let this happen?"

"How could I not? I'm not about to stop Congress. At this point, anyway. What has Mrs. Lincoln said to you?"

"She's shocked, and I feel somewhat responsible. After all, Henry Wikoff was—is—my friend. That's why I'm willing to go through the embarrassment of defending him in the uniform of a general, so help me . . ."

"God," concluded Seward piously. He opened a drawer in his desk and removed a folder, marked "Mrs. Lincoln." He opened it. "I think I have a fairly clear idea of the lady's expenditures on the White House. Major French gives me copies of all the bills, both paid and outstanding. There is one unpaid bill here, presented by a Mr. Carryl, that is for a sum larger than the entire sum Congress appropriated to renovate the mansion. There is also a rug that cost ten thousand dollars. There is another rug that cost twenty-five hundred dollars. There are something called 'patent spring mattresses.' There are wallpapers that cost—"

"But all this is for the White House, which belongs to the nation. None of it is for Mrs. Lincoln personally." Sickles rehearsed, as it were, a defense.

"There is another file, for her expenditures in New York—for herself." Seward rummaged in the drawer.

"But *not* paid for with Federal money."

Seward smiled. "No. Just not paid for at all. I'm afraid that the poor woman has a compulsion to spend money. It is a madness, like gambling."

"I wouldn't know, Governor." For the first time Sickles smiled; and the two men made a date for a game of poker at the Old Club House with the Barons Schleiden and Stoeckl. "Now I must go see my client at the Old Capitol. How do I get in?"

Seward scribbled a note. "All you need," he said, airily, "is a word from me." He gave the slip of paper to Sickles. "You know, Dan, that sooner or later your friend will have to tell the committee the truth."

"No, Governor. He won't even have to tell them the truth. But he will have to tell them something."

Seward nodded, approvingly. "Good boy. I am sure that there are all sorts of people lurking about the Mansion who could have got their hands on the President's message, and passed it on."

"That's what I was thinking," said Sickles. He paused at the door. "How much does Mr. Lincoln know?"

Seward frowned. "Unless Madam has told him, which is unlikely, I shouldn't think he knows anything other than the fact that Wikoff has been accused, which is all *we* know." Seward paused; then added, "Isn't it, Dan?"

"Yes, Governor. That's all we know. Well, I must see the Chevalier. And then I must practise my gentle arts on my old colleagues in the House."

"You do that, Dan. Meanwhile, let's not forget that there is a spy . . . a second spy, loose in the Mansion. Who can it be, I wonder? One of the servants?"

"Or one of the groundsmen?"

"Capital," said Seward, waving good-bye to Sickles, who marched from the room, head high, as if leading an army into battle.

For the third day in a row the President had not joined his family at lunch, and so Mary herself brought him exactly what he had asked for, and no more—bread with honey from the comb. She avoided the crowd in the corridor by slipping through the side doors from the oval sitting room into the Reception Room, which was empty, and then into the President's office, where she found her husband at his writing table between the windows, feet on a straight chair. Nicolay was at his side, with a stack of books.

"Molly!" The face was tired; the eyes, too. "Come on in. I'm sorry about dinner. But there's no time to eat."

"You'll eat this, Father." Mary put the plate down. Lincoln sat up more or less straight.

"Leave the books, Mr. Nicolay, and hold off the hungry hordes for the next five"—he looked at Mary—"ten minutes."

"Yes, sir." Nicolay left the room. Lincoln absently smeared honey on a fragment of bread. Mary picked up a sheaf of papers. "*On Military Genius*," she read. "I think General McClellan should be reading this, not you."

"Since he's still abed, I have to look after his shop as well as my own. Fact, I've been thinking about borrowing that army of his, and going for an excursion in Virginia."

"I wish you would. Because, left to himself, he'll never move, except to run for president, which he is busy doing at this very moment."

"Well, I think it's actually typhoid fever that he is busy doing at the moment. But I must admit a lot of Democrats are getting in to see him, while I can't." Lincoln picked up the book which he had been reading. "Listen to this: 'War is the realm of uncertainty: three quarters of the factors on which action in war is based are wrapped in a fog of greater or lesser uncertainty. A sensitive and discriminating judgment is called for, a skilled intelligence to scent out the truth... and the courage to follow this faint light wherever it may lead.'"

"You have the courage, God knows. And the judgment," said Mary.

Lincoln began, slowly, to munch the bread and honey. "I've also got that fog of uncertainty. And I've got a general that won't see me."

"McClellan won't see *you*?" Mary was still angry over the snub that the general-in-chief had administered the President.

Lincoln shook his head. "Every time I stop by, they tell me he's sleeping. I suppose I rile him too much."

"Replace him!"

"With what?" Lincoln drank water from a brown-glazed cup.

"Anybody!"

"I can't take just anybody. That's the problem. I've got to have *some*body." Lincoln gave her a sidelong glance. "What's wrong, Mother?"

"The Chevalier Wikoff has been arrested." It was Mary's usual policy with her husband to come straight to the point, except on money matters, where she simply lied as best she could.

"I know. Is he going to tell the committee that it was you who gave him the message?" Lincoln's voice was calm and untroubled; and so all the more troubling for Mary.

"If he does, he will be lying!" Mary felt her cheeks grow warm.

"People do lie, Mother." With a napkin Lincoln mopped a spot of honey from his desk.

"I thought he was my friend." Mary was bleak.

"I'm sure he was. I'm sure he is. But he's also Mr. Bennett's man at the White House. We can never be too careful here."

"I know. I know. I'm sorry."

"Don't be. I'm afraid I'm just as careless as you in these matters. I seem constitutionally unable to keep a secret. Anyway, I don't think that Mr. Wikoff wants to harm you."

"*I* can't be harmed, Father. I don't matter. But you can be harmed."

Lincoln smiled. "Well, if that's all that's bothering you, I'm not going to lose a moment's sleep over who's been purloining my messages to Congress, which I tend to leave all around the house, anyway. But more important"—Lincoln picked up a sheaf of papers—"are these bills that keep coming in, and coming in. Major French says that you've spent nearly seven thousand dollars *more* than Congress gave us, all to buy flub-dubs for this damned old house!"

"But, Father, the house was falling apart! Nothing has been spent on it for fifty years, and so I . . ."

"So you're trying to spend all at once what the other presidents did not spend for half a century? Mother, I can't get the money to buy enough blankets for the soldiers and here you are spending ten thousand dollars on a carpet. On a carpet! Why, you can buy a fine house back home for that money, or ten thousand blankets, or . . ."

"Father, I know I've been . . . I've been . . ." But no word came to her. "I'll stop. I have stopped. You'll see. The worst is over. I swear it is."

Lincoln nodded, somewhat wanly, Mary thought. Now deeply penitent, she started to explain the necessity of each of her purchases, as well as the innumerable economies that she had practised. But Lincoln had pulled the bell cord beside his table and Hay entered the office. Lincoln turned to Mary. "We have a surprise visitor, from Springfield."

"I'd better go."

"No, stay a moment and say 'hello' to Billy."

"Billy?" In the doorway now stood Mary's true nemesis, William Herndon, Lincoln's law partner. Tall and gray and uncouth, Herndon was nine years younger than Lincoln; and the same age as Mary. Although Herndon was indisputably brilliant—and far better read than Lincoln—he was, to say the least, eccentric. For one thing, he was often a heavy drinker. For another, he was radical in his politics—a fiery abolitionist. It was often said by the Springfield "scrubs"—as the ordinary folk were known—that Herndon was Lincoln's last direct connection with them, a connection that Mary would very much like to sever. When Lincoln married, he had moved into the ruling class of not only Springfield and Illinois but of Lexington and Kentucky, leaving Herndon behind with the sort of people that Lincoln had originally represented as a Whig legislator from Sangamon county, the scrubs.

"Well . . . Well!" Herndon stared at his old law partner, affecting bedazzlement at the change in his estate. Lincoln crossed to Herndon, and shook his hand in both of his.

"Come on in, Billy." Lincoln smiled, mischievously, at Mary. "Mother, here's Billy, large as life, as the preacher said, and twice as . . ."

"So I see. Good morning, Billy. I mean Herndon. Mr. Herndon. Sir." Mary grew colder and more correct with each version of her enemy's name.

"Mrs. Lincoln." Herndon was altogether too easy for Mary,
278

who noted that his beard was now a somewhat exaggerated duplicate of Lincoln's own. Doubtless this was good for business. Herndon still displayed the eighteen-year-old sign "Lincoln and Herndon" in front of his Springfield office; and it galled her that Lincoln allowed this because, as he'd say, not entirely to tease her, "One day we'll be going back, and I'll want to practise law again."

Lincoln sat Herndon down in front of the fire, while Mary remained standing, like a statue of Rectitude, at the writing table. She was formal. "I was sorry, sir, to hear of your wife's death in the summer just past."

"It was a hard death, Mrs. Lincoln. A hard death. But then phthisis always is. The lungs get coughed up bit by bit, like red rose petals."

"A very fanciful description," said Lincoln, while Mary shuddered. "How do you get on now, Billy?" asked Lincoln. "You've got—what is it? Five? No, six children to bring up."

"Well, it is not easy, Lincoln. I mean Mr. President. I mean . . ."

"Your Majesty suits Mother and me just fine." Lincoln drew up a chair beside the fire. On the one hand, Mary resented Herndon's presence, no matter how brief, in their splendid new life; but, on the other, she had to be grateful for anyone who could distract her husband, even for a moment, from what she was only just beginning to realize was a burden beyond the capacity of any one man to bear, much less the high-strung, melancholic, Richard the Second sort of man that she had married, a fragile creature who seemed now to be living off some inner source of energy unknown to her even as it, literally, consumed him before her eyes. Mary somewhat softened. "Do you have a proper woman to look after the very little ones?"

Herndon nodded. "From that point of view, I'm all right. But it's very hard to be a father without a wife. Fact, that's sort of why I'm here."

Lincoln shook his head. "I think you got it backward, Billy. Washington's a fine place for a woman to find a husband but a terrible place for a man to find a wife—that doesn't belong to someone else, that is."

"In this city, gentlemen outnumber the ladies ten to one," said Mary, producing a smile. There was no sacrifice that she would not make for her husband, who had made—and would be obliged to keep making, she thought, glumly—so many for her.

"Oh, I've found the lady, thank you. Remember Major Miles, who lived in Petersburg?"

Lincoln nodded. "I hadn't realized he was dead."

"Is there a widow?" asked Mary, trying to recall the family.

"No, no. He's alive all right. Worse luck. It's his daughter Anna I want to marry."

Lincoln frowned. "Isn't she that..."

"... very pretty girl, who was here a couple of years with Congressman Harris and his wife. She's uncommonly beautiful; and wise beyond her years."

"So wise, in fact, that she's willing to marry an old man like you, with six kids?"

Herndon rose to his partner's bait. "Well, at least there's no mortgage to pay off."

"You must be twenty years older than that child." Mary had indeed met the Miles girl; and found her as vain as she was pretty. It would, of course, serve Billy absolutely right to be married to her.

"*Eighteen years*, Mrs. Lincoln," said Herndon, with a droll look at Lincoln. "Anyway, it was my Mary's last wish that I get someone to take her place as soon as possible."

"But such a *young* wife?" Mary could not resist the opening.

"*My* Mary was never one for detailed specifications. There's only one rub." Herndon turned to Lincoln. "Major Miles is not as enthusiastic as I am about the possible linking of our two great families."

"Plainly, he is shortsighted." Mary could tell that Lincoln was perfectly enthralled by Billy's problems. "So we must bring him around. But how?"

"Well, Anna—she's got a really good head on her shoulders, that girl..."

"And an uncommonly pretty head, too." Mary added.

"That, also. Anyway, Anna's older sister is married to a man called Chatterton, a good Republican, who voted our way..."

"But is now, temporarily, out of a job?" Lincoln looked expectantly at Herndon, who nodded. "So if I were to give Mr. Chatterton, who is a loyal Republican..."

"... but not a radical like me..."

"More of a moderate, like me?"

"That's it, Lincoln. I mean Your Majesty."

"So if Mr. Chatterton were to be appointed to some Federal office, Anna would then advise her sister, who would advise their father that in exchange for this Federal office, Anna's hand in marriage would be yours."

"That's about the size of it."

Lincoln slapped his knee; and roared with laughter. "Billy, you never don't cheer me up."

"Why, Father, I thought that you were sick of people who want jobs with the government."

280

"I am. But this is different. This is purest Billy." Lincoln pulled a card from his vest; and scribbled a note. "Here, Billy. Give this to Mr. Smith, the Secretary of the Interior. There's always something open down there." He turned to Mary. "Just think, Mother, here we are able to play Cupid..."

"With the government's money?" Mary felt that she ought, in some way, to redress that balance which had so recently gone against her "flub-dubs."

"I'm sure Mr. Chatterton is no worse—*can* be no worse—than any of my other appointments. Besides, we are making it possible for Billy to marry, and that is the most sacred gift in my... Sacred?" Lincoln stopped; and frowned. "But isn't what I'm doing the greatest crime of all? Billy, you know about such things. Am I committing simony?"

"I haven't looked up that word in a coon's age. It has something to do with the popes, doesn't it? Selling sacred indulgences, or something."

"It *sounds* horrendous," said Mary, collecting the remains of the bread and honey.

"Well, as I am not the Pope, I guess a little simony can't hurt us." Lincoln rose; as did Herndon.

Mary bowed. "I'm sorry, sir, we won't be able to have you for dinner this week."

"But, Mother..." Lincoln began.

"That's all right," said Herndon. "I'm just here for a few days, to commit some simony, and go straight home."

"Come back tomorrow, and tell me how it went." As Lincoln led Herndon to the main door, Mary left through the Cabinet Room door. The appearance of William Herndon at the White House, even for a moment, struck her as the worst of omens.

Chase thought it the best of omens, if not too palpably coincidental, that as he sat in Seward's study late Sunday evening, Cameron, who had come to see him earlier, had now come to see Seward, who looked at Chase suspiciously, when the man-servant announced the Secretary of War.

"I told him that I would be here with you," said Chase, innocently. "Doubtless he wants to see us both together."

Cameron looked more than usually pale as he hurried in, breathing heavily. "I walked from Willard's," he said. All in all, thought Chase, Cameron had been wise not to take a house in Washington, preferring the barrooms and the parlors and the barbershops of Willard's, where he could prowl like some lord of the jungle.

"Sit down, Mr. Cameron, sit down." Seward filled a crystal glass with brandy, which Cameron took, without comment.

"As you see, I came straight here..." Chase began.

But Cameron spoke through him. "After I got back to Willard's, I had some supper. Then as I was crossing the lobby, one of the White House ushers gave me this." Cameron held up a sheet of paper. "The President has condescended to propose me as minister to Russia. He wants to send my nomination to Congress tomorrow."

"But you haven't yet resigned, have you?" Seward himself had written the somewhat curt letter that Cameron now held in his hand. Lincoln had agreed with Seward that it ought to bring about the long-desired resignation.

"No, I haven't resigned." Cameron drank the brandy as if it were water. Chase averted his eyes. "I'm also perfectly willing to continue in office. But only if I am to be the true head of the War Department."

"That could be difficult," said Chase, "now that General McClellan is beginning to rise..."

"...slowly," interjected Seward.

"...slowly," Chase repeated, "from his sick bed. As we agreed earlier this evening, you are well out of it, Mr. Cameron. Also, Saint Petersburg is crucial to us now that we are having—or, thanks to Mr. Seward, have *had*—so many problems with England. The Czar is currently pro-Union; and you are the one statesman who can keep him that way."

"True." Seward looked grave; he was, Chase noticed, slightly, but only slightly, drunk. "There is even a chance, as you know, of military aid from Russia." Seward improvised freely. Cameron became somewhat calmer; and then Seward, suddenly inspired, said, "I think you should go to the President tomorrow and accept this high post on condition that a fellow-Pennsylvanian take your place."

"Stanton?"

Seward nodded. There were times when Chase was obliged to admire the skill of his not entirely moral colleague. It was all-important to Lincoln—and to Seward—that Cameron not turn against the Administration. Cameron had a history of turning on presidents whom he had served. Although he himself was of no great importance, the fact that he currently controlled the politics of the state of Pennsylvania made him, potentially, a formidable adversary. Fascinated, Chase watched the master of New York hypnotize with a cobra's skill the master of Pennsylvania. "You—and you alone—will be able to make the difference between Holt and Stanton. And once Stanton is chosen, why, it is as if you were still in the Cabinet, for he is now a Pennsylvanian and a part of your own powerful constituency."

The fact that Stanton was a Democrat who had come, originally, from Ohio seemed to make no difference. Cameron had begun to nod. "You think he will listen to me?"

"Listen to you!" Seward spread his arms theatrically; and swayed slightly in front of the glowing fire. "He will do as you tell him. Also, if I may make the suggestion, give him a letter of resignation, dated a week or so ago. He will then give you an antedated receipt, and Mr. Nicolay can send that to the wire-services, to show that your promotion to Saint Petersburg"—Seward enriched each syllable of that city's name with positively ecclesiastical unction— "was planned by you as well as by the President."

"That," said Cameron, somewhat flatly, "will get me off the hook."

"Speaking of hooks," Seward glanced at the clock on the mantelpiece, "I am expecting General Butler any minute now. He has just come in from Fortress Monroe."

"Did he come *through* the blockade?" asked Chase. The fact that the Confederate navy had been able to seal off the Potomac River had been a source of much embarrassment to a nation that had been threatening, only two weeks earlier, to fight a war at sea with England. Currently, the rebel blockade was keeping the city in short supply of all sorts of northern manufactures, not to mention fuel.

"I think he came overland." Seward was shaking Cameron's hand vigorously. "See the President first thing tomorrow. I'll come in and help out, if you want me."

"That's good of you, Mr. Seward." Cameron frowned. "You ought to send Butler on his way as fast as you can. He's about the worst of our political generals."

Chase laughed somewhat nervously. "Well, let's leave Mr. Seward to order him off at once." He turned to Cameron. "I have my carriage. I'll take you to your hotel."

During the short carriage ride, Chase did his best to soothe Cameron, who seemed willing to be soothed. After all, Chase reflected, as the Czar of Pennsylvania entered Willard's, there might come a time when he himself would need the support of the Pennsylvania organization. All in all, Chase decided that he had behaved very well, considering the delicacy—and importance—of the matter.

On an equally delicate, if less momentous matter, John Hay was determined not to behave well, as that was his mission. The President had told him "to look after Mr. Herndon"; and so he had. They dined richly at Wormley's, where General McDowell was also at dinner with a half-dozen foreign observers, amongst them a British peer whom Hay had met with Mr. Russell of the London *Times*. General McDowell drank quantities of water to go with the quantities of food that he ate. Meanwhile, his guests did their best to keep up with the tall slender peer, who drank bottle after bottle of claret, despite the disapproving eye of his host. Mr. Herndon said that he was not drinking at all this trip but, perhaps, he would have one of Wormley's special mint juleps— where Wormley found mint in the winter was perhaps the only well-guarded secret in Washington. Hay himself drank only one glass of wine during the dinner, whose two principal features were a thick terrapin soup and canvasback duck, which Herndon had never tasted before.

"They're at their peak November tenth," said Hay, who had got to know a number of the capital's serious gourmets. "The best birds are the ones from certain Maryland marshes where wild celery grows, which is why the flesh has a celery taste." Hay was aware that Herndon was more apt to be able to taste the bourbon in the julep than the celery in the duck. But he was going to "look after Mr. Herndon," as ordered.

Back in Springfield, Hay had not known Herndon at all. He had seen him often at the courthouse or in the street, as he went to and from his office in the main square. Herndon had been particularly active when Lincoln was President-elect, with an office in the state Capitol. Later, Herndon had found a hideaway in a side street where Lincoln was able to work on his inaugural address with only Herndon in attendance. Now Herndon had a new partner. "A bright young man, who'll do for me, I hope, what I did for Lincoln all those years."

"What was that, exactly, Mr. Herndon?"

"Well, I was the one who read up on the cases. Lincoln preferred the courtroom and the circuit and, of course, politics always came first with him."

"Always?"

"Always since I knew him, and I reckon long before, too. I think of that ambition of his like some sort of little engine tick tick ticking away, and never stopping..."

This was a strange simile, thought Hay, who quite liked it. But then Herndon had a way with language that was all his own. "I can't say I think much of his Secretary of the Interior, Mr. Caleb V. Smith." Herndon adverted for the third time that evening to the subject. He had taken Lincoln's card down to the Interior Department, where he and Smith had promptly quarrelled over politics. "I am a radical through and through and that time-
284

server is a conservative, like most of the Cabinet. Anyway, when I saw we were not in the most perfect harmony, I shut up. But it was too late by then. When I asked for a place for my friend, Mr. Smith led me from office to office, pausing at each one, and asking the chief clerk, 'Is there room for another clerk?' and, of course, the answer was always no."

"Well, you'll see the President tomorrow, won't you?"

"Oh, I'll be back. I think I'm asked to dinner. At least he asked me. She didn't. Poor Lincoln, with that woman. I don't know how he abides her. It has been a desolate marriage, I'd say."

Like everyone in Springfield, Hay knew that law-partner and wife did not get on. Certainly Herndon had never been invited to any of Mrs. Lincoln's Springfield receptions since the time when he had said of her dancing that she was "as graceful as a snake," a reptilian image that highly appealed to Hay the poet but immensely irritated the Hellcat.

From McDowell's table, the peer of England—whose name Hay could not recall—sent over a bottle of port, by way of the mulatto Wormley himself, who was always gracious to Hay, and called him "young master," without too much irony.

Hay and Herndon toasted the peer across the room; and General McDowell raised his own tumbler of water, ostentatiously, thought Hay. "I have promised by wife-to-be, if to be she is, that I shall"—Herndon drained in one slow practised swallow the rich port—"stop drinking once she has consented to be my wife. I must say I thought highly of General McDowell until tonight. I had no idea that he was temperance. A bad thing in a general, to my mind."

"He is so much of a teetotaller that when he fell off a horse and was knocked unconscious, the doctor who tried to pour brandy down his throat could not get it past his clenched teeth."

"I would treat such a doctor in a more magnanimous way." Herndon offered Hay a bad cigar, which he refused. Herndon lit up. "I've often thought that certain phlegmatic types, like Lincoln, need alcohol but, poor fellow, he has no taste for it. If he had, I'm sure he'd not go mad the way he does."

"Go mad? The President?" Hay had not heard this before.

Herndon nodded, as a liveried Negro removed the remains of the duck. "It was the year before I joined Lincoln's firm, Logan and Lincoln; it was back in 'forty-two. Then Logan left in 'forty-four and I've been Lincoln's partner ever since. Anyway in 'forty-one, Lincoln was in the state legislature, and all set to marry Miss Todd, when he just went mad. He was crazy as a loon, according to Joshua Speed, his old friend. Tried to kill himself. Took to his bed, wouldn't eat. Wrote a poem called 'Suicide,' which he sent off to the *Sangamo Journal*, where it was published. Then he called off the wedding with Miss Todd, thinking of which was probably what drove him crazy."

"You mean he didn't want to marry her?" On this score, Hay did not need much convincing. He himself could not imagine anyone in his right mind marrying Mrs. Lincoln, but if what Herndon said was true, it was only when Lincoln was out of his mind that he had had the sense to reject her and then, sanity returned, he had the bad judgment to marry her a year and a half later.

"What really brought on the . . . madness?"

Herndon shook his head. "I can't say. Because I have no data. There has always been talk that Lincoln loved another woman. But he has never mentioned any such thing to me. So it is only conjecture on my part. But I think the hell of their life together, and there is no other word, comes from the fact that she knows he loved—still loves—another, and not her."

"Why, then, did they marry?"

"He could not have the other." Herndon poured himself more port. "Or so they say. But he could have Mary Todd, of the grand Todd family. He could move up in the world, which he did, with some help from her family, not that they ever cared much for him. But except when he was in one of his fits of madness, the ambition was always there, you see, driving him up and up and up."

"Fits? Were there other times when he was mad?" Hay could hardly believe that the eminently sane if sometimes highly melancholy Tycoon that he saw, intimately, at close hand, could ever have been anything other than the sanest man who ever lived. But, of course, Hay could never imagine Lincoln young—or being anything other than the Ancient that he knew. "I never saw him more than in low spirits, which he was after he lost the Senate race to Douglas. But back in 'thirty-five, in Menard county, they still talk of a time when he was crazy, as the people in that region understand craziness or insanity. That was about the time that he wrote this little book called *Infidelity*, all about his lack of faith in the Bible and the Trinity and the Immaculate Conception of Jesus and the rest of it. Anyway, a friend of his, a Mr. Hill, who owned a store—this was in New Salem, in the wintertime—made him throw the only copy—I hope it was the only copy—in a stove, and burned it up."

"The President is an atheist?" Hay had always been aware that Lincoln almost never made any reference to Christianity, while his Sunday excursions to the Presbyterian church were largely

286

ceremonial; yet God and the Almighty and Heaven did keep turning up in his speeches, even without Seward's prompting.

"No, not an atheist, as far as I understand the term. He's sort of a deist, like Jefferson and most of the founders. I think he has his own religion, of the grandest and noblest type. He believes in an overruling Providence. But to a devout Christian, I suppose, he would still be an infidel."

Somewhat sleepy from the port, Hay walked Herndon home to his hotel, Brown's, on Pennsylvania Avenue. The cold rain that had been falling earlier had stopped; and the night was clear and would have been cold had not the port kept them warm. In fact, so warmed was Herndon that before Hay knew exactly how it had come about, the two men were standing in the dark slush of Marble Alley, ringing Sal Austin's bell.

In the vestibule Sal greeted Hay warmly; and bowed to Herndon, who bowed, graciously, to her. "The red parlor is all right this evening." This meant that it was safe for Hay to go into the parlor on the left, as there would be no one there that he knew, and if someone who might know him should come in later, Sal would usher him into the purple parlor. By now, she knew everyone who was in the Administration and the Congress; and she was careful to maintain pseudonyms and disguises. Nevertheless, Hay pulled his soft felt hat over his brows and pushed up the collar of his jacket so that all that was visible of him were his long silky moustaches, whose satisfying presence acted as total insurance against any man ever again calling him Sonny.

Behind a small palm tree rising from a ceramic cachepot, Herndon and Hay stationed themselves. Herndon sat on a loveseat with room for a lover in addition to himself, while Hay sat in a straight chair; the girl of his current choice, one Penelope from Cleveland, would not be able to receive him for half an hour. Meanwhile, handsome creatures glided past them, smiling at Herndon, winking at Hay. At Herndon's request a tall slender girl with red hair and skin like milk brought them a bottle of bourbon. "I hope you won't mention that I've been drinking when you're with . . . our friend." Herndon poured himself a tumbler of whiskey.

"On condition that you don't mention to him where it was I took you." Hay was amused that the appearance of temperance was of more concern to Herndon than a revelation of wanton venery.

"Oh, I don't think our friend would be too shocked by this." Herndon looked around the elegant parlor where army and naval officers decorously paired off with the young ladies of the establishment. There was seldom much noise in Sal's parlors, other than the black pianist who was, on occasion, accompanied by one of the girls who played, most soulfully, the violin. "Not," said Herndon, "that there was ever anything like this in Springfield in our day, or even now."

"There's Chicago," said Hay, who had made the rounds of that city during the election.

"Yes, there's Chicago. But I don't get there much. I fancy the young red-haired waitress," said Herndon.

"Shall I . . . tell her?" Hay felt like a procuress.

"In a moment." Herndon put his feet up on a stool. "What's the tariff?"

"Depends on how long you stay. About fifteen dollars, usually. Sal sometimes will make a special price." Actually, Sal charged Hay a mere five dollars for what he always called "room and board"; he then paid the girl what he liked. Herndon sipped bourbon; and watched the comings and goings. "You know Joshua Speed, don't you?"

Hay nodded. Speed was a friend of Lincoln's, who had once lived and practised law in Springfield. He was known to be one of the Tycoon's few intimates, if such a closed man as Lincoln could ever be said to have had an intimate friend.

"Well, Speed told me this story of Lincoln. About 1839 or '40, Speed was keeping a pretty woman in Springfield, and Lincoln, desirous to have a little, said to Speed, 'Speed, do you know where I can get some?' and Speed said, 'Yes, I do and if you'll wait a moment, I'll send you to the place with a note. You can't get *it* without a note or by my appearance.' So Speed wrote the note, and Lincoln took it and went to see the girl . . ."

Hay cleared his throat, nervously, and murmured, "Maybe, sir, you ought not to use his . . . uh, the name."

"What?" Herndon was a bit deaf; then he nodded. "I see what you mean. My voice carries, don't it? Anyway, Lincoln . . . I mean, *he* handed the girl the note after a short 'How do you do,' etcetera. Lincoln told his business, and the girl, after some protestations, agreed to satisfy him. Things went on right. Lincoln and the girl stripped off and went to bed."

Hay was beginning to think that he was dreaming. He looked about him in the dimly lit parlor. Fortunately, no one was within earshot. Occasionally, he and Nico had speculated on what sort of life the Ancient had led before his marriage. But as there had been no data, as Herndon termed it, to go on, they thought of Lincoln as having always been a very ancient man indeed, and not concerned with fleshly as opposed to political unions.

"Before anything was done, Lincoln said to the girl, 'How much do you charge?' 'Five dollars, Mr. Lincoln.' Mr. Lincoln said,
288

'I've only got three dollars.' 'Well,' said the girl, 'I'll trust you, Mr. Lincoln, for two dollars.' Lincoln thought for a moment or so and said, 'I do not wish to go on credit. I'm poor and don't know where my next dollar will come from and I cannot afford to cheat you.' Lincoln, after some words of encouragement from the girl, got out of bed, buttoned up his pants, offered the girl the three dollars, which she would not take, saying, 'Mr. Lincoln, you are the most conscientious man I ever saw.' So Lincoln went on his way and never told Speed what had happened but the girl told him and he told me later." Herndon chuckled. "That's very like him; out of conscience, he ends up getting *it* for nothing."

"I had no idea," said Hay, weakly.

"He was young, once. Just like you." Herndon frowned. "But then he married that woman, and he has been true as steel to her ever since, poor man. He was—is—a man of powerful passions when it comes to women, but powerful control over himself. I've always said that he has saved the honor of more women than any other man I ever knew. The way they would fling themselves at him. Still do, I suppose..."

"I wouldn't know," said Hay, as Sal approached him.

"You wanted to see Dr. Prettyman?" she said. "He's here."

Hay thanked her; and excused himself. Dr. Prettyman was seated in Sal's office, going over the medical records of the girls; once a week, he checked them all for venereal disease. Prettyman was considered the best in the city for what, Hay often wondered, that was worth. Since the troops had arrived, there was now an epidemic of venereal diseases in the city. Earlier in the week, Hay had developed a curious symptom which he showed Dr. Prettyman, who examined him with all the swift aplomb of a butcher at the Center Market. "Nothing to worry about," he said at last, to Hay's relief. "You've got a slight strain. That's all. Try not to drive yourself too hard in the service of Venus." Hay buttoned his trousers; and the ubiquitous copavia salve was mentioned as a palliative.

Hay returned to the red parlor, where he found Herndon, eyes shut, but not asleep. "You saw the doctor?"

Like so many deaf people, Herndon could always hear what one did not want him to hear. "Yes," said Hay. "But nothing's wrong. He comes here regularly, to check the girls. That's why I prefer this place to the others. You can feel safe—well, reasonably safe, anyway."

Herndon nodded. "That's about all anyone can ever feel in such matters. They say there's a lot of syphilis here, thanks to the army and all. God knows there was a lot of it in Illinois back in the 'thirties, when Lincoln had it."

"Mr. Herndon!" Hay reached for the bourbon bottle and poured himself a tumblerful.

"Of course, he was a mere boy at the time. Your age, I'd say. Yes. It was about the year 1835. Mr. Lincoln had gone over to Beardstown, where, during a devilish passion, he had connection with a girl and caught the disease. Lincoln told me this. Then about the year 1837, Lincoln moved to Springfield and took up his quarters with Speed; they became very intimate. At this time I suppose the disease hung to him and, not wishing to trust our physicians, he wrote a note to Doctor Drake, in Cincinnati, the latter part of which he would not let Speed see, not wishing Speed to know it. Speed thought the letter had reference to Lincoln's crazy spell. But the note to Doctor Drake, in part, had reference to his disease and not to his crazy spell."

"I suppose he was cured?"

"Well, you never can know for sure with such a thing. But four years later he was all set to get married, and he would never have married if he thought he was not cured. Of course, he called off the marriage, due to the crazy spell. But then he got married, finally." Herndon was now drunk. But unlike most drunks that Hay was acquainted with, he did not slur his words or lose his train of thought other than to rely somewhat more than usually on ellipsis. "Lincoln's totally blind to his children's faults, you know."

"I know," said Hay. As a part of his recovery from the summer ague, he had been sent to the New Jersey seaside with Madam and Robert, whom he liked, and the other two...

"I have felt many a time that I wanted to wring the necks of those brats..."

"Amen," said Hay. The bourbon had now reached his own head.

"But little Eddie died—three years old—and the one they call Tad is not right in the head, with his palate misformed." Herndon frowned. "I wonder at times..." Herndon stopped. The red-haired waiter-girl had returned. Herndon rose, unsteadily, and offered her his arm.

As Herndon left the parlor, Hay had the sense that he himself must be very drunk or, perhaps, asleep and dreaming. But if he was not dreaming, then a concerted effort must be made to get Mr. Herndon safely married—and sober—in Springfield.

Mary's view entirely coincided with Hay's, though for different reasons. With a martyr's good grace, she had invited Herndon to dinner in the family's dining room. The only other guest was Congressman Washburne. Lincoln was in good form, telling stories of the early days in Springfield. Herndon was in less good form. Mary noted that the eyes were bloodshot and that his hands shook. When Lincoln asked Herndon about his evening with John Hay, he said, "We ate too much at Wormley's, where we saw General McDowell drinking water, a somber sight."

"I hope you imitated him, Billy." Lincoln gave Herndon a mischievous sidelong look. "These are somber times."

"Well, I *shall* be imitating him soon, anyway," said Herndon. "Once safely married, I join the Order of Good Templars."

"What's that?" asked Lincoln.

"A temperance group that fights the demon alcohol with a vengeance, which will at last be mine, now that our affairs are all in order."

"Did you find a job for Mr. Herndon's friend?" asked Mary, with sweet interest.

Lincoln nodded. "I took Billy over to the Indian department, where we found one of Mr. Buchanan's appointees who was eager to be set free from the national service, so Mr. Chatterton is now an agent for the Cherokee Indians, and Billy will soon be a Good Templar."

"I am sure it is *never* too late," said Mary, aware—too late— that she had given great offense to Herndon; and, worse, that she had embarrassed her husband, who now turned to Washburne, and asked for news of Congress.

"We wait for news of you," said Washburne. "When does the army move?"

Lincoln slumped in his chair; and shook his head as the waiter offered him a huge silver dish on which rested a roast loin of pork that deeply appealed to Washburne. "I'm getting set to issue an order to the effect that by the end of February, no later, the army must be in Virginia. But if McClellan is still sick in his bed . . ." Lincoln stared absently at Washburne, who was helping himself to the roast.

"I thought *you* were general-in-chief now." Washburne carefully stacked the slices of pork to one side of his plate so as to diminish the effect of what otherwise might have looked to be uncontrolled greed.

"Oh, I am that." Lincoln sighed. "I also think that I could probably set the army in successful motion. But then I remember that I am only a politician, and must listen to generals, who are never ready to move. The people are impatient. Chase has no money. McClellan has typhoid fever. In the West, Buell and Halleck seem unable to move in concert." At length, Lincoln complained of the dilatoriness of his expensive generals, and

291

Washburne listened; and helped himself to the last course, apple pie.

"You have other... maybe cheaper generals," said Washburne, his mouth full.

Lincoln nodded. "I've been meeting the past two nights with McDowell and Franklin, trying to decide what to do if the rebels happened to attack the Army of the Potomac; trying to decide who should command."

"What does Mr. Stanton advise?"

"He's not yet part of our councils. He's been too busy examining the War Department's expenditures." Lincoln grimaced. The waiter removed the last plates.

"The Augean stables?"

"Exactly. Unfortunately, our new Hercules is asthmatic..."

Ghostlike, Nicolay appeared in the doorway. "Sir, your... guests have arrived. They're in the Reception Room."

"You should be in bed, Mr. Nicolay." Lincoln put down his napkin; and got to his feet.

"I'm going to bed now, sir. It's the *winter* ague I've got," he added, wanly.

"Poor Mr. Nicolay," said Mary, with some small compassion for her enemy. "Anyway, I now see why it takes two full-time secretaries so that Mr. Lincoln can have at least one secretary at work in the office."

"Mr. Stoddard," said Nicolay, with quiet satisfaction, "has just taken to *his* bed. Potomac fever we think." Nicolay left the room.

Mary rose. "Oh, poor Mr. Stoddard! I must go look after him." They were all on their feet.

"Look to your own health, Mother. This is a sickly place." As Lincoln turned to go, Herndon drew him to one side. Neither Mary nor Washburne could hear what the two partners were discussing but Mary was quick to see her husband's mischievous half smile. Then, to her horror, she saw Lincoln remove from his pocket several greenbacks, as the new money had been promptly nicknamed; and give them to Herndon.

Mary glided toward the two men with, she hoped, genuine reptilian speed as well as grace. "What's that for, Father?"

"Well, Molly, I was just showing Billy some of the new money that we're going to print so much of. Now, here's Mr. Chase's honest face on the one-dollar bill, which everyone gets to see, and here I am—proposed, that is—on the two-dollar bill, which has a sort of rare look to it, doesn't it?"

"Certainly rare by my standards," said Herndon. He turned to Mary. "I'm twenty-five dollars short. His Majesty has graciously

292

advanced me the sum, which I will repay from the proceeds of our next fee. We're still owed a fair amount, you know."

"I see," Mary began but her husband did not allow her to finish.

"You know," said Lincoln, "I asked Mr. Chase why he had put himself instead of me on the one-dollar bill, clearly the most in use of the two denominations, and he said, 'As you are the President, you must be on the more expensive bill; and I on the less.'"

Lincoln and Herndon and Washburne laughed. Mary did not. She not only disliked the idea that money should be lent to Herndon, but she had also been deeply affronted to see Chase's face so conspicuously displayed on the currency. "He is running for president!" she had exclaimed when she saw the one-dollar bill. For once, Lincoln had agreed with her; but he also thought it wondrously funny, "To run for president on the money!"

Now Lincoln was showing Herndon the elaborate signature of Mr. F. E. Spinner, the Treasurer of the United States. "We're in luck with him, because no one on earth can ever forge the way he signs himself. It is a truly resplendent signature, all those curves and slashes."

"He don't sign each one," said Herndon. "That's from a metal plate."

Lincoln frowned. "What do you mean?"

"That's from a metal engraving. Can't you tell? God knows, we've been around a lot of print-shops in our day, you and I."

Lincoln had gone pale. "I am the greatest fool," he said. "I thought Mr. Chase ordered the money printed up and then Mr. Spinner signed it, and made it legal."

"Well that *is* the way it's done," said Washburne, "only it's all on metal plates."

"And they can print as much as they please?" Lincoln shook his head. "Mr. Chase and I must have a talk. There must be safeguards. Suppose a thief got into the Treasury and..." Lincoln stopped. He shook hands with Washburne and bade him goodnight; then he took Herndon by the arm, and said, "There's a carriage waiting for you at the south portico; I'll walk you down."

"Mrs. Lincoln," Herndon bowed.

"Mr. Herndon," Mary nodded. Thus, they parted.

At the south portico, Lincoln stood a moment, shivering in the cold damp wind. A corporal held open the door to the carriage that would take Herndon to the depot. The night was clouded and dark, and the only lights to be seen in the distance were those of the camp fires within the White House grounds.

"Behave yourself, Billy," said Lincoln, shaking Herndon's hand.

"You look to your health, Lincoln. You're too thin, and this is a *truly* sickly place."

"Yes, Billy. It's a truly sickly place indeed. Good-bye."

"Good-bye."

Thus, the partners parted.

In the President's Office Chase presided at one end of the table while Generals McDowell and Franklin sat at the other end. The quartermaster-general, Meigs, sat next to the President's chair. Although Seward had been present at the previous two meetings, he had this evening sent his apologies. While they waited for Lincoln to join them, Meigs told Chase that they now all inclined to McDowell's view that the army move against Manassas rather than Franklin's proposal—an echo of McClellan's secret Urbana plan—to move south along the water routes to the east of Richmond. As Meigs explained McDowell's plan, Chase could not help but wonder at the essential oddness or perversity of men. If he had had such a defeat at Manassas as McDowell had sustained, no power on earth would get him to return to that ill-fated place. But, presumably, McDowell felt that the only way to erase the infamous defeat at Bull Run would be with a famous victory in the same place. Certainly he had responded coolly to Lincoln, who had said with great kindness after the original debacle, "I still have confidence in you, General." To which McDowell had replied, "I see no reason why you should not." On the other hand, McDowell had lost Chase's confidence; and Chase had been and still remained his friend in a way that Lincoln was not.

Alone, the President entered the room. Everyone rose. He motioned for them to sit. He himself sat not in his usual chair but next to Chase, who was somewhat surprised that neither secretary was present. "Mr. Seward cannot join us," said Lincoln. "But we have another visitor, who shall be here any minute." Then Lincoln turned to Chase and asked, in a low voice, "I had no idea that our greenbacks are not *each* signed by the Treasurer."

Chase was stunned by the President's naïveté. "But how could he sign each one? The first issue of ten million dollars in various denominations would have taken him more than a year to sign, particularly with that signature of his."

"I know. I know." Lincoln was distracted. "I did not understand. But this thing frightens me. I mean *anyone* can get into the Mint and start printing money."

Chase's jaw set. "Sir, from the beginning I warned you that this scheme of issuing fiat money, with nothing but the government's word to pay *in specie* one day, was unConstitutional—"

"That sacred instrument, as I pointed out at the time, is mute on the point in question." Lincoln was sharp. "Besides, Congress is the initiator in money matters, and they wanted such an issue, as did you."

"I accepted the necessity because I saw no other way of financing this war." Chase prayed that the others in the room could not hear what they were saying, because if the word were to circulate that the President, whose face was on the two-dollar bills, had no idea what the greenbacks actually represented, the entire fragile currency of the United States would go crashing. But the generals were huddled together in their usual world of high intrigue. "But I did insist that we attach our money-machine to the creation of an internal revenue system and a national banking act and . . ."

"You have been meticulous," Lincoln interrupted him. "I have not. But we must ensure the safety of the Treasury's printers."

"Sir, if you have faith in me and in Mr. Spinner . . ."

"I have every faith. As does the public. But . . ."

"But, sir, we must delegate authority." Unlike Seward, Chase seldom interrupted the President. But now he was angry. "You must trust us to be able to appoint honest printers, and clerks to count the money and carriers to dispense it across the nation."

John Hay stood in the doorway. "General McClellan," he said. McDowell, Hunter and Meigs got uneasily to their feet, as did Chase and the President, who crossed to the doorway where the pale Young Napoleon now stood. Almost tenderly, Lincoln put his arm about the little man's shoulders and drew him into the room. Hay vanished. The meeting would go unrecorded.

The President's tenderness was plainly lost on McClellan, who greeted the President—and everyone else—with a scowl. Once seated, Lincoln said, "While you were ill, I called these gentlemen together to give me advice on the conduct of the war. I also asked them to draw up tentative plans for an advance into Virginia, which General McDowell has done, at my order."

Chase noted the dark suspicion with which McClellan glowered at McDowell; so did McDowell, who said, "I proposed, sir, during your illness, that elements of the Army of the Potomac move on Manassas . . ."

"A strategy which I had, previously, rejected; and still do." McClellan's voice was as strong as ever, Chase decided; and he wondered, idly, if McClellan had actually been stricken with typhoid fever. Certainly, his recovery had been uncharacteristically swift.

Lincoln turned, expectantly, to McClellan, who crossed his arms on his chest, in imitation of Napoleon; then lowered his head, and was lost in thought. There was a long silence. Finally, Chase whispered to Lincoln, "Is he really recovered?"

"So he tells me." At the other end of the table, Meigs was whispering to McClellan, who simply shook his head. Meigs spoke again, and Chase heard McClellan say, "No. He can't keep a secret."

Chase glanced at Lincoln out of the corner of his good eye. Had Lincoln heard? Yes, the President had heard and understood the reference; and was not pleased.

Chase cleared his throat. The room grew silent; the whispering stopped. Chase spoke: "General McClellan, we are happy to see that you are now able to resume your duties. Since you do not like *our* plan of action, I suggest that you tell us *your* plan."

There was a moment of silence, during which General McDowell caressed his paunch as though it were a skittish horse in need of soothing, and the President drummed the fingers of his left hand on the table.

Chase found McClellan's attitude mysterious. During the general's illness, Chase had communicated with him on a number of occasions. Chase had also made it as clear as he dared that one man ought not to be in command of all the armies as well as of the Army of Virginia. Personally, Chase would prefer McClellan as general-in-chief and McDowell, perhaps, with the fighting army. But McClellan was not to be advised, while his rudeness to the President was unforgivable, no matter how sorely tempted he might be by a first magistrate who was both indolent and fussy. In Chase's view, Lincoln was, often, an extremely irritating and vacillating man and if he, as a fellow-politician, found the President maddening, what on earth would a military man think of such a commander?

Plainly, not much, as McClellan now proceeded to demonstrate. "Mr. Chase, I have my reasons for not wanting to discuss my plans with this group." McClellan's fierce eye was now on McDowell, who continued to caress his belly.

Why, Chase wondered, would McClellan not tell the President what he had already told him about the Urbana plan? In due course, President and Cabinet must know. As for Lincoln's inability to keep a secret, McClellan was himself not precisely the sphinx. Chase now affected the new highly reasonable voice that he had only lately learned from the bankers. It was a voice both confiding and noncommittal. It was also a voice that in no way reflected Chase's fiery evangelical spirit. But the Lord's work must be done, and if it meant sounding like Jay Cooke selling watered stock, so be it. "General, whatever your grounds, we have devised a plan which you reject without giving us an alternative. Surely..."
296

General McClellan sat up very straight. He turned to Lincoln. "If Your Excellency, as my Commander-in-Chief, *orders* me to divulge my strategy, I shall do so."

"No, no. I won't do that, of course."

"Thank you, sir." McClellan was swift. "I should like to repeat, however, in reference to our recent conversation about the necessity of liberating East Tennessee, that I have ordered General Buell to prepare for an advance."

Lincoln nodded. "Well, that is something, I must say." Then Lincoln was on his feet; and the highly, to Chase's mind, unsatisfactory meeting was at an end.

As Chase walked down the dim second-floor corridor with McDowell at his side, he prayed for guidance. At church the previous day, he had not taken communion as he had found himself too subject to temptation to sin. He wished now that he had had the consolation of the Eucharist.

"Very awkward," said McDowell, as they descended the empty staircase. The gaslights in the main entrance hall were dimmed; and Old Edward was sound asleep in his chair at the door.

"I wish," said Chase, "that Mr. Stanton had been there."

"Do they get on—Mr. Stanton and our general-in-chief?"

Chase nodded. "Stanton tells me that he is devoted to McClellan."

"Devoted? Well, that is the sort of emotion that commanders like to excite in the bosoms of others, particularly their superiors."

"I fear that the President's devotion to McClellan is being sorely tried."

"Mr. Chase." McDowell paused at the foot of the stairs. The only sound in the hall was that of Old Edward, snoring in his chair. McDowell murmured in Chase's ear. "I think—between us—that McClellan is a fool."

Chase was startled to hear the other state so clearly his own most private fear. "I pray you are wrong."

"Oh, I do a lot of praying, too, Mr. Chase. And I say this only to you in confidence. After all, for me to say it to anyone else would sound as if I were jealous of a fellow-officer when I am, justifiably, anxious for the country."

Chase nodded. "I, too, feel the same way." But Chase left the matter at that. He was not about to confide to General McDowell his own total lack of faith in the President, whom fate had selected to shatter forever the Union and delay, perhaps for a generation, the abolition of slavery.

4

OLD EDWARD DID NOT STIR FROM HIS CHAIR AS DAVID ENTERED
the White House. "Go upstairs. Second room to the left," said
the doorkeeper.

"Yes, Mr. McManus." David crossed the entrance hall as slowly
as he dared. He had never seen so much activity in the Mansion.
Men in shirt-sleeves were arranging floral wreaths over the doors.
Trestle tables were being set up in the state dining room. Silver
and plate were being uncrated by an army of waiters. As David
climbed the stairs, a dozen naval officers descended.

The second-floor corridor was crowded, and David could see
John Hay at the far end, looking into the waiting room. The other
secretary was sick in bed. At Thompson's, the health of the Mansion's residents was much discussed. Currently, the two children
were ill; and David had been entrusted with their medicine.

Keckley received him in the room where the oldest boy, Willie,
lay. Mrs. Lincoln sat beside the bed. She did not look up as David
entered, but continued to talk in a low voice to the child, who
looked pale but lively enough.

"Thank you." Keckley took the package from David.

"Anything else I can fetch you?" asked David, admiring the
loops of material that hung most royally from the posters of the
bed, rather the way they had hung in the play *Cleopatra*, one of
his favorites.

"No. That's all." Keckley reached into her apron pocket and
gave him a coin. As David made his way down the stairs, he
passed the head groundsman, John Watt, going up them.

"Good morning, Mr. Watt."

"Good morning, David." Watt was an amiable man, well-
disposed to the Confederacy. He was also said to be one of the
richest men in Washington because of his shrewd management
of the White House grounds, which he regarded as his own private
plantation. All Washington knew of Watt's arrangements to sell
produce to a half-dozen restaurants and hotels, including Willard's
and Wormley's. Over the years, attempts had been made to get
rid of him; all had failed. Watt was a hero to David.

To Mary, Watt was a comfort. She received him in the upstairs
oval sitting room. "How are the boys, ma'am?" Mary knew that

Watt genuinely liked Willie and Tad; played with them by the hour; taught them to ride and shoot.

"It's the fever." Mary frowned. "I don't wonder. This house is so cold. I think they are better, sir. Oh, I wish I could call off this reception!" Mary did indeed regret the inexorable nature of her first reception in the entirely refurnished and repaired Executive Mansion. Tonight was intended to be her justification to the world for the money that she had spent. Certainly, never in the history of the Mansion had the state rooms been so gloriously decorated. She had seen to that. She had also made an innovation which had, by and large, been much praised: instead of opening the rooms to anyone who chose to come look at the President, she had invited five hundred of the most brilliant personages in the land. She had also eschewed the services of Washington's ubiquitous Gautier and sent for New York's finest chef and caterer, M. Maillard. But now both boys were ill; and the Chevalier Wikoff was locked up in the basement of the Old Capitol prison; and she needed money.

As always, Watt was understanding. "In President Buchanan's time, we often used the stationery fund for . . . other uses."

"I know." Mary was hard. "I have asked Mr. Hay for some of it. He has said no." Hardly a day passed now without some sort of scene between Mary and one or the other of the President's secretaries. Stoddard tried to be helpful but he was no match for Nicolay and Hay.

"It's always Mr. Hay, isn't it, ma'am?" Watt looked grim, and chewed the ends of his moustache. "He's in league with Major French—against us."

Mary did not entirely appreciate the "us." But it was certainly true that her only ally in the Mansion was Watt. Periodically, efforts were made to get rid of him as well as of his wife, a stewardess on the Mansion's payroll. So far, Mary had been able to rout their common enemies. Now Watt wanted to counterattack. "After all, why should you allow a mere boy to tell you what you may or may not do with White House funds? Funds which are almost never used for what they're supposed to be used for because of the way the times change while the wording of the old appropriations don't."

"I've always thought Mr. Hay was stealing the funds for the horses' feed." Although it was Watt who had put the idea in Mary's mind, she had since made it her own. "I know that he was supposed to pay the supplier directly, but never did. I shall bring charges!"

"I wouldn't do that, ma'am." Watt was cautious. "Not yet, anyway; we must give him a bit more rope." Watt stood up. "One

299

way to get some money quick and easy is to sack one of the stewards and then you yourself can collect his salary which will keep on coming every month."

Mary was astonished at the simplicity of this plan. "*I* can do that?"

"Miss Harriett Lane did it all the time when she was mistress here."

Mary saw the vista beginning to brighten. "I shall see to that, Mr. Watt. Thank you, sir." Mary drew a letter from her reticule. "You remember Mr. Waterman, whom we met in New York City last fall?"

Watt nodded. "A very rich man, they say. And most loyal to you and the President."

"See that this gets to him." Mary gave Watt the letter. "I don't want it sent from the White House."

"I'll get it to him by courier, ma'am."

"Thank you, Mr. Watt." Mary smiled. It was good to have one friend at least. But Watt had something on his mind. "I've been to Old Capitol prison," he said.

"How is he?"

"They've practically got him in chains. He's in a sort of closet..."

"This is all Mr. Seward's doing! God, that man is vile!"

"Yes, ma'am, he is. Five days from now, Mr. Wikoff will go back before the House Judiciary Committee. They will ask him how he got a copy of the President's message."

Mary began, faintly, to see a corona of flame around Watt's head. Could this be The Headache? "He will not answer them, will he?"

"I don't know, Mrs. Lincoln. But I think that you should speak to the President."

The flames flared like the sun during an eclipse. "I cannot, sir."

But Seward could speak to Lincoln; and did. Lincoln listened carefully, feet on the writing desk, a handkerchief in his left hand which he used to rub ink from the fingers of his right hand. He had spent the morning signing military commissions, an endless task made even more disagreeable by a singularly oily paper that resisted ink.

Seward paced the office, as if it were his own. "Anyway, Dan managed to get the Committee so enraged that they're now threatening to bring charges against *him*, for contempt of Congress, and throw him into the Old Capitol, too."

"It would appear that General Sickles was not the best of all possible defense attorneys." Lincoln stared, thoughtfully, at Seward. "Why did you pick him?"

"Mr. Wikoff chose him." Seward was prompt. "But I trust Dan. He's loyal. He's clever. He's popular in Congress..."

"So popular that they are about to lock him up? And just think what that will do to us! A brigadier-general, a former congressman, arrested!" Lincoln threw down his handkerchief. "When does Wikoff testify?"

"February tenth."

"What will he say?"

"What he has already said, that he is sworn to secrecy."

Lincoln sighed. "That will not do, Mr. Seward. That will not do at all."

"Then should he name someone?"

Lincoln nodded. "I think he will have to, unless we can arrange something with the Committee, to get them to drop the matter."

Seward felt the slight voluptuous tingle that always preceded, nowadays, any exercise of inherent powers. "I believe you could, simply, order them to drop the investigation; and they would have to comply."

"I suppose I could. But then we'd never hear the end of it. No, we must find a way to approach the chairman of the Committee."

Seward and Lincoln discussed in considerable and unflattering detail the character of one John Hickman, a Pennsylvania politician who had left the Democratic Party to become not only a fierce abolitionist Republican but the sworn enemy of all moderates, beginning with the President. It was agreed that Seward would try to involve Thaddeus Stevens in the affair. Meanwhile, every effort must be made to get from Wikoff the truth. "Because," Lincoln said, "he plainly stole the message. Now since that is a crime, he pretends that he was given it, which is not a crime. But by his silence, he indicates that the giver of the message was Mrs. Lincoln, which makes her the criminal. But she did not give it to him. I am certain of that. So either he will have to confess to theft—and I to carelessness—or he must tell us who it was that really gave him the message."

Seward said, "I think I have an idea."

"Good. But don't tell it to me. I'm not made for secrets."

Seward smiled. Actually, he had never known a man so secretive as Lincoln when it came to keeping to himself the direction that he planned to take in some great enterprise. On the other hand, Lincoln tended to be quite free with the secrets of others. Seward paused at the door. "How are the boys?"

"The fever lingers. Willie is particularly weak. I hate the winter here," he added, as if that somehow explained the darkness of the times.

Seward said good-bye, and left through the door into the Cabinet Room, avoiding the usual mass of supplicants. He was reasonably certain that Mrs. Lincoln was the guilty party. He was also certain that there was an interesting way out of the imbroglio, one in which a number of birds might crash to earth as the result of a single flung stone.

Mary had ceased to think of Wikoff. She trusted Watt's ingenuity. More to the point, the whole world had now been concentrated into a single pier glass, in which she was at last able to see the result of her two hours' labor with Keckley. The mirror reflected a white satin gown, trimmed with black Chantilly lace. There was a yard-long train. Shoulders and arms were bare, in imitation of the French empress; and, wonder of wonders, she did not for once look to herself to possess any more than a mere sufficiency of flesh. A white-and-black wreath of crepe myrtle crowned her head. She was unmistakably the Republican Queen.

"It is beautiful," said Keckley, a shadow in the mirror behind her that was now joined by a taller, thinner shadow.

"Well, our cat has a long tail tonight." Mary turned, smiling, to greet her husband, still in his shirt-sleeves. Lincoln picked up the long train; and whistled.

"Father, it is the latest style."

Lincoln stared at her low-cut dress and shook his head. "I'd be happier if more of the tail was up there at the neck, and less on the floor."

"I don't advise you about generals."

"Every day you do..."

"Well, then, if I do, you never listen to me; so I'll not listen to you."

"I suppose that is a fair trade." Lincoln let the train drop. "I told the musicians there'd be no dancing."

Mary nodded. "I think Willie is better. I was just with him. Tad is cold, he says."

"What does the doctor say?" Lincoln proceeded to pull on his coat, with Keckley's aid.

"All is well, he says. But this ague is a new one, he says, not like the others. I wish," said Mary, staring at her reflection as if it were that of someone else, "there was some way of cancelling all of this, so that I can look after the boys."

"I'm here, Mrs. Lincoln." Keckley held open the door. "I'll be with them the whole night. So you go down there, and show those secesh ladies the flag, which is just what you are—and Mr. Lincoln, too."

"No, Mrs. Lincoln is the flag. I'm just the flagpole." Lincoln
302

indicated Mary's dress. "By the way, why is the flag black and white tonight?"

"Mr. Seward says we should be in half mourning for Prince Albert. That's how it's done, among us sovereigns."

Lincoln laughed. "Well, I reckon we *are* sort of temporary ramshackle sovereigns at that."

"Speak for yourself, Father. Ramshackle!" Keckley fastened Mary's pearl necklace at the back. Then Mary turned, sweeping her train with her left hand while with her right she took her husband's arm. "I think it's time, Father."

There was a fanfare from the Marine Band as they appeared at the head of the stairs. Then they descended to the strains of "Hail to the Chief."

The East Room was as splendid as Mary had dreamed that it would be. Beneath the gaslit crystal chandeliers, the diplomatic corps were lined up to the right of the entrance, gold and silver braid glittering, while, to the left, were the military and the politicians and the crinolined ladies in all their jewels. Mary's sharp eye noticed that Mrs. Crittenden was laden with diamonds like an Eastern idol, while Miss Chase wore mode-colored silk and no jewels at all.

As the President and Mrs. Lincoln made their stately circuit of the room, many of the ladies curtseyed at their appearance; and all the diplomats bowed low. We *are* sovereigns, thought Mary contentedly; and not so ramshackle as all that.

In the center of the room, they stopped. To the President's left stood a military aide and the chief of protocol from the State Department, ready to announce each of the guests. For once, Mary knew them all; or at least their names. The French princes were the first to pay their respects; then the diplomatic corps, according to seniority, filed past.

Suddenly, a slender young man with a moustache shook the President's hand and said, "Mr. President, I wonder if you remember me? I'm your son, Robert."

Lincoln blinked his eyes; gave a slow smile; lifted his left gloved hand and gave the boy a slight cuff on the cheek. "That's enough of that," he said. From the next room, the Marine Band played a polka, to which no one could dance that night.

Robert bowed to Mary, who gave him a low curtsey. She noted how he had entirely grown up in the year that he had been at Harvard. He was self-contained, strong-willed and somewhat shy; more Todd than Lincoln. He wanted to join the army. Although she had, thus far, successfully forbidden it, she lived in terror that one day Lincoln would let the boy do what he wanted. Lately, the newspapers had begun to speculate on the eventual military

303

status of the Prince of Rails. It was Mary's prayer that the war would end before Robert had graduated from Harvard.

At eleven-thirty, as the party moved into the entrance hall, two stewards came forward to fling open the doors of the state dining room in order to reveal Maillard's masterpieces of the confectionary art. Unfortunately, the doors were locked; and the key was missing.

Mary found herself standing at the locked doors between the President and General McClellan. "Madam President, we seem delayed," said McClellan, plainly enjoying the mismanagement.

"Oh, but *we* shall advance, sir, soon enough." Mary smiled at the Young Napoleon. "We always like to set the example," she added.

From behind them, a voice cried out the words of a recent newspaper editorial, "'An advance to the front is only retarded by the imbecility of commanders!'" There was a good deal of laughter, and the Young Napoleon carefully joined in. Lincoln looked down at McClellan and said, "I hope, General, they don't mean the Commander-in-Chief."

"They don't know what they mean, Your Excellency."

A key was found and the doors were opened. At the center of the state dining room, Maillard had created a fountain, supported by water nymphs of nougat and surrounded by marzipan beehives filled with marzipan bees, producing charlotte russe. Elsewhere, venison, pheasant, duck and wild turkey were displayed, while an enormous Japanese bowl contained ten gallons of champagne punch.

Just back of the punch bowl, Seward and his diplomatic cronies Schleiden and Stoeckl stationed themselves and conspicuously made up for the abstinence of so many of the principal figures of the still essentially rural and pious republic. Then Dan Sickles approached; and Seward drew him to one side, to inquire of Wikoff.

"He's very uncomfortable. So he's apt to say anything, just to get out of the Old Capitol." Sickles twirled his moustaches. "He asked for my old cell. But he was refused."

"Have you seen Hickman?"

Sickles grimaced. "Not very likely. He's threatening to hold me—*me*—in contempt of Congress. Do you know John Watt?"

Seward looked surprised. "The head groundsman?"

Sickles nodded. "I've been talking to Major French about him. It seems that he's been robbing the White House ever since the days of President Pierce. Years ago, French tried to get rid of him but Watt always covers his tracks. Now he's working pretty close with Madam."

"I see." Seward began to see a great many things all at once; and the vista was ominous indeed. "Major French has some sort of . . . evidence?"

"Yes." Sickles dipped his crystal cup straight into the punch bowl to the horror of Mrs. Gideon Welles—a New England virago, in Seward's prejudiced view. "He has enough evidence to send John Watt to prison for larceny, both petty and grand."

"Well, I like them both, Dan. Particularly together. This is *solid* evidence?"

"Solid, Governor."

"Now, then, is she . . . ?" Seward looked across the room. Mrs. Lincoln was holding court to Sumner and Trumbull and the French princes.

"No, she's not involved. At least not in what Major French showed me. On the other hand, when she took Watt to New York with her, it is said he helped her raise money for herself from . . ."

"That's only 'said,' Dan." Seward was peremptory. He had his own sources of information in New York. Mrs. Lincoln had more than once begged money from businessmen. She had also promised political favors to at least one known enemy of the Administration. In Seward's privileged position as the unofficial chief censor of the United States, he had read a good deal of Mrs. Lincoln's correspondence. But since Seward regarded information as the source of all political power, he was not about to discuss any of this with Sickles. "Do you think we can put Mr. Watt in jail?"

"For a long time. And best of all, Governor, *legally.*" Sickles added with a grin.

"I don't like your tone, Dan. I get the impression that you may possibly, in unpatriotic moments, suspect that due to the present danger to the Union, I sequester the innocent out of malice or even mad caprice."

"Governor, I'd never hint such a thing."

"Even so, I feel it, Dan. It's in the air. Something unspoken. But then I am an uncommonly sensitive man, as you know. I writhe under the lash of criticism . . ."

". . . as do the editors you lock up for lashing you . . ."

". . . *pro bono publico.*" Seward was enjoying himself. He was also beginning to see a way out of the dilemma. "It was Mr. Watt who gave the Chevalier Wikoff the President's message."

"Why?" Sickles began the cross-examination.

"Because Mr. Watt was on a retainer from the *Herald* . . ."

"That would be criminal."

"True. I shall modify the evidence. Out of *friendship*, he gave the Chevalier . . ."

"He can't *give* anyone the President's property. That's theft."

Seward nodded. "I haven't done a cross-examination in years, as you can see. Well, then, Mr. Watt happened to see a copy of the message lying on a table, as who did not? Since he has a perfect memory, can visualize page after page of Holy Writ at a single glance, he memorized certain passages from the message and then, out of friendship to the Chevalier and mistaken devotion to the President, he recited the passages to Wikoff, who wrote them down and sent them to the *Herald*."

Sickles finished the punch in one long swallow. "I think, Governor, that I've restored you to your old brilliance as a trial lawyer, who is never surprised by what his client says."

"Yes," said Seward, thoughtfully. "But Mr. Watt is not yet our client."

"He will be if he knows that Major French means to bring charges against him and that I can get those charges dropped *if* he confesses to having told Wikoff about the message."

"What is to stop Major French from charging him anyway?" asked Seward.

"Mrs. Lincoln. The President. I don't think that Major French is so zealous to see justice done as he is anxious to see Mr. Watt gone from this place."

Seward patted Sickles's shoulder. "You have threaded the eye of the needle."

"Like a rich man? Or a camel?"

"It is the camel that passes through each time. But so boundless is the Lord's mercy, even the rich man may find salvation."

Twice, during the dinner, Mary visited the boys. She found Keckley seated beside Willie, who was asleep; he was breathing heavily but normally. Mary touched his face: the fever lingered.

"The crisis should have come," she said.

Keckley was soothing. "It is never the same, particularly with this kind of fever, which the doctor says is new to him." Lincoln joined them.

"There is no difference," said Mary.

Lincoln's huge hand rested, gently, on Willie's face, quite covering it. "He is no worse," he said. "That is something."

"Call the doctor . . ." Mary began, but Keckley shook her head. "Let them be for the night. Let them sleep. You two go back to your business."

Lincoln smiled. "Well, at least you know what it is we do down there. In spite of the music and all, there is no party or pleasure in this house, ever. Only business."

Mary wondered whether or not her husband knew that eighty of those that she had invited had refused to come because they thought it frivolous in time of war to celebrate, or as the truly evil Ben Wade had scribbled on his card of invitation, which he had sent back to the White House: "Are the President and Mrs. Lincoln aware that there is a civil war? If they are not, Mr. and Mrs. Wade are, and for that reason decline to participate in feasting and dancing."

Despite the feasting, the Civil War continued; and, twelve days later, John Hay sat with the President in Secretary Stanton's office at the War Department, and waited anxiously for dispatches. Apparently, McClellan had taken to heart Lincoln's insistence on the importance of East Tennessee. Buell's army had won an engagement at Mill Springs in Kentucky, while elements of Halleck's army, which had been permanently settled in Missouri, as Lincoln had despairingly put it, were now on the move. An Illinois brigadier-general, Ulysses S. Grant, had then captured Fort Henry on the Tennessee River. He was now at the Cumberland River, twelve miles away, laying siege to Fort Donelson. If Donelson were to fall, Nashville and eastern Tennessee would once more be a part of the Union.

On February 14, Grant's first attack on Donelson was repulsed. On February 16, as Lincoln and Stanton and Hay had been studying the map of Tennessee, a telegram from Halleck at St. Louis was brought them: Grant had refused to come to terms with the Confederate General Buckner. "No terms except unconditional, immediate surrender can be accepted," Grant had told the rebels. "I propose to move immediately upon your works."

When this message had been read aloud by the wheezing Stanton, Lincoln had said, with wonder, "Can this be one of *our* generals?"

"Yes, sir. And he's crazy to be where he is." Stanton had held his chest as if to push all the air out—or hold it in. Hay was never sure which. "Buell can't come to his aid. The roads are impassable, all mud. Now he faces Fort Donaldson . . ."

"Done*l*son," Lincoln had said, peering at the spot on the map.

But the next day in the same room, Hay witnessed what was, in effect, the Union's first true victory of the war. General Grant's message to General Halleck was read aloud by Stanton, whose wheezing had abruptly ceased. "'We have taken Fort Donelson, and from twelve to fifteen thousand prisoners.'" Stanton turned to Lincoln, "Will you announce this, sir, to the people in the reception room?"

"No, Mr. Stanton. I leave that pleasure to you. You've deserved it."

So it was Stanton who opened the door to the anteroom, where some fifty army officers and newspaper writers were gathered.

When Stanton read them Grant's telegram, there was cheering. Then Stanton proposed three proper cheers for General Grant, and the entire War Department resounded with the noise. Hay saw two rats hurry from the anteroom into the relative quiet of the Secretary's office.

A moment later, McClellan and his glittering foreign aides swept into the reception room. To Hay's astonishment, McClellan was roundly cheered. Then, with quiet modesty, the Young Napoleon addressed those present. Hay saw that a writer from the Washington *Star* was taking down every word. McClellan had noticed the same thing; he spoke slowly and deliberately. "In a moment, I shall join President Lincoln in the office of the Secretary of War. I shall report to him what you already know. In little more than a week, the Union has won five decisive victories." There was more cheering at this; and the Count of Paris picked his nose, lost in thought. "I, personally, was able to give each commander his orders for each day in five separate parts of the country, thanks to the miracle of the telegraph. Modern warfare has now come of age. Little did Alexander or Caesar or... Napoleon," the head lowered a moment, a frown creased the youthful brow; he did indeed resemble the Young Napoleon—the Third, thought Hay, sourly, "suspect that one day a great general could conduct a war on five—on *fifty* different fronts—and design five—or fifty—victories exactly as if he were face-to-face with his commanders in the field. Today eastern Tennessee is ours. Tomorrow... Virginia, and peace!" In an ecstasy of cheering, McClellan, alone, entered Stanton's office. Hay shut the door behind him.

Lincoln looked amused; bemused, as well. "I must congratulate you, General, for putting a fire under Halleck. I thought he was frozen solid there in St. Louis."

"It was not easy, let me tell you, Your Excellency." As always, Hay wondered if McClellan knew how much this title annoyed the President; and if he knew, as how could he not, why did he persist, except to mock Lincoln to his face?

McClellan marched up and down the room explaining his Western strategy, while Stanton wheezed and fumed; and, finally, intervened. "General, you can take a lot of credit, of course. But you did announce to the press that Fort Donelson had fallen six hours *before* General Grant had actually seized the fort."

"A minor misunderstanding, Mr. Stanton, nothing more." Hay wondered if there was a fraying of the friendship between McClellan and Stanton—or what everyone had been led to believe was a friendship. Lately, Stanton had been even more irritated by McClellan's slowness than Lincoln. Of course, Stanton's usual state was one of irritability. But then he worked harder than any man that Hay had ever known. He was also said to be as resolutely honest in business dealings as he was totally treacherous in personal ones. Could it be, Hay wondered, that now that the friendship with McClellan had served its purpose and Stanton had been made Secretary of War, a division between them was bound to take place? Particularly, if McClellan failed to prosecute the war with the sort of vigor that Stanton fiercely demanded and Lincoln somewhat wistfully desired.

After further tributes to his own exploits by proxy in the West, McClellan spoke of what was now the agreed-on strategy in Virginia. When McClellan had finally taken the President into his confidence and shown him the plans for the taking of Richmond by water, Lincoln had vetoed the enterprise. It would be far better—and safer, said the President—to seize Manassas; and cut the lines of communication between the north and the south, as well as the east and the west, of the Confederacy while maintaining the defense of Washington, which would, otherwise, be at the mercy of the rebels should the Army of the Potomac be shifted to the lower end of Chesapeake Bay. But, gradually, against his better judgment, Lincoln had given way to McClellan.

"Now, Your Excellency, we are ready to move. All we need is your order to provide us with ships to transport the army south." McClellan's right hand had found its way, irresistibly, into his tunic. Then, legs wide apart, he stared at the President, who was now leaning against the wall, carefully flattening first one shoulder blade and then the other in a rocking motion that indicated to Hay deep thought as well as physical discomfort.

"I shall see to the order, of course. And now, with these victories in the West, we should be able to close most swiftly the circle of death . . . of victory, I mean . . ." Lincoln's voice trailed off. Hay had almost never seen the Tycoon lose his train of thought. But in the last few days Lincoln had been unusually distracted by the illnesses of Willie and Tad, the business of Wikoff and Congress, the constant tension with McClellan.

"Halleck wants more men in the West," said Stanton, eyeing Lincoln curiously. "He also wants a unified command, under himself."

"We cannot spare the men," said McClellan promptly. "Certainly not on the eve of what is about to be the final engagement of the war. As for a unified command in the West . . ."

"I shall address myself to that presently," said Lincoln, picking up his hat from its place on Stanton's desk. He turned to Stanton. "How is your child?"

Stanton's eyes filled suddenly with tears; he was no longer the ferocious master of endless detail. "We are fearful. He took the vaccine well enough the first day. But now there are hideous eruptions all over his body."

"How old is he?"

"Six months. He is christened James."

"They can be surprisingly strong at that age."

"So we pray. And yours?"

"I do not know." Lincoln turned, bleakly, to McClellan. "We shall speak in a few days, about your ships."

"Yes, Your Excellency."

Hay held the door for Lincoln, who passed through, eyes on the floor. This was sometimes a deliberate tactic in order not to see those who wanted to be seen by him; but today the Ancient seemed to want to be invisible—even gone.

At the door to the White House, Old Edward said, "Mr. President, Mrs. Lincoln would like to see you. She's with the boy."

"Is the doctor here?"

Old Edward paused. Then he nodded: "Yes, sir. In point of fact, he is."

Lincoln ran up the stairs like a man half his age. Hay turned to Old Edward, who said, "Madam told me I was not to distress him. But when he asked about the doctor..."

"How is the boy?"

"Oh, Mr. Hay, he is dying! Can't you feel it in the house? Like a cold wind."

Mary sat holding Willie's hand. Keckley stood behind her, as if prepared, in turn, to hold her hand. The doctor was trying to get Willie to take medicine; but the boy's mouth was firmly shut. He was conscious; but seemed too weary from the struggle to speak. As Lincoln approached, Willie tried to smile. The doctor took advantage of this sign of life and got the spoonful of medicine past his lips.

"You see, Father, how well he is doing?" Mary had now held back her own tears for so long that she wondered if some part of her might not, presently, drown.

"I do. I do." Lincoln sat on the bed and, lightly, ruffled the boy's hair. "You'll be down for the parade next week. General McClellan's holding a review, just for us. A hundred thousand soldiers, he says. About the biggest parade that's ever been held in the world."

Willie nodded; swallowed hard to get down the medicine; shut his eyes. Lincoln looked at Mary across the bed. She turned her head to one side. She had been young when Eddie left them. She had been able to have more sons; and did. But she was not young now; and never again would there be anyone in her life resembling Willie, for of all the children he was the one who was closest to her, the one that she had always envisaged at *her* bedside when she lay dying, old and widowed and forlorn, save for him. Now she saw an image of herself, as clear and precise as the freshest daguerreotype; saw herself old, widowed, forlorn—and quite alone.

Lincoln turned to the doctor, who spread his hands, as if letting Willie go. Then Nicolay appeared in the doorway; and motioned to Lincoln, who left the room. Mary preferred to be alone with Willie. The enormity of her grief was as unique and as unshareable as it would be at the end of her own days.

Seward apologized to the President. "At such a time..." He shook his head.

"At such a time, at such a time..." Lincoln stared into the burning coals of the grate. "I cannot believe that he is going."

"He is not gone yet."

"No." Lincoln's sigh was close to a moan. Seward had never seen the President so—unlike himself. But then, with an effort, he was himself again; or a fair facsimile. "Let's get down to it. You have spoken to Mr. Hickman?"

"Yes, sir. We have all spoken to him. He has been studying Watt's testimony; and he does not believe it."

"How can he disprove it?" Lincoln straightened the painting of Jackson above the mantel.

"I doubt if he can. But he told me that he intends to hold hearings. Wikoff will be questioned again and again, and so will John Watt, not the happiest witness that I have ever dealt with. Hickman also tells me that the Committee will call other witnesses."

"I see." Lincoln turned around, his face suddenly harsh. "He will call Mrs. Lincoln."

"Yes."

"Well, Governor, you and I are going to pay Mr. Hickman a call."

"But he's at the Capitol now..."

"So? This is not England, where the sovereign may not set foot in the House of Commons. I can wander in and out of the Capitol as I please."

Seward was alarmed. "Is this wise, sir? What if the press should discover that you had gone before a committee...?"

"We'll take our chances."

At Stanton's insistence, the President's carriage was now always accompanied by a company of cavalry. "I feel like a parade," said

311

Lincoln, as the carriage and its escort clattered loudly down Pennsylvania Avenue.

"You feel what?" asked Seward.

"... like a parade," shouted Lincoln. "When Mother and I go driving we can't even talk, for all the noise."

At the Capitol, the President and Seward were received by a very surprised Sergeant-at-arms, who ushered them into the vast gilded office reserved for the Speaker of the House. A moment later, Mr. Hickman joined them. He was a smiling, hard man. "Well, sir, this is quite an honor for us," he said, shaking Lincoln's hand.

"Indeed it is," said Seward, lighting his cigar, as if to emphasize that he was in some not entirely polite establishment.

"I understand," said Lincoln, "that you do not accept Mr. Watt's testimony that it was he who told Mr. Wikoff about my message to Congress."

"Well, sir, I find it hard to believe that he would have so good a memory for something that he had only looked at, very briefly, once, or so he told us."

"I," said Seward, "in my youth, could learn some thirty legal citations in the space of half an hour."

"But you, Mr. Seward, are one of the great lawyers of the age. You are not a professional gardener."

"Actually, the law *can* be approached as if it were a kind of garden," said Seward. "You must recall where and when you plant each seed..."

Lincoln raised his hand; and Seward was still. "I accept the story, Mr. Hickman, and I—not you—am, in this case, the plaintiff since the message in question was mine."

"In a sense, sir, that is true. But this is wartime, and we must be ever-vigilant, all of us, you at your end of Pennsylvania Avenue and we at ours."

Seward started to speak; but then chose to cough instead. Lincoln spoke: "The Congress, Mr. Hickman, has every right to question the official actions of the Executive, but I do not see this as an official matter. If I choose to lodge a complaint, I would do so through a civil court, as would you if you were robbed, which I was not."

"Naturally, sir, we here take a different view. Should there be Confederate spies at large in the White House, surely we would be negligent in our duties not to find them."

"Mr. Hickman," Seward was growing annoyed, "the secret service reports both to the general-in-chief of the armies and to the Secretary of State. Surely, Congress is not about to set itself up over General McClellan and me, and go searching for spies on its own, without the means to apprehend them?"

Hickman continued to smile. "Mr. Seward, the Constitution *does*, in a sense, put us over you. Certainly, it puts us, collectively, on the same level as the President. Of course, we can't—or we don't—hire our own detectives as you do, but we can question suspicious personages, and we have the power to jail them, if we choose."

"Mr. Hickman." Lincoln's voice was mild; but his expression was remote and cold and, to Seward's now experienced eye, chilling. "I want you to send for all of the Republican members of the Judiciary Committee. I'd like to speak to them."

Hickman's smile began, slightly, to fade. "But the Committee's not in session today, and I don't know who's here in the Capitol or on the floor or gone home..."

"Tell the Sergeant-at-arms to fetch us as many Republican members of the Committee as he can rustle up."

"But, Mr. President..."

"Now," said Lincoln.

Hickman left the room. Lincoln looked at Seward; then, suddenly, he smiled. "You know, Governor, all of this reminds me of the time when I was out on circuit, back in 'thirty-nine..." As Lincoln told his story, the members of the Judiciary Committee began to assemble. Seward admired the skillful way that Lincoln kept drawing out the story so that, by the time the Committee was all assembled, he could conclude it to much laughter.

The half-dozen representatives now circled the President like so many Lilliputians, thought Seward, about to tie up Gulliver. Hickman threw the first rope. "Gentlemen, this is highly irregular, of course, for a president to come down here and ask to see a committee. But," the smile was again in place, "these are irregular times."

"So they are, Mr. Hickman." Lincoln was the soul of amiability. "Gentlemen, we are all of us, I hope, patriots. We are also, all of us, Republicans. The two need not be the same thing but we must act as if they are." There was a nervous laugh from one member; and total silence from the rest. "Now I am, for better or worse, the head of the Republican Party, whose majority in Congress is considerable. I know that there are some who think I am a usurper, and that Governor Seward here is the true head of our party, but he'll be the first to tell you that that is not so. Or he had better be the first." With that, Lincoln detonated genuine laughter and Seward's laugh was loudest of all since there was nothing in this for him to laugh at.

"Well, I am here as the Republican leader—and President—to tell you that I believe John Watt's story, and that I want you to believe it, too. Otherwise, in the middle of a war which we are only, this very day, beginning to win—Fort Donelson has fallen . . ."

There were spontaneous cheers from all but Hickman.

". . . you will deeply embarrass me personally if you persist in allowing every sort of gossip and troublemaker and secret secessionist to use your committee to make newspaper sensations. You will damage our brand-new political party. You will put at risk our majority in this House come November's election. Finally, you will give great comfort to the rebels at the South. Well, I am telling you what you *can* do. But I know that you will not do it, because I know that I can count on you—as Republicans and as Unionists—to do the right thing."

Seward admired Lincoln's unexpected mastery of what was, in principle, a hostile group. They might all call themselves Republicans, but the word was too vague to describe a former Democrat turned Jacobin abolitionist like Hickman or a former Whig moderate like himself—or the President, for that matter.

Finally, Hickman said, "You guarantee, sir, that Watt's story is true?"

"Oh, Mr. Hickman, I guarantee nothing on this earth that I've not experienced firsthand, and even then the sharpest eye can fail you. I *think* Watt's testimony is true. I also think that there will never be a story more interesting, nor to the dramatic extent that some would like."

Seward saw that Hickman was furious but there was nothing now that he could do. Lincoln's reminder to the Committee members that they would be up for reelection in nine months' time had neatly done the trick. To damage mortally the leader of their party would so help the busy Democrats that a number of those present might be abruptly removed from public life. "Thank you, Mr. President," said Hickman, "for your courtesy—and your candor."

Lincoln was now shaking each congressman's hand. "Thank you, Mr. Chairman, for letting me drop in on you like this. Or to quote the preacher who said . . ."

As Mary Hurried down the corridor to Willie's bedroom, Watt suddenly stepped in front of her, as if he'd materialized from nowhere like a ghost. Mary cried out with surprise; and some alarm. Watt was pale and grim. "Mrs. Lincoln," he began.

"Mr. Watt, no one's supposed to be in this part of the Mansion. My boy is very ill . . ."

314

"I know. I'm sorry. I did what I was told to do. I did what they forced me to do."

"I'm sorry, Mr. Watt. I can't talk now." At the far end of the corridor, she saw Nicolay, watching her with some curiosity.

"My wife has just given up her job as stewardess. I have resigned as chief groundsman. I was supposed to receive a commission in the army. But it was revoked today. I shall go off the payroll at the end of the month. Now, I have done everything that I could..."

"Mr. Watt, you will always have a friend in me, as well as in our common friends at New York City. The greenhouse that you have always dreamed of, the one that we saw in Fourteenth Street, is available..." Mary spoke rapidly; and to the point. She had rehearsed this speech before. She told Watt that she was grateful to him for his support; and that she would repay him. When Mary had finished, Watt gave a little bow.

Mary tried but failed to smile. Then she crossed into Willie's room, where one of his playmates was seated solemnly beside the great bed. Willie's eyes were shut.

"Has he spoken?"

The boy shook his head. "But he recognizes me sometimes. He squeezes my hand a little."

Mary sat in a chair next to the boy, whose presence plainly comforted Willie in his rare conscious moments.

Mary now had the sense that she was dreaming; and that she had been dreaming for quite some time. Soon she would wake up and all would be well. They would be back in Springfield; and she would report, over breakfast, her nightmare that Lincoln had been elected President and that the Union had been dissolved and that Willie was dead—no, dying—no, alive—still. That morning the doctor had said that there was no longer anything to be done. But that was the way things were in nightmares, and she was an expert on dreams and their significance. Dreams work mainly in opposites, she knew. Willie dying meant Willie thriving.

Finally, it was Keckley who told Hay that he should fetch the President from the War Department. When the cries from the living quarters of the Mansion had begun, Nicolay ordered everyone out of the waiting room and told Old Edward to stand guard at the top of the stairs to fend off all intruders.

Hay hurried across to the War Department, where he found Lincoln in Stanton's office. Since Nashville was about to be part of the Union, Lincoln had spent the morning working on a statement welcoming East Tennessee back into the Union. But when he saw Hay in the doorway, he let the papers in his hand fall to the floor. Stanton looked at Lincoln, somewhat

315

irritably; looked at Hay, and understood. Stanton began to choke from asthma. Lincoln stood up, his eyes on Hay, who could not speak. Lincoln nodded, and Hay was relieved that he had not been obliged to tell the Ancient that the boy was dead.

The Mansion was silent. Hay assumed that Mrs. Lincoln had been drugged by now. Certainly, no one could have endured much longer her cries, which were neither screams nor sobs but an eerie keening, addressed to the underworld itself; to that voracious darkness which had robbed her yet again.

Hay stood in the doorway and watched as Lincoln crossed to the bed, where lay the small shrouded figure. Slowly, Lincoln pulled back the sheet. The boy's eyes had been closed; the hair combed. Delicately, with a forefinger, Lincoln touched his son's brow. Keckley pushed a chair in place so that Lincoln might sit. As he lowered himself into the chair, Hay saw that the tears had begun to flow down leathery cheeks that looked as if they had never before known such moisture. "It is hard," Lincoln whispered. "Hard to have him die."

Then Robert entered the room. Lincoln looked up at him, for a moment disoriented. "The doctor has given her morphine. She is asleep." Lincoln looked back at Willie. Robert started to go to his father; but then thought better of it. He left the room.

Lincoln addressed the dead boy, in a voice that was oddly conversational. "We loved you so."

In tears, Hay left the room, bumping into Robert, who said, urgently, "We must get my aunt here, as fast as possible. Can you telegraph her?"

Hay blew his nose; and used that gesture as an excuse to dry his eyes. "Of course. Which aunt?"

"Elizabeth Edwards. She is the best with Mother. You must tell her to start today. Because if she doesn't . . ."

"If she doesn't, what?"

"If she doesn't, my mother will go mad."

5

As Chase held out his mug to receive the fresh coffee, the ship gave a sudden leap and the coffee came toward him, slowly, it seemed to Chase, making an arc from spout to what was no longer cup but his own unprotected face. Fortunately, a second shudder of the ship caused the jet of coffee to avoid his cheek; even so, he could feel its warmth, as it made its way to the deck with a splash not entirely drowned out by the sound of water cascading off the Treasury cutter's bow.

Chase looked down the table at the President, who was holding onto the edge with one hand while in the other he held a fork that had been aimed at a plate which was now skittering along the table, depositing its contents impartially between the lap of Stanton and that of General Viele. Once the mess-boy was certain that all of the coffee had left the tin pot, he put it down on the table, where, as waves again struck the ship's bow, the pot retraced the course of the presidential plate and struck Lincoln full in the chest.

"I don't think," said the First Magistrate, thoughtfully, "that I'm all that hungry, anyway."

The commanding officer of the *Miami* apologized. "I'm sorry, sir. It shouldn't be this rough. But you never know with the Chesapeake."

"How much longer," gasped Stanton, "before we are at Fortress Monroe?"

"By eight this evening, sir."

Stanton shut his eyes. Lincoln smiled, wanly. Chase felt vigorous; and alert. But then this was *his* ship: a cutter of the U.S. Treasury, and the President and the Secretary of War were his honored guests.

Chase turned to the captain. "I'm sure *we'll* be able to do justice to this delicious meal that your cook has prepared for us," he said, graciously; then, to his alarm, he saw that a second mess-boy had appeared from the galley with a tureen of steaming soup. "But I would suggest that we forego the . . ."

A great wave broke over the bow; and the soup was foregone. Happily, it missed the President, who was now the color of chalk. "I believe," said Lincoln, "that I shall lie down for a while." With

317

the aid of the captain, the President lurched across the salon to a long locker on which a pallet had been placed. Here he stretched himself out and shut his eyes. Stanton staggered to his feet and hurled himself toward the mess-boy, who caught him in midflight, and deposited him on a second locker, where he lay, gasping softly, eyes red-glazed behind the pebble glasses.

"That seems to leave just us, General," said, Chase, cheerily, to Viele, who seemed at ease. As best they could, they dined. Meanwhile, the plate and cutlery had taken on a sinister life of their own. "Rather like a spiritualist's séance," Chase remarked. Lately, conversation with the dead had become the rage at Washington; and the city was filled with mediums of all sorts. It was rumored that Mrs. Lincoln had summoned to the White House a particularly fashionable medium; and that she had been able to speak to Willie, the only bright—or even sane, if gossip was to be believed—moment in her bereavement.

The White House had been in deepest mourning ever since the child's funeral, which had been held, three months earlier, in a storm so terrible that Chase had been put in mind of one of those Shakespeare plays where all the elements do conspire to presage some terrible—*more* terrible, that is—tragedy.

General Viele discussed the previous month's seizure of Fort Pulaski, just outside Savannah; and Chase said that he only prayed that McClellan would be inspired by the numerous Federal victories all around the country; and himself move. General Ben Butler had occupied New Orleans. General John Pope had seized a crucial island in the Mississippi River, known, somewhat ingloriously, as Island Number Ten. General Grant had sustained great losses—some thirteen thousand men when he was surprised by the rebels at Shiloh Church on the Tennessee River. Grant had managed, barely, to survive. Subsequently, he had been denounced by a former commandant of the United States Military Academy as a common gambler and drunkard. Lincoln had ignored the denunciation.

But Lincoln could hardly ignore the denunciation of McClellan from the radicals in Congress; and of himself and Stanton from the reviving Democratic Party in the North. When he had finally ordered McClellan and the Army of the Potomac into action, he took the occasion to remove McClellan as general-in-chief on the ground that he could hardly command all the other armies while he himself was in the field. McClellan had accepted this loss of command with rather more serenity than Chase had anticipated. Halleck was given the Western command and, to please the radicals, Frémont was revived and given something called the Mountain Department.

Between March 17 and April 5, 1862, more than one hundred thousand Federal troops were moved by water down the Potomac River to the so-called Yorktown peninsula, a marshy strip of land between the York and the James rivers, dominated at its eastern tip by Fortress Monroe and at its center by Yorktown, that historic village where the War of Independence had been, finally, won—by the French fleet. Now the rebel troops occupied the remains of the British fortification at Yorktown.

McClellan's "Urbana plan" had been abandoned when, in a surprise movement, the Confederate Army had abandoned Manassas and Centerville in order to regroup along the Rappahannock River, thus making it impossible for McClellan to effect a successful landing anywhere near Urbana. McClellan had then announced that he would use Fortress Monroe as the center of his operations, first, against Yorktown; then against West Point, some twenty-five miles southeast of Richmond; and, finally, against Richmond itself. In a joint operation with the navy, under the command of Commodore Goldsborough, McClellan would now put a prompt end to the rebellion.

Unfortunately, modern naval science had deranged McClellan's plan. The Confederate navy had succeeded in raising a forty-gun Union frigate, sunk at the beginning of the war so that it might not fall into their hands. The frigate's hull was then plated with metal, while a cast-iron ramrod was attached to its bow. On the morning of March 9, this frigate—renamed the *Merrimack*—had sunk two Union ships in the Hampton Roads just off Norfolk, and had driven the *Minnesota* aground. Chase had never seen Stanton so entirely demoralized.

"They will sink every Union ship in every Union harbor!" Stanton had then sent word to the northern ports to be on their guard against this terrible new weapon. "There is no doubt," he had said in a dramatic voice, "that this one ship will be able to destroy the city of Washington." But, as Welles kept reminding them, a Union ship of equally radical design was on its way to the rescue. This curious flat metal ship had a revolving turret, containing cannon. On the evening of March 9, the *Monitor* engaged the *Merrimack* (the Union press did not recognize the rechristening) in an inconclusive battle, which did not end until the *Merrimack* withdrew to the safety of Norfolk harbor. Nevertheless, the fact that the *Merrimack* still existed made any sort of naval operation more than usually hazardous.

McClellan had now laid siege to Yorktown. During April, he erected elaborate batteries with which to destroy the enemy's fortifications. The expense of McClellan's engineers alone had given Chase many a sleepless night. Although McClellan claimed to have only ninety-three thousand men, Chase believed that he had a hundred fifty-six thousand men. But no matter how many men he had, he was always certain that he was outnumbered by the enemy. Hence, the elaborate preparation for a siege which had ended two days ago, when the Confederate Army simply abandoned Yorktown; and it was then that Lincoln decided that the time had come for him to pay McClellan a visit. Thus far, the Army of the Potomac had taken only two Confederate strongholds—Manassas and Yorktown; and each had been given up by the enemy. Worse, at Manassas, the famed, feared fortification turned out to be logs of wood painted black to resemble cannons.

Side by side, Chase and General Viele clung to the ship's railing, and watched the waves precede them; the wind was leeward now. "We are making excellent speed," said Chase, quietly expert—*his* cutter.

"A summer storm." Viele pointed to the dark receding clouds in the distance. "Weather's fickle."

"It will," said Chase, cocking an old salt's eye at the pale sun, "still be light when we make landfall."

In absolute dark, the *Miami* anchored off Fortress Monroe. Fortunately, at sunset, the waters of the Chesapeake had grown as still as glass and the cutter was, thought the contented Chase, exactly like a painted ship upon a painted ocean.

The President was now in good spirits. Although Stanton's eyes were bothering him, even he was amiable, as they were helped from the cutter into a tug that would take them to Commodore Goldsborough's flagship, the *Minnesota*.

In absolute stillness, the tug came alongside the towering, floating wooden fortress, ablaze with lights—a tempting target, Chase could not help but think, for the *Merrimack*.

The ship's side looked to Chase like a mountainside, smelling of tar and burnt gunpowder. A ladder of incredible fragility descended from the ship's deck high above them. A sailor stepped forward and held the bottom of the ladder. He looked, expectantly, at Lincoln. "You first, sir?"

Stanton's authoritative voice sounded in the night. "Naturally, military etiquette requires that the President go first. Then the Secretary of the Treasury. Then the Secretary of War. And the others, each according to rank."

"On the theory," said Lincoln, steadying the two parallel guiding ropes which flapped against the ship's side, "that should the ladder *not* hold, each of the remaining officers would move up one rank." On that sardonic note, the President put one large foot on a rung of the wooden ladder; and like, thought Chase, disrespectfully, the Original Ape, Lincoln rapidly ascended the ladder.

Then Chase put a foot carefully on the nearest rung and, slowly, pulled himself up. The warm May night enveloped him like a shroud. He knew that if he looked down at the dark sea, he would fall and drown. So he looked ever upward at the shining stars, not to mention the kerosene lamp a sailor on deck held, presumably to light his way while, simultaneously, blinding him. But the perilous journey finally ended; and Chase was able to take some pleasure in the gasps and groans of the Secretary of War, who lurched up the ladder calling out, piteously, for aid.

Commodore Goldsborough was a stern self-confident officer of what Stanton liked to call "the old school, which means you can teach him nothing now that school's out." The Commodore showed the great officers of state into the low-ceilinged wardroom, where lamps made bright the dark wood interior. He was particularly attentive to Chase, who had once considered marrying the Commodore's wife. In Chase's youth in Washington, he had got to know the Attorney-General William Wirt, a famous lawyer who had begun his career as one of the prosecutors of Aaron Burr for treason. Wirt's five daughters had enthralled Chase. But duty—and necessity—had made marriage impossible then. Nevertheless, he still enjoyed the company of Mrs. Goldsborough; and the Commodore.

Lincoln shook hands with a number of naval officers, who seemed genuinely pleased to gaze upon Old Abe. The President's continuing popularity with the military forces was a mystery that Chase had yet to solve. It was not as if they ever had any dealings with him as opposed to McClellan, who worked mightily—and successfully—to make the army love him; or Stanton, who worked equally hard—and successfully—to make himself feared. But, somehow, the vague, gentle President had captured the imagination of the troops in a way that the face on the one-dollar bill, Salmon Portland Chase, had not. But then Lincoln was not an abolitionist politician. Like Lincoln, the troops were fighting for the Union, while Chase was fighting for the abolition of slavery and the glory of Christ. Curiously enough, Stanton had, lately, come round to Chase's view. At least, he had started to go to church; and read the Bible; and question Chase at length on the fine points of Scripture. But then Stanton's baby son was dying, most horribly; nevertheless, a soul might yet be saved.

"I do not think, sir, that the entire rebel army can save Richmond." Commodore Goldsborough had spread out a number of maps of the peninsula on the wardroom table and the visitors peered at the various points of interest. "General McClellan is now here—at Yorktown. His advance guard has moved to Williamsburg and so, from there, to Richmond, using the York river—here—as his line of communications."

321

Lincoln put his finger on the Chickahominy River, a wriggling line that split the peninsula in two parts. South of the river was Richmond. North of the river was Yorktown. "I assume that once General McClellan is established at Williamsburg, he will keep the army south of the river, which strikes me as a good thing because if he puts the army north of the Chickahominy, he will, sooner or later, have to cross the river, a hard thing to do with the entire rebel army between him and Richmond."

"I'm not in his confidence to that extent," said the Commodore. "I do know that he has, this morning, landed four divisions here at West Point—which is north of the river. I believe that he will hold that position until General McDowell's corps descend from Manassas to Fredericksburg to rendezvous with him at West Point. He needs reinforcements."

"Reinforcements?" Lincoln spoke with a certain wonder. "I cannot believe that General McClellan has too few men for the work at hand."

Stanton then turned to the Commodore, and fired questions at him. Why had the *Monitor* not sunk the *Merrimack* during their first engagement? Why had the *Monitor* not pursued the *Merrimack* at least to the beginning of Norfolk harbor? Why had the newly arrived *Vanderbilt*—a former yacht of the eponymous Commodore now heavily iron-clad—not been brought into the general engagement? With growing temper, the Commodore explained to Stanton the various logistical and tactical difficulties involved, while Stanton, whose own temper never ceased to grow choleric when confronted, harangued the Commodore on the importance of destroying the *Merrimack* by any and every means. The ship represented a mortal danger to the Union.

As the two men pushed the map back and forth between them, Lincoln walked over to the nearest porthole and looked out at the rectangular Fortress Monroe on its promontory. Chase joined him. Neither had seen this legendary fortress before, this solid anchor to the Union's effort in the South. "It should be fair tomorrow," said Lincoln, indicating the clear black sky in which shone a white, small moon.

"I wish I understood better the naval dilemma," said Chase, as the voices of the Commodore and Mars, as Lincoln had taken to calling Stanton, sounded in the background. Chase noted that Stanton's voice was now uncommonly dulcet; always a sign that he was working himself into a real fury. "But I do not."

"Nor do I," said Lincoln. "But I shall want to see these ships in action tomorrow. We'll try to call out the *Merrimack*, and see if the *Monitor* and the *Vanderbilt* can't sink her or drive her to

322

ground. This thing is so new to us—ships made of iron-plate, with turrets that move around, like tin cans on a plate."

"The London *Times* is now predicting the end of wooden navies."

"In that case, I suggest we invest in a lumberyard. The *Times* usually gets it wrong."

There was a stir at the door to the wardroom; the commanding general of Fortress Monroe, John E. Wool, made his entrance. He was a grim, lean old man who had served with Winfield Scott in the War of 1812. Slowly but precisely, he saluted the President; then he introduced his staff.

General Wool also had a number of telegrams from McClellan, addressed to Stanton, who thanked him and withdrew to a corner of the wardroom to read them, while the old man took the President and Chase to one side. There were a number of polite but pertinent remarks about the weather. "The rains have been seasonable but unusually intense, and we have been obliged to build corduroy roads to and from Yorktown." Chase nodded solemnly; he had only recently learned that a corduroy road was one in which planks of wood or branches of trees were set down in the mud of the roadway in order to provide sufficient traction for wheeled vehicles to pass. It was a laborious and costly process. Naturally, McClellan took pleasure in the corduroy road, as he did in any engineering task. He should be back in the railroad business, thought Chase sourly, connecting the east coast to the west, the perennial ambition of a thousand entrepreneurs; and one to which Lincoln often adverted. But as long as the President gave no Federal money to any of the entrepreneurs, Chase did not grudge him his daydream of a railroad line from New York to California.

"What condition are the men in?" asked Lincoln.

The old man frowned. "They arrived in April, as fine an army as I have ever seen. But then the weeks spent before Yorktown took their toll."

"In what sense?" asked Chase.

"The fever, sir. Half the army is ill." Wool turned to Lincoln. "We feed them quinine the way you feed horses hay. The air of these marshes is poisonous in the extreme."

"So the army is not what it was. And the fever beats us." Chase recalled that after the death of Lincoln's son, the President had taken to his bed—for the first time—with Potomac fever; and so had Stanton. Chase alone of the Cabinet seemed exempt from Washington's fevers. But then he had served a term in the Senate, and was almost as inured to the climate as a native.

"It is not that bad, sir. But the advance does not go as swiftly as it ought."

"Tell me, General, how many rebels were there at Yorktown, all this month?"

Although Wool looked somewhat embarrassed, Chase did not feel in the least sorry for him. He had suspected all along the answer the old general now gave. "At the most there were never more than ten thousand men. They waited until all our earthworks and roads and artillery batteries were in place, and then they moved out."

"So we outnumbered them ten to one," said Lincoln; and Chase knew then that McClellan's career was finished unless, in a swift and totally uncharacteristic blaze of activity, the Young Napoleon were to seize Richmond and end the war.

"Tactically, less than ten to one, sir. But certainly four to one."

"We could have broken through?"

Wool nodded; but said nothing. Stanton joined them, telegrams crumpled in one hand. "General McClellan is upset that McDowell has not reinforced him."

"That sounds familiar," said Lincoln. "Is he well established at West Point?"

"As of this morning, yes. There are no later dispatches. Tell me, General Wool, is there any information from Richmond?"

"Yes, sir. There is panic in the city. The Confederate... I mean the rebel congress has adjourned. All the government files—and the gold from the Treasury—are loaded on railroad cars. They expect to lose their capital."

"We are so close," said Lincoln, softly. "So very close."

The next day the President did his best to hasten the end. He stood with General Wool and Commodore Goldsborough on the wall of Fortress Monroe, facing due south across the James River to Sewell's Point, a pale yellow-green promontory in the misty light. To the right of the point was the entrance to Norfolk harbor, where the *Merrimack* lay in wait. The Union ships were now in a line close to the point. The *Monitor*—looking very odd to Chase's eye—waited nearby, turret aimed at the harbor mouth.

"It would be a good thing," said the President, removing his hat, to Chase's relief, as he made a perfect tall target when he stood, unmistakably his giant self, against the sky, "if we were able to sink the *Merrimack* today."

"Yes, sir," said the Commodore, plainly uneasy. "But we are not certain if that is possible..."

Stanton was curt. "It is two iron-clad ships to one. Not to mention our wooden ships..."

At that, there was a terrible roar, as the Union ships opened fired on Sewell's Point. During the intervals between bombardments, Lincoln tried to extract from General Wool the strength of the garrison at Norfolk. General Wool conceded that no one knew for certain but there had been a rumor that when the rebels abandoned Yorktown, they had also abandoned Norfolk.

"But you are not certain?"

"No, sir."

"Then," said the President, "I suggest that we do our best to find out, and should there be no great garrison, occupy the town."

"Naturally, sir, our intelligence will . . ."

There was a cry from the soldiers farther along the high wall. The *Merrimack* had come into view, low and sleek and ominous.

"The *monster!*" said Stanton, as if there was indeed something supernatural about the curiously iron-plated, prowed ship. As the Union's wooden ships began to move out of range, the *Monitor* swung in an awkward arc toward the *Merrimack* while its turret turned in order to sight the monster, which moved, first, directly toward the *Monitor* but then, abruptly, swung to starboard and disappeared round Sewell's Point.

"That was *not* the battle that I had in mind." Lincoln spoke with some disappointment. He turned to Wool. "I'd like a good map of the Norfolk area."

"I'm afraid, sir, there is no such thing."

"We can get you a pilot's map, sir," said Goldsborough. "They are exact—reasonably exact—for this area."

Lincoln turned to Wool. "As I see the exercise, we must move as quickly as we can with all available men to Norfolk. Speed is necessary because we must occupy the Navy Yard before the *Merrimack* can stop us or escape or whatever."

Chase thought the aged general looked more than usually aged as the full morning light came glittering across the water—the famous Hampton Roads.

"I can produce six regiments, sir. They are here and at Camp Hamilton and near the town of Hampton."

Lincoln then said that he would like to review the troops; and a dozen orderlies hurried off to send the word to the surrounding camps that the President was coming to inspect them.

Chase and Stanton and Viele rode behind Lincoln through the ruins of the town of Hampton, put to the torch by the retreating rebels. As Lincoln would approach a regiment, lined up for inspection, Chase and Stanton would remain to one side while the President, accompanied by General Wool and the regiment's commander, would ride past the rows of men in dark, dingy blue uniforms. At the first regiment—in a muddy field outside Hampton—the President appeared awkward and tentative and most, thought Chase, sternly, unmartial. But then, as if Lincoln himself had come to the same conclusion, the President removed his top hat; and when the men got a fair look at the familiar, lean, bearded face of the President, a spontaneous cry went up for "Old Abe" and Chase was both moved and alarmed. If Lincoln could carry the military vote in the next election, he would be electable and if he was electable, he and not Chase would be nominated. Grimly, Chase watched a Lincoln he had not seen before—a smiling and almost youthful war god, cantering past lines of uniformed cheering men.

But Chase's moment of glory came that night. Aboard the *Miami*, Lincoln and Stanton had studied with Chase a pilot's map of the Norfolk area. General Wool had suggested that a landing be made close to Sewell's Point, but Chase had found on the map what looked to be a well-protected place close to the city. "Surely," said Chase, "this is more practical and the men will be less exposed to fire, if there is any."

General Wool had finally got word that although Norfolk was being evacuated, no one knew how many troops remained on the other side of the Elizabeth River to guard the Navy Yard. Chase had then gravely measured the distance on the map—held at a distance of one inch from his left eye—from the landing place that he preferred to Norfolk. "Less than nine miles," he had said. "And there appears to be a good road."

General Wool continued to look uncommonly aged—and superior. "These pilot maps are never to be relied on when it comes to inland roads."

"In that case," Chase had declared, the fierce blood of a hundred generations of Christian warriors now coursing through his large, rejuvenated frame, "let us go ashore *now*, and ascertain the condition of the road, and the principal features of the landing place."

Before General Wool could object, Lincoln had said, "I see no reason why we shouldn't at least send a ship's boat ashore, to scout Mr. Chase's landing place."

The *Miami* was now some five hundred yards off the coast. The moon blazed in the sky and had Chase been able to see anything at all with his new and more than usually unsatisfactory spectacles from Franklin's, he would have been able, quite alone, to determine the state of the shoreline. As it was, a boat was sent to the shore. Then, while Lincoln and Stanton stood beside Chase on the deck—*my* deck, he thought—the ship's boat suddenly turned back.

"I think they've sighted an enemy picket," said Lincoln, the only one of the three statesmen who could see objects in the distance. At best, Stanton was nearly as blind as Chase. At worst,
326

as now, he was suffering from opthalmia. He had already confided to Chase that he was probably going blind. Chase had quoted Scripture; and Stanton had been, Chase was certain, comforted.

The ship's boat was now beneath the deck. An officer called up, "We have found an enemy patrol, sir."

"Come aboard," said Wool.

"Not so fast," said Lincoln, peering across the moon-spangled water to the dark tangle of low trees back of the driftwood-strewn beach. "Someone looks to be waving a white flag. And there are colored people coming down to the water. *Unless*, of course, I am hallucinating."

General Viele now trained a telescope on the shore. "The President is right. We have a welcoming committee. They seem to be colored and as far as I can tell they are all women."

"Then let us go ashore," said Lincoln. "We shall be well-met by moonlight."

Stanton's wheezings began; then ceased. "This could be a trap," he warned. But Lincoln, backed by Chase, overwhelmed Stanton and Wool; and so the three statesmen got into the tug and were rowed ashore. "After all," as Lincoln pointed out, "no one is about to open fire on three sedate old lawyers out for a midnight excursion on the waters."

"More to the point," said Chase, "no one will know it is us."

So it proved. The women paid no attention to the three lawyers but they were most attentive to Generals Wool and Viele, and they assured them that they were in favor of the Union, not to mention the abolition of slavery—their own condition. Yet when General Wool proposed to the women that they be taken across to Fortress Monroe and freedom, they said that they preferred to stay home, and be freed in due course. They did confirm the rumor that the day after Yorktown had fallen, the rebel garrison had begun to abandon the city. But there was still a detachment of troops at the Custom's House, while no one knew whether or not there were troops at the Navy Yard, where the *Merrimack* was tied up.

Lincoln and Chase strode up and down the beach, while Stanton sat on a piece of driftwood, applying cologne from a pocket flask to his whiskers. "This looks," said Lincoln, finally, "as good a place as any on the map, Mr. Chase."

"That is what I thought when I located it on the chart." Chase wanted the discovery to be remembered always as his.

"Yes, you've chosen well. We'll send the troops ashore first thing tomorrow under"—Lincoln lowered his voice—"the ancient Wool. I am amazed he is still in the service."

"I should like to go ashore with him." Chase cast what he

hoped looked like an eagle's eye at where he was fairly certain the road to Norfolk ought to be.

"By all means, General Chase. I'd go with you, too, only Mr. Stanton is already beginning to threaten me with house arrest."

"Well, sir, you are a conspicuous target," said Chase, so cocking his one adequate eye that he could make out with some clarity the tall, thin, top-hatted figure beside him, black in the white moonlight. The President was unmistakable—except to the slavewomen, who were kindly but ignorant.

The next morning when Chase again set foot on the shore, General Viele and an orderly were waiting for him. "You will want a horse, Mr. Chase? Or a carriage?"

"A horse, General." Chase had never felt so alert; yet he had not slept all night in his excitement. Was it too late, he wondered, to resign from the Treasury and accept the commission of major-general, in command of the Ohio troops? With a victory or two in the field, and his face on the one-dollar bill, he could take the nomination from Lincoln, assuming that that kindly, modest man would even want to stand in his way. Chase felt a genuine liking for Lincoln on this cool May morning, as he rode toward Norfolk, General Viele at his side and a squad of dragoons behind them. Along the road, the colored people were lined. There were cheers for the Union army; and an occasional homemade Union flag was displayed. There was also sullen silence from the occasional white person glimpsed, and Chase was suddenly aware of what a very large, not to mention tempting, target he himself presented in his frock coat, surmounted by the second most-famous face in the United States, which included, in his case, the rebel states, where his greenbacks were often used as tender. If shot by a sniper, he could think of no end more worthy of a Christian warrior.

"General Wool has gone on ahead with four regiments," said Viele.

"I thought there were to be six." Chase began to wonder whether or not their informants had been accurate. Could it be that there was still a *large* rebel garrison in Norfolk? Could this be a trap?

"I don't know why the other two regiments were not sent over." Viele did not think much of Wool. Neither did Chase, when, on the outskirts of Norfolk, they found the bridge, which had looked so integral on the map, newly destroyed. Worse, up ahead, the sound of artillery. "The rebels are still here," Chase observed, as coolly as possible.

"So it would appear." Viele reined in his horse. Chase did the same. The dragoons fanned out on either side of them. Over the flat spring countryside, the Union forces were stopped at the river's edge. Rebel artillery was in place to the east of the town on a low wooded hill, as well as in place beyond the burned-out bridge, where earthworks had been raised and bayonets now gleamed.

"We have been misled." Chase was conscious of the sun's heat on his bald head. At that moment two Union generals approached from the direction of the rebel earthworks. They paused to confer, respectfully, with Chase.

One general said that he thought the number of rebels in the works up ahead were few, but that he had counted at least twenty-one major guns, and so, all in all, they had best turn back and consider flanking the works. The other general favored an out-and-out assault. Chase decided that they had best turn back.

On the road, Chase met General Wool at the head of a regiment. As the general conferred in the now dusty roadway, Chase crossed his arms on his chest, as he had seen McClellan do so often. He tried to think of some novelty that would save the day, but as he could think of nothing at all he gravely endorsed General Wool's plan to send General Viele to Newport News for an additional brigade. Meanwhile, the Union regiments were reassigned; yet all were under General Wool, to whom Chase was now, reluctantly, attached.

As the newly reorganized Union army wheeled back toward Norfolk, fire and smoke appeared from behind the earthworks. A moment later a squad of Union cavalry rode up to report that the rebels had evacuated the earthworks and set fire to the barracks. The Union cavalry had already breached the works.

"Norfolk is ours." Chase spoke with quiet satisfaction to Wool as, side by side, they rode into the abandoned fortress. The barracks—mere huts for the most part—were already ashes; and the worst of the smoke had been dispelled by a cool west wind. The troops rode through fortifications where the great guns were still in place; loudly, they cheered their victory.

In the distance, the steepled town of Norfolk seemed empty of all life except for a delegation of civilians who were coming toward them. Chase sat very straight astride his horse, aware that he was now surrogate for the Commander-in-Chief. Beneath a tall elm tree a stout white-haired man got out of a closed carriage; and removed his hat to General Wool. "Sir, I am here, as mayor of Norfolk, to surrender to you, peacefully, our city. If I may, I should also like to introduce to you the aldermen, who have come with me; and present you with the key to our city."

Wool looked at Chase, who nodded and said to the mayor, "I shall receive the key, in the name of the President. I am," he added, quietly, "Secretary Chase."

"Well, sir, I ought to have known you from those greenbacks we see every now and again."

Chase smiled politely; and dismounted. He was stiff in every joint. Beneath a large tree, the mayor, a loquacious Southern gentleman, introduced the city worthies to Chase and Wool. The mayor was careful to make the point that: "Personally, I was for fighting to save the city but the Administration at Richmond decided otherwise, and so we must throw ourselves on your mercy and hope that you will respect property and persons, according to the immemorial laws of the United States."

Although Chase made a short, decorous speech, he was somewhat amazed that twice during his well-chosen, even compassionate words, Wool had looked at his watch. Chase then accepted a large rusty key, alleged to be that to the city if not to its citizens' hearts. Then the mayor proposed that they all repair to City Hall. He turned over to Chase and Wool the fine carriage in which he had arrived. "It was used by *our* commanding general," he said, somewhat bleakly, "until this morning."

Once inside the carriage, Wool said, "We must find out about the Navy Yard. I think they are trying to delay us while the *Merrimack* escapes."

"To where? The Union fleet is waiting off Sewell's Point. The *Monitor* is ready. No, General, the *Merrimack* will not escape. I am certain of that."

At City Hall, the mayor attempted a second speech to a small, grim crowd of elderly white men and hot-eyed crinolined women but Chase, politely, cut him short. Then Chase appointed General Viele military governor of Norfolk; and ordered the Union flag to be raised over the handsome Custom's House, a Greek-revival building of considerable charm. Meanwhile, General Wool ascertained that the Navy Yard was still occupied by rebel troops. "We shall move against the Yard tomorrow," he said, as he joined Chase and Viele in the mayor's office.

"The President thinks we have been too slow," said Viele. "When I was at Newport News, collecting the brigade, he sent for me to come see him at Fortress Monroe. He wanted to know what we were doing back on that side of the water. I told him that I had come across to get the brigade. He wanted to know why all the available regiments had not been sent over in the first place." Viele looked at Wool, who frowned but did not answer. "I said I did not know, and then he took his hat off his head and threw it on the floor. He was, gentlemen, in one hell of a rage!"

"The President?" Chase was startled. He had never seen Lincoln anything but controlled—phlegmatic and rather listless, if the truth were known.

"Yes, sir. Anyway, he wrote out an order sending all available troops to Norfolk."

"He will be pleased," said the old general, "that Norfolk is ours this day. And that the Navy Yard will be ours tomorrow. Now, Mr. Chase, I suggest we avail ourselves of the carriage, and return to the *Miami*, leaving Norfolk in General Viele's competent hands."

The moon had begun to fade when Chase found himself in the parlor of the house where the military commander of Fortress Monroe lived—when not moved out by the President. In the parlor, Chase found a familiar uniformed figure, Governor Sprague, who was holding enthralled a group of naval officers. When Sprague saw Chase, he leapt to his feet. "Mr. Chase, sir. It is good to see you. The President's gone to his room. So has Mr. Stanton, who's now gone blind. I'm aide to the chief of artillery, with McClellan. I was at Williamsburg. We whipped them. Now McClellan's moving out. But he's got to have reinforcements . . ."

Unable to think of a polite way to stop the staccato sentences of the boy-governor, Chase turned to one of the officers and said, through Sprague's lurid description of the battle for Williamsburg, "Tell the President that I am here, with General Wool. Norfolk has fallen."

This stopped Sprague, to Chase's serene delight, which was even further enhanced by the arrival of the President, who pounded him on the back with pleasure when he told him what had happened. The President's happiness was only somewhat marred by the fact that the Navy Yard was still in Confederate hands, and that the *Merrimack* was still at large. "But we cannot have everything, I suppose," he said to Stanton, who had joined them, eyes streaming with ophthalmiac tears. Then Lincoln turned to Wool. "You should make a concerted effort to take the Yard tomorrow. Failing that, keep the *Merrimack* bottled up; and out of the Hampton Roads. Now, gentlemen," Lincoln turned to Chase and Stanton, "we've been away from Washington too long."

"At this rate, sir," said Sprague suddenly, "you could probably end the war before the week is over."

Lincoln laughed. "Well, Governor, there is such a thing as beginner's luck, which I am not about to press any further. Since General McClellan is only twenty miles from Richmond, I shall let him finish things off properly." Lincoln turned to Stanton. "Have you a ship for us?"

"Yes, sir. The *Baltimore*, ready to leave at seven in the morning."

"We shall be ready." With that Lincoln disappeared to his room and Chase, well pleased, went to the room assigned him by General Wool, and slept so well and so heavily that he did not hear the explosion in the night. At breakfast, he was told that the rebels had fired the Navy Yard; and blown up the *Merrimack*.

"In one week, thanks to the President," said Chase to Kate at breakfast, two days later, "we took Norfolk, destroyed the *Merrimack* and secured the Virginia coast."

"You must take all credit, Father. You chose the landing place. You accepted the key to the city..."

Chase nodded and hummed a few bars of "A Mighty Fortress Is Our God," as a quantity of sausage slowly settled in his stomach. It was good to be home again.

"What else did Governor Sprague have to say?" Kate's hair, that morning washed, was shrouded now in a towel that looked like some exotic Venetian turban.

"He was more talkative than informative. He was commended officially by General Hooker, at the battle of Williamsburg—or skirmish, I suppose it should be called. By now he's back in Providence, I should think."

"It's a pity they don't give him a proper command."

Not for the first time did Chase wonder whether or not Kate really liked the little millionaire, who plainly worshipped her in, admittedly, his own highly curious way. "I fear that Governor Sprague lacks the principal prerequisites of a modern general."

"You mean that he did not attend West Point?"

"I mean that he has not practised law like the best of us generals."

Kate laughed. "I sometimes think there is probably nothing to being a general but common sense. And luck," she added, motioning to the butler to pour her father tea.

"He did tell me that he'd be coming here to live, if he does not get a proper command."

"What will he do here, when all those cotton mills of his are up there?"

"He controls the Rhode Island legislature." Chase filled up his teacup with sugar. "He will have them elect him to the Senate. That means his term would begin next March."

"*Senator* Sprague." Kate looked at her father, thoughtfully. "He would be useful here, wouldn't he?"

"Oh, yes. The Administration needs all the help it can get with Ben Wade and his friends..."

"I was thinking ahead, Father, to 1864..."

Chase nodded. "Yes, Kate. Senator Sprague would be useful, if the times should require a different president." Chase looked at Kate, and realized, from her expression, that she would, in due course and entirely for his sake, marry William Sprague IV.

6

ON THE BACK PORCH OF THE OLD CLUB HOUSE, SEWARD LAY
in a hammock, eyes shut, and ears attuned only to the chatter of
birds in the flowering backyard, where huge roses in full bloom
made the air heavy with their scent. Congress had dispersed three
days earlier, and Seward felt like a free man again, no longer the
target of Ben Wade the Bluff and all the other Jacobins who now
held him totally responsible for the slowness of the war effort, not
to mention the vile continuation of slavery everywhere on earth.

As Seward rocked slowly back and forth in the hammock, he
thought, longingly, of sending a detachment of troops to surround
the Capitol while Congress was in session. There would be a mass
arrest. He himself would speak to the assembled members of the
two houses—would they be chained to one another? He left that
detail for a later daydream. But, for the present, he was seated in
the Speaker's chair, and smoking a cigar as the terrified members
of the Congress stood before him, guns trained on them from
soldiers in the gallery. Naturally, he would address them pleasantly; he might even make a joke or two. Then he would explain
how no state could support, in time of war, the luxury of such a
large, unwieldy and often dangerously unpatriotic band of men.
Therefore, it was with true sorrow that he was dissolving the
legislative branch of the government. Most of the members would
be allowed to return home. Unfortunately, there were a number
who would be obliged to stand trial for treasonable activities.
Senator Wade would, of course, be given every opportunity to
defend himself before a military court. But should he and the
other Jacobins be found guilty, they would, of course, be hanged—
in front of the Capitol. Seward was debating whether or not the
gallows should be placed at the east or the west end of the Capitol,
when the servant announced, "Mr. Chase to see you, sir."

Seward opened his eyes; and there was Chase, in a white linen
jacket, looking reasonably cool on such a hot day. "Forgive me
for not stirring," said Seward.

"You are forgiven," Chase pulled up a chair and sat at the foot
of the hammock—like a physician, thought Seward, motioning
to the servant to light his cigar for him. "I've been enjoying the

333

peace and the quiet, now that Congress has gone, and we've only the war to worry about."

Chase nodded. "They take up so much time, our old colleagues. I am told that Ben Wade has announced that the country is going to hell."

"I can only hope that he gets there first," said Seward.

"Things are coming to a climax, Mr. Seward." Chase stared at the small figure in the hammock so like, with its short legs and large nose, a parrot fallen from its perch.

"You mean with McClellan?" Seward knew what Chase meant: the freeing of the slaves was now a matter of great urgency. But *whose* slaves? That was the problem. Meanwhile, England and France were more than ever pro-rebel; each nation taking the high line that the Lincoln Administration was essentially indifferent to the fate of the black man, a subject of no particular interest to either power but a highly convenient rationale for supporting the South—and the breakup of the youthful American empire.

Currently, the radical Republicans were threatening to abandon the Republican Party and the Lincoln Administration. Some of the Jacobin firebrands in Congress—yes, he would have them chained to one another, and the executions would take place on the north side of the Capitol—were insisting that Seward, as Lincoln's evil genius of moderation, resign immediately and that the Joint Committee, together with Chase, free the slaves, sack McClellan and together prosecute the war. Seward was never entirely certain to what extent Chase was involved in these devious plots. He did know that Chase tended to agree with whatever any of the radicals had to say about the President or himself.

"I was not thinking of McClellan, though he is a part of the problem." Chase had come to detest the Young Napoleon. Ever since he himself had delivered Norfolk into the Union's hands, Chase had lost all awe of the military. Some organizational ability, a degree of common sense—and courage—were all that was needed. McClellan had only the first. Chase had all the rest; and so did any number of civilian leaders. Even Lincoln was better equipped to conduct a military operation than McClellan, who had got within six miles of Richmond; and then had failed to take the city, though his army outnumbered the rebels at least five to one; and the rebel commander, Joe Johnston, had been seriously wounded at Seven Pines, one of the few real battles of the so-called Peninsula campaign. Johnston had been succeeded by Robert E. Lee, the friend of the Blairs.

During June and July, McClellan continued to ask for more troops. He claimed that Lee had two hundred thousand men, ready to crack the Union army. Actually, Chase had learned that
334

Lee's army was closer to eighty-five thousand men. In desperation, Lincoln had slipped out of Washington and gone up the Hudson River to the military academy at West Point to confer with Winfield Scott. The result had been that Halleck was soon to arrive as general-in-chief while General John Pope—also from the Western army—was now the commander of a new Army of Virginia, to protect the capital and hold off the alarming "Stonewall" Jackson, who ranged at will up and down the nearby Shenandoah Valley. Finally, with Pope approaching Richmond from the west and McClellan from the east, the city was bound to fall.

McClellan's troops were still divided by the Chickahominy River; and the rains were falling, and the creeks were swollen. But then while everyone was predicting that with a single stroke McClellan could take Richmond, Lee attacked McClellan; and McClellan lost what little nerve he had. After denouncing the President and Stanton, the Young Napoleon retreated to the James River and set up a new headquarters at Harrison's Landing.

Since the Confederate government was now conscripting men, Lincoln sent Seward, secretly, to New York City to meet with the Northern governors and ask them to petition the President to call for more troops. As there was now no great general eagerness to enlist in the Union army, the day before Congress adjourned those men between the ages of eighteen and forty-five might be liable for military duty.

But Chase had not come to Seward's house to discuss McClellan. He had written off McClellan and he knew that Lincoln would, presently, replace him. Chase had total faith in John Pope, a dedicated abolitionist, who had made an excellent impression on the Joint Committee. The war would come to its predestined end. "But, Mr. Seward, we cannot remain silent any longer on the subject of slavery."

Chase got the full benefit of Seward's single, bright parrot's eye—the nose made it impossible for Chase to see both eyes at the same time of the recumbent Secretary of State.

"Silent? Mr. Chase, we chatter of nothing else. Even the President is beginning to sound like an abolitionist. I told him it would do no good to try to talk to those border-state congressmen. But he thought he had to. So last week he told them he'd pay three hundred dollars a head for each of their Negroes; and they said no."

"They did not *all* say no." Chase had thought Lincoln more than usually feckless in the way that he had handled so difficult a business. Lincoln had appealed to their patriotism, which was irrelevant since they were all on the Union's side, more or less willingly. Lincoln had then made the curious point that as long

as they maintained slavery within their borders, the states in rebellion would always feel that one day the border-states would
join them; but should slavery be abolished and the slaveholders
compensated, the rebel states would not continue to fight much
longer. Like so many of Lincoln's attempts at logic, this essay had
left Chase as cold as it had a majority of the border-men present.
"But I suppose it is hard for the President to forget that he is a
Kentuckian, and that Mrs. Lincoln's brothers are all at war against
us."

"I think the President is peculiarly able to rise above his brothers-
in-law," said Seward, swinging his hammock in a sort of semicircle, which made Chase dizzy to watch.

"I wish he would rise the entire way in this matter."

"You would free all of the slaves within the Union?"

"Yes, Mr. Seward, I would."

Seward was enjoying himself. "And in those states that are in
rebellion?"

"I would have the military commanders free them, as each
rebel state is brought to heel."

"The military commanders rather than the President?"

"I think," said Chase, judiciously, "that is the practical way."

"I see." Seward saw that for all of Chase's passion on the subject
of abolition, he did not want the President to get any of the credit
for so noble a deed. On the other hand, he would not object to
Lincoln taking whatever blame might be handed around.

"I think, Mr. Seward, it is up to us to guide the President in
this matter. He will not act of his own accord . . ."

"You may be surprised, Mr. Chase."

Chase looked at Seward expectantly. "What form will the surprise take?"

"I think that Mr. Lincoln is thinking hard, and that means
that he is about to make a move."

"You are in his confidence, of course." Chase was polite; but
no more. He knew that if Seward had his way, nothing would be
done until after the congressional elections in the fall. As Chase
rose to go, Seward got out of his hammock with a surprisingly
youthful spring.

"Would that we had a Cromwell!" Seward exclaimed, as he
led Chase into the house.

"You?" asked Chase, who had often heard Seward go on in a
similar vein.

"Or you. Or even Lincoln."

"I am sure *he* could never rise to the stern . . . necessity."

"Could you, Mr. Chase?"

Chase mopped his brow. The interior of the house was even warmer than the back porch.

"It is tempting, in a war, to give the leadership to one man. But once the war is over, he must, of course, be executed promptly."

"*I* would avoid that," said Seward, merrily.

"*Et tu, Brute?*" said Chase, thinking not of Shakespeare but of Scripture and of Christ's suffering on the cross that man might be redeemed through His blood. Now *that* would be a mighty, worthy fate.

Hay was at the window of Nicolay's office when the Secretary of the Treasury emerged from Seward's house. "They are plotting," he said to Nicolay. "Chase and Seward are up to something."

"We shall survive." Nicolay was on his feet. He was en route to the cool wilds of Minnesota. Once Congress had gone home, half the secretary's work mysteriously ceased. Hay watched as Chase drove away in his carriage. Then the newest streetcar, an open affair for summer days, passed in all its cream-and-white splendor beneath the White House and a number of well-dressed gentlemen and ladies waved at the President, wherever he might be; and Hay waved back.

"I think," said Hay, half to himself and half to the busy Nicolay, "I shall call on Miss Kate."

"Isn't the boy-governor in town?"

"No. He's at Corinth, I think. He's asked the Tycoon to allow him to explain to Halleck how to wind up the war in the west."

"When does Halleck get here?" Nicolay's carpetbag was now filled up with papers.

"The twenty-third, he says. He keeps delaying. If I were to be general-in-chief, I'd come running." Hay sat at Nicolay's desk. "Miss Kate is more than usually agreeable this summer."

"Then beware. *She* is plotting."

Lincoln entered the office. "Well, Mr. Nicolay, you are off today, I see."

"Yes, sir."

"I hope you'll get a glimpse of Miss Therena Bates."

"If there is a chance, between the Chippewas and the Cheyennes, I will."

"Yes." Lincoln frowned. "You'll have your work cut out for you. As if we didn't have enough to do, we're about to have us an Indian war. Present my compliments to Chief Hole-in-the-Day."

"I will, sir."

"Offer him your scalp," added Hay, aware that Lincoln had drifted off. Absently, the President had walked over to the table strewn with newspapers. "It is ominous," he said, picking up the

337

New York *Tribune*, "that I've not heard from Horace Greeley for a week."

"Perhaps," said Hay, "he is ill."

"Oh, we should have heard *that* news," said Lincoln, glancing at the editorial page. "'A great man is fast sinking,' we'd read. Well, he favors last week's Confiscation Act, but he says it don't go far enough. How much further can Congress go than to say that the slaves of any person found guilty of treason are free?"

Both Nicolay and Hay realized that whenever Lincoln asked questions of a newspaper, he did not expect either of them to speak in the editor's place. Lincoln next addressed a number of ringing questions to James Gordon Bennett; and then threw down the *Herald*. "I ought not to read these people," he said; then added: "Anyway, our Railroad Bill seems popular."

"But the *New York Times*," said Nicolay, "wonders how, in the middle of the most expensive war in history, you'll be able to pay for a railroad line from coast to coast."

"It's only from western Iowa to San Francisco..." Lincoln looked, for a moment, wistful. "You know, I really hope to take that train one day. I dearly want to see the Pacific Ocean. It is my last passion." He turned to Nicolay. "Have you a copy of General McClellan's letter to me, the one he gave me at Harrison's Landing?"

"Yes, sir." Nicolay touched the strongbox on his desk. "I keep it here, locked up."

"You keep it under lock and key, too, John," said the Ancient to Hay; then he bade Nicolay farewell; and returned to his own office, where Tad promptly started to bang a drum. "My son," they heard the President's mild voice from the corridor, "could you not manage to make less noise?"

"That boy's run wild since Mrs. Edwards went home." Hay had his own ideas about the way in which children should be brought up, and the Lincolns failed entirely to meet his standards. Tad was seen, was heard, was everywhere underfoot.

"I'd hoped she would stay longer," said Nicolay.

"Not even she can take the Hellcat."

"The scenes never stop." Nicolay shut his bag. "I don't envy you, Johnny."

"Do you think she's mad?" This was a recurring dialogue.

"She is certainly not like other people. She is two people..."

"She is Hell. She is Cat. And she is the Hellcat. That's *three* people." Since Willie's death, Hay had gone out of his way to be sympathetic and helpful, but nothing could allay Madam's suspicions, compounded, as always, by urgent demands for money. Since Watt continued, mysteriously, to work at the White House under a cloud rather larger than a President's message to Congress, she had turned more and more to the urbane Major French, whose urbanity with each passing month was more and more tested. Meanwhile, she was in darkest mourning. The Marine Band was no longer allowed to play on summer evenings in the President's Park, while the bedroom in which Willie had died was now off-limits for her as was the downstairs Green Room, where the boy had been embalmed. The President bore his own grief stoically—although Nico had told Hay that immediately after the Ancient had left the death-bed, he had come, in tears, to Nicolay's office and said, "Well, Nicolay, my boy is gone. He is actually gone. Gone," he repeated, as if he could not believe what had happened. But there it ended. After that, he shared his grief with no one, as far as Hay knew.

Nicolay was at the door, carpetbag in hand. "I shall think of you, Johnny, from time to time. Beware the fair Kate."

"Like the Medusa."

"You'll enjoy the coming surprise. I wish I were going to be here."

"Surprise?" Hay usually knew everything that Nicolay knew. But, lately, he had noticed that the Ancient and Nicolay were often alone together in the President's office; and that whenever he had entered the room, they would fall silent.

"You'll see. Now I must go. You have the key to the strongbox. All else is in order." Nicolay shook Hay's hand firmly; and left the room. Ten minutes later, Hay realized that Nicolay had forgotten to give him the key to the strongbox. Hay hurried downstairs, but Nicolay's carriage had already departed for the depot.

The surprise occurred at the Cabinet meeting on July 22. At first Hay feared that he would not be included, but the President, at the last moment, said that he would want notes of what the others said.

The room was bright; and the air hot. Flies buzzed in and out of the open windows. Lincoln had loosened his tie; and the corded brown neck looked as if it might have belonged to Chief Hole-in-the-Day. All the Cabinet was present save Blair. After a few bits of business, Lincoln removed a document from his pocket; and put on his glasses. But instead of looking at the pages in his hand, he stared at the gaslight fixtures that depended from the ceiling. "I think that we are, in many ways, about at the end of our rope on the plan of operations that we have been following—politically as well as militarily. We are to face a difficult election in November. There's a possibility we may lose Pennsylvania, Ohio and Indiana. Meanwhile, our French friends are busy across the border in Mexico, stirring up trouble, and our British friends

339

are letting the rebels use their shipyards, in violation of our agreed-upon neutrality. In one year, Mr. Chase tells me the public debt has gone from ninety million dollars to a half billion dollars. Personally, I cannot visualize either sum. But I know that we cannot go on much longer as we are without victories in the field and in the world's political arena."

Lincoln glanced at the papers in his hand. Hay could not for the life of him guess what the Ancient was up to. But Seward knew; had indeed discussed the matter with the President. Chase suspected; and was now most uneasy. In a sense, he himself could—with a stroke of Lincoln's pen—lose his moral superiority to Lincoln. "As you know, I have said, more than once, if I could preserve the Union by freeing *all* of the slaves everywhere, I would do so. If I could preserve the Union by freeing *none* of the slaves, I would do so. If I could preserve the Union by freeing *some* of the slaves but not others, I would do so. Well, I have not the political power to do the first. I have not the inclination nor the need to do the second. So I shall now do the third, as a military necessity."

The silence in the room was made all the deeper by the buzzing of the flies—and the bluebottles that swept like artillery shells past Hay's face. The Ancient had at last seized the moment. Chase was very pale; and perturbed. Seward was in another, pleasanter world, gazing out the window. Stanton scowled. Welles sweated beneath his wig. Bates looked sorrowful. Smith looked indifferent. "I should tell you that I have myself prepared a proclamation of emancipation. I shall, in due course, publish it. And it will be the law. I have not asked you here for your advice, though once I have read you what I have written, you may certainly comment."

Lincoln then proceeded to read a most adroit document. To the slaveholding states within the Union, he promised to ask the Congress to provide some means of giving financial aid to those elements which favored the gradual abolishment of slavery. But for those states that were in rebellion against the Union, "I, as Commander-in-Chief of the army and navy of the United States, do order and declare that on the first day of January, in the year of our Lord one thousand eight hundred and sixty-three, all persons held as slaves within any State or States wherein the Constitutional authority of the United States shall not then be practically recognized, submitted to and maintained, shall then, thenceforward, and forever be free." The President put down the pages on the table; and removed his glasses; and rubbed his nose.

Blair entered the room, apologizing for being late. Lincoln indicated, silently, that he read the draft of the proclamation, which he did; not happily, thought Hay.

Linclon turned not to Seward, as protocol required, but to Chase. "We all spoke yesterday, Mr. Chase, about a number of military orders that I have had in mind on the question of what is to be done with those Negroes from the rebel states who are now free of their masters, and I think we are all pretty much agreed that they may be employed by us as laborers, and so on. All of us supported the plan to colonize the Negroes in some tropical place except you."

"Yes, sir." Chase cleared his throat; he was suddenly aware that he was nervous, and he wondered why. "I have never taken to the idea that we simply remove three million Negroes from this continent, and send them to Central America or across the Atlantic to Africa. If nothing else, the cost of moving them would be prohibitive."

"Well, I have tabled the matter, at your insistence. On the other hand, I part company with some of you on the arming of former slaves. I think that this would have a most incendiary effect in the border-states, and not affect the rebels much one way or the other."

"There, sir, we differ." Chase looked to Seward for aid, but there was none; looked to Stanton, who was with him in this matter, but Stanton chose silence. "As for the proclamation that you have read to us, I would prefer that you leave to the various commanding generals the task of freeing—and arming—the slaves, as these Negroes come within their jurisdiction. But since you are averse to this, I give my entire support to the proclamation, in its place."

The President nodded. "Thank you, Mr. Chase." Then he turned to Montgomery Blair. "You missed yesterday's meeting, but you now know the gist of it; and you have read the proclamation."

"Yes, sir." Blair's naturally fierce face was made more ferocious by the bright sun that caused his eyes to shine like polished gray marble. "I think you know my views. I want all the slaves freed at the *end* of the war; and then I want every last Negro shipped off to Africa or New Granada or wherever we can find a country for them. The people, Mr. Chase"—Blair turned his glare on the bland Roman bust of the Secretary of the Treasury—"will find the money to transport them from this continent where they never should have been brought, which is why this war is the Judgment of God on us for bringing them here in the first place."

"That's very eloquent, Mr. Blair." Lincoln was dry. "And much my own view, but the issue at hand is the proclamation. What is your view of it?"

"My view, sir, is that if you publish it, we will lose the No-

341

vember election, and you will be faced with a Democratic Congress."

Lincoln seemed taken aback by Blair's directness. But before he could speak, Seward broke in. "I fully support the proclamation, which the President intends to publish in any case, and I think it will do us more good than ill, particularly in our relations with the European powers. But I would suggest, Mr. President, most respectfully, that as we are plainly *not* winning the war—and going bust in the process—that you postpone the proclamation until you can give it to the country supported by military success. Otherwise, the impression will be, in the light of so many reverses, of our last shriek on the retreat."

Lincoln stretched his arms, always, Hay knew, a sign that he was past the worst of some encounter. "I think that's eminently sound advice, Governor, which I shall take." Lincoln gave the pages to Hay. "Mr. Hay, put this away in the strongbox." Hay felt slightly ill. *Where* was the key? "We shall keep all of this a secret until such time as I am able to celebrate a victory. What news"—the Tycoon turned to Stanton—"of General McClellan?"

"The Great American Tortoise remains in place."

"He is consistent," said the President, wearily. "Well, soon we shall have General Halleck here as general-in-chief. At West Point, he is known as Old Brains, and he is, yet again, General Scott's choice. I've also been reading General Halleck's *Elements of Military Art and Science*; it is most serious, most serious."

The conversation turned to General Pope, who was everyone's idea of a fighting general. Chase had got very friendly with him; he had even shepherded the fiery general around the Capitol, where he had made an excellent impression on the abolitionists. Pope's father had been an Illinois district judge in whose court Lincoln had practised. But Lincoln had done nothing to promote him. Pope had succeeded quite on his own in the West, under Halleck. While Lincoln was with Scott at West Point, Stanton had summoned Pope to Washington and offered him the command of a new army, to be known as the Army of Virginia, with McDowell and Frémont and Banks under him. Pope had accepted the command. He was a magnificent-looking man with a vast beard. Unfortunately, he took an immediate dislike to McClellan, who reciprocated. As a result, the armies of Virginia and of the Potomac were now commanded by two rivals. Thus far, Lincoln chose not to notice the irritabilities of his commanders. But then after Hay had read the letter that McClellan gave Lincoln at Harrison's Landing, he had come to the conclusion that the Ancient was a saint. Unable to take Richmond, McClellan had had the audacity to present the President with a letter filled with political advice to the effect that the noble war to preserve the Union must not be fought against the Southern people or their property, which included slaves. It was plain to Hay that this document was intended to be the platform from which McClellan would run for president in 1864. It was also plain to Lincoln, who made no comment other than a wise smile when others made the same comment.

Chase thought *himself* a saint for concurring so wholeheartedly in Lincoln's plan to emancipate the slaves of the rebel states. Granted, he had no alternative, for the President had been uncharacteristically firm. Lincoln had assembled the Cabinet in order to tell them what he intended to do. Since Seward was plainly behind him, pulling the strings, Chase was outnumbered. More than ever, he was convinced that Seward was the mind of the Administration to the extent that such a haphazard and themeless government could be said to have a mind. Since he himself was not permitted to create grand strategy, he could at least continue to be the voice of conscience—seldom heeded, of course, by these conscienceless politicians.

As the conversation became desultory, Chase struck one of his themes. "In the matter of the currency..."

Lincoln gave a long sigh; and all the others save Stanton smiled.

The President's inability to cope with even the idea of the national finance was a sign, if nothing else, of his incompetence, thought Chase, who did understand the precarious nature of fiat money in general and of the so-called greenbacks in particular. "I know," said Lincoln, "that in the matter of the currency, we have, always, too much of it, which means too little of it. This is highly metaphysical, as my old law partner, Billy Herndon, would say."

Hay had a sudden image of Herndon at Sal Austin's; and he wondered if the old man had married the young girl that he had been courting; and if he had, he wondered if Herndon had given up whiskey, as promised. He hoped so, for the Tycoon's sake.

"I did not mean to advert to the metaphysical," said Chase, with what he hoped was a polite smile. "I did not want to bring up again to the Cabinet my personal desire to have printed on our bank notes the same phrase that I devised for our coinage. I mean, of course, 'In God we Trust.'"

"Surely," said Bates, a constant antagonist in these matters, "the Constitutional separation of church and state makes such a phrase highly irregular if not illegal."

"Well," said Lincoln, getting to his feet, "if you are going to put a Biblical tag on the greenback, I would suggest that of Peter and John: 'Silver and gold have I none; but such as I have give I

343

thee.'" In the ensuing laughter, the President withdrew to his office and Chase realized that, once again, he had not managed to get a straight answer from the President on an issue of signal importance to every God-fearing Unionist.

Seward put his arm through Chase's, a gesture that Chase deeply disliked but endured, as he did so much else, for his country. "The President is not the free-thinker you may suspect he is."

"I suspect nothing." Chase was aware of the smell of stale cigar smoke from the small figure at his side; also, a hint of port upon the breath.

"Well, you have your emancipation," said Seward comfortably, as the two men made their way down the crowded hallway. Every step or so, a petitioner or well-wisher stopped one or the other or both. Seward's responses were merrily elliptical. Chase's responses were gravely vague.

"It is not *my* emancipation. There are still the border-states. *I* would have freed all the slaves everywhere."

"Then I pity *your* poor Secretary of the Treasury, because he'd never sell another Treasury bond anywhere on earth."

Chase gave Seward what he hoped was a cold eye; certainly, it was an eye that was nearly blind in its central vision. On the other hand, the peripheral vision saw everything with fine clarity.

Saw Kate, radiant, in the front parlor, with the young Ohian general who had just moved into the house for the summer. He sprang to his feet as Chase entered the room. He was tall, with blue eyes and a quantity of curling golden hair as well as an equally golden beard. When Kate had suggested that he had gilded at least the beard, he had cut off a lock, suitable, he said, for analysis or a locket or both. Kate had declined the trust on the ground that he must be as true as gold, if not steel, to his young wife, Lucretia, back in Hiram, Ohio. If only, Chase had thought more than once, William Sprague had half the charm and learning of James A. Garfield or, put another way, if only General Garfield had a tenth of Sprague's fortune, he would indeed, at the age of thirty and unmarried, be a suitable son-in-law. But nothing is ever as it should be. Garfield was married; and poor.

Kate presided over lemonade; asked her father what had happened at Cabinet; listened attentively to his report, which did not include the secret emancipation proclamation.

"I'm receiving today," said Kate, finally, as Chase drank deeply of the lemonade. "I said I'd be home to what's left of the town, now that Congress has gone."

"Well, there's the military left," said Chase.

"Worse luck," said Garfield. "Everything's beginning, at last, to happen and I'm here in the city—waiting."

344

"Well, it's nice for us, if not the war," said Kate.

"You won't wait long," said Chase. But he stopped speaking while the manservant dressed in a linen coat with gold braid and gold buttons—Kate's latest innovation—put out cakes on a tea-stand. When the man was out of earshot, Chase murmured, "I think I've got you the Florida command. But it's a secret."

"That's what I most want!" The youthful face was animated—Apollo, the ladies called General Garfield. "The war will be decided when the western troops join the eastern troops *below* Richmond."

"But, first, we must wait for General Halleck to arrive. He'll make the final decision. Stanton likes him, and the President *thinks* that he will like him."

"Oh, he's first-rate, Old Brains. A born general-in-chief, if not a born field commander. Everything that we've won in the West was actually won by Grant..."

"...and Pope," said Chase.

"Your latest enthusiasm," said Kate.

"Pope, too," said Garfield, politely. "But I was with Grant at Shiloh, on the second day, the bloody day. I saw the way he was pounded and pounded..."

"...the way he killed and killed," said Kate, shuddering.

"Yes," said Garfield, "that is what we do in a war."

Kate's guests began to arrive; and Chase withdrew to his study, missing John Hay, who arrived just as the sun began, gloriously, to set.

Hay had seen Kate several times during the summer. They had gone three times to the theater, twice in the company of others. But the last time, the two of them had attended an operetta, followed by supper at Wormley's. Hay found Kate endlessly attractive in her person. He found less attractive the shrewd political mind that never ceased to plot, so reminiscent of the Tycoon if Herndon were to be believed; and certainly reminiscent of her father, who was constantly alert to his own advancement. Yet Hay liked the way that Kate would often ask him a direct question of the sort that no lady would but a politician might.

Hay now sat beside her, aware that the saffron light of the setting sun had turned each to gold. In the front parlor, the bebuttoned servant was lighting candles. "We must go riding Sunday," said Hay; he could feel the heat of her forearm on his left hand which now clutched, modestly, his right elbow.

"Oh, Atalanta's being shoed then, poor beast!" Kate looked at him and her ordinarily golden-hazel eyes were now like Spanish doubloons in the spectacular last light of day. "But during the week, if I haven't gone North..." As she raised her arm to indicate that Garfield should join them, the smooth skin touched Hay's fingers for an instant and he felt an electrical shock to his system.

Garfield, all gold to begin with, looked somewhat brazen in the light. Hay found him amiable enough; but then Hay was also somewhat jealous. Of course, Garfield was older than he—thirty, at least; and married. But Garfield, who had been a state legislator, was now a distinguished general; and the President's second secretary felt very small in that glittering presence. Worse, Garfield possessed a most good-humored if highly generalized charm. "I know your uncle," he said to Hay's surprise. "I saw him last in Columbus, where we all used to live." He turned to Kate, who smiled at him as if, thought Hay, she were in love, always a sign, he now knew, that she was not. Kate Chase loved only her father; and, perhaps, herself.

"Some of us lived there more happily than others," she said. Kate turned to Hay. "If Atalanta's shoed in time, we could go riding in the afternoon."

"I'm always at your disposal," said Hay.

"The one man who is not." Garfield was amiable. "You keep late hours at the White House. I've seen your lights on at midnight—and after."

"The confusion never stops," said Hay, affecting a weariness that he only occasionally felt.

"How is Mrs. Lincoln?" asked Kate, with a worried frown that Hay had come to know meant that she was up to mischief.

"She's at the Soldiers' Home now, she and the boy."

"Still in deep mourning, they say." Garfield seemed genuinely sad.

"She speaks to the child." Kate's frown did not alter. "I know. I've met Mrs. Laury, the medium. Apparently, the boy is happy on the other side."

Garfield responded in Greek. The voice was musical; and the accent precise. But then he had been a professor of Greek and Latin literature before he went into politics.

"What is that?" asked Kate, not as "finished by school" as Hay had supposed.

"It is Achilles in the underworld," said Hay. "He is telling Odysseus he would rather be a serf among the living than king of all the dead."

"What paragons I know!" Kate was enchanted; and, thus, enchanting. But the golden evening light had gone. The candles were now lit. Through the windows fireflies flashed in the backyard. William Sanford presented himself to Kate, who smiled, and said, "We were speaking Greek, Captain Sanford."

"Well," said the rich young man, "that's Greek to me."

"Oh, three paragons!" Kate exalimed; then leapt to her feet. "It is General Pope!" The hero of the hour was indeed in her parlor; but not to see her. Plainly a busy and preoccupied man, he greeted the guests en masse and disappeared into Chase's study. As the door closed, Garfield said, "There's the key to the lock. He is our best general—in the West, at least," he added with a politician's care.

"Better than Grant?" asked Hay, genuinely curious. He could not make up his mind which set of generals was worse—the West Pointers who had spent their careers making money in the railroad business or the politicians on horseback, looking for renown. Although Grant was a West Pointer, he had gone into the saddlery business, where he had attractively failed.

"He's a better all-round general than Grant. But Grant is best in the field. I know you disapprove, Miss Kate, of how he never lets up but that's the way it's done. The two sides lost more men at Shiloh than were ever before lost in a single day of modern warfare. That was because Grant would not retreat, even though the rebels had the advantage."

In Chase's study, Pope was saying the opposite. "Grant is hopeless. When not drunk, he is in a sort of stupor. At Shiloh, he was surprised by the enemy. He was unprepared. He barely survived. He is no general. But then McClellan's worse."

Chase nodded. "I have come to the conclusion, General—and this is just between the two of us—that McClellan has no intention of harming the South in any way. If possible, he would like them back in the Union by 'sixty-four, so that he could then get their votes as the Democratic candidate."

Pope combed his thick black beard with thick red fingers. "I would not be surprised if you are right. Certainly, he has acted curiously. Imagine being within six miles of Richmond, and not taking the city. I don't think he wants to fight at all, and your reason is the best I've heard—cowardice to one side. But I mean to fight. I've told the troops not to worry about lines of escape and all the rest of it. We shall see only *their* backs, I promise you, I said." Pope strode up and down the study, and Chase felt confidence at last—or at least for the first time since McDowell. He thanked Heaven yet again that the general who would defeat the South was a dedicated abolitionist; and partisan to him.

Pope wanted to know exactly where Lincoln stood on the matter of abolition. "I shall be inheriting thousands of black souls as I lead the Army of Virginia into Virginia. What am I to do with them?"

For an instant, Chase was tempted to tell him what he had sworn not to tell—about the Emancipation Proclamation. But that weak instant passed. "I would," said Chase, voice very low, "in the wake of victories—and I expect *you* to take Richmond with or without McClellan's aid—*I* would free the slaves on my own initiative and include them, if possible, in your army, even arm them if you choose. That is what *I* would do, of course. I concede that. It is not what Mr. Seward would do."

"Which means the President?"

"Which means the President." Chase nodded. The seed had now been planted. He prayed that it would take proper root and flourish. Lincoln's Emancipation Proclamation would then be a legislative afterthought to Pope's bold freeing of the slaves.

"I understand you, Mr. Chase."

"I think we understand each other, and what Heaven commands us to do. In my small way, I know what it is like to conquer an enemy city—as I did at Norfolk—and to see the black slaves all around me, beseeching me to strike their chains. But I had not the authority that day. You will. Your victories in the field will be your orders."

"I shall not disappoint you, Mr. Chase." Pope took Chase's hand in both of his. They were allies, committed to Heaven's work.

During their solemn pledge, William Sanford proposed to Kate in the front parlor. "I plan to leave the army the first of the year. We could go to France. There is a house there I've had my eye on since before the war. At St. Cloud, near Paris. We could have a wonderful life. I'd study music. You would be at court, if you wanted that."

Kate's eyes glowed in the candlelight. "You are good to ask me, Mr. Sanford. I am honored. I am touched. If there was no war, and if my father were not so deeply involved in public affairs, I cannot think of a happier life..."

"It is Governor Sprague, isn't it?" Sanford scowled; the rosy lips pouted.

"Oh, it's no one, I promise you, but my father and me," said Kate with, for once, perfect candor. Then General Pope swept through the room; and out into the night, and his destiny.

Hay was now at Kate's side. He had a fair notion of Sanford's conversation. The younger set in Washington was much aware of Sanford's passion for Kate. Some thought she should marry him; and never again worry about money for herself or her father. Others thought that she should settle for Sprague and *his* money, and remain with her father. Hay thought that she would make *him* an admirable consort, even though there was no money at all between them, and he was not certain that he had the knack of making it. "How do you like your new commander, Captain

348

Sanford?" Hay asked Sanford the question but looked at Kate, who was staring, idly, at Garfield.

"General McDowell likes him well enough," said Sanford, who was still on McDowell's staff. "But General Frémont won't serve under an officer he outranks. So Frémont has quit."

"That's a bit of luck," said Hay, aware of his tactlessness; after all, the President had done everything in his power to keep content the absolutely incompetent but highly popular Frémont, who had been the first Republican candidate for president; thus, outranking, in a sense, the second candidate, Lincoln.

"That's what General McDowell thinks." Sanford continued to stare at Kate, who looked more than usually lovely and un-touchable—but not untouching, for Hay could still feel on the back of his hand the smooth skin of her arm.

"What is the plan?" asked Kate. "Or is that secret?"

"We know very little," said Sanford, glancing at Hay. "The Army of Virginia will probably join up with the Army of the Potomac and together they'll occupy Richmond."

"I'm sure," said Kate, "that that is *not* what will happen. By design or plain incompetence something else is bound to take place, and the enemy already knows everything."

7

DAVID HEROLD, ENEMY OF THE UNION AND OCCASIONAL SPY—far too occasional for his taste—made his way through the crowded Center Market. The first cool wind of autumn was in the air; and the first hogs had been slaughtered. The pig-ladies were all of them busy, each at her stall beneath the vast roof of the market which was neither enclosed nor open air. The entire high structure was a fretwork of beams set in brick half-walls. The market was the center not only for the women of Washington, but many of the ladies, too. Everyone came to look at the produce from the surrounding farms as well as every sort of fish—preserved, fresh and alive in tanks. There were barrels of oysters from the Chesapeake, but none from the Rappahannock, now lost forever to the Union capital, thought David, well pleased that the latest Confederate victories had deprived the Yanks of the world's best oysters.

Chickens dead and alive overflowed Mr. Henderson's stall, where several Henderson women, bright-eyed and beak-nosed, wrung the necks of living chickens; then plucked and eviscerated the corpses with extraordinary speed and skill, all the while smiling to themselves like cannibals sated. Ladies in crinolines and huge hats stood alongside black women in bandannas. The Center Market made sisters of them all. Where a thousand men and women sold quantities of food, no degree was observed other than that of food-seller to customer. David's mother had known some of the countryfolk all her life. One old woman from Fairfax had sold fruit not only to David's mother but to his grandmother and great-grandmother as well. As a result, there were always barrels of apples going bad in the cellar of the Herold house.

"I reckon you're looking for a stewing chicken, for your mother." Mr. Henderson began each meeting in the same way; and with the same words. Then he would motion for David to join him in the back of the stall, where he would produce a number of plucked chickens and he would caress them as he and David talked, their voices low—not that any voice lower than a shout could be heard on a bright Monday market morning in September.

"We've taken Harper's Ferry back," said Mr. Henderson, bright eyes on the crowd of women who had gathered around his wife in order to pinch and poke the superior-to-all-others Henderson fowls.

"They say General Lee's headed for Philadelphia." David repeated the latest rumors. "And only McClellan can stop him, which means there is nothing to stop him."

"He's gone from the town?"

David nodded. "Week ago today. I took some medicine over to his house, and almost broke my neck on these telegraph lines he's got running all along the floors and up the stairs. He was fixing to go, I could tell from what he was saying to these aides who kept coming in and out, and he was blaming Old Abe and the Pope for the fix he's in."

"*General* Pope, Davie," said Mr. Henderson. "No need to involve the papists just yet. There being a few good ones, like John Surratt, God rest his valiant soul." Both David and Mr. Henderson had attended the old man's funeral the previous month. He had died happy in the knowledge that the Yankees under General Pope had been beaten a second time at Bull Run by Lee and Jackson, who were now invading Maryland on their way to Pennsylvania.

"Well, we've helped save Richmond, you and me, by feeding Mr. Pinkerton till he's like to burst with all sorts of nonsense. Now if General Lee can set up shop in Philadelphia, the war is over and we have won."

David was pleased; and displeased. He had yet to play a gallant

350

role. He had kept his ears open. He had delivered Thompson's medicine and, in the process, he had managed to steal copies of orders which he liked to believe were crucial to the war but, actually, he had yet to come across anything like a real secret on the order of the one that Bettie Duvall—now vanished—had ridden all one night to give General Beauregard. But, as Mr. Henderson said, you never know what might prove useful to the government at Richmond. So David gave whatever he came across to Mr. Henderson; and he was rewarded with kind words and, occasionally, money. He now lived, once again, with the widow in the Navy Yard. But he was growing mortally sick of ham. He had visited Sal Austin a number of times, ostensibly to chat with her on a Sunday afternoon but, actually, to try to discover who frequented her parlors and her beds. But Sal was discreet. Fortunately, the girls were not; and he learned that John Hay, a regular customer, was currently enamored—if that was the word— of Azadia, a beautiful, half-Indian girl, who confessed that she quite enjoyed the President's secretary. "Like going to bed with a schoolboy—or you," she had added, as they lay side by side on the wide bed, watching the summer light stream through half-closed shutters, listening to church bells. Sunday morning was the only time that he could properly enjoy, at a special rate, Sal's premises.

When David questioned Azadia—most cunningly, he thought to himself—she had been talkative. Unfortunately, Hay had not been talkative. But Hay had told her of the President's outrage at McClellan, who had told Mr. Stanton that Pope could get out of his own scrape at Bull Run; and then let Pope's army be destroyed. Hay had also said that there would soon be a great change in the war. When David had repeated that to Mr. Henderson, the chicken-man actually cackled. "The change is," he said at last, "we went and won!"

But Mr. Henderson was not cackling now. "The next few weeks will decide this thing. We have some good people inside the War Department. But we've got nobody near Mr. Stanton, who's sickly as can be I hear . . ."

"Asthma, opthalmia, chronic bilious fevers." David could identify each Washington worthy's every ailment. Only Old Abe seemed immune to everything save constipation; and a single slight attack of the fever after his son died. On the other hand, the President had started losing weight; and he was growing gray. But that, David had concluded, was more the result of a losing war than of anything vital being eaten at inside him. "I'll do my best," said David. "Only the Stantons never use Thompson's. I don't know why."

"Find out who their doctor is. Get Thompson to work on him. I want you in and out of the Stanton house."

"I'll try." They parted among the stewing chickens. David then walked to the Surratt house, where he knew he'd find Annie alone.

Annie was on the parlor floor, polishing furniture. She gave a cry, as he entered. "Knock on the door, Davie!" she said. "You scared me half to death. With the streets full of wild soldiers and even wilder niggers . . ."

"Then lock your door. What's happening in Surrattsville?"

Annie put down her cloth, and sat in her mother's rocking chair; she resembled, somewhat, that highly voluptuous woman. "John will take over as postmaster the first of the month. That'll keep him busy, except when he's really busy. You know, he rides back and forth all the time to Richmond."

"I know." David was bleak. "I don't get the chance, ever, but he does."

"Well, he is where he is and you are where you are, which is worth a lot to us. Anyway, he was just now South, all the way to Fortress Monroe, where they were waiting for General Burnside, who was coming up from North Carolina, and the question was *where* was Burnside's army going to go? If they were to stay in the vicinity, then he and McClellan would attack Richmond. But if they went on up to the Rappahannock, then that meant McClellan would be ordered back to Washington and Richmond would be safe, and Lee would be able to move up north. Well, John overheard two barge captains talking, and they said that they'd been ordered to take Burnside's men to the Rappahannock. So John rode, fast as he could to Richmond, with the news."

"Now he's back at the post office."

"For the time being. Mother's busy with the farm. I'm fixing up this place so we can take in lodgers and make some money now Father's gone."

During this, David moved so close to Annie that he could smell the lilac water she liked to splash over her clothes, not to mention the lemon oil that she was rubbing into the furniture. When he tried to kiss her, she laughed; struggled; kissed. Then she told him either to leave her alone or help her clean up.

As David left the house, he wondered at the curious laws that governed men and women. Where Azadia was all his whenever he liked, to do what he wanted with, Annie would never be his without marriage, while the ham-lady—well, he was hers. On the other hand, if he were John Hay, everything would be his, including, if what the newspapers said was true, Kate Chase.

But at that moment, no one was John Hay's nor was he anyone's. He was in Stanton's office, seated on a straight chair opposite

352

the long sofa on which lay the Tycoon, feet on one sofa arm, head on the other, with a gray felt hat pulled over the eyes as if he no longer wanted to see anything or anyone, ever again. Stanton sat behind his desk, heavy jaw set, red eyes blinking. General Halleck was at the large map of Maryland. It had been Hay's unkind observation to Nicolay that Old Brains was just that: brains that had grown too old to be of any use to their owner, much less the country. He had taken over as general-in-chief. He had sent Pope and the Army of Virginia to rendezvous with McClellan and the Army of the Potomac so that, together, they would seize Richmond. Instead, Pope had been defeated at Bull Run; and McClellan recalled to Washington. Halleck had been hopeless in the crisis; and Lincoln had not been much better.

For the first time, Hay had begun to wonder if the Ancient, for all his virtues, had the right temperament for a war leader. Or, put the other way around, the rebels had produced a half-dozen first-rate generals and the Union none, with the possible exception of Grant, who was currently bogged down in the West. Was it possible that the Southern military superiority was due to a more intelligent political system? Certainly, the Northern president either gave his generals too much freedom or too little, while his decision to withdraw McClellan from a position twenty-five miles east of Richmond was not only arbitrary but foolish. With Richmond no longer threatened, Lee was now free to invade the Union; and that was exactly what he was doing.

Henry W. Halleck turned from the map and stared, lugubriously, at Lincoln. He was a paunchy man, with a gray puffy face in which were set two large, singularly glassy eyes. It was rumored that he was addicted to opium; and smoked pipes of it late into the night. The old brains, however, were contained in an impressively large place, thought Hay, eyes resting on the high domed forehead made even higher as the wiry gray hair receded, doubtless in terror of what lurked beneath that dome, those inexorable brains. "So there the armies rest for the moment. Lee on this side of Antietam Creek and McClellan on the other. Yesterday's battle has been described by General McClellan as a complete victory. Today he should finish off Lee, and that will be the end of Lee's invasion. Because an army that has invaded the enemy's territory and suffers a defeat and is cut off"—the professional note, which had crept into Halleck's voice, had much the same effect on Hay as a metronome—"invariably is a prelude to an overall surrender, as you may recall when Fabius Cunctator turned back Hannibal."

"I recall it as if it were yesterday," said the President, beneath his cap.

"I am suspicious of this 'complete' victory," said Stanton. "One never knows with McClellan."

"Well, we know that he commands those heights here at Sharpsburg." Halleck touched the map with a long dirty forefinger. "We know that Lee fell back after yesterday's fighting. So today will determine whether or not McClellan follows the President's order and destroys Lee's army, or whether Lee will withdraw safely to Virginia."

The President removed his cap. He sat up, swinging his legs to the floor. "I'm well pleased so far. As you know, I never wanted to use McClellan again, but the only other general who was available refused the command."

"Burnside was slow to attack at Sharpsburg," said Stanton, glancing at the pile of telegrams from the Army of the Potomac.

"So General McClellan tells us." Halleck's dislike of McClellan had an abstract purity. For Halleck, thought Hay, McClellan was an incorrect theorem that ought, simply, to be erased from the blackboard. But Lincoln had been tolerant with the little man; and now he was well pleased with him. "The present danger, as I see it," said Halleck, "is the nearness of the rebel army to Washington. Stonewall Jackson holds Harper's Ferry. He is between our army and this city. If Lee were to join with Jackson, they could seize Washington before McClellan got here."

Lincoln frowned. "There is no doubt Little Mac has a permanent case of the slows. How many men has he got on the Antietam?"

"He began with close to ninety thousand. This morning the first estimate of casualties is fifteen thousand men . . ."

"My God!" Lincoln shut his eyes. "It is worse than Shiloh."

"It is the bloodiest engagement of this war," said Halleck, "or of any modern war. The rebels have sustained almost as many casualties, or so we have been told."

"They have fewer men, fewer resources." This had been Stanton's line from the beginning.

"I had no idea," said Lincoln, "of the cost." There was silence, as the President appeared to daydream. Hay often wondered what the Ancient's daydreams were like. Often, for no apparent reason, he would simply drift off and be no longer present in spirit; then he would return as suddenly as he had departed, all business again. This time, the business was numbers. "I keep trying to reckon the size of the rebel army. By now, McClellan has convinced himself—if not me—that they've got a million men, all set to go. He has said that Lee's army on the Antietam is twice the size of his. I don't believe it, particularly if General Halleck is right that the bulk of their army is still south of here, which I'm not all that sure of. I still remember those logs at Manassas, painted to look like cannon. I think we have it over them, in numbers, two, maybe three to one."

"We get our reports from Mr. Pinkerton's Secret Service," said Stanton.

"Where does *he* get his numbers from?" asked Lincoln.

"Spies, observer balloons, deduction." As Halleck proceeded to analyze Pinkerton's reports favorably, Hay could see that Halleck had lost, yet again, the President's attention. But the latest dispatch from the Army of the Potomac caused the Tycoon to sit up. "'Lee's army retreating into Virginia.'" Stanton read the original of the telegram. "'Maryland is saved.'"

"That is well done," said Lincoln. Halleck and Stanton exchanged a glance, which Hay caught. In their eyes, nothing that the Young Napoleon did could be done well, even when he had gained a victory. Nevertheless, the object of the exercise had been accomplished: Lee's invasion of the Union was at an end. The Tycoon got to his feet. "Now that we've got the victory we've been waiting for, I can issue my proclamation of emancipation."

For some weeks, Hay had been arranging for a number of Negro leaders to meet with the President. The idea for the meeting had long been in Lincoln's mind. He had known few colored people. He wanted to hear their views on a number of subjects. Now he sat at the head of the table in the President's Office, staring as curiously at the well-dressed colored men as they stared, with equal curiosity, at him. Hay took notes.

The Tycoon began by confiding to them that he intended to issue his proclamation in the next few days. When he had explained its contents, the leader of the group, E. M. Thomas, said, "This means, sir, that slavery will still continue in the border-states of the Union?"

"That is right."

"So," said a large man, "you are really freeing the slaves in the Confederacy as a means of punishing their owners for secession."

"Well, that is a part of it, yes. Actually, I have not the authority to abolish slavery in the Union. I can only do it in the rebel states as a wartime measure. Once the war is over, I expect slavery to be abolished as the result of an amendment to the Constitution, which I would be happy to initiate if I am in this chair."

The large man chuckled. "Well, sir, a half-loaf is still nourishment for a starving man."

Lincoln smiled, perfunctorily; and began, from habit, "Or as the Baptist preacher said . . ." He stopped himself. "Gentlemen, I want your advice, and I want your help. Congress has given me a sum of money toward the colonization of New Granada in Central America. The agricultural land is rich, there are coal mines, and it is empty. If you choose, it can be filled up with your people."

Lincoln paused, as if he expected some sort of delighted response; but there was none. Hay noted that the black, the beige and the yellow faces were all equally stony. The Tycoon was, if nothing else, as sensitive as a perfect barometer to the human responses of others. He now sat back in his chair and began to speak, as if thinking aloud; a sign that he had already made his case to himself. "Why, you may ask, should the people of your race be colonized? Why should they leave this country? This is, perhaps, the first question for proper consideration. Well, you and we are different races. We have between us broader differences than exist between almost any other two races. Whether it is right or wrong, I need not discuss." Lincoln paused. One of the Negro men seemed ready to open a discussion; but then he thought better of it.

The President continued. "This physical difference is a great disadvantage to us both, as I think. Your race suffers very greatly; many of them by living among us, while ours suffers from your presence. In a word, we suffer on each side." Hay could see, once again, the Tycoon's powerful logic begin to gather force; he could also see, from the faces in the room, that something other than Lincolnian logic was going to be needed. "If this is admitted, it affords a reason, at least, why we should be separated. You here are freemen, I suppose."

"Yes, sir," said E. M. Thomas. Hay wondered why, at this point, the President's logic needed to ask a question whose answer he already knew.

"Perhaps you have long been free; perhaps all your lives. Nevertheless, your race is suffering, in my judgment, the greatest wrong inflicted on any people. But even when you cease to be slaves you are still a long way from being placed on an equality with the white race." Lincoln turned his cloudy gaze on the large man, a minister from New York. "The aspiration of men is to enjoy equality with the best when free, but on this broad continent not a single man of your race is made the equal of a single man of ours."

Hay wondered what the fiery Negro leader Frederick Douglass would answer to that. So, perhaps, did the Ancient, who closed the argument. "Go where you are treated the best, and the ban is still upon you. I do not propose to discuss this, but to present it as a fact with which we have to deal. I cannot alter it if I wanted." Hay wondered if Lincoln *would* want to alter it. Although
356

Lincoln had a true hatred of slavery, as much for the brutal effect it had on the masters as on the enslaved, he was unshaken in his belief that the colored race was inferior to the white. Hay concurred; but Hay's belief was not unshakable. He had long suspected that, given the same advantages as a white man, a Negro was probably every bit as capable. The fact that Lincoln had always found it difficult to accept any sort of natural equality between the races stemmed, Hay thought, from his own experience as a man born with no advantage of any kind, who had then gone to the top of the world. Lincoln had no great sympathy for those who felt that external circumstances had held them back.

Nicolay disagreed with Hay; he felt that this *had* been Lincoln's view, but was no longer. The two secretaries often argued about the matter. Lincoln himself never cast the least ray of light on the subject. He wanted the Negroes freed, and he wanted them out of North America. He now proceeded to make his case to the jury, which was plainly hostile. He spoke of the evils done the white race by the institution of slavery: "See our present condition—the country engaged in war—our white men cutting one another's throats—none knowing how far it will extend—and then consider what we know to be the truth. But for your race among us there could not be war, although many men on either side do not care for you one way or the other. Nevertheless, I repeat, without the institution of slavery, and the colored race as a basis, the war could not have an existence. It is better for us both, therefore, to be separated." Lincoln paused; eyes shut. He seemed to be staring at that wall of marble in his mind from which he read his finished texts.

The minister from New York said, "Mr. President, it is one thing to offer a new country a thousand miles away to men who have been slaves all their lives, and quite another thing to propose that people like us pull up stakes and leave our homes for the wilderness, no matter how rich in coal mines and farmland. After all, this is our country, too. Some of our families go back to the very beginning, so why on earth should we leave home to go and settle this wilderness Congress has given you?"

Plainly, Lincoln was taken aback by the minister's directness. But he rose to the challenge. "Why else have I asked you here except, as I have said, that I need your help? I am quite aware that many of you have no desire to go. But if intelligent educated men such as yourselves don't go, then how will the former slaves manage to organize themselves? How will they support themselves?"

E. M. Thomas took the President's rhetorical question for a real one. "Well, Mr. President, for three centuries they have done

357

a fine job of supporting themselves *and* their white masters, so I think we can assume that if they are not obliged to sustain a white population in luxury, they will be able to look after themselves nicely."

Lincoln's jaw set in a fashion that was rare with him; and the presage to the sort of storm that was all the more terrible because it was so seldom unleashed on those who had provoked it. "I do not mean to put this harshly," he said with his usual mildness, "but I think there is some selfishness here. You ought to do something to help those less fortunate than you. It is exceedingly important that we have men at the beginning capable of thinking as white men and not those who have been systematically oppressed." Hay noted that one of the beige faces smiled at the phrase "thinking as white men"; because he was more white than colored?

"I do not," said Lincoln, "ask for much. Could I have a hundred tolerably intelligent men with their wives and children, and able to 'cut their own fodder,' so to speak? Can I have fifty? If I could find twenty-five able-bodied men, with a mixture of women and children—good things in the family relation, I think—I could make a successful commencement. I want you to let me know whether this can be done or not. This is the practical part of my wish to see you."

E. M. Thomas was courtly. "We appreciate this opportunity to meet what our slave-brothers call Uncle Linkum..."

Lincoln laughed. "I am told that at the South, every other colored boy baby born since 1861 is called Abe."

"You've been told the truth," said Thomas. "And it is not only in the South that our sons are being called Abraham. You have been chosen to do the work of the Lord in some way that is strange to me, when I look at you like this—a man so worn down by Fate."

Hay looked at Lincoln, who had become suddenly very still; absorbed in the writing on the marble wall? Then Lincoln got to his feet, as did the others. He was genial. "Take your full time about this," he said, as he shook Thomas's hand. "There is no hurry at all, I'm sorry to say. But we must be prepared."

When the last of the colored men had left the room, Lincoln said to Hay, as a convenient surrogate for himself, "Why would any colored man want to live in this country, where there is so much hatred of him?"

"Perhaps they think that that will change, once slavery's gone."

Lincoln shook his head. "There are passions too deep for even a millennium to efface."

But Chase disagreed and, most courteously, on Monday, at a meeting in the White House, he registered his objection to the colonization scheme: "Except, perhaps, as a means of our obtaining a foothold in Central America." Lincoln had, as courteously, noted their difference of opinion. But the President's mind was now made up; and he had called together all the great officers of state to tell them that he would now release the Emancipation Proclamation. Of those present, only Blair made any demur. He thought that the effect would be bad in the border-states and in the army. He reminded everyone, yet again, that there would be a congressional election in two months' time.

The President was now on his feet, towering over the seated Cabinet ministers and assorted political chieftains. "You know, when the rebel army was at Frederick, I determined, as soon as it should be driven out of Maryland, and Pennsylvania was no longer in danger of invasion, that I would issue a proclamation of Emancipation. Naturally, I wish that we were in a better condition. The action of the army against the rebels has not been quite what I should have liked best."

Chase and Stanton exchanged a look. Only that morning, Stanton had told Chase how McClellan's inability to move in time had allowed Lee to retire to Virginia, virtually victorious in what had been, the Confederates now declared, no more than a punitive raid on the enemy's territory.

Lincoln seemed to divine how opposed the room was to a proclamation, which he was not, he had said, about to alter. "I know that many others might, in this matter, as in others, do better than I can." Lincoln looked at Chase; and smiled. Chase dropped his eyes, modestly. "And if I were satisfied that the public confidence was more fully possessed by any one of them than by me, and knew of any Constitutional way in which he could be put in my place, he should have it. I would gladly yield it to him." Chase glanced at Seward, who sat across from him, in full angular and aquiline profile. What a crafty little man! Chase thought. In effect, he was the president; but how he exerted his influence over Lincoln was a mystery yet to be pierced.

Lincoln suddenly made a startling admission. "I am quite aware that I have not so much the confidence of the people as I had sometime since. On the other hand, I do not know that, all things considered, any other person has more." Again the gray eyes rested, almost quizzically, on Chase, who felt the blood rise in his neck. "In any event, there is no way in which I can have any other man put where I am. I am here. I must do the best I can, and bear the responsibility of taking the course which I feel I ought to take."

"With that, the President read us the proclamation." Chase was at the window of his office, watching not without a simple pleasure the autumnal rains wet the passers-by as well as, more ominously, the ambulance-carriages of the Sanitary Commission, which had formed a cortege along Pennsylvania Avenue, bearing to hospital the wounded from Antietam. The losses were greater than suspected. The Union was now bemoaning the loss of blood as well as of money.

Henry D. Cooke sat on the sofa beneath the painting of Hamilton. Chase always found Henry D.'s presence comforting. They had been good friends even before Cooke became editor of the *Ohio State Journal*, where he had supported Lincoln rather more strenuously than the state's governor, Chase, had bargained for. But all that was now behind them. Henry D. was the head of the Washington branch of Jay Cooke and Company, a highly successful bank, with many distinguished depositors, among them the Secretary of the Treasury himself. Although Jay Cooke had made Chase a number of personal loans, Chase had paid them off most scrupulously, excepting the matter of the coupé, which Chase had accepted, finally, as a gift for Kate. Jay Cooke was a shrewd investor; and Chase allowed him a free hand with his finances. The previous year Cooke had lent Chase thirteen thousand dollars, which had now grown, magically, to fifteen thousand dollars: nearly twice his annual salary. Without Jay Cooke, Chase could not survive financially, nor could the Union. It was Jay Cooke who had taken over the selling of war bonds, not to the bankers, who were out to bleed the Treasury, but to ordinary citizens. Jay Cooke's ability to sell issue after issue was a source of wonder to Chase, who understood all too well the fragility of the paper money that they had so blithely invented. But Jay Cooke's mastery of publicity had made enticing the bonds; and thus the war was financed. Meanwhile, Henry D. remained in the capital as a link between the financial genius and the Treasury head, who now spoke, seriously, of resignation. "I don't see how I can remain any longer in this Administration." Chase turned from the rain to the gaslit interior of his office. "The President is losing what popularity he had. Seward encourages him to keep McClellan and all the other incompetent generals simply because they are fellow-moderates, and agreeable to the border-states. Imagine fighting a war with the enemy's generals commanding your army! Well, that is exactly what Lincoln is doing."

Henry D. was soothing. "McClellan can't last much longer. Brother Jay is selling your war bonds in astonishing quantities; and we should do well in the November elections."

"No." Chase had already worked out the Republican losses. "We shall lose more than forty seats in the House, and what can

360

I do? I am already being held accountable for other people's blunders and errors of policy. I think I should resign, now."

Henry D. shook his head vigorously. "Where would this Administration be without you?"

"Look at where it is *with* me?" Chase sat at his desk. "Yes, I have been able to finance the war, thus far. But how can we keep on selling bonds without victories? Pretending that Antietam was a victory did not fool the marketplace. No, I must go."

"Where?"

"Back to the Senate. If I resign now, I can be returned at the next election."

"I would not do it, Mr. Chase." Henry D. was firm. "You are the second most powerful man in the country . . ."

"After Governor Seward." Chase could not restrain his bitterness. "But I am a true abolitionist, a . . . a radical, as we are called. Well, I am not ashamed to be what I am. But I am ashamed to belong to an Administration that is indifferent to everything that I hold dear. Has there ever been a document more cynical than the President's proclamation? Or a policy more misguided than that of shipping the freed slaves as far away as possible?"

Chase had been shifting papers on his desk. Suddenly, he uncovered his new treasure and his mood lightened. There on a sheet of notepaper were the British royal coat-of-arms and the legend "Windsor Castle" at the top of a letter addressed to President and Mrs. Abraham Lincoln. In Queen Victoria's own handwriting, she advised the Lincolns of the marriage in July of her daughter the Princess Alice to the nephew of the Grand Duke of Hesse. Chase stared, lovingly, at the positive signature: "Victoria R."

"Mr. Lincoln gave me this." Chase held up the letter. "I must say, as a man, he is the soul of kindness and originality, for all his weakness and want of policy. It is very rare to find a holograph letter by the Queen. I was much moved when he said that I could have it. I shall hang it next to Gladstone's, which should please neither of them."

Henry D., again, objected to the notion of Chase leaving the Cabinet. "Certainly, it will be a blow to my brother Jay, if you go."

Chase duly noted the significance of his banker's objection. "Yet I would still be able, after two years in the Senate, to secure the Republican nomination for president."

"That's possible, Mr. Chase. But if I were you I'd stay where you are, out in front of the pack with your face on the one-dollar bill." On that particular note, they parted.

Chase did not seriously intend to resign, tempting as the prospect was. He was aware that his present position was preeminent;

on the other hand, he ran the risk of being so identified with Lincoln and Seward that when he did win the nomination he would be defeated at the general election by the Democratic candidate. He called for his carriage.

In an undecisive and somewhat querulous mood, Chase sent his coachman into Mrs. Douglas's house to see if she was at home. At the door, a maid shook her head. The coachman returned to the carriage. "Mrs. Douglas is not home. The main wants to know who wants her." Chase took out a one-dollar bill, and tore it in half. The part with his picture on it he gave to the coachman. "Give the maid my card."

As the carriage rattled across F Street, ripped up to accommodate new railway tracks, Chase wondered whether or not remarriage was a good idea. As long as Kate was with him, it was pointless. They were—the two of them—a happy couple. But, presumably, she would marry Sprague; and move out. Then what would become of him? Adéle Douglas, widow of the Little Giant, was the handsomest of Washington's ladies; and highly congenial. She would make a superb First Lady; in fact, had the Democratic Party not split in two in 1860, she would now be that lady and Stephen Douglas would still be alive. It was Chase's view that men who get what they want in the world seldom die, prematurely, of pneumonia in Chicago.

At Sixty and E, Chase was greeted by Kate, only recently home from Philadelphia, and William Sprague, just arrived from Providence. "Mr. Chase, did you talk to Mr. Hoyt?" That was the greeting the Secretary of the Treasury received from his putative son-in-law.

"It's good to see you again, Governor." Chase was serene as he shook the young man's hand. "I trust Katie is doing the honors?"

"Oh, I am bearing up against the governor's onslaught. I now know more about the fluctuations in the price of cotton than I had ever dreamed possible."

"Oh, it's bad. Mr. Hoyt said he was going to see you today." Sprague stared, accusingly, through his pince-nez.

"Whoever Mr. Hoyt is, he did not, I fear, see me. Or if he saw me, he did not talk to me. We have been busy all day freeing the rebel slaves." Chase sat in his rocking chair. Slowly, he rocked back and forth until his mood began to harmonize with the chair's regular pleasant motion. He tried to recall who Hoyt was, the name was familiar; the connotation unpleasant.

"I guess he couldn't get in to see you." Sprague frowned. "It's like this. Harris Hoyt is from Texas. But he's good Union man. He's got a letter from Johnny Hay, recommending him to everybody. He's all right, let me tell you."

362

But Mr. Hoyt was not all right. Chase suddenly remembered a most disagreeable meeting with a tall Southerner, who claimed to be recommended by the President. The man had wanted a permit to sell Texas cotton to the New England mills. Since this was expressly forbidden by a law that was now being enforced with some rigor by the Union's naval blockade of the rebel states, Chase had said that there was nothing he could do. The man had then become excited; had said that he would report what Chase had said to his partners, of whom one was Governor Sprague. Chase had ordered Mr. Hoyt out of his office with the stern admonishment: "I wish you to understand that these gentlemen don't control me."

Chase stopped rocking. "Yes, Governor, I do recall Mr. Hoyt. I thought his tone to me was somewhat . . . offensive."

"Oh, he's Southern. You know what they're like. But he's a loyal Union man. He says the cotton's there at Galveston, piled up on the docks. Bale after bale of it. We need that cotton, Mr. Chase. Fact, if we don't get it, the mills will shut down all over Rhode Island—all over New England, and all of the out-of-work workers will go and vote Democratic."

Chase seldom thought of Sprague as any sort of a logician but he was obliged to agree with this brutal political analysis. For some time, the Cabinet had been divided on the issue. He himself had thought that where it was advantageous to the Union, trade permits should be given to responsible parties. The President inclined to the same view. But Gideon Welles had taken an unrelenting line. There must be no trade at all with the enemy, particularly now that the much-expanded navy was beginning seriously to isolate the rebel states. "Yes," Welles had said, "it will hurt us in New 207England but it will kill them in the South. To make any exceptions now will simply prolong the war." Stanton had sided with Welles. Seward had given the subject no thought. Chase let the majority prevail, but at the price of being tormented by the boy-governor, who kept on cannonading him with dire statistics until the appearance of General Garfield in the parlor was like the rising of the sun after a night of terrible gloom.

The two young men had not met before. Kate told each about the other. Sprague was distracted. Garfield was his usual radiant self. "I have been, again, to see General Hooker at the insane asylum."

"He's crazy, too?" asked Sprague, brightening at the thought. "He commanded me at Williamsburg."

Garfield laughed. "He appears sane. He was wounded in the foot at Antietam, and they have put a number of officers in the asylum, to recuperate. He is positive that if he could have stayed

363

another three hours on the field at Antietam, our victory would have been complete."

"He's a very confident and forceful man," said Kate. "I quite like him. Father and I went to see him yesterday." She turned to Sprague. "He said that he was with McClellan when the order came to withdraw from the Peninsula, and that he told McClellan to disobey the order and let him take Richmond. McClellan agreed but then, just as General Hooker was finally ready to attack the city, McClellan ordered him to leave the Peninsula. Hooker was furious because he knew that he could have occupied Richmond just the way that Father took Norfolk."

"Last week," said Chase, the martial mood again upon him, "I asked Mr. Welles to let me volunteer to take the fleet up the James River. He thought there was merit in the idea."

"I *know* there is," said Garfield. "You have the presence and, Heaven knows, the intelligence to command. After all, what are the rest of us? I'm a college president, a classics professor . . ."

"And a politician," said Kate, with every appearance of fondness.

"Well, I'm a businessman, about to go bust." Sprague was on his feet. He excused himself. "Must see these men at Willard's."

"You're welcome, as always," said Chase, benignly, "to stay here."

"Yes," said Sprague; and departed.

"An abrupt young man." Chase smiled at Garfield. "But he means well."

"Do you think so, Father?" Kate frowned. "He does go on and on about those trading permits."

"Who wouldn't," said Garfield, "in his place? With all those empty mills."

"About Eastern Florida," began Chase, as Kate presided over fresh tea. "The President is now willing to create a department of Florida with Mr. Thayer as its governor, and you as the commanding general—*major*-general."

"This is your doing!" Garfield was delighted. "How do I thank you?"

"Do your duty. That is all." Chase was quietly Roman.

Kate was practical. "You could then bring Florida back into the Union, and come here as its senator." Kate gave Garfield tea. "The way they are about to do with those westernmost Virginia counties. Father, what is that new state to be called?"

"When last we discussed the matter, it was decided to name the new state West Virginia."

"How dull!" Kate handed her father his heavily sweetened tea. "Those Norths and Souths were bad enough. Now we are getting

Easts and Wests. Like the streets here: A and B and C and D. And First and Second and Third . . ."

"Ah, but the avenues, Miss Kate!" Garfield dried his golden beard with a lace-edged napkin. "Pennsylvania and Massachusetts and Rhode Island . . ."

"There is a peculiar lack of imagination in this place. At least back home we have Elm and Oak and Pine streets. Father, why is Washington so dull?"

"Dull? I thought that we both found the city uncommonly interesting—even too interesting, at times." Chase picked up the latest copy of the *Revue des deux mondes*. He had become interested in spiritualism, which the French had also taken up with their usual intrepid cleverness.

"Oh, *our* lives are interesting. I only meant why is there no sense of mystery or romance or even much history here? Just the corner of Sixth and E and . . . and the Patent Office!"

"It's still a new city," said Garfield. "It's still a new country."

"Surely a century is long enough to have produced something to go with Lafayette Square, and *he* died practically yesterday. I would like," said Kate, thoughtfully, "a cathedral, a serious Gothic cathedral . . ."

"You shall have it!" Garfield was exuberant. Why, Chase wondered, had this admirable young man got himself married at such an early age?

"It will be located on a hill somewhere," said Kate, "and it will be approached by Chase Avenue."

"Oh, come now, Kate! I don't really want to be an avenue." Chase wanted, actually, to be a city. After all, even the highly corrupt Senator Dayton had had a now-thriving city named for him. Chase, Ohio, sounded right. But was he perhaps too modest? There were bound to be at least a dozen new states in the next few years. If he were to be president, might he not be a state, after all? Particularly if he gave his particular blessing to one of the territories that currently aspired to statehood. But then if there was a state called Chase might there not be one called Lincoln or Seward? Someone had actually suggested that West Virginia be named Lincoln. Although Chase had been quick to make light of the proposal, for an instant he had known fear.

Happily, Kate and Garfield were adding opera houses and palaces and libraries to the city, and naming them after the worthies of the day. It was Kate who was inspired to christen the pink marble (in imitation of Venice's doge's palace) Cotton Exchange, Sprague Hall.

Chase wondered what she really thought of the man who was

365

bound to be, more soon than late, her senatorial husband—and source of endless wealth.

But the source of endless wealth had convinced himself that he was soon to be ruined by the blockade. Harris Hoyt did nothing to allay Sprague's fears as they drank gin together in the long barroom at Willard's, and watched Zach. Chandler get slowly and quietly drunk by himself at the opposite end of the room.

"Just how firm is Mr. Chase's no?" asked Hoyt.

"About as firm as can be. Who the hell is General Garfield?" Sprague let, first, the end of one moustache float in the glass of gin; then the other. When each had been thoroughly soaked, he chewed the ends and drank the gin, interestingly strained by facial hair.

"I don't know one Union general from another. Did you make the point how important it is to get cotton out of the South when it can be done without giving aid and comfort to the enemy while providing relief to the Union?"

"Made the point ten times. I should make a speech on all this."

"I wouldn't." Hoyt was alarmed.

"I don't mean on our Union-relief dodge. I'm not crazy, Hoyt. No, a speech on the necessity of *limited* trade, for the Union's sake."

"Well, you're still the governor of Rhode Island. Go back to Providence and make the rafters ring."

"Can't." Sprague shook his head sadly. "He's been shot."

"Who's been shot?"

"Fred Ives. He writes for the *Post* back home. Well, last week he was shot at Sharpsburg."

Hoyt was mystified. "So what's that got to do with you giving a speech?"

"He writes them for me. That's what that has to do with my making a speech. You don't think I wrote all that stuff in the magazines about Bull Run, do you? It was Fred. I think the world of Fred. Always have. Always will." A single alcoholic tear appeared behind the pince-nez. "Listen, I've talked to my cousin Byron. He's pretty much running the business. He thinks it's too risky."

Hoyt shrugged. "Of course, it's risky. But I don't see what else you can do. Or I can do, for that matter. The deal is simple enough. I bring into Galveston arms and ammunition for the rebels there, and then they will let me install as much cotton-carding machinery as I like. They'll then help me get the cotton out to you."

"Through the blockade?"

"Through the blockade." Hoyt smiled a bright pirate's smile. "After all, it's my neck."

"That don't matter." Sprague was to the point. "But it's my money."

"Well, that's an exchange in your favor. All I'm asking for is one hundred thousand dollars..."

"What I spent on that regiment." Sprague sounded wistful.

"Yes, sir. With that money, I can buy up a lot of Confederate money for next to nothing right here in town. Then my friend Charles L. Prescott here, who's a shipfitter and an engineer, will buy the necessary ships..."

"Your friend where?"

"Down the bar. See the red-haired fellow? Drinking alone next to Senator Chandler. That's him."

"Zach. Chandler's a drunk." Sprague ordered more gin; then he dried his moustaches with his sleeve. "All right, Hoyt. You'll get the money from Byron and me. But you've got to start fast."

Hoyt motioned for Prescott to join them. Prescott had already found a schooner in New York. "It's a sweet ship, Governor. Called *Snow Drift*. We could load all... our gear in New York and then go on to Havana, which is Spanish and neutral, and then from there to Galveston."

"Through the blockade," said Sprague.

"Through the blockade." Hoyt smiled, as if happy at the thought of danger.

"There's not that much in the way of a blockade," said Prescott. "The Yankees have only got around one hundred ships in all, and there's over three thousand miles of Confederate coast. I've slipped through many a time. Fact, that's how I'm here right now in enemy country."

"*Enemy* country?" Sprague gave the red-haired man an icy stare. Hoyt was quick. "He's Texan, too. But he's a good Union man."

"Yes." Sprague stared at Zach. Chandler, who was having trouble getting off the barstool. One of the colored waiters hurried over to him, and took his arm. Since the drafting of men for the army had begun, there were no longer many white waiters at Willard's. "We go up to New York tomorrow," Sprague commanded. "Byron's there, waiting. I'll take you to the bank. I'll want to see this schooner." Sprague set his pince-nez firmly on the bridge of his well-shaped nose. "If you get caught, I never heard of you."

"I hope before then your future father-in-law will have given us a trade permit."

"You can hope anything you like, Hoyt." Sprague rose. "We'll

367

take the cars at noon. You know what it means, your shipping arms to the rebels?"

Hoyt looked innocent. "I know it's the price that they asked me in exchange for my receiving a charter to establish a cotton mill."

"Whatever," said Sprague, even more flatly than usual. "Bringing arms to the enemy in wartime is treason. They shoot you for that, if they catch you."

"Well, Governor, we *are* Texans. Technically, we could call ourselves patriots, trying to get arms to our own people. So for us it's not at all like it is for you, sir, a Union man, a governor and a general and soon-to-be a senator. I mean, sir, if there's any treason being committed..."

"I don't know you. That's the way it'll be, if you get caught." Sprague left the barroom. Zach. Chandler looked him full in the face, but plainly did not recognize his future colleague, which was just as well.

8

MARY SAT AT A ROUND MAHOGANY TABLE. ACROSS FROM HER was the Roman emperor Constantine, in the plump form of Mrs. Laury of Georgetown. Constantine was Mrs. Laury's personal friend in the world of the dead, and if not otherwise engaged, he was wonderfully cooperative in delivering and transmitting messages between the world of light where he existed and that world of darkness and pain where the living are. "I saw Willie only this morning," said Constantine, whose deep voice was entirely different from Mrs. Laury's ordinary fluting tones. "He wants to know about his pony, and has Tad learned to ride it yet?"

"Oh, yes! Tad needs help, of course. But tell him the pony's fine, and every day Tad rides, with Mr. Watt next to him, to keep him from falling off. Did you ask Willie if he has seen little Eddie?"

Mrs. Laury-Constantine nodded gravely. By the light of the single candle on the table, Mrs. Laury looked very like a Roman emperor ought to look if he happened to be an elderly woman with dyed auburn hair. "At first they did not know each other. How could they? But in the world of light all things are clear at last and, suddenly, the two boys knew each other, and they were
368

so excited and thrilled...Oh!" Mrs. Laury-Constantine's voice dropped to an even lower register. "There is danger."

"What danger?" Mary shuddered. "Danger to whom?"

"To the President. There is a dark cloud over him. A deep darkness. Danger."

As the two women sat in the small parlor of the stone house next to the Soldiers' Home, Lincoln was riding alone, toward the Soldiers' Home. In the bright moonlight, he was a perfect target, while Seventh Street was nothing more than a deserted country lane at this hour. As the horse—called Old Abe, too—trotted past a grove of willow trees, the wind suddenly stirred the moonlit branches. Menacing shadows danced. The horse shied. As Lincoln leaned forward to soothe the skittish horse, a shot rang out. Lincoln's hat was blown from his head. Reflexively, he lay forward atop the horse; and spurred him into a rolling canter. There was no second shot.

Both horse and Lincoln were breathing hard when they arrived at the stone cottage. The sergeant on duty helped the President dismount. "You've had a mighty good run, sir," said the man, somewhat disapprovingly: the horse's flanks were steaming in the moonlight.

"Yes. You'd better walk Old Abe around a bit, to cool him down." The President entered the cottage.

"Father!" Mary greeted him at the door to the parlor. "Where's your hat?"

"I seem to have mislaid it. Is that Mrs. Laury?"

"Yes. Come in. Sit down. Talk to her. Though it's actually the Emperor Constantine *I've* been talking to. He's been with Willie, who's met Eddie at last."

"Well, that must be nice for the codgers." Lincoln sat at the table.

"Oh!" Mary frowned. "He says that there's some sort of danger, involving you. There's a dark cloud over you. Isn't that right, Constantine?"

Mrs. Laury-Constantine nodded gravely. "There is a plot to take your life, Mr. President."

"I'm sure that there are quite a few, Emperor. I read about them every day in the papers. People like such sensations. But then you know how it is—or was, back in your day, too."

"Father! Don't joke. The Emperor has some very good advice, too. Don't you, sir?"

Mrs. Laury-Constantine spoke in a stern voice. "You must replace a general who will not fight. You must replace a member of the Cabinet who would be president. You must beware of a small man with a large nose..."

"Well, Mr. Chase is a large man with a small nose, so that rules him out..." Lincoln began.

But Mary stopped him, irritably. "It's Seward. Who else? And don't joke about these things. The Emperor Constantine thinks that Mr. Sumner would be a splendid secretary of state, and so do I."

"What about Mrs. Laury?"

"Mrs. Laury is in a trance, and she will remember nothing of what's been said between Constantine and us."

Ward Lamon was at the door to the parlor, holding the President's top hat. "Mr. President, I found your hat."

"Oh, good. Excuse me, Emperor." Lincoln joined Lamon in the entrance hall. "The hat fell off in the road, when the horse shied."

"No, sir," said Lamon, grimly. "It didn't fall off." Lamon held up the hat. From left side to right side, three inches above the brim, a bullet had made its way. "That bullet just barely missed you."

"Take the hat away, Ward," said Lincoln in a low voice. "Show it to no one. Tell no one."

"On one condition, sir. That you will never again ride out here, or anywhere else, without guards."

Lincoln nodded, gloomily. "I see now that I'll have to."

"Pinkerton says there are at least three plots against you."

"If Pinkerton says there are three that means one and a half. He doubles the enemy's numbers from habit." Lincoln put his forefinger through the bullet hole. "From the size of the hole, I'd say that's from one of our new rifles. The problem, Ward, is not my being killed. If that happens that happens and there's no way to stop it. I am a fatalist in this matter. But there is one recurring plot that I don't much care for, and that is being captured by the rebels and held for ranson."

"All the more reason for guards at all times, especially when people know in advance where you're going to be going."

Lincoln nodded. "I agree. If I could prevent the government from paying a ransom for me, I would. But I know what sentiment is at such times. They would go and pay no matter what I might want."

"How much, do you think, the rebels would ask for you?"

Lincoln smiled. "It's not how much, Ward. It's how many. They want their men back. The ones that we're holding prisoner. Sooner or later, they'll run out of men. Something we never will; and that's how we'll win. Well, to exchange one secondhand president for a hundred thousand soldiers, now that would be very tempting to Jeff Davis, or whoever decides such things at Richmond." Lincoln gave the hat to Lamon. "Funny how Old Abe—the horse, not me—knew that there was a rifle, trained on us. If he hadn't shied when he did . . ."

On quite a different horse, the President, as Commander-in-Chief, rode toward Harper's Ferry, situated in its dramatic gorge and ringed, no less dramatically, by the tents of the Army of the Potomac. Soldiers' washing hung on lines between the tents. The sound of the blacksmiths never ceased. A man with a banjo sang a plaintive song, addressed to one Juanita.

The October noon was intense and clear; and flocks of birds wheeled in the bright blue air, on their way south, a direction that Lincoln duly noted when he turned to Washburne, who was riding beside him: "Let's hope the Young Napoleon is inspired by those birds to move in a southerly direction."

Washburne laughed. "You're about the only bird big enough to get Little Mac to move."

Washburne had been delighted when Lincoln had asked him if he would like to pay a call on the army above the Antietam River. Except for Stanton and Mrs. Lincoln, no one knew that the President had left the city. "Spur of the moment," said Lincoln, vaguely, as they travelled by the cars to Harper's Ferry, accompanied by a dozen officers, mostly from the Western command. Lincoln wanted their professional impression of what McClellan was doing and not doing. Thus far, the West had provided the Union with its only good news; and Washburne's constituent, Ulysses S. Grant, was now Lincoln's favorite general. Washburne had been tact itself in explaining Grant to Lincoln. But then Washburne could not explain to himself the extraordinary military success of a man who had spent a dozen years failing. There were times when Washburne wondered if there might not be two Grants. One was the intermittently hard-drinking, somewhat grubby little man whom he had known in Galena; the other was the hero of Fort Donelson and Shiloh.

Lincoln had hoped to take McClellan by surprise but the Little General had been duly warned that the President was approaching; and now the two men, each at the center of a phalanx of aides, were riding one toward the other over a stubbled cornfield, where bright-colored leaves swirled in the wake of horses' hooves.

The huge Ward Lamon rode in front of Lincoln while the small detective Pinkerton rode to his right. Washburne remained at the President's left as the two groups met at the center of the field. McClellan and his officers smartly saluted the President, who raised his new hat a moment; and then replaced it.

Washburne had not seen McClellan in some months. The

little man was somewhat plumper than he had been; and the eyes were, not surprisingly, anxious. He took Pinkerton's place to the President's right.

"Welcome, Your Excellency, to the Army of the Potomac." The voice was as firm and as commanding as ever. "You'll want to see the battlefield, of course, at Sharpsburg."

"Yes, I'd like that, I think." Although Lincoln was genial, the two men hardly spoke as they rode. Washburne tried to overhear what they did say; but failed. At one point, McClellan seemed to be describing his famous victory; and the President seemed to be listening.

The sun was setting splendidly over the Maryland Heights, when dinner was served them on tables in front of McClellan's tent. A separate tent had been provided for Lincoln alone; but Lamon had insisted that he spend the night with the President, derringer at the ready. In the next tent, Washburne was billetted with three colonels from the Western army. Washburne's questions about Grant were answered directly. Yes, he drank, occasionally. But whenever things got out of hand, Mrs. Grant would be sent for; and all drinking ceased.

They dined by starlight, and Washburne ate all the pheasant that Lincoln chose not to eat. As usual, the President ate frugally— a slice of bread and a piece of burned beef; and that was it. Washburne thought Lincoln too thin and too frail. Yet when Washburne had taken Lincoln's arm to help him across a muddy creek, the muscles of the President's arm were like steel cords.

McClellan did most of the talking during dinner. "I have not— at present—the horses to pursue Lee. But I will have them in a week at the most." He glanced at Lincoln out of the corner of his eye. Lincoln made no response. "The problem has always been numbers. My army has seldom been as large as Lee's. I think Mr. Pinkerton will agree."

At the far end of the table, Pinkerton nodded. "That's right, General. Also, there's a lot of conscription going on at the South now. We get reports from Richmond every day. Pretty near the whole male population is under arms."

"You see the problem, Your Excellency."

"Well, I see a number of problems, General." Lincoln sat back in the thronelike chair that had been taken from a nearby house. Washburne knew that the army was now in the habit of taking anything that it wanted from anyone, loyal or rebel. War is not good for character, he thought, starting in on a squirrel stew of uncommon delicacy. McClellan lived well, if nothing else.

But it was something else that was on Lincoln's mind. "There is a feeling in the country that we are simply bogged down here,
372

and that Lee could be dispatched in no time if this army would only move..." Lincoln raised his hand to stop the usual complaints about inadequate manpower and supplies. "I know that you need this and that for... *your* army," the delicate prick of the "your" was characteristic of Lincoln when angry or exasperated, "but you do have more men, ready to go, than does Lee at this moment. You also have perfect weather. Here we are, only the second day in October. You have at least four, perhaps six weeks of good weather in which to drive Lee out of the valley and back to Richmond."

"When I am ready, sir, I will do just that. I suspect we shall meet, Lee and I, at Winchester, and that the war will end with one swift stroke." Washburne stopped listening to McClellan; and he had the sense that Lincoln had done the same.

The next morning, at dawn, Lincoln himself awakened Washburne, who had slept fully clothed on a cot. Lincoln motioned for Washburne to join him for a walk about the camp. Although McClellan was still abed, the private soldiers had been roused. Some were shaving; but most were not. As Lincoln passed among them, many shook his hand. Lincoln then led Washburne to the top of a low hill overlooking the encampment. As the sun's rays struck the red earth, a ghostly mist rose from the ground. "Do you know what all this is?" Lincoln pointed to the rows and rows of tents, as far as the eye could see.

"Why, it's the Army of the Potomac."

"No, Brother Washburne. It's General McClellan's bodyguard."

"Then he is hopeless?"

Lincoln nodded. "He is hopeless—for our purposes. He has his good points. He's a superb organizer. But he can't fight."

"Or *won't* fight?" It was Washburne's view that, for political reasons, McClellan did not want to crush the South.

Lincoln's mind was moving along much the same track. "In five weeks the country votes," he said. "If McClellan doesn't move before then, and if we don't have victories..." Lincoln stopped.

Washburne filled in. "We'll lose control of Congress. And there will be all hell to pay. Do you think that McClellan might actually want us to lose to the Democrats?"

"I can't read his mind. I don't know. I do confess that there are times when I *suspect* him of bad faith. But I have no proof. Then when I'm with him, I think, well, maybe I've underestimated him."

Lamon appeared on the hilltop. "There you are, sir," he said, accusingly. "You got away from me."

"Well, if I'm not safe here in the middle of the army, we must surrender all notions of security."

As they started down the hill, Washburne saw a photographer and his assistants setting up their paraphernalia in front of McClellan's tent. "I guess you're going to have your portrait taken with Little Mac," said Washburne; and he laughed when Lincoln gave a comical moan. "Well, this is a judgment on you, Mr. President, for never allowing any photographer to go through Springfield without making a picture of you. I have never known a man to so like having his picture made."

"Now that is unkind, Brother Washburne. No one who looks like me could ever be vain."

"Then you must be doing some sort of penance, with all those pictures of you all around the country."

Lincoln chuckled. "Well, it is true that I am a politician as well as a statesman, and we like for the folks to look at pictures of us, just so they'll know we're really all right, without horns and tails."

But later that day, Lincoln was obliged in the flesh, as opposed to the safety of a glass plate, to convince a number of men that he was indeed not the devil abroad in the land. At the town of Frederick, McClellan had assembled an army division for the President to review. Washburne took it as a good omen that the troops seemed pleased to have the President among them; he also felt that the President took far too seriously McClellan's constant references to "my army." If McClellan inspired loyalty, that was part of his task. As for the recurring rumors of a military coup, Washburne had never given them much credence even though Burnside had reported to a friend, who had told Stanton, that a number of McClellan's closest aides often spoke of the necessity of a military solution to the political problem at Washington. Apparently, there had been wild talk of sending Congress home; locking up the President and Cabinet; then, under McClellan, peace would be made with the South. Lincoln found some novelty in the idea of McClellan as dictator. "At least he would be the first general to overthrow a government without ever having won a battle. Of course, if he were to win some great victories, I might just help him chase us all out of town."

A platform had been built near the ruins of a farmhouse, and here the President took the salute of the troops. When they were again in formation, he made them a graceful little speech, something he always had difficulty in doing impromptu. Washburne, who was seated next to the President, noticed that Lincoln's hands trembled as he spoke. But the voice itself was as clear and firm as a tenor trumpet, each syllable as clearly pronounced as if it
374

were chiselled on stone. Lincoln's best speeches were those that he had himself written and rewritten; sometimes he took weeks over a single paragraph. "My mind does not work quickly," he used to say to Washburne. Certainly, he had taken his time on the speeches that he had made in the course of the debates with Douglas. Those speeches were often learned by heart; certainly, each argument had been worked out in precise detail. At such times, Lincoln did seem to Washburne like a rail-splitter. The ax was his logic, going methodically and rhythmically to work on the subject's wood. "But I never go to make a speech that I wish it wasn't over," he had said to Washburne on more than one occasion. "Also, it is an agony for someone my height to stand by a table that comes up to my knee, trying to read a speech through glasses that are never much help, by the light of a candle that shines straight up into your eyes." Lincoln would shake his head comically. "It was no accident that the Little Giant was a better orator than me. He was built a lot closer to the folks—not to mention his text."

But Lincoln's words now flowed effortlessly in the bright October light. He paid homage to the bravery of the troops; and to the loyalty of the people of Frederick—a mild insincerity, Washburne thought, since many of the town's inhabitants had been delighted to welcome the Confederate army. As an election was approaching, Lincoln pointed out that it was not proper for him in his position to make a serious speech. But he felt obliged to say how proud he was of the army—there was no mention of its commander—and of the good citizens of Frederick "for their devotion to this glorious cause; and I say this with no malice in my heart for those who have done otherwise."

To three cheers from the army, the President and his suite departed for the next army corps. Washburne again rode beside Lincoln, who was relieved the speech was done. "After all, I don't want to appear to be electioneering."

"But you are. We all are now."

Lincoln frowned. "We don't have much choice. I'd hoped McClellan would do the campaigning for us. I'd hoped that between now and the election, he'd move against Lee. But he won't."

"He said he would."

"He won't. When I get back, I shall order him, officially, to cross the Potomac and give battle to the enemy."

"Then when he doesn't?"

Lincoln simply shook his head.

"Do we let the soldiers vote?" Congress had been arguing this matter all session. Republicans were eager that Republican soldiers vote; and Democrats were eager that Democratic soldiers vote.

But the logistics of getting the men home was complex, to say the least, while many states refused to allow the soldiers to vote in the field.

"I don't see just what we can do." Lincoln was genuinely puzzled. "The only fair thing would be to send all the troops home. But then what happens to the war? Send the ones that we know are for us?" He shook his head; then he added, with a smile, "I will say that Mr. Stanton, although an ex-Democrat, is a dynamo for our cause. A week before the election, he's going to release just about everybody he and Seward and the generals have locked up."

"Just in time for them to vote Democratic?"

"Just in time to bring Horace Greeley into line. I'm afraid we're going to get a fair whipping in the press and at the polls, but Stanton says not to worry because of the border-states. He says that the army in those states will do what has to be done to get us the votes we need."

"By shooting all the Democrats?"

Lincoln chuckled. "Something along those lines. Stanton is a very determined man." The President reined in his horse. They were now opposite a large farmhouse on whose porch a dozen wounded men lay on pallets. Lincoln turned to his colonel-escort. "What's this, Colonel?"

"Confederate prisoners, sir. Wounded at Sharpsburg. We'll be sending them on to Washington once we've finished shipping our own wounded back."

"I think I'd like to take a look at these boys," said Lincoln. "And I'm sure that they'd like to take a look at me."

"No, sir!" Lamon was firm.

"Yes, Ward." Lincoln was firmer. "You stand outside, with Mr. Pinkerton, while Mr. Washburne and I, two harmless Illinois politicians, pay these Southern boys a call."

Lamon cursed not entirely under his breath; but did as he was ordered. The colonel led Lincoln and Washburne up the steps and into the house, which consisted, at this level, of a single large room lined on both sides with cots. At least a hundred men and boys lay on the cots, some missing arms or legs or both. Some were dying; others were able to limp about. The smell of flesh corrupting was overpowering; and Washburne tried not to breathe. But Lincoln was oblivious of everything except the young men who were now aware that a stranger was in their midst. The low hum of talk suddenly ceased; and the only sound in the room was the moaning of the unconscious.

When the colonel started to call the men to attention, the President stopped him with a gesture. Then Lincoln walked the length of the room, very slowly, looking to left and right, with his dreamy smile. At the end of the room, he turned and faced the wounded men; then, slowly, he removed his hat. All eyes that could see now saw him, and recognized him.

When Lincoln spoke, the famous trumpet-voice was muted; even intimate. "I am Abraham Lincoln." There was a long collective sigh of wonder and of tension and of...? Washburne had never heard a sound quite like it. "I know that you have fought gallantly for what you believe in, and for that I honor you, and for your wounds so honorably gained. I feel no anger in my heart toward you; and trust you feel none for me. That is why I am here. That is why I am willing to take the hand, in friendship, of any man among you."

The same long sigh, like a rising wind, began; and still no one spoke. Then a man on crutches approached the President and, in perfect silence, shook his hand. Others came forward, one by one; and each took Lincoln's hand; and to each he murmured something that the man alone could hear.

At the end, as Lincoln made his way between the beds, stopping to talk to those who could not move, half of the men were in tears, as was Washburne himself.

In the last bed by the door, a young officer turned his back on the President, who touched his shoulder, and murmured, "My son, we shall all be the same at the end." Then the President was gone.

Hay admired the tactful way in which the Tycoon had convinced Madam that she ought, for her health as well as her shopping, to spend election week in New York City, at the Metropolitan Hotel, with Tad and Keckley and John Watt, who still worked at the Mansion though his name no longer appeared on the payroll. When Madam wondered whether or not such a trip might be considered a flaw in her mourning for Willie, the Ancient had said that the mourning would continue no matter where she might physically be; after all, he had worn *his* band of mourning while at Antietam and Frederick, Maryland.

On the day that Madam was to leave, she summoned Hay, through Stoddard, who looked more haggard than usual. "What's it about?" Hay asked; but if Stoddard knew, he was not about to spoil Hay's suspense; he was not telling.

Madam was telling. Most telling, thought Hay, as he stood respectfully in the upstairs Oval Room while Madam explained to him her plan. "You know the difficulties that we have had in maintaining the Mansion as it ought to be." Hay acknowledged that rumors had come his way to that effect. But Madam was not listening. Whenever the subject was money, she tended to speak rapidly, as if she herself had become like one of her mediums and the words of some long-dead demon of avarice were now tripping off her tongue. "Today one of the stewards—James Trimble—has told Mr. Watt that he will leave us, as of the first of this month. I see no reason why his name cannot be left on the Mansion payroll, and his salary continue to be collected."

Hay realized that it was not a dead demon but a living one named Watt who now spoke with Madam's tongue. "But how can money be collected in the name of someone who is no longer here?" Hay blinked his eyes; innocently, he hoped.

"It has been done since Washington's time." Hay was always amazed at Madam's ignorance of American history in general and of that of the Mansion in particular, whose first occupant had been not Washington but John Adams. "It was certainly done during Mr. Buchanan's Administration, and Mr. Pierce's, too . . ."

And any other president who had had the bad luck to employ John Watt, thought Hay. "I must look into this, of course, Mrs. Lincoln."

"But I'm leaving today, and so is Mr. Watt. The fact that the steward Trimble is no longer here must *not* be sent on to the Treasury. Otherwise"—she was now sweet reason itself—"they will stop the salary from coming to the Mansion."

"Who, in theory, do you see collecting the money in Trimble's name?"

"I shall collect it, of course. The Mansion is *my* responsibility, after all. The money is for the nation, Mr. Hay, not me."

"I wonder how that will look to Congress."

"Why should it look like anything to Congress, Mr. Hay?" Madam was now beginning her transformation to Hellcat. The breath came fast. The cheeks had turned a dull brick-red. The eyes were wide open and glassy. She moved abruptly up and down the room like a bird trying to escape—from herself? "After all, Mr. Hay, this is not exactly unusual."

"Well, I don't know about past administrations, of course . . ."

"I mean, sir, *this* Administration. You yourself are here under the falsest of pretenses. Since Congress does not give the President the money to pay for two secretaries, he has, illegally I daresay *you* would call it, given you a clerkship at the Interior Department to pay you for your work here, which Congress has not authorized. I fail to see the slightest difference between my using Mr. Trimble's salary to help pay for the Mansion and Mr. Lincoln using the Interior Department's money for you to work here."

Hay was stunned by so much specious logic. "There is a difference," he began.

"None!" The Hellcat finished. "There is none, sir. It is the same. The wording for appropriations remains always the same even though the original uses for the money are altered." Hay recognized the familiar echo of perfect government corruption in that by-rote-repeated sentence. "You would not allow us to touch the stationery fund, which the First Lady customarily spends as she sees fit, as did my predecessor, Miss Lane. You leave me no choice but to use the steward's salary, in this same way that the President uses the Interior Department salary . . ."

At that moment every bell in the Mansion began to ring. "My God!" exclaimed the Hellcat, covering her ears. "What is it?"

The question was the same in every part of the White House. Even the President, standing in his shirt-sleeves at the door to his office, said, "What is it?" to Edward, who did not know, nor did Nicolay. But Hay suspected. He hurried up the steep stairs to the attic where all of the Mansion's bells were controlled and there, as he had suspected, he found Tad manipulating the network of cords and wires. Somehow, the child had managed to set every bell off at once. Hay gave the delighted Tad as serious a shaking as he dared; and called for help. "It's really very easy," said Tad, as one of the White House maintenance men started to work on the confusion of wires. "Buy you have to know how, of course, it all works, which I do and Johnny here don't."

The carriage that drove to the depot First Lady, First Brat, Elizabeth Keckley and John Watt was not at all mourned by the secretaries, who watched the carriage turn right into Pennsylvania Avenue.

"It was a stroke of genius, getting her out of here for the election." Nicolay held close to his stomach a sheaf of hostile editorials.

"Or for any other time. Guess what she's asked for?" Nicolay guessed wrong. Hay told him. Nicolay whistled. "Watt's behind this," said Hay, summing up.

"We really must get rid of him before . . ."

"He gets rid of us," said Hay.

"Before he embarrasses the Tycoon." Nicolay placed the unfavorable editorials next to the stack of favorable cuttings, which was very small by comparison. "The problem is that Mr. Watt lied to save the Hellcat; and she is loyal. I'm told he's been able to buy himself a greenhouse in New York City."

"Perhaps he'll retire of his own accord." But even as Hay said this, he doubted it. "We must get him an army commission."

"Over Stanton's corpse, I fear."

The newly repaired bell rang in their office; Hay went into the President's office. The Ancient was gloomily reading court-martial documents. They came to him at the rate now of thirty thousand

379

a year, and there were days when he and the two secretaries did no other work but study whether or not Private Ezra Smith had really been asleep on duty, and so must be shot dead. Lincoln was generally inclined to mercy, particularly with what he called "the leg-cases," men who had run away when guns were fired at them. "It is a sensible reaction," Lincoln had once observed. "And very much my own. I have a good deal of moral courage, I think, but faced with a battery of guns up ahead, I might just find me a nice tree to rest behind." Stanton was for shooting everyone. Lincoln was for sparing anyone where there might be an extenuating circumstance. "After all, if you take a coward and put him in front of a firing squad, you'll scare him to death anyway." Although the President made his jokes—like a tic they sometimes were, thought Hay—he grew grayer and bleaker on those days, as now, when he was obliged to play God and determine who was to live and who was to die. From the beginning, the military had insisted that if cowards were not dealt with harshly and publicly, there might be no army left at all. So at the end of this particular day, there might be a hundred men who would die because the Commander-in-Chief had chosen not to pardon them.

"Here, John." Lincoln gave Hay a stack of orders. "These are the ones that I've pardoned. The rest . . ." He sighed; and stretched until the vertebrae cracked. Hay wanted to bring up the subject of Watt, but when he saw how wan the Ancient was he let the matter go. He and Nicolay would have to handle this one together. "Sit down, John, and tell me about Springfield and Cincinnati."

Hay had just returned from two weeks in both cities, as well as in his hometown of Warsaw, Illinois. "Well, sir, there is not a good word said of McClellan anywhere, even by the Democrats."

"And of me? Is there a single good word said—or, maybe, two?"

"There is all the usual talk, sir. There are still people who think that Mr. Seward and General McClellan are running the government and that if you would only get rid of them, we'd win the war."

Lincoln nodded, vaguely. Hay wished that he could tell him something that he did not know; but this was rare. Lincoln had a habit of asking strangers seemingly idle questions which, like a trial lawyer's cross-examination, were not idle at all but very much a part of his ongoing education in a thousand matters. He called his meetings with strangers "public-opinion baths." Lately, he had been nearly drowned in them. Everyone gave him advice. "How will the voting go back home?"

"It won't be easy, sir. Our best Republicans are all in the army, while the smartest Democrats are all working to win the state."

Lincoln nodded. "And I am criticized for putting too many Democrats in high places. I should have doubled the number; and doubled the blame. I suspect we'll lose Illinois," he added in a matter-of-fact way. "Did you see Billy Herndon?"

"Yes, sir." Hay smiled. "During the summer he married the fair Miss Anna Miles. He told me that she is a Democrat and pro-slavery but that he has, by masterful argument, changed her mind entirely."

"Poor Billy. But then," Lincoln added drolly, "poor Miss Anna. She's got her a handful, with Billy and all those children."

"They refuse to call her Mother."

"Well, she's about the same age as the older ones. Is he a Good Templar now?"

"Yes, sir. He has foresworn the demon rum; and preaches against it."

"That is to the good. I've often thought that if he had not so . . . handicapped himself in life, he might have been the American Voltaire."

"Do we really need one of those, sir?" Hay feigned a bumpkin's innocence.

"Now, John, you must never ask a politican such a question just before an election."

On Election Day, there was rain. Lincoln received the returns in Stanton's office, while Hay sat nearby at a clerk's desk, sorting the telegrams and arranging them according to state. Lincoln lay on the sofa; eyes shut. Stanton, in his shirt-sleeves, wheezed and moaned and addressed God, threateningly. Since the death of his baby son, James, he and God were in constant communication. Washburne sat in a rocker, keeping track of the vote. At regular intervals, military aides would come from the Telegraph Room next door. If the message was significant, Stanton would read it aloud and then Hay would file it with the others.

The loss of New York State came as no surprise to Lincoln; but it was a matter of bitterness to Stanton, who had persuaded a friend, the politician-general Wadsworth, to run for governor. Now Wadsworth was defeated, and the Democrat Horatio Seymour was elected. "It is tragic!" Stanton cried.

"And, like all classic tragedy, to have been expected," said Lincoln on his sofa. "There are one hundred thousand New York men in the army, most of them Republicans, away from home; and unable to vote."

"Wasted!" exclaimed Washburne; he was surprised at the extent of the Republican defeat in New York.

"Well, not entirely wasted," said Lincoln, with the beginning of a smile. "Mr. Stanton here has placed those very same loyal
381

Republican New Yorkers all around the border-states, where they will make sure that we get proper majorities."

Stanton struck his desk a great blow. "We will, too! In Delaware alone, I've got three thousand men supervising the polling places."

"And Tennessee?" Lincoln—as Jupiter—enjoyed teasing Mars.

"Oh, General Grant will follow your orders to the last comma. You told him 'to follow forms of law *as far as convenient.*'"

"Did I say that?" Lincoln pretended surprise.

"I hope you put it even more strongly," said Washburne, who had now noted Tennessee's clean sweep for the Republican Party. "There is nothing like the presence of bayonets to get the pro-slave element to vote right."

"Well, I did send General Grant a message, saying that we should elect only men of good character, and loyalty to the Union, like our military governor Andy Johnson."

"Between Johnson and Grant, this should be a highly bibulous election for Tennessee." Washburne could not resist the comment.

"Well," said Lincoln, "we must give old Andy credit for going against his own state's wishes and staying put in the Union when all the others skedaddled off to the South, like Breckinridge. I don't know why Andy is so loyal to us but he is, and I'm grateful."

Between messages, they discussed McClellan. Washburne was curious about the nature of the political advice that McClellan had given Lincoln at Harrison's Landing. But Lincoln only smiled. "I've locked all that away," he said.

"But what," asked Washburne, "did you think of this unsuccessful general, giving *you* advice?"

"Nothing," said Lincoln. But then his face lit up. Hay saw a story coming. "I will say that it made me think of the man whose horse kicked up and struck his foot through the stirrup, causing the man to say to the horse, 'Well, if you are going to get on, I'm going to get off.'"

As the night wore on and the news from around the country got worse and worse, Lincoln discussed his favorite Shakespeare play, *Macbeth.* "Even though I have never seen it in a version I liked, not that I've seen all that many plays, of any sort."

Lincoln was quoting from the fifth act when the loss of Pennsylvania was announced. Lincoln then spoke of the West, as if by hopeful association. "If I am remembered for anything, and if we lose this war, I shall be, I pray, totally forgotten."

"We . . . win . . . !" Stanton was now in the throes of a serious asthma attack; but since those present were so used to them, no one showed the slightest concern.

"I *think* we'll win, too, Mars," said Lincoln. "Only it's not

382

done yet. But if, say, we lose, I will take pride—posthumous, I'm sure—in just two things. The railroad across the continent..."

"Jay Cooke and Company are ready to start selling shares," said Washburne, who was more than ready himself to subscribe, "for what they call the Northern Pacific Railway, which doesn't exist yet, of course."

"What matters is that there will be, one way or another, a railroad that joins the whole Union into one... union. Without such a railroad we have no nation, in the modern sense..." The President sat up in the sofa. "What was that again about Jay Cooke, Brother Washburne?"

"There's a rumor going around that he wants to get into the railroad business, in competition with Union Pacific."

"Well, the more the merrier. If he can sell railroad shares the way he sells government bonds, we will have our railroad pretty fast."

A messenger arrived with a stack of telegrams, which Stanton was now in no state to read. He gave them to Hay, who read them quickly; then feeling like the messenger who was bound to be executed for the news he brought, he announced, "As of the latest returns, we have lost Ohio and Indiana. Wisconsin is split. New Jersey remains Democratic."

There was no sound in the room but the rain beating on the window; and Stanton's gasping. Hay had never seen the Ancient look so sad or sound so confident. "The other thing," he said firmly, ignoring message and messenger, "that we can take credit for is the Homestead Act. No other nation has ever done such a thing, giving a man a rich farm of at least a hundred and sixty acres in the Western territories, with no conditions other than he farm it for at least five years. We will gain five, ten, twenty million good farmers from Europe, and fill up the whole West."

It was close to dawn when they were joined by Seward, red of face from what must have been a long convivial evening. He had followed the returns through the wire-services. "Well, Mr. President, as midterm congressional elections go, this is not a great victory. But all is not lost."

"Well, Governor, maybe not all, but a great deal is lost, you must admit." Lincoln was now on his feet, restlessly pacing the room. Washburne's eyes were shut. Hay was trying to figure out the provisional if not the final vote for the Congress. Stanton now looked to be dead behind his desk.

"I've worked it out, Mr. President. We control the Senate, naturally. And we shall control the House by eighteen votes."

"That means," said Lincoln, "the Democrats have gone from forty-four seats to seventy-five."

"But we hold our majority, thanks to Michigan, Kansas, Iowa—which I thought we'd lose—Minnesota, Oregon and California."

Lincoln shook his head. "They gave us the additional seats, but it is the border-states, thanks to Mr. Stanton, and New England, that control the Congress. But..." Lincoln struck his right fist into his left hand. "Oh, it is hard! We lost New York and the other great states because our best people are away at war, and because the press does everything to inflame the average person against us."

"It is not for want of us trying to shut down those voices of treason," said Seward, magniloquently. Hay rather hoped that he would make one of his dazzling, tipsy speeches.

But Lincoln spoke through him. "What we have had to do we have done and I hope that we have done it fairly. I have suspended *habeas corpus* throughout the Union, and on January the first I shall free the slaves in the rebel states. Yet I am told that I do not go far enough. Oh, it is hard!" Lincoln turned to Stanton, who had now returned to a blue-faced lazarene sort of life. "Mr. Stanton, tomorrow you will relieve General McClellan, as commanding general of the Army of the Potomac."

"With pleasure, sir; and relief," said Stanton, in a normal voice.

"This is great news," said Washburne.

"I could not do it before the election for fear people would think that I was bowing to the radicals, who've been asking for his head."

Seward was suddenly uneasy. "By the same token," he said, allowing himself to strike slightly the Jesuitical note, "there will be those who say that you did not dare remove him *before* the election for fear that you would lose the support of the moderates, not to mention the lovers of slavery—and of McClellan—in the border-states."

"Whatever I do, Governor, will be misconstrued by most." To Hay, the Tycoon seemed now to be relieved at last of some heavy burden. "In any case, I gave McClellan every possible opportunity. Fact, I made a little bet with myself. If McClellan didn't cut off Lee on the way to Richmond, which could easily have been done in the last two weeks, then he did not mean to bust the enemy, for whatever reasons. Well, he did nothing, as usual. And now he is gone."

Stanton had already written out the order of dismissal. He himself left the room to see that it would be taken, as rapidly as possible, by courier to McClellan.

"Who will take his place?" asked Washburne.

Hay looked at Lincoln, aware that the President had now spent months talking to generals, communicating secretly with Winfield

Scott at West Point, asking Halleck pointed questions. With Lincoln's eerie bad luck in military matters, Old Brains was now no more than a head clerk. After Pope's debacle at Bull Run, Halleck had simply given up. Once again Lincoln was his own General-in-Chief, supported vigorously by Stanton, the only good thing to have happened to the Tycoon since the war began. But as Hay had said to Nico, two sly lawyers do not an Alexander make; and both agreed that Lincoln's political skill and strength of character were of no use to him when dealing with generals. He simply did not have the experience to know which commander was capable and which was not. He had endured McClellan because Little Mac was good at drill; and a born engineer. Also, there were urgent political reasons for keeping him on; reasons that had now vanished beneath the stack of telegrams on Hay's desk.

Lincoln had trusted McDowell; but then obliged him to go into battle with a green army. Lincoln had accepted Pope at Pope's own high evaluation of himself; also, Pope was pleasing to Chase and the radicals. Now the Ancient was faced with a choice between Ambrose E. Burnside and Joseph Hooker. Neither general liked or trusted the other. It was all too reminiscent, thought Hay, of the McClellan-Pope rivalry, which had led to the Union's worst disaster.

If nothing else, Burnside was, a splendid-looking figure, with ferocious, much-imitated moustaches that connected with the whiskers at his ears. This extraordinary display of facial hair was now known far and wide as "burnsides," and much imitated. Burnside had been Governor Sprague's choice to lead the first of Rhode Island's regiments. Later, he had served with distinction in North Carolina. The previous summer, Lincoln had offered him McClellan's place, and Burnside had declined it; partly because he was then on friendly terms with McClellan, and partly because he did not think that he had the competence to direct an entire army. He was not yet forty years of age; he was a martyr to chronic diarrhea. But Burnside did think of himself as a fighting general, and Lincoln inclined to such men.

Joseph Hooker was in his forties; and his career had followed the by-now-usual pattern for nonpolitical generals. He had graduated from West Point; fought in the Mexican War; resigned from the army and gone west to California, as had Halleck, whom he detested. Hooker was reputed to be a heavy drinker as well as a bold, even reckless, conversationalist. He was close to Chase, always a bad sign in Hay's eyes. Chase's wooing of generals was one of the scandals of the city. Whenever a general looked as if he might indeed be the leader the war required, Chase would draw close to him and befriend him. If the general was also politically correct in Chase's eyes, the Secretary of the Treasury would then go to work on Ben Wade and the other Jacobins of the Joint Committee. All this, Hay knew—and, presumably, Lincoln knew, so that the winning general would stand at Chase's side in the election of 1864.

During October, another of Chase's protégés, William S. Rosecrans, had been given command of the Department of the Cumberland. Previously, under Grant, Rosecrans had done moderately well at the battles of Corinth and Iuka. There were times when Hay thought that the secret master of the armies of the United States was Salmon P. Chase, who, in turn, affected to believe that the actual master of the nation was Seward. In political circles, little credit was given Lincoln for anything, which, in Hay's eyes, was probably a good thing for the present. Let Chase and Seward take the blame for the Union's long series of military defeats. Sooner or later, the Tycoon would assert himself. The war would be won. He would be reelected; and Hay would be a poet—or something.

The President was at the map of Maryland when he answered Washburne. "I have chosen Burnside to take McClellan's place. He is a fighting general, you know. I have faith in him." But Lincoln sounded, to Washburne, curiously listless.

As they crossed to the Mansion, a small crowd cheered the President on the Republican victory. Then Lincoln paused to speak to the secretary of the Senate, who was also the editor of Washington's daily *Chronicle*, John Forney, known to the Democratic northern press as "Lincoln's dog." "It will be a difficult year for us in Congress," said Forney, sadly.

"Well, that seems to be the usual condition for us," said the President. Hay clutched the telegrams; and tried not to yawn.

"What did you feel when we lost New York?" asked Forney. This was easily the most idiotic question that Hay had heard since the last journalist had questioned the President.

But Lincoln rallied nicely. "Somewhat like that boy in Kentucky who stubbed his toe while running to his sweetheart. The boy said he was too big to cry, and far too badly hurt to laugh." Those in the street all laughed at this; and Lincoln bade them good-night.

As they entered the Mansion, Hay asked, "Did you have that prepared, sir?"

"Have what prepared, John?" Lincoln was bent over, studying each step as they walked up the main staircase.

"What you said to Mr. Forney."

"Oh?" Lincoln glanced at Hay; like someone just awakened from sleep. "*What* did I say to him?"

"You said you felt like the boy who stubbed his toe..."

"Too old to cry, too hurt to laugh," Lincoln finished. Then he smiled. "Sometimes I say those things and don't even know I've said them. When there is so much you *cannot* say, it's always a good idea to have a story ready. I do it now from habit." Lincoln sighed. "In my predicament, it is a good thing to know all sorts of stories because the truth of the whole matter is now almost unsayable; and so cruel."

9

THERE WAS IN THE CAPITAL NO DRAWING ROOM MORE ENTIRELY agreeable and stimulating to Seward than that of Mr. and Mrs. Charles Eames. Mr. Eames had been, in earlier years, a publisher of the Washington *Union*, a Democratic newspaper long since vanished. The Eameses themselves had vanished for four years, during which time he was American minister to Venezuela. They returned to Washington in the last golden secesh days of the Buchanan Administration; and thanks to Mr. Eames's charm and to Mrs. Eames's New York wit they conducted what was, in effect, Washington's only salon in the European sense. To be at home with the Chases was a far grander experience; but the house of the Chases was, simply, the elegant command headquarters of the next president, and the guest lists at Sixth and E were altogether too calculated, in Seward's amused view, to amuse him. But one was invited to the Eameses only if one were amusing or wise or, like William Seward himself, both.

When Seward stepped into the drawing room, Mrs. Eames gave him a delighted smile and a small curtsey. "*Monsieur le Premier*," she murmured reverently.

"Do rise, my dear. I know how exciting it is for you to see me like this, power radiating from my fingertips. But do battle with your natural awe." Seward took her arm comfortably, and surveyed the room. Of the twenty or so guests already arrived, Seward remarked, contentedly, "There is not one uniform. That is a relief, let me tell you."

"The only military men we know, Governor, live only to fight. They are either in the field—or safely, heroically, under it."

"Do you actually know *any* men of this sort?"

"Yes. And they are all Democratic politicians. And here is their queen."

They were joined by Mrs. Stephen Douglas, widow of the last leader of the entire Democratic Party. Seward was much taken with Mrs. Douglas's charm, Southern though it might be. As there had been much speculation in recent months that should Kate Chase marry Governor Sprague, Chase himself would marry the widow Douglas, Seward felt free to inquire if this would be the case.

"Oh, I don't think so!" Mrs. Douglas turned slightly away so that Seward might better view her famous profile, whose high, curved forehead and straight, perfect nose had inspired legions of newspaper writers to classical allusions—usually mistaken, Seward would duly note. Mrs. Eames went to greet the Baron and Baroness Gerolt and their large but handsome daughter Carlota.

"I think you'd make a splendid couple," said Seward, enjoying the profile, as it began, delicately, to flush.

"I esteem Mr. Chase highly," she said.

"And is not Miss Kate—your prospective stepdaughter—glorious?" Seward liked nothing better than to make lighthearted mischief.

"Oh, is *that* the word?" Mrs. Douglas gave him her full face; and full smile. He noted that the teeth were not as regular as those of a Greek goddess. But then she need not eat marble. "Glorious," she repeated in her soft voice. "Well, yes, she *wants* glory."

"Meaning she desires it, or lacks it? Our old verbs have so many meanings."

"And you know them all." But Mrs. Douglas was not about to be drawn out on the dangerous subject of Kate. "Mr. Chase did pay me a call one day when I was out. So he left me, as his card, half a one-dollar bill, with his picture on it."

"Such elegance!" Seward was delighted at the thought of the ponderous, Bible-quoting, hymn-singing, monomaniacal (on the subject of himself and the presidency) Chase tearing up dollar bills and leaving them as calling cards on beautiful ladies. He would have to tell the President, who had not had much to laugh at since the beginning of the third and last session of the Thirty-seventh Congress of the United States on December 1, 1862. In the last ten days, the full weight of the Republican Party's loss at the election had been felt. As a result, the radicals were now crying out for Seward's head; and Chase was not so secretly inciting them. Once Seward ceased to be premier, Chase would take his place, with the blessing of Congress and the acquiescence of the weak and now weakened Lincoln. Seward's thoughts, always mercurial, were turning dark indeed, even as he smiled at Adéle
388

Douglas; but she lightened his mood with her response to Chase. "I sent him back his unusual calling card, with a note saying that I did not accept money from gentlemen."

Seward laughed wholeheartedly. Mrs. Douglas, pleased to have made him laugh, said, "As the eyes and ears—not to mention gaoler—of the government, what has become of my poor aunt, Mrs. Greenhow?"

"We exchanged her and a number of other lady spies some time ago..."

"I know. I was so grateful. But I thought it better not to put anything in writing to you. Yes, I know you sent her to Richmond. But then what happened to her?"

"*You* don't know?" Seward wondered if Mrs. Douglas might not be lying. There were times when he felt that, except for a few hundred outlander politicians like himself, Washington was the actual capital of the rebellion.

"If I knew, Mr. Seward, I would not ask." This was dignified.

"According to my spies—and they are, literally, spies—Mrs. Greenhow is now living in Paris, paying court to the empress, and intriguing to get the French to recognize the Confederacy or, failing that, to annex all of Mexico, a bone of contention between Mr. Mercier, over there, and me."

"My aunt is so—vehement." Mrs. Douglas shook her head. Then she embraced the Baroness Gerolt while the Baron greeted his crony Seward.

"Well, Governor," said Gerolt in his heavily accented English, "I have written my government today that the war will be finished one way or the other before the first of the year."

"One way, Baron, yes; but why the other?" Seward took the teacup that a maid brought him.

"Berlin requires me to sound neutral."

"I wish London required the same of Lord Lyons. I tell you the British legation should be called the rebel legation. I think you may be right," Seward added, in a low voice. "We seem to be preparing for the final confrontation in Virginia. Lee and all his army are at Fredericksburg, or so I read in the newspapers."

Gerolt laughed. "I am told, through *our* newspapers, that our new chief of Cabinet very much admires the way that you arrest editors but he dares not do the same in Prussia because he says that, unlike you, he is devoted to freedom of speech."

"Mr. Bismarck has a nice wit."

"We think so, privately. Also, privately, he is fascinated by this war of yours."

"He can come and take it away with him any day of the week, my dear Baron. It is all his."

"I shall transmit your proposal. Meanwhile, I have sent him your latest book."

Seward had just published a volume of his speeches and correspondence as Secretary of State. He had been heavily criticized for doing such a thing while in office; and in wartime. He had even been accused by Sumner of levity and cynicism and indifference to the abolitionist cause.

John Hay bowed low to Seward. "Premier," he said.

"Young man." Seward acknowledged the obeisance with a wave of his long pale hand.

"Baron." Hay shook hands with the Prussian, who smiled benignly. "Miss Carlota has done me the honor of saying that she will come to the theater with me, if I have your consent."

"I will telegraph Berlin."

As Hay and Gerolt chatted amiably, Hay watched Seward, who was surveying the room with his usual quizzical air. Hay wondered how much Seward knew of the plot to remove him. Resourceful and clever as the little man was, he had grown more and more estranged from his one-time colleagues in the Senate, where the chiefs of the anti-Seward cabal were located.

Shortly after McClellan's removal, Senators Wade, Hale and Fessenden had called on the President to congratulate him. The meeting had been pleasant enough; but there had been a number of pointed references to Seward's lack of zeal in the matter of abolition. Lincoln had chosen to ignore, through deflection, these comments. Now something was stirring at the Capitol. Ben Wade had been quoted as saying that the war could never be won until Seward was sent away and a lieutenant-general—a true Republican—placed in command of the entire nation, as dictator. Who this potentate should be, Wade did not say. But Chase was always a magical figure for the senatorial members of the Joint Committee on the Conduct of the War.

Mrs. Eames led the Prussian minister away. Seward turned to Hay. "I sometimes wonder what is the use of growing old. You learn something of men and things but never until too late to use it." Seward sighed, theatrically. He had used almost the exact same words to Hay in the autumn as preface to the latest human folly that had allegedly come his way—military jealousy. He had been appalled that McClellan, envious of Pope, had let Pope go down in flames at Bull Run. Now Seward was on another not-too-dissimilar tack. "I have only just begun to understand what ambition will do to a man."

"You mean Mr. Chase, sir?"

"Johnny!" Seward feigned shock. "I never speak ill of a colleague; or of anyone. It is my custom to speak only in wise gen-
390

eralities, occasionally decorated by the odd aphorism or insight so annoying to Senator Sumner. But I do believe Mr. Chase is altogether too frequent a visitor to the Capitol. Mind you, during the redecoration—so tastefully if expensively done—I can see his eagerness to observe how the Treasury's money is spent. Now that it looks as if they may actually put a permanent dome over the rotunda, I realize that he has a proprietary feeling—even one of kinship, since the dome is bound to resemble his own noble head, and yet why does he forgather with the Jacobins, who detest his Administration? And why was he observed yesterday in the Speaker's chamber, staring at himself in a gold-framed mirror and—thinking himself alone—saying to his reflection, with solemn unction, 'Mr. President Chase'?"

Hay roared with laughter at the image. Seward grinned mischievously. He had said all that he had intended to say on the subject but he had sent Hay a signal. Seward was one of the few people who knew that Hay often wrote Washington stories, anonymously, for the New York newspapers. Hay's speciality was inside information about the Administration, which seemed, at first, to be scandalous but then proved to be subtly favorable to the President. He often published in the World, a newspaper noted for its virulent hatred of Lincoln. It gave Hay a good deal of pleasure to know that the editor never suspected that he was being manipulated by the President's own secretary. Meanwhile, Hay and Nicolay had seen to it that journalists of every sort had been given military and civilian posts in different parts of the country so that they could then write stories favorable to the Administration for their old newspapers.

During Hay's first year in the White House, he had thought it a good idea to keep his own stories secret from the Ancient. But since Thurlow Weed and Seward both knew—it was Weed who had made the arrangements with the World and the Journal—Weed had promptly blabbed to the President, who had been troubled. "Is it proper?" he had asked Hay.

"Is it proper, sir," Hay had answered, "that we are never allowed to answer our critics in those papers?"

Lincoln had let the matter drop; and Hay continued his secret journalistic career. He had been amused to learn from Seward that the son of the American minister to the Court of St. James, Henry Adams, was doing exactly the same thing; and only Seward knew about both young men. But then only Seward probably knew everything worth knowing on earth, thought Hay, who said, "I wonder if the readers of the World might be interested. I'm sure the editor, Mr. Marble..."

"What a terrible man is Manton Marble!" With that, Seward,

inscrutable as Ignatius Loyola himself, crossed the room in order to torment M. Mercier about Mexico. Hay had received his instruction. He was to expose the Chase cabal against Seward and, ultimately, the President.

Mr. Eames joined Hay at the fireplace. Coal burned and hissed in the grate. The parlor was warm; but Hay was always chilly now. He stood with his back to the fire as his host complimented him on the President's message to Congress, which Nicolay had allowed Hay to deliver, in person.

"I thought some of it even poetic," said Eames. "Highly poetic."

"Even Shakespearean?"

Eames smiled. "That is a little lofty, perhaps. But the last lines had their echoes." The Tycoon had labored for weeks on the message, the first since his party's electoral set-back in November. The ending had been beautiful. "Fellow-citizens, we cannot escape history. We of this Congress and this administration will be remembered in spite of ourselves. No personal significance or insignificance can spare one or another of us. The fiery trial through which we pass will light us down, in honor or dishonor, to the latest generation."

But there had been many objections made to the principal theme of the message, the buying of the slaves by the government; and then their colonization elsewhere. Hay thought Lincoln somewhat obsessed on the subject of colonization, while Mr. Eames thought that Lincoln was under some sort of hallucination about the nature of the war itself. "Mind you, I'm an old Democratic editor, and so I see things with a half-Southern eye. But when the President thinks that the rebellion will end if we compensate the slave-owners with money, he totally mistakes what the war is about."

"What, then, is it about?" Hay had often wondered. No explanation had ever seemed to him entirely plausible. It was like the fever; it came for no reason and left for no reason.

"I thought Mr. Lincoln understood that better than any man, at the beginning. It was the principle that the Union cannot be dissolved, ever."

"But it had been dissolved before he was inaugurated."

"So he started the war in order to put the Union back together again. That is what the fighting is all about. But now he seems to have shifted over to the slavery side, and there he is wrong—in my humble view. He tells us that in the thirty-eight years between now and 1900, the government can sell bonds and pay off the slave-owners. Well, perhaps, it can. But what makes him think that any Southerner will put down his arms because the government is willing to pay him for his slaves? The South is not fighting for slavery, Mr. Hay. The South is fighting for independence. You can buy all their slaves, and they'll take the money. But they will not come back into the Union except by force."

"You think it has gone so far?" Hay had not heard a supporter of the Union present so confidently—and plausibly—the Southern case.

"Oh, Mr. Hay, the cost! Think of all the blood that has been shed, and think of all that will be shed; and then ask yourself, will any man say that he has fought in so terrible a war just for the right to keep slaves? No, he will say that he fought to keep his country free; and he will mean it."

Certainly, John Surratt meant it, as he and David crossed Pennsylvania Avenue, the wet snow swirling all about them. John described what had happened the day before on the Rappahannock. "I was supposed to come straight here. But then all hell broke loose, starting Saturday in this terrible fog, and going on till yesterday when the Yanks retreated back across the river. They lost three times the men we did. I know. I saw a lot of the fighting from near Marye's Hill, where our artillery was. We made a trap for Burnside; and he fell into it."

The two young men entered Sullivan's Saloon, just off the avenue, now filled with ambulance carriages. Although the saloon's owner had been born in Ireland, he was entirely dedicated to the Confederacy. But since practically everything that Sullivan said was posed as a joke, Pinkerton's men had given him no real trouble, while he, in return, had made all sorts of trouble for the secret service, passing on false information, usually having to do with the vast size of the Confederate armies.

David and John sat at the back of the bar, near the Franklin stove. The floor was strewn with sawdust turned to mud as a result of wet boots, spilled beer and the spittle of tobacco-chewers. Though it was noon, gaslights hissed cozily from the low ceiling and the free lunch was now being set out by a mulatto waiter, as loyal to the Confederacy as his employer. David helped himself to a boiled egg while Sullivan himself brought them mugs of beer. The front of the bar was crowded with what looked to be countryfolk of the sort who brought their produce to the Center Market, which was what many of them did. But there were also a pair of night-riders, drinking whiskey and talking to each other in low voices.

Sullivan sat with John and David; he listened with fascination to John's account of the Union army's defeat at Fredericksburg. "What happens now?" Sullivan asked, when John paused for a moment in his delighted if somewhat awed account.

John shrugged. "I guess General Burnside will stick there in the mud till spring. Or he'll retreat to here." John shook his head. "A year ago they were almost in Richmond and now they can't even cross the Rappahannock, sixty miles away."

"They can't fight, which is lucky for us," said David, repeating what his friends were always saying.

"Oh, they can fight," said John. "You never saw anything like how wave after wave of them went up that hill only to get blown to bits by the cannon in the breastworks. They don't have one good general, that's what is lucky for us. They also don't have us night-riders," he added in a whisper. "We've got Pinkerton so full of misinformation now that he truly thinks General Lee has a million men under arms, and that we're fixing to kidnap Lincoln."

"Why don't we?" asked David.

"There's no point. We're winning. Lee's going to be in Philadelphia by summer. When that happens, the war ends."

Sullivan nodded. Absently, he cleaned the rough wood of the table with a rag. "One of the wild boys took a shot at Old Abe last August on Seventh Street road, and when the Colonel heard what he had done he was mad as could be." The nameless Colonel was someone whom David had yet to see, that he knew of. He was the link between Richmond and the Confederate agents in Washington. Sometimes David thought that Sullivan himself might be the Colonel; certainly, he quoted him often; and seemed to know him.

"Why was he mad?" asked John. "It would be a righteous thing to shoot the man who thinks he's going to free our niggers."

"It may be righteous, but the Colonel said that with President Lincoln in charge of this war, it is as good as won for us."

John laughed. "Well, he may have a point there. But if the time comes to kill him we'll let Davie here do it."

"Me? How?"

"Put poison in his medicine. That's how. Couldn't be simpler."

"But Mr. Thompson would know it was me." Actually, David had often thought how easy it would be to poison the President— or anyone else who frequented Thompson's. As it was, between Mr. Thompson and himself, a number of untimely deaths had taken place due to carelessness in the prescription department. Fortunately, as Mr. Thompson liked to say of the medical profession, "Theirs is the only other profession that is allowed to bury its mistakes."

"Anyway, for now," said Sullivan, "Mr. Lincoln is the South's chief weapon. We must treasure him."

The South's treasure was awake most of that night. He lay on the lounge in his office and received a series of callers. Hay was present when, toward midnight, Governor Curtin of Pennsylvania appeared. Curtin had come straight from Fredericksburg. Lincoln rose to greet him. Hay had never seen the Ancient so ancient and fragile and distraught.

As the excited Curtin paced the room, Lincoln half stood and half lay against the mantelpiece. Hay noted that in this position Lincoln's head and the portrait of Andrew Jackson were side by side; and they looked alike now—Old Abe every bit as old as Old Hickory.

"I saw our men torn to pieces before my eyes. Yet they kept on advancing. I've never seen such bravery. Or such butchery."

"I know. I know." Lincoln rubbed his eyes from weariness. "What are the casualties, thus far?"

Curtin removed a sheet of paper from his pocket. "I was given this by General Burnside's adjutant. These are the estimated losses for each of the grand divisions. General Sumner's. About five hundred men killed. About five thousand wounded . . ."

"Dear God! That is only *one* division?" Lincoln was now the color of the dead fire at his back.

"Some eight hundred missing." Curtin continued, "General Hooker's division. There are more than three hundred dead. And three thousand wounded. And eight hundred missing."

"This is too much, Governor. Far too much. The country cannot endure these losses. I cannot endure them. Oh, this was madness!" Lincoln struck the mantelpiece with his fist. "To attack." He struck it again. "In winter." And again. "Across a river. With the entire rebel army entrenched and waiting. It was a trap." Lincoln turned from the fireplace. "I see it all now. I did not see it then. Burnside insisted. You understand? So Halleck and Stanton and I gave way. You must give way to a general who fights . . ."

"Fights, sir, but does not think. The man is incompetent. Worse, he knows that he has not the competence to command a great army. He asked you, he told me himself, not to appoint him."

Lincoln was now walking about the room as if in search of some hitherto unseen door through which he might escape. Hay recalled Herndon's story of the time that Lincoln had been mad. Was there to be a repetition?

As Lincoln moved frantically along the wall, feeling his way like a blind man, Curtin continued his account of the dead and the wounded and the missing. Hay tried to divert him, with a gesture of "no." But Curtin ignored him. He too seemed to be on the verge of madness. "And so this defeat cost us, finally, sir, in dead and wounded and missing, roughly fifteen thousand men. I saw the wounded from one of our Pennsylvania regiments. I saw young boys of fifteen with their stomachs hanging out of them. I saw . . ."

"*You* saw, sir?" Lincoln opened and then shut the door to the Reception Room with a crash. "Think what *I* see! Think how I must watch as all this blood fills up this room and now is near to drowning me. You have no responsibility, sir, no oath registered in Heaven. Well, I do!" Lincoln's voice had gone so high that it broke on the word "do." Hay leapt to his feet. "Mr. President," he said in what he meant to be a soothing voice; but his own voice broke with emotion. Dumbly, the three men stood in a circle at the room's center.

Lincoln glared for a long moment at Curtin, who took a step backward, as if alarmed by what he saw in the President's eyes. "I am sorry, sir. To distress you like this. I only wanted to answer your questions. I am overwrought, I fear. Because of what I saw. Certainly I would give anything to deliver you of this terrible war."

"Me?" Lincoln shook his head like a man who has suddenly awakened from a bad dream. "Oh, Governor, I don't matter. I am done for anyway. I was chosen to do a certain work, and I must do it, and then go. But I do need help. There's no doubt of that." The Ancient's face lightened; as did his mood. Hay saw that he was about to tell a story; and was deeply relieved. "This reminds me, Governor, of an old farmer out in Illinois, who had two mischievous boys called James and John. Or maybe John and James. Anyway, the farmer bought a mean-tempered prize hog, and penned him up, and told the boys they were to stay clear of the pen. Naturally, James let the hog out of his pen the next day and the hog went for the seat of James's trousers, and the only way the boy could save himself was by holding onto the hog's tail. So they went round and round a tree a number of times until the boy's courage began to fail, and he shouted to his brother, 'Come here quick and help me *let this hog go*.'" Lincoln chuckled. "Well, Governor, that is exactly my case. I wish someone would help me let this hog go." On that amiable and characteristic note, Lincoln bade Curtin, "Good-night."

After the governor had gone, Lincoln stood staring into the remains of the fire.

"Shall I have them make a new fire?" asked Hay.

"No, John. You go to bed now. Let Edward guard the fort. All is well now. That is, all *will* be well. Because, you see, it is like this. Should we lose the same number of men tomorrow as today, and they the same. And we the same the day after, and they the same. And so on, day after day after day, we shall have won. For we have more lives to give than they do, and we shall
396

keep on giving these lives of ours until—yes, *all* of them, if need be—are dead."

Before Hay went to his room, he crossed into the living quarters, where Lamon sat at the door to the President's bedroom, armed to the teeth, and sound asleep. "Mr. Lamon," Hay whispered. Lamon raised first his derringer; then his eyelids. "Tell Mrs. Lincoln to get the President to bed. He's about at the end of his rope."

Lamon nodded. He rapped three times on the bedroom door. From within Madam's wide-awake voice sounded. "Yes, Mr. Lamon?"

"We think you should get the President to his bed."

"Yes," said the voice. Hay went into his own room, where Nicolay snored softly.

Mary opened the door to the President's office. Lincoln was stretched out on the lounge, reading a book. "Why, Mother, what are you doing up so late?"

From the sound of her husband's voice, she could tell that he was indeed at the edge of his strength. "You come to bed, Father. It's no good staying up all night."

"But they keep coming to me from Fredericksburg; and I must listen to them all."

"No, Father, you must not listen to them all. You've listened to too many, as it is. The battle is over. There is no more news tonight. Come on."

Lincoln got to his feet. He put down the book. "It is by Artemus Ward," he said. "Powerful funny."

"I know, Father." She took his arm; and led him into the dimly lit hallway. Edward was at his desk. "You go home, Edward," said Mary.

"Yes," said Lincoln. "We're shutting up shop for the night."

"Good-night, Mr. President."

As Lincoln and Mary passed the guard on duty, he saluted the President and said, "Good-night, sir. Sleep well."

"Thank you. Thank you, my boy."

But once husband and wife were in their bedroom, Lincoln shook his head and said, "I'm better off awake tonight."

"Don't be foolish! You can hardly keep your eyes open, you are so tired."

"True. But I don't dare sleep."

"Are your dreams so bad?"

"Yes, Mother. They are so bad."

But, in the end, Lincoln slept; and it was Mary who stayed awake the night to comfort him, if need be. She knew the horror of dreams.

Chase read the newspaper article, with lips pursed. Then he gave it back to Ben Wade. "I fear that for all his good qualities, the President lacks dignity."

"Dignity!" Wade threw the newspaper into the brass spittoon beside his chair. "Imagine on a day as tragic as Fredericksburg to compare his position to that of a boy with a pig by the tail. Well, I'm for helping him let it go. So is the Senate. We've just held our Republican caucus."

"With what result?" Chase pretended that he did not already know.

"Well, our faction carried the day. The moderates want both Stanton and Seward to go. But we said the departure of Seward was enough for now. With Seward gone, the Cabinet can be reorganized."

"Seward is too much a politician for my taste." Chase arranged the papers on his desk in a neat line with the top of the blotter. "He has a sort of back stairs influence on the President that strikes me as dangerous. They constantly . . . joke with each other."

"Oh, he's a card, the governor," said Wade. "But I don't mind the jokes so much as I do the way he acts on his own, without consulting the President or the Cabinet, like that letter of instructions he wrote to Adams in London, mocking us abolitionists. Then, he goes and publishes it in that damned fool book of his. When Sumner showed the letter to Lincoln, he said he had never seen it before, and that it didn't reflect his own policy. Now *that* is serious."

"Seward does as he pleases. But then so do many of the other Cabinet ministers. Our meetings are a mockery. The real business is decided between Lincoln and Seward at the Old Club House, over brandy. The rest of us are seldom consulted. Worst of all, I suppose," said Chase, coming to the point, "is not so much the fact that Seward is the master of Lincoln. After all, someone must fulfill that function; and Seward is the leader of our party. No, the problem is much more serious. Mr. Wade, Governor Seward does not believe in this war. That is why we sustain one defeat after another. He has always thought that, somehow or other, the Southern states will return. Now that there is the possibility of a war with France over Mexico, he will try to abandon our civil war for an external one."

Wade nodded. "That is also my view, Mr. Chase, and that is why we have been meeting in the greatest secrecy. We have now drawn up our terms, which we'll present to Mr. Lincoln tonight." Ben Wade looked most pleased with himself. "I am sure that they will come as a surprise to Mr. Seward."

But Seward had already sustained his surprise at home. New York's senator, Preston King, had left the caucus while it was in session; and he had gone straight to his old friend Seward with the news. Seward had acted promptly. "I will not let them embarrass the President," he said; and wrote on a slip of paper: "Sir, I hereby resign the office of Secretary of State, and beg that my resignation be accepted immediately." Then Seward shouted to his son in the next room. "Fred!"

"Yes, sir?" Frederick Seward appeared in the doorway.

"We're resigning, the two of us. Write out your resignation, and give it to Senator King."

The young man did as he was told; he was every bit as cool as his father. Then King went across to the White House and gave the President the message. King explained what had happened. Lincoln thanked him, politely. But when King had gone, Hay could see that the Tycoon was about to become very Tycoonish indeed. "They want me out," he said. "I'm half tempted to oblige them."

"Half tempted, sir?"

Lincoln saw Hay as if for the first time that day. "Somewhat less than half. I'll see the senators at seven tonight. Then call a Cabinet meeting for tomorrow morning."

"Yes, sir."

Seward was expecting the President. In fact, he had been sitting at his study window, looking out at the cold muddy expanse of Lafayette Square, and waiting for the tall, slouched figure to cross from the Mansion to the Old Club House accompanied by two soldiers from Company K of the 150th Pennsylvania Regiment, known as "Bucktails," now permanently assigned to guard the President. Just as the gaslights were being lit along the avenue, the President appeared.

Seward opened the door himself; and showed Lincoln into the study. The President took off his top hat and placed it on the head of Pericles, a marble bust on a column that ornamented one corner of the room. "Well, our friends have been busy on the Hill." Lincoln poured himself a glass of water from a crystal decanter, and helped himself to an apple from the sideboard where Seward's numerous restorative bottles were kept. Then the President sat beside the fire and turned his gaze upon Seward, who noted that Lincoln had aged a decade in the last month; plainly, a number of harsh additional years were now about to be added to that unhappy decade. Midge rested her head on the President's knee and gazed up at him with deep solicitude.

"You know," said Seward, "this may be difficult for anyone to believe, but I cannot wait to get back home to Auburn and private life. This is no joy to me, what we do here."

"Well, that's all very well for you, Governor. But I am like the starling in Sterne's story: 'I can't get out.'"

"What will you do?"

"I'm not sure yet. Naturally, I will listen to the senators. I've already had the pleasure of an interview with Thaddeus Stevens, who believes that only you stand between us and victory in the war."

Seward shook his head, with true wonder. "I am the author of the notorious—not to mention revolutionary—concept that there is 'a law higher than the Constitution,' and though our Constitution may allow for slavery, that higher law does not. Now our Jacobins consider me indifferent to the issue and, secretly, pro-rebel."

"Mr. Seward, the inability of men to grasp an obvious truth is a constant in political life. I seem to spend most of my time explaining what should be obvious to all. Now what is obvious to me is that you are of no particular interest to the Senate. But I am. They wish to remove me; and they don't know how. So they strike at you."

"Well, I am gone. So when they tell you tonight that you must throw me out, you can say that the governor, with that largeness of spirit and grace of character for which he has been ever known, has withdrawn to his ancestral acres in New York, where his prayers will never cease to rise to Heaven that the Union be reassembled as of old."

Lincoln laughed. "Your forensic powers are what they always were."

"Yes," said Seward, grimly, "and I wish that I still had the right to appear in the Senate, like Cicero, and drive these Catalines into the night."

"I think there'll be no need." Lincoln was about to say more; but did not.

Seward was now intensely curious. "What will you tell the senators?"

"I shall listen a good deal. I shall be listening particularly for Mr. Chase's voice."

"You will hear a good deal of it. He and Ben Wade are the chief conspirators."

"I know. On the subject of the presidency I sometimes think Mr. Chase is a bit crazed. Well..." Lincoln put his feet on the fire-tender. The great black shoes always made Seward think of a pair of coffins for babies.

"Governor, I think it most unlikely that I shall be reelected.

We have had one disaster after another, and I am held—quite rightly—responsible." Midge turned her back on the President and curled up in front of the fire.

"But these things change rapidly. A victory or two, and you will be a hero again." But Seward agreed, privately, with Lincoln's estimate of the matter. As a political force, the President was burnt out; and nothing could reignite the fire. The collapse of Burnside in the mud of Virginia was the end of the Administration. The fact that the pusillanimous Senate now dared to dictate to the President was a sign that all true authority was gone.

"It seems pretty plain that McClellan will be the Democratic candidate; and I suspect that if he is, he'll be the president; and if he is the president, this entire bloody and costly enterprise will have been for nothing because he will make a quick and shameful peace with the South, and slavery will continue a while longer."

Seward nodded. "In New York City, at this very moment, the bosses are fixing it for him to be the candidate. If he wins, which I doubt, he'll do as you predict."

"If things are as bad in 'sixty-four as they are now, I shall not even try to be nominated by our party. That means it will go to Mr. Chase . . ."

"Heaven forbid!"

"It has been my experience that Heaven can be highly unreliable," said Lincoln. "Well, there are worse men than Chase. But since the country will never accept his extreme views on slavery, McClellan will beat him."

Seward was drawn to one of the decanters. Political intrigue so stimulated him that he craved the soothing properties of port.

As Lincoln was staring into the wood fire, Seward watched him closely. Whatever the President's shortcomings as a war leader, he was a master politician. It takes one, thought Seward, sipping the port, to understand another. But Seward was not prepared for what came next. "Tell me about Horatio Seymour."

"Well, he defeated our man pretty soundly in New York. Thurlow Weed likes him, though he is a Democrat. Weed thinks he'll make a good governor. And, of course, he is a strong Union man. Why?"

Lincoln still stared into the fire. "I have it in mind to support Mr. Seymour for president in 'sixty-four."

Seward put down his port glass so hard that the crystal nearly broke. "A Democrat?"

"If our party fails to win the war, the Democratic Party will win the election. Since McClellan would be as disastrous a president as he was a general, we must see to it that the Democrats

401

come forward with a strong Union man, whom we can support, openly or secretly or whatever."

"You have given this a lot of thought?"

"Well, since November fourth, anyway."

"Have you talked to anyone else about it?"

Lincoln nodded. "I've talked, in strictest confidence, with Stanton. After all, he's a Democrat himself. He likes McClellan even less than I do. He could use the War Department to help Seymour, while I could bide my time to the last minute; and then support Seymour."

"You astonish me, sir."

"Well, Governor, these are highly astonishing times. Anyway, talk this over with Weed; and no one else." Lincoln got to his feet. "Now I must get ready to do some listening." He patted Seward's shoulder. "You have behaved nobly, Governor. The thing is not over yet."

"Precisely my advice to you, sir, when you start talking about supporting Seymour for president."

"Well, we have to look ahead, don't we? That's what the people hire us to do." Lincoln paused; then smiled. "Naturally, I shall expect Mr. Seymour to see to it that New York fulfills its draft quota."

"*Quid pro quota?*" Seward was amused by Lincoln's exquisite political craftsmanship.

"Governor..." murmured the President, with a hint of reproach; and he was gone. Hay had never seen Lincoln quite so subdued as he was when the nine senators harangued him about the shortcomings of his Administration. Even Sumner was harsh in his estimate of the Administration's conduct of foreign policy, not to mention Lincoln's ignorance of Seward's letters to the American minister at London. Worse, in the midst of a war, Seward had seen fit to publish a volume of his diplomatic correspondence, filled with malicious observations about the abolitionists and, most ominous of all, strewn with asterisks to show where even more alarming sentiments had been originally written and then excised.

The Ancient mildly replied that all such letters were read to him by Seward but, offhand, he could not recall the ones in which Seward made what Sumner said were disrespectful remarks about Congress. Lincoln agreed that it was tasteless of Seward to have published the correspondence. Actually, Hay was reasonably certain that Seward had indeed shown Lincoln many of his remarks; and that Lincoln had concurred in them. On the other hand, the Ancient was somewhat disingenuous when he said that Seward read him every dispatch. For quite some time, Lincoln had left all but the most important of foreign dispatches in Seward's hands.
402

At the beginning of the Administration, Lincoln had insisted on reading all letters to him; and all letters sent in his name. He now largely ignored the vast flow of paper in and out of his office.

After three hours, the President got to his feet; and the meeting was over. He took from Ben Wade the memorandum of the caucus. "I'll study this very carefully, of course. And we shall be in communication with each other some time tomorrow." On a reasonably cheerful note, the senators filed out of the room. Then Lincoln gave Hay the memorandum. "Put this in the strongbox, John."

"You won't be studying it very carefully, sir?"

"Oh, it is engraved on my heart!" Lincoln's half smile was enough to convince Hay that the Tycoon was preparing a counterattack. As Hay said to Nicolay, in describing the meeting, "They made a mistake that Machiavelli always warned against. If you strike at a prince, you must kill him."

"Even so, I wonder," said Nicolay, more apprehensive than Hay, "how he'll get out of this one."

At seven-thirty the next evening, the senators, less Wade, returned to the White House at the President's invitation. Meanwhile, the Cabinet, less Seward, had also been summoned. During the late afternoon, the senatorial memorandum was withdrawn from the strongbox; and the Tycoon had indeed studied it for some time. Hay could see his lips move as he spoke to himself not the words on the page but his responses to them.

The aged moderate Senator Collamer led the senatorial delegation, which Hay ushered into the President's office. The Cabinet were next door in the Reception Room, guarded by Nicolay. Earlier in the day, Lincoln had seemed at the end of his strength; and Hay had overheard him tell a friend that he had never been so distressed by any event in his life as he had been by the senatorial ultimatum. But now Lincoln appeared serene; and sublimely courteous, as he welcomed the senators. Edward had already placed extra chairs around the office.

The Tycoon invited the senators to sit, while he remained standing in front of the fireplace, Andrew Jackson scowling over his right shoulder. Hay noticed that the lean, dour Fessender of Maine was counting the extra chairs; plainly, he was puzzled by their number.

"Gentlemen, you have given me a lot to think about since last night." The Tycoon took the memorandum from the mantelpiece. "It seems to me that the heart of your argument—as opposed to your criticisms of Governor Seward and me—is the following." Lincoln put on his glasses and read: "The theory of our government, and the early and uniform construction thereof, is that the

403

President should be aided by a Cabinet Council, agreeing with him in political theories and general policy, and that all important public measures and appointments should be the result of their combined wisdom and deliberation. This most obvious necessary condition of things, without which no administration can succeed, we and the public believe does not now exist . . .'"

Lincoln stopped and looked over his glasses for a moment, as if about to add a remark of his own. But then he continued, with the ghost of a smile on his lips. "'. . . and therefore such selections and changes in its members should be made as will serve to the country unity of purpose and action, in all material and essential respects, more especially in the present crisis of public affairs.'" Lincoln put the pages back on the mantelpiece; and removed his glasses. "Now I could, of course, put the case to you that the Constitution nowhere obliges the President to listen to his Cabinet, or even to have such a thing if he chooses not to. Naturally, the great departments of the state require officers to run them, and these officers are chosen by the president, alone, to help him execute his office. But the notion that these officers from a high council to which the president must pay heed is entirely foreign to our Constitution and our practices."

Fessenden now cleared his throat.

"Yes, Senator Fessenden?" Lincoln was amiability itself.

"The nature of the Cabinet is not, like so much else, entirely spelled out in the Constitution, but, if I may remind you, President John Quincy Adams in dealing with *his* Cabinet used always to put to a vote every major proposal."

"Well, that was Mr. Adams's way, no doubt. But no other president has regarded the Cabinet as anything more than a group of men who serve at his pleasure. Sometimes he wants their advice; and sometimes not. When he—"

"But, sir," Fessenden broken in, to Hay's annoyance though not, visibly, to Lincoln's. "We have made the case in our memorandum that these are extraordinary times. We are in the midst of a terrible war. We must have unity everywhere."

"I quite agree, Senator. In fact, the very reason that you gentlemen are here tonight is a proof of how serious the times are. In ordinary times, if you were to come to a president with orders to him to remake his Cabinet and then to obey that Cabinet's decisions, you would be shown the door—not to mention a copy of the Constitution. Properly speaking, you have no business at all here with me in a matter which concerns the executive only, and the legislative branch not at all." The Tycoon maintained a kindly smile. The senators sat very straight in their chairs. "But we are in a crisis. I believe that you have come to me in good
404

faith, wanting to help, and I shall so respond." Lincoln turned to Fessenden. "I know that you, personally, prefer the British parliamentary system to our own and that you would like members of the Cabinet to sit in Congress and answer your questions. This may be a better way of doing things than ours, but we cannot do it without, first, holding a new Constitutional convention, something not entirely practical at the moment."

"But, sir," Fessenden was resolute, "without going to such an extreme, a united Cabinet that is consulted by you is not an impossibility."

"It is, I would have said, a reality." Lincoln was demure. "I realize that there has been much talk to the effect that I am controlled by my 'premier,' Governor Seward; and that I seldom consult the Cabinet on Major issues; and so on. Well, I have decided to indulge you, Senator Fessenden. You would like for our government to have a question time for the ministers, on the order of the British parliament. So I shall now oblige you. I have asked the entire Cabinet—except for Mr. Seward—to sit down here with you; and you may question them to your hearts' content as I listen—and learn." Lincoln pulled the bell cord. Then he turned to Fessenden. "I am sure your committee does not object to this extra-Constitutional meeting."

Hay saw that Fessenden was too confused to speak. Fessenden looked at Collamer, who shrugged. Fessenden nodded to Lincoln. Meanwhile, Nicolay had opened the door to the Reception Room, and Chase, followed by the other ministers, entered the room. The senators were now most uneasy. The Cabinet had known since morning about the confrontation. Chase had done everything possible to avert it while the legalistic Bates had been deeply annoyed.

Once everyone was seated, Lincoln made a mild little speech. There had been talk that the Cabinet did not meet often enough; that views contrary to his and to those of Mr. Seward were stifled; that true unity was never sought. "Now it is my impression that as we meet twice a week and discuss everything, we are a true unit. The fact that we do not always agree with one another is the reason that I selected this Cabinet. I know that some of the senators are urging me to appoint a Cabinet of men who all think as the senators here do. But this does not strike me as wise. A president must hear every sort of argument. He must listen to the moderate majority as well as to the radical minority." Lincoln gazed, rather sleepily, at Fessenden, who scowled at the floor. Lincoln resumed. "So let us—President and Cabinet—reveal openly to the senators how we work."

Blair went on the attack. With all the biting contempt of which

405

that turbulent clan was capable, he questioned the right of the senators even to inquire into such matters. Executive and legislative were forever separate. Certainly, if his old friend President Jackson were in the chair, the senators would be out on the street. But since a gentler man was in the chair, Blair would assure the senators that whatever gossip they might have heard—and he looked straight at Chase, whose eyes were shut as if better to attend some inner celestial hymn—every member of the Cabinet was invited to have his say. "Personally, I disagree with Government Seward on almost every subject, but to say that he is not earnest in the prosecution of the war is a downright lie!"

There was a nervous stirring among the senators. A seraphic smile now appeared on Chase's lips. Within that sculpted dome, thought Hay, there must now be not only a heavenly choir but at least one archangel, praising him for fighting so many of the Lord's battles on earth.

"In any case, gentlemen," and Blair glared at Fessenden, "there can be no *plural* executive in this country. There is one president and one commander-in-chief, and he is chosen by the people and if you should try to defy him in the exercise of his legitimate office, you do so at your peril."

Although Fessenden disagreed at much length, he made no headway against, to Hay's surprise, old Bates, a constant conservative complainer, who disapproved of almost everything that Lincoln did. But Bates was the closest thing to a Constitutional lawyer in the room; and every argument and precedent that Fessenden put forward Bates struck down, to the particular embarrassment of Sumner, who had come armed with his usual eloquence; but now chose silence. "All in all," Bates summed up, "this committee had better not meddle in these matters."

At last, the Tycoon was ready for the *coup de grâce*. He lifted, as it were, his executioner's ax. "I think, to indulge the committee, the Cabinet should answer the principal charge that has been brought—that I do not consult them." Sweetly, thought Hay, the Tycoon turned to Chase, whose eyes were now open, the celestial music only a memory. "Mr. Chase, as the highest-ranking member of the Cabinet, I think it might be useful for you to tell the senators just how we run our shop."

There was no sound at all in the room. Everyone present knew that it was Chase who had most inflamed the radical Republicans with his revelations of Seward's sinister influence on a president too weak and too evasive to allow full discussion of the great issues. Now, thought Hay, Lincoln had arranged this elaborate trap for Chase; and no matter what Chase said or did, the trap had sprung on him. If he told the senators in front of the Cabinet what he

406

had been telling the senators in private, the members of the Cabinet would not only call him a liar but a traitor to the President and the Administration. If he denied before the Cabinet what he had told the senators in private, he would lose the support and the respect of those radical Republicans who had wanted him for president. For sheer political craft, Hay had never seen anything so neatly done. One way or the other, with a single bold confrontation, the Tycoon had disarmed his rival.

But Hay was also obliged to concede that Chase handled himself with dignity, cutting, as best he could, his losses. "I did not come here tonight expecting to be arraigned like this before a committee of the Senate."

"This is no doing of ours," said Fessenden, irritably. "You are not being arraigned by us. We came here tonight to meet with the President. This unusual"—Fessenden turned to Bates and positively quoted—"unConstitutional, as some would have it, meeting has come as a surprise to us. It is the President's doing."

"That is true," said Lincoln. "I thought it the only way to clear the air, even if it bends the Constitution a bit, to have us all meet like this. Now, Mr. Chase"—Lincoln's dreamy gaze was entirely contradicted by the hard set of the wide mouth—"do you feel that there has ever been any important issue, dealing with your department, say, that I have ever myself decided without your counsel? Or allowed another to decide?"

"No, sir. In respect to the Treasury, I have been supported by you at all times. Only . . ." Chase was beginning to rally; but Lincoln interposed.

"I am sure," said the President, "that the committee will be relieved to know that the ablest Secretary of the Treasury since, uh, Gallatin, is not subject to arbitrary presidential whims."

"Naturally, on other issues, I feel that sometimes we are not sufficiently consulted . . ."

"Such as?" asked Blair.

"That is, we are not *thorough* in our discussions."

"Could you, Mr. Chase, think of one important measure that we did not all of us discuss at length?" Lincoln's tone was so conciliatory that if Hay had not known the Tycoon better, he would have thought him lawyer for the defense rather than the prosecution.

Chase began now to stammer. "I speak, sir, of thoroughness, which in the flow of events we sometimes lack, nor is there always, as I would like, a canvass of the members, in *every* case, that is, I mean."

Hay looked at Fessenden, who was staring, open-mouthed, at Chase. Hay looked at Sumner, who had placed one hand over

407

his eyes as though to hide from his own clear and noble gaze all signs of human vanity and folly; at Collamer, who looked old and weary and unsurprised; at Trumbull, who was furious—at Chase.

Once Lincoln had given Chase the rest of the rope with which to hang himself, he dropped the subject; and Chase again closed his eyes, no doubt, thought Hay, in prayer.

"I think that you gentlemen now have a clearer idea of how the Cabinet works. It is not perhaps the monolithic unit you would like but it is hardly a place where arbitrary decisions are made by me—or by Mr. Seward."

"I take the point," said Fessenden, "that a president need not consult his Cabinet at all. But I urge you, sir, that in wartime, which this is, that there be greater consultation."

"With different councillors," said Trumbull.

"You have, perhaps, an ideal Cabinet that you would like me to appoint?" Lincoln sat down in his chair, plainly tired from so long standing.

"We believe Mr. Seward must go," said Wade.

"*We* is it?" Lincoln affected surprise at the pronoun. "Then, perhaps, we—I use the presidential we—should poll the senators present, and the Cabinet, too, as to whether or not Mr. Seward should resign. Mr. Sumner, how vote you?"

Fessenden was quick to avoid any sort of canvass. "I don't think it proper for us to discuss the merits or demerits of a member of the Cabinet in the presence of his associates."

"But that is what we have been doing for several hours now," said Lincoln.

Chase gratefully seized on Fessenden's sudden tactical demur. "I agree with Senator Fessenden, Mr. President. And I suggest that the Cabinet be allowed to withdraw so that you may with more... ease discuss its composition." Chase rose majestically. Lincoln nodded, casually; and the members of the Cabinet departed. Hay noted with some interest that that alleged constant schemer, the Secretary of War, had said nothing at all.

Chase's collapse under the President's questioning had ended the present assault on the Administration. Although the senators still agreed that Seward must go, the case against him now seemed vague indeed. Lincoln ended the meeting by thanking the senators for their patriotic concern and weighty advice.

It was now one in the morning, and the Ancient was showing signs of fatigue. He was like, thought Hay, one of those bullfighters he had read of. Or, perhaps, more to the point, a bull who had outwitted both matador and picadors.

As the senators milled about the room, Hay was close enough to Lincoln to hear Trumbull mutter indignantly in the Tycoon's ear, "Chase sang quite a different tune with us before!" Lincoln smiled; and said nothing.

Fessenden remained behind, after the others had left. Hay made himself invisible at his small table beside the door. "Mr. President, you have asked my opinion about Seward's removal. I never really answered you because there is a rumor that he has already resigned, and if he has, that's the end of that."

"I thought I told you last night that he'd resigned," said Lincoln. "Fact, I have the resignation in my pocket. But I haven't made it public, *and* I haven't accepted it."

"Then, Mr. President, the real question is whether or not you intend to ask him to withdraw his resignation?"

"Yes," said the President; and his ordinarily restless body was now very still in its chair.

"You have heard us on the subject. Since Seward has asked to go, it will be upon your head to keep him. He lost my confidence long before you appointed him and had you consulted me in advance I would have advised against appointing him."

"Well," said Lincoln, thoughtfully, "I didn't have the opportunity to consult you."

"I realize that, sir. But you knew my views—our views— through Mr. Trumbull. We took it for granted that you would advise with us before you made your Cabinet, but you did not. Now, on this issue, whether you should accept the resignation of Mr. Seward, would you like me to consult my fellow-senators?"

"No," said the President. "I would not." He unfolded himself from his chair until he towered over the slight New Englander. "I want to have good relations. That is why I have done something tonight that no president has ever done before, and I pray that none will ever be obliged to do again. I have let you into the heart of the executive, to see us as we are. But that is the most I can do to show good faith and openness."

"You are aware, sir, that a majority of our caucus want Mr. Chase at the helm of a cabinet composed of new members, who will prosecute the war with a single will."

Lincoln looked down at Fessenden. The left eye had begun to droop with weariness but the voice was very hard and very clear. "That is what you and your friends may want, Mr. Fessenden. But that is not what you will get. Becuase," Lincoln suddenly smiled without the slightest trace of amiability; a smile, thought Hay, reminiscent of the wolf as it bares its teeth, "I am the master here. Good-night, Mr. Fessenden." Lincoln took the senator's hand.

The shaken Fessenden, bowed; and said, "Good-night, Mr. President." When Fessenden was gone, Lincoln dropped like a felled tree onto the lounge. "There are times when I wish I was dead," he sighed, "and this is one."

"It was a famous victory, sir." Hay was elated. "Mr. Chase was tonguetied."

"But these famous victories do mightily drain the victor; and I'm not in the clear just yet. Tomorrow... 'And tomorrow and tomorrow...'" As the Ancient recited his favorite Shakespeare aria, Hay knew that more surprises awaited Mr. Chase and his fellow conspirators.

As for Chase, he sat alone in his study, beneath the framed holograph of Queen Victoria's letter, composing his own letter of resignation from the Cabinet. He had been made a fool of by Lincoln in front of his senatorial allies. Further, he had known from Stanton that Seward had already resigned; and that Stanton might, *pro forma* if nothing else, do the same. It was clear that if the Cabinet was to be begun anew, presumably with himself as its chief, they must all, of their own free will, depart. As Chase signed his name with a flourish, he could not help but cringe at the way that Lincoln had forced him to back down; and to contradict himself. Actually, the truth of the matter was as he had told the senators. They were by no means always consulted, and the meetings were usually casual to the point of incoherence. But Lincoln knew that Chase dared not say this in front of his colleagues, none of whom liked him except the highly unreliable Stanton. Whatever Chase had said, the others would have denied. The blood was beating in his temples as he sealed the letter.

The blood was again beating in Chase's temples when he obeyed a presidential summons to join Stanton and Welles in Lincoln's office. Chase sat beside Stanton on a sofa facing the bright fire. Welles sat on a sofa to one side. The three men chatted, awkwardly. Stanton had been to see Seward. "He seems pleased with himself. He had a copy of the *Herald*, which says that I'm the next to go after what happened at Fredericksburg. Apparently, if it were not for my hostility to McClellan, the war would have been won a long time ago. Apparently, I refuse to support Burnside because I am a Democrat..." Stanton continued in this self-pitying vein, much to Chase's disgust. The political future of one Edwin M. Stanton was, perhaps, the least important aspect of the current crisis, while the failure of Chase was inextricably bound with the unique moral issue of the abolition of slavery. There was a profound difference between them, thought Chase sourly, glancing at Welles, who looked, as always, to be disapproving of him.

410

Nicolay announced the President. The men rose. Lincoln seemed no more rested than he had been at one o'cock that same morning. He took a chair beside the fire. "Well, Mr. Chase, that was quite an ordeal for all of us last night."

"For *me*, certainly." Chase had vowed not to show his indignation; and, promptly, gave way to it. "I had not expected to be so questioned before the world."

"Hardly the world," said Welles.

"The world we deal with will know every word that was said. Not," Chase added, "that there was anything said that any of us need be ashamed of. I spoke, as always, from the heart."

"While Senator Fessenden spoke from what sounded to me like some sort of conspiracy," said Lincoln. "That is what most disturbed me. If they force me to let Seward go, then I lose the majority of our party which is moderate like Seward—and me. If I were to keep Seward and you, Mr. Chase, were to go, I would lose the radical element of the party, which is also the most brilliant. I must have both elements in the Cabinet. I have also been well pleased with both of you, and the balance you have given me."

"Well, sir, I shall perfect your balance." Chase sat up very straight; he was aware of Stanton's anxious wheezing at his side. "I have prepared my own resignation."

To Chase's amazement, the President leapt to his feet. "Where is it?" he asked, without one word of surprise or sorrow or compliment.

"I have it here with me." Chase removed the envelope slowly from his pocket.

Lincoln practically tore the envelope from his hand. "Let me have it!" Then Lincoln read aloud the gracious and dignified two sentences of resignation, signed S. P. Chase. Lincoln clapped his hands, gleefully. "Well, that cuts the Gordian knot all right!"

Stanton then began to gasp; and speak. "Mr. President, as I told you day before yesterday, I am prepared to tender my own resignation..."

"Nonsense, Mars. I don't want yours. Go back to work and find me Burnside." He waved the letter. "This is all I want. This is all I need. Now I've got me perfect balance, as the farmer said when he put the second pumpkin in his saddlebag."

"I don't understand," said Chase, who understood only that he had been, in some obscure way, outmaneuvered yet again by the President.

"You and Seward have both resigned. So the Cabinet doesn't lean too far one way or too far the other. It is just the way every farmer likes his saddle. It is just the way *I* like it."

Chase rose with, he hoped, Roman dignity. "It has been an honor, Mr. President, to have served you in these harrowing times, and to..."

To Chase's amazement, Lincoln had consigned his dignified and gracious resignation to the fire. Then the President took from the mantelpiece a second sheet of paper, which he also burned. As the four men watched the edges of the letters curl into red and yellow flame, Lincoln said, "You are both soldiers in a war. I am the Commander-in-Chief. I need you both. Will you desert?"

Although Chase could barely speak, he was able to force from his throat a negative pleasing to the President, who had for the moment so entirely routed him.

10

"I WISH, SIR, TO CROSS THE RAPPAHANNOCK AT THE PLACE I have noted on the map." Burnside crossed his arms and stood, a monument to defiance, the unfinished monument to Washington behind him in the distance.

Lincoln looked at the map; looked at Burnside. "You would move now?"

"As soon as possible. But one thing stops me."

"The weather?" Lincoln looked out the window at the unseasonably warm drizzle that fell on the mud-sea that had once been the White House lawn. It was the first day of January, 1863. The President was already dressed for the long day's reception, which would also mark the official end of Mary's mourning.

"I am content with that, sir. No, it is my officers, particularly General Hooker. I have not their support. Hooker makes trouble. He speaks of the need for a dictator here in Washington; and for another in the field."

"Well, that is novel at least. Most of our would-be dictators only favor one." Lincoln pushed the map away. "Mr. Stanton and General Halleck will be joining us in a few minutes. I have certain misgivings about recrossing the river in this weather..."

"Should those misgivings seem to you to be justifiable, then, sir, I think you should relieve me of a command that I never wanted." The highly agitated Burnside kept folding and unfolding his arms, and tugging his huge moustaches.

"I am sure that it has not come to that, General." Lincoln was mild.

But Burnside was not. "It is plain that what I've lost, I won't recapture—the esteem of my commanders. I suggest that I go. I also suggest that Stanton and Halleck also go, as they have lost the confidence of the country. I have put all this in a letter to you." At that moment, Edward showed in Stanton and Halleck.

Burnside looked straight at Stanton and said, "Sir, I have written a letter to the President." Burnside produced the letter from his tunic. "In which I have asked to be relieved of the command of the Army of the Potomac. I have also made it clear to the President that I believe you, sir, and you, General Halleck, should both be removed from office, as you have lost not only the confidence of the country but that of the officers in the army." Burnside gave Lincoln the letter.

Stanton maintained, for him, great calm. "I don't see, General, how your failure at Fredericksburg is in any real way our responsibility, even though we have, as your superiors, shouldered it. It's true that there are those in the country who would like all of us gone, including the President, but I doubt if these people are in any way a majority. If they are, we shall all be dismissed in due course."

During this, Lincoln sat carefully reading Burnside's letter. Meanwhile, the general was working himself into an even higher emotional state. "I should think, Mr. Stanton, that the divisions between you and General Halleck would be enough for one of you, at least, to want the other one gone just as the feud between you and General McClellan caused him to go."

On this, Lincoln looked up from the letter. "*I* dismissed McClellan, not Mr. Stanton."

"But, sir, McClellan was constantly undermined by Mr. Stanton. Everyone in the army knows that. As for General Halleck, I can only say that he must not find it easy to work with Mr. Stanton, who, back in California, called General Halleck a perjurer when he was superintendent of the New Almaden quicksilver mine."

"General Burnside," Stanton's voice was agreeably low and controlled, "your knowledge of ancient—and arcane—corporate history is uncanny. But it is modern military history that we are trying to make. Keep to the task at hand; and do not concern yourself with the relations between General Halleck and me."

"Sir, it is a fact that your personal relations with people color everything you do, and that no general can ever take the field confident that he is protected at his rear from you."

"Gentlemen." Lincoln folded the letter, and gave it back to

413

Burnside. "I will not accept this letter, written in such heat, and out of such understandable distress. Let us act as if none of this took place."

"But, sir, it has!" Burnside was vehement.

"Well, then all the more reason for us to pretend that nothing has happened. Anyway, I have no intention of losing three men so useful to me, not to mention the nation." Lincoln got up and arranged the map of Virginia on the table. "Gentlemen, General Burnside wants to cross the Rappahannock as soon as possible, below Fredericksburg. Here on the map." Stanton and Halleck looked at the map. Burnside looked at himself in a mirror, and pushed at the edges of the great moustaches. "I myself worry about the weather at this time of the year. But I will leave it to you to decide, General Halleck."

"I must consider the matter, sir." Halleck was more than ever lugubrious.

"Of course. It is not a decision to be made in an instant. I hope, General Burnside, you will stay for the reception."

But Burnside chose to return to the army. "You know my views, sir," were his parting words.

"Indeed I do," said Lincoln. When Burnside was gone, Lincoln turned to Halleck. "What do you think?"

"I think," said Halleck, carefully and mournfully, "that I would rather that the decision to cross the river *not* be mine."

Lincoln frowned. "General Halleck, I called you here and made you general-in-chief just so that you would be able to make this sort of decision for me."

Halleck's watery eyes focussed on the President. "Sir, if you are not satisfied with my performance..."

"Enough! Enough!" Lincoln turned from the map. "I am sick of resignations. Come, gentlemen. Let's go to Mrs. Lincoln's reception."

Seward and his son prepared for the reception by getting in order the Proclamation of Emancipation, which, at some point that day, the President would sign.

As Secretary of State, Seward had already signed the document; an agreeable piece of work, he thought, although Lincoln had once again left the Deity out of the original draft. But this time it was Chase not Seward who had inserted Him. Chase had produced the final paragraph: "And upon this act, sincerely believed to be an act of justice warranted by the Constitution, and an act of duty demanded by the circumstance of the country, I invoke the considerate judgment of mankind, and the gracious favor of Almighty God." Lincoln had then slyly added the phrase "upon military necessity" after the word "Constitution." He was still not
414

ready to be linked to the abolitionists. The freeing of the slaves was a military act and nothing more, as the President demonstrated when he proceeded to exempt not only a number of Louisiana parishes, as a favor to a Louisiana congressman who was a Unionist, but seven Virginia counties in and around Norfolk, where the pro-Union elements had persuaded the President that slavery ought to be maintained.

Seward had thought Lincoln typically illogical; but he had made no issue of the matter. On the other hand, Chase had balefully said that it was by no means certain that Lincoln's Louisiana friend would even be allowed by Congress to take his seat in the House. Lincoln had been much irritated by this; and said that he would not be dictated to by Congress. As a result, slavery still flourished in those parts of Louisiana and Virginia under Union control, as well as in all of the border-states.

The abolitionists hated the document for its inconsistency. What was the point to freeing slaves in another country when you would not free them in your own? Many of the moderates were displeased because they feared turbulence among the Negro population in every part of the Union. Nevertheless, Seward felt the document more useful than not. After all, it had been carefully designed by him, as well as by Lincoln, to influence, favorably, the European powers.

"Fred, fetch me the Great Seal of the United States." Seward now slipped on his frock coat. Then father and son—and the Great Seal in its small leather case—went across the avenue to the White House, where carriages were still coming and going at a great rate.

The sky was now clear; and the day warm as spring. Old Edward showed them into the main hall, filled with bemedalled diplomats and bejewelled ladies. "The President says, will you please be waiting for him upstairs in his office." Bowing amiably to right and left, Seward and son went up the stairs. In the President's office they found Hay. Then, a moment later, Lincoln and Nicolay entered the room. The President peeled off his white gloves and said, ruefully, holding up his huge right hand, "I've been shaking hands for three hours, and I'm swollen like a poisoned pup."

"Well, sir, relax your fingers. It is a pity we have no pianoforte for you to play. The limbering finger exercises are, to me, a joy, after I have been at large amongst the democracy," said Seward, arranging the document on the table while Fred withdrew the Great Seal from its container and Hay lit a kerosene burner so that the red wax for the seal could be softened in a miniature pan.

Lincoln made some flourishes in the air with a pen. "Now,"

415

he said, poising the pen over the page, "everyone is going to look at this signature when it is reproduced in the papers, and they are going to say, 'Was he nervous or hesitant?' not knowing that my hand and arm are sore. So I must write slowly and carefully, like this." With that, he carefully inscribed his name in a bold dark ink. Then he frowned at the result. "It looks a bit tremulous," he said.

"It is splendid, sir," said Seward. "Now, Fred, the seal." Duly, and a bit messily, the red wax was dribbled onto the parchment and the seal impressed.

"Now, sir, you are immortal," said Nicolay.

"At least you are immortal for one entire edition of the New York *Tribune*," said Seward, blithely.

"Let us see what the London *Times* will say." Lincoln turned to Hay. "John, have you that cutting from the *Times*, when I announced that I was going to release the Proclamation?"

Hay found the cutting in one of the pigeonholes of the desk; and read aloud: "'Is Lincoln yet a name not known to us as it will be known to posterity and is it ultimately to be classed among the catalogue of monsters, the wholesale assassins and butchers of their kind?'"

Seward chuckled. "Oh, they have a sulfurous way with them, our loving cousins."

"Plainly, the *Times* has a window onto posterity. Proceed, John."

Hay continued: "'The Emancipation Proclamation will not deprive Mr. Lincoln of the distinctive affix which he will share with many, for the most part foolish and incompetent, kings and emperors, caliphs and doges, that of being Lincoln—The Last.'"

Lincoln chuckled. "I don't know whether they mean I'm to be the last American president or just the last one named Lincoln."

"Can I come in?" It was Robert at the door.

"My heir-apparent!" Lincoln exclaimed cheerily. "With no affix at all."

"All hail the Prince of Rails!" Seward exclaimed; and all proceeded to hail the bewildered Robert, who then put himself in Hay's hands, and together they made the rounds of Washington's New Year's Day parties.

The most elaborate of the open houses was that of Mr. Stanton, who greeted the young men with grave politeness; as did his non-smiling white-faced wife. Hay looked about for the urn containing the ashes of the first wife, but saw no receptacle that seemed suitable for such rich earth. Robert stood with Hay in a corner of the parlor, and as the people came and went—much the same group that had called on the President—he complained to Hay.
416

"I want to leave Harvard; and enlist. But every time I bring up the subject, Mother..." He did not finish.

"I can imagine," said Hay, who could. The Hellcat had never been so impossible as during the last weeks of her mourning. Fortunately, she seemed genuinely to like visiting the hospitals; and so, accompanied by Keckley and Stoddard, she was kept away from the Mansion for hours at a time, distributing fruit and flowers from the White House conservatories; and allowing peace to reign in the living quarters. Over Christmas she had been kept especially busy by Mrs. Caleb Smith's decision to give every man in hospital a splendid dinner as her farewell to Washington: Mr. Smith had quit the Cabinet in order to become a judge. Smith had been replaced as Secretary of the Interior by his assistant, John Usher, another nonentity from Indiana.

As there were more than twenty hospitals in the District of Columbia, the government ladies had all worked hard as waiters, Madam not excepted. But when she was not so employed, there were stormy scenes in the Mansion. She had never forgiven Hay for not allowing her to pocket the steward's salary. She had also kept on Watt, though he was not on the official payroll. Nicolay and Hay were presently conspiring to capture Watt for the army but, thus far, he had evaded their net. Currently, Watt was the owner of a greenhouse in New York City's Fourteenth Street; he also performed mysterious errands for Madam.

A colored man brought two plates on a tray. "Mrs. Stanton wants you to try the game-pastries," he said.

As the young men tried the pastries, Lord Lyons made his entrance, accompanied by a slender youth whose black coat set off the minister's gold braid and feathers. "How has she been?" asked Robert, mouth full. Hay took two glasses of punch from a passing tray.

"Well, she keeps busy visiting the wounded." On the subject of Madam, Hay was always tactful with Robert.

"I hear she talks to Willie."

"Quite often; and to her two half-brothers. One was killed at Shiloh..."

"That was Sam. Aleck was killed at Baton Rouge. 'Little Aleck' she called him. She used to say to me that Little Aleck was like her own firstborn, as if I were not." Robert was morose. Hay wondered whether or not Robert had any liking at all for his difficult mother—as opposed to sympathy. "It is not easy for a highly emotional woman like my mother to live such a life as she has done with my father."

"I thought it was wonderful for her; and everything that she
417

wanted. Besides, he is remarkably good to—and good with— her."

"Well, he is open with her, I guess."

"He is not open with you?" Hay was genuinely curious. The Ancient's passion for the late Willie and the ever-present Tad was a considerable strain on everyone. But Robert was another matter. He was seldom mentioned by his father; and he was seldom home.

"Father is amiable with me, as he is with everyone. But I rather think he dislikes me."

Hay was startled. "That is not possible."

"Oh, everything's possible, Johnny. He hates his past. He hates having been a scrub. He hates all this rail-splitter nonsense, even though he uses it to ingratiate himself with the folks. He wanted me to be what he couldn't be. He wanted me in the east, and at Harvard, and to speak without a midwestern accent. You know, they laughed at the way he spoke when he came to see me at Exeter and started a speech with 'Misturr Cheermun.'"

"But then they applauded him." Lincoln's success on his New England tour was now legend.

"Oh, yes. He can win over any audience. But he does not like to seem a bumpkin." Robert finished his glass of punch; looked sad. "You know that was the only time we ever talked, as two men might. He told me I was going to have all the world he had ever wanted, but I probably wouldn't have as good a time as he had had..."

"Good time!" Hay thought of the Ancient after Fredricksburg, nearly out of his mind with fear and grief and weariness. "Do you know what his days are like in this place?"

"He meant then. When he was young. On the circuit. He started to tell me how he had always dreamed...But I never found out what the dream was because some of the boys from school joined us and, of course, he had to perform, and so he asked if anyone had a banjo, and someone did, and he sang comical songs. We've never really talked to each other since."

"He's very proud of you," said Hay, wondering if this was the case.

Robert wondered, too. "He shows no sign of it. He treats me like a minor politician from Cambridge, Massachusetts. But then he has always been cold that way."

"Not with me."

"You're one of his arms, Johnny. No one is cold to his own arm. But I'm his replacement on earth; and, thanks to him, we are now totally different from one another."

On this melancholy note, the two young men made their way to the Chase household, where Kate, all in white with real flowers
418

in her hair, made a great play for Robert, who responded delightedly, while Hay listened as General "Fighting Joe" Hooker, in town for the day, declared, "The problem is Halleck. Has always been Halleck. Has been Halleck, as far as I'm concerned, since we were in California together. How can I take charge in the field with Halleck here in Washington, undermining me?"

Hay decided that the famous fighting general was somewhat under the influence of alcohol. But the ladies present were enraptured by their hero; and even Ben Wade listened to the general with every appearance of respect.

At the other end of the parlor, Chase decorously courted Mrs. Douglas while keeping a somewhat nervous eye on his general. He was aware that Hooker had been making the social rounds that day. Every important official was at home to callers on New Year's Day, according to an old Washington custom. Although Chase, as befitted the exponent of austerity in wartime, served neither food nor drink, while the Speaker of the House wisely served only coffee, other houses specialized in alcoholic punches and eggnogs. Hooker had plainly permitted himself to be made too much of. Happily, it was only a matter of time before Burnside would be replaced by Chase's general. They were a winning team, he had decided some time ago when Hooker had privately pledged himself, without any urging, to support Chase for president. Chase only wished that his general was less talkative and more discreet. Hooker was constantly criticizing his superiors, a bad habit. Chase decided that he would bring up the matter when they were next alone.

"Is that Mr. Lincoln's son?" asked Mrs. Douglas, pointing to the short moustached young man talking to Kate.

"Indeed it is. Very much grown up. There is criticism, of course."

"That he is not in the army? Well, if I was Mrs. Lincoln, I'd keep him out forever."

"But then you have secessionist tendencies, Mrs. Douglas." Adèle Douglas was the best-looking woman of her age in Washington, he thought, by no means for the first time. They, too, could be a winning team. But Kate had said, no. On the other hand, should Kate move out of his house, would he not be obliged to marry? Mrs. Douglas's shoulders, he noticed, were like those of the Medici Venus, a plaster cast of which had haunted him in youth, largely because he had been warned never to look at it, even though the goddess stood brazenly in the lobby of a principal Cincinnati hotel.

Thaddeus Stevens joined them; and launched a Ciceronian period. "Well, Mr. Chase, I suppose that you and Mr. Lincoln have had a joyous day celebrating the freeing of all those slaves that you cannot free and the continuation of the enslavement of those that you could free."

"I have not been celebrating, sir. I was stunned at the exception of those Virginia counties. Because"—he turned to the superb Mrs. Douglas—"when I regained Norfolk for the Union, I promised the Negroes of Norfolk, right in front of the Custom's House, that all of them would be freed. Now, of course, nothing has changed."

"The President is really a sort of shyster," said Stevens.

"You put that too harshly, Mr. Stevens," said Chase, reprovingly.

"But he has put it well, I think," said Mrs. Douglas. "I can't think that there is much of anything for the true abolitionists—and I'm certainly not one—to celebrate."

But on North Twelfth Street, in the heart of the Negro encampment, bonfires had been lit; and hymns were being sung. Together David and John Surratt looked out over the ramshackle shanties and fragile tents, made to appear even more insubstantial by firelight. Most of these colored people were from the Confederate states; and they had freed themselves. Technically, they were "contraband," to use the military euphemism. Over a thousand of the ten thousand in the city lived here at the city's edge.

David and John were armed. But only for self-defense, for, as John put it, "We won't ever have to do anything to these niggers, as the Yankees are fixing to kill them all." Like most natives of Washington, David had been amazed by the Union soldiers' hatred of all Negroes. By and large, Southerners got on well with them. After all, they grew up with niggers; and they liked—even loved—the ones who kept their place. But the Yankees seemed to hate the very idea of blackness; proof, to David, that Yankees tended to be a bit on the crazy side. After all, wasn't that what the war was supposed to be about? how the institution of slavery gave the South an advantage over the North's so-called free, if ill-paid, labor. Yet hardly a day passed that blacks were not beaten up, even killed, by soldiers. The convalescent men at the Soldiers Rest were the most vicious in this regard; possibly because they were the most bored.

"We dare not lose this war," said John, as he and David left the Negroes, now singing "Jesus Christ Has Made Me Free."

"Why not? Not that there's much chance of our losing."

"Well, just look at them; those apes! And then think of them all free, the way they are now, right here in this city, thanks to Old Abe. My God, Davie! Don't you realize how they damn near outnumber us in half the South?"

"But if they were really free, they'd all go North."

John shook his head. "The Yankees are too smart. They won't let them anywhere near their states. No, we're the ones who are going to end up having to live with them, and *they'll* be the masters then. He's gone pretty far, Mr. Lincoln has," said John. Suddenly, a dozen wild horses came cantering down the dirt avenue. David and John leapt to safety on the porch of a farmer's house.

"Why," said John in a low voice, "don't you poison the President?"

"But you was just saying he was the best thing we got on our side."

"I'm changing my mind."

"What does the Colonel say?" Both David and John spoke of the Colonel as if they knew him.

"He says, no. For now, anyway." John frowned. "He's bound to change."

"Well if he does, then I'll go and kill Old Abe." David had never before been so excited by anything that he had himself said.

But Lincoln, unaware of the ongoing threat from nearby Thompson's Drug Store, continued to please the shadowy colonel. Grant's assault on the rebel stronghold at Vicksburg had failed; and he had returned to his base near Memphis. He was planning to dig a canal through the peninsula across the river from Vicksburg so that the navy could then go around the Confederate batteries that had made the river impassable at this point. Meanwhile, Grant's rivals—particularly the political generals—continued to accuse him of drunkenness.

Lincoln called in Washburne at the end of January. Washburne found the President in a surprisingly good mood; and said so. "Well, if I am, it is for no sensible reason, Brother Washburne. Perhaps I have really taken leave of my senses. They say that when you go truly mad, you never know it."

Washburne cleared his throat; and wondered at Lincoln's wisdom in mentioning a subject of such personal delicacy.

"Anyway, Brother Washburne, I think the time has come for you to go down to Memphis and renew your acquaintanceship with General Grant, and then give me some idea of how he is doing, and if he is doing it sober or drunk. If drunk, I shall distribute casks of whiskey to all my generals. If sober, I will be relieved."

"I'll go as soon as this session's out of the way."

"Congress." The President looked out the window at the tents of his Pennsylvania regiment, pitched on the long-since vanished lawn. "I hear you want to tax the banks..."

"Well, they're holding all those greenbacks of yours. At the very least, we should tax them."

"We are in debt seven hundred twenty million dollars." Lincoln shook his head. "I cannot fathom such an amount. But Chase is unfazed." Lincoln then questioned Washburne in some detail about a speech made in the House by Clement L. Vallandigham, a recently defeated representative from Ohio. When first elected, Vallandigham had been a Douglas Democrat. But since the beginning of the war, he had been leader in the House of those antiwar Democrats known as the Copperheads. He held that Lincoln's war measures were illegal and unConstitutional and so far worse than the defection of the Southern states.

"It was a stormy speech," said Washburne, who had a grudging admiration for the fiery youthful enemy. "He said George Washington was also a rebel, and that we are all descended from rebels against an oppressive and tyrannical government."

Lincoln chuckled. "It will be interesting to see how history deals with that great cruel tyrant James Buchanan, against whom those states went into rebellion. What other marvels did he display?"

"The war is not free labor against slave labor so much as it is about two attitudes toward life, and that the Southrons and the Yankees are like the Cavaliers and the Roundheads in England, born antagonists."

Lincoln nodded. "I would not entirely disagree."

"He also said that if New England so disliked slavery, *they* should leave the Union."

"He is most humorous." Lincoln whittled at a pencil with his pocketknife.

"He made one novel point. He said that if the South does maintain its independence, the entire northwest will go with them, and they will together form a great nation."

"I wonder if there is any basis to that." Lincoln swept the pencil shavings from his lap; and put away his knife. "Well, this is his last session, I'm happy to say."

"Oh, we'll hear more from him," said Washburne.

Nicolay appeared at the door. "It's General Hooker, sir."

"Send him in." Lincoln rose. "When Congress adjourns, go down to Memphis for me, and scout the situation."

"Yes, sir." Washburne left as Hooker, bright of eye and red of cheek, marched into the office; and saluted the President smartly.

"General Burnside has given you your orders?"

"Yes, sir. But I wanted to speak to you before I accept the command of the Army of the Potomac."

422

"That is sensible." Lincoln sat now on the window-sill, the gray-steel sky behind him.

"I had—I have great esteem for General Burnside..."

"We all do. He has been under a great strain. Yesterday when he was here, he wanted to resign from the army. But I would not let him. I'm sending him to Ohio."

"Naturally, I have had my disagreements with him." Hooker now left the chair that Lincoln had placed him in and began to march from chair to window-sill and back to chair; he grew more and more ferocious with each trip. "I don't know whether you were told that when I criticized him for this last madness, the so-called mud-march, when he nearly wrecked the army, that he wrote out an order dismissing a number of high-ranking officers, starting with *me!*"

"I heard about this. He was not himself, of course. No one can remove you except the War Department—or me."

"Did you also hear that when someone suggested that I might resist the order, as I would have, he said he'd have me hanged?"

Lincoln nodded, sadly. "This, too, was reported to me. I then sent for him, and relieved him of his command and told him to give you your orders, as the new commander."

"I think he is mad, sir."

"But you also have the greatest esteem for him, don't you? As do I." Lincoln's slightly mocking tone did not penetrate Hooker's martial self-absorption.

"Fortunately, he is now gone. I will take his place, but on one condition."

"Oh?" Lincoln looked mildly surprised. "And what is that one condition?"

"General Halleck *must* go, sir."

"Why *must* General Halleck go?"

"Because he will do anything to harm me, once I am in the field. We were adversaries in California..."

"A turbulent state, plainly," said Lincoln. But Hooker was not listening to the President; he was entirely intent on his retreat from window to chair.

"He did harm to McClellan; and harm to Burnside. I refuse to put myself in a position where he can put the knife in my back." Hooker turned and faced Lincoln, vulnerable back now to the door.

"Well, General, I am not about to relieve General Halleck because of some personal animosity on your part. But I will arrange that you report directly to me from the field; and not through General Halleck. That way he cannot, as you say, put a knife in your back. Is that satisfactory to you, sir?"

"Yes, sir, that is satisfactory. I accept the command."

"Thank you." Lincoln got off the window-sill, and went to the pigeonhole desk and removed a letter, which he gave to Hooker. "Read this at your leisure, General. Since we are on the subject of satisfactoriness, I must tell you that there have been times when I have found you less than satisfactory. I have listed those times. I have also written out my views on a number of subjects."

Hooker's florid face grew dark. "I, not satisfactory? In what way, sir?"

"You talk too much," said the President, equably. "Yes, I know that I talk too much, too, but I don't ever say much of anything. I just tell stories, and make a noise and keep my own counsel. Now I have recorded in the letter those comments of yours that I do not like, nor want ever to hear again."

"I am stunned! And, on my honor, I am outraged that you should think... What has been reported to you?"

"Your constant attacks on your fellow generals have not gone unremarked. Witness, General Burnside's ill-advised attempt to remove you from the army. You were the same with McClellan. Now, you yourself are the commander and I'm afraid that your past spirit may turn upon you. You must repair your fences or, as the farmer said..."

Hooker was not ready for a Lincoln story. "I have never said behind any man's back what I would not say to his face."

"Then I would enjoy hearing you tell me how I should be removed, by force, from my office, and the government turned over to a military dictator, like yourself." Lincoln smiled, benignly, as he spoke.

Hooker began to stammer. "I have said no such thing. Not like that, anyway. Not about *me*, certainly. Or any other general, by name, taking your place. Perhaps I said *you* should be more forceful, more like a dictator. But I never said..."

Lincoln raised his hand. Hooker fell silent. "Only those generals who gain success can set up as dictators. That seems to be one of the few absolute laws of history. What I now ask of you is a military success, and I will risk the dictatorship."

"Sir, you will have your military success. That is a promise. As for the dictatorship..."

"Don't give it a second thought," said the President, amiably; and then he sent Hooker to see Stanton. Once the general was gone, Lincoln entered the Reception Room, where Seward stood at the window, watching the hogs being slaughtered at the base of Washington's monument.

"Well, Governor, it's Hooker."

"You've given him the Army of the Potomac?"

Lincoln nodded. "I think he is a fighting general. I don't much like his character. He intrigued against McClellan and Burnside, and now he's after Halleck..."

"I thought politicians were vain and treacherous," said Seward, settling in a chair. "But we are like cherubim and seraphim compared to military men."

"I can't say I feel much like a cherub today, Governor." Lincoln leaned against the door and pressed his back hard against the wood to relieve the aches and pains of age.

"Well, you look seraphically bright," said Seward, who indeed thought Lincoln looked less than usually haggard. "You realize, of course, that you have made this appointment without consulting your Cabinet." Seward was mischievous.

"Surely, I consulted all of you, and we took a vote, and I abided by the majority, as I always do." Lincoln was equally mischievous.

"Well, one thing," said Seward, "Chase won't go to Ben Wade, complaining. Hooker is Chase's man."

"So I gather. So I gather." Lincoln shut his eyes; and smiled. "I must say that the presidential ambitions of Mr. Chase are like a horsefly on the neck of a plow horse—it keeps him lively about his work."

But although Mr. Chase's presidential aspirations were now growing in intensity—the election was only a year and a half away—he was subject to a distraction that touched upon another of his passions. One of the Treasury clerks was William O'Connor, a literary young man whose pro-abolition novel, *Harrington*, had much pleased Chase. The previous day, O'Connor had asked Chase if he would consider for a clerkship a man mysteriously considered by O'Connor to be a great poet. "He comes to you, sir, with a letter of introduction and commendation from Ralph Waldo Emerson." At the mention of this letter, Chase agreed to see the infamous Walt Whitman.

On a cold morning, as Chase stood in front of the coal fire in his office, warming his hands, the large, gray-bearded, pink-faced, blue-eyed poet, dressed somewhat theatrically in Southern planter style, was shown into the room by O'Connor, who made the introductions and then tactfully withdrew.

Chase stared at Walt Whitman; who stared at Chase. The immorality of Whitman's very bad book of poetry had been much discussed in Columbus a few years earlier. Emerson's endorsement of a poet whose horrifying emphasis on the sexual in man was equalled only by his absence of any talent for versification gave credence to the recurring rumor that the great Emerson was now senile. Nevertheless, thought Chase, senile or not, Emerson could still sign his name.

"Mr. Emerson has spoken of you to me with such admiration."
The poet's voice was husky; the accent common New York.

"I gather he has written me a letter," said Chase. "In his own
hand," Chase heard himself add, somewhat ridiculously.

"Oh, yes! He has also recommended me to Governor Seward
and to Senators Sumner and King. I have seen the senators. Mr.
King showed me the Capitol the other day. Not in one's flightiest
dreams has there been so much marble and china, gold and
bronze, so many painted gods and goddesses..."

"I have often thought that the new decorations are somewhat
too opulent and pagan for a Protestant republic." Chase wondered
if Whitman had brought Emerson's letter with him.

Whitman nodded. "I was somewhat surprised. But then I
thought, well, the republic is no longer young, and so the inside
of the Capitol is now every bit as sumptuous as the interior of
Taylor's saloon in the Broadway, which you doubtless know."

Chase felt an involuntary shudder go through him. The man
was plainly a beast. "I am temperance, sir. I have never set foot
in anyone's saloon. About Mr. Emerson's letter..."

"I seldom go to Taylor's. Poets cannot afford the tariff. Anyway,
Mr. Sumner has been most kind, and he said that he would speak
to you. I have also been to the White House, and though I did
not meet Mr. Lincoln, I talked to the young secretary—such a
handsome manly lad—John Hay, who is a poet, too; and a charming one. He asked me to sign his copy of *Leaves of Grass*."

Chase had heard tales of John Hay's attendance at disorderly
houses. He was glad that Kate only flirted idly with the young
man, who was plainly debauched.

Whitman was now describing his part-time job as a copyist at
the Paymaster's office. "It's only an hour or two a day. Then I
make the rounds of the hospitals. I bring what gifts I can afford
to the wounded. I write letters for them. Comfort them. My own
brother George was wounded at Fredericksburg. That is why I
came here, to see him. I was also robbed of all my money the
first day in town, but then I ran into Mr. O'Connor, and now I
live in his rooming house..."

"Is Mrs. Whitman with you?"

"No, my mother lives in Brooklyn. She is not well. So it is
important I get employment. Mr. Emerson thinks that I should
continue as a journalist, but hacking on the press here is not really
practical..."

"In Mr. Emerson's letter, does he mention *what* you might do
in the government's service?" Chase thought this approach subtle
in the extreme.

"Well, here it is," said Whitman. He gave Chase the letter.

426

On the envelope was written "The Honorable S. P. Chase." Inside was a letter dated January 10, endorsing Walt Whitman highly for any sort of government post; and signed, Chase excitedly saw, with the longed-for-but-never-owned autograph "R. W. Emerson."

"I shall give Mr. Emerson, and yourself, sir, every sort of consideration," said Chase, putting the letter in his pocket where it seemed to him to irradiate his whole being as if it were some holy relic.

"I shall be truly grateful. As will Mr. Emerson, of course." Chase shook Whitman's hand at the door and let him out. Then Chase placed the letter square in the middle of his desk, and pondered what sort of frame would set it off best.

O'Connor entered during this happy reverie. "Well, Mr. Secretary . . ."

"What?" Chase looked up. Then he recalled the business at hand. "I must tell you, Mr. O'Connor, that it is my view that Mr. Whitman is a decidedly disreputable person, based on what he himself has written, presumably about himself."

"Oh, sir, he is a splendid original man—and a great poet."

"I defer, Mr. O'Connor, to your personal knowledge of him. But what might the press do to us here if it were known that I was harboring the author of pages—or leaves, as he would term them—that one could not allow a lady to read or even a young man of—susceptible nature? Far better a single page of your *Harrington* than all Whitman's leaves of, so appropriately named, grass. Anyway, until now I have nothing of Emerson's in his handwriting, and I shall be glad to keep this."

The first secretary then ushered Jay Cooke into the office. "Thank you, Mr. O'Connor," said Chase. "I am sure that Mr. Seward can find a place for his one-time constituent."

As the door closed behind O'Connor, Jay Cooke said, "Mr. President!"

"Oh, don't tempt the gods! It is too soon to do more than hope."

427

11

It was Mary Todd Lincoln's second visit to Corporal Stone of Lexington, Kentucky, late of the rebel army. She had known him as a boy. He was an exact contemporary of Little Aleck. Mary sat in a straight chair beside his cot, which was at the end of one aisle in the main display room of the Patent Office. Next to the cot a glass-enclosed piece of complex machinery, patented in an earlier time, somewhat screened them from the view of the curious.

Corporal Stone was red-haired and soft-spoken; he had lost both legs at Chancellorsville in Virginia, where the Union army, under "Fighting Joe" Hooker, had been outfought by General Lee and driven back across the Rappahannock.

"But it will be hard for us, losing Stonewall Jackson like that." General Jackson had been accidentally killed by one of his own snipers.

"Did you know General Jackson?" Mary arranged the small bouquet of hothouse roses in a mug on the table beside his cot. She tried to inhale only the odor of the roses and not that of the chamber pots that seemed never to be emptied.

"Oh, I saw him. But I never spoke to him. He was a strange sort of man, very religious." Corporal Stone smiled, reminding her of Aleck. She smiled back; and tried not to weep. "One of the boys here was with him, and he said that when God sent down one of the archangels to take "Stonewall" up to Heaven, they couldn't find him anywhere. So they went back to Heaven, and there he was, already. He had outflanked them."

"Our men fight well, don't they?" said Mary absently.

"You mean us Confederates, ma'am?" Corporal Stone looked at her with some amazement.

"I meant... us Kentuckians," said Mary. "That is all that I meant. But I ought not to have said it, for I am loyal to the Union."

"Back home, they say you are really with us, secretly."

"No, I am not. But what has happened to us all grieves my heart. I have lost two brothers. I may lose more."

"I have lost two brothers and two uncles and now—two legs."

"It is tragic."

428

"Well, I knew what I was doing, and how it might end. I was at the Phoenix Hotel..."

"Where Mr. Breckinridge always boarded." Mary wondered where Cousin John was. He had been at Shiloh; he was now a general. Little Emilie's husband, Ben Helm, was serving under him. Lately, there had been no news of either of them.

"...I remember it was a Thursday evening, September 19, 1861. The first Yankee soldiers arrived in Lexington. Well, when they marched past the hotel, one of our hotheads fired on them from a window. No, it wasn't me, Mrs. Lincoln. But that was when I went and joined up with John Hunt Morgan..."

"...the Lexington Rifles, I remember. He is kin to us, too, I think."

"We are all kin, which is maybe the problem. Anyway, fifty of us Lexington boys, under Captain Morgan, headed down the Versailles Pike to the Green River, and we've been fighting ever since, and Lexington has been under Yankee military law ever since, and ever your stepmother don't dare speak out against the Yankees."

"I doubt that," said Mary, a trifle grimly; she had no liking for her father's second wife, a woman of great determination, to say the least. "I was told that after her son Sam—my half-brother—was killed at Shiloh, some Yankee-sympathizer was blaming John Morgan for getting you Lexington boys to go join the rebels, and Mrs. Todd said to a large gathering, 'I wish there were ten thousand John Morgans.'"

"Well, she *is* a Todd," said Corporal Stone; and laughed.

"By now, yes, I suppose she is. We all knew John Morgan, all his life."

Keckley came toward them. Mary rose. "When you are well, I shall try to get you sent home."

"Bless you, Mrs. Lincoln."

Mary and Keckley were then joined by a hospital matron from the Sanitary Commission. She guided them through the various halls of the Patent Office, which was now one vast incongruous hospital. Unmovable inventions still remained where they had always been on permanent exhibition, surrounded now by the highly impermanent ever-mutable flesh of wounded men. Mary delivered flowers and fruit; and spoke to this one and that one.

The matron was filled with complaints. The hospital had been overwhelmed after the defeat at Chancellorsville. "I thought Fredericksburg in December would destroy our whole system. But this is worse. They keep coming and coming, the wounded." She was a stout woman from New England. "We have no more room here.

We are trying to take over a floor or two of each hotel, but the politicians fight us."

"Would that *they* were here," said Mary, bitterly. "And these boys at home and well."

"My sentiments, Mrs. President. But I do wish—if you will forgive me—the President ends this war before we lose all the young men in the country."

"We may well lose them all at the South," said Mary. They had stopped in front of a huge iron plow, invented, if that was the word, by General Washington. "There are fewer boys there than at the North."

"We've mixed them, as you've seen. We are supposed to keep the prisoners separate. But we can't. There are too many now. I wonder how much longer this will go on, our being defeated all the time."

"My husband must find a general first. Unfortunately, the best ones are all on the other side." Mary smiled. "I ought not to say that. I dare say I shall read in the New York *World* that I was speaking treason, but I have lost interest in the vampire press."

"Would that they would lose interest in you, ma'am," said Keckley, guiding Mary to the door.

The search for a general was about to begin again. While Mary was at the Patent Office, General Hooker was at the White House with the President. Once again Lincoln perched on the window-sill and once again "Fighting Joe" marched up and down the room. But the nature of the march had entirely changed from their earlier meeting. Hooker was now defensive and ill-at-ease, while Lincoln seemed worn out.

"I am certain," began Hooker, with no great display of certainty in his manner—he had been knocked unconscious when a Confederate shell hit a pillar of the porch on which he was standing, and the pillar had fallen on him, and he had been unconscious for hours. Once recovered, he had given up drink and without drink there was, everyone said, no longer a "Fighting Joe" Hooker but simply another incompetent Union general named Hooker, whose headquarters, according to the military son of the American minister to London, was like a brothel-casino. In fact, so addicted was Hooker and his immediate staff to the flesh that Washington's army of prostitutes was now known as Hooker's girls or, for short, Hookers.

"I am certain," said Hooker, "that I can once again cross the Rappahannock, and while Lee is still regrouping, I can strike at Richmond."

"I will follow you in this, of course," said Lincoln. "But, for the moment, I'd be happier if you were simply to stay where you

430

are and hold off the enemy until we have worked out some large design. Meanwhile, I have now been twice to see you in the field. I have talked to the various commanders, and what I feared might happen has begun to happen. As Burnside lost the support of his commanders—of which you were one—so now you are losing their support."

Hooker stopped his pacing. The pale eyes stared at the President, more like those of a frightened rabbit than of a predatory fighting animal. "Who has spoken to you against me?"

"I cannot tell you. But it is now quite general."

"Do you wish to replace me?"

Lincoln shook his head; and slid off the window-sill. "I'm not in the habit of throwing away a gun just because it has misfired once. But, for the moment, I am content not to go firing at just any target."

"I think, sir, you should consult *all* the ranking generals of the army and not just my rivals within the Army of the Potomac." Hooker was once more his fighting self. "You will find me held in the highest esteem."

"As you are still in command, it is plain that I, too, hold you in the highest esteem." Lincoln rang the bell. "We shall be in communication, General."

A dark-skinned John Hay entered the room. He was just returned from South Carolina, where he had seen his ill brother Charles; and from Florida, where he had investigated the military and political situation for the President. With Lincoln's blessing, Hay had been looking for a possible congressional seat once the newly reattached-to-the-Union east Floridians again held elections. Lincoln was eager to bring the Southern states, or those portions of them that were in Federal hands, back into the United States so that they could send loyal Republican representatives to Congress. If none were to be found among the sullen natives, then a number of John Hays would have to be sent to the various regions; and duly elected. Lately, it had become a matter of some urgency to regularize the returned states or fragments of states because the radical Republicans took the line that the states in rebellion were out of the Union and should be treated as an enemy nation's conquered provinces.

But Lincoln's line was unwavering. The Union was absolutely indivisible. No state could ever leave it; therefore, no state *had* ever left it. Certain rebellious elements had seen fit to make war against the central government, but when those elements were put down all would be as it was and the Southern states would send representatives to Congress, exactly as they had done in the past. Thaddeus Stevens was now openly challenging this policy; and there were, Hay could see, storms ahead for the Tycoon.

When Hooker had gone, Lincoln stared at the door through which the general had passed. Then he said, "You know, John, they say that if that pillar which fell on him at Chancellorsville had killed him, the war would have been shortened." Lincoln smiled. "Naturally, I have never said anything so unkind."

"Naturally, sir. Will you replace him?"

Lincoln shook his head. "There is no point... now."

Hay gave the President the latest folder of dispatches from the War Department. Lincoln's face lit up almost immediately. "Listen to this. Grant is now just below Vicksburg. Halleck sent him an order to join his army with that of General Banks to the south of him. Actually, that was my inspiration, not Halleck's. But I enjoy giving credit to others. They like it so much. Now Grant tells Halleck that to bring the armies together would delay his operations against Vicksburg, and then he says, 'I could not lose the time.' There is a lesson here somewhere," said Lincoln, putting down the folder. "Where I pick the generals and have them here in my own front yard, nothing goes right. But out west, where I don't do much of anything, things go like a house on fire. I shall ponder the moral of this."

Hay found that others were also pondering the same moral. He arrived at Chase's house a few moments after General Hooker had left. Apparently, Hooker had gone straight from the Manison to the house of his political mentor. "He stayed just long enough to compliment Kate on her engagement to Mr. Sprague. Then he went into Mr. Chase's study for an hour, and now he is gone." Mrs. Eames's bright eye saw everything; she also understood what she saw. Mrs. Eames and Hay stood in an alcove massed with every sort of May flower. Hay noted that Kate was rather more slender than usual and rather more pale than usual. Decorously, she moved from group to group, as did Senator Sprague. They moved separately.

All of Washington's grandees were on hand, as well as a number of financial men, including the brothers Cooke, who were now openly at the center of Chase's campaign for the presidency. Since Lincoln was equally aware that his Secretary of the Treasury was now trying to secure the nomination, there were times when Hay regarded the Tycoon's patience with Chase as greater even than that of Job's with God. On the other hand, he knew that Lincoln always liked to have enemies nearby in order to keep an eye on them. But did he not mind the fact that they were also able to keep *him* in view?

"I think they are well matched," said Mrs. Eames. "In every sense."

Hay looked at her, and saw the delicate ironic smile. "They *complement* each other," said Hay judiciously. "Her beauty and his money."

"Her father and . . . his money."

"The money seems to be the key element," said Hay.

"Well, this is a marriage. And," Mrs. Eames added, "this is Washington."

For Sprague, money was of urgent interest. He stood at the buffet in the dining room, listening to a former congressman from Texas, who said, "I've just received a letter from our friend Harris Hoyt."

Sprague stared blankly at the man. "Our friend . . . who?"

"Well, you must've met him somewhere, Senator, because you gave him a letter of recommendation to General Butler in New Orleans."

"I gave out a lot of those when I was governor. Friends of friends. Cotton business?"

"That's right, sir."

"Where is he now?"

"Well, he took a ship, he told me, from Havana. He was going to Galveston but the Yankees got there first. So he landed in Mexico at Matamoros, and then he went on to Houston, from where he wrote me this letter. He says he's got a cotton mill now, and he's making money."

Sprague looked glum. "I wish I had some of that cotton."

"Surely your prospective father-in-law can give you a Treasury permit."

"He can. But he won't."

Chase said, yet again, that after the President's proclamation in March there could be no trading with the enemy. Chase and Sprague had withdrawn to Chase's study.

"The cotton's more use to us than the money is to them." Sprague had found a decanter containing port; and he filled a glass. Chase was aware that Sprague often drank more than he ought but he put this down to the young man's long fatherless youth and subsequent bachelorhood. "I'm going to buy this," said Sprague.

"Buy . . . what?" Chase looked, anxiously, at the decanter, an inheritance from Bishop Chase.

"The house here. Sixth and E. I've worked it out with Kate. She doesn't want to be separated from you. So now she won't be."

Chase was stunned with delight. "Come now," he said, at last.

433

"You cannot move in with a father-in-law at the very beginning of your marriage."

"We're not. You're moving in with us. That is, you're staying put. The only thing that's changed is you won't have to pay rent. I made a sweet deal with the owner."

"My dear boy..." Chase was genuinely moved. He had been dreading this marriage for twenty-three years. Finally, when he knew that it must be now or never, he had tried to accustom himself to the idea of moving to a smaller place nearer the White House where he could at least try to compete with Seward for the President's ear. Now all was beautifully changed because nothing was to be changed.

Sprague struck the philosophic note. "I guess you know I have my faults. Katie knows, God knows. We've had our problems these last two years. Mother thinks Katie's too good for me. But then she thinks everyone's too good for me."

At Providence, Chase had met Fanny Sprague, the most formidable matriarch in all New England. Fanny's contempt for her son William was chilling. But then Fanny's admiration for Kate redressed, somewhat, the balance in Chase's eyes. "Your mother is a most... exigent parent."

"She's a terror all right. Anyway all *my* defects come from drink. Whatever in my life that I may have done wrong comes from that. My life has been an excited and eccentric one. I know that. But now, with Katie, I've found a remedy. With good health and disposition, I have more hope for the future than I ever thought I would."

There were genuine tears in Chase's eyes, as Sprague finished both his soliloquy and the decanter of port at the same time. "I know that the two of you are bound to be happy. I like your manly admission of your weaknesses. She has hers as well, as do we all. Don't expect perfection from her. She has had an unusual life, with an unusual attachment to a father; and no attachments to anyone else—before now. She is the Sleeping Beauty. You are the Prince. But then, after the awakening, there is... breakfast, and ordinary life, and desires in conflict. Understand her as you understand yourself, and you will both be happy." Chase was well pleased with the happy inspiration of the Sleeping Beauty. After all, it was true, in a way. Kate had never loved or even thought that she had loved anyone on earth except her father, who had, selfishly, kept her in thrall. Now, graciously, he let her go. As for himself, he might yet marry Adèle Douglas. He would need a hostess in the White House. He would also need company once Kate had got used to marriage and motherhood and a life that would, eventually, be apart from his own.

Jay Cooke entered the study. "I'm sorry, Mr. Chase," he said, when he saw Sprague. "I thought you were alone."

"No, no, Mr. Cooke. Come in."

"I don't think Katie looks too good," said Sprague, frowning. "She's lost weight. I think I'll take her north."

"Mrs. McDowell has asked us all to Troy, New York," said Chase.

"Dull place," said Sprague, leaving the room.

"An unexpectedly *thoughtful* young man," said Chase, straightening the frame of Queen Victoria's holograph letter. Originally, he had planned to put the Emerson autograph between those of Longfellow and Tennyson but then he had had second thoughts about keeping a valuable letter addressed not so much to him as to the Secretary of the Treasury and so, with a sad heart, he had handed it over to the Treasury archives; just as now he gave Jay Cooke a check made out not to the Secretary of the Treasury but to S. P. Chase, a man who must always be above suspicion, for the nation's sake. "This dividend, Mr. Cooke, comes from a stock which I do not actually own. Therefore, I cannot accept it."

"As you have done in the past?" Jay Cooke took the proffered check. "Do you have a new banker?"

"No, no, Mr. Cooke. Our relationship continues. I shall bank with you, as always. I shall also rely on you, as always, to keep the ship of state afloat financially. But now propriety is all-important."

Cooke nodded, gravely. "Shall I stop raising money for your campaign next year?"

"I had not realized that you had been so engaged," said Chase, a bit uneasily. He had never actually discussed the details with Jay Cooke.

"Oh, we are at it all the time, a group of us. We want you elected, and that costs money nowadays."

"Naturally, I will regard any sums raised toward that end as a public and not a private matter."

"Good." Cooke folded the check and put it in his pocket. "The money don't belong to me. So I shall lay it aside for future consideration. Meanwhile, I assume your usual needs will be taken care of by Senator Sprague."

Chase felt his cheeks grow warm. "My usual needs will be taken care of by me. I've just sold the last of my farms in Ohio. Since Senator Sprague is buying this house, I shall be relieved of paying rent, a considerable expense. But that is the limit of his kindness."

"He is worth twenty-five millions," said Jay Cooke, respectfully.

"Is he? The subject has not come up—at least, not so specifically. Let us join the guests."

Hay was being questioned by a handsome young congressman from New York, who had not been reelected the previous November. "What is she really like?" was the burden of his questioning. But Hay could think of no interesting answer. "I think she is sad at the moment." Both men looked at Kate, who was now presiding over a tea urn.

"I don't think," said Roscoe Conkling, "that I'd enjoy being married to a fool like Sprague. Do you know her well, Mr. Hay?"

Hay shook his head. "I have seen a good deal of her since we both came to Washington. But I still have no idea at all what she is really like."

"She fascinates me," said Conkling.

"You are too late, Congressman."

"So it would appear. I don't suppose it helped, my leading the fight in the House against her beloved father's banking scheme."

"He is certainly the beloved father."

"With an elephant's memory." As Conkling moved away, Hay wondered whether or not the rumors were true that Conkling was a member of the secret congressional cabal whose aim had been, since Fredericksburg, to impeach and remove from office Lincoln. Only once had the Ancient mentioned this conspiracy to Hay; and in the most elliptical way. "They would have Hamlin for president for a year; and then what?" Nicolay thought that Simon Cameron, recently returned in disgust from Russia, was also involved. But, thus far, no overt move had been made; and the Thirty-eighth Congress had now adjourned until December, much to everyone's relief. Currently, the ineffable Horace Greeley was telling everyone that only the presidency of General Rosecrans could save the country.

Hay went to Mr. Chase to say farewell. As relations between Chase and Lincoln deteriorated, all the greater was the appearance of warmth between statesman and youthful secretary. Chase was quarrelling with Thaddeus Stevens, who was leaning heavily on his cane. "Ah, Mr. Hay! Mr. Stevens here is tormenting me yet again about the currency."

"Mr. Chase, there is nothing wrong with your currency. It is a good green color; and you, sir, are the handsomest man in public life as well as the most honest. In fact, whenever I see your incredibly youthful countenance staring at me from beneath the dollar sign, I feel secure. But then when I read the Treasury's latest promise to the moneylenders, the National Banking Act which your friends in Congress passed over my broken body, that you will redeem in gold—in precious gold—the principal on your bonds, I shudder, for you have too much favored the unfortunate moneylenders who were clamorous lest the debtor should the more easily pay his debt. Say that I am right, Mr. Hay?"

"I always *say* that you are right, Mr. Stevens," said Hay to what many suspected was the leader of the secret cabal.

"A wise youth. I may also say, Mr. Chase, that when it takes one hundred and seventy of your dollars to buy one hundred dollars of gold, I grow anxious; and tend to tear my hair." Delicately, he touched the chestnut wig.

"Well, sir, the war must go on until the rebellion is shut down, so we'll keep on putting out paper until it costs a thousand dollars for breakfast."

"I agree about the rebellion."

Hay said good-bye to Kate at the door. For an instant, they were alone. "Are you happy?" he asked, to his own surprise.

"I don't think that I am supposed to be." This was the surprising answer to his impertinence. But then she gave him, suddenly, the famed mischievous smile. "But Father is happy; and that is all I ever want."

Hay was halfway down E Street when it occurred to him that it was not Kate who managed Chase, as everyone assumed, but Chase who managed Kate; and in his lust for the presidency he had thrust his daughter into a loveless marriage so that he might have Sprague's money.

12

IT WAS ONE OF MARY'S NUMEROUS ECONOMIES TO KEEP A COW on the front lawn of the White House. But in the summer of 1863, the cow, though seemingly in good health and appetite, ceased to give any milk, and Mary and Watt often visited the cow's fenced-in corner of the lawn to discuss its condition.

One hot morning in June, as Company K drilled in the driveway and Mary and Watt and a dairyman were contemplating the cow, a carriage containing old Mr. and Mrs. Blair and their son Montgomery pulled into the driveway. When Mr. Blair saw Mrs. Lincoln, he ordered the carriage to stop. The Blairs greeted the First Lady; and Mrs. Blair, a vigorous white-haired lady, leapt from the carriage to announce dramatically, "We have fled from Silver Spring!"

"My God, what has happened?" asked Mary.

"The rebels are in the area," said the Old Gentleman grimly. "Some say they are going to move on to Washington..."

"So we have fled!" Mrs. Blair seemed to be enjoying the image of herself in flight. "I wanted to ride my new hunter into town, but Mr. Blair said no. So some rebel may have himself the best hunter in all Maryland."

"Is the President in the Mansion?" asked Montgomery Blair.

Mary nodded. "Go and tell him. I'll be right in."

Washburne had been with the President since breakfast; he was now on his way back to Illinois, with a number of messages from Lincoln to various political operatives. Washburne wondered if he would ever see the President again. In the last six months, his old friend had become spectral-thin. The face was sallow; and he had developed a tremor in one hand. The left eyelid was now almost always half shut in a curious wink. "I cannot sleep any more," he said. "General Lee has murdered sleep for me."

"Take laudanum. Take something."

Lincoln shook his head. "Even when I do sleep and don't dream, which is seldom, I wake up tired. There is a part of me that will never be rested again. How strange..." Lincoln stared at the portrait of Jackson. "You know me well. You know how most of my life I wanted to be here. I wanted to be the president. I think it was in my bones and blood from birth. I wanted to be here so that I could sort out a country already founded but in need of so much."

"Henry Clay's 'internal improvements'?" Washburne had yet to find any politician who had had the slightest influence on Lincoln save Clay; and that was indeed slight.

"Harry of the West was blessed, finally, never to have got to this place, particularly at such a time as now. I am president of part of a country, with a fire in front of me, the war; and a fire behind me, the Congress and the Copperheads. It is a white elephant I have got on my hands."

"Well, you wanted to ride it," said Washburne, with less sympathy than he intended.

"Yes, I wanted to ride it; and so I shall, to the end." Lincoln picked up a sheet of paper from his desk. "A petition to me. I am told I must let Mr. Vallandigham return; and that banishment is not American."

The former congressman had been arrested by General Burnside, the commanding general of the Department of Ohio. He had been charged with preaching treason. Although Washburne had thought the whole business deeply embarrassing for the Republican Party, Lincoln had supported the arrest with the state-

438

ment: "Must I shoot a simple-minded soldier boy who deserts, while I must not touch a hair of a wily agitator who induces him to desert?" Lincoln had then ordered Vallandigham sent to the South.

"We shall hear a lot more from Mr. Vallandigham," said Washburne.

"No doubt," said Lincoln. "On the other hand, banishment, un-American as it is, is probably preferable to a firing squad, the usual resolution of such cases in wartime."

Hay announced the presence of three Blairs in the family sitting room; and Lincoln and Washburne went to greet the refugees.

Washburne marvelled at Lincoln's endless patience with the Old Gentleman. Lincoln deferred to him at all times; no doubt influenced by the fact that here was the last living friend and adviser of Andrew Jackson, ever ready to advise the great man's successors.

"It is plain to me that General Lee means to attack the city at any moment," said the old man. "What better time? Hooker is down at Manassas. Lee is in the valley . . ."

"That's not quite the case, Mr. Blair," said Lincoln. "If all goes well, Hooker is crossing the Potomac at Edward's Ferry and headed for Frederick city. So the Army of the Potomac is between us and the rebels, who are now moving on to Chambersburg."

"Chambersburg!" Mr. Blair was astonished. "That is in Pennsylvania."

"So it is; and so it has always been." Lincoln was impassive.

"This is a raid then, on our territory?"

Lincoln shook his head. "No, sir. This is an all-out invasion. From what we can tell, which is not as much as we would like, Lee's goal is Harrisburg and then Philadelphia."

"That will be the end, won't it?" Mrs. Blair sat very straight in her chair.

"Oh, not the end. But it will mean that England and France will recognize the rebels. It means that the Copperheads will defeat us in next year's election; and then they will make a peace with the South; and all our efforts will have been for nothing."

"It does not seem possible," said the Old Gentleman and, for once, he said no more.

At eight-thirty that evening, Stanton sent word to the President that he would like to see him at the War Department. As usual, Hay thought he saw assassins behind every tree; as usual, Lincoln paid no attention to anything save his own thoughts, which seldom, from what Hay could tell, dwelt on the matter of personal safety.

As Lincoln preceded Hay up the stairs of the dimly lit War

439

Department, a young lieutenant, rushing down the stairs, crashed head-on into the President, who fell back against the railing, the wind knocked out of him. When the lieutenant saw who it was, he cried, "Oh, God! A thousand pardons!"

"One is enough," said Lincoln. "Now if only the rest of the army could charge like that."

Stanton was alone in his office. As Lincoln and Hay entered, Stanton gave Lincoln a telegram. The Ancient looked at it; and gave it back to him. "Why?" he asked, "has General Hooker seen fit to resign now, of all times?"

"General Halleck, I suppose. Hooker wanted to withdraw the garrison from Harper's Ferry because he thinks Lee outnumbers him. But Halleck said he was not to leave Harper's Ferry unguarded."

"So in the midst of an invasion our commanding general quits on us. There are times, Mars, when I would like to shoot every single general in the Union army."

"It is a tempting prospect; and it would probably shorten the war. What shall be done?"

Lincoln was grim. "First, we shall surprise 'Fighting Joe.' I accept his resignation. Second, I am appointing General George Meade to take his place."

"Yes, sir." Stanton left the room. The President rocked in his chair. Hay wondered just what the political reaction would be to Meade, who was a Democrat and so anathema to the Jacobins in Congress, not to mention to Hooker's mentor Chase. On the other hand, Meade was a competent general—if such a thing existed in the Army of the Potomac; he was also a Pennsylvanian, which might inspire him to fight well in his native state.

"I expect General Meade to fight well on his own dunghill," said the President, inelegantly, at next day's Cabinet. Seward admired the way that the very same president who had so eloquently asserted to the senatorial delegation that his Cabinet was in all things consulted, now flatly told them what he had already done with no discussion of any kind. Chase started to speak; but then thought better of it. Seward was now making it his particular task to keep track of Chase's intrigues. On the day Seward had learned that a clear majority of Republican senators lacked confidence in him, he abandoned whatever lingering ambition he might have had to be himself a candidate in 1864. Since his own political career was now over, he contented himself with being an appendage of President Lincoln. Since he enjoyed his office if not his dependency, he had decided to do everything possible to reelect Lincoln. At the moment, this would not be an easy thing to do. The President had lost the confidence of the country, while the so-called Peace Democrats were everywhere on the rise. Chase would also have huge financial resources, thanks to his prospective son-in-law and Jay Cooke. Chase also had an excellent organization in place. Almost every one of the thousands of Treasury agents in each of the states had been selected by Chase with an eye to next year's elections.

Seward began, ever so delicately, to plot, while Stanton made the case for the conscription of more men. "We have our enrollers going from house to house. We know where the men are. We know—or will know—who is able and who is not. We know who can pay the three-hundred-dollar fee for a replacement and who cannot. I think we can now use the pretext of an all-out invasion as a means of raising a million troops."

The President looked unhappy. Seward asked Stanton how many men the last call had brought to the colors. Stanton scowled. "We have had our problem with Governor Curtin. We want men who will serve for three years, or the duration of the war if that is less. The governor says he cannot guarantee to raise any troops on those terms. He wants, as of today, to call out fifty thousand militia for sixty days, to defend Pennsylvania. I have said no. That is not good enough."

"But it is better than nothing at the moment," said Seward. A sudden warm breeze stirred the papers on the Cabinet table. The wind had shifted and the smell of rotting animals and excrement and stagnant water from the canal nearly overpowered President and Cabinet. "It is a pity," said Lincoln, after Hay had shut the windows, "that the war has interfered with that excellent plan to build the presidents a house on the outskirts of town, away from the canal and the swamps."

"What would we do with the White House if the president is moved, let's say, to Silver Spring?" asked Seward.

"Why, it would make a splendid State Department, something you've always wanted; and then you could preside over the canal, as it is filled with foreign objects." Lincoln turned to Stanton. "We'll compromise with Governor Curtin. Let's aim for one hundred thousand men from Pennsylvania, Maryland, West Virginia and Ohio for six months."

"But, sir, if we back down in this matter . . ."

"I don't see much choice. You feel out the Governor."

Chase waited until the Cabinet was officially adjourned; as always, it had been a most unbusinesslike and informal affair. When the President had said all that he wanted to say, he simply got up and either left the room or went off in a corner with one or another of his ministers. This time Chase caught him at the door to the President's office. "Was it entirely necessary to accept General Hooker's resignation?"

"Well, Mr. Chase, I don't see what else I was to do. Oh, for a moment, I debated whether or not to have him shot for desertion . . ."

"But surely his resignation was a means of drawing your attention to the disagreements between him and General Halleck."

"My attention has already been drawn in that direction—several times a day, in fact. Mr. Chase, when a man's native country is being invaded and we are all in peril, he does not play games of this sort. I know you are fond of General Hooker, and I am sure he has his good points, but I cannot easily overlook his supreme selfishness." Lincoln smiled; but this did not in any way mitigate what Chase could plainly see was a most uncharacteristic rage.

"I only pray that General Meade is capable of this command," said Chase, backing away both physically and figuratively from the President.

"There are many such prayers, I suspect, at this hour."

During the next week, the President, for all practical purposes, lived at the War Department. The telegraph office now seemed to be simply an extension of the Commander-in-Chief, like his large ears. Hay was surprised that the usually frantic Stanton had become calm and orderly. General Halleck, on the other hand, seemed more than ever like the head clerk of a bank which was about to default.

The Ancient was ancient and weary; but calm. He followed the movements of Lee and Meade on a map of Maryland-Pennsylvania. As the reports came in, blue pins for the Union forces and yellow pins for the rebels were moved this way and that on the map. Lee had begun by spreading his forces across Pennsylvania. The city of York had surrendered. Lee was now in a hurry to seize the state capital, Harrisburg; then, rearmed and provisioned from Union stores, he would move on to Philadelphia, doing battle with Meade en route. Halleck's original orders to Meade were that he must at all times be the shield for Washington, as well as the cutting edge of the Union's response to invasion. Beyond that, Meade was very much on his own.

"What sort of man is he?" Lincoln would ask from time to time, as he paced the room; and waited for news.

Stanton did not know much about him. "He's from Philadelphia, a powerful family, a friend of the Biddles," said Stanton, always impressed, Hay knew, by the patriciate. "He is called the Snapping Turtle. He is uncommonly bad-tempered, they say."

"A general after your own heart, Mars."

442

"Or stomach," said Stanton. "My alleged bad temper comes from the lungs, while General Meade's is from the stomach. He is dyspeptic."

"The interiors of these generals!" Lincoln then proceeded to analyze the direct and indirect effect of Burnside's chronic diarrhea on the course of the war.

By Wednesday, the first of July, the yellow pins were coming together at Cashtown and Gettysburg in Pennsylvania, while the blue pins were at Pipe Creek, Maryland, some fifteen miles from Gettysburg. At midday, on the first of July, Halleck entered Stanton's office. From the expression on his face Hay knew that the run on the bank had begun. "Both armies have now come together at Gettysburg," said Halleck. "The battle has begun."

On July 2, Lee tried to break the Union left; and was repulsed. The President was more and more on edge. When senators came to see him, he would explain what was happening in the serenest of terms. But when they were gone, the pacing and fidgeting would begin again; and his fears would be expressed. At the end of the day, Madam stopped by on her way to the Soldiers' Home.

"Does the battle still go on?" she asked, looking at the map.

"Yes, Mother. More fiercely than before. Today our losses have been pretty bad."

"This is General Sickles's corps, isn't it?" Hay had noticed how quickly Madam had absorbed a degree of military lore. In April she had insisted on going with the President to see General Hooker and the army at Falmouth. She had asked a thousand questions; and remembered at least nine hundred answers. Like everyone else in Washington, Madam was something of a military strategist.

"Yes, Mother. That's Sickles's corps; or at least that's where we think it was. He has been wounded."

"Badly?"

Lincoln nodded. Stanton entered with a number of dispatches, which he gave to Lincoln, who glanced at the first; then shook his head as if by shaking it he could rid himself forever of the information just received.

"What is it, Father?"

"Casualty estimates. Thus far, ten thousand men. And mostly from Sickles's corps."

Mary looked at Lincoln; and wondered what it was that sustained him. She had watched, day by day, as the war whittled him away. He seldom ate or slept or, worst of all, laughed. Then she looked back at the map. "This town is significant because of all these roads, isn't it?"

Stanton looked surprised. He came close to the map and studied it carefully with his small watery eyes. "Well, there *are* a lot of roads, yes."

"But look," said Mary, suddenly interested. This sort of detail always fascinated her: it was like working closely with a good dressmaker and a complicated pattern. "Note," she said, "the main road here to Baltimore and the one here to Philadelphia; and this one to Harrisburg. Why, this town is at the very center of everything in Pennsylvania."

"You know, Mother, you may be right." Lincoln also peered at the map. "I can't say that any of us here at the highest command post of all ever noticed anything much except a dot called Gettysburg." Lincoln turned to Stanton. "We must get Old Brains to analyze this for us."

Stanton's response was a snort. "It is an accident," he said, "if the town is of any strategic importance."

"But *someone* must have known." Mary was quite thrilled with her new dignity as warlord and tactician. "These places are not chosen at random, are they?"

Lincoln chuckled. "I have a hunch they are, Mother." He touched the map with one long finger. "You see, General Meade was down here. And Lee was up there. And now they have gone and met between those two places—at Gettysburg."

"Let us pray that we do not lose this all-important town," said Mary, all-importantly, as she left. Lincoln said that he would try to join her later at the Soldiers' Home.

As Mary drove alone in the back of the presidential carriage, she thought of money. She had failed to get any of the twenty thousand dollars a year that the President's secretaries disbursed for stationery and other office items. Major French was being increasingly difficult over her latest absolutely minimal expenditures for the Mansion. Watt was her strong right arm; but he had been conscripted in the army. Without Watt as go-between, she would have no one who was able to collect money from any of her usual sources in New York City. For some time, in exchange for government favors, Mary had been able to raise sufficient money to keep her personal debts more or less under control. In June, she had spent a week at the Continental Hotel in Philadelphia, where Simon Cameron called on her. He had made it plain, without actually saying a direct word, that money could be raised in exchange for political favors. Although she had not committed herself she had been tempted.

Fortunately, Lincoln suspected nothing. He had never reproached her for the Wikoff affair. In fact, she had only learned by accident that he had actually gone to the Judiciary Committee to beg them to accept Watt's testimony. She had been horrified;

444

she had reproached herself; she had apologized to her husband, who had said, "Molly, there are so many really terrible things for us to fret over, let's let this one slip away." But she had never forgiven herself.

Idly, Mary wondered what had become of the Chevalier, who had so adroitly used her. She wondered how badly his friend Dan Sickles had been wounded. She wondered why the driver of the carriage had allowed the horses to break into such a fast trot. She looked up just in time to see the driver's seat detach itself from the carriage, plummeting driver and seat into the road.

Mary rose in order to get out of the open carriage. But the horses were now runaways. She did not dare throw herself out. She cried out for help. But they were already in the woods that surrounded the Soldiers' Home and there was no one in sight.

Then the carriage swung in a swift arc from out behind the berserk horses and collided, with a huge hollow sound, against the trees; and like the snuffed wick of a candle, Mary's mind went out.

Seward was with Lincoln at the Mansion when the word came that Mrs. Lincoln had been injured and taken to an army hospital close to the Soldiers' Home. For a moment, Seward felt that Lincoln himself might have to be taken to hospital. He slumped back, as if his heart had suddenly ceased to beat. But then he rallied. "Come on, Governor," he said. In the outer office, Lincoln told Nicolay where he might be found. "Tell Stanton to send all dispatches to me at the hospital."

As the carriage, with its cavalry guard, clattered into Seventh Street Road, soldiers saluted their Commander-in-Chief; and a few civilians raised their hats. Lincoln responded with absent-minded waves of his right hand alternating with touches to his hat's brim. "Fate does nothing by halves, does it, Governor? Here we have the greatest battle of the war going on, and my wife's lying unconscious in a hospital, and I am feeling none too well myself in this poisonous swamp of a city."

"When we win the war, let us move the capital to the north." Seward thought it best to strike as light a note as possible. He understood now his friend's moods. Although Lincoln's depressions were deep, well-timed laughter could often bring him out of one. "I propose my own town of Auburn. A salubrious climate. No fetid canals. No malaria or bilious fevers."

"What," said Lincoln, suddenly smiling, "about Toronto?"

"Ah, you want to make an old man happy!" Seward exclaimed, pleased to have elicited the smile. "It would be a dream come true to annex Canada! And if you promised people that you'd move our capital up there, what Canadian would complain?"

Mary lay in a hospital bed at the corner of a long room crowded with wounded men. Ropes had been put up all around her bed to which sheets had been attached, providing her with some privacy. Lincoln and Seward stepped inside the tent. Keckley was seated beside the bed. She rose when she saw the President. "She is still unconscious."

"Molly?" Lincoln spoke directly into Mary's ear; but she did not stir. Disconcertingly, thought Seward, Mrs. Lincoln's eyes were wide open; and she had a polite smile on her lips. The white turbanlike bandage that covered her head made her look not unlike the White House portrait of Dolley Madison.

Lincoln turned to Keckley. "What does the doctor say?"

"It is not serious. She comes and goes. All her faculties are in order. The only fear, he says, is infection of the wound. She must have a nurse full time. I've sent for Mrs. Pomroy."

Lincoln nodded. "When can we take her home?"

"Perhaps tomorrow."

The presence of Lincoln in the ward was causing a considerable furor, and Seward thought that the sooner they left, the better. But Lincoln told Keckley to go take some air and rest while, "I hold the fort."

So Seward sat on one side of the bed and Lincoln sat on the other, and soldiers on crutches would come stumping by, trying to get a glimpse of the President through a crack in the sheets. Lincoln and Seward spoke in low voices across Mary's unconscious form. "Meade is now waiting for Lee to attack," said Lincoln, grimly. "Our generals always wait to be attacked. It is not their nature to attack first."

"There is Grant." Seward wished that he had not, on doctor's orders, been obliged to give up snuff: the air in the hot stuffy ward was beginning to make him ill.

"He does not move for now. He is stopped at Vicksburg. You know, back in April, I sent Washburne out to see him. Apparently the rumors are true. He does get drunk now and again but he has an adjutant who gives him all hell when he does; and if things look too bad, they send for Mrs. Grant. Washburne stays in close touch with the adjutant. So all is well." Lincoln fiddled with his glasses. "I like Grant. He doesn't worry and bother me. He isn't shrieking for reinforcements all the time. He takes what troops we can safely give him, and does the best he can with what he has got. If he takes Vicksburg . . ."

There was a scratching sound on the sheet. Then a colonel from the War Department tiptoed into the makeshift tent. Not certain how to comport himself, he gave the President the dispatches and tiptoed away. Lincoln read quickly. "Lee is attacking.

Meade will stay where he is. He does not know whether his own operations will be defensive or offensive." Lincoln sighed. "Surely, they are both."

"Or neither. You should get some rest, Mr. President."

"No. I'll stay here until Mrs. Pomroy takes over. But you go on home, Governor. After all, this is the hour of the day when you expect *your* reinforcements."

Seward chuckled. "It is a pity you are not more like General Grant and me."

"The thought sometimes occurs to me that I am, in this case anyway, truly pitiful."

As Seward departed, a youthful military doctor hurried into the tent. "I'm the doctor, Your Excellency. Captain Rewalt. From Pennsylvania. I dressed her wounds. There is some danger of infection . . ."

As Seward made his way out of the ward, he was smartly saluted by the colonel from the War Department. "Sir, should I wait for the President? Or go back to Mr. Stanton's office?"

"I suggest you wait for him. I'll borrow Mr. Lincoln's carriage; then send it straight back. What actually happened to Mrs. Lincoln?"

"The coachman—he broke an arm but he's all right otherwise—says that someone took all the screws out from the driver's seat and then glued the seat back on, knowing that after a certain amount of jiggling, the thing would fall off."

Almost every day Pinkerton brought Seward rumors of plans to assassinate the President. Most were straightforward threats to shoot him. This attempt was unusually ingenious, planned from within the White House. "The seat was . . . altered today?"

The colonel nodded. "Between the morning when Mrs. Lincoln drove into town from the Soldiers' Home to the Mansion and when she drove back."

Seward thanked the colonel and got into the carriage. Obviously, whoever had arranged for the accident had access to the White House stables.

The next day, Mary was conscious. She was moved back to the White House, while the President, in effect, moved into the Telegraph Room of the War Department. Here he followed the battle in Pennsylvania. Although reports were conflicting, the enormity of the losses on both sides was soon apparent. Plainly, this was no ordinary battle.

Hay was constantly on the move between Mansion and War Department. Nicolay was now president *de facto* while the president *de jure* tried to direct a three-day battle from the Telegraph Room, whose floor was now covered with flimsies, the yellow copy-sheets of incoming telegrams. Stanton and Halleck would occasionally join the President. Hay was impressed with how entirely directionless the two men were. To the messages from the clattering machine they simply responded with cries and expletives, with moans and sighs.

Lincoln, at least, had an objective. Lee's army must now be destroyed once and for all. Lee was far from home, and he was, in Lincoln's view, outnumbered. Best of all, he was giving ground to Meade. Strange new names were coming off the wire. Seminary Ridge and Cemetery Hill were often reversed: charges were made up Cemetery Ridge and down Seminary Hill; then there was Culp's Hill and Round Top Mountain. During the long sultry day, Hay tried to visualize these places; but failed. Of those who visited the Telegraph Room, only Stanton had ever been to Gettysburg; and he remembered nothing but the courthouse, where he had defended an embezzler.

By nightfall, Lee had been driven off. "Now we have got him!" Lincoln's eyes glowed. He turned to Halleck, who was in the room. "Send Meade word that he is to pursue the enemy, and cut him off before he reaches the Potomac."

Halleck scratched his arm; and rolled his watery eyes. "I don't think, sir, that at this hour of the night, after many thousands of casualties, and many hours of hard fighting, any general could begin a pursuit..."

The telegrapher gave a start. "Mr. Lincoln, a message from General Meade. He is congratulating the Army of the Potomac for having defeated, I quote him, sir, 'an enemy superior in numbers and flushed with pride of a successful invasion, that had attempted to overcome and destroy this army.'".

"What a strange tone!" Lincoln frowned. "I suppose it is always good to say the enemy is superior in number even when he is not, but why speak of a successful invasion, when it is now not? Why say that the enemy has attempted to overcome and destroy us when that is what we must do to him? Go on."

The telegrapher continued. "'The commanding general looks to the army for greater efforts to drive from our soil every vestige of the presence of the invader.'"

Lincoln leapt from his chair. "Drive the invader *from our soil!* My God! Is that all?"

"It is a very great deal, sir," said Halleck.

Lincoln rounded on Halleck; and for a moment, Hay caught a glint of true violence in the Tycoon's eyes; but then the usual iron control returned. "You will, General, in due course—by tomorrow morning, that is—tell General Meade that he is to pursue Lee. We have the rebels within our grasp. We have only to stretch forth our hands and they are ours. The war, General Halleck, must now come swiftly to an end." Lincoln then dictated a congratulatory message to the Army of the Potomac. When this message had gone out on the wire, Lincoln turned to Hay and said, "Well, I can now go to bed. But, first, Mr. Chandler," he gestured to the telegrapher, "send a message to my son. Three words, 'Come to Washington.' Sign it with my name; and charge the message to me, personally. Goodnight."

As they crossed the avenue, the Tycoon was both tired and febrile. He could not let go the phrase "our soil." "Of course, Pennsylvania is our soil. But so is Virginia. So are the Carolinas. So is Texas. They are forever our soil. That is what the war is about and these damned fools cannot grasp it; or will not grasp it. The whole country is our soil. I cannot fathom such men."

Hay could not help but think that few men could fathom Lincoln's passion for the Union, which had become, for him, the ultimate emblem of all earthly if not heavenly divinity.

The next day—propitiously, the Fourth of July, an Independence Day which the capital had already decided to celebrate to the fullest—Stanton announced that Lee's army had been turned back at Gettysburg; and was now retreating south to the Potomac River and Virginia.

The President waved to the crowds that had assembled in front of the White House; and watched the fireworks; and kept Mrs. Lincoln company. He was highly annoyed that he had not yet heard from Robert.

"There is bad blood," said Nicolay to Hay, "betwen the Hellcat and the Prince of Rails." Side by side, they were preparing answers to the various congratulatory telegrams that had begun to arrive at the White House.

"Is the cause of this blood gone bad the beautiful Miss Hooper, daughter of the dry-goods magnate of Georgetown, whose flashing eyes ensnared our Robert at the last Yuletide season, specifically, in the parlor of Mrs. Eames, when he confessed to me, sotto voce, that he would like to see her elevated to Princess of Rails?"

"God forbid! That really would kill Madam, if she knew. No, it was over those two midgets that Mr. Barnum brought to the White House."

"Tom Thumb and his bride, who looked not unlike a miniature Madam. That is, Tom Thumb looked like Madam, not his beauteous consort."

"Well, before the reception for the two Thumbs," said Nicolay, "Robert told his mother that he would not be joining them. When she asked him why not, he said, 'My notions of duty, perhaps, are somewhat different from yours.'"

Hay whistled softly. "That's what Harvard does to you, Nico. They should've sent him to Brown. He will become more and more intolerable."

"But then," said Nico, lapsing into his original language, "Robert *ist unser Prinz.*"

The Tuesday Cabinet meeting had been a most gloomy affair, thought Chase. The President had described at length his efforts to get Meade to pursue Lee. But Meade still remained at Gettysburg. "He could have been in Hagerstown by now. Lee's army is still north of the Potomac, which is in flood. So there is the bulk of the enemy army, trapped between us and the river."

"What does General Halleck say?" For some time, Welles had been urging the President to send Old Brains off to retirement. On this one point, Chase and Welles were in perfect accord.

"General Halleck is very short with me," said the President, sadly. "The troops are not yet ready, I am told. And the general in the field always knows best. So I drop the subject."

The new Secretary of the Interior, Mr. John P. Usher, plump and fair, an Indiana lawyer who had been assistant secretary to the departed and unmourned Caleb Smith, was interested in the progress of the enrollment of conscriptable men. Stanton was rather short with *him*, thought Chase. "We've got no full reports yet. They are still in the field, as our generals say. But we have millions of able men to draw on; and the rebels don't."

"But will they let us draw on them?" asked Usher.

"They—whoever they are—have no choice," said Stanton.

Seward got up from the lounge where he had been stretched out full-length during the entire Cabinet meeting; a perfect symbol, in Chase's view, of the general slovenliness of the Administration. He wished Ben Wade could be somehow present but invisible. "Has anyone any idea what our losses have been?" asked Seward.

"At Gettysburg, they were—" Stanton began.

But Seward interrupted him. "No, I mean for this last year. We have been fighting pretty steadily since the Peninsula, and we've been sustaining great losses. There's been Fredericksburg and Chancellorsville and Antietam and now Gettysburg. We've been taking quite a pounding..."

"So have the rebels; and they don't have the men we do." Stanton tugged at his wiry beard and blinked his red-glazed eyes. "We calculate our losses to be about the same as theirs, which is desperate for them, but not for us."

"Even so," said Usher, "won't these losses of ours somewhat chill our drive to conscript more men?"

Chase looked at Lincoln, who was now present only in the

flesh. The President's eyes were those of someone lost in a waking dream.

Stanton coughed and wheezed with irritability. "To conscript is to conscript, Mr. Usher. It makes no difference whether or not the man conscripted is chilled by our losses."

Bates, with a gentle smile, said, "Mr. Stanton is trying to say that if anybody resists the draft, he'll be hanged, and I, as Attorney-General, will have to justify these hangings under the Conscription Act."

Seward sat on the lounge combing his hair, a habit which greatly annoyed Chase; and not simply because he himself was now almost entirely bald. "I revert to my original question, Mr. Stanton. What have been our casualties during this last year?"

"One hundred ten thousand men killed, missing or wounded," said Stanton. "Naturally, I don't have all the figures from the West."

Lincoln got to his feet; and bade them farewell. Chase asked if he might remain and discuss the new bond issues. Together the two men went into the President's office. Chase found Lincoln as vague and tentative as ever when it came to financial matters. Fortunately, he had always given Chase a free hand. But there had been problems lately, and the price of gold had been rising. Chase was concerned that Gettysburg might not in itself be a large enough victory to encourage the financial markets, not to mention the speculations in gold. Suddenly, Gideon Welles flung open the office door. Wig askew, Welles stared at them, red in the face and out of breath.

"Well, Neptune, you seem to have got a look at some sort of terrible sea monster," said Lincoln. "Sit down. Here, take some water."

Welles drank the water that Lincoln poured out for him. Then he announced, in gasps, "Message. From Admiral Porter. In the West. Vicksburg has fallen."

"Which way?" asked Lincoln, as if unable to believe that there could be good news of such magnitude.

"Our way. On July the Fourth, after a siege of eighty days. Grant allowed the Confederate garrison, some thirty thousand men, to go home—on parole, as he put it. Then he occupied the city. The Mississippi River is ours."

"I cannot comprehend it!" Lincoln shook his head with wonder.

"I must say that I always believed that we would, sooner or later, take Vicksburg," said Chase, serenely elated. "And win the war."

"No, no, Mr. Chase. You misunderstand me. What I cannot comprehend is that the winner of the war's greatest victory has

451

not reported it to me and to the nation. Usually, my generals tell the press about their victories while the fighting is still going on." Lincoln was on his feet. "Come on, Neptune, we must send the word to General Meade. I shall try to inspire him, as Grant inspires me."

As the President and Welles appeared in the waiting room, Hay and Nicolay applauded the Commander-in-Chief, who gave mock-solemn bows to left and right. Then the Tycoon and Welles hurried off to the War Department, leaving behind them Chase, who observed to no one in particular, "This is proof of the justice of our cause."

As Chase moved like some great ship down the hall, Hay turned to Nicolay and said, "Did you hear what Ben Wade said about Chase? 'He's a good man, but his theology is unsound: He thinks there is a fourth person in the Trinity.'"

From one end of the Union to the other, church bells rang and orators spoke and newspapers praised the victor of Vicksburg. To Hay's amusement, there was a mass return of all those grand politicos who had fled the city with the adjournment of Congress, many of them in the conviction that the city would be in rebel hands before Congress was due to meet again. Sumner and Fessenden and Chandler were again visitors to the Mansion. General Sickles, less one leg, was at a friend's house in F Street. When General Hooker arrived to comfort Sickles, he was promptly arrested under a War Department order forbidding general officers to come to the capital without special permission. It was said that Old Brains himself had arranged the arrest of his enemy.

At sundown, the President was serenaded in front of the White House. The Ancient then proceeded to make what Hay thought was easily the worst speech that he had ever heard him make, full of cracker-barrel phrases, as well as the odd comment that three presidents had died on the Fourth of July, a matter of some irrelevance to the fall of Vicksburg. "He is worn out," said Hay to Nicolay, as they made their way through the crowd to Willard's and supper.

"So am I," said Nicolay. "But I shall soon be in the Rocky Mountains, breathing proper air, while you are strangling here in the heat."

"I wonder if Robert will come or not." There had been no response to the first telegram. The Tycoon had sent off a second one; presumably, Robert was now en route. Madam was feverish: the infection had spread.

When the Cabinet met next on Tuesday, July 14, the euphoria of Vicksburg had begun to evaporate. Lincoln was cold and de-
452

liberate. "General Meade, on Sunday night, against my advice, held a council of war to ask his commanders what he should do next."

Seward sat in the President's usual chair, his knees under his chin. Seward had other things on his mind. Unlike the President, he had already written off Meade. Union generals assigned to the Army of the Potomac invariably became cowardly or worse.

Seward saw a much greater danger at hand. The day before, in New York City, a well-organized mob had wrecked the house of the Republican mayor; burned a dozen buildings, including the draft office; murdered dozens of Negroes; hanged a captain of the state guard and severely wounded the Superintendent of Police. They then assembled barricades in First Avenue between Eleventh and Fourteenth Streets, as well as in Ninth Avenue. All to show their fury at the Conscription Act. Since dawn, Seward had been trying, unsuccessfully, to get word to his friend Archbishop Hughes, the only man who could control the almost-entirely Irish mob. Even though many of the Irish were just arrived in the United States, to a man they hated both Negroes and the Republican Administration. Ordinarily archbishop and governor kept them in line. But someone very shrewd indeed had been at work. Shortly after the available New York militia had left the state for Gettysburg, the mob had struck. The city's fifteen hundred policemen were soon routed; telegraph offices were seized and the wires cut, while railroad and streetcar lines were disrupted. Carefully, the city was isolated from the rest of the state and country.

Seward could not, for the life of him, figure out who was behind this remarkably well-executed revolution. There was a rumor that Vallandigham was in the city; but Seward doubted if that Copperhead demagogue had the skill to overthrow so vast a city. But who had? Or was it simply a spontaneous uprising on the part of a citizenry enflamed by such newspapers as the *Daily News* and the *World*, which day after day, denounced the government, the draft and the Negroes.

Seward thought, somewhat wryly, of the secret overtures that he and Thurlow Weed had been making toward Governor Seymour, Lincoln's choice as the Democratic-Unionist president. Luckily, Seymour had proved to be vain and dull, a highly resistible combination in Seward's view. Worse, on the Fourth of July, Seymour had told a large audience at New York's Academy of Music that the government was destroying the rights of the citizens with midnight arrests, the shutting down of newspapers, the suspension of *habeas corpus* and the right of trial by jury. Nicely, the governor lit the fuse; and the city went up in flames.

Lincoln was now comparing General Meade to McClellan,

the beginning of the end for Meade, thought Seward. "Meade is making the same mistakes. Like calling for a council. I warned him that no council has ever wanted to fight; and I am afraid that the one he has called is no exception."

Stanton entered the room. "May I see you, sir?"

Lincoln moved into his office; and Stanton followed, shutting the door behind him. Seward looked about the table at his colleagues. "Let us have an informal council behind the President's back. As of this morning, how many here agree with me that we should have shot or, perhaps, hanged Vallandigham?" The response was properly bloodthirsty. Even Chase was moved to denounce in harsh terms the President's unaccountable leniency. They were exchanging items of news or gossip from New York City when Lincoln and Stanton returned.

Usher asked Stanton if there was bad news. Stanton gasped a negative. Then Welles asked if there was any truth to the rumor that Lee had already crossed the Potomac into Virginia. Stanton said, "I know nothing of Lee's movements."

"Well, I do," said the President; and he gave Stanton a hard look. "If Lee has not got all of his men across the river by now, he soon will." Lincoln turned back to Stanton. "I want to see Halleck. At the War Department." Without a word, Stanton left the room.

"About the rioting in New York City," Seward began.

But Lincoln cut him off. "I don't think we're in any mood— or at least I am not in any mood—to continue this meeting. I've now got two volcanoes on my hands."

"How do you plan," asked Bates, "to answer Governor Seymour's request that the draft be suspended in New York City?"

"I don't know," said the President; and he left the room with Welles, who walked him part of the way across the White House lawn. Just as Welles was about to return to the Navy Department, Lincoln stopped in his tracks and took his arm. "Mr. Welles, there is something excessive strange here. There is bad faith somewhere. General Meade has been pressed and urged by us to pursue Lee and cut him off. But only one of his generals favored an immediate attack. What does it mean, Mr. Welles? Good God, what does it mean?"

"Did you ever directly order Meade to attack?"

"I urged. I exhorted. So did Stanton, I think. Halleck was always waiting to hear from Meade."

"Halleck was only four hours away by rail from Meade. Why didn't he go to him at Gettysburg and tell him that he was to attack?"

454

Lincoln did not answer. The bright sun made his face more than ever sallow; and the eye sockets were now cavernous.

"Sir, I think that General Halleck is the problem. He is inert, at best. At worst, he is not competent."

Lincoln sighed. "Halleck knows better than I do. He's a military man, has a military education. I brought him here to give me military advice. It's true that his views and mine are widely different. Even so, it is better that I, who am not a military man, should defer to him rather than he to me."

Welles shook his head. "I disagree, Mr. President. Halleck has *no* ideas, that I ever heard of. He originates nothing. You have the overall view of the war in your head, with all its ramifications, political and military. You must never fear to give the lead to those who must be led."

Lincoln seemed not to have heard any of this. He spoke as if to himself. "When we got word that Vicksburg had fallen, and the Potomac was in flood, and Lee was desperately waiting for the waters to fall so that he could cross, I saw that the rebellion was at an end. But the generals voted not to attack him, and now the war goes on and on—and on."

Then Lincoln turned, abruptly, and set off, alone, to the War Department. Welles crossed to the Navy Department. Mrs. Lincoln's cow moaned. One of the Bucktails asked the cow to shut up. The heat was intense. Gnats filled the summer air.

Robert Lincoln entered Nicolay's office as Nicolay was preparing to depart for the West. Hay had already moved into Nicolay's office. "Well, the prince at last!" Nicolay exclaimed.

"What became of you?" asked Hay.

"I was caught in the rioting. The beginning of it, anyway. Luckily, I had a friend at the Fifth Avenue Hotel who had his own carriage. He got me across the city to the ferry before they stopped the service. I was on the last cars for Baltimore." Robert looked thirty years old, thought Hay, somewhat enviously; and he sounded like a Boston Brahmin. "Where are they?"

"Your father's at the War Department, as always," said Nicolay, giving Hay a small key. "To the strongbox. Don't lose it." Nicolay turned to Robert. "And your mother's now out at the Soldiers' Home. She's better, they say. The infection's clearing up."

"Everything's happening at once down here."

"We try never to have an idle day," said Hay, blithely.

"Isn't the town awfully crowded for summer?" Robert studied the stack of newspapers. They were from everywhere in the Union; and Richmond, too.

"Vicksburg," said Nicolay, with some satisfaction. "All the fainthearts have come to town to rally round the victorious president."

Robert inquired after mutual acquaintances but Hay knew that he was interested in only one, the daughter of the hardware magnate; and so Hay took a deep breath and said, "Miss Hooper is to be married this month."

Robert swallowed hard; inquired if Mr. Watt was to be found; was told that Mr. Watt had gone to the army.

"What started the rioting?" asked Hay.

"Who knows?" Robert was vague; his mind elsewhere, in Georgetown. "At first, it looked to be organized. The Irish were all set to kill every Negro in the city. Oh, they are animals!"

"The Negroes?" asked Hay, mischievously.

"No, the Irish. Damned drunken papists!" Robert was very much the Boston Brahmin. "They are calling this a rich man's war and a poor man's fight."

"They are not so far wrong," said Nicolay. "It's certainly not fair to let a man stay out of the war because he's got three hundred dollars to pay for someone else to go. There's bound to be trouble."

"There *is* trouble," said Robert. "It's like the French Revolution, what's going on up there, with people being hanged from lampposts." Edward announced that the carriage was ready to take Robert to his father. "Well, I'd *give* three hundred dollars to be allowed to fight."

"Give it to your mother," said Hay. "She'll let you join up in a flash." Hay was icily aware that he had gone too far. But Robert only laughed; and left.

"That was hardly tactful." Nicolay frowned.

"I'm sorry. I couldn't help myself. Anyway, I don't think he knows about Madam's mysterious ways of raising money. Curious, how little like either of them he is."

Nicolay took down the map of Pennsylvania from which all pins had been removed. "I think he's very much a Todd."

Hay suddenly recollected a conversation that he had had with Herndon on his last trip to Springfield. "Old Herndon says that he believes that all the rumors about the Ancient being illegitimate aren't true but that the Ancient himself told Herndon that *his* mother—someone called Hanks—was illegitimate, and the daughter of a Virginia grandee."

"Mr. Herndon is very good at quashing rumors that no one else has heard." Nicolay did not take a friendly view of the President's law partner.

Hay was thoughtful. "I don't think he ever lies. But he does like to speculate. He thinks that the Ancient knows who his real grandfather is, but he would never tell Herndon."

"The Ancient is nothing if not wise."

"So Herndon is now of the opinion that the shadowy grand-

456

father is none other than that great advocate of slavery, the aristocratic John C. Calhoun."

"God help us!" Nicolay was appalled.

"'They even,' said Herndon happily, 'look alike.' Is that for your book or mine?"

Hay and Nicolay had each had, on his own, the idea of writing a biography of Lincoln. Lately, they had been discussing such a book as a joint effort.

Nicolay shut his desk. "Upon the two of us, John, must fall the noble task of telling the world who Abraham Lincoln really was. This means that we are obliged to leave Billy Herndon out."

"But, Nico, do we know who he really was—or is?"

"We know what we know, which is a good deal, I think."

"I wonder," said Hay. "The Tycoon is a mysterious man; and highly secret."

"That's because he's smarter than anybody else. Nothing mysterious about that. Where's the key?"

"Here in my watch pocket."

"Guard it well; and the Republic, too."

"To the death, Nico."

Hay sat with the Tycoon in the President's Office, waiting for Seward to usher in the latest delegation from New York. Lincoln sat on the window-sill, gold glasses on the end of his nose; and read from Artemus Ward: "'Any gentleman living in Ireland who was never in this country, is not liable to the draft, nor are our forefathers.'" Lincoln chuckled, and looked at Hay over his glasses. "That has the statesman's ring to it." Then he read on. "'The term of enlistment is for three years, but any man who may have been drafted in two places has a right to go for six years. The only sons of a poor widow, whose husband is in California, are not exempt, but a man who owns stock in the Vermont Central Railway is.'" Lincoln threw back his head, and roared with laughter. Hay marvelled at the Tycoon's power of recovery. Whatever fire that kept this extraordinary engine going was plainly unquenchable if fuelled by laughter. "'So also are incessant lunatics, habitual lecturers, persons born with wooden legs and false teeth, blind men, and people who deliberately voted for John Tyler.'" Hay and Lincoln were now both laughing, uncontrollably, as Edward opened the door and announced, solemnly, "The Secretary of State, Senator Morgan and Mr. Samuel J. Tilden of New York."

Seward had heard the laughter; saw the copy of Artemus Ward. "I shall want that next," he said to the President.

"It is a tonic, let me tell you. President Tyler died, didn't he?"

"A year ago January, in Richmond. He'd just been elected to

the rebel congress. Mr. President, allow me to present Senator Morgan, whom you know, and Mr. Tilden, whom you don't."

Lincoln shook hands with each man; and to Tilden, a small, spare, cleanshaven man of about fifty, he said, "You were an associate of Martin Van Buren . . ."

"*He* died a year ago this month," interjected Seward, settling into his usual place at table.

"I know that, Governor." Lincoln turned to Tilden. "You worked with Mr. Van Buren?"

"I helped him as best I could during his presidency. I wrote many briefs for him." Tilden stifled a belch. Senator Morgan had assured Seward that although Mr. Tilden's acute and chronic dyspepsia had ruled him out as a candidate for office it did not prevent him from being an adroit manipulator behind the scenes.

"Well, I did not support Van Buren in 'forty-eight but he was plainly the best of the lot, as it turned out. And once upon a time he had favored Negro suffrage, too." Lincoln chuckled. "When I read that out to Judge Douglas, a Van Buren man through and through, I thought he'd have a fit. 'Where did he say that?' he asked in front of this huge crowd. So I gave him the book, open to the passage, and the Judge said, 'I want nothing to do with that damned book,' and threw it on the ground."

Seward allowed Lincoln a few more reminiscences; then he brought up the subject of the meeting. "We were able, Archbishop Hughes and I, to turn off the mob on the third day." Seward felt that he deserved full credit for having so bombarded the archbishop with telegrams that His Eminence had been obliged to summon the faithful to his house on Madison Avenue, where he had scolded and soothed a crowd of some five thousand men, mostly Irish. As a result, the city was tranquil—for the present.

"The danger now, Mr. President," said Senator Morgan, "is the reopening of the draft offices. Governor Seymour has done what he could to placate the immigrants, but they are in a devilish mood. He would like a clear statement from you that the draft will at least be postponed in the city."

"He will never get that, Senator. If you postpone the draft in one state, you will give other states the notion that they, too, can have postponements."

"But you do realize, sir, that the city will explode again if you try to impose conscription." Tilden watched Lincoln's face intently: one lawyer testing another.

"I do not impose conscription, Mr. Tilden. Congress does. The Conscription Act was much debated and thought out. It is not perfect. The Constitution is not perfect either. But at least the Conscription Act was passed almost unanimously. It is the
458

law; and I must execute it." Seward thought that Lincoln must, presently and characteristically, soften his line. But, to Seward's surprise, Lincoln grew even more hard and legalistic. "To that end, ten thousand infantrymen are on their way to the city. Also, several artillery batteries."

"You will place the city under martial law?" Tilden probed.

"In effect, Mr. Tilden, the whole Union is under a kind of martial law; as it is wartime. Now I know that you and Governor Seymour and a number of other Democrats think that we have torn up the Constitution down here. But we are simply trying to salvage it, and the nation." To Seward's relief, Lincoln finally struck the conciliatory note. "Tell the governor that the principle to which I propose adhering is to proceed with the draft while, at the same time, applying"—Lincoln paused for a strong word; found one that Seward thought too strong—"*infallible* means to avoid any great wrongs."

"This," said Tilden, eyeing the bait, "is to be interpreted as giving a certain leeway to New York's conduct of the draft?"

"*I* did not say that. But I cannot control every interpretation put on my words."

"Yes," said Tilden, nodding. Seward was pleased. The two distinguished lawyers had understood each other.

But Senator Morgan had not got the point. "What do we say when demagogues cry out against the three-hundred-dollar exemption? 'Rich man's money against the poor man's blood,' they say. You know there is a lot of communist sentiment in the city; and all this just heats it up."

"To have an army, you must first have men." Lincoln was reasonable. "Ideally, they should be volunteers. Otherwise, we must have conscription. After all, other countries—republics as well as monarchies—have it. The exemption seems to me a fair enough thing. At least it brings money to the Treasury, which helps the war."

Senator Morgan was not pleased. "Why can't you wait until the Supreme Court has determined whether or not the Conscription Act is Constitutional?"

"Because I don't have the time, Senator. The war grows bloodier with each day. The rebels are conscripting every male who can walk; and they send them off to be slaughtered like cattle. Are we so degenerate that we cannot, with our greater numbers, raise an adequate army through a lawful draft?"

"Then you refuse, sir, to wait for the Supreme Court to rule?" Morgan was now very tense.

Seward looked at Lincoln, who, for no perceptible reason, was smiling. "Sir, I will not wait upon anyone. The time for argument

459

is past. If this is not agreeable to you, then we shall just have to see who is the stronger."

Seward felt an involuntary shudder in his limbs. He was also ravished by the irony of the moment. For nearly three years, a thousand voices, including his own, had called for a Cromwell, a dictator, a despot; and in all that time, no one had suspected that there had been, from the beginning, a single-minded dictator in the White House, a Lord Protector of the Union by whose will alone the war had been prosecuted. For the first time, Seward understood the nature of Lincoln's political genius. He had been able to make himself absolute dictator without ever letting anyone suspect that he was anything more than a joking, timid backwoods lawyer, given to fits of humility in the presence of all the strutting military and political peacocks that flocked about him.

The two New Yorkers also appeared to have some inkling of who the man was that they were dealing with; or being dealt by. Senator Morgan fell silent, while Mr. Tilden belched softly. The President then read a page or two from Artemus Ward, lightening the mood.

As the meeting ended Tilden looked up at Lincoln and said, "Mr. Van Buren had the greatest respect for your tenacity and your general judgment in this war."

Lincoln could not resist the obvious joke. "My 'general' judgment has been on the whole pretty bad. But I am tenacious all right. I am glad he appreciated that."

"He was also much amused," said Tilden, ignoring the joke, "when he recollected an adjective you once used to describe *his* presidency."

Lincoln frowned. "What was that?"

"'Monarchial,' Mr. President. He was much tickled by the word, as coming from you. In fact, at the end, Mr. Van Buren felt that you were bent on outdoing him."

Lincoln laughed, showing all his white teeth. "Well, if I am monarchial, it is the times that shoved the crown on my head. Anyway, when the war is won, I'll lose my crown fast enough, and probably my head, too. And, frankly, between us, I am heartily sick of both."

How *does* such a sovereign lay down his scepter? Seward wondered, as he walked down the main stairs of the Manison, Senator Morgan to his left and Mr. Tilden to his right.

"Mr. Lincoln seems," said Tilden, thoughtfully, "a man of good will."

"Oh, Mr. Tilden!" Seward exclaimed, "I can testify to that! Mr. Lincoln's will is very good indeed. In fact, his will is all that we have here."

460

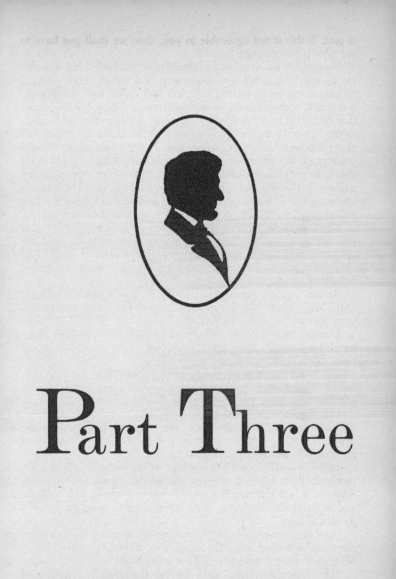

Part Three

1

ON A COLD GRAY AFTERNOON, DAVID REPORTED BACKSTAGE at Grover's Theater. He was suffering, so Mr. Thompson had been told, from the smallpox, which was now sweeping the periphery of the city, particularly in the Negro sections and around the Navy Yard. Actually, David was in excellent health; but he had decided to reserve for himself the month of October. He had saved a certain amount of money. He was now living at home again, a quieter place since two—or was it three?—of the sisters had moved out of the house and into matrimony or its appearance. Although the ham-lady was angry with him, Sal Austin could always be counted on to give him odd jobs to do around Marble Alley, where he was paid in kind. He also worked at Mr. Ford's theater from time to time; as well as at Mr. Grover's new establishment, which had opened with much excitement the previous week, a brand-new theater fashioned from the ruins of the old National Theater in E Street between Thirteenth and Fourteenth Streets. Mr. Grover was a pleasant man, though a Yankee from western New York. He knew David by sight—as opposed to Mr. Ford, a Marylander, who knew him by name.

The backstage entrance was in a narrow alley just back of E. The scenery for the next night's play was still in its wagon. E.L. Davenport and J. W. Wallack, two actors David admired, were embarked upon a season, whose highlight would be a single charity performance by Charlotte Cushman as Lady Macbeth in *Macbeth*, a play that David disliked almost as much as he did the famous Miss Cushman, a tragedienne who looked like an elderly mare; and always stayed with Mr. Seward when she was in Washington. Had she been less hideous and he less old, there would have been a scandal. As it was, no one at all cared.

Backstage, the manager shouted to David to help out with the third-act set, which was yet to be assembled. A dozen stagehands were arranging tables and chairs and putting scenery in order. The painted flats suggested a production both opulent and exotic. Kerosene lamps lit the back of the theater to reveal a jungle of ropes and high, perilous walkways, of furniture and scenery flats. Expensive gaslight was only used during performances.

As the curtain was now up, David could just make out the

newly remodelled interior of the theater, ghostly in the dim light from backstage. There was the usual smell of glue and wood shavings and cheap paint; later, during performance, there would be the heady smell of sweaty actors and perfumed actresses and the acrid burnt-oxygen odor of calcium light mingled with that aromatic dust which seemed to cover everything during a performance. David could never get enough of the theater backstage or, for that matter, out front in the audience.

To David's surprise, he found himself working with Edward Spangler, one of Mr. Ford's regular stagehands. "But the boys needed some help back here tonight, so Mr. Ford looked the other way." Spangler was a slow-talking Marylander; although red of face from drink, he was highly reliable and much in demand.

David helped Spangler assemble an arbor of green paper leaves glued to a fragile wooden trellis. "What's the play?" asked David, who almost never read newspapers; and had not been near the theaters in a week.

"*The Pearl of Savoy*, whatever that is. Nine scene changes, I think. And they want a horse in this act but I don't think Mr. Grover's going to let them after what happened last week."

"What happened?"

"Well, what happened was what always happens when you let a horse up on a stage."

David giggled, appreciatively. "I saw that when Forrest was here, in Shakespeare."

"Well, they don't want to see it tonight. So the heroine will say, 'Lookee, now, there's yonder white steed in the gloamin'! I must go and mount it.' Oh, you should see this one." Spangler whistled.

"Who is she?"

"Davie, I don't know, never know, their names. I just like their looks, or not, as the case may be. You want some work at Ford's?"

David nodded; carefully, he put the arbor right-side up. "I'm taking time off from Thompson's. He thinks I'm sick, which I am—of that drugstore of his."

"Don't ever give that up," warned Spangler to David's annoyance. Apparently, a life spent as a prescription clerk in the back room of a Fifteenth Street drugstore seemed perfection to everyone that he knew. At least his secesh friends knew that he had another life, but Spangler, though himself secesh, knew nothing of nightriders and the Colonel, of Mr. Henderson and Surrattsville. He simply thought that David Herold had a good job, suitable to his station in life; and should keep it.

"What's at Ford's?" asked David, not wanting to go into the sore subject of his current employment and limited prospects.

464

"Old Junius Brutus's boy is going to play for two weeks, starts first of November. I was pretty fond of his father. Fact, I built most of his house for him near Baltimore, at Cockeysville, when Johnny was a boy."

"Is he really the youngest star in the world?" asked David. They were now carrying what looked to be a moss-covered stone wall to its place at stage right.

"Danged if I know, Davie. Why?"

"That's what the sign said when he played here last spring. I saw him in *Richard III*. But I couldn't tell how young he was, with the whiskers and the nose and all."

"Well, he's a star, I guess. Not like his father. Now old Junius Brutus Booth was the greatest actor I ever saw and certainly the craziest, while young Junius Brutus is the greatest tightwad as a manager I ever saw. Edwin's the real actor of the family, while Johnny's just—Johnny. I reckon he's twenty-three or four now."

Suddenly, David felt his usual pang when he thought of what he might have been. The pang was sharpest whenever he thought of actors, particularly the young, handsome ones, because they not only knew and worked with actresses but all the girls looked up to them. In April, at Grover's, John Wilkes Booth had been a success, and for weeks the young ladies of the city talked of no one else, as they bought his photograph in the shops.

But Spangler preferred to speak of old Booth. "There was no one like him on the stage; or anywhere else. He was an Englishman who settled over here forty years ago, not far from Baltimore. He had ten children; and never killed a living thing."

Spangler reached into his back pocket and removed a flat bottle of homemade corn whiskey. David took a polite sip; but even that made his throat burn. Spangler drank deeply. Although he was never not drinking, he was never drunk at work. "Old Junius Brutus kept every sort of animal on his farm but never killed even a chicken. Once when he was west he found a stack of dead birds in a field, and he hired a gravedigger to fix them a grave, and got a preacher to say a funeral service."

"Was he crazy?"

Spangler frowned; then pushed David to one side as a huge gate almost ran them down. David looked about to see which of the principal players had arrived. But so far, only the old character people were behind the canvas in the wings, making up.

As the two men put together an Italianate fountain, Spangler said, "Well, he was crazy *some* of the time. But he was a noble soul. He believed in this old Greek Pie-thuh-gorus, who said you shouldn't kill things because they might haunt you or something. Now when he was drunk in the theater . . ." Spangler chuckled.

465

David recalled a story of old Junius Brutus. "Wasn't he the one who died for a long time on stage, and then got up and said to the audience, 'How did you like that?'"

"*Othello*." Spangler nodded. "Then there were times when he'd have his sword in his hand and he'd go after the other actor and he'd really try to kill him; and they'd all have to go and sit on him to quiet him down."

"I thought you said he never killed anything."

"That was sober. Drunk he was a terror. Once he was so bad that they went and locked him in his dressing room, raving from drink. But he had a friend who would come and bring a bottle and stand outside the locked door while old Junius Brutus put a straw through the keyhole and slurped up the whiskey from the other side."

"Was he as good an actor as his son Edwin?"

"Well, he was a lot stranger, I guess. Once, he befriended this horse-thief in Lexington, Kentucky. But he couldn't save him. So after the man was hanged, old Junius Brutus got ahold of the body and gave it a Christian burial, after first taking off the man's head, which he went and cooked to the bone. Then always, ever after, he used that skull whenever he played Hamlet in that scene with the skull."

David shuddered with delight. "That is downright ghoulish."

Spangler nodded. "It's also kind of ghoulish that to this day when Edwin plays Hamlet *he* uses the same horse-thief's skull."

In the foyer of Grover's Theater, Hay and Kate Chase (Sprague-to-be in less than two weeks' time) held court beneath the hissing gaslights. Ladies in vast crinolines promenaded up and down. This season the colors were vivid but deep—mostly burgundy reds and forest greens; and deepest black for widows not yet merry but no longer in full mourning. Kate wore green velvet; and a frown. Hay had been pleasantly surprised when she had proposed that he take her to the theater; and then to Harvey's Oyster Saloon. "My bachelor days are almost over," she had somewhat startlingly said. But then, as Hay told Nicolay in an exuberant moment, "She is her father's son."

Hay and Kate stood against the wall beneath a copy of a copy of the celebrated painting of Mrs. Siddons. As people came up to pay Kate their compliments, she was her usual regal self. Hay also received a good deal of deference from men twice and three times his age. All in all, it was a very fine thing to be the second secretary to a president during a war when everyone in the nation wanted something from the government. The tidal waves of money that Chase had sent forth into the world from his printing press at the Treasury were now, like the tide at full moon, sweeping back into the capital, where decorous honest-faced gentlemen with gray hair and beards and kindly smiles had forgathered to scoop up in their buckets as much of the green paper sea as they could. Simon Cameron, the first lord of corruption himself, approached them. "Ah, Miss Kate, what a union it is!"

Kate gave him a sidelong smile. "Surely, General Cameron, with eleven states gone out of it..."

Cameron laughed. "You know which union I mean. How fortunate Governor Sprague is!"

"You will not be at the reception?" Since Kate was now a full-time political manager, invitations to Sixth and E were sent out in a spirit of perfect calculation. Alone of the enemy camp, Hay was invited regularly. But Kate liked to tease him; and he her. She also liked to quiz him about the President; but he never told her anything of the slightest use. In fact, he often let slip an occasional false fact in order to confuse the Chase faction, which was now headed by a corrupt Kansas senator named Pomeroy; and, of course, the brothers Cooke and Senator Sprague.

"I am *only* here," lied Cameron in his thin whispery voice, "to celebrate your nuptials."

"How good you are!" Kate gave him the full radiance of her eyes, now pale as agate by gaslight.

"What news," asked Cameron of Hay, "from the West?"

"I was there only two weeks," said Hay. He had been sent to Ohio and Illinois by the President to keep an eye on the state elections. Neither Lincoln nor Stanton had made the same mistake that had been made in the disastrous November elections of the previous year. Regiments from the doubtful states were sent home on furlough to vote. When General Grant refused to send his forty thousand Ohio troops back home to vote, Stanton had arranged for them to vote in the field; something without precedent. Needless to say, the forty thousand voted almost unanimously for the Republican Party; and Ohio state was once again Republican. Except for New Jersey, the states were now all Republican. But Congress, reflecting the previous year's election, still had a strong Democratic opposition.

"Well, Mr. Hay, I'm glad the President followed my advice on bringing some of the troops home to vote. We would've lost Governor Curtin back home, if we hadn't. Not," and Cameron glowered, "that that would be any true loss in itself." Cameron disappeared into the crowd.

General Dan Sickles, on crutches, paid his compliments. Lately, he and Hay had become most friendly. Sickles was very much enjoying himself as the hero of Gettysburg. "I won't be able to

467

dance at your wedding, Miss Kate," he said, eyes bright. "But I'll be stamping one leg during the quadrilles."

"I shall be cheering *you*, General Sickles. And weaving you a wreath of laurel."

As Sickles stumped off, Hay said, "It is amazing the change in his character since he lost that leg. It's as if all the scandal had been washed away, and he's reborn, a hero."

"But he has always been a hero. Any man who kills his wife's lover is a hero to me." Kate held up her fan to hide the lower part of her face so that Hay could not tell if she was serious or not.

"But everyone says that Mr. Key was *not* her lover."

"It is the thought, Mr. Hay, that excites me." They were then joined if not by lovers by a young man and a young woman visibly enamored of him. Though Bessie Hale was still in her twenties, she looked middle-aged. She was plump; had more than one chin; blushed easily but not evenly. The young man was none other than the youngest star in the world, John Wilkes Booth. Both Kate and Hay had seen him in the spring at Grover's, where he had played, most athletically, *Richard III*, a play in which his father and two brothers had distinguished themselves. Everyone thought it daring of Wilkes, as he was known, to compete with famous father and older brothers. Devoted theatergoers felt that he had not really competed, as he was not of their class. But the theater had been sold out during his engagement. If nothing else, the combination of famous name and extraordinary beauty had indeed made him if not the youngest world star, at least a popular performer.

"Oh, Katie!" Bessie was red and white in the face with excitement. Of all Washington's girls, it was she who had netted this longed-for beauty. "You know Mr. Wilkes Booth. We saw him here together. Remember?"

"How," said Kate, demurely, "could I forget the handsomest man in America?"

Booth bowed low over Kate's hand. He *was* handsome, thought Hay, irritably. The hair was dark and curly—storm-tossed, romantically, like Lord Byron's. The skin was pale and smooth, while the moustache was like Hay's, but where Hay's was somewhat gingery and wiry, Booth's was smooth and dark and silky. The brow seemed carved in ivory, while the lustrous eyes were the color of palest honey. The hand that shook Hay's hand was surprisingly large and muscular for so short a man; but then Booth was as muscular as an acrobat, as anyone who had seen him cavort about the stage could testify. In *Richard III*, he had leapt some fifteen feet from stage-mountain to stage-field in search of a horse

468

to exchange for his kingdom. Hay had never so much disliked anyone on first sight. But Booth was a charmer; and charmed Kate, easily; and Hay, gradually. He spoke of the play they were to see, *The Pearl of Savoy*. "If acted well, it has its moments. I saw it in Richmond when I was playing there."

"Richmond?" Kate's eyes widened. "You play in the enemy capital."

Booth's teeth were white and even; was he *all* perfection? Hay wondered. "That was two years before the war. I was only nineteen..."

"The *youngest* star...?" Kate was inquiring.

"Well, I was young. And I was a lead. But it was Mr. Grover who made up that billing for me last spring. Anyway, I liked Richmond because they put up with me. It's not like New York, where everyone says that I am raw and crude and not as good as my father or brothers. Apparently, I'm supposed to wait until I'm old; or my brothers stop. Anyway, it is true, Miss Chase, that you are the most beautiful young woman in Washington. As Miss Hale," he turned tactfully to Bessie, "warned me."

"Are they not the most beautiful couple?" breathed Bessie. "Katie and..."

"Me?" asked Hay, innocently.

"No, Mr. Booth. Not," added Bessie, whose father was hostile to Lincoln, "that Mr. Hay hasn't his own wholesome charm."

"Wholesome," murmured Kate. "The very word."

"Perhaps Mr. Barnum should put the two of you in his circus," said Hay, unable to control himself. "You could stand side by side on the stage, like statues, and everyone would worship."

"Do you think they really would?" asked Kate with every appearance of seriousness.

"Oh, yes!" Bessie was all seriousness and without jealousy. "What a sight!"

"*Pay* to see us?" Kate was persistent.

"Mr. Barnum can get people to pay to see absolutely anything," said Hay, noticing that Booth's physical perfection was marred by his own initials crudely tattooed in ink on the back of one hand.

"I am willing, Miss Chase." Booth's eyes gleamed. "We shall appear all in white, like Greek gods."

"As reproduced in marble or in plaster?" Hay was benign.

"Oh, Mr. Hay, like clouds from Olympus," said Kate, well pleased with her conceit—and conquest.

Hay and Kate took their seats in the so-called presidential box, also occupied by Lord Lyons and members of his staff. Lyons made much of Kate and saw to it that she sat in the presidential rocker, with the best view of the stage, though even the best view from the box was none too good. In order not to appear monarchial, both Grover and Ford had built, to the left and right of the stage, in the first gallery or dress circle, large boxes that could be divided into two if necessary. These boxes were so angled that the occupants were not visible to the audience since curtains screened whoever sat in them; only the actors on stage had a good view of who was in the box, while the occupants' view of the stage was somewhat skewed. Lately, since Madam's mourning had ceased, the Lincolns had become devoted theatergoers. Madam preferred opera; the Tycoon Shakespeare—and farce. So sometimes he went alone or with Hay to his Shakespeare, while she went with friends— often Senator Sumner—to her Italian operas and German operettas. Usually, at the last moment, Lincoln would ask Hay to see if Grover or Ford would allow him to slip, unnoticed, into the theater; usually, both managers were delighted to be of service. Lincoln would wait in a side street until the curtain had gone up. Then he would hurry upstairs to the box, a policeman at his side. Lamon was often in attendance.

"What," asked Kate, as the overture began in the pit, "does the handsomest man in America see in Bessie Hale?"

"Adoration."

"Oh, *that.*" Kate was cool. "I should have thought that he was oversupplied with that commodity."

"Perhaps it is her intellect." Hay hastily removed his feet which had been nearly sliced off by Kate's sudden vigorous rocking of the presidential rocker.

"I must say it is mysterious," said Kate, looking about the box.

Lord Lyons thought that she had spoken to him. "What is mysterious, Miss Chase?" asked his lordship, the usual small smile at the corners of his lips.

"Masculine beauty and its effect on women—and others," said Kate, delicately nudging Hay.

But Lord Lyons was never to be caught out. "You allude to my own beauty, of course; and its universal effect. Personally, I find it a burden. But, as a diplomat, it has its uses. In the service of my country, I do dazzle deliberately."

"'*Mine* eyes dazzle,'" quoted Kate, allowing him the round.

"But," Lyons finished off the quotation, "he did not die young, despite Washington and its fevers."

The previous March, when Lord Lyons had appeared in full uniform to announce the marriage of the Prince of Wales to a Danish princess, the President had received the solemn news most solemnly; and then he had said to Lord Lyons, "Go thou and do likewise."

Grover's new curtain with its painting of a bust of Shakespeare
470

now rose; the lights dimmed. Attentively, Hay followed the play, which was highly romantic and highflown. During an emotional scene of lovers parting, he heard a gasp beside him. He turned and in the half-light from the stage saw that Kate had a fist to her mouth as she tried, unsuccessfully, to stifle sobs. Tears flowed. She saw him look at her; she shook her head, as if to say that she could not stop and that he must look away, which he did.

Later, at Harvey's Oyster Saloon, beneath the huge immobile fans, Kate made no allusion to her tears; nor did Hay. They sat at a table in a corner and ate oyster stew. "The first Rappahannock oysters in two years," said the smiling waiter, ladling from a pewter tureen the steaming contents into thick china bowls. Waiters came and went across the white-and-black tessellated marble floor, heels clicking like those of Mr. Barnum's Spanish dancers. At the table opposite, General Dan Sickles presided over a group of senior officers and handsome ladies, none his wife but each someone's respectable wife—highly refined but absolute lines of propriety were drawn in certain rooms at Harvey's; in others not, as Hay had enjoyed from time to time. Once he had even brought Azadia from Sal's to the upstairs room. To those whom he happened to know, he introduced her as the daughter of Governor Seymour of New York. If word of this caper had got back to the Ancient, he had said nothing to Hay. But then on the subject of the ladies, the Ancient was always mute if never deaf. He very much enjoyed dancers; and he and Hay would both ogle them as they stood, enticingly, in the wings, waiting to go on. Once, both President and secretary had been entranced by the same pretty dancer, until the Tycoon had noted her enormous feet. "I fear," he had murmured, "no beetle would have a chance with her." The unobstructed—and uninhibited—view of backstage was the only advantage of the presidential box.

"Where do you go after . . . afterwards?" Neither Hay nor Kate alluded directly to the coming wedding.

"We go to Providence to see . . . *Fanny.*" Kate pronounced the name comically. "My prospective mother-in-law is a lady of much energy."

"I know. I used to see her when I was at Brown. She is a dragon."

Kate did not acknowledge Fanny's dragonhood. "Then we go to Ohio, where Father wants me to be seen by all. You know, they call me 'Kate the Shrew' in the newspapers back home. I can't think why. Am I shrewish?"

"Hardly. Perhaps," Hay lowered his voice to a conspiratorial whisper, "they envy you."

"Oh, surely, not that!" Kate put down her spoon with a crash

471

on the marble-topped table, much ringed by a generation of steaming oyster stews. "And I so simple, so unadorned, so self-effacing . . ."

"Plain, too," said Hay, thinking of Booth.

"True. My nose is too pug, according to General Garfield."

"He told you?"

"No, he told his wife, who told everyone else in Ohio."

"He is a blackguard . . ."

"Call him out."

"I shall. A blackguard; and afraid of you."

"No one is afraid of me." Kate frowned. "I wish they were."

"I am."

"Oh, you! When will *you* marry?"

"I am only a boy."

"Boys grow up, occasionally."

"If you had waited for me, I would have married you." Hay could not believe what he had said.

But Kate could believe it. "There was no time, ever, for us," she said, reflectively. "There is not much time for anyone, really. We must all move with such haste toward . . . our goals."

The Washington correspondent of the Cincinnati *Gazette*, Whitelaw Reid, stopped at their table. Kate achieved a dazzling smile for the friend and partisan of her father while Hay gave him a quick wink. Reid was only a year or two older than Hay, and though the two young men were in opposing camps, they enjoyed each other's company. After the usual compliments, Reid asked Hay whether or not Frank Blair, Junior, would be returning to Congress.

The Blair impasse, as it was known at the White House, had, lately, grown more than ever impass-ive. Frank Blair, Junior, had refused to give up his seat in Congress; he had, also, refused to give up his command in the field. Currently, as a major-general, he was serving with great distinction under Sherman in the west. Since Blair himself would never give up either place, the President or Congress must decide for him.

"I have no idea," said Hay, who knew that the Tycoon had already made up his mind. Blair would come back to Congress, and help organize it for the Administration. He would be proposed for Speaker. If elected Speaker, he would resign from the army and remain in Congress. If he was not elected, he would re-join Sherman and Grant, who were well pleased with the only politician-general, in Sherman's phrase, "worth a damn."

"He's certainly making a lot of commotion," said Reid, smiling at Kate. "The speech at St. Louis—"

"—was vile!" Suddenly, Kate was no longer the languorous

472

bride-to-be but an angry politician. "To attack my father for trade permits with the enemy when he does nothing, nothing at all, for Governor Sprague who is desperate for a permit. Oh, how I would like to see Mr. Blair on the nearest gallows!"

Hay looked at Kate; and saw that she was serious. Reid saw the same; and excused himself. Kate turned to Hay. "They are as good as rebels, that family, and why Mr. Lincoln indulges them is beyond me."

"Well, they are moderates like the President."

"I thought Mr. Stanton had relieved General Blair and..." Kate suddenly stopped—aware that she was not supposed to know of a curious exchange between President and Secretary of War. After the St. Louis speech, Stanton had relieved Blair of his command. Lincoln had then ordered Stanton to reinstate him. There had been much confusion, not to say embarrassment, all around. Both Hay and Nicolay assumed that Stanton was now working, secretly, in Chase's interest. Whatever the Tycoon may have thought, he did not say. But he had been angry with Stanton. The Blairs, needless to say, were up in arms. They had vowed to destroy Chase and Stanton and all their other enemies. Should they succeed in this, Hay had told Nico, North America would again be a primeval wilderness.

"There was," said Hay, mildly, "a misunderstanding. Anyway, General Blair is still a general and he's still a congressman and he'll be taking his seat this winter with the others."

"My father is a saint," said Kate, refusing more stew from the tureen. "He forgives his enemies."

"You don't?"

"I don't."

"But you don't have any."

"Oh, but I do." Kate's smile was radiant. "I live for my enemies."

As they were finishing their stewed Rappahannock oysters, David Herold began his humble fried Chesapeake oysters. He could not believe his luck. After the theater, he had gone with Spangler to Scala's restaurant and bar. While he and Spangler were sitting at the end of a long table, drinking beer and watching the various theatricals at their supper, Wilkes Booth and a slender, pretty, blond girl came into the restaurant. Scala greeted them warmly: and showed them to a table in the back.

"That's not the girl he was at the theater with." During the performance, David had spotted Booth in the audience.

"I guess he's gone changed his tie, you might say," said Spangler, with a broken-tooth grin. "I never saw such a boy for girls or, I reckon, so many girls for just one boy. Even when he was

473

still growing up, there was always girls hanging about him. He's always had his pick."

"Oh, that is rich, isn't it?" David stared at the dark actor and blond girl; and he wondered what it would have been like had he, not Wilkes, been Junius Brutus's son. Certainly, he would not have had to work as a stagehand or a prescription clerk. He would have been an actor, too. As he stared at the young actor, he was suddenly aware that there was a physical resemblance between Wilkes Booth and himself. Each had coal-black curling hair and pale eyes. They could have been twins, he thought, were it not for his own slightly bucked two front teeth and ruddy coloring, so unlike the alabaster pallor of the youngest star. They were hardly twins; but they could have been brothers.

"He's secesh," said Spangler, himself devoted to the Confederacy though not one to do anything about it.

"So why don't he go home and fight for us?"

Booth himself answered David's question at Sullivan's later that night. As Booth and the blond girl left Skippy's, Booth had greeted Spangler warmly; and introduced the young woman, Miss Turner, to "Old Ed Spangler, who practically brought me up back in Maryland." The girl had smiled sweetly; and said nothing. When Spangler invited them for a drink, Booth had said that he must accompany Miss Turner home but he might join them later. When David mentioned Sullivan's Saloon, Booth had looked knowing.

They sat in the back of the long barroom, only half filled at this late hour. Sullivan had recognized Booth. "A great honor, sir. You'll be wanting privacy, I know," he said. Sullivan indicated a group of Yankees at the bar. Sullivan's smile was merry; but the look he gave David was one of warning.

Spangler and Booth and David sat at a table with pinewood walls on three sides. Booth ordered a bottle of French brandy, and three glasses. David had never seen anyone drink as much as the actor; and hold it so well. He himself drank sparingly, while Spangler got drunk.

"I promised my mother I wouldn't go fight," said Booth, fixing slightly bloodshot eyes on David. "Why haven't *you* gone?"

"They want me here. At Thompson's Drug Store. You see, I get to run errands. I get to go to the White House and the War Department and Mr. Seward's house and General McClellan's house when he was here. I find out things for the Colonel."

"You know the Colonel?" Booth had now lowered his voice from stage whisper to real whisper.

"No, sir. But he gets word to me and I to him, if it's important."

"I don't know him," said Booth. "I'd like to. I think sometimes I know who he is. Canada."

"Canada?"

Booth nodded. "That's where we have some of our best men. They gather information. They deal with England and France and our friends in New York."

Spangler had been running his black thumbnail up and down a deep crack in the table. "Davie's a night-rider, too. You tell Wilkes here about your rides."

David blushed. He had boasted, from time to time, of dangerous rides to Richmond through the Yankee lines. Actually, he had never been sent farther than Fredericksburg. But he was not about to admit to Booth that he had been lying to Spangler. So he half shut his eyes in order to look mysterious; and said, "Oh, we're not supposed to talk about the rides. Anyway, I don't go that often."

"What route do you take?"

Booth's question was unexpectedly to the point.

"It varies, sir. But I generally cross through Maryland at . . . Surrattsville."

Booth nodded. "I've heard of the Surratt family there. I know a lot of people in the area, and I know some of the roads. But not all of them."

"I was in Surrattsville last Easter." This was true. Annie had invited David to spend the holiday with her family. The Surratt house contained not only rooms for rent and a bar, but also the post office where John was postmaster—and would be postmaster until next month when, on November 15, he was to be replaced. Currently he was in Washington looking for a job. Several members of the Marine Band had also spent Easter with the Surratts. They were all ardent secessionists.

David proceeded to repeat to Booth one of John's most hazardous rides to Richmond, adding details freely. As he talked, Booth grew more and more interested; and drank more and more brandy. David could not believe that he, David E. Herold of the Navy Yard and Thompson's Drug Store, was holding enthralled the handsomest actor in America. There was not a girl in Washington who would not have given her most precious possession— very nearly, anyway—to be where he was, facing the pale beautiful Wilkes Booth, so like a somewhat flattering if older mirror image of himself.

When David had finished, Booth poured himself more brandy and said, "If I were not so known, that is what I would be doing. But we all do what we can where we are. The Colonel's right. You're in the best place possible at Thompson's."

"I know," said David, sadly. He had been thinking, most seriously, of giving up his job. He was sick of the work and although he enjoyed exaggerating the importance of the information he was able to collect, he knew that he was really of no use to the Confederacy, not like John Surratt, who still rode nights to Richmond.

"Does Thompson know you're a stagehand, too?"

David shook his head, which had begun, slightly, to ache from brandy. "He thinks I've got a light case of the smallpox. He thinks I'm home in bed."

"Good. Then you can work for me at Ford's. I start rehearsing tomorrow. I'm booked for two weeks."

"I'd like nothing better, sir."

"Call me Wilkes."

"Yes, sir. Wilkes."

"I taught that boy to shoot," said Spangler, pointing an unsteady finger at Booth; then his chin dropped on his chest and he slept.

"I'm a good shot, too, thanks to old Ed. My father thought the world of Ed Spangler. So you really know the roads well in that part of Maryland?" Booth then asked about the various back roads to Richmond. David told him what he knew, adding honestly, "John Surratt's the one who can help you most. He lives there, and he rides most nights; or did till recently. He's in the city now."

"I'd like to meet him." Booth pulled out his watch. "I have a lady waiting for me."

"Is that the lady from the theater?" David was made bold by brandy.

Booth laughed. "Mine is the most ravished body since the Trojan War—or Byron's anyway. But I've not yet been out-and-out raped. No, Davie, the lady at the theater is Miss Hale, daughter of the senator from New Hampshire, and a source of many sweet nothings and a few hard facts about Yankee naval affairs, as her father is chairman of that committee. I learn from her things we need to know, while she learns from me—what it is to love!"

"So it is the other, Miss Ella."

"It is Miss Ella who waits for me in room Twenty-nine of the National Hotel. You come there, too. No, not now, Davie. Tomorrow, at eight in the morning. We'll have breakfast in the dining room." Booth finished the last of the brandy. The ivory of his face was now coral pink, and the eyes were slightly glassy. But the voice had not become in any way loud or slurred; rather, it had become very low and precise, as he whispered to David, "You must poison Old Abe, and soon."

"That's what John said." David was startled; did Booth know John? And if he did, why did he not say so?

476

"I know the arguments against." Booth's voice was that of Iago now; or, rather, of his brother Edwin playing Iago. "That he is good for us because he is so poor a President. This is true, of course. But the Yankees are starting to win victories in the West."

"Nothing like ours . . ." David began.

"Nothing like ours. But we are short of men. Listen, David, the reason why we must kill him now is very simple. If he lives, he is bound to be reelected next November; and the war will go on and on, and we will run out of men long before the Yankees do."

"But whoever they elect, the war will go on."

Booth shook his head. "If Lincoln is not the candidate, the Democrats will win, and the new president, McClellan, will make peace on our terms."

"Is he really one of us?" David had heard for years that McClellan was a Knight of the Golden Circle, a secret society of Northerners in sympathy with the South.

"I cannot say." Wilkes Booth rose. "But I know that if he is president, he will give us what we want. So . . ." Booth raised an eyebrow. "Good-night, Davie. Say good-night to Old Ed, when he wakes up. Or good morning, it that's more suitable."

"Good-night, sir. Wilkes." Booth was gone. David was surprised at how calm he himself was. He had been taken into the confidence of the famous star, who had asked him, in the most agreeable way, to murder the President. In theory, David was perfectly willing to remove Old Abe from the vale of tears in which all were at present dwelling. But how? You did not put arsenic into a laxative. The President would taste it, and spit it out. Even if Lincoln did happen to take it and die, everyone would know that someone at Thompson's Drug Store had poisoned his blue mass. Of course, David could just disappear as soon as the delivery was made to the Mansion. But where would he go? He did not fancy serving in the Confederate Army. Half the haggard ragged young men in Washington—not to mention at Sullivan's—were deserters from the Confederate Army or captives who had been let go after taking the oath of allegiance to the Union. On the other hand, if he did succeed in poisoning Lincoln, he would be a hero at Richmond. So perhaps he really would take a night ride through the lines, and report to President Davis that his rival was dead; at David's hands.

But what, he wondered, would be the best poison to use? It would have to have little or no taste; and act quickly. Ideally, its effects should resemble a familiar illness like bilious fever or the smallpox . . .

*   *   *

"You don't think it's the smallpox?" Mary stood beside Tad's bed while the doctor took the boy's pulse. Tad's face was flushed with fever; and his usual odd babble was now incomprehensible even to Mary as he drifted in and out of fever-dreams.

"It's too soon to say, Mrs. Lincoln. I doubt that it is. But we'll know by tomorrow, when the symptoms start or, let us pray, don't start."

"My God! Poor Taddie!"

Lincoln appeared in the doorway. "What is wrong?"

"The smallpox!" she cried.

"No," said the doctor. "There are no true signs as yet. Simply a fever."

Keckley appeared. "Come, Mrs. Lincoln, you must get ready for the wedding."

"No. I shall not go! Nor will you, Father. Not with Taddie so ill."

"He is not that ill, Mrs. Lincoln," said the doctor.

"You hear that?" Then Keckley motioned for Lincoln to remove Mary, which he did. More and more did Keckley manage Mrs. Lincoln, with the President's connivance.

In the bedroom, Lincoln dressed for the wedding; but Mary did not. "You can say Taddie's ill. Or I'm ill. Or I'm still in mourning. Tell the Chases anything. I don't care. I won't go."

"As you like, Mother." Lincoln stood in front of the pier glass and tied his white cravat.

"You ought not to go either." Mary watched her husband's reflection in the mirror. He was now far too thin; but he would not eat. Tonight he had refused his favorite dish, fricassee of chicken with biscuits and gravy.

"Mr. Chase is my Secretary of the Treasury."

"He is your rival for the nomination. He works against you every day. He's as busy as a . . . as a . . ."

"As a bluebottle fly. Wherever there's something gone bad or rotten, he lays his eggs."

"He'll be nominated, Father. He'll be elected!"

"May we never have a worse president," said Lincoln, idly. He changed the subject. "I can find out nothing about Little Emilie. She's not in Lexington. I suppose she's still at the deep South someplace."

Mary's eyes filled with tears. "Poor Ben. Poor Little Sister, a widow at her age."

"There are many young widows now. It is the brutal fashion."

Mary helped Lincoln into his coat. "I have lost three brothers," she said, more with wonder than with sorrow.

For Chase, this was a day of both wonder and sorrow; of pride, as well. Kate seemed to radiate light from her own person. She wore a gown of white velvet and real point lace; and a veil into which had been worked orange flowers. On her head, she wore not a tiara but a crown of diamonds and pearls, the gift of Sprague. Everyone had remarked that she was now even more splendid than the French empress.

Fifty friends were in the rear parlor, which had been decorated in red and white and blue. Later, five hundred guests would come for the wedding reception. In the rooms upstairs, Gautier and his waiters had laid out a splendid buffet. For the last time, Chase was a hundred dollars overdrawn at the bank. From now on, as Sprague had made clear, all expenses as Sixth and E would be met by him.

In the sealed-off front parlor, an altar had been placed before the fireplace, where stood a clergyman in full vestments. Sprague and his cousin Byron stood to the left of the altar, while Chase, sporting a new silk grenadine waistcoat from France, stood next to Kate, his arm through hers. Nettie, also in white, was bridesmaid. In silence, they waited until the hands of the clock settled at thirty minutes past eight; then servants threw open the doors between the parlors.

There was applause from the guests when they saw the brilliant tableau. Kate suddenly shuddered. Chase looked at her from the corner of his right eye, whose peripheral vision was perfect. She appeared, as always, serene. Perhaps she had felt a draft. Certainly, this was a happy moment for the two of them, since they would never now, on this earth at least, be separated.

The minister proceeded to marry Kate Chase to William Sprague the Fourth. Chase then gave his daughter to Sprague, whose cousin gave him the ring which he, eventually, got onto her finger. Once they were married, it was Chase not Sprague who kissed the bride. "God blesh you, my child," he heard himself, with horror, lisp.

As the room filled up with people, from the dining room the Marine Band struck up "The Kate Chase Wedding March," written especially for the occasion.

Seward arrived with his daughter-in-law. "We shall see," he said, rather roguishly, "just who is here and who is not."

But to Seward's disappointment, the entire Cabinet was in attendance, except for Montgomery Blair, now the sworn enemy of Chase and all his works. The President was planning to come, Hay assured the premier, as they watched Kate do the quadrille with Mercier in the dining room, where the entire Marine Band had been crowded into one small alcove.

"It is curious," said Seward, as he was shoved back against a

479

wall, "how reluctant we are in these states to acknowledge that grand entertainments are now the rule not the exception."

"You mean, sir," said Hay, "there are no ballrooms?"

"I mean exactly that. We empty the bedrooms to accommodate the buffet tables, and we turn the dining room into a place to dance."

"And the front parlor," said Hay, "into a chapel."

Seward laughed delightedly. "Exactly! What other nation's minister of the treasury would not have his own private chapel, frescoed by Michelangelo?"

To Seward's surprise, Henry D. Cooke approached him as if they were the best of friends, and Henry D. himself not under a cloud no darker than a Union soldier's tunic. Hay slipped away: he wanted no part of Mr. Cooke.

"Mr. Seward!" Henry D. shook the premier's unenthusiastic and so entirely limp hand. "I have wanted to talk to you for some time now about all that nonsense back in Ohio."

"Surely Mr. Stanton is more apt to be . . . useful when it comes to what you call nonsense and the world calls embezzlement."

Henry D. took this calmly. "There has been no trial, Mr. Seward, so we don't know what my partner really did as opposed to what the Democratic papers say that he did."

"In July," said Seward, suddenly precise, "he was arrested by General Burnside for having stolen government funds." Lincoln had been appalled when the word reached Washington of the arrest of F. W. Hurtt, who, together with Henry D. Cooke and Isaac J. Allen, owned the *Ohio State Journal*, a pro-Lincoln newspaper in the state's capital.

Earlier in the year, Hurtt had turned the paper's editorship over to Allen; then he had been commissioned an army captain and stationed at Cincinnati. As an army quartermaster, Hurtt then proceeded to steal everything in sight. Unknown to Henry D., Seward had read letters between the partners. From these letters, it was clear that Henry D. was not only very much aware of what was going on but he may well have diverted government funds to Hurtt. Fortunately, the scandal had not affected the October election. Hurtt was now due to go to trial in February. Chase had asked the President to intervene, which had delighted Seward. Let Chase appear as Hurtt's sponsor, and that would be the end of Chase's increasingly furious drive for the presidency.

To Seward's amazement, Henry D. now said, "We think it might be a good idea if our partner Mr. Allen were to go abroad for a while. Since the consulship at Bangkok is unfilled, my brother and I wondered if you might not send Mr. Allen there."

Seward had spent the better part of a lifetime in never being taken aback. But this was dizzying. "Mr. Cooke, in the midst of a scandal involving God knows how many people, you would have me... the Administration, that is... assign a post of honor"— Seward quite liked the phrase, particularly when applied to swampy Bangkok—"to one of the principals?"

"Well, Governor, it's not all that bad—just yet, anyway." Henry D. was cool. "What we have to remember is that my brother, Jay, single-handedly, is financing this war."

"He himself is not doing too badly out of the war." Seward knew that Chase often passed on to Jay Cooke news of military victories or defeats before the press reports, so that Cooke's bank could then buy or sell bonds and gold in advance of the market. Seward had wanted Lincoln to expose this practise, but Lincoln had taken the line that there was nothing illegal in what might be no more than indiscretion. On the other hand, if Seward could prove that Chase was being paid for information, that was another matter. To date, Seward had found no instance of outright dishonesty on Chase's part.

"Jay's business is open to inspection," said Henry D. "He has nothing to hide. But the point is this. We are all Republicans. We're going to have enough trouble next year with the Democrats without a major scandal in Ohio. Drop the charges against Hurtt, and he'll go abroad. Send Allen to Siam."

"And what about you, Mr. Cooke?" Seward cocked an eyebrow. "Shall I make you minister to Spain?"

"Oh, I'd like that, Governor. But I'm otherwise engaged with... my brother."

"And with Mr. Chase," Seward could not resist adding.

"We think the world of Mr. Chase," said Henry D., smoothly. Then the butler in the front parlor shouted, "Ladies and gentlemen, the President!"

Lincoln stood tall and fragile in the doorway. The President looked most elegant, thought Chase, as he hurried forward to greet the First Magistrate. But Hay, in the second parlor, thought that the Ancient was looking most unwell.

Chase said, "Welcome, sir! Our joy is now complete. Katie..."

Mrs. William Sprague and consort were duly presented to the President, who gave Kate a small package, which she opened, to reveal an ivory fan. "I brought it myself, since someone forgot to send it along with your other presents." Lincoln smiled at Kate, who opened the fan and exclaimed, "It is very beautiful."

Congratulations were given and received. Wedding presents were discussed. Chase had been amazed by the extent of the presents, not to mention the value—over one hundred thousand dollars' worth had been the estimate of a Treasury aide.

Then Fanny Sprague, small and imperious, fell upon the President. "I would vote for you," she said, "if women could vote. But I suppose you'll go let the niggers vote before we do!" Chase maintained his dignity, as did the President, who observed, "You know, back in Illinois, I sort of favored giving the ladies the vote."

"But now you've changed. You do something about it!" She rounded on her son.

"I can't, Mother."

"Yes, you can. But you never do anything right. Why is there such a draft in here?"

The style of the son had plainly been formed by the mother, thought Chase. Happily, the President was amused. "Perhaps we'll give the vote first to the white women and then to the Negro women. Then we'll include the Negro men..."

Sprague abandoned new wife and old mother; and went upstairs, where he found what he wanted in the first of Gautier's well-stocked rooms. As Sprague received a glass of the Widow from a waiter, he was joined by Hiram Barney, the collector of customs at the port of New York. Barney was a Republican attorney, who had raised thirty-five thousand dollars for Lincoln's campaign in 1860, for which he had been rewarded with the lucrative collectorship. Although Barney was a member of the Treasury Department, he was not yet a part of the Chase-for-president movement. Nevertheless, Barney maintained the most friendly relations with Chase; he had even lent him five thousand dollars. In exchange, Chase had threatened to resign if the President should insist on Barney's replacement. Lincoln had given way, even though he feared that the Administration would one day be embarrassed by Barney, whose conduct of his office was slipshod, while his political views were radical, and so anathema to New York's Republicans.

Barney was also a friend of Sprague's; and of Harris Hoyt. "He's escaped," said Barney in a low voice, as he allowed a waiter to carve him a number of slices from a Virginia ham so thoroughly cured that it was more black than red. "The doctor says I am not to eat salt," he said, chewing the ham slowly. "But I am disobedient. He is in Matamoros, Mexico."

Sprague looked at Barney; and said nothing. During the last spring and summer, thanks to Hoyt, a fair amount of cotton had found its way from Texas to Rhode Island. It was Barney who had helped Hoyt get his guns through New York customs. Officially, the guns were intended for the Spanish provincial government at Havana. In due course, guns and cotton mill had arrived in Texas by way of Havana and Matamoros, a port just below Confederate-held Galveston. Hoyt had immediately gone to General Magru-
482

der—late of Jamestown—and got his permit to establish a cotton mill. Magruder had then asked for a further ten thousand stand of rifles in exchange for which Hoyt would be exempted from impressment for two thousand bales of cotton, to be exported to A. & W. Sprague & Company. But since Hoyt did not have the rifles, he decided to run for it, with the cotton. Shortly before he was about to sail, Hoyt was arrested at Magruder's order. Now, somehow, according to Barney, he had escaped; nor did Barney say how it was that he had heard the news, but, "He'll be in New York some time this winter."

"Damn fool," said Sprague, finishing the champagne. "Bad enough for that ship of his to get caught in the blockade. Now he goes and ruins himself with the Texans. He can't go back. So what do we do?"

"Let us hope that the war will end soon." Barney was not helpful.

"Lucky there was nothing about any of us on that boat they caught. What was it called?"

"*America*," said Barney, mouth filled with ham.

"Well, we made sixty percent on our investment in Hoyt." Sprague brightened somewhat. "That ain't too bad."

The buffet rooms began to fill up with guests. Hay suddenly found himself in front of the wedding cake, where stood Bessie Hale and the actor Wilkes Booth. "I saw you last night," said Hay to Booth. "You were Romeo."

"He is always Romeo," breathed Bessie.

"Mercutio has the better part." Booth was somewhat sour. "Romeo is a hopeless sort of character to play. But he's what people want." Hay had admired Booth's agility. The actor had climbed like a squirrel to Juliet's balcony. Later, he had leapt off a ten-foot wall and the audience had cheered him.

"Why aren't you playing tonight?" asked Hay, aware that the Tycoon was now at the other end of the room, holding a glass of champagne in his left hand while pumping hands with the right.

"Tonight I'm producing. It's a play called *Money*. The theme," said Booth with a small smile, "is whether or not a girl should marry a man for his money."

"Why," asked Hay with, he thought, sublime innocence, "did you put that play on tonight of all nights?"

"Because," said Booth, with equal innocence, "it's the only one in my repertoire in which I don't appear. I wanted to come here, with Miss Hale and observe . . ."

"The real thing?"

"Now, Mr. Hay!" Bessie exclaimed. "They are perfectly matched, Katie and Mr. Sprague."

483

Booth glanced toward the door where Lincoln stood. "I saw him the other night—and you, too. In the box."

Hay nodded. "We enjoyed you in *The Marble Heart*." Actually, they had all been somewhat bored; and Mrs. Lincoln had nodded off.

"It was a dull performance," said Booth. Hay was always amazed at how actors knew, instinctively, if they were good or not; or, rather, if the audience was with them or not. "I'd hoped the President might have come last night. He is said to know Shakespeare well." Hay was not about to say that, after *The Marble Heart*, there was no further enthusiasm at the White House to see the world's youngest star. Also, the Tycoon did not much care for *Romeo and Juliet*.

"Would you like to meet the President?" asked Hay, politely.

Booth shook his head. "He looks much too busy and too tired to talk to an actor. So, what do *you* think of the songs?"

As an innovation, Booth had added modern sentimental songs to the various plays in his repertoire. He had been much criticized for doing this; particularly in *Richard III*. Hay said, truthfully, "I thought they were charming last night."

"You see?" Bessie turned to Booth. "I told you to take no notice of the *Sunday Chronicle*, which is practically a rebel paper, anyway."

"They called me a second-class actor," said Booth. "Did you see the article?" He turned to Hay.

Hay nodded. "I must read everything. But at least the press is a lot kinder to you than to my employer. Second-rate would be high praise for Mr. Lincoln from Horace Greeley."

"Others think," said Booth, "that if Lincoln is reelected he will be another Bonaparte. He will make himself king."

Hay laughed at the absurdity. "You must have been reading the Chicago *Times*."

Booth nodded. "I was. Curious," he said, agate stare turned toward Bessie. "The *Times* was the only paper that preferred my Romeo to William Wheatley's Mercutio."

"A sound paper," said Hay.

Booth suddenly smiled. "A sound paper," he repeated.

In the crowded first parlor, Chase was also concerned with the soundness of the press. "I can't think where these rumors come from," he said to Ben Wade. "I have in no way encouraged any one to put me forward as president. Yet they keep printing these stories like . . . like . . ."

"Like greenbacks," said Wade, his usual sneer now an amiable snarl, in honor of the nuptials. Chase had always counted on Wade as an ally. But, lately, he had sensed a certain reluctance
484

on Wade's part to commit himself. Certainly, each was a radical in regard to abolition and to the reconstruction of the once-conquered Southern states. Each was from Ohio. Each despised Lincoln. But Wade's manner to Chase had subtly altered since that confrontation between Cabinet and Senate which had not been, Chase knew, his finest hour. Lately, Senator Pomeroy had been sounding out Wade and the other powerful radicals in Congress. All preferred Chase to Lincoln and yet...

"I see you in one place and one place only, Mr. Chase," said Wade, abruptly.

"Naturally," Chase began his usual demur, "I do not put myself forward..."

"Naturally," said Wade, bluntly. "Because you can't. I see you as Chief Justice of the United States."

"Oh." Chase was entirely defeated. In dark moments, he had also seen himself in that high isolated place, out of the swift currents of history. But he could not believe that Wade was saying this to him at a moment when their faction of the party had no other alternative to Lincoln, who could not, in any case, win reelection. "There exists," said Chase, rather weakly, "a Chief Justice."

"But he is eighty-six. He has been fading rapidly for more than a decade. You know, all through Buchanan's Administration I prayed most earnestly for the life of Chief Justice Taney to be spared and, by God, I'm a little afraid I overdid the matter."

Chase laughed politely at Wade's favorite joke. None of their party had wanted Buchanan to appoint another pro-slavery, pro-states-rights Chief Justice. Fortunately, the old man had survived Buchanan's presidency; now, if he were to die within the next year, Lincoln would appoint his successor. Should Taney live more than a year, Chase, as president, would make the appointment. Chase was direct. "Frankly, Mr. Wade, I had always thought that if the appointment were mine to give, you would be my choice."

Wade looked as surprised as Wade could ever look. Then he said, "I am very moved, Mr. Chase." He had recovered his usual coolness of manner. "Am I to take this as the beginning of a trade?"

"Oh, no, no!" But Chase was pleased with the turn of the conversation. "I do not trade, of course. I merely expressed a personal sentiment that is also general."

The President was now leaving. "I seemed to have stayed two hours," he said to Chase, as Wade smiled up at him. "But then I wanted to take the cuss off the meagerness of my party of one."

"I hope Mrs. Lincoln is well." Chase was polite.

"She has her ups and downs. That bang on the head last summer still bothers her."

Ben Wade said, "Sir, I was just telling Mr. Chase what a splendid Chief Justice he would make."

Chase felt as if deep in the cellar beneath his feet a charge of dynamite had been set off. As he swayed, he wondered why others did not respond to the vibrating floor. Weakly, he said, "I told Senator Wade that *he* was my own private choice."

"Well, Mr. Wade," said Lincoln, a half smile on his lips, "you would both look mighty nice up there on that dais in the Capitol. While Mr. Chase here"—Lincoln looked down at Chase, who looked up at him, blindly, like a child expecting a kiss—"would adorn any office in the land, including the one which I, temporarily, hold so"—Lincoln's head now turned from Chase's uplifted face to that of Ben Wade's—"unworthily."

"Hardly, sir!" Chase heard himself strike the sycophantish note. "You inspire us all."

"Then come with me next week to Pennsylvania, where I'm going to need all the help that I can get, helping our greatest orator, Edward Everett, inspire the nation."

"What is happening in Pennsylvania?" asked Wade.

A servant was now helping the President into his topcoat. "We are dedicating a cemetery at Gettysburg, right on the battlefield. Governor Seward and Mr. Stanton are coming with me."

"If only I could," said Chase. As he started to describe the next week's business, the President took his hat and stick. "I have said farewell to the young married couple. Now I say it to you, Mr. Chase. Mr. Wade."

"I wish I could go with you, sir," said Chase to the President's back.

"Let the politically dead," said Wade in a voice that Chase knew that Lincoln could hear, "bury the dead."

Shocked, Chase hurried to lead the President out the front door and into the street where, late as it was, hundreds of people still watched as the carriages came and went.

When they saw the President, silhouetted, unmistakably, in the door, there was a cheer. He raised his hat. "It is for the *living*, Mr. Chase," he said serenely, "that we honor the dead. They are well out of it, as we shall be, in due course." He looked at Chase; and smiled. "Politically—or otherwise." Then Lincoln got into the presidential carriage; and drove off.

2

AT THE LAST MOMENT, MADAM DECIDED THAT SHE COULD NOT leave Tad, who was still sick, while Stanton said that he must stay at the War Department in order to follow Grant's attack on Chattanooga. So, in the end, Seward and Blair and Usher were the only members of the Cabinet to accompany the President. The ubiquitous Lamon was, as always, at Lincoln's side, while, for once, Nicolay decided that he, too, would like an outing; so both secretaries attended the President at Gettysburg.

The morning of November 19, 1863, was warm and still. Indian summer had set in. The celebrated old orator Edward Everett had already sent the President a printed copy of his speech. "My God, John!" Lincoln had said, as he sat in the special railroad car. "He will speak for two hours." Lincoln had handed the thick pamphlet to Hay; and taken off his glasses.

"I suppose that is what he's always expected to do." Hay had decided not to read what he would be obliged to hear.

"A splendid old man." Lincoln had held in one hand a single sheet of White House notepaper on which he had written half of what would be, he said, "a short, short, short speech," dedicating the cemetery. "You know, I have heard of Everett all my life, and he has always been famous, and yet I never could find out why."

"Our greatest orator?"

"Greater than Clay or Webster?" Lincoln had smiled. "No, he is just famous, that's all. There are people like that in public life. They are there, and no one ever really knows why."

They were all there the next morning on Cemetery Hill. There were seven governors, among them Seymour and Curtin; many diplomats and members of Congress. A platform had been erected, with a tall flagpole next to it. In the warm stillness, the flag hung listlessly. A military band played. A crowd of some thirty thousand people had already gathered when, finally, at ten o'clock, the presidential procession came into view, and the military band struck up "Hail to the Chief."

Lincoln rode at the head of the ragged column of notables. He sat very straight on a sorrel horse too small for him. He was like some huge effigy, thought Hay, who rode with Nico behind him. It was odd that the biggest man in the country should also

487

be among the very biggest—or at least tallest—of men. Seward looked sublimely sloppy at the Tycoon's side. Trousers pulled up to reveal thick, wrinkled gray stockings, the premier was blithely indifferent to how he or anyone else looked.

Earlier that morning, Nico had gone to the house where the President had spent the night; and he had stayed alone with the Tycoon for an hour. "What news?" asked Hay. The procession was now stopped by crowds singing, "We are coming, Father Abraham." Hay could see Lamon furiously shouting orders; but no one listened. The people wanted to see and touch the President.

"Tad is improved," said Nico.

"That is earth-shaking. What else?"

"A battle has begun at Chattanooga. Grant is attacking. Burnside is safe at Knoxville; he does not attack."

"How is the Tycoon?"

"He just finished rewording the speech an hour ago. He complains of dizziness."

Alarmed, Hay turned to Nico. "Oh, God! You know, in the train, he told me that he felt weak."

Nico nodded. "There's something wrong. I don't know what."

But if there was something wrong with the Ancient, there was nothing wrong with the Tycoon, who sat dutifully through Edward Everett's extended version of Pericles's commemoration of the Athenian dead. But where Pericles had been very much to the Attic point, Everett was to a myriad of New England points.

As the beautiful voice of Everett went on and on, Hay looked out over the battlefield. Trees had been smashed into matchwood by crossfire, while artillery shells had plowed up the muddy ground. Here and there, dead horses lay unburied; as they were not yet turned to neat bone, the smell of decomposing flesh intermingled with the odor of the crowd was mildly sickening. Now, in the noonday sun of an airless sort of day, Hay began to sweat.

When Everett sat down, Lincoln pulled out his sheet of paper; and put on his glasses. But there was a musical interval to be endured; and so he put away the paper. The Baltimore Glee Club intoned a hymn especially written for the occasion. A warm breeze started up, and the American flag began to snap like a whip cracking. Opposite the speaker's platform, a photographer had built a small platform so that his camera would be trained straight on the President when he spoke. He was constantly fiddling with his paraphernalia; raising and lowering the cloth hood at the back, and dusting his glass plates.

Finally, there was silence. Then Lamon stood up and bellowed, "The President of the United States!"

Lincoln rose, paper in hand; glasses perched on his nose. He was, Hay noted, a ghastly color, but the hand that held the paper did not tremble, always the orator's fear. There was a moment of warm—if slightly exhausted by Everett—applause.

Then the trumpet-voice sounded across the field of Gettysburg, and thirty thousand people fell silent. While Everett's voice had been like some deep rich cello, Lincoln's voice was like the sound that accompanies a sudden crack of summer lightning. "Fourscore and seven years ago," he plunged straight into his subject "our fathers brought forth upon this continent a new nation, conceived in liberty and dedicated to the proposition that all men are created equal."

That will please the radicals, thought Hay. Then he noticed two odd things. First, the Tycoon did not consult the paper in his hand. He seemed, impossibly, to have memorized the text that had been put into final form only an hour or so earlier. Second, the Tycoon was speaking with unusual slowness. He seemed to be firing each word across the battlefield—a rifle salute to the dead?

"Now we are engaged in a great civil war, testing whether that nation—or any nation, so conceived and so dedicated—can long endure."

Seated just to the right of Lincoln, Seward began actually to listen. He had heard so many thousands of speeches in his life and he had himself given so many thousands that he could seldom actually listen to any speech, including his own. He, too, noted Lincoln's unusual deliberateness. It was as if the President was now trying to justify to the nation and to history and, thought Seward, to God, what he had done.

"We are met on a great battlefield of that war. We are met to dedicate a portion of it as the final resting place of those who have given their lives that that nation might live." Seward nodded, inadvertently. Yes, that was the issue, the only issue. The preservation of this unique nation of states. Meanwhile, the photographer was trying to get the President in camera-frame.

"It is altogether fitting and proper that we should do this." Lincoln was now staring out over the heads of the crowd to a hill on which a row of wooden crosses had been newly set. For an instant, the hand that held the speech had dropped to his side. Then he recalled himself, and glanced at the text. "But, in a larger sense, we cannot dedicate, we cannot consecrate, we cannot hallow, this ground. The brave men, living and dead, who struggled here, have consecrated it, far above our power to add or to detract." Lincoln paused. There was a patter of applause; and then, to Seward's amazement, a shushing sound. The audience did not want to break into the music until it was done.

Seward studied the President with new—if entirely technical—interest. How had he accomplished this bit of magic with his singularly unmellifluous voice and harsh midwestern accent?

Lincoln was now staring off again, dreamily; this time at the sky. The photographer was under his hood, ready to take the picture.

"The world will very little note nor long remember what we say here; but it can never forget what they did here." The hand with the text again fell to his side. Hay knew that the Tycoon's eyes had turned inward. He was reading now from that marble tablet in his head; and he was reading a text written in nothing less than blood. "It is for us, the living, rather, to be dedicated, here, to the unfinished work that they have thus far so nobly carried on. It is rather for us to be here dedicated to the great task remaining before us; that from these honored dead we take increased devotion to that cause for which they here gave..." Hay was aware that the trumpet-voice had choked; and the gray eyes were suddenly aswim with uncharacteristic tears. But the Tycoon quickly recovered himself. "... the last full measure of devotion; that we here highly resolve," the voice was now that of a cavalry bugle calling for a charge, "that these dead shall not have died in vain; that the nation shall," he paused a moment then said, "under God..." Seward nodded—his advice had been taken.

Nico whispered to Hay, "He just added that. It's not in the text."

"... have a new birth of freedom, and that government of the people, by the people, for the people, shall not perish from the earth."

Lincoln stood a moment, looking thoughtfully at the crowd, which stared back at him. Then he sat down. There was some applause. There was also laughter at the photographer, who was loudly cursing: he had failed to get any picture at all.

Lincoln turned to Seward and murmured, "Well, that fell on them like a wet blanket."

In the last of the presidential cars, Lincoln stood on the rear platform. He waved to the assembled crowd with his right hand while his left hand clutched Lamon's arm. Nicolay and Hay stood just back of the President. In the elaborately appointed car there were red-and-green plush armchairs with lace antimacassars, a long horsehair lounge and, everywhere, much inlaid wood and crystal and brass. A green Brussels carpet covered the floor, while the rows of brass spittoons shone like gold.

Politicians crowded the car, each eager to get the President's attention. Like a man in a dream, Lincoln had gone through a lunch with Governor Curtin, followed by a reception, followed
490

by a sermon at the Presbyterian church. Then he had boarded the six-thirty evening cars to Washington. Now, as the train pulled out of the Gettysburg depot, Lincoln and Lamon stepped into the car. Sweat was streaming down Lincoln's pale yellow face; the eyes were out of focus; the wide mouth trembled. Lamon looked almost as ill, from fear. "Boys," he whispered to the secretaries, "get these people out of here. Don't let them near the President."

Lincoln said nothing. Propped up by Lamon, he stood swaying with the movement of the train. Nicolay led the disappointed Simon Cameron from the car while Hay asked Seward if he could persuade the others to go. The President had work to do, said Hay. There was news from Stanton. Seward got the point; had seen Lincoln's face. Exuberantly, he proposed to his fellow-politicians a banquet in the restaurant-car.

When the car was cleared, Lamon picked up Lincoln, who must have weighed no more than a farmer's scarecrow to such a powerful man, and carried the half-conscious President to the lounge, where he stretched him out. Nicolay found a blanket and placed it over the shuddering form.

"What is it?" asked Nicolay.

Lamon shook his head. "I don't know. The fever, I think. Malaria?"

"But he has never had it," said Hay, a lifelong victim of that recurrent disease.

"Well, he can always catch it, I reckon," said Lamon.

Lincoln's eyes were now shut. Lamon found a towel, which he wetted from a water carafe; then he placed the towel on the Ancient's face. Suddenly, Lincoln said, in a clear voice, "Something has gone wrong." He took a deep breath and slept; or fainted.

As agreed, David met Booth in front of the bulletin board in the National Hotel lobby. Here, as at Willard's, wire-service dispatches were posted up at regular intervals, and there was never a moment when a crowd was not gathered to read the latest news from the front or from Congress or, now, from the White House, where the President had been ill for some days with scarlatina. No one was allowed to see him outside of the immediate family. There were rumors that he was dying.

David had not seen Booth since their first meeting. It was Miss Ella Turner who had appeared at Thompson's. As she ordered throat lozenges from David, she whispered, "Our friend says to meet him in the lobby of the National at noon." Then she was gone.

Booth was at the bulletin board. A place called Lookout Mountain in Chattanooga Valley had just fallen to "Fighting Joe" Hooker.

Apparently, under Grant, "Fighting Joe" had finally learned to fight. The rebel army was now in retreat. Booth turned on David with a scowl. But then when he recognized him, scowl was replaced by brilliant smile. "Davie, I'm glad to see you! I'm leaving today." Booth led David to one of the lobby's full windows, where two leather armchairs, side by side, commanded a view of a rank of hacks in Pennsylvania Avenue. A light, curiously feathery snow was falling. Since Congress was at that moment in session, the lobby was deserted save for palm trees in ceramic cachepots. Through a nearby door, barbers and shoeshine boys could be seen practising their necessary arts.

"My God, Davie, you are a great man in Richmond!" Booth's voice was low; but his face was ablaze with excitement.

For an instant, David could not believe his ears. He, David Herold, a great man?

"How did you do it? What did you use? Or is that a secret? If it is, I shall respect it and ask no more."

David started to tell the truth; and then saw no reason to alter his usual policy in these matters. Since last he saw Booth, there had been only one opportunity to poison the President. Two days before Lincoln went up to Gettysburg, Old Edward had come over to Thompson's with a list of prescriptions for the Lincoln family. David had already decided that the taste of cyanide, added to the blue mass, would be barely detectable, and swift-acting. He would, of course, vanish from Washington as soon as the poison had crossed the avenue. But Old Edward had said, "No more blue mass, Mr. Thompson. Mrs. Lincoln has decreed castor oil to make himself's bowels move. So castor oil it is." At such short notice, David could think of nothing that could be added, safely, to that clear viscosity. Admittedly the taste of castor oil would have neutralized even arsenic's bitterness, but the clarity of the mixture would have betrayed the presence of a granulated poison. So pure castor oil had gone to the President. Then, a few days later, when the President became ill, David assumed that now his time had come. But he was not allowed to prepare any of the medicines for the White House because Lincoln's own physician chose to work with Mr. Thompson in the back room. Together they had prepared a number of mixtures in the hope of curing what was, at first, a mysterious disease, involving high fever and a body rash like scarlatina—or poisoning. The mystery was solved when the symptoms changed to those of smallpox. Needless to say, the White House would not admit what it was that the President had. There were already sufficient rumors that he was dying to depress the sale of war bonds and inflate the price of gold. So scarlatina was the official illness.

492

"I can't really say just what it is . . . what it was I used," said David, taking the cigar that Booth offered him. "But, like you see, he didn't take anywhere near enough of the medicine. If he had, he would've been dead on the way up to Pennsylvania."

"There will be other chances. You are unsuspected?"

David nodded, with what he hoped was a secret sort of smile in spite of the bucked teeth that made even his subtlest smile turn into a silly grin. "No one's got the slightest idea I'm involved because the medicine was a patent one, which means none of us mixed it. Also, the symptoms are pretty much like the smallpox, which half the town has got. I did hear his doctor talking to Mr. Thompson," David was inspired to invent, "and there's still a chance he'll die."

"My God, Davie! You are a treasure. There will be statues to you one day, and that is a promise." But then Booth frowned. "If we win, that is. I'm going up to Pennsylvania tonight. I've got some oil fields that I mean to sell. Then I go to Canada to talk to the Confederate commissioners. If Lincoln dies meanwhile, you are to go straight to Richmond, where I will join you. But if he lives, stay here and wait for orders from me—or the Colonel."

"Do you really know the Colonel?"

Booth nodded. "I *think* I know him. Anyway I know how to reach him, and he me." Booth leapt to his feet. He always leapt. But then David had noticed, with admiration, that offstage Booth was the same as on. "Come on to the bar. We must celebrate."

There was no celebration at the White House. Hay worked on the presidential message to Congress, which Lincoln and the department heads had more or less assembled. Technically, it was a report on the Union's state during 1863. But as a result of Lincoln's illness, the Tycoon had not been able to pull together all the strands. So Stanton's report on the war was a separate message, while Usher's report on the Interior had to be rewritten. The only new note was Lincoln's first intimation of how he would go about reconstituting the South. In the teeth of such radicals as Wade and Sumner and Stevens, he would admit to full citizenship anyone who swore an oath of allegiance to the Union. When a tenth of the voting population of any of the rebel states chose to accept the Emancipation Proclamation, they could send a delegation to Congress. On this point, the radicals were prepared to fight Lincoln. For them, eleven states had ceased to exist when they left the Union. Once defected, those eleven states were to be treated as occupied enemy territory; and their leaders punished. In Lincoln's view, as they had once been part of the Union and would be so again, it was a somewhat metaphysical waste of time to fret over just *where* it was that they had been in the meantime.

493

Once the rebellion was crushed, he stood on Article Four of the Constitution, which empowers the president to grant protection to the states *in* the Union. Seward had objected to this construction on the ground that as everyone, incuding Lincoln, had been so free with the Constitution lately, this was hardly a tactful argument since it raised yet again the delicate question of *in* versus *out*. Unhappily, Lincoln agreed to forget about Article Four.

While Hay assembled the message with help from Seward and Bates, Nicolay was again the *de facto* president, receiving supplicants, answering mail, sparing as much as possible the Tycoon, who could do business for no more than an hour or two at a time.

Stoddard was now in command of the newspaper cuttings, an important matter since the election year was at hand. Although the Tycoon had said nothing publicly of his plans, he was now set to run again on the ground that, for all the faults of his Administration, it was probably better not to go and swap horses in midstream—an image that Hay had thought somewhat lacking in majesty.

But then the absence of majesty much concerned Lincoln's numerous critics in the press. Stoddard read aloud to Nicolay and Hay from some of the newly arrived newspapers. From England, Charles Francis Adams had sent a copy of the London *Times*, which described the dedication at Gettysburg as a ceremony that was "rendered ludicrous by some of the sallies of that poor President Lincoln."

Nicolay put down his pen. "Was there anyone there from the London *Times*?"

"Who knows?" said Stoddard.

"They make it all up, anyway," said Hay, suddenly aware that, as President and Cabinet were all lawyers, the three secretaries were all journalists; and yet they were hardly able to control, as they should, the press, short of actually arresting editors—Seward's peculiar delight.

"'Anything more dull and commonplace it would not be easy to produce' says the *Times* of the President's speech."

"What does the Chicago *Times* say?" asked Hay.

"What don't they say?" Stoddard picked up a cutting from the table.

"'The cheek of every American must tingle with shame as he reads the silly, flat, and dish-watery utterances of the man who has to be pointed out to intelligent foreigners as the President of the United States. And neither he nor Seward could refrain, even on that solemn occasion, from spouting their odious abolition doctrines.'" Stoddard looked up. "Did Governor Seward speak?"

494

"No," said Hay. "But he *ought* to have spoken and if he *had* spoken, that is what he *ought* to have said, according to the *Times.*"

"Well, the Chicago *Tribune* says, 'The dedicatory remarks of President Lincoln will live among the annals of man.'"

"That is fair comment," said Hay. "Did you know that Edward Everett was a friend of Lord Byron?"

"What has that to do with anything?" Nicolay placed the last of the letters for Lincoln's signature in a folder.

"I was interested," said Hay, who had been most surprised when, the night before the ceremony, the old man had sat before the fire of a Gettysburg magnate and regaled visitors with unusual memoirs. "He knew him at Venice, fifty years ago. He said he was charming but immoral."

"Here is something interesting," said Stoddard, who had no interest in Byron. "The *Ohio State Journal . . .*"

"Henry D. Cooke's paper?" Nicolay turned to Stoddard. In disarray, Nico's beard was like that of a goat in the wind, thought Hay, trying to think like Byron, tragically (from the Greek word for goat song).

"The same. And of Captain Hurtt, now in prison. The present editor, one Isaac J. Allen, writes: 'The President's calm but earnest utterances of this brief and beautiful address stirred the deepest fountains of feeling and emotion in the hearts of the vast throng before him, and when he had concluded, scarcely could an untearful eye be seen, while sobs of smothered emotion were heard on every hand.' Is that what happened?"

"No," said Nicolay.

"Actually, if it was on every hand that sobbing was heard, the sob then got smothered, and no one could hear," said Hay, pedantically. "Anyway, I'll bet he's consul at Bangkok before he goes to prison." Late the previous night, Seward had regaled Hay and a number of cronies with the high misdeeds of the proprietors of Ohio's leading newspaper.

"Gentlemen." In the doorway stood the President. The clothes hung from him as if they contained not flesh but a wooden framework. The cords in the neck were like ropes. The face was sallow and sunken. But the eyes were cheerful and alert. "I have risen, as the preacher said, when he left the widow's house."

The secretaries greeted their employer with much warmth. He had been so seldom in their office during the last three weeks that the business of the presidency was beginning to overwhelm even Nicolay, who ordinarily quite liked governing the United States.

"The doctor says that I can move around, but I must remember that I am made out of glass. So I will keep visitors to the minimum. Mr. Nicolay, bring me the message to Congress."

"Yes, sir."

"Have you all been vaccinated?"

"Yes, sir," said Hay.

"I wonder if it does any good." Lincoln took the lengthy message from Nicolay. "By the way, I did not have the smallpox but varioloid, which is the same thing but doesn't sound quite as bad. Anyway, it was nice, for a change, having something that I could give everybody." Lincoln started to go; then paused.

"As you know, Mrs. Lincoln's half-sister, Mrs. Emilie Helm, is here in the house. As she is the new widow of a . . . of a Confederate general"—this was the first time that Hay had ever heard the Ancient use the word "Confederate"—"I would simply not let on anything to the press, if they ask you about her."

"We haven't, sir," said Nicolay.

"She is a comfort to Mrs. Lincoln," said the President; and left the room.

But at that exact moment Emilie was something less than a comfort. Although Mary had had few visitors during the President's illness and Emilie's visit, she had made an exception in the case of her old friend Dan Sickles, who had just come stumping into the upstairs parlor, accompanied by the senator from New York Ira Harris. Mary had received them graciously; and introduced them to Mrs. Helm, who was now looking almost healthy again.

The previous month, Emilie Helm and her young daughter had arrived at Fortress Monroe, where she had asked for a pass so that she could go home to Lexington, Kentucky. As the law required, Mrs. Helm was told that she could have the pass if she would sign the oath of allegiance to the United States. When she refused, the commandant had cabled the War Department, which in turn had asked Lincoln what was to be done with his rebel sister-in-law. "Send her to me," he had said. Mary had been delighted. The two women had now wept a great deal together; spoken of their common dead; avoided politics. Mary had begged Emilie and her daughter—Tad's age—to stay on through the summer at the Soldiers' Home. Emilie had been tempted.

Now Sickles was eyeing the young woman most curiously, while Harris glowered. Mary realized that she had made an error in presenting Sickles to Emilie, while Sickles had compounded the error by bringing the uninvited and unsympathetic New York senator into the private rooms.

"You must have had a most difficult time, Mrs. Helm," said Sickles, arranging his stump on a footstool.

"It is not easy," said Emilie, politely, "travelling with a child

496

in wartime. But then Brother Lincoln insisted that we stop off here on our way home to Lexington."

Harris said, "I believe your husband served under my old colleague Breckinridge."

Emilie nodded. "Yes, General Helm was with Cousin John—to the end."

"Are you a cousin of Mr. Breckinridge, too?" Harris seemed surprised.

"My mother is, yes. I don't know," said Emilie, mouth beginning to set, "about the 'too.'"

Mary intervened. "Cousin John was a great figure in all our lives, always. It was a tragedy when he..." Mary stopped herself. There was now nothing that she could say which was not, potentially, embarrassing, one way or the other.

"I *thought* very highly of Mr. Breckinridge," said Harris solemnly. "We were friends, even. How is he, Mrs. Helm?"

"I would hardly know. My husband was killed three months ago, and I have heard nothing more of those who served with him."

"I suppose," said Harris, "life is very hard now at the South."

"I have not noticed any particular change." Emilie was much calmer than Mary would have been under such questioning.

"Well, the blockade must stop you from getting all sorts of goods..."

"Oh, our ships always seem to get through your blockade." Emilie smiled, sweetly. "Charleston harbor has never been so busy."

"How is dear Mrs. Sickles?" asked Mary, quickly—too quickly, since by common consensus the lady was never mentioned in polite company, not so much because her husband had killed what may or may not have been her lover, but because he had then returned to her and, worse, she to him.

"Oh, Teresa is blooming. She's in the Ninety-first Street house. In New York." Sickles was airy. "How is the President?"

"He is up and around, and recovered. He held one Cabinet meeting last week, which tired him out. It was *not* the smallpox as the papers say. Only varioloid, and general tiredness."

"It's a pity," said Emilie, "that you can't take him away to Lexington for a week or two of good air."

"I don't think he could leave the Telegraph Room for a day. He wants news of the war almost before there is any."

"Well, he must have been pleased about Chattanooga," said Harris. He looked at Emilie, challengingly. "The rebels ran from us like so many rabbits."

Emilie responded in swift kind. "If that is true, Senator Harris, it must have been the example that you set them at Bull Run and Manassas and Chancellorsville and Fredericksburg . . ."

Mary felt the beginning of a severe headache. Senator Harris's mouth was now ajar, while Sickles's pale eyes glittered dangerously.

"We do not dwell on such things here, today." Mary was babbling; and continued to do so until she thought that the moment had passed.

But it had not. Abruptly, Senator Harris turned on her. "Why isn't your son Robert in the army? He's old enough and fit enough."

"He is finishing at Harvard . . ."

"He should set an example," said the senator, inexorably.

"He will, sir, in due course." Mary was beginning to feel faint. "He has wanted to go for some time."

"Well, all he has to do—" began the senator but Mary broke in, "Sir, he is not a shirker as you seem to imply. It is true that I have only recently lost one son . . ."

"But not to the war, Mrs. Lincoln," said Harris. "Now I have only one son, and he is fighting for his country, with my blessing." He turned to Emilie. "If I had twenty sons, they would all be fighting the rebels!"

Emilie rose to her feet. "If I had twenty sons, Senator, I promise you that they would defeat all twenty of yours, with *my* blessing."

Mary stood up. "Gentlemen, it was good of you to call," she said. She did not offer her hand to either man. As they withdrew, Mary turned to Emilie. "I am sorry, Little Sister. It is so bitter here."

"It is bitter everywhere."

But a moment later, Sickles was again in the room. "Can I see Mr. Lincoln for a moment?"

"Isn't he in his office?"

"They said he is lying down."

"If Mr. Lamon will let you into the bedroom, you can see him, of course."

As Sickles stumped down the corridor, Emilie said, "I cannot stay, Sister Mary."

"You must! Don't take this seriously. It will be different at the Soldiers' Home, where we aren't exposed to everyone. It will be just us and Willie and Aleck and Ben, too, though I've not seen him yet. But the others have seen him and told me."

Emilie shook her head, as if she had for a moment lost her hearing. "What was that? About Ben and Aleck?"

"Willie comes to me every evening. He stands at the foot of my bed. He is so . . . so full of light. He smiles at me and he tells me about all the others who have joined him. He has seen your

498

Ben, who is well and happy. Sometimes Aleck comes with Willie, and little Eddie's been twice to see his mamma. He remembers me. Imagine, Emilie! After all these years he remembers me, and he so young when he crossed over."

Emilie took Mary into her arms as if she, Mary, were the youngest sister—indeed, the child. "I am glad for you," she whispered. "I am so very glad that they come to you like this."

But Dan Sickles was not glad. As he hurtled about the President's room on his crutches, he described Emilie's conversation to Lincoln, who lay, fully clothed, on his bed. When Sickles had finished both talking and hurtling, Lincoln observed, "The child has a tongue like all the rest of the Todds. It is unwise to take on any of them in a dispute."

"Sir, it is unwise of *you* to have that rebel in this house!" Sickles struck the bed's carved footboard with the flat of his hand.

Lincoln sat up as if he himself had been struck. "It is not your place, General Sickles, to advise or assist my wife and me in whom we choose to invite to our house, as we have invited *you*, despite criticism."

"I am sorry, sir. I should not have spoken like that, but..."

"No, you should not have." Lincoln was icy. "Anyway, it's no fault of the child that she's here. That was all my doing, as so much is."

On the fourteenth of December, Lincoln wrote out a pass for Emilie Todd Helm and her daughter, Katherine, to return to Lexington. "I've also written out the oath of allegiance," he said, with a smile, "and a pardon."

"I've done nothing that I need to be pardoned for, Brother Lincoln."

The family was seated at the breakfast table; at least, Lincoln and Mary and Emilie were seated. Tad and Katherine were staring out the window at Tad's goats.

"Oh, sign it anyway, Emilie," said Mary. "It's just a piece of paper."

"I can't. I'm still loyal to Ben; and to our country."

Mary shook her head, wonderingly. There was, again, a sense of total unreality. "Will we ever again," she asked, "wake up from this nightmare?"

Lincoln tore up the document; and said to Emilie, "When I heard that Ben had been killed, I felt like David in the Bible when he was told of the death of Absalom. 'Would God I had died for thee, O Absalom, my son, my son!'"

"Now you will leave me again," said Mary to Emilie. "Is life to be borne?"

There was no answer to that in the room. Then Tad said,

"No," in a loud voice to his cousin; and shouted to his father, "She says Jeff Davis is president and I say you're president. You *both* can't be president, can you?" Tad's turn of mind was often legalistic.

"No," said Lincoln, smiling, "we can't. And that's what this big trouble is all about. Anyway, Tad, you know who your president is and Katherine knows who her Uncle Lincoln is; and that's quite enough."

It was more than enough for Mary, who fled the room. She had suddenly seen the nimbus of fire about her husband's head. She was going mad again; and this time she might not return.

3

ELIHU B. WASHBURNE FAILED TO BE ELECTED SPEAKER OF THE House of Representatives despite Lincoln's secret assistance. The anti-Lincoln Schuyler Colfax, a smiling man of imperfect honesty, won the post and Washburne did his best to appear philosophical as well as statesmanlike. Once Washburne had lost, he himself put Colfax's name in final nomination; thus, the vote was unanimous. There now was a good deal of work to be done, and a number of new members to help with it, among them an eloquent newspaper editor from Maine called James G. Blaine and Major-General James A. Garfield, the hero or *a* hero, of the battle of Chickamauga.

But the focus of interest in the Congress was the arrival, January 12, of Major-General Frank Blair, Junior. As a result of Stanton's best efforts at the War Department and Thaddeus Stevens's in the House, Frank Blair had ceased to be a general; but he was still a member of Congress.

Lean and tall, with a thick red moustache and beard, Blair made a dramatic entrance into the chamber, and the galleries applauded while Garfield averted his head—Blair was still in uniform, while Garfield wore mere statesman's black. The business of the House stopped for ten minutes. Blair complimented the Speaker, who welcomed Blair, as did a number of border-state congressmen. The rest opened up their newspapers or sat at their oaken desks and caught up on their correspondence. Thaddeus Stevens limped from the chamber in order to avoid the sight of Blair, even temporarily triumphant.

Washburne led Blair to one of the sofas that lined the semi-circular chamber. As the business of the House continued about them, Washburne began to do the President's work. Lincoln was aware of the Blair capacity for divisiveness. As Speaker, Blair would have been of great use to Lincoln; otherwise, he was better off in the army. Of all the political generals, Blair was the only one to have inspired a modicum of admiration in either Grant or Sherman, the two professional soldiers who now stood above all others in the country.

"You've nothing to worry about from Grant," said Blair, ostentatiously stretching out his long booted legs on the new carpet. Washburne saw that Blair had not removed his spurs on entering the Capitol; they now made tiny holes in the carpet.

"Worry?" Washburne pretended not to know what Blair meant. Actually, as Grant's congressman, not a day passed that Washburne was not asked by press and politicians about the availability of General Grant for president. Certainly if Grant were the Republican candidate, he would beat McClellan. But, as Washburne liked to point out to the radicals, Grant was a Democrat who had supported Douglas. If Grant were to oppose McClellan for the Democratic nomination, most people thought he would win. Certainly, Lincoln thought so. Lincoln also thought that Grant could get, if he chose, the Republican nomination. In a contest of any kind with Grant, Lincoln felt that he would probably lose. Currently, the press was puffing Grant, who had made no public comment.

"Grant wants only to fight. The last thing he wants is to be a politician." Blair was definite. But then he was always definite.

"I find that hard to believe," said Washburne. Congress was already beginning to fill up with generals; and the war was far from over. Yet Washburne often felt like an impostor on the subject of Grant. He was acknowledged, as Grant's congressman, to be an authority on the subject, but in actual fact he barely knew the man. Luckily, at the beginning of the war, he had proposed Grant for brigadier-general simply because Grant was a West Pointer who happened to be living in Washburne's hometown of Galena. Grant had been, and continued to be, grateful to his congressman. Recently, at Lincoln's request, Washburne had sent for a friend from Galena who was known to be close to Grant. The friend had reported to Lincoln that Grant would support him for a second term. The President was relieved. But the *New York Herald* continued its campaign for "the people's candidate, Ulysses S. Grant."

"What does the President want me to do?"

"That is up to you." Washburne was tactful.

"I think," said Blair, "I should go back to the army, if Stanton will let me. I'm told that there is a new law, which means that I've lost my commission for good by coming here today."

"That's true. But the President's willing to write you out a new commission whenever you want it, and you can go back to your corps."

"Will he do this?" Blair gave Washburne a hard look.

Washburne nodded. "I speak for him."

Blair was relieved. "Then I'll do some work here; and go back. I assume Grant will be assigned to the East."

"I don't know. I do know the President wants to put him in command of all our armies."

"What about Old Brains?"

"He will serve under Grant."

Blair whistled. "That'll be trouble. What about Meade?"

"I think the President will want Grant to take over the Army of the Potomac, where all is quiet, as usual."

"Grant wants to stay in the West. You know his plan. To strike at Atlanta and Savannah. Then move north to Richmond."

"Sherman can do that while Grant takes on Lee in Virginia. But I am not in the confidence of the War Department." Washburne turned to Blair, who was now staring at the back of Stevens's wig: the owner had returned to his seat. "One thing we're all curious about. Why didn't Grant telegraph Stanton the news about Vicksburg? Why did we have to wait three days before we heard about it, and then it was from an admiral?"

Blair grinned. "Because the wires from Grant's headquarters to Washington had been cut."

"Well, it's no great thing to repair the wires, particularly with the rebels all dispersed."

"Oh, Mr. Washburne, don't you know about us in the West? It isn't the rebels who cut the wires to Washington, it's General Grant."

Washburne was stunned. "Grant cuts his own wires?"

"To Washington, of course. Since we never know what damn fool orders Stanton or Halleck or Old Abe, bless him, may be sending us, whenever there's a real crisis brewing, like the fall of Vicksburg, Grant just breaks off all communication until it's over."

"Don't tell the President," said Washburne.

"Oh, I'll tell him, or Grant will. It's Stanton who must never know. He'll have us shot."

Then Washburne got down to the principal business between them. "Your speech at St. Louis last fall caused a certain sensation here, as you know."

"I took the nigger question head-on, I'll say that." Blair looked
502

grimly satisfied with himself, an almost habitual expression, thought Washburne, who made it a point to deal with the Blairs, singly or collectively, as if with a leaking cask of dynamite on a hot summer day. "The problem isn't slavery, which is ending, and would have ended without a war. The problem is the Negro, who must leave our shores."

"Of course," said Washburne, who had no great interest in Blair's racial views. "Naturally, you caused a stir; and your brother, Monty, did the same when he spoke at Rockville during the election." Montgomery Blair had elaborated on his brother's remarks. He, too, had spoken of colonization as the only answer to the racial problem. He had denounced Sumner and all the abolitionists who opposed the removal of the colored population, painting a horrendous picture of a future nation of hybrid mulattoes if the North did not make common cause with the loyal white Southerners, while punishing only turbulent seditious politicians and slave-holders. "Treason was not committed by any state," said Monty Blair, echoing Lincoln in private, "but by the individuals who made use of the states and attempted to dismember the government."

"I know that we speak for the President," said Blair, "and hardly anyone but us dares to go up against Sumner and Greeley and the rest."

"But you do. You do." Washburne began to caulk, as it were, the barrel of dynamite. "I think what interested many of us here were your allegations against certain Treasury agents in Missouri . . ."

"Allegations? I have the proof, Mr. Washburne. They are up to their eyes in corruption. And so is Chase himself, selling permits to trade with the enemy."

"It is interesting," said Washburne, quickly, the dynamite contained and now ready to be used in a controlled way, "what you have to say about Mr. Chase. Perhaps you could elaborate." Thus the fuse was lit.

Chase looked about his half-furnished office and was half-pleased. The pearl-gray carpet of his first days as Secretary had long since been drowned in tobacco juice; and removed. Now a newly tessellated marble floor waited for an Axminster carpet, currently being woven especially. Although the teakwood furniture, recovered, was still in place, new gilded furniture was being fashioned in Philadelphia by a cabinetmaker highly vouched for by Jay Cooke. Most satisfying of all, in Chase's view, was the recently completed marble bathroom adjacent to his office. Of its useful sort, it was unique in Washington; and much envied by the First

Lady, who often alluded to it—euphemistically of course—as the subject was not a polite one.

The young Ohio journalist and war correspondent Whitelaw Reid sat on the sofa beneath Hamilton's portrait, a copy of Chase's elegant little book *Going Home to Vote* in his hand. For some time, Reid had been helping Chase with his speeches. When Chase had taken his triumphal swing through the west in October on behalf, officially, of the Republican Party, Reid had gone along in order to write of the statesman in the loftiest of terms and of the man in the homeliest and most appealing ones.

Reid had described the loving way that the people had hailed Chase as "Old Greenbacks," a name that seemed to him to be far more resonant and appealing than "Old Abe." To compete with the cunningly wrought image of "Old Abe the Rail-Splitter," one John T. Trowbridge had now assembled yet another book about Chase: the dangerous phrase "campaign-biography" was never used by the conspirators. Since on more than one occasion, at the age of twelve, Chase had ferried passengers across the Cuyahoga River, it was Trowbridge's inspired notion to combat the image of the rail-splitter with that of a humble, hard-working child. The result was now on Chase's desk. Entitled *The Ferry Boy and the Financier*, the book made Chase somewhat uneasy. Although Chase never lied, he preferred to tell only as much of the truth as was useful. Would the occupation of several days in his twelfth year truly compete with Lincoln's largely mythical yet entirely adult rail-splitting? Much had been made, and would be made again, of the fact that of all the presidents, Lincoln alone had worked for a living with his hands *after* he was grown. But Trowbridge's work was in print; and could not now be altered.

Senator Pomeroy of Kansas sat in the chair beside the secretary's desk. Pomeroy was at the head of the thus far secret committee to secure for Chase the Republican nomination. Others said to be on the committee were Senators Sumner, Wade, Sherman and Sprague as well as Congressman Garfield, while of the nation's great editors, Horace Greeley supported Chase. On the other hand, the abolitionist William Cullen Bryant did not.

"Mr. Greeley thinks that with Hiram Barney at the customs, you'll have the entire New York delegation. He thinks it's easy." Pomeroy was a smooth creature not at all to Chase's liking. Pomeroy was thought to have obtained his own election to the Senate by corrupt means. But he was a splendid political manager, according to Sumner, who would not know, and to Wade, who would. Chase had not told either Pomeroy or Greeley that Hiram Barney, his own appointee, was for Lincoln.

"Nothing is easy, Senator," said Chase, returning to his chair.

"Mr. Lincoln thinks the same. He is worried about you. He is worried about Grant. He told a friend of mine that if 'the disaffected elements in the party,' his exact words, 'should be combined in one strong candidate,' he would be done for. Well, Grant ain't a candidate; and you are..."

"No, no. I am not, in any *ordinary* sense, a candidate or..."

"That's right. That's right." Pomeroy spoke through him. "Anyway, we're fixing to bring together all the disaffecteds, which is just about everybody. Now I think we should follow up Senator Sherman's little pamphlet 'The Next Presidential Election'..."

"He was much criticized for sending that out under his frank," said Chase, staring at his own face as it looked up at him, winsomely, from the pages of *The Ferry Boy and the Financier*.

"He was; and he don't give a damn, if you'll forgive me. But he was writing *against* Lincoln, and not in favor of you. Now our committee has it in mind to do something a bit more dignified, putting forth *your* views and so on; and then letting it sort of leak into the press."

"I should not want to see it in advance, of course," said Chase. "I am a member of the Administration still. But I do think—and I will say so openly any time and anywhere—that the practise of the last thirty years should be adhered to. No president should serve two terms. In fact, I would pledge myself to be a single-term president."

"That will be much admired, sir," said Whitelaw Reid.

At the door, a clerk announced Mr. Henry D. Cooke. As Henry D. entered the office, he looked about to see who was present. When he saw only loyalists, he said, "Well, Frank Blair has done it."

"Done what?" asked Pomeroy.

"He's just asked for an investigation of the Treasury Department. He wants a committee of five to investigate what he says is a long list of crimes or allegations of crimes committed by Treasury officials and by..." Henry D. sat down uninvited on the sofa beside Reid.

"By *me*?" Chase was pleased at his own coolness under what was, after all, as real fire as ever came a soldier's way.

"By you, sir," said Henry D.

"What am I supposed to have done?" Chase tried to recall a relevant passage from St. Paul's correspondence with the Ephesians; but failed.

"I'm sure that Frank is pretty vague," said Pomeroy, who had lived through so much of this sort of thing, but, unlike Chase, as the guilty party.

"Yes, he was vague as to specifics. But he is saying that he has

505

reason to believe that you have given—or sold—permits, secretly and illegally, to various businessmen in order to trade with the enemy, and that if this is true and if the enemy has been aided, then you must be impeached and tried for treason."

Chase felt, for an instant, as if he might faint—with fury. Then he tried to console himself with the marvelous irony of it all. He may, at times, have gone to the outer edge of propriety but no further. On trade permits he had been impeccable, as his own son-in-law knew most bitterly. "I believe," said Chase, focussing his anger, "that it is now necessary for us to destroy Mr. Frank Blair, Junior, and break once and for all that... infernal family." Chase rang for his secretary. When the man appeared, Chase said, "Bring me the *specified* Frank Blair file, the Vicksburg file and the *specified* Montgomery Blair file." The secretary disappeared. Chase turned to Pomeroy. "We shall see to it that General Blair is charged with defrauding the government at Vicksburg. I shall also explore, one by one, his shady associates in Missouri. As for Montgomery Blair..."

Pomeroy raised his hand. "Now then let's hold our horses for a moment. I agree, Mr. Chase, that you should pile up all the ammunition you can. But we hold it for now. We keep our powder dry for now." Pomeroy turned to Henry D. "Blair has asked for a committee of investigation, you say?"

"Yes, Senator. There's been no vote yet. But..."

Pomeroy smiled. "If there's been no vote yet, that is the end of that." He turned to Chase. "Privately, the Speaker opposes Mr. Lincoln's reelection. Privately, he supports you. Publicly, he dislikes the Blairs, as who does not? Between the Speaker and General Garfield, there will *never* be an investigation. Consider the resolution as dead. I know the votes we got. The House will split seventy-something to sixty-something in your favor."

In a sense, Chase was relieved. But, in another sense, "How will it look if my friends block an investigation of my department?"

"Why like nothing at all, Mr. Chase. Just yesterday's wind across the lonesome prairie."

"It would be good to be exonerated—" Chase began.

But Henry D. finished for him, "—but a bad idea to have the business of the trade permits gone into. You have done nothing illegal, Mr. Chase. But we have seen to it that, by and large, permits go only to men who are loyal supporters of your candidacy. That's what Blair hopes to reveal—at the least."

"I agree," said Pomeroy. "It wouldn't look too good, even though there is nothing unlawful in helping friends." Pomeroy was on his feet. "I shall start circulating our views." He held high the manuscript in his hand as though it were Excalibur.

In Chase's eyes the pamphlet was indeed well done, the work of a New York journalist named Winchell. The case against Lincoln's renomination was made with dignity and cogency. First, Lincoln would lose to the combinations arrayed against him. McClellan would be a formidable candidate. If Grant were to enter the field, as a Democrat, there would be no contest at all. Second, another term of shilly-shallying might bankrupt the nation, as the war dragged on. Third, patronage was now out of control; only single-term presidents could control this. Chase somewhat doubted the logic of this point, as he himself had increased the number of clerks in his department more rapidly than that of any other, including the War Department. But his political managers thought the sentiment sounded well. Fourth, Chase was the better man, the better administrator and the purest in the management of public affairs. Chase subscribed wholeheartedly to this estimate of himself; therefore, the Blair charges were all the more galling and dangerous. Fifth, the more Lincoln's partisans tried to promote his renomination, the more opposition there would be to his unsuccessful Administration. For these reasons, the supporters of Chase had now started a national organization, with a Republican National Executive Committee at Washington, whose chairman is Senator Pomeroy.

"I shall send this circular out to every corner of the country," said Pomeroy.

"You better get it out quick to Pennsylvania," said Henry D. "I've just heard from my brother that Simon Cameron is rounding up endorsements of Lincoln from every Republican member of the legislature, which he owns."

"Is not Thaddeus Stevens at work for us?" Chase had been assured by that irritable and irritating but entirely honest man that he would be able to deliver Pennsylvania to Chase.

"Ever since Mr. Stevens denied saying that Simon Cameron wouldn't steal a red-hot stove, there is a war between them."

Chase thought of the night that he had found the most graceful of departures for Cameron from the Cabinet. But the perfidy of men no longer surprised him. "I had thought Mr. Cameron still angry at the President for removing him from the Cabinet."

"He is convinced," said Henry D., "that his departure was your work and Seward's."

"I shall never again do a good deed!" Chase exclaimed.

"You will, you will, Mr. Chase," said Pomeroy at the door. Again he held up the circular. This time as a torch to light them down the corridor of history. "And as the president."

* * *

Seward and his son read the circular with disbelief. The entire text had been published in the *National Intelligencer*. "He will have to resign," said Fred Seward.

"But he won't," said his father, as he lit, with shaking hands, the first cigar of the day. The ruins of breakfast lay before him like Troy, he thought, blowing smoke at the ham rind; he was Odysseus.

"Perhaps he didn't know," said Fred, tentatively.

"Oh, politicians never *know* anything. But I don't see the point to it. Cameron's already delivered us Pennsylvania. Sprague can't even deliver Rhode Island, and Ohio—his home state—is doubtful. There is, of course, Horace Greeley. Amen."

"Amen," said Fred, dutifully.

Seward went straight to the White House while Fred went on to the State Department. As usual, they were obliged to climb over blocks of marble and sheets of iron for the new Treasury annex, while across the street, in all its brand-new white-marble glory, stood the bank of Jay Cooke and Company, separated from the Treasury by Pennsylvania Avenue, down whose center the Washington Horse-car Company's carriages clattered through the half-frozen mud, a company that had been financed by Jay Cooke. If nothing else, thought Seward, Chase was fortunate in his friends.

Seward found Nicolay alone in his office. As a newly commissioned major in the Adjutant-General's department, Hay was in Florida, searching for a congressional seat, with the President's blessing. On Nicolay's table was the *National Intelligencer*. "Has he seen it?" asked Seward.

"No, sir. I took it in to him. I told him what it was, and he said he'd rather not read it."

"Is that all?"

"Well, he had a funny dream last night, which I won't spoil for you since he's telling it to everyone this morning." Nicolay looked at the clock. "The hordes are not let in until nine o'clock now, which gives him two hours to think and write."

The President was neither writing nor, apparently, thinking, when Seward entered the office. He was seated in his big chair in front of the freshly made fire, feet on the fender and eyes shut. He had still not recovered the weight from the smallpox attack. But his color was normal; and the energy had returned.

"Sit down, Governor," he said, opening his eyes and then shutting them again. "I had the most comical dream last night and I was just trying to put myself asleep again so that I could bring on another one as good. By and large, my dreams tend to be on the gloomy side."

"What was it?" Seward pulled up a chair so that his own feet

508

could rest on the fender, which meant that he was at least three feet closer to the fire than the President.

"Well, I dreamt I was in the Blue Room, receiving the folks, as is my Constitutional duty and wondrous pleasure, when people started making offensive remarks about my appearance."

"They would not dare!"

"But dare they did. One said, in a very loud voice, 'Old Abe is a very common-looking man.' Well, everyone laughed, and I felt obliged to rise to the challenge. So I then said, 'Common-looking people are the best in the world: that is the reason the Lord makes so many of them.'"

Seward laughed. "That's pretty good for a man asleep."

"Rather neat, I thought."

"I'm also happy to hear that, in your dreams at least, the Lord of Hosts is invoked."

"So now you see what stuff my dreams are made of. Yes, Governor, I've heard about the circular. No, I haven't read it, and I'm not going to."

"I suppose Chase will now resign—again." Seward watched Lincoln's face with his usual fascination—fascination because the expression told him so little of what was going on in the man's mind.

"He has written me a letter, which I *have* read." Lincoln gave Seward the letter. "I can't imagine that it's meant to be private."

Seward read the letter quickly; saw the admission of guilt in the sentence: "I had no knowledge of the existence of this letter." Chase then admitted that although he had several times met with a number of gentlemen who wished to put him forward, he had neither encouraged nor discouraged them. He realized, however, that "if there is anything in my action or position which, in your judgment, will prejudice the public interest under my charge, I beg you to say so. I do not wish to administer the Treasury Department one day without your entire confidence." Seward put down the letter. "He has resigned."

"Not exactly. He wants me to tell him to go."

"You won't?"

Lincoln sighed. "I understand him, I suppose. You know, Governor, it is a terrible thing when this presidential bug starts to gnaw at a man."

"So I've been told, Mr. President," said Seward, cocking his head at the man who had forever displaced him in history.

"Yes, I reckon you do at that. God knows *I* know firsthand. We may land here by chance—but it is not for *wanting* to land."

"What will you answer him?"

Lincoln smiled. "I think I'll let him stew a bit. I've sent him a note to say that when I have the time I'll give him my views."

"I am sure that there is darkness at Sixth and E this morning." As Seward rose to take his leave, an usher showed in Frank Blair, now in civilian clothes. Seward affected delight at the vision of the Blair clan's most dashing villain. Blair was equally insincere. Seward departed.

Blair also had a copy of the Pomeroy circular in his hand. "Yes," said Lincoln, "I know all about it."

"What are you going to do?"

"That depends, General. That depends." Lincoln motioned for Blair to sit in the chair just vacated by Seward. Blair moved the chair back from the fire so that he was side by side with the President, who observed, "I don't suppose you'll ever get your committee of investigation."

"No," said Blair. "Chase's people are too strong. But I can still speak out."

"Yes, there's no doubt about that." Lincoln gazed thoughtfully into the fire. "I had the most comical dream last night..." He began.

"Was it something to do with perfidy embodied, as I think of Mr. Chase?"

"No. It was on quite a different tack. I'll tell you some other time. What is the exact nature of your... evidence of the misdeeds of Mr. Chase and his agents?"

"I've already left a copy of my notes with Mr. Nicolay. There are other pieces of evidence which I prefer to keep to myself for the time being."

"I see." Lincoln cleaned his glasses with the back of a kid glove that had been placed, mysteriously, in a waistcoat pocket. "Now, Frank, it is a very grave matter to suggest that the Secretary of the Treasury is guilty of corruption."

"I know it. That is why I think that I now must present a full and detailed account to Congress."

"Naturally, this will harm Mr. Chase."

"That is the object of the exercise." Blair indicated the circular which he had let drop to the floor. "In the light of Chase's treachery to you, do you object?"

"Well, let us say that, as of today, I am more inclined to study your bill of particulars than I would have been yesterday." Lincoln stared through the now-polished lenses of his glasses. "Frank, it is one thing to give out legal trade permits to your friends and supporters as patronage, and another to sell them and pocket the money. It is disloyal and unethical of him to do the first but it is
510

not illegal. The second is a crime. Has Mr. Chase committed a crime?"

Blair nodded. "I believe he has in several instances. But I must admit that it is hard to prove. When Jay Cooke gives him five thousand dollars to help him in his campaign and then Cooke receives, in turn, a higher commission for the war bonds he sells, is that corruption?"

"It is shadowy, Frank. You wanted to know whether or not I thought you should come back to Congress or stay in the army. I said that if you could become Speaker instead of Colfax, I thought it a good idea. Otherwise, you are more valuable in the field."

"Well, it's all decided now. Stanton has taken away my commission. I am out of the army."

Lincoln raised his left eyebrow, which also raised to a normal height the heavy upper lid. "If I sign my name to a piece of paper, you are once again a major-general in command of an army corps."

"You would do that?"

"I think I *must* do that. Once this problem is unsnarled."

"Then I had better present to Congress my charges against Mr. Chase."

"If you feel that those charges can be upheld, I think it is your duty, embarrassing as it will be for the Administration."

"Oh, I'll keep my sights on Chase. Don't worry."

"Unfortunately, I am employed by the people to worry about everything. But I think Mr. Chase has made your task—and my embarrassment—a good deal easier with this circular. By allowing himself to be put forward in such a furtive way, he has distanced himself from me . . ."

"Distanced? He's gone and stabbed you under the fifth rib!"

"Yes." Lincoln turned and gazed thoughtfully at Blair.

"I understand you, Mr. President," said Blair at last.

"Yes," said Lincoln," I think you do, Frank."

Blair suddenly grinned. "Monty says the reason why you wanted me to come back to Congress was to destroy Chase."

"It is curious how you Blairs see only the darkest motives in men, while I try only to dwell upon the true and the good." The left eyebrow now suddenly dropped, obliging the left lid to cover, for an instant, the eye. The effect could not have been more like a deliberate wink.

At the State Department, both of Seward's eyes had shut in a most uncharacteristic blink of amazement. Dan Sickles was stretched out on the sofa, his stump arranged rather unattractively on the bolster that Seward often used as a pillow for his frequent naps. "What," said Seward, opening his eyes again, "do the letters say?"

"I haven't seen them. But Isaac Newton tells me that there are three of them, and that in all three Mrs. Lincoln makes it clear that she has received or expects to receive money for political services rendered."

"Dear God in Heaven," whispered Seward to a deity who, plainly, was capable of anything.

"They are clever," said Sickles. "They wait until four months before the Nomination Convention, and then they ask for money, knowing there is no time for the President to maneuver in."

"Does he know?"

"I don't think so. The infamous Watt knows Mr. Newton, as one farmer knows another. Since Mr. Newton is now head of the Agricultural Bureau with access to the President, Watt approached him. Newton then asked me what to do. As Watt now lives in New York, I said I'd speak to you."

Seward nodded. "You did the right thing. We must keep the President out of this."

"If we can. He's the one who'll have to pay, after all."

"How much?"

"Twenty thousand dollars for the three letters," said Sickles. "Otherwise they will be published before the Convention, and Mr. Chase will then be nominated."

Seward began to whistle to himself, a most imprecise sort of whistle as his pendulous lower lip did not precisely meet the upper. Then he asked, "Does Mrs. Lincoln know?"

"No."

"That's a blessing. Dan, I want you to go to New York. I want you to have a chat with Mr. Watt. Isn't he supposed to be in the army?"

"He was. But now he isn't. He's operating a greenhouse. He feels that he was ill-treated over the Wikoff business."

"He is apt to be worse treated in this matter." Seward was prepared to take a considerable gamble. If it failed, the Administration might well be at an end. "When you get to New York, I want you to call on my friend Simeon Draper. You know him?"

Sickles nodded. "He's the Seward-Weed man for the city."

"That's one way of putting it, I suppose. He's generally known as the Collector of the Port of New York. But I do use him for delicate matters. For instance, when I am obliged, as Secretary of State, to order the arrest and detainment at Fort Lafayette of anyone suspected of treason, Mr. Draper arranges the matter quietly with the Superintendent of Police, and the traitor vanishes until such time as I choose to release him—after the election, in this case."

Sickles swung his stump over the sofa's edge. He smiled, and twirled his moustaches like an actor. "I trust that I will have in my pocket an order for the arrest of one John Watt, who, while at the White House, purloined state papers, and gave them to the enemy?"

"You will have it as soon as the ink is dry," said Seward, writing rapidly on his official stationery.

"What if Mr. Watt has given copies of the letters to others?"

"They are simply copies—of forgeries. They prove nothing. It is the originals that concern us." Seward signed his name with a flourish. "The originals you must get from Mr. Watt."

"What if he refuses to give them up?"

"Dan, have you ever been inside Fort Lafayette?"

"No, Governor, I am happy to say that I've only been detained for murder in Washington's highly civilized if verminous cells."

"Well, it's a fearsome place, the Fort. Ask Mr. Draper to describe it to Mr. Watt in great detail. Also"—Seward rolled a cigar between the palms of his hands—"a man can simply die of the fever in no time at all in one of those dark, damp, hideous, hopeless dungeons. It is truly amazing how a man can suddenly take ill and just... die, while he's there in the spidery slithery dark."

"Yes, Governor." Sickles, well pleased, took the warrant and put it in his tunic.

Five days after the publication of the Pomeroy circular, Frank Blair rose in the House of Representatives and began an attack on what he called the Jacobins in his native Missouri. But as Blair spoke, the powerful voice ringing throughout the chamber, the attack went beyond those Missouri abolitionists who sought to undermine the Administration. "I say here in my place and upon my responsibility as a Representative that a more profligate administration of the Treasury Department never existed under any government, that the whole Mississippi Valley is rank and fetid with the frauds and corruptions of its agents; that 'permits' to buy cotton are just as much a marketable commodity as the cotton itself; that these permits to buy cotton are brought to St. Louis and other western cities by politicians and favorites from all over the country and sold on 'change' to the highest bidder, whether he is a secessionist or not, and that, too, at a time when the best Union men in these cities are denied permits."

Washburne, from his front-row seat, saw that a number of Senators had come over from their side of the Capitol to hear the voice of the Blairs raised against Chase. One was Sprague, who stood at the main door, listening carefully.

Blair was now attacking the so-called trade stores, which Chase had established in those sections of the seceded states that had been occupied by Federal troops. "These trade stores are given to political partisans and favorites, who share the profits with other men who furnish the capital, Mr. Chase furnishing capital to his friends and partisans in the shape of permits and privilege to monopolize the trade of a certain district."

Chase sat at his desk, reading Blair's speech with a sense that he might, suddenly, burst. "'Some of them, I suppose, employ themselves in distributing that "strictly private" circular which came to life the other day which informs us that the friends of Mr. Chase have been secretly forming an organization in his favor all over the country and which charges the Administration of Mr. Lincoln with corruption. None knew better than the friends of Mr. Chase at whose door does that corruption lie as their efforts to stifle investigation here so plainly prove.'

"It is monstrous," Chase said to Jay Cooke, who was staring through the light rain that fell now between the Treasury and his bank. "There are no specific charges of any kind. Just . . ." Chase could not finish; his heart was pounding; he had just become fifty-six years of age, and he had the sense that at any moment life could take wing from his aging body.

"Well, Pomeroy's circular hasn't helped us," said Cooke. "That's for sure. But we'll be hanging Mr. Blair in due course, and in the same place."

"But the damage that this does me! True or false don't matter when this speech is spread all around the country. I must resign."

"Don't you think that you should wait to hear what the President has to say?" Chase knew that Jay Cooke did not believe in anticipating trouble. But then Cooke did not understand how politicians communicate with one another.

"Mr. Cooke," said Chase, lowering himself into his teakwood throne, to be abdicated more soon now than late, "we have already heard from Mr. Lincoln."

"He's written you?"

"No, he has not written me. He has sent me his message through Frank Blair."

Jay Cooke shook his head with disbelief. "He controls Frank Blair?"

"Mr. Lincoln, in his strange, shifting, weak way, controls almost everyone. You see why I cannot stay."

"Wait for his letter, Mr. Chase."

The President had finished the letter in question and was re-reading it when Robert, home from Harvard, came into the office. Lincoln handed him the letter and said, "How does this sound to
514

you? It is to Mr. Chase, who thinks he should resign over the Pomeroy circular."

"He should. Don't you agree?"

"Read."

Robert read; then asked, with some wonder, "You've *never* read the circular?"

"No. There are some things it is often better not to know."

"Just curiosity would drive me to look at it."

"I think I lack that bump," said his father.

Robert finished the letter. "You're keeping him in the Cabinet?"

Lincoln nodded. "In a sort of casual way. I think Frank Blair has pretty much taken the wind out of Mr. Chase's sails. He can never win the nomination now. Find a messenger and send this over to the Treasury." Robert took the letter and left the office. Seward entered from the Cabinet Room.

"Well, Governor, I've just gone and patched things up with Mr. Chase."

"After ordering his execution on the floor of Congress."

"Well, you know the Blairs." Lincoln stared vaguely out the window at the truncated monument to the first President, dirty white against the dark wintry sky.

Seward took a deep breath; and then he told Lincoln of John Watt and the three letters. He was now happy to report that Sickles had been successful. Threatened with Fort Lafayette, the price had dropped from twenty thousand to fifteen hundred dollars, which Sickles had paid. Seward had the letters. As long as the war was on and *habeas corpus* suspended, Watt could never speak out. Once the war was done, it made no difference.

As Seward spoke, Lincoln leaned against the window frame; his face did not change expression, but since the face in repose was always deeply melancholy, he seemed now, to Seward's eye, a graven image of sorrow. He showed no surprise at any part of the story. When Seward was finished, Lincoln said, "Have you the letters?"

Seward gave the three letters to Lincoln, who promptly put them, unread, in the fireplace, where they swiftly turned to ash. Then Lincoln went to his writing desk and wrote out a personal check in the amount of fifteen hundred dollars and gave it to Seward. "Repay Sickles or whoever provided the actual money."

"Yes, sir."

There was a long silence as Lincoln stared into the fire and Seward examined, yet again, the furious face of old Andrew Jackson, so very like, in expression, that of Mr. Blair, Senior. Finally, Lincoln said, "You know, Governor, that I do not ever discuss personal matters with anyone, as they tend to be painful for me

515

and I see no need to share the pain. But as you have become so intimately involved with my family, I think I should give you my view of all this, and that is that the... caprices of Mrs. Lincoln, I am satisfied, are the result"—Lincoln rubbed the back of his hand across his eyes, as if not to *see* what he was about to say—"of partial insanity."

Since nothing that Seward could say on the subject would be of any use, he simply replied, "I am glad we could be helpful. The episode is over."

"Well, *this* episode is over."

In the front parlor of Sixth and E the political managers of Salmon Portland Chase had just accepted, somberly, the end of a crucial episode. All pretense that Kate did not involve herself in politics had been dropped. It was she who stood before the fireplace like the conductor of an orchestra, while Chase slumped passively in his usual chair and the brothers Cooke sat side by side on a loveseat. Sprague poured himself brandy from a decanter. In the five months that he had been married, he had several times given up drink for good. Senator Pomeroy folded and refolded a handkerchief, as if it were the Union's own sacred flag.

"I cannot believe that Ohio has deserted us." Kate was white with anger.

"Well, they have," said Henry D. "I always said one of us should have gone back last month and rallied the legislators..."

"But Father was there himself in October. I've never seen such crowds, and now they have all turned against us."

"I've written my friend Mr. Hall of Toledo a letter saying that I wish no further consideration of my name." Chase himself did not find it hard to believe that his old friends and allies had turned from him to Lincoln. That was the nature of politics. Lincoln was the president; and the president controls the party apparatus. Six months earlier, when the military news was bad, Chase might have prevailed. But since the war was now going well, the Republicans were not inclined to switch horses in the midst of history's stream. On the other hand, there was an excellent chance that the people of the country might be inclined to elect a Democrat in November. Already Chase had received a hint or two from leading Democrats displeased with McClellan. But Chase knew that it would take a political miracle for him to gain the Democratic nomination; and miracles were in peculiarly short supply at Sixth and E.

"We did our best, Mr. Chase." Pomeroy folded his handkerchief yet again. "We are nowhere near finished, of course. I have talked to many Republican leaders, and they believe that our strategy should be to lie low for the time being, while working with the Frémont faction in the party. Then, at the convention itself, we should be able to stop Lincoln. Once he is eliminated, who else is there but Mr. Chase?"

"That seems sound," said Jay Cooke; he turned to Chase. "What was the President's response to your letter about the circular?"

"He waited until *after* Frank Blair's attack on me, then he wrote to say that he agreed with me that neither of us could control his friends and that I should remain at the Treasury." Chase had wanted to tear up the letter; but dared not. He knew now that he would have to remain where he was and endure in the most public way the humiliation of one who had tried and failed to supplant a rival who had, in the most public way, outwitted him. Within three days of the publication of the circular, Lincoln had arranged for the Republicans in the Ohio legislature to reject their native son, Chase, and unanimously support the President. Within five days of the circular's publication, Lincoln had inspired Frank Blair to accuse his own Secretary of the Treasury of corruption. Then, two days later, Lincoln wrote Chase his friendly but, to Chase, highly condescending letter—of victory.

"Was all that stuff of Frank Blair's about trade permits true?" asked Sprague suddenly.

"Certainly not!" Sprague's wife answered for her father. "That people sell permits back and forth to one another is something Father cannot control. Certainly *he* does not benefit."

"We have a pretty good case against Frank Blair now," said Henry D. "We'll spring it on him next month. In the House."

"Too late," said Kate.

"Revenge is never too late," said Senator Pomeroy with a gentle smile. "We shall also show that he and Lincoln are in cahoots to destroy Mr. Chase. Some good will come out of it, never fear."

Chase listened to his friends talk as if he were, somehow, present at his own funeral. Everything was now past tense. Henry D. was off to Europe for a rest cure: or to avoid indictment in the Hurtt affair. Jay Cooke was winding up the affairs of the Chase campaign in which some ninety thousand dollars had been spent. Sprague continued to finance Sixth and E, but he was now less than generous when it came to political funding. As Chase had feared, Kate and Sprague were ill-matched. She was too intelligent; he too dull. She was also far too distracted by her father's collapsing political future to give Sprague the attention that he needed. As Chase listened to the far-off funereal voices, he composed his political epitaph: "I believe that I would rather that the people should wonder why I wasn't president than why I was."

Meanwhile, Washburne was staring at the one man in the United States who could be elected president by acclamation, burying Lincoln and all the rest. The short, slight man was at the reception desk at Willard's. Washburne had just come from the barbershop when he heard General Ulysses S. Grant say to the clerk, "I'd like a room. For myself and my son here." The son was a weedy boy of fourteen, who was staring about the crowded lobby with a certain wonder.

The clerk said, wearily, "I'm sorry, sir, but we've got nothing at all except a small room on the top floor."

"Well, we'll take what we can get." Grant filled out the registration card. The clerk took it; glanced at it perfunctorily; then said, without the slightest change in his manner, "You shall have the presidential suite, General Grant. It will be free within the hour, if you don't mind waiting."

"No," said Grant, "I don't mind. We'll get something to eat."

"I'll join you," said Washburne.

"Well, how did you know I'd be here?" asked Grant, a smile just visible beneath the thick brown beard.

"I didn't. I was in the barbershop. Where's your escort?"

"I don't have one. I've only got two staff members with me, and they've checked into the National. This is my son Fred."

Washburne shook the boy's hand warmly; and was relieved to see that he had not inherited his mother's startlingly crossed eyes. As they walked through the lobby, Grant said, "Since there was nobody from the War Department at the depot, we just hailed a cab and came on here."

They entered the large dining room. Washburne told the head waiter that they would like a quiet corner, which was found. In that huge, noisy, roast-meat-smelling room, no one paid the slightest attention to what was easily the shabbiest of a hundred Union officers at table. Even the two stars on each shoulder strap excited no interest: Washington was filled with major-generals.

But Grant was about to be a lieutenant-general; and Washburne took seriously his role as the congressman of the Union's greatest general. "I finally got the bill through the House, allowing for such a rank to be revived. It was not easy."

"I suppose not." Grant did not seem very interested. The pale-blue eyes were alert but somewhat bloodshot. Washburne wondered if the general might have been drunk on the cars from Nashville. At the moment he was drinking quantities of water and eating bread as they waited for the waiter to bring them the day's soup. Fred was chewing his nails and counting the number of generals in the room.

"Well, there hasn't been such a rank since George Washington. Winfield Scott's lieutenant-generalcy was more . . . emeritus?"

"Brevet," said Grant, precisely.

"That's the word. Garfield thought the honor too great for any man while the war is still going on."

"Did he?" Grant smiled, and chewed bread.

"He did. Anyway, I got the bill through and tomorrow the President will give you your commission. We don't anticipate any trouble from the Senate."

"I have a condition of acceptance," said Grant. "I will not make my headquarters here."

Washburne was surprised. "But you will be commanding all the armies..." The soup arrived.

"I can do that from the west." Grant proceeded to eat the soup like a man digging a ditch. The spoon was there to empty the plate, and so the spoon was used; and thus the plate was emptied. He was, as soldier and man, all of a piece, thought Washburne.

"You know there is a lot of speculation going on about you." Washburne paused so that Grant might ask, of what nature? But the general simply stared at the spoon, which now lay in the center of the empty soup plate. "Speculation as to whether or not you'll be tempted to run for president in the fall. Certainly, the Democrats would nominate you, and perhaps even the Republicans." This was not, Washburne realized sadly, the most subtle political approach that he had ever made. But Grant was not a man for the usual political ellipsis.

"I've said I don't want the job." Grant looked up from the plate. "I hate this city. Sherman warned me against Washington." Grant lowered his voice so that Fred could not hear. "Worse than Sodom and Gomorrah," he said. "Besides, I like what I'm doing. Tell Mr. Lincoln he has nothing to fear from me."

This was almost too direct for Washburne's taste. "Well, I'm not sure exactly what General Sherman had in mind in his characterization of Washington, but this is a city devoted to intrigue, and with an election approaching, it is more than usually mephitic."

Grant was now carefully slicing up the entirety of a steak, preparatory to eating it. Fred reported that five major-generals and eighteen brigadiers were in the dining room. "But you outrank 'em all, Pa."

"If the President wants me to, and the Senate agrees, I do. Otherwise, I don't." Grant was not about to tempt fate.

"The President is curious to know if politics tempt you. You know, perhaps, *after* the war..." Washburne was amazed at his own maladroitness. Plainly, there was something in Grant's blunt, matter-of-fact nature that brought out a certain crudeness in his own.

"Well," said Grant, speaking and chewing at the same time,

"I do have a certain political interest for after the war. If I survive this business, I mean to run for mayor of Galena and, if elected, I intend to have the sidewalk fixed up between my house and the depot."

Suddenly, there was a cry, "General Grant!" To Washburne's amazement and Grant's discomfiture, half the diners in the room were now converging on their table. Grant had been recognized. He stood at his place and shook hands until it was plain that he was not going to be allowed to finish his dinner. Suddenly, he blurted out, "Let's go, Fred." With that, the general, followed by Fred and Washburne, cut through the crowd to the lobby, where Grant said to Washburne, "I think I'll hide out in my room now."

"But you'll be seeing the President this evening, won't you?"

"I'm not invited." Absently Grant continued to shake a series of proffered hands while never once looking up to see to whom the hands belonged.

"It's the weekly reception. Everyone's invited."

"Oh." Grant seemed to think a moment. Then he said, "What time?"

"I'll come and pick you up at nine-thirty. We'll walk over together."

"Can I come, Pa?"

"No," said General Grant.

At nine-thirty, Grant's two aides were waiting for him at the White House portico. One of them said, "Word's got around that you might be here. There's quite a crowd in there."

Grant looked at Washburne, as if to ascertain what to do next. Then he entered the Mansion first.

In the entrance hall, guests were milling about. At first, the arrival of three shabby officers and one rumpled familiar member of Congress interested no one. Also, when it came to generalissimos, the capital was used to white-haired or at least grizzled commanders. At forty-one, Grant's hair was still entirely brown— and all his own, unlike that of Gideon Welles, who was the first to recognize Grant as he and Washburne made their way to the Blue Room, where the President and Mrs. Lincoln were receiving their guests. Welles bowed to Grant, who gave him a half salute. Grant insisted on joining the long line in front of the Blue Room. When Washburne suggested that he go straight in to the President, Grant said, "No." Grant seemed very fond, Washburne decided, of that monosyllable.

As Grant stepped up to the President, Lamon started to ask him his name so that he could make the presentation, but Lincoln had recognized the small figure. "Why," he said, with a smile
520

that was all white teeth, "here is General Grant!" He shook Grant's hand warmly. "Well, this is a great pleasure for me."

As Grant mumbled something in reply, Lincoln motioned for Mary to come forward and shake the general's hand, which she did with genuine interest. "We have looked forward, sir," she said, "to seeing you here, sir, for quite some time." Then the line disintegrated, and everyone rushed into the Blue Room. Washburne was shoved to one side, and only the formidable Lamon was able to keep the Lincolns from being physically overwhelmed, while only the quick-thinking Seward saved Grant from being trampled.

From nowhere, Seward had suddenly materialized at Grant's side. Small as Seward was, he could, through gestures alone, appear to occupy a large space or, in this case, create a sufficient space about himself and Grant. Arms flailing the air, Seward shouted, "This way, General! To the East Room!" He then propelled Grant out the door, followed by everyone else. In less than a minute the Lincolns were left alone with Lamon.

"I have never seen anything like that!" Mary was truly astonished.

"Well, it's the first time the folks have ever got a look at a really successful general," said Lincoln. "It's sort of like Tom Thumb all over again."

From the East Room, there was a sound of cheering. "Come on, Mother, we may as well see the sights, too."

The Lincolns arrived at the door to the East Room just as Seward was coaxing the red-faced Grant onto a sofa, where he now stood, swaying slightly, in plain view of everyone. "Father," said Mary, deeply alarmed, "he is running for President!"

"Well, Mother, he has said that he has no such base ambitions."

"*Everyone* says that." Mary could not believe that here in the Mansion the President was entirely ignored, while what looked to be a dry-goods clerk was staggering about on a newly reupholstered crimson sofa, and everyone in the room was cheering him and trying to shake his hand, while Seward more than ever resembled an eccentric parrot, hopping about the hero of the hour. "They would nominate him, wouldn't they?" Mary was upset.

"If he were to win the war for us before June, of course they would. But as that's only four months from now, I don't think he's apt to defeat General Lee all that fast. If he does, of course, I'll help him get elected."

"Don't say such a thing!" The thought that Lincoln might not be reelected was the worst of Mary's night terrors. She was close to thirty thousand dollars in debt, and now, without John Watt to help her borrow money in New York, she was at a loss how to pay her personal bills, many of them years overdue. As long as it looked as if she would be First Lady for another four years, she could intimidate her creditors. But at the first sign that her husband might be defeated, they would fall upon her like wolves. Keckley had begged her to tell the President; but she could not. He had already had to endure so much on her account. Could she bear, she wondered, to part with the new diamond-and-pearl earrings that she was wearing? They had cost three thousand dollars. She touched one of them with her forefinger. She thought of the matching brooch which she had declined to buy. She *could* show restraint, she knew. Besides, one of the Republicans who owed so much to Mr. Lincoln might buy it for her. Since so many men that he had appointed to office had made fortunes, it was only justice that they provide for her when she was financially embarrassed. One of them, William Mortimer, had just given her a gold-and-enamel brooch with forty-seven diamonds. She still had friends. But would they remain friends if the President were not reelected? The thought made her shudder.

Seward was now proposing three cheers for the victor of Vicksburg, and the East Room echoed with a thousand voices, including Lincoln's if not Mary's. Then Grant got off the sofa. As the crowd that circled him tried to shake his hand, he visibly shrank from them. "I don't think he's running for president just yet," said Lincoln, whose practised eye was taking in the scene. "He's too scared of the folks. But once he gets the knack of handling them, there'll be no stopping him."

"Let us hope that that won't be until after next November."

Lincoln nodded. "Let us hope so. Because there is nothing on this earth quite as useless in a war as a general who is running for president. On that subject, I am the world's greatest—and saddest—authority."

Seward took the same view. Clearly, Grant was as ambitious as all the others and like all great men and a good many not so great, he had no modesty. He had been spoken of as a presidential candidate ever since the battle of Lookout Mountain. The American public had a curious appetite for military leaders in politics and though Seward tended to deplore this peculiar craving, he would cater for it if he had to. If Grant won the war, he could be groomed. But did Grant truly understand his situation? That was the question.

Lincoln seemed to think that Grant did. The two men were seated in the President's office. In the next room, Cabinet and interested parties were gathering for Grant's investiture as lieutenant-general in command of all the armies of the United States.

"Grant *seems* a sensible fellow," said the President, holding up a plaster copy of the curiously ugly gold medallion that Congress had ordered to be struck in the general's honor.

"They are all sensible until..."

"Until the presidential grub starts to gnaw." Lincoln put away the plaster disk. "I didn't have many words with him last night but I think he understands that he needs me, as president, as much as I need him as general. He has had victories. But he's also had defeats. I covered up for him over Shiloh. If he is to be... what he would like to be"—how typical of Lincoln, thought Seward, to leave unrevealed his own deepest estimate of Grant—"we must support each other. Thanks to me, he holds George Washington's rank. Now he must be worthy of it."

"He must win the war, of course," said Seward, adding, pointedly, "He *himself* must win the war, not any other general. Will that be a problem?"

Lincoln smiled. "Why, Governor, you make me feel like Napoleon with a hundred brilliant field-marshals, when all I've got's one general and a half."

"Named Sherman?"

Lincoln nodded. "Grant thinks more highly of Sherman than I do. Last night Grant was eager to go back to Nashville and continue his plan to strike at Mobile and Atlanta, but I talked him out of it. The heart of the rebellion is at Richmond and the victory to be won is over Lee. He grasps that now."

"He will move here?" asked Seward.

Nicolay now was at the door. "Everyone's ready, sir."

"I'll be right in." Lincoln picked up a sheet of paper. "I want this to sound exactly right on both sides. I gave him a copy of my little speech last night, and I told him he should write out his answer since the wire-services will carry everything we say. I suggested that he say something that would make the other generals feel a bit less envious..."

"You will have us in there for several hours."

"Something *brief*, I said. Also, I felt that he should, somehow, praise the Army of the Potomac, since that is our principal... weapon."

As it was, Grant followed neither of the President's suggestions. After the President's gracious presentation of the commission, with an "under God" added by Seward, Grant rose and read, with difficulty, from a piece of paper on which he had scribbled a number of lines with a lead pencil. Grant invoked Providence rather than God; and praised the armies but not their commanders. Seward found the performance disappointing.

Chase barely listened; his mind was elsewhere. Grant was Lincoln's general; and would never be his. Since his own career seemed at an end, he was not much interested in the ascendant stars of others. He tried to console himself with a Pauline homily but only the cadences of Jeremiah sounded in his head.

When the meeting broke up, Lincoln introduced everyone to General Grant and his son Fred. Then Grant and Lincoln and Nicolay went into the President's office. If Stanton or Halleck were distressed at being overlooked, neither showed it.

Lincoln came to the point. "The object of the exercise is now Richmond—and the defeat of General Lee. I know that you would rather be in the West, but it is too far away for you to take personal charge of such a great undertaking."

"I agree. I would like Sherman to take my place in the West."

Lincoln nodded; then he said, "General Halleck has resigned as general-in-chief. So you are now that as well."

"I would like him to continue," said Grant, "if he would, as chief of staff to me. He can coordinate matters here better than I, since I don't expect to be in Washington all that much."

Lincoln's left eyebrow slowly raised. "You will not take a house in the city then?"

"I'll have to find something for Mrs. Grant and the children. They will have to move here now. But I will live with the Army of the Potomac."

Lincoln clapped his hands, eyes to Heaven or Providence. "I have waited three years to hear a general say that!"

Grant ignored this moment of Providential rapture. "I shall keep General Meade where he is."

Lincoln frowned. "The Joint Committee wants him replaced. They want Hooker to replace him, because Hooker is a good abolitionist."

Grant said, "I'd better go talk to General Meade now."

"I'll send for him."

"No, I'll go to him. Besides I want a look at the Army of the Potomac. If that is all...?"

Lincoln shook Grant's hand. "I have only one suggestion, General. Wherever Lee's army is, there you should be, too."

"That is about right, sir." Grant left the office.

When the door had shut behind the new lieutenant-general, Lincoln said to Nicolay, "At least he is not like any of the others." Then he added, as ever cautious, "No matter *what* he proves to be like."

4

SHORTLY BEFORE MIDNIGHT, MAY 13, JOHN HAY WAS FINISHING an entry in his diary when the door to the bedroom swung open, and there stood the Ancient in his nightshirt. "I saw your light on," he said.

The Ancient had taken to roaming about the White House late at night: sometimes he wore an old wrapper, sometimes nothing but a topcoat, sometimes just his shirt, which was now all bunched up in the back, giving him the look of a highly comical sort of ostrich with long, brown, bony legs.

The Ancient settled comfortably on the corner of the bed, the usual War Department dispatches in his hand. "Well, the rebels have just abandoned Spotsylvania, and Grant keeps moving. I've never seen anything like it, the way he keeps on, no matter what!" The Ancient's face grew somber, as he added, "And no matter what his losses."

Ten days earlier, Grant had begun his move into what was known as the Virginia Wilderness. He had sustained astonishing losses. Some thirty thousand Union men were dead or wounded. But then Lee had suffered equally; and Lee had fewer men. What Grant could not win in a set battle, he would win through numbers and endurance. The country had been both horrified and thrilled by this dreadful new kind of warfare: not that either country or President had been taken into Grant's confidence. At one point, Grant and his army of one hundred twenty thousand men simply vanished without a trace, and Stanton's difficulty in breathing became even more pronounced, not to mention contagious, for even the Ancient grew short of breath. But now the reports had begun to come in. There had been a head-on battle between Grant and Lee at Spotsylvania Court House. Grant had a two-to-one advantage. After great losses on both sides, Lee had withdrawn.

"One thing about General Grant, he doesn't turn back," said Hay, shutting his diary.

Lincoln nodded. "I believe if any other general had been at the head of that army, after such losses, he would have been high-tailing it back across the Rapidan by now. But he grinds on and on, and when he gets hold of a piece of ground, he acts like he inherited it. Poor Wadsworth," he said suddenly; and shut his eyes. Among the casualties of the Wilderness had been General James S. Wadsworth, a good friend of the Ancient. Wadsworth had left the army to be Republican candidate for governor of New York. Defeated by Horatio Seymour, he had gone back to the army. "There is... there was... no other like him. He was not in the army for glory or personal advancement. He was there because he thought it the right thing to do; thought it his duty. In this world of calculating Iagos, he was truly noble. He was also the only general who wanted to cut off Lee after Gettysburg, but Meade..." The Ancient stopped; let that be ancient history. "Now, John, you are a poet—"

"Oh, sir! If only I were."

"No. I liked that poem you wrote about Key West." The Ancient settled himself comfortably on the pillows and Hay, dizzy with fatigue, realized that the Ancient, like Coleridge's Mariner of the same affix or prefix, intended to recite poetry. "I was thinking about *Hamlet* while I was waiting for news from Grant. Now it is fashionable to admire Hamlet's 'To be, or not to be' soliloquy, but I have never cared for it, save the last part: 'The undiscover'd country' is most chilling. I have always preferred 'O!, my offence is rank...'"

Lincoln gave the entire speech. He then demonstrated how most actors misunderstood the irony and bitterness of Richard III's "Now is the winter of our discontent..." He acted Shakespeare rather more subtly than most actors—at least those arias that appealed to him. Half an hour passed. Did the Ancient never sleep anymore? Hay tried to keep his eyes open; but failed. He had now missed most of Richard II's "Let us sit upon the ground, And tell sad stories of the death of kings." The Ancient laughed; and got off the bed. "Go to sleep, Mr. Hay. I seem to have lost the knack for sleep lately."

"Well, sir, the amount of underpinning you have seems to have improved." Hay indicated the legs, which were somewhat less bony than they had been just after the bout of smallpox.

Lincoln nodded. "I now weigh a hundred and eighty pounds." Thus, thought Hay, "Honest Abe" had finally lied to him. "Goodnight."

At Sixth and E, Honest Abe was not only a sulfurous epithet but a hideous irony. Chase sat alone in his study, waiting for news from Cleveland of a convention composed mostly of his admirers, fellow radicals who wished to undercut the Republican Party's regular convention, where Lincoln was expected to be renominated if Grant's name was not, somehow, put in nomination.

In regard to Lincoln, Chase's fury—there was no other word,

save, perhaps, his own word "wrathy" to Jay Cooke—was now absolute, just as the Blairs' control of the President was now absolute. Admittedly, Chase's allies had blundered in the matter of Frank Blair. The "evidence" of Blair's corruption at Vicksburg had been somewhat clumsily forged, as Blair himself had pointed out in a fiery speech on the floor of the House, where he attacked Chase and all his works and minions. But then, most pointedly, the President, instead of supporting his own colleague, sent for Blair, gently chided him for "kicking over the beehive"; and sent him back to the front as a major-general.

Chase's usual allies were now speaking more and more of Grant as a replacement for Lincoln. To Chase's sorrow and surprise, they had taken his withdrawal from the race with more seriousness than loyal friends ought to have done. He did not enjoy being told that he should wait for the death of the Chief Justice. Besides, even that ghoulish watch might not prove fruitful. Since relations between him and the President were so strained, Lincoln was now perfectly capable of appointing an inferior man Chief Justice. For once, Chase was truly eager to resign from the Cabinet. Unfortunately, Lincoln needed him; and so the uneasy relationship continued. Once Lincoln was reelected, Chase would be dismissed if he had not already gone on his way to the Chief Justiceship—or home to Ohio. The unfairness of life could only be borne, thought Chase grimly, by a rapt contemplation of the Savior's agony.

Kate swung open the door to announce: "They've nominated Frémont. There were only about four hundred people at Cosmopolitan Hall. They've all gone home."

"Well, let us hope *he* fights the good fight." Chase was startled by his own indifference.

"Oh, it is all a joke, says Mr. Sumner."

"Sumner entered the study. Chase rose to greet his friend and ally who had recently managed to deal so well in morals and so ill in politics that he had helped, with his Olympian advice, to shipwreck Chase's career. I mistrust all generals," said "Sumner. "But Grant could be nominated at Baltimore."

"If he agrees," said Kate. "And he won't. Anyway, he's bogged down in Virginia, just like McClellan. There he is, nine miles or whatever from Richmond, but Lee won't fight."

"Still, Grant is the man of the hour," said Sumner, unperturbed, as always, by inconvenient detail. "The common people trust and revere him."

"But should *we*?" asked Chase, in a tone sharper than he had ever before used to Sumner. "Ought we? Who is Grant? Where

527

does he stand on abolition? Where does he stand on the read-mission of the conquered states?"

"I only make the point that he can defeat Mr. Lincoln," said Sumner. "If he can be captured for the Republican Party."

"There is no such thing," said Kate. "Have you heard what they mean to call the convention at Baltimore?"

Sumner frowned. "Surely, it is the Republican . . . Well, the *National* Republican Party convention?"

"No, Mr. Sumner. The word Republican will not be used at all because of us. Mr. Lincoln has decreed—"

"The Blairs, Katie," Chase interposed.

"The Blairs," Kate corrected herself, "have renamed our party. It is now the National Union Party."

"This is unspeakable!" Sumner shook a lock of straw-colored hair from his eyes. "This also means that we are now absolutely obliged to hold our own convention—a *Republican* convention."

For some time, Chase's allies had discussed, in a more or less desultory way, the possibility of breaking away from the Blair-Lincoln party. The Frémont convention had been a futile enterprise, if only because of Frémont himself. But a full-scale convention of true Republicans, endorsed by Governor Andrew of Massachusetts and Governor Curtin of Pennsylvania, and directed by the congressional leadership might very well eliminate the Blair-Lincoln element. Sumner had now caught fire. "We shall wait until after the Democrats meet at Chicago. That will be the end of August. Then we shall persuade poor Mr. Lincoln to step aside, so that we can call a new convention for late September. It should be somewhere in . . ."

"Ohio," said Kate. "Cincinnati, I should think."

"Exactly! Then"—Sumner threw his arms wide as if to embrace both Chase and the world itself—"*you* shall take up our fallen standard!"

Chase felt the first stirring of hope in some time. "It is conceivable," he said, "that, by then, the country will turn to us."

"Oh, Father! Where else? Who else?"

"*In hoc signo*," intoned Sumner, "*vinceremus.*"

President Chase, thought Chase. It was again a possibility. So near at hand!

The actual President sat at his desk, reading a report of the Frémont convention, which Seward had brought him. Seward had been alarmed. But Lincoln had been amused. He was particularly amused, he told Seward, to read that although thousands had been expected to fill up the Cosmopolitan Hall, there had been only four hundred casual men who had wandered into the building and said that they were delegates. "Four hundred," said
528

Lincoln, putting down the report, and reaching for a copy of the Bible which he kept in the same pigeonhole as Horace Greeley's correspondence. "That strikes a note, Governor." Lincoln riffled through the Bible until he found what he wanted. He read aloud, "'And every one that was in distress, and every one that was in debt, and every one that was discontented, gathered themselves unto him; and he became a captain over them: and there were with him about four hundred men.'" Lincoln shut the Bible; took off his glasses. "I should be surprised if Frémount ever gets around to running. No, Governor, I'm more concerned about these meetings they're holding in New York to honor, as they put it, General Grant."

"Should they know what happened yesterday, I wonder how great the honoring will be." There was a division within the Administration whether or not to release the full figures of the defeat that Grant had just sustained at Cold Harbor in Virginia. He had made a frontal assault on Richmond's northern defenses; and had been thrown back by Lee. Thus far, the press had only reported that Grant had not succeeded in taking Richmond. Stanton had seen to it that the enormity of Grant's defeat was kept from the country. In a single operation, Grant had lost fifty thousand men, more than half the fighting army that he had taken into the Wilderness. If the country were to learn of this, Seward had said, there would be no nomination of Grant for president by any party. But Lincoln had taken the view that anything which might cause the country to lose confidence in Grant would also bring down the Administration and elect McClellan. "He's just about our last hope, Governor. Besides, I believe him when he says he isn't a candidate."

"The Missouri delegation is pledged to vote for Grant on the first ballot."

"But all the others will be voting for me." Lincoln seemed unconcerned by Missouri's display of Blairish disloyalty or eccentricity. "I'm sending Nicolay to Baltimore. He'll have a word with the Missourians."

"Will he spread the word about Cold Harbor?"

Lincoln shrugged. "I hope it won't be necessary."

"With some of our Grant-honoring New Yorkers, I think it will be necessary."

"Then he will do it," said Lincoln, obviously prepared to go further in secret than in public. "What word from New England?"

"Weed is busy." In principle, Lincoln favored the renomination of the 1860 ticket of Lincoln and Hamlin; therefore, publicly, he would support no one. Privately, Lincoln was working with Seward and Weed and Cameron to deny Hamlin the renomination. "The

Maine delegation will support Hamlin, as favorite son. But Massachusetts will go mostly for Dickinson, my fellow New Yorker." Seward was more amused than alarmed at the current Byzantine strategy of the radicals to remove him from the Cabinet by electing a New Yorker to the vice-presidency on the ground that two such high offices could not be filled by natives of the same state.

"Welles says that Connecticut will be for Andrew Johnson." Lincoln stared out the window at the blazing green summer foliage. The year's weather had been bizarre. At the end of March, snow had covered the city for the first time in anyone's memory, destroying the spring flowers. Now June was equatorial in its heat. All things are out of joint, thought Seward. "Sumner is our greatest ally," he said. "But he doesn't know it, which is always a pleasure. He wants Hamlin to leave the Vice-Presidency so that he can then go home to Maine, where he will replace Sumner's enemy, Fessenden, in the Senate, while Dickinson, as a New Yorker . . ."

Lincoln sighed. "Sumner exhausts me. Anyway, one burning house at a time. I must have a vice-president in sympathy with my views, which Hamlin is not."

"To say the least." The issue of Hamlin's possible corruption had never been alluded to by either Lincoln or Seward. Some months earlier, the two men, each on his own, had come to the conclusion that the next vice-president must be a Democrat and a Unionist and a Southerner. Cameron had also concurred. Cameron had then approached Ben Butler, whom Chase had wanted as *his* running mate.

Ben Butler had declined the honor. "At forty-six," he told Cameron, "I'm far too young to spend four years being bored to death listening to senators make stupid speeches."

The second choice was Governor Andrew Johnson of Tennessee. He had been loyal to the Union. He agreed with Lincoln's policy of readmitting the rebel states once ten percent of the population had taken the oath. He was popular in the North. Seward knew that Lincoln had sent Dan Sickles on a tour of the South, and that Sickles had given a good report of Johnson, whose virulent hatred of the slave-owners had made Lincoln uneasy.

"Naturally, I must not be seen to have any preference," said Lincoln for the hundredth time.

"What happens if things start to slide toward Dickinson?"

"I've given Lamon a letter which he is to show the delegates only if it is absolutely necessary. But I think, between Weed and Cameron, we will have Johnson without much fuss." Lincoln chuckled. "Of course we can never really count on anything, can we? I can never forget that I was nominated at a convention where two thirds of the delegates wanted the other fellow."

"Me."

"You."

Nicolay entered the room; and gave Seward a dispatch. Lincoln asked after Lamon, who had been thrown from a carriage two days earlier and suffered a number of broken ribs. "He just took the cars for Baltimore."

"He is made of iron," said Lincoln. "When do you go?"

"This evening, sir. With Mr. Cameron." Nicolay left the room.

Seward looked up from the dispatch. "Mexico," he said, eyes glittering as always when he considered that prize-to-be. "The Emperor Maximilian is having his problems."

"President Polk's version of the Monroe Doctrine is not one of them," said Lincoln wryly.

"You know the radicals in Baltimore are going to make Mexico an issue. First, Maximilian is a French puppet. Second, France is on the side of our rebels. Now, you know my dream—"

"The United States as master of the entire earth. From China to Spain. From the North Pole to the South Pole. All ours!" Lincoln laughed. "Well, Governor, when it comes to territory, I am much more modest. All I want is Richmond, just sixty miles away."

"There is a way to end this war gloriously." Seward could not resist sharing his latest dream with Lincoln. "We will buy the slaves, as you've suggested, and we'll colonize them, as you've suggested, in Central America. I am certain that the South will agree to those terms at this point *if* we then unite, as one entire nation again, and our combined armies under Grant and Lee sweep across the Rio Grande into Mexico, driving the French from this hemisphere, and then we move into Central and South America, driving out the Spanish and the Portuguese. Oh, I see such a glorious logical *American* solution to all our problems!"

Lincoln shook his head in mock dismay. "How do I persuade Sumner and Ben Wade and Zach. Chandler to go along?"

"Shoot them!" said Seward, exuberantly.

"Well, if *you* sign the order, Governor, and I can prove that I was totally incapacitated at the time..."

Hay appeared in the doorway. "Sir, something that says it's the delegation from South Carolina wants to see you. I think they are a swindle, sir."

"Send them in, John. They won't swindle me."

As the delegation, which included several Negroes, entered the room, Seward departed through the Cabinet Room. He had been entirely serious about his solution to the war. He had also sent a message through to Richmond, and he knew that his idea was

531

now being seriously discussed in the highest Confederate circles. Grant and Lee; and then the world.

Major John Hay enjoyed wearing his uniform at the Eameses. "It is not that I exactly fight in it," he said, "but I feel that I *could* fight in it." He and Mr. Eames were in an alcove of the drawing room where a crude painting of Simon Bolivar hung, a souvenir of Venezuela. "You should leave the fighting to others," said Mr. Eames. "The real war is here in Washington."

"Certainly it is a war of its sort," agreed Hay, aware that the once and perhaps future warrior Chase had just entered the room.

"The President must be pleased with what happened at Baltimore." Eames seldom couched questions as questions, diplomatically allowing the other person not to answer if he chose.

"Oh, yes. He seems well pleased with Governor Johnson as a running mate. He's not entirely happy with all the platform, but then no one ever bothers much with platforms." Nicolay had come back, tired and bored, from the convention. He had reported to Hay that no one had recognized the President's hand in the choice of Johnson. Cameron had arranged matters with his usual skill. Missouri had cast its votes for Grant; then switched to Lincoln, who was chosen unanimously. The speeches had been tedious but, mercifully, short; there was less drinking than usual. Last-minute details of Grant's defeat at Cold Harbor had chilled, said Nicolay with a smile, the ardor of his admirers. Lately, the Tycoon had been so much serenaded at the White House that he had come to the conclusion that the only entirely painful form of speech-making was responding, vapidly, to a serenade.

"What news of General Grant?" Mr. Eames did pose this as a direct question.

Hay responded with equal directness. "He has moved south and west of Richmond. He hopes to take Petersburg. If he does, he will be able to cut off Richmond from the rest of the South."

"But he has been stopped."

Hay nodded. The Tycoon had taken the news well enough. But Hay could see that he was, each day, more and more reminded of McClellan, who had got himself bogged down in much the same place. Fortunately, Grant had not made his headquarters at Harrison's Landing. Instead he had picked City Point, a minuscule port on the south bank of the James River, some ten miles from besieged Petersburg. "As long as Grant stays where he is, Lee must stay there, too, or give up Richmond. Meanwhile, our Western generals are moving east." As Hay spoke, he watched Chase approach Julia Ward Howe, the celebrated poetess who had been in the city for some time, giving elevated lectures on "Moral Trigonometry" and other complex issues. The town was making

532

much of her. But then she had become nationally famous by putting new words to that old drinking-song to which the words of "John Brown's Body" had been, briefly, attached. Now, once again, John Brown had been detached, as it were, from the living music and Mrs. Howe's "Battle Hymn of the Republic" had replaced him with a poetic exuberance that had caused some laughter in Washington's literary circles where the phrase "the evening's dews and damps" gave much pleasure. Hay far preferred the works of the scandalous old Walt Whitman, who was still skulking about the city's hospitals, looking after wounded boys and writing occasional puff-pieces for the press in which the good gray poet, Walt Whitman, was ecstatically praised by the author, Whitman himself. When Hay got the chance, he often enjoyed evenings with such Washington litterateurs as John Burroughs and William O'Connor, both Treasury clerks and friends of the unemployable-by-Chase Whitman.

At the moment, however, Chase was in his element with a poet he could entirely admire. "Knowing, Mrs. Howe," he said to the small plump-faced woman with her braids of hair like coronets of reddish mouse fur, "that I would have the honor of seeing you tonight, I took the liberty of bringing with me your very first volume of verse in the hope that you would give me a *dedicace*."

"With pleasure, dear Mr. Chase." Julia Ward Howe took the thin volume that Chase offered her, and together they withdrew to a writing desk where she inscribed his name and her name on the title page of *Passion Flowers*. "It is curious the affection that one so often, even misguidedly, feels for a first effort," Mrs. Howe observed, blotting the two names firmly and returning the book to Chase, who felt the collector's peculiar joy at having acquired something so deeply longed for.

"You need never feel that your affection for these verses is misguided. My daughter Katie used to read them aloud to our literary group in Columbus."

"Your daughter is a Renaissance lady, Mr. Chase. One sees in her something of Queen Elizabeth. Yes, of Gloriana herself. She has all the gifts—and she has the will! It is the implacable will that makes all the difference, as I demonstrate in my essay 'Equalities'..."

They were joined by the Assistant Secretary of the Treasury, Maunsell B. Field, an invaluable aid to Chase. Field was something of an exquisite, who parted his hair in the middle, which Chase did not approve of. But Field's devotion to his master was absolute. Field was also very much at home in the world of the fine arts: it was he who had redecorated Chase's office, designed the much-envied marble bathroom, and chose the pattern for the Axminster rugs. When Chase was in New York City, Field saw to it that the Secretary met the highest society. Field had known every important visitor to the United States from Baron Renfrew—alias the Prince of Wales—to Jenny Lind. Needless to say, he was on the best of terms with Julia Ward Howe, and this formidable lady now included him in her general remarks on the nature of the will.

As Mrs. Howe spoke, Chase, too, pondered the nature of the will. The Assistant Treasurer at New York, the able John J. Cisco, had just resigned. Chase wished the appointment to go to Field, who longed to spread, as it were, his wings in the more glittering atmosphere of the notorious great metropolis. Chase would have preferred to keep Field at Washington, but to have a man of such loyalty in New York was no bad thing since Hiram Barney's defection to Lincoln, who, most ungratefully, wanted Barney to resign in order to appease the state's moderate element.

At first, the President had made no particular objection to Field's appointment, but he insisted that the two New York senators must concur in an appointment so important to their state. Senator Morgan and Chase had had several meetings. Chase had been the soul of graciousness and conciliation. He had agreed to appoint Senator Morgan's first choice; but the gentleman in question had declined the honor. Chase had agreed to Morgan's second proposal; but again the honor was declined. Chase had then written the President, proposing Field. Lincoln had said that he could not make the appointment without "much embarrassment" because Senator Morgan was firmly opposed to it. Since three additional names had been proposed by the New Yorkers, surely Chase could select one. As of that morning, Chase had neatly, if temporarily, resolved the matter by persuading Cisco to remain in office for three more months. Simultaneously, he had received a disturbing letter from Lincoln, refusing Chase's suggestion that they discuss the matter face-to-face. Lincoln wrote that he saw no point to a discussion on the mysterious ground "that no man knows so well where the shoe pinches as he who wears it." Am I, Chase wondered, the shoe that pinches? Or is it the New York element that Lincoln wishes to appease?

Chase liked the tone of the letter not at all. Lincoln had said, right out, that Mr. Field was not the proper man for an office that Senator Morgan wanted to make a political machine of; worse, the President had refused even to discuss such an important matter with the Cabinet officer directly involved. Chase had responded with quiet firmness. He was sorry if he was a source of embarrassment—he had seized on the operative word—to the President.
534

Because if this were the case, and Chase's position should prove to be disagreeable to the President, he would resign that position with real relief. Actually, if he were to leave office, now was the time. The national finances were more than ever unsatisfactory. The price of gold was sky-high. The costs of the war could only be met through taxation; and Congress was not about to impose the necessary taxes in an election year.

Julia Ward Howe was now explaining the French Revolution to Mr. Field, who was enraptured. Chase pretended to listen but his mind was on other matters, of which not the least was the variety and quality of the leather with which he would bind *Passion Flowers*.

Across the room, Mr. Eames told Hay that he had read his poems and that he was a real poet. "When your present work is over, you must apply yourself to poetry. Anyone can be a man of action. But hardly anyone can write a line that will live down the ages."

"I am not *that* gifted," said Hay, almost meaning it. He knew that his recent poems were good; he also knew that his talent was for comic verse; and no comic line had ever managed to get from one generation to the next, much less make its way through the ages.

"You will never know who you are until you are on your own and, of course, married. Yes, you must marry." Since Mr. Eames had made a happy marriage, he inclined to fervor on the subject, particularly when dealing with contented young bachelors. "In fact, the earlier a man gets used to marriage, the better it is for him. Delay too long..." Mr. Eames shook his head at the horror that might lie in store for one who had married too late to get the knack of it—like the Ancient, Hay suddenly, perhaps disloyally, thought.

The next morning disloyalty was the theme at the White House. At nine, the Tycoon sent for Hay; he was at his writing desk, rereading a letter that he had just written. "What time does the Senate meet today?" he asked, without looking up.

"Eleven, sir."

"I want you to be there when they open shop." Lincoln looked up; and smiled. "It is a big fish this time. A salmon, in fact. Mr. Chase has resigned for the third or fourth time—I've lost count—and I have accepted his resignation. I could not take much more of him."

Hay was stunned. Chase had seemed so entirely part of their Washington landscape that it was inconceivable that he could, with a stroke of the Tycoon's pen, cease to exist. It would be like

535

the view from the window, without Washington's unfinished monument. "Is it about the Field matter?"

"Yes."

"Who will succeed Mr. Chase?"

"Dave Tod. He's my friend, with a big head full of brains. He's also a Douglas Democrat."

"But does he know about finances?"

"Well, he was a good governor of Ohio, and he made himself a fortune in business. I'm willing to trust him." Lincoln gave Hay the message for the Senate. He then placed Chase's letter in the pigeonhole marked "C." "I suppose, sooner or later, there is bound to be a resignation that is accepted."

"Why did you accept this one, sir?"

"How could he and I have gone on after all that has happened between us? Also, the sense of his letter to me is, 'You have been acting very badly. Unless you say you are sorry, and ask me to stay and agree that I shall be absolute and that you shall have nothing, no matter how you beg for it, I go.' Well, he is gone now."

Hay told Nicolay what had happened. Nicolay shook his head with disbelief. Then he said, somewhat grimly, "If I had the money, I'd buy gold today."

Hay rode alone to the Capitol in the presidential carriage. Early as the day was, the sun was hot, while with each shallow reluctant breath, Hay was haunted by the ghosts of the millions of cats who had given their lives that the nearby canal might exude its distinctive odor.

At the door to the Senate chamber, Hay paused. While the chaplain exhorted the Almighty, the senators fanned themselves listlessly; the galleries were empty. When the chaplain finally boomed forth his "Amen," John Forney turned to Hay. "Is there a message? From the President?"

Hay nodded; and gave it to Forney.

"Is it urgent?"

"Look and see."

Forney looked and saw; and whistled. Hay hurried back to the carriage. He did not want to be caught in the storm that was about to break over Congress.

As the carriage passed Seventh Street, Hay saw Azadia coming out of a milliner's. He took off his hat in order to hide his face; but he was too late. Azadia smiled; and curtseyed. He waved his hat politely. He knew that she knew who he was. Would she talk? Perhaps Mr. Eames was right. Perhaps he should marry. But who? After all, at present John Hay was the most important young man in Washington, not counting the Prince of Rails, who was at

Harvard. But when the Tycoon's first term ended, he would be no one at all. Both Nicolay and Hay had told the President that after four years he should break in new secretaries. The Tycoon had been sad but not grief-stricken. He had also realized that if either man was to have a proper career, he must start soon. Each thought that he might edit a small-town newspaper; and go into politics. Meanwhile, Major Hay might yet see action in the war; and then return to Florida and, as a new congressman, escort that exotic state back into the Union. He had not been discouraged by his recent failure to get elected; nor had the Tycoon, who thought it worth a second try.

At Sixth and E, Chase was helping Sprague write his somewhat belated answer to the Blair attack. Sprague had been silent during the furor that had followed upon Blair's assault. Presently, on July 4, Sprague would rise in the Senate and answer each of the charges, including the ones against himself as the recipient of a trade permit from his father-in-law. Chase reread their common work with satisfaction. "I believe the case well made," he said. "But," he quoted from scripture. "'Oh, for more faith and clearer sight! How stable is the City of God! How disordered is the City of Man!'"

Sprague's only answer was, "I wish I had Fred Ives here. He can write a speech like nobody's business."

Chase thought this somewhat tactless in the light of the composition at hand, which was largely his own doing. Kate joined them in the study. "Father, the carriage is ready. You won't have breakfast?"

"No, I said I'd break my fast with General Schenk and General Garfield." Although Chase was not able to see her features clearly, he was able to detect her pallor and thinness. Ever since the collapse of his presidential campaign, Kate had been withdrawn and listless. Their only hope now was the still unofficial convocation of true Republicans in September. If Grant had not shown interest by then, there would be a powerful movement among the Republicans to replace Lincoln. As always, Chase was ready to do what duty required.

Duty with Generals Schenk and Garfield was done at breakfast at the National Hotel. Chase then drove to his office, where he found a message from Senator Fessenden. Could he come immediately to the Capitol? Chase drove through the African heat, softly singing to himself a lament for Zion's city, and rereading a memorial from Fessenden on the repeal of the so-called Gold Bill.

Alone, Chase crossed the echoing rotunda where two soldiers were testing the acoustics by singing a martial song. Chase stood and waited until he was recognized; and shook hands all around.

537

Then, as a former senator, he entered the Chamber, where the business of the day was proceeding in a desultory fashion. As there were a number of finance bills coming to vote, his presence was unremarkable. Chase shook more hands and then withdrew to the nearby cloakroom, a long, narrow space where, in comfortable leather chairs, the Senate's real work was done.

A Vermont senator cornered Chase. "Fessenden's not back yet. I can't speak for him, of course, but I'm against any increase in taxes. The people won't support it."

While Chase spoke soothingly of the need for taxes in wartime, Fessenden joined them. But before he could discuss the Gold Bill with Chase, a messenger approached him and said, "Sir, you're wanted on the floor."

Fessenden excused himself, as did the Vermonter. The messenger looked at Chase curiously. Then he asked, "Sir, have you resigned?"

Chase was so startled that he both stammered and lisped. "I have tendered, yes, my resignation. But I have not heard that it was accepted."

"It was accepted, sir. I'm sorry to say, sir. The President has already sent the Senate the name of your successor."

"And . . . and . . ." Chase's humiliation was now complete. He was obliged to ask a Senate messenger the name of his successor. "Whose name did the President send over?"

"Governor Tod, sir. Oh, I am sorry, sir."

"A distinguished and honorable man," said Chase, appalled. "And, of course, a Democrat."

There was subdued panic in the opulent soon-to-be-vacated office at the Treasury. Field was, literally, wringing his hands, something that Chase had only read of. "It is a calamity, Mr. Chase! And *I* am the cause."

Chase quite agreed with both sentiment and analysis; but he chose to rise above mere emotion. "My days have been numbered since the Baltimore convention, when I ceased to be of any more value to the President." Then Chase read the President's letter: "Your letter of resignation of the office of the Secretary of the Treasury sent me yesterday is accepted." Chase felt faint. Could these terrible words be at last before his eyes, each relentlessly formed by the familiar hand? "Of all I have said in commendation of your ability and fidelity I have nothing to unsay; and yet you and I have reached a point of mutual embarrassment in our official relations which it seems cannot be overcome or longer sustained consistently with the public service." That was that. Because he had refused to allow the Treasury to be a part of the spoils system as practised by the New York politicos, he was now sacrificed.

Chase wrote Stanton—his one ally—a note hoping that he would not resign, too, out of sympathy; which meant, of course, that he hoped he would.

At the White House, Washburne was apopletic. "Of all times to let him go, this is the worst!" Washburne marched about the room waving his arms, while the President sat meekly at his writing table. "We have no tax program. The currency is collapsing. Whoever is secretary of the treasury must know how to raise one hundred million dollars a month, which Chase could do. Grant has turned into McClellan—temporarily, I pray. The war news is all bad, and the Jacobins are threatening to hold a Republican convention in September to put up their own candidate, who will now be Chase!"

Washburne had a great deal more to say; and said it. Then Hay announced the presence of the entire Senate Finance Committee in the Reception Room. Since eleven o'clock that morning, Hay had decided that the Tycoon had made a major error in letting Chase depart at a moment when the country's finances were in total disarray, while Washburne was positive that their ramshackle Union party could very easily split in two, making it possible for the Democrat McClellan to win.

Finally, Lincoln rose. "Brother Washburne, don't fret. All is for the best, believe me. Now I just saw our friend Congressman Hooper in the waiting room. I'm not going to have a chance to talk to him today, but I know he's a friend of Chase, and he's a friend of yours. Tell him that I'd be obliged if he were to call on Mr. Chase this afternoon, and reassure Mr. Chase that my esteem for him continues unabated, despite our... embarrassments." Lincoln smiled at the word. "He is also to say that I recall very well Mr. Chase's remark to me that the one *other* office that he would most like in all this world is that of chief justice, and that I have it in mind, should Mr. Taney ever die, to appoint Mr. Chase."

Washburne's wrath at Lincoln suddenly evaporated. "You would do this?"

Lincoln nodded.

"Well, if he thinks that you will make him chief justice, I don't suppose there's much chance of his trying to run against you this year."

"I would reckon none at all. So you go talk to Mr. Hooper, while I let the senators in there tell me my business." Lincoln opened the door to the Reception Room. Washburne could hear the sounds of men rising and greetings being exchanged. Then he sought out Mr. Hooper in the crowded waiting room; and the netting of Salmon Portland Chase began.

If the Tycoon had made a mistake in letting Chase escape from the Treasury at a desperate moment in the country's finances, he certainly did not show the slightest unease with the five senators from the Finance Committee. In fact, it was their chairman, Fessenden, who seemed most distraught. "I cannot imagine a worse time, sir," he echoed Washburne, "to let him go." The hard, thin New England face looked, to Hay's unaffectionate eye, like that of an undernourished goat. "We have the Gold Bill before Congress. We have the various tax and trade proposals. We have need of Mr. Chase's wise counsels."

"I'm sure you do," said Lincoln, amiably, omitting the expected "we." "And I'm sure that he will share them with you."

"But as secretary of the treasury, he could have salvaged our position. Now *you* have let him go." Senator Conness glared at the President.

The Tycoon spread wide his arms, as if to show that there was nothing up either sleeve. "How was I to stop him? This was his third or fourth resignation."

"You should have appealed to his patriotism," said Fessenden.

"*Should* I have?" Lincoln was ironical. "Well, I seem never to have you at my side when I need you, to tell me what I should be doing. Anyway, Governor Tod has been nominated by me. You now have the duty and responsibility of passing on his fitness."

There was a confused conversation about the merits of Governor Tod. Hay could see that the committee did not dare reject so powerful a politician but that Fessenden was displeased. Finally, the Tycoon ended the meeting with the announcement that he could not in justice to himself or to Tod withdraw the nomination.

But that evening Tod telegraphed to say that he must decline the office, as his health was not good. "Well, that was unexpected." The Tycoon was morose.

Hay was anxious. "I think the Senate's holding a night session, and I think that they might just reject Tod. So don't you think I should . . ."

"Yes," said the President.

The Senate side of the Capitol was ablaze with gaslight; numerous senators and lobbyists were ablaze with drink. But Fessenden was all cold, sea-green, Robespierrian sobriety. Hay met him at the swinging doors to the chamber. "Governor Tod has declined the post. The President thought you should know."

"Well, that shows the governor's got better sense than I thought. Who's next?"

"I don't know, sir."

At ten-thirty the next morning, Fessenden was seated in Hay's
540

office when an usher whispered to Hay that the President wanted him.

Hay found the Tycoon in a buoyant mood. The departure of Chase had rejuvenated him. The President gave Hay an envelope. "Here, John, take this nomination down to the Senate. I think they'll be pleased, for once."

"Who is it, sir?"

"Fessenden."

Hay was astonished. "Why, he's in my office right now."

"Well, that's a nice coincidence, isn't it? Personally, I think the choice is inspired, if I say so myself. He's chairman of the Finance Committee. He knows the problems. He is a radical, but he lacks the usual petulance and vicious fractionalism of the breed. He's also going to have a hard time getting reelected back in Maine if Mr. Hamlin decides to go to the Senate." The Tycoon was indeed delighted with himself; and Hay thought that he had every reason to be, *if* Fessenden accepted.

"You may go in, Senator," said Hay to the dignified Yankee, who little knew what fate had in store for him.

At Sixth and E, slipcovers had been placed over all the furniture and steamer trunks crowded the vestibule where once all that glittered in Washington had glittered. Kate moved like a ghost through the hot, dusty rooms. Since Sprague had ceased, for the moment, to drink, he tended to dourness. Kate had wanted to retreat as rapidly as possible to Europe, but Sprague thought that they should go instead to Newport, Rhode Island, now that Congress was adjourned. Sprague's speech defending Chase had been a great success, only slightly marred by the fact that Chase had ceased to be Secretary of the Treasury five days before. In any case, since Sprague now anticipated a change in the laws regarding the purchase of Southern cotton, he did not dare go abroad. Kate gave way, more from physical than from moral weakness.

The world has turned unreal, thought Chase, as he made his way through the shrouded furniture to his study, where Senator Sumner waited for him. There were few visitors nowadays. Only Stanton from the Cabinet had been—or so he said—sorry that Chase was gone, erased, as it were, from power if not from History's dusty tablets. The rest of the Cabinet had responded to his departure with indecent rejoicing. Pomeroy and Garfield were loyal—and Sumner, whose bodyguard was just out of earshot in the second parlor. "Oh, my friend! My friend!" Sumner appeared to have tears in his eyes.

"It is over," said Chase, with what he hoped was Roman dignity and brevity. For once, the "is" was "is" and not the dreaded inadvertent "ish."

541

"You have been with Fessenden?"

Chase nodded. "I do what I can to help him settle in. He is worthy, I think. We both agree that the American people may revolt should we place a tax on their incomes of more than ten percent, but he will hold as steadily to this course as ever I did."

Sumner nodded. "Where will you go now?"

"Home to where I was born—the White Mountains of New Hampshire. I must think..."

"While you restore yourself, we shall be at work for you here. There is now a plan to hold a new convention at the end of September. Then..." Sumner clapped his hands.

But Chase was torn. As the true Republican candidate for president, he could destroy Lincoln. But then would McClellan not destroy him and all the work that the abolitionists had accomplished? Of course if he did nothing he would probably be chief justice. But was it *right* to do nothing to prevent the reelection of a president whose idiotic notion to colonize the Negroes outside North America was not only immoral but would wreck the national economy? Was it right *not* to oppose a pro-Southern President who had only that week refused to sign Congress's Reconstruction Bill, which was an outright attack on his own amnesty for the rebels' program? Was it right to permit Lincoln to allow the rebel states, defeated in battle, to return to the Union as if nothing had happened and with slavery, in some way, continued or even briefly condoned?

Chase appealed, silently, to the Lord of Hosts to show him a sign; but all that he got was an historical analogy from Senator Sumner. "Of all the rulers of recent times that I can recall Lincoln is most like Louis XVI. The storm is all about him, but he does nothing."

"I had not thought of him as Louis XVI, but it is quite true that when he likes to say 'my policy is to have no policy' or 'I do not control events, events control me,' he certainly resembles that... headless monarch."

"Just as you resemble the king's brilliant finance minister, Necker. And I predict that, like Necker, he will be forced to ask you back."

"If Lincoln were king, I might agree," said Chase. "But he is not king but politician. And I am gone for good."

5

ON SUNDAY, JULY 10, 1864, SHORTLY BEFORE MIDNIGHT, JOHN Hay was awakened by Robert Lincoln getting into his bed.

"What's happened?" was Hay's first sleepy response.

"Stanton," said Robert; he wore only his shirt. "We were all ordered out of the Soldiers' Home. The rebels are at Silver Spring. God, I hate this place." Then Robert turned onto his side and went to sleep; and slept, thought the now wide-awake Hay, like his father. All night long there were sighs and moans; so unlike Nicolay's familiar snoring, rhythmic as a steady rain. But Nico was at the west, enraging the Indians; and now Robert lay in Nico's place.

At dawn, Robert sprang out of bed, fresh and rested, while Hay was exhausted. As they took turns shaving at the single mirror in the bathroom, Robert asked if the Canterbury girls were still performing *The Bushwhackers of the Potomac*, a singularly lewd production which they had both enjoyed several days earlier. In fact, thanks to Hay's Virgilian knowledge of Washington's circles of infernal pleasure, they had actually met and supped with a number of the girls. Hay knew where at least one of them was always to be found. But, "We may all be leaving the city today," he said.

"Oh, I don't think Father has any intention of budging." Robert carefully reshaped the corners of his moustaches.

"Look," said Hay, pointing out the window. Back of the Smithsonian Institution, a gunboat rode at anchor. "That's for the evacuation of the White House."

"The unspeakable Stanton?" Robert tended to blame the Secretary of War for keeping him out of the army when, actually, it was his mother who had seen to that.

"The War Department, anyway. For once, Stanton isn't tearing his hair out. But things are bad. Yesterday the rebels whipped us at Monocacy Birdge..."

"Why, that's practically here in town!" Robert frowned. He had nicked his chin. There was now a drop of blood forming. Hay found it interesting that such an important defeat had *not* been mentioned by the Ancient to his family at the Soldiers' Home. But then Madam was easily excited.

Hay proceeded to alarm Robert. "Rebel pickets were seen last

543

night in Georgetown, while the Blairs have fled yet again from Silver Spring."

"You know, in a way, it would be nice if they burned this bloody city to the ground," said Robert, the Boston Brahmin. Carefully, he dried his face with Hay's only towel, leaving a thin streak of fresh blood on the clean side. "It was a terrible notion, having the capital of the country in this stinking swamp—and in the South."

"Well, the swamp certainly stinks today," said Hay, as a warm summer breeze filled the bathroom with a particularly sickening odor of stagnant canal, jasmine and offal from the slaughterhouse.

"Anyway, you'll be up in Saratoga, cutting a swathe," said Hay, folding the towel to hide the royal blood. Robert had just graduated from Harvard. Madam had attended the ceremonies. Now he was enrolled in Harvard Law School because Madam had said that if he were to go into the army, she would go mad. Since no one doubted her word, Robert was the most famous and sullen "shirker" of the war.

"At least, Father says I can go down to Fortress Monroe next week and *watch* the war."

Hay found the Tycoon in his office, spyglass in one hand, studying the river for signs of the reinforcements from Grant at City Point. The Tycoon was as angry as Hay had ever seen him. "What goes on in Stanton's mind is sometimes unfathomable to me. He obliges me to flee in the middle of the night from the Soldiers' Home, and now he's trying to evacuate me from the capital."

"I think that was Admiral Porter's idea."

But Lincoln had put down his telescope. "I can get no news from the War Department. No one seems to know where the rebels are. When I ask Halleck—"

Edward ushered in the Postmaster-General, whose Blairian rage made Lincoln's anger seem like high good humor. "General Jubal Early's men are now burning my house at Silver Spring. They are burning my father's house. But first the bastards stole everything they could get their hands on, from the silver to all my father's papers. You can see the smoke from here."

"We seem to have been outsmarted again," murmured the Ancient.

"It is Halleck. He is a coward. He is a traitor. He should be hanged." There was much more of this Blairesco to which neither Lincoln nor Hay gave much attention. As callers began to arrive, Lincoln did his best to try to understand what had happened.

Apparently, Jubal Early and John C. Breckinridge had been given an army of no one knew how many men. They had come swiftly up the Shenandoah Valley, seized yet again Harper's Ferry and, yet again, isolated the capital; then, on Saturday, they had defeated General Law Wallace at Monocacy Junction, and burned much of Silver Spring. They were now encamped two miles north of the Soldiers' Home, with only the somewhat ramshackle defenses of Fort Stevens between them and the Seventh Street Road, at whose terminus was the White House itself. Hay began to look with a more friendly eye on the nearby gunboat.

Grant's troops were expected to arrive sometime during the early morning, but no one knew when. "If they are not here by noon, it is all over," said Blair. "Because we don't have the men to stop them. How," he exclaimed, "could this have happened?"

Lincoln's response was that curious mocking smile which Hay had noticed at other moments of crisis. "I think, Mr. Blair, we should first find out *what* is happening. The 'how' we will explore at our leisure."

Blair gave a sudden cry of rage. "My father's papers! The letters from Andrew Jackson! From Henry Clay! All gone!"

"I think I may have written him, too," said Lincoln, who was again at the window. Then he beamed: "Here they come! The transports from City Point." He turned back into the room. "I think I'll go down and meet our rescuers."

"But if General Early breaks through Fort Stevens—" Blair began.

"We'll have a real fight on our hands, won't we?" The Tycoon motioned for Hay to accompany him; and motioned for Blair to stay. In the outer office, there was a messenger from the Treasury. "Sir, before the telegraph went out, gold was being quoted at two hundred eighty-five dollars. Mr. Fessenden wants to know what we should do."

"Personally, I would shoot every last devilish gold-dealer. But since I'm not allowed to, tell him that we'll shoot rebels today, and then the price of gold will fall back."

Pennsylvania Avenue was dusty and full of flies. The streetcars had ceased to run. For once, there were no soldiers in view. Every able-bodied man, and a good many from the hospital who were not, had gone to the various forts that encircled the city. "The city is never so tranquil," observed the Tycoon, "as when it is being besieged."

"It also helps that Congress has adjourned."

"Yes, that is a blessing." To Hay's amazement, Lincoln was now more interested in Ben Wade's bill, which had passed both houses of Congress, than he was in the danger at hand. It was as if he knew, instinctively, what was truly dangerous and what was not. A rebel raid on the capital was embarrassing. But unlike

Blair, he was not unduly agitated. Although he had made up his mind some time ago that the war would be absolutely won, he was still not certain on what terms the Union would then be restored. He knew what *he* wanted; but he also knew that he was in a minority within his own party's vengeful congressional majority.

As the sky to the north grew dark with smoke from Silver Spring, and the sounds of artillery and rifle fire echoed in the valley between Seventh Street Road and the Capitol, Lincoln spoke of the radical problem. "They are trying to force me to devastate the rebel states, which I will not do. Naturally, I will punish certain individual rebels but I cannot—and I will not—punish a whole people. That's why I shall stick to my ten-percent formula."

"But Congress has rejected that."

"So I must use what weapons I can. In wartime, my proclamations must be obeyed. As President, I could not free the slaves. I had not the right; and neither has Congress. But as a *military* necessity, I could free them; and did. Now I want a Constitutional amendment abolishing slavery, which will take care of that problem once and for all. I'm also satisfied that we now have acceptable government in Louisiana and Arkansas."

"But Congress isn't satisfied; and Congress can keep the Louisiana and Arkansas delegations from taking their seats."

"Well, the whole thing is very curious. Since I accept a part of Ben Wade's bill, I won't veto the whole. But since I don't accept the rest of it, I won't sign it."

"So what happens?"

"Well, if I don't sign it, it isn't a law. So I guess I'll just stick it in my pocket."

"Is this Constitutional, sir?"

Lincoln smiled. "There is no Constitutional question that I know of."

Hay was convinced that Lincoln's refusal to act directly in regard to the Wade Bill was a not-so-subtle declaration of war on the radical faction of the party, who were now certain to put up their own candidate for president. As Frémont was already a Republican candidate and Lincoln a National Union candidate, the addition of a radical Republican—Mr. Chase?—would split three ways their party and the Democrat McClellan would win, as a minority president, in just the same way that Lincoln had won in 1860 when the Democrats broke in two. On the one hand, Hay admired the Tycoon's formidable response to Congress; but he also saw only too clearly that barring some extraordinary military victory, Lincoln would soon join James Buchanan and Frank-

546

lin Pierce and all the other one-term mediocre presidents of the last third of a century.

At the Sixth Street wharf, they stopped. The first of the transports was now drawn up to the dock. As Lincoln climbed onto a small reviewing platform, the disembarking troops began to cheer. Lincoln raised his hat. The cheering was taken up by the men in the second transport; the sound was thunderous. As always, Hay was mystified by the magical effect that the Ancient had on the troops. Since they had no way of fathoming him except through newspapers, which, knowingly or unknowingly, misrepresented him, it was nothing short of miraculous that Old Abe or Father Abraham could inspire so much affection. Of course, it did not hurt that he looked very much like that somewhat ambiguous cartoon figure "Uncle Sam."

Lincoln had now removed his hat, which he held in his left hand. As he stood, very straight for him, brown face glowing, wide mouth smiling, he waved with his right hand to the men who filed by him down the gangplank. Presently, he was joined by the Sixth Corps commander, Major-general Horatio Wright, who saluted him; and said, "Reporting for duty, sir."

"We are relieved, General," said the Tycoon. "In every sense."

Lincoln might have stayed there all morning had not the stern Lamon appeared with the President's forgotten military escort. "I shall resign, sir, if you go off like this again," grumbled Lamon.

"I'm sorry, Lamon. But we could not stay put, Mr. Hay and I." Lincoln then turned to General Wright. "I think, General, you should install yourself at Fort Stevens as soon as practical."

"That is my plan, sir."

"If the rebels were to make a push now, before you get there, there could be a lot of breakage at the Capitol, which we've only just finished fixing up."

When General Wright asked where the rebels were mainly concentrated, the President said that no one knew but he suspected at Silver Spring, just three miles north of Fort Stevens. As Lincoln and Hay, surrounded by the President's cavalry guard, rode back to the White House, Lincoln said, "There is only one danger now . . ." He stopped, to take a satisfied look at the Capitol's new dome.

"The rebels will steal everything that's not nailed down." Hay knew that this had been going on for several days: guns, horses, silver, gold, food . . . The nearby towns of Rockville and Tennalytown had been stripped by the rebels; and the frightened inhabitants had fled to Georgetown, where they were obliged to sleep in the open.

"No," said Lincoln. "It is the seventeen thousand prisoners that we're holding at Point Lookout. That's what Lee wants more than anything, and that's what he must never get."

The next day all the telegraph lines to the city were down, and the railroads were blocked. For the second time in the war, the capital was isolated. But this time, the mood was cheerful at the White House. The President himself had visited Fort Stevens the day before; and he had watched as Early's men exchanged fire with the newly arrived Union troops. It was the first action that the Tycoon had seen during the war.

After a brief noon meeting of the Cabinet, Lincoln was eager to return to the action; and Major Hay was eager to go with him. But it was not Hay but Madam who went forth to battle on the afternoon of July 12.

Although Mary had been suffering from a bilious attack, the thought of a military outing cleared her head most wondrously. The President had said, firmly, that under no circumstance was she to go with him to Fort Stevens, while Lamon had said that under no circumstance would he allow the President to return to Fort Stevens. So, as a compromise, all three now rode up Seventh Street Road, with a company of cavalry, sabres drawn.

For Mary, the thought of battle was, mysteriously, a tonic. Mysteriously because the most homely of thunderstorms could set her to screaming, usually from beneath the nearest bed. Now Mary would face real guns with real bullets. Defiantly, she wore a dark-red dress. "To disguise my bloody wounds," she had said to Keckley, who gasped.

Lamon spoke to neither President nor First Lady. Furious at the needless risk, he simply glowered at them.

A mile before the Soldiers' Home, the street became a road and then a dusty trail through sparse unsettled woods.

"That's where my carriage struck the trees!" Mary recalled, without panic, the swift deathlike darkness. "Did they ever decide who it was who loosened the driver's seat?"

Lincoln shook his head. "There are so many people in and out of the stables."

"There *were*," said Lamon.

As they passed the Soldiers' Home, they could smell the smoke of burning houses up ahead; and hear artillery's peculiar slamming sound.

A cart piled high with furniture passed them, with a large farmer and larger wife in the driver's seat. Behind the cart, a half-dozen children shepherded a procession of livestock. The President raised his hat to the farmer and his wife, who stared, stonily, at the source of their ruin.

"How ungracious!" Mary exclaimed. "How ungrateful!"

"Well, Maryland has never been exactly my state," said Lincoln, putting his hat back on.

"How could General Grant have let this happen?"

"Well, he *is* down near Richmond, Mother. This is more General Halleck's department."

"He's hopeless, too!" Mary could never understand Lincoln's tolerance of bad generals. Mary's original high hopes for Grant had ended when he lost more men at Cold Harbor than anyone had dreamed could be lost in so short a time. The man was a butcher—of his own men. For some time, Mary had had her own ideas of how the war should be prosecuted but no one took her seriously. As for Halleck, everyone agreed that he was hopeless but there he remained at the War Department, with his huge watery, drug-dilated eyes. Others might suspect that Halleck used opium, but Mary *knew* that he did. After all, there was little that she did not know about drugs. For years doctors had liked to experiment with her during The Headache and its painful aftermath.

As for Stanton, he had made clear his true allegiance. He had asked Chase to be godfather to his new daughter. Worse, they sang hymns together. Mary was positive that Stanton was working secretly for Chase. Why else did the war go so badly? Lately, Mary had sensed that her husband was beginning to resign himself to defeat in the coming election. The thought made her frantic. At present her debts were more than his annual greenback salary of twenty-five thousand dollars a year—worth, before tax, less than ten thousand dollars in gold, which he would not take. For Lincoln to be both an ex-president and a bankrupt—thanks to her—was more than she could bear. Fortunately, she was now most subtly at work on Mr. Thurlow Weed to get a mutual friend, Abram Wakeman, appointed surveyor of the port of New York, a rich post which Wakeman was more than willing to pay her for. She would then be able to settle her accounts with the New York stores, particularly with A. T. Stewart, who was long-suffering, but not eternally so. With each Union reverse, not to mention hint that the President might fail of reelection, the bills had become more urgent and their tone more insolent. But once Wakeman got his job, Mr. Stewart's account would be promptly settled. Meanwhile, she had her eye on a black camel's-hair shawl from India that Stewart had offered her for only three thousand dollars. As the carriage drove up to Fort Stevens, Mary wondered if she might not, with luck, be shot this very day through that source of all her pain and anguish, the head.

Fort Stevens proved to be not so much a proper fortress as a series of earthworks. Mary had envisaged something with stone

549

walls and parapets and towers, on the order of Fortress Monroe. Instead, at the Fort's center, there was a mound of earth like a loaf of bread on its side, shored up by wooden latticework. Artillery was in place to left and right.

As the fort commanded the countryside to the north, she was able to see the butternut-gray of the rebels in the pinewoods up the road, and in the two small farmhouses which had, until two days ago, been in the Union and were now, thanks to Jubal Early, out of the Union.

Just back of the earthen breadloaf, the presidential carriage was met by General Wright, who looked with some displeasure upon Mary. "There are rebel sharpshooters, Ma'am, all around us."

As if to demonstrate his point, there was a sudden volley from the two houses; to which the Federal troops responded. Mary noted that most of the Union soldiers were from Massachusetts. "Sir, I shall stay well back," she said, politely. Then she accompanied the President to the top of an earthwork where wooden shields provided an irregular parapet. From this altitude, they could see a green, dusty landscape beneath a gray, smoking sky.

"You know who is just a mile from here?" Lincoln pointed to the woods that served as cover for the main body of rebels.

Mary knew. "Cousin John Breckinridge. I suppose he's come to take over the White House for the Davises."

"Well, he's just one day too late, thanks to General Grant."

A surgeon from a Pennsylvania regiment showed them the sights; and gave his opinions: "As I see it, sir, this is more in the nature of a raid now. Once all the men General Grant sent are here, they will high-tail it into the brush. But I'm sure that if General Wallace hadn't held them up for one whole day, fighting the way he did at Monocacy Bridge, they would have swept right into town, because there never were enough of us to—"

The surgeon did not finish what had promised to be a lengthy analysis. Rifle fire sounded. The surgeon gave a sudden cry and fell in a heap at Mary's feet. To Mary's amazement, she did not herself scream. Instead, she looked down at the man whose face was now twisted with pain. "Sir . . . ?" she began.

But two orderlies had appeared. The surgeon looked up and said to Mary, "It is not serious. My left ankle's struck." To the orderlies: "Help me up. Do forgive me, Mrs. Lincoln."

"Of course, sir. I am sorry, sir." Mary was uncertain as to what was proper battlefield etiquette. Then Lincoln put his arm around her. "I think you better go back to the carriage."

"Oh, no, Father! Not now. I want Cousin John to get a good look at me. Remember how I told him they'd have to fight me
550

personally before we gave up the Mansion? Well, give me a gun, and I'll start shooting."

"Mother, you amaze me."

But Mary was ravished with excitement. "No, Father, I mean it. I was a marvelous shot as a girl. I could kill a squirrel at thirty yards—through the eye."

"You *are* bloodthirsty. But things grow..." Simultaneously, the Federal artillery went off to the left and the right of them; and acrid smoke made their eyes stream. Lincoln motioned to a young Massachusetts lieutenant-colonel to escort Mary back to the carriage. Half blinded by smoke and half deafened by cannon, she was now not unwilling. Nevertheless, Mary felt cheated that Cousin John had not seen her on the parapet, firing directly at him.

Lincoln stood alone, looking out between two wooden palings. Sharpshooters on both sides went about their lethal work. General Wright moved up and down the fortifications, giving orders. The sight of the President plainly gave him no pleasure. But Lincoln had now turned to a fresh-faced lieutenant. "You came yesterday from City Point?"

"Yes, sir," said the young man, with a smile that suddenly enlarged, before Lincoln's eyes, to a scarlet mass as the bullet that struck the center of his face caused him to pitch forward, dead, some three feet from where the President stood. With that, as if from nowhere, the tall young officer who had escorted Mrs. Lincoln back to the carriage seized the President. "Get down, you damned fool!" he exclaimed; and he shoved Lincoln below the parapet. As the President landed on the base of his spine, he observed, "Well, Colonel, since you put it like that..."

The snipers had now got their range. There was also an excellent possibility that they had recognized the only six-foot-four-inch American president in the world. They were now firing in regular volleys. The young officer squatted beside the President. "What is your name?" asked Lincoln.

"Holmes, sir. And I wish you would leave us to our work."

"Holmes. From Massachusetts. No relation to Oliver Wendell Holmes?"

"I am his son, sir."

"How curious! I am a great admirer of his verse." As the sniper fire continued about them, Lincoln recited from Holmes's poem "Lexington."

"'Green be the groves where her martyrs are dying!
    Shroudless and tombless they sunk to their
    rest...'

That's the part," said Lincoln, gray eyes suddenly misty, "where I always find it so hard to go on."

"I never learned it, sir. But then my father quotes himself so much better than I can—and so often—that I leave the recitations to him."

"I once thought that I had some gift for poetry. I suppose all young men do at a certain time of life. But Blackstone knocks it out of you."

"That's what will knock it out of me, sir, if the next bullet I get does not."

"You have already been wounded?"

"Yes, sir. At Ball's Bluff."

They were then joined, not by General Wright, who had been disturbed by the arrival of a second general and a fresh brigade, but by Gideon Welles and Senator Ben Wade.

Although Lincoln remained seated, his back to the parapet, he proceeded to introduce the two men of state to Lieutenant-colonel Oliver Wendell Holmes, Junior. "We have been discussing his father's poetry. Come join us."

"I prefer," said Ben Wade, sourly, "to get a look at the battle."

"It's not really all that interesting," said the President, matter-of-factly.

Wade took a heroic stance between the two parapets. But when a sudden fusillade of bullets swept his way, bluff Ben Wade, with an astonishingly youthful leap, removed himself from the line of fire.

"I warned you there was not much to see." Lincoln was grinning. Nervously, Welles straightened his wig as if it were a helmet. Colonel Holmes excused himself. Lincoln continued. "I stood for some time up there, to see what it was like, being fired on. I cannot say that it is a likable sort of experience. Yet Mrs. Lincoln when she was up there wanted to go get a gun and start firing back."

"I'd like to do the same," said Wade, his bluff grim self again. "It is a marvelous thing to kill rebels."

"Well, I'm sure General Wright will lend you a rifle." At that moment, orderlies rolled the dead young officer onto a stretcher. The face was now no longer recognizably a face. As the stretcher passed them, Welles shuddered and Wade scowled. "I was talking to that boy when he was shot," said Lincoln. "He was standing right next to me. One second he was a splendid young man. The next... he was that." Orderlies and stretcher were now out of sight. "We are engaged, gentlemen, in a most grievous work, and I wonder if we had known the true cost at the start whether we would ever have undertaken it."

"There is no doubt in my mind, as to the justice of our cause, and the evil of theirs," said Wade.

"Well, if we are *not* in the right, I should want to die this very instant," said the President. "Naturally, I *believe* we are right, Mr. Wade. But I wish I had your absolute certitude, and lack of any doubt about the evilness of the other."

"I wish you did, too, Mr. Lincoln."

"You are impertinent, Mr. Wade," said Gideon Welles, whose temper was even worse than Stanton's; and so more reined in.

"Well," said the President, smiling, "what he says is certainly pertinent to his own passion, which is to punish all rebels."

"You would *not*, Mr. Lincoln?" Wade was challenging.

"I would punish some; but not others. They are, after all, despite this great trouble, still citizens of the United States."

"They are no longer a part of the United States. They are foreigners, whom we are conquering."

"If they are not in the Union always, then where are they? If they are truly out of the Union, why do we fight them? I'm afraid we cannot indulge ourselves in this interesting metaphysical question because, Mr. Wade, if you admit that they are foreigners, then there is no United States, and if that is so, then I am no President and you are no member of Congress..."

A battery of artillery drowned out the rest of Lincoln's voice. When it ceased, Wade said, ominously, "We must change your mind, Mr. President."

Lincoln rose. "In this one instance, that is neither possible nor—I warn you—wise."

General Wright was now at hand. The light had begun to fail. Fireflies, incongruously, glowed in the Seventh Street Road alongside the flashes of rifle fire. "Gentlemen," said the general, "I must ask you to leave. Mrs. Lincoln has already gone back to the Mansion with Mr. Lamon. I swore to him, sir, that I would get you safely home."

"Your oath will be respected, General. My compliments for this day's work."

Together, in Welles's carriage, Lincoln and his Secretary of the Navy drove from the battlefield, accompanied by an armed guard. Ben Wade followed them, alone, on horseback.

"I reckon," said Lincoln to Welles, "that this will be their last raid from the Valley, so if General Wright follows up, we can cut them off before they cross the Potomac. And that will be the end of Jubal Early."

But, as usual, no one followed up. By July 14, Jubal Early and John Breckinridge were gone, and the railroads functioned once again, and the telegraph lines were reconnected, and the mail and the newspapers from around the country were arriving as usual. The Ancient expressed his disgust to Hay; as did the national press.

For the first time, Hay conceived that there was an excellent chance that the Tycoon would be defeated for reelection. Yet things could be worse, said Montgomery Blair at the next meeting of the Cabinet. Thanks to John Breckinridge, the house of the Old Gentleman at Silver Spring had only been looted but not burned, while "*My* house" said Monty Blair, "was both looted and burned." Apparently, this was to even the accounts. "We burned the house of the governor of Virginia. Now they burn my house. Next we shall burn one of theirs—"

"Where does this lawlessness end?" asked Usher, whose favorite question was the rhetorical.

"The Eumenides are the key," said the classicist Blair, mystifying Usher and amusing Seward, who added, "and Mr. Lincoln is our Apollo."

"No," said the President, "Horace Greeley will be the peacemaker." He had before him on the table half the contents of the Greeley pigeonhole. "Brother Greeley, after telling me that I don't prosecute the war hard enough, now thinks that I am too unyielding! He has been in communication with what he says are two bona-fide rebel negotiators and that they would like to know on what terms we would make peace." The Ancient sighed. Hay felt sorrow for anyone who had to deal seriously with Horace Greeley, a voice still of great consequence, connected with a brain that had long since ceased to function save in sudden spasms of despair.

"I have decided that I shall go through the motions of dealing with these unofficial official peace commissioners. I've drawn up a 'to whom it may concern' letter, setting forth our terms for peace." The Ancient put on his glasses, which were steamed over from the heat; then, to the buzzing of flies and the soft snores of the Attorney-General, he read, "'Any proposition which embraces the restoration of the Union, the integrity of the whole Union, and the abandonment of slavery, and which could be proposed by and with an authority that can control the armies now at war against the United States, will be received and considered by the executive government of the United States, and will be met by liberal terms on other substantial and collateral points, and the bearer or bearers thereof shall have safe conduct both ways.'" The Ancient put down the note; and removed his glasses. As a rule, heat did not appear to affect him, but despite the momentous excitement on the Seventh Street Road, he had become, lately, more and more listless as every tide ran against him. He seemed,
554

thought Hay, to be merely going through the motions of the presidency, as if he knew that in a few months he would be gone from office, and the great decisions would be made by another.

"The real or imaginary rebel peacemakers—you never know with Brother Greeley—are at Niagara, on the Canadian side. Governor, what do you think?"

Seward had now abandoned the Cabinet table for the lounge, where he proceeded to stretch himself out to the fullest measure of his short length. "Give Greeley his chance. It will shut him up for a while. Also, since he is bound to do something stupid, why not lead him on?"

Fessender looked at Seward's recumbent form with much the same disapproval that his predecessor had. Both Hay and Nico felt that there was something about the office of secretary of the treasury that made its incumbent inordinately formal and self-important. "Mr. President. Will you receive these commissioners here?"

"If they will come. But there seems a hitch. I think Brother Greeley wants to involve himself." Lincoln gazed at the ceiling. Despite the heat and his own general lassitude, Hay could see that the Ancient was beginning to spin one of his webs. "I think he should. In fact, I want him to have all public credit for this peace mission . . ."

"And all the public credit for its failure when the commissioners turn out to be bogus or uninstructed or opposed forever to the abolition of slavery." Seward could always read that part of Lincoln's mind which was most like his own: the practical politician.

"Well," said Lincoln, "something along those lines. Anyway, I'm sending Major Hay here to New York City to deal with Greeley." This was the first that Hay had heard of his mission. The Ancient gave him an intentional wink from the hooded left eye. "After all, Major Hay is aiming for a career in journalism one day, and I have decided that a week or two with Horace Greeley will be an education for him—even an 'open sesame.'"

Montgomery Blair was not pleased. "You make it a condition, for the first time, that the abolition of slavery is one of our absolute terms, not to be negotiated. Is this wise, sir?"

"It may not be wise, Mr. Blair. But it is consistent with my message to Congress and with my own proclamation in response to the Wade Bill. After all, I have asked for a Constitutional amendment abolishing slavery."

"*That* is wise," said Blair. "Because you are giving the rebel states an opportunity to end the war and return to the Union and then, as eleven states, deny the abolitionists the two-thirds vote that they will need to amend the Constitution in order to abolish slavery." Blair spoke, sonorously, for history; then he spoke, nervously, to Lincoln, "But can you really have it both ways?"

"Both ways, one way, no way." Lincoln shook his head. "I have, as a military necessity, freed the slaves in the rebel states. I cannot take that back."

Suddenly, Stanton coughed. He had spent the entire meeting reading dispatches from the various fronts. But, apparently, he had been following this last exchange. "Sir, what will your political opponents say to this? There is a powerful peace-at-no-matter-what-the-price movement in the country, particularly at the North, particularly in New York City, where our next draft of men could bring on the worst riots yet. Now if it looks like you are willing to prolong this war until the South *voluntarily* abolishes slavery, the Democrats will carry every state in the North, and we will hold onto nothing but the border-states, thanks to the army."

Hay wondered if even the border-states were secure. On August first, Kentucky would hold an election. Stanton was currently arresting all sorts of Democratic politicians as "disloyal," including the candidate for an important judgeship. The Democrats had promptly responded by substituting another candidate; and Lincoln had then declared martial law throughout the state.

The Ancient was now mopping his face with a handkerchief. Hay felt sorry for him; pity and awe, too. This was the stuff of tragedy. The overreacher soon to be felled by his own hubris—if not by the gods by *vox populi*. "I have evolved," repeated Lincoln, "as we all have during this big trouble. I have never been an abolitionist. But now all our party, like it or not, must be abolitionist."

"Would you really give the freed Negroes the vote?" asked Blair, disingenuously.

"Well, Monty, you know that I, like you, favor colonization . . ."

"But there are now freed Negro slaves in Louisiana." Blair was inexorable. "Would you let them vote?"

"The very intelligent ones, I suppose." Lincoln was growing more and more evasive. He will not, Seward decided, from the comfort of the lounge, be reelected. He himself would be genuinely happy to go home to Auburn. But what would become of this strange ambitious man? Seward could hardly imagine the Commander-in-Chief of the greatest military force earth had ever seen arguing cases before a Supreme Court that he himself had chosen. "The very intelligent Negroes," Lincoln said, again. "And the ones who have fought in our army. What news," he addressed Stanton, turning off the subject, "from General Sherman?"

"He is laying siege to Atlanta. It will be a long siege, he says."

556

"And General Grant wants more men in Virginia," said Lincoln, almost to himself. "It is just like three years ago. Except I was not so tired then."

"Mr. Jefferson Davis is a lot tireder," said Montgomery Blair and, for once, Hay approved of Blair's last word.

6

ON THE SECOND OF AUGUST, 1864, SEWARD, DRESSED NOW FOR the tropics in baggy wrinkled cotton pantaloons and a light shirt two sizes too large for him, sat with the President in Stanton's musty office and listened to the reports from Pennsylvania. On July 30, Jubal Early's army had reappeared at Chambersburg, where he held the town for a ransom of two hundred thousand gold dollars. When this money was not paid him, he burned Chambersburg to the ground. That same day, Lincoln, unaware of what was happening, went down to Fortress Monroe to meet Grant. That same entirely disastrous day, an elaborate tunnel that Grant had constructed beneath the Petersburg fortifications had blown up, doing little damage to the rebels but causing 3500 Union losses. Grant had admitted to Lincoln that the entire scheme had been harebrained. It was Seward's surmise that neither man was at his best that ill-omened day. Now between the turbulence over the draft—Lincoln had just called for half a million more men—and the success of the rebel raiders within sight of the Capitol's new dome, the Union's fortunes, not to mention fortune as precisely defined by the currency, were at rock bottom.

From the beginning Seward had thought it a mistake for Lincoln to concentrate the entire command of the armies in Grant, who would not now leave the siege of Petersburg just west of Richmond. Although Grant was a splendid general in the field, he could not be expected to understand the confusion of overlapping commands and stern military incompetence at the capital, where Old Brains thought old thoughts while Stanton acted as a sort of frantic conductor on a runaway set of railroad cars. No general could deal with such resourceful raiders as Early's so far to the north of Grant and the bulk of his army.

When Washington was beleaguered, Grant had refused pointblank to come to the city on the ground that Lee would interpret this as a slackening of Grant's siege, the object of Lee's strategy.

Since Halleck had been deprived of authority and Lincoln had sworn not to interfere with Grant's decisions, Early had escaped from General Wright, who had never been ordered to do anything beyond driving him from Washington.

"I think," said Lincoln at last, "that we had better send for General Grant. He must take a look at our situation and decide what's to be done. We can't keep on asking him all the time to loan us men. We must have a proper army here."

"We also need a proper general to command that army," said Stanton. "Grant still wants to send us Meade."

Lincoln frowned. "On the ground that Meade is now so unpopular with the Army of the Potomac that he might as well come up here and offend everyone else?"

"My spies tell me," said Seward, chin resting on the high window-sill back of Stanton's desk, "that General Grant has been drunk since July 27, at about noon."

Lincoln and Santon both, for once, stared at Seward as if he had gone entirely too far.

"I have not heard that," said the President, finally. "I can also personally testify that on July 31, he was sober, if somewhat low in spirits. I make, for once, no joke."

"I hear that rumor all the time," said Stanton, "and tend to disregard it. Who told you, Governor?"

"That is for me to know, as they say. But if true, and I believe it is, as of July 27 . . . Anyway, it is worrisome."

"Yes," said Lincoln. "It is."

A messenger arrived with a communication from City Point; it was almost as if Grant's spirit—or spirited spirit, thought Seward—was aware of this conversation. The general proposed that he come to Washington by way of Monocacy Junction, where an army was currently being somewhat haphazardly assembled in order to deal with Early. Meanwhile, Grant proposed that there be, first, a united command of all forces at the capital and, second, a single overall divisional commander whose task would be the destruction of Early and the sealing off of the Shenandoah Valley. Grant had already ordered to Washington the one officer capable of accomplishing what was necessary.

"General Meade," said Seward, turning from the window.

"No," said Stanton, peering through suppurating lids at the telegram, "it is General Philip Sheridan."

"He is a child," said Seward.

"No," said the President, "he is a boy, which may be what we're looking for. Grant swears by him as the best cavalry officer we have."

"He is far too young," said Stanton. "We must dissuade General Grant."

"Or let him persuade us."

"How old *is* he?" asked Seward.

Stanton turned the pages of a notebook until he found the name. "Well, it says here, thirty-three, but—"

"The same age as Our Lord." Lincoln looked, piously at Seward, who crossed himself like Archbishop Hughes. "I think the problem is," said the President, judiciously, "that he is so small. Sheridan's a foot shorter than me, and looks like a skinny boy with a beard glued on."

At the Center Market, a boy—with no beard glued on (but had there been one handy he might thus have disguised himself, so nervous was he)—stood among the corpses of a regiment of pullets, listening to Mr. Henderson describe the next attempt upon the President's life. Ever since Lincoln's alleged near death from poisoning, David had found himself treated with a new dignity at Sullivan's and elsewhere. The fact that the attempt had failed did not discourage his fellow patriots. After all, a man could do no more than try. Through Mr. Sullivan, David had been congratulated by the Colonel himself. Meanwhile, unsigned cryptic letters arrived for him in care of Sullivan. Several were postmarked Canada. Wilkes Booth remembered him.

Deftly, Henderson removed the insides of a pullet. "The plan now is to shoot him first chance we get."

"But why bother when he's going to lose the election anyway?" David had grown somewhat fond of the man he was now thoroughly convinced that he himself had almost poisoned.

"He's wily, says the Colonel. He could win yet. But dead, he won't win for sure. We have an arrangement with McClellan, you see."

"I know," said David, who knew nothing but what he heard in the saloons. When it looked as if old Jubal Early was going to take the city, David had been instructed to join a group of wild boys at Lookout Point and just as Early entered the city, they were to charge the stockade where the prisoners were being held. But Early had never got beyond Seventh Street Road; and seventeen thousand Confederate soldiers were still penned up like . . . chickens, thought David, listening carefully to Mr. Henderson's low cluck while Washington's housewives crowded about the Henderson women, and poked the chickens and complained of prices. David looked at his watch. This was his morning to make deliveries. He had to be back at Thompson's by noon.

"We can't take no chances now, says the Colonel. Things are bad for us. We got almost no men left, and the Yanks won't make any more prisoner exchanges. We was counting on that." Mr. Henderson regarded the chicken's liver in his hand, as if it were a purple jewel of great price.

"So why not catch Old Abe and hold him for ransom?" David had always been intrigued by the possibility. Of all the mooted plans, this one had seemed the most sensible and to the point. The Yanks would give up a lot of Confederate soldiers to get back Old Abe.

"The Colonel thinks that Seward won't make no exchange for Old Abe. He thinks it's pointless. He also says that Richmond says that the foreigners won't like it if we do that and we need the English to keep on helping us out with boats. I don't know. Anyway, we're killing him real soon. What I want to know is, what are his movements now?"

"Well, he still takes blue mass," said David, making a joke that Mr. Henderson affected not to hear. "He's out at the Soldiers' Home most nights. Mrs. Lincoln and the two boys and the nigger woman are all out of town and so is Johnny Hay. Old Abe's pretty much alone most of the time. He rides or drives in from the Soldiers' Home about sun-up and goes back when it's dark. But there's always troops with him now—the Bucktails, they call them."

"Marshal Lamon?"

"Most times he's with him. But sometimes he's not." Since Lamon was U.S. Marshal of Washington, Mr. Henderson regarded him with more fear and respect than any president.

"Lately, when Old Abe's been at the War Department at night, he'll go back to the Soldiers' Home without Lamon. He's sure a big man, isn't he? Lamon—with all those guns."

Mr. Henderson nodded. He wiped his hands with a bloody cloth. "You keep an eye out during the next week or so. If you think Old Abe is going to be late one night, or if you hear Marshal Lamon won't be with him or anything useful, tell it to Sullivan and he'll pass us the word."

David saw that his evenings would be ruined. Recently he had got to know a girl who made up packages in Shillington's Book Store. Since she was an orphan living with an aunt, she was free as air; and as fickle. Lately, she had allowed him to take her to respectable places to eat, where she ate a great deal and spoke disapprovingly of girls who got involved with Yankee soldiers or frequented places where drunks and druggies were to be found. David had expected to unite himself with her in the ham-lady's back room where he currently slept, paying for the privilege in cash not person. Now David would be obliged, night after night, to lurk about the Mansion and the War Department until Old Abe decided to go to bed, which, sometimes, he didn't do at all.
560

When there was a battle on, he was apt to spend the whole night at the War Department.

As if Mr. Henderson understood his problem and took pity on him, he said, "There's a groom called Walter in the White House stables. He's the one who gave Mrs. Lincoln that bad fall, by mistake. You say you know me. You tell him you'd like to know, when he knows, if the carriage—or better yet a horse—is to be got ready late. That will give us some warning."

This was better. "I reckon I can keep track of Lamon from Thompson's, where you can see everybody who comes and goes to the Mansion. But why worry so much about him? Bullet's going to kill him, too, ain't it?"

Mr. Sullivan strangled the neck of an old hen so deftly that the hen never experienced so much as an instant of premonitory despair. "Lamon's not careless. Old Abe is. Lamon always sees to it that Old Abe's got a wall of troops around him, which makes him hard to hit. Left to himself, Old Abe just moseys along."

David agreed that this was the case. Once the President had actually wandered all alone into Thompson's. Mr. Thompson had been profoundly excited. What might he do for His Excellency? But Old Abe had just smiled and said, "Nothing at all, Mr. Thompson. I just came in because I like the smell."

Mr. Henderson was now plucking the hen so rapidly that a cloud of feathers hid both hen and hands. "We tried to take care of General Grant when he was here last week. But we never got close enough."

"I saw him," said David. "He looked like he had been on a real drunk. He came riding hell-for-leather up the avenue with this little fellow Sheridan aside him." David had been impressed by Sheridan's youth. But young and dashing as he was, Sheridan would be no match for old Jubal Early, the first Confederate hero since "Stonewall" Jackson's death.

"We went and put a bomb inside Grant's headquarters at City Point. It went off the very day he got back from here." Almost tenderly, Henderson laid out the now nude hen on the white marble butcher's slab. "Had he gone into his headquarters just five minutes earlier..." Mr. Henderson shook his head. Anyone observing them, thought David, would have thought that Mr. Henderson was saying a prayer for the hen's departed soul.

At Sullivan's, David was greeted by a number of midmorning drinkers. David wanted to discuss with Mr. Sullivan how best to get information to him, but the Irishman was not to be found and the bartender had no idea when he would be back.

David stood side by side with a night-rider at the bar, each with a foot on the low brass rail. The night-rider gave David a plug of tobacco to chew on, and David duly chewed. Once his mouth had filled up with nicotine-induced saliva, he spat at the nearest spittoon more than a yard away, and made a perfect bull's-eye; he gave back the plug.

"That's fine shooting," said a soft Southern voice with a touch of Irish brogue. David turned and saw a ragged youth of the sort the town was full of now. A piece of rope held up faded trousers that were unmistakably butternut gray. "You take the oath?" asked David, the usual polite introduction this season at Sullivan's.

"Well, I got caught by the Yanks who went and locked me up until I said to myself, well, I'm Irish anyways, so I took the oath. Mr. Sullivan's been real nice to me."

Although the night-rider was not about to be nice to a Confederate soldier who had renounced the sacred cause, David couldn't help but think that had it not been for the accident of his job at Thompson's, he might be this boy, living on handouts and looking for work. He bought the young man, Pete Doyle his name was, a beer. They talked a while of the war but David could see that Pete had lost what little interest he might have had in it. "I'm looking for work," he said. "I've been to the horsecars. They say there might be something someday soon. But I don't know. There's so many like me in the town." He pushed back his thatch of gingery hair. If he hadn't been so smelly, David might have taken him off to the ham-lady.

But at that moment, a tall, stooped figure appeared in the bar. He was well known to the patrons of Sullivan's, who had first taken him to be one of Pinkerton's spies until Sullivan said, no, that despite the creature's Yankee accent and eccentric ways, he was William de Latouche Clancey, the editor of a small pro-Confederate magazine in New York City, currently on the run from military prosecution. David had seen him a number of times at the bar. Although Sullivan personally tolerated Clancey, he had warned David and the other young men to steer clear of him because "He'll leap at you like you was a glorious young colleen fresh from Cork." As it was, a number of penniless youths had indeed been leapt at—successfully. Currently, one of them was using copavia and blaming his disease on Clancey. Sullivan was not sympathetic. Since the young man had been fairly warned, the fault was his.

"There you are, my Davie!" honked Clancey, who had learned all the names of the regulars.

"Be careful, Pete," whispered David.

But Pete just grinned happily as Clancey put a long skeletal arm about his shoulders and ordered beer for his new friend Pete. The night-rider left in disgust. "How marvelous to encounter one who has come through the fires of a righteous war unscathed!" Clancey, who had long since given up on David, peered into Pete's innocent face, on whose cheeks proper whiskers had yet to grow.

"Well, I didn't see all that much fire before I went and got captured and took the oath."

"Oh, you are modest! The one quality that I love above all others, save love of country!" The beer arrived. "Let us drink," said Clancey, eyes popping as he contemplated his tender quarry, "to the death of Lincoln, and the inevitable victory!" David also drank to that. Then, as it was past noon, he left the bar. Mr. Thompson did not like to be kept waiting.

Senator Sumner did not like to wait either. He had sent Nicolay a message: Could he see the President as soon as possible? Sumner would meet Lincoln anywhere except at the White House, where journalists might see them together. With a degree of mischief, Lincoln had suggested that the most convenient place would be at Governor Seward's Old Club House. The Senator had agreed; but the meeting must be private, he said. When Lincoln asked Seward if he might use his house, Seward had been much amused. "I shall stay at my desk, fighting the Emperor Maximilian and all his works, while the two of you plot in my study, with only Pericles as witness."

Lincoln nodded, and picked at the single boiled egg that dominated the great crested plate on his desk. This was the lunch that he himself had ordered. Seward suspected that the President might stop eating altogether were it not for Mrs. Lincoln. Certainly, when she was away, as now, he made no pretense of any interest in food. The President's one indulgence was water. During the day, he made numerous visits to the water-cooler in the corridor; and there he would drink cup after cup of water as if it were the finest hock. "Mr. Sumner will probably try to compete with Pericles," said Lincoln, finishing, with an effort, the egg.

"Do you think he will mention the well-known secret meeting in New York?"

"I think he will speak of nothing else." Lincoln poured himself yet another glass of water from the brilliant Waterford glass carafe. Seward woundered if the President had any idea of just how much money his wife was spending of public as well as of private money. Certainly, the newspapers were keeping careful track of her visits to the stores in New York and Philadelphia. But those were not the sort of stories that Lincoln would ever look at. Currently, the press was making much of the fact that while viewing the dead on a battlefield, Lincoln had asked Lamon to sing him some ribald songs. The story was curiously repellent; and so believed by many.

563

But Lincoln would not read any version of the story, much less answer it. "In politics," he had said to Seward, when the subject came up, "every man must skin his own skunk. These fellows are welcome to the hide of this one. Either I have established the sort of character that gives the lie to this sort of thing, or I haven't. If I haven't, that is the end."

The end seemed now to be approaching, thought Seward, as he watched Lincoln dry his lips with a napkin. For the first time in some months—well, hours—Seward wondered what might have happened had he and not Lincoln been elected in 1860. The war would certainly be over by now, due, if nothing else, to Seward's superior guile. He would have seduced the South back into a more voluptuous, if not perfect, Union. But at what cost, he could not hazard. Certainly, if he had had to bear what Lincoln now bore, he might have resigned and gone home to Auburn. There were times when Lincoln seemed to him like some bright, swiftburning substance that, once ignited, could not be extinguished until it had burned itself entirely out, according to its own peculiar and circumscribed by time, nature.

"Will Horace Greeley publish your correspondence with him?"

Lincoln shook his head. "I insisted that certain passages must be deleted. I felt that he would only aid the rebels by giving too gloomy an aspect of our case—not to mention the Democrats. He has backed down. I don't think he wants them published, anyway. They make him look more than ever a fool. Hay writes me that the Niagara meeting was a comedy of errors. The so-called commissioners had no authority, and Mr. Davis is not about to agree to any terms. As usual, Greeley wasted everyone's time; and nothing came of it."

"He was at the secret meeting last week."

Lincoln suddenly smiled. "You know, when Johnny Hay was leaving Greeley's office at the *Tribune*, guess who was coming in the door?"

"Mr. Chase?"

"You have second sight, Governor. But I attach no importance to that, as long as Mr. Taney lies on his deathbed—interminably breathing, to be sure!"

"Well I don't want to cry out like Cassandra—how Mr. Blair brings out the classicist in me!—but, if you'll forgive me, I think you've fallen into a trap. I don't think Greeley had the slightest interest in those two rebels at Niagara. I think he was trying to smoke you out as an abolitionist, and I think he succeeded. He got you to state, more plainly than ever, that if the South does not absolutely abandon slavery as a pre-condition of peace, the war will go on. As a result, there's been all hell to pay in New

564

York. Archbishop Hughes is tearing his hair—or, I guess, to be more precise, his miter—to bits, and my good Irish supporters are now saying that they will never fight for any nigger's freedom."

"They do precious little fighting as it is." Lincoln's face set. "They are the least disciplined and most cowardly of our troops. They are welcome to support McClellan, and an instant bad peace." Lincoln pushed back his buckthorn chair from the table. "You are right, I suppose, about Greeley smoking me out. But I was already out after the Reconstruction proclamation, and the last message to Congress, and the reply to Wade."

"You have never before said that if the South were to come to you and say 'we will lay down our arms and rejoin the Union,' that they could not do so until they set free their slaves."

"If they rejoin the Union, those slaves *are* free—freed by me."

"As a military necessity. Well, that necessity will have gone."

"Naturally, we would hold a convention of some kind if they were to return, as you suggest. I have always been for reimbursing the slaveowners. Everyone knows that."

"Oh, *I* know what you mean. But will the archbishop's parishioners understand? Greeley has lined you up with the abolitionists, and there will be hell to pay."

Lincoln smiled wanly. "I am very much used to that foul currency, Governor." Lincoln pushed the plate away from him. "I have always admired Greeley. He helped put me here—perhaps not a cause for general rejoicing or, for that matter, even personal. Now he is like an old shoe—good for nothing. When I was young out west, we had no good shoemakers, so once a shoe got old the leather would rot and the stitches wouldn't hold and that was the end of it. Well, Greeley is so rotten now that nothing can be done with him. He is not truthful; the stitches all tear out."

In Seward's study, Sumner stood, immaculate, before the flower-filled fireplace. In the hallway the ubiquitous bodyguard saluted the President as he entered the study, alone. "Well, Mr. Sumner, it is strange to see you here, in enemy country, and not at Mrs. Lincoln's house." Lincoln was amiable. Sumner constrained.

"Sir, I have never been so saddened in my life, as to meet you here."

"Oh, come now! Governor Seward is profane at times, and temperance holds no delights for him, but he is not the devil, you know."

"Oh, I did not mean that, sir. Far from it." Sumner straightened his light-blue coat, whose silver buttons shone in the summer light like new-minted coins. Lincoln was, as always, disheveled. "By the way, I have just had a charming note from Mrs. Lincoln, at Saratoga Springs. She is an accomplished letter-writer, an accomplished lady. I must confess to you that I go to her salon voluntarily, and not from mere sullen duty."

"Well, Mr. Sumner, we hope to see a lot more of you in the next four years when, I expect, foreign affairs, your specialty, will be occupying us more and internal troubles less." Lincoln was coolly provocative.

"Oh, sir, *that* is the crux!" Sumner arranged himself in front of Pericles. One lock of blond-gray hair fell across his own marblelike brow. He looked every bit as historic as Pericles; but then he had once declared that even alone, in the privacy of his own house, he would never strike a pose that he would not be willing to strike before the nation in the Senate chamber.

"We shall have to deal, sooner or later, with the French in Mexico. Naturally, I shall follow, as always, the lead of your Committee on Foreign Affairs. Then there is the matter of Spain—"

"Defeat!" Sumner spoke each syllable as if it was itself a word of such awfulness that Heaven might open up and lightning strike them both.

Lincoln had settled into Seward's own armchair. "You mean yesterday's election in Kentucky?"

"Sir, I mean for our party and our cause in November."

"I will admit that things do not go exactly well for us—"

"Or for the cause that we adhere to. Sir, it is not just politics that are involved. If it were . . ." With one hand, Sumner made a leveling gesture to express his contempt for all human pettiness. "But there is something larger. There is the morality and the rightness of our cause. The freedom and the enfranchisement of the Negro has been the lifework of many of us. Now that work is about to be undone if not forever for at least a generation, because McClellan will make peace at any price and the price we already know. Human freedom for the black man, human dignity for the black man . . ." The famous orator's voice had begun to resound in the small study.

Lincoln broke in before it got out of control. "Now, now, Mr. Sumner, let's not go leaping overboard, as the steamboat captain said to the widow. General McClellan isn't elected yet—"

"Pennsylvania will go for McClellan by a hundred thousand majority." Sumner could be as briskly political as anyone else. "I heard that from your own partisan, Cameron."

"That is as of today. But the election is a hundred days from now. Things can change."

Sumner put his hands on his knees; and sat very straight. "Yes, that is what we all want, for things to change. I have been delegated by certain Republican leaders to request you, most respectfully, most . . . affectionately, if I may be personal . . . to withdraw as the candidate of our party, so that we can then unite behind someone who can win the election in what is, actually, less than a hundred days from now."

Lincoln's half smile was in place as he stared, absently, at Sumner, who was finding it difficult to hold his monumental pose as his plump thighs were now resting on the chair's extreme cutting edge. "Naturally," said the President at last, "I have heard of the meeting in New York City—"

"Which I did not attend." Sumner slid back in his chair.

"But Brother Greeley and a number of other influential abolitionists were all there, as well as Mr. Bryant's son-in-law. I gather that it is your—their?—your, I see, wish to hold a second national convention next month in order to select a new Republican candidate."

Sumner addressed not Lincoln but Pericles. "Obviously, if you were to step aside, voluntarily, and allow us to unite behind someone else, there is no doubt we could defeat McClellan, whose main support comes from those unthinking elements which are, simply, sick of the war and care nothing for its morality." Sumner turned to Lincoln.

The President's left eyebrow had so ascended that now left eye perfectly matched right. When this phenomenon occurred, the habitual dreaminess of the gaze was metamorphosed to the hunter's glare, which he now turned on Sumner, who sat back in his chair as if, for safety's sake, to increase the distance between them. "I do not follow your logic, Mr. Sumner. If you select an out-and-out radical Republican like Mr. Chase—or yourself even— you will split this two-headed party that I have done my best for years to hold together. The moderates—of which I am one— will desert you, while the peace-at-any-price folks will vote you down, and McClellan in."

Sumner removed a white, scented, cambric handkerchief from his sleeve and touched each of his now lightly glistening temples. "I cannot speak as to the likely choice of a convention not yet called. But I am reasonably certain that my friend Mr. Chase would *not* be selected. After all, we do want to beat McClellan, and that could be done with a greater military man, like Grant or Butler or Sherman, with someone like Admiral Farragut as vice-presidential candidate."

The now brilliant gray eyes were staring straight at Sumner, who squirmed slightly. "I am no expert in these things." The voice was even. "But in the past, from George Washington to Andrew Jackson to Zachary Taylor, victorious generals were elected president only after they were victorious and their particular war was won. This war is still going on—and on. McClellan may win against me by default, because the people cannot endure another day of war. That is a possibility. But he cannot prevail as a military hero, because he is not one. He is simply a failed general, whom I was obliged to discard."

"Sir, General Grant could have had by acclamation the nomination that you won at Baltimore. All he had to do was put himself forward."

"Well, he *was* put forward. By Missouri, and he did not get any other votes."

"The convention, of course, was managed by you—"

"What else would you expect a man whose work is only half done to do? Of course, I controlled the convention. After all, I am our party's leader."

"You lead one wing—"

"The larger wing, Mr. Sumner."

"I know that, sir. That is why I beg you to stand aside, as a patriotic duty for which you will be forever remembered, and let us win the election with, let us say, Grant."

"So it is Grant." The half smile was gone; the glare remained. "I do not think that he will make the race. He has not yet finished his appointed task. He certainly will not run against me."

"Sir, all the more reason that you withdraw, that you . . . that *you* nominate Grant, as the better man. Then, your place in history secure, we can finish the greatest task of all." Sumner stopped abruptly. The only sound in the room was the musical chiming of the clock in the hall. For once, even the flies were still.

Finally, Lincoln spoke. "I was unanimously nominated at Baltimore by our party. Now you want me to withdraw from the contest in order to make room for a better man. I wish I could. I mean that, Sumner. Because I am sure that there are many better men than I for this work. But they are not here, and I am here. Now let us say you find this better man, and I step aside. Can he—endorsed by your hollow if pure true Republicans—unite the party and then the country? I think it most unlikely. The factions opposed to me would fall to fighting among themselves, and those who now want me to make room for a better man would get one whom most of them would not want at all. My withdrawal would probably bring on confusion far worse than anything we now know. God knows, I have at least tried very hard to do my duty, to do right to everybody and wrong to nobody. There are those who say I prolong the war because I lust for power. Well, that is nonsense, as you know. I may once have wanted—even lusted—for power, but all that has been burned away. There is nothing left of me. But there is still the President. He must be

568

allowed to finish the work that he was chosen to do. So leave me in peace. Once that is done, you and your better man are welcome to my dangerous place. In fact, you and your better man can come to my funeral, for I have known for some time now that when this conflict is over, I end."

The President got to his feet. Sumner also rose. So did Seward's dog, Midge, who had been sleeping, unobserved, beneath her master's desk.

"I am sorry," said Sumner, gravely shaking the President's hand.

"So am I, Sumner. But then sorrow is something we have an abundance of."

Seward had been sitting on a bench in Lafayette Square. As soon as he saw statesman and muscular shadow depart, he hurried home, where he found Lincoln stretched out on a sofa in the study, eyes shut. Midge's greeting of Seward was so noisy that Lincoln opened his eyes and said, "I have just been asked to withdraw as a candidate."

"For what reason?"

"Patriotic, I think. The premise was suitably vague."

"They will put up—who?"

"They will try Grant."

Seward poured himself brandy. "They are insufferable fools."

"Insufferable, they are. Foolish...?" Lincoln's voice trailed off, as from exhaustion.

"I concede that we *could* lose," said Seward. "But as long as our army occupies the border-states, and the reconstructed rebel states, we can squeak through—I think. After Kentucky, I'm not so sure."

"That does not strike me as exactly what I meant when I spoke of government by the people." Lincoln was suddenly droll; he sat up, and the huge feet crashed onto the floor.

"It may not be by the people but it is certainly *for* the people, since you insist on using rhetorical triads, though God alone knows what *of* the people means, since no government can be anything else but of them, unless the lions and the tigers take over."

"Or the race of eagles..." Lincoln murmured, half to himself, half to no one at all.

As Seward did not understand the reference, he did not ask for an explanation. In any case, he had a constitutional dislike of being told things that he did not know, as opposed to ferreting them out. "The only danger, as I see it, is General Grant deciding to run."

"I don't think there's any chance of that, unless he's taken Richmond, in which case I'll be like the fellow who didn't especially want to die but if he had to, well, that's the way he'd like

569

to go." Midge rested her muzzle on Lincoln's knee. He scratched her ears, as required. "But there's one curious thing I noticed when Grant was just here. We got onto the subject of the election—I can't imagine how! Anyway, when I said what a splendid team I thought he and I were, he didn't say a thing."

"That is ominous." Seward knew that in politics nothing speaks more loudly than the unspoken. "You think that he will not endorse you?"

"I know he won't. Oh, I can understand why. If I'm defeated, he will be obliged to work with the next president. He won't want an enemy in the White House, though I can't see him lasting a day with McClellan." Lincoln was now ready to leave. "But I was still somewhat hurt that he did not respond."

"There is time." Seward was soothing.

"No, Governor. There is no time left. Or rather, this is the time. Well, now I must go back to work."

"And I must let Midge take me for my evening stroll."

At the Mansion, Thaddeus Stevens was coldly vehement. "We are pleased with Andy Johnson, we are not pleased with any Blair."

Zach. Chandler went even further. "The only way the true Republicans can be got to vote for you and not Frémont, or whoever they come up with at Cincinnati, will be the elimination of the Blairs from your Administration."

"But there is only one Blair in the Administration," said Lincoln, reasonably.

"He must be gone before the election," said Simon Cameron, "if we are to hold our own in Pennsylvania."

"Hold our own?" Lincoln repeated.

"As opposed to lose outright," said Stevens; the stiff wig set off his hard white face like an oaken frame.

"I am not convinced, Mr. Stevens, that my reelection depends on whether or not there is a Blair in the Cabinet." Lincoln towered over the three men, who were lined up on the sofa opposite the fireplace.

"Then let us say, sir, that the vigor with which the party leaders work for you in Pennsylvania will be affected if Mr. Blair stays." Stevens was icy.

Lincoln was amused. "There is useful vigor, and there is useless vigor, Mr. Stevens, as you well know."

This reference to Stevens's attempt to swing Pennsylvania from Lincoln to Chase was duly noted by all, and appreciated by all save Stevens, who said, "Without us, Mr. Cameron and me, working together, as peculiar as that combination must look to the innocent—if such exists—eye, you will not carry Pennsylvania and without Pennsylvania you will not win the election."

"That is my view," said Cameron, staring at Stevens with familial dislike.

"You must get rid of Blair." Chandler was harsh. "Now!"

"So you mean to dictate to me my Cabinet?" Lincoln appeared more bemused than angry. "Does this mean that I am now your puppet? that once elected, thanks to this peculiar combination, *you* will govern?"

"Surely, the giving up of one measly Blair does not constitute puppethood," said Stevens.

"It's more like a bargain," said Cameron, yawning.

"I take a different view, gentlemen. For four years this or that faction had tried to govern me, and none has succeeded. Naturally, I want to be reelected since I have not done what I set out to do." Lincoln turned to Cameron. "I am also quite capable of making a bargain, as you know." Cameron nodded pleasantly; he was quite incapable of embarrassment even at this direct acknowledgment of the way that he himself had come to the Cabinet. "But I am not about to allow any faction to dictate to me who is and who is not in my Administration, or to be told that I must or must not do certain things."

"We had hoped you would be a little more easy with us," said Cameron, frowning. "You know it's not as if we had us a real political party, and everyone knew what he had to do. We are just a hodgepodge, more or less united behind you."

"Then I hope you will be more united, because if you are less, we all lose. In any case, gentlemen, rather than accept the disgraceful terms you would force on me, I would decline the office."

"That seems to be that," said Stevens, getting to his feet.

"Yes," said Lincoln. "That is that."

The two Pennsylvanians shook hands—Stevens grimly, Cameron mournfully. Chandler remained behind. "There is something they don't know that I do."

"What is that, Mr. Chandler?" The sun was setting now behind the monument, and Lincoln's eyes kept straying to the billows of rose and saffron clouds as they flowed across the sky.

"I have spoken to General Frémont. He told me to tell you that he will pull out of the race, *if* you drop Monty Blair."

Lincoln studied Chandler's huge, homely brick of a face, where colonies of whiskey-broken veins had left their memorials as red crosshatchings. "I'll keep that in mind, Mr. Chandler."

Chandler nodded; and took his leave.

It was dark when Lincoln mounted his horse. Then, at the center of a company of cavalry, he rode out to the Soldiers' Home, by way of Fifteenth Street, where a huge transparency proclaimed: "The Star of Canterbury Never Sets." Stanton had so devised the

President's horseback excursions that, due to the physical bulk of the cavalrymen on either side of him, the President was not visible to anyone in the street.

At the turnoff to the low hill on which stood the Soldiers' Home, Lincoln reined in his horse; and dismissed the escort. For a moment horse and rider were an integral part of the dark stillness of woods and warm, windless, starless night. Once the sound of the retreating cavalry escort had ceased, only crickets and tree toads sounded. For a moment, Lincoln took deep breaths of the scented summer air.

Then, finally, reluctantly, he rode up the driveway to the stone gates of the Soldiers' Home. When he was halfway to the gates, a rifle was fired; and the horse bolted through the gates at a panicky gallop. In a grove of cedar trees where peacocks now shrieked, a soldier grabbed the horse's reins and coaxed it to a standstill.

As Lincoln dismounted, he said, casually, "He got the bit in his teeth before I could draw rein. I'm glad you caught him, Nichols. I was getting set for a fall."

"Something startle him, sir?" asked Nichols; he had guarded the President before.

"No, no." Lincoln ran his hand, absently, through his hair.

"You've lost your hat, sir."

"So I have. Well, good-night; thank you."

Lincoln went inside the stone cottage, where he was greeted by the orderly assigned to him. Lincoln asked for tea, an unusual request for him. He then sat in the small parlor of the cottage, and began to read by kerosene lamp a copy of Artemus Ward. But before the first smile, much less laugh, had been produced, Nichols appeared, carrying Lincoln's hat. "We found this, sir, in the road."

"Oh, good. Put it in the hall."

"Sir." Nichols held the hat so that Lincoln could see clearly two small round holes an inch below the crown. "This is where the bullet entered; and here is where it came out," said Nichols.

"I heard a rifle shot." Lincoln was neutral. "I thought it was a coon hunter, maybe, in the woods."

"It was a *hunter*, sir, in the woods."

"That is the second good hat that I have lost in this fashion. Strange how he—or they—always aim at the head, which is so hard to hit, and not at the body, which is so much easier a target." Lincoln gave the hat to Nichols. "Say nothing of this to anyone. Particularly, say nothing to Marshal Lamon."

"On condition, sir, that you will not send your escort back *before* you are inside these gates."

Lincoln smiled. "A bargain? Well, today has been bargain day
572

all day, and I guess that's how it will end. All right, Nichols, I will grant your wish. Now burn the hat. I want no one to see it."

"Yes, sir." Nichols left.

At the Cabinet the next morning, Seward found the President distracted. Although the Seward-Weed machine did not want Roscoe Conkling to return to the House of Representatives, Lincoln favored him; and Seward had given way. The morning was unusually humid and hot even for the African Capital, as Seward had taken to calling Washington.

The President moved restlessly about the room. Seward sat slumped in his chair. Stanton combed his beard with two fingers, always finding new and interesting—even Gordian, thought Seward—knots. Blair seemed as if he were not present, no doubt in anticipation of when he would indeed be gone. Fessenden, the new boy, sat very straight; and paid close attention to everything. Nicolay was in and out. Bates had already said that he would be going home after the election, no matter what the result. Usher was present but, to Seward, permanently invisible. Welles made notes. It was rumored that, as a one-time literary man, he was keeping an elaborate journal, which would destroy them all.

It was Fessenden who was first with the latest ominous news. "I have just learned that General Butler is prepared to run for president on a ticket with Ben Wade." Seward found Fessenden's disapproval of his former senatorial colleague and ally most pleasing; but then Seward always enjoyed the sight, no matter how familiar in politics, of even the mildest leopard-spot-changing at season's change. Senatorial Jacobin was now staunch loyalist.

"Ben Butler," the President began; and ended. The subject plainly tired him. Seward wondered, idly, if any of the presidents had been as cross-eyed as Butler or, for that matter, as peculiarly ugly? Old Abe was indeed Apollo next to the squat political general who had earned the nickname "Spoons" Butler, the result of having seized all the valuables that he could get his hands on when he was at New Orleans. Should the radical Republicans be stupid enough to nominate Butler and Wade, Seward knew that their makeshift party would go the way of the Whigs; and McClellan would win.

There was a general exchange of political information; and all the news was bad. Weed had told Seward that if the election were held as of this day, August 23, 1864, Lincoln would lose New York by fifty thousand votes; and that was without Butler in the race.

Lincoln read a note from Washburne, who was at Chicago: Illinois was, for the moment, lost. Blair remarked, sourly, that with Cameron and Stevens in charge of Pennsylvania, the Keystone State could also be written off.

Lincoln sighed. "It is curious. We have no adversary as yet, and we have no friends. I suppose this is a unique situation." He took his seat at the center of the table; and glanced at a letter. "Mr. Raymond of the *New York Times* thinks that I am now identified as an abolitionist, thanks, I suppose, to Horace Greeley. He thinks that the only way I can win is to offer—immediately—peace terms to Mr. Davis, on the sole condition of acknowledging the supremacy of the Constitution. Everything else, including slavery, to be decided at a national convention."

"Shameful!" said Stanton, tearing his fingers loose from his beard, and stifling a cry of pain.

"One sees his point," said Bates. "You have gone and made it an absolute pre-condition of peace that the South abolish slavery. Perhaps that question was better left moot."

"I freed the slaves as a military measure only." Lincoln was now on the verge of changing a whole set of very black spots, and Seward hoped devoutly that he would go through with the metamorphosis. But Lincoln dropped the subject; he turned to Nicolay. "Have you the memorandum?"

Nicolay gave the President a sheet of paper, folded in half and sealed. "I would like you gentlemen to indulge me," said Lincoln. "Will each of you sign his name on the back of this paper."

"What are we signing away?" asked Seward. "Our lives and sacred honor?"

"Nothing so priceless," said Lincoln. "It is just in case . . ." But he did not say in case of what. As requested, the seven men signed.

On August 29, the friendless President at least gained an official adversary when the Democratic Party nominated George B. McClellan for president at Chicago. Lincoln and Seward sat in the Telegraph Room of the War Department as the news came through. From time to time they were joined by Stanton, who could now neither see without weeping nor breathe without choking.

As the news of McClellan's nomination came clattering into the room, everyone expected, at the least, a *pro forma* joke from the President. But there was none. Lincoln sat on a plain wood chair so low that his knees touched his chin while the huge hands grasped his shins.

Finally, Seward broke the silence. "I think they may have done themselves in, allowing Vallandigham to play so large and visible a part. After all, he is as close to being a traitor as the war has produced."

Lincoln nodded; but said nothing. Plainly, that curious mind
574

was elsewhere, threading a labyrinth that led, at the very least, thought Seward, to a whole herd of minotaurs. Seward was already preparing, in his own less curious but no less subtle mind, a series of attacks on the Democrats for having accepted as a delegate the banished traitor Vallandigham, who had written a peace-at-any-price platform for McClellan, the warrior, to stand and run on.

The telegrapher reported that Governor Horatio Seymour would deliver the official notification of nomination to General Mc-Clellan. Meanwhile, the convention was eager to hear Mc-Clellan's response. For the first time, Lincoln smiled. "I hope they don't all decide to stay in Chicago until they hear from him. If they do, they had better start looking around for permanent lodgings."

Seward laughed, more from relief that the President was himself again than from amusement. "One thing," said Seward, "the Democrats are even more divided than we are. The New Yorkers and McClellan mean to continue the war for the Union, ignoring the slave issue, while the Vallandigham people want an instant peace. I suspect that long before the election, their party will have split in two."

"As ours is doing now?" Lincoln was quizzical.

"It should be noted that the group that met two weeks ago in New York with an eye to holding a new convention was supposed to meet again tomorrow. But my spies tell me that they have no plan to meet. I suspect even Horace Greeley has accepted the fact that you are all that we have."

Lincoln made no response.

Four days later, David Herold was staring, somewhat vacantly, out the window of Thompson's. In the back room, Mr. Thompson was trying to achieve yet another tonic for Governor Seward, whose morning malaises no longer yielded to the usual mixture of elm bark and bicarbonate while Seidlitz powders had long since been abandoned.

As David watched, he saw the familiar figure of the President cross from the War Department to the Mansion; he was accompanied by Gideon Welles and Marshal Lamon. Sadly, David thought of the recent opportunity that had been missed by a matter of inches, if Mr. Sullivan's story was true. Everyone was now agreed that it was curious indeed that a man who wandered about as freely as did the President could not be more easily shot. Plainly, Old Abe was a lucky man.

But David did not know how lucky Lincoln was. As the President walked, he held in his hand the flimsy copy of a characteristically dry telegraph message from Grant at City Point: "A dispatch just received from Superintendent of Telegraph in Dept.

of Cumberland of this date announces the occupation of Atlanta by our troops. This must be by the 20th Corps, which was left by Sherman on the Chattahoochee whilst with the balance of his army he marched to the south of the city."

At the corner of Pennsylvania Avenue, the three men paused as the horsecars went by. A number of riders recognized the President. There was a mixture of cheers and boos. Cheerfully, Lincoln raised his hat.

"Every last one will be cheering you tomorrow," said Lamon, as a single red maple leaf floated toward them on the cool autumn wind.

At the gate to the Mansion, they were stopped by a messenger on horseback. He gave the President a second flimsy. "Mr. Stanton said you would want to see this, sir." The messenger saluted; and departed.

Lincoln glanced at the message; then broke into a great smile. "It is from Sherman himself. He says 'Atlanta is ours and fairly won.' Well, Neptune, I think I shall now declare a day of thanksgiving in honor of Sherman."

"Don't forget Admiral Farragut. The navy's occupied Mobile Harbor."

"Neptune will be celebrated as well as Mars."

"And Jupiter?" asked Welles, as they walked up the driveway to the portico. "What of him?"

"Jupiter," said Lincoln, "has regained his thunderbolts."

Nicolay met them on the portico. He, too, had heard the news. He shook the President's hand as if they had not been together all morning.

"You will be elected unanimously!" In Nicolay's excitement "will" had become "vill"; he was again a six-year-old Bavarian child, newly arrived in America.

Old Edward also shook the President's hand. "A number of those newspaper writers are upstairs," he said. "I have told them that you are much too busy winning the war to see them."

"I shall tell them exactly the same thing," said Lincoln; and repeated aloud the magical phrase: "'Atlanta is ours and fairly won.'"

7

IN THE PRESIDENT'S BEDROOM, HAY HELPED LINCOLN ARRANGE
the pier glass so that the light from the window struck it head-on.
Lincoln then pushed the mirror back and forth until he got the
exact angle that he wanted. "Yes," he said. "That is just about
the way it was yesterday." He squinted at his own reflection. "And
the way it was back in Springfield." He pulled an armchair in
front of the mirror and placed it just off-center. Then he seated
himself. "Now, John, you stand so that you can look in the mirror
and see me but so I don't see you." Hay kept moving, tentatively,
to the right until Lincoln told him to stop. "You can see my
reflection?"

"Yes, sir."

"Now then . . ." Lincoln stared intently at his reflection in the
glass. Hay noticed that the Ancient's hair and beard both needed
trimming; he was also thinner than ever and, more than ever,
thought Hay, a doughnut-brown.

Lincoln cocked his head; and shut one eye. Then he shut the
other eye. Then he frowned. "I cannot see it," he said at last. "It
is the strangest thing. You see nothing?"

"No, sir. Only you, in the chair."

Lincoln was disappointed. "Yesterday I thought it was happening again, the way it did four years ago at Springfield. For an
instant, I saw myself twice, one image was clear; the other was
paler and shadowier. In Springfield, it looked as if I was sitting
next to my own ghost."

"Do you believe in ghosts, sir?"

Lincoln smiled. "No, I'm too earthy for that. But don't tell
Mrs. Lincoln. She gets great comfort from charlatans. If she thinks
Willie comes to her every night, let her think it. But I *am* interested
in phenomena—physical phenomena. I'd hoped to demonstrate
this one, with a witness. Because if I saw me and my other self
and you did, too, why we would both be scientific ring-tailed
wonders. But I don't; and you don't."

"What makes the effect, do you think?" Hay also believed in
phenomena; a category that could include almost anything, not
to mention everything.

"Well, I was planning how to find out. I suspect it is the way
577

that the light strikes upon the glass, doubling the image, but I tell you the *effect* is just like you are seeing your own ghost." Lincoln stood up. "I will say that I do put some faith in dreams. But then dreams are the self talking to the self. I have one recurring dream that always comes to me the night before some great event. I just had it the night before Atlanta fell." Lincoln stared at himself in the mirror, as if it were indeed the ghost of himself that he saw; or, perhaps, he was the ghost addressing the mirrored, still-incarnate flesh. "I am on a raft, without a pole or a rudder of any kind. I'm at the center of a river so wide that I cannot see either shore, and since the current is a swift one, I am drifting... drifting... drifting." He stared dreamily into the looking glass.

"Then what happens?"

"Then...? Oh, I wake up." The Ancient smiled. "To find that while I was dreaming, the raft has come triumphantly aground, and Atlanta is ours and fairly won."

"Did you dream your dream the night before last? When Sheridan was massacring Jubal Early at Winchester?"

"No. I think the dream is rationed. Only turning points require its presence."

The President then went to the Friday Cabinet, while Hay went to Nicolay's office. Nico was in New York, trying to find Thurlow Weed, who had recently vanished. Stoddard was at the small table that Hay himself used when Nico presided over the secretary's desk. The usual pile of correspondence had been dumped, as usual, on the floor. The latest consignment of newspapers was stacked on the central table. Back and forth, in the hall, supplicants marched. Some asked to have a word with Major Hay. Hay enjoyed the handsome women; often they flirted with him. Yet Nico claimed that no woman had ever once flirted with him. Hay had said that was because they could see, upon his brow, in letters of fire, the sacred name, "Therena."

"Look!" Stoddard's usual worried frown had shifted to a scowl. He gave Hay an official-looking sheet of paper, which proved to be a letter from Frémont, posted the day before, September 22. Frémont was withdrawing as a candidate for president. He would support Lincoln. Nevertheless, he could not approve Lincoln's course, which had been a failure... Hay read no further. He hurried across the corridor, stumbling over an admiral, who reached for his sword. But before Hay was stabbed through, he was safely inside the Reception Room. All heads turned toward him. Silently, he gave the Tycoon the message. Silently, the Tycoon read it. Silently, Hay left the room.

Seward did his best to guess the contents of the letter. Obviously it was important, or Johnny would not have broken in on them like that. If it had had anything to do with the military, he would have given it to Stanton or Welles first. So the message was political. But Sherman and Farragut had knocked the bottom out of the Chicago nomination convention. McClellan was finished. There was still a faint possibility that the radicals might yet nominate Butler, who was more than willing. Perhaps that was it. Meanwhile, Seward was very much aware that Montgomery Blair had been glowering at him ever since the beginning of the meeting. Although the Blairs tended, as a family, to glower on principle, Seward was uncomfortably aware that today he alone was the innocent object of the family's collective wrath.

Lincoln ended the Cabinet with a reading from Petroleum V. Nasby's latest book of drolleries. Everyone laughed uproariously at the jokes except Stanton, who muttered, to Seward's amazement, "Goddamn it to hell!" Plainly, Chase's work of Christian conversion was not complete in the case of the War god. As the meeting broke up, Seward started toward the President, but before he could get to him, Monty Blair was at his side; and the two men vanished into the President's office.

As Lincoln shut the door to the Reception Room, he said, "I'm sorry it had to happen so suddenly."

"So am I." Blair held a letter in his hand, signed by Lincoln. "This was waiting for me when I came in from Silver Spring."

"I had no choice, Monty. Your father also agrees."

"I will write out my official resignation this afternoon. I see Seward's hand at work."

Lincoln shook his head. "He has nothing to do with it. I let Chase go, and offended all the radicals. Ever since, they have been after me to let you go—Anyway, we must unite the party, and when it comes to a lot of folks, you and Frank are like a suit of red underwear to a bull."

"Then I go."

"Monty, if it could have been otherwise, I would keep you with me to the end. Your kindness to me has been uniform; and I am deeply grateful."

"As I am to you," said Blair.

"What will you do now?"

"Make speeches for you. What else can I do?"

"That is the most, certainly. I am grateful; and will not forget." On that note, they parted.

Hay entered the office. "Is it true Mr. Blair is resigning?"

"Yes, John. It is true."

The moment that Frémont withdrew from the race, Blair was let go. Plainly, the Tycoon was now beginning to behave like

Machiavelli; and about time, thought Hay. "You knew about Frémont already?"

Lincoln nodded. "I was told last night. Mr. Stanton has just given me this." Lincoln unfolded a telegram. "'John G. Nicolay, unemployed, has been drafted into the army at New York City. Signed General Dix.'"

"My God! Poor Nico. What do we do?"

"*We* don't do anything except keep quiet about it. I've sent word to Nicolay, through Dix, to buy himself, as secretly as possible, a substitute."

"Let's hope Mr. Greeley doesn't get word of this."

"He is the least of our problems now." It was true. Ever since the disaster at Niagara Falls, Greeley had been all-out for Lincoln. In person, Hay had found the famous editor odd, but charming. Once it was clear that the peace-mission was nonsense—disavowed even by Jefferson Davis—Greeley had come around to Lincoln. The *Tribune* was now entirely pro-Lincoln; and had been so even before Atlanta—or B.A., as Nico now termed the dark ages of the Administration, while A.A. designated the new victorious era. It also had not hurt that Greeley had, somehow, got the impression that if Blair should leave the Cabinet, he would be the next Postmaster-General. In fact, when the Tycoon had been asked recently by a number of New Yorkers if he would consider Greeley, they had been told that, after all, another editor by the name of Benjamin Franklin had been pretty successful in the job. Greeley, who lusted for public office, had taken the bait; and his editorials now oozed honey.

Seward was at the door. Lincoln motioned for him to come in. "Hold back the crowd for another twenty minutes," he said to Hay, who shut the door behind him. Seward congratulated Lincoln on letting go Blair. "Now I assume that we shall soon be joined by Horace Greeley, the heir of Franklin, as the Pope is of Peter."

Lincoln laughed. "I'm afraid that is not meant to be. I've just sent a telegram to William Dennison in Ohio, to the effect that *he* is now Postmaster-General; and I want him here quick."

Seward frowned. "He is a friend of the Blairs."

"He is a friend to man, Governor," said Lincoln sweetly.

"How will Greeley take this?"

"I never committed myself to him. Anyway, the worst is past, as far as the *Tribune* goes. Unless Butler runs, they have no one else but me. The problem in that area—*your* area in more ways than one—is not the *Tribune* but the *Herald*."

"James Gordon Bennett." Seward pronounced the three names as if they were the witches in *Macbeth*.

"The very man." Lincoln opened the window. The wind was from the north; and the air, for once, fresh and wholesome. Lincoln took a deep breath. "I am told that now that he has got all that money can buy, he would like those things that money cannot buy."

"What on earth can they be? And if they are on earth and not in Heaven, tell me."

"Well, I'm not exactly up on these matters either, but I believe something called social position means a lot to him—or to his wife."

Seward nodded. "I am sure that it does. But that's for sale, too, like everything else in New York."

"Maybe the price is a mite high or maybe he doesn't want to wait. We need the *Herald* on our side."

Seward nodded. "They could easily support McClellan—or the Emperor Maximilian, for that matter."

"This can come from you, Governor, as Secretary of State: For Mr. Bennett's editorial support, he can be minister to France or wherever he would like to go."

Seward whistled. "That's a big price."

"That's a big circulation the *Herald*'s got. Since Bennett and Weed are now on speaking terms, I suggest you use Weed to get the word to him."

Seward had never seen Lincoln quite so direct in his indirection. "What happens if the *Herald* supports you, and you are reelected?"

Lincoln grinned. "Well the Emperor Napoleon will just have to spend four years looking at two of the most crossed eyes he ever saw. He may find the sight horrifying but it will be better than a war over Mexico."

"Perhaps," said Seward, "he can have both Mr. Bennett and a war."

"No, no. At current inflated prices, one Bennett is the equal to one war. We cannot afford both. Besides, we must first win *our* war."

"And election..."

"And election," said Lincoln. "I begin to feel that we may have got—almost—to the other side of the Jordan."

Chase was very much on the wrong side of his Jordan River; and saw no way across. But Sumner did. That morning, October 12, the spirit of the Chief Justice of the United States, Roger B. Taney, fled its eighty-seven-year-old earthly envelope. "I tell you for certain, Mr. Chase, that you have my support. You have Mr. Fessenden's support. You have, best of all, Mr. Stanton's, and he is more with the President than any other man."

"But Seward is not with us." Chase was filled with melancholy, unlike the plaster bust of himself on the mantelpiece. While still at the Treasury, Chase had, most graciously, he thought, allowed a sculptor to make a plaster bust of his features which would then be cast in bronze, to be paid for by a subscription of Treasury employees. Since the bust would be the property of the nation, forever on display in the Treasury's main hall, it had never occurred to him that there would be the slightest objection. But misfortunes tend to flock together. Maunsell Field was now fearful that this bust might never be cast, as the subscription was, thus far, inadequate, and his successor, Mr. Fessenden, indolent. "Seward, I am told, wants Montgomery Blair, who hates him with a true passion."

"We ignore Mr. Seward's chicaneries. We ignore Mr. Blair's. They are nothing to us."

"Welles favors Blair." Chase's mood was as dark as the twilight now gathering. Unoccupied all summer, the house was damp and uninviting; the fireplaces did not draw properly; the chimneys needed cleaning. Kate was at the North, suffering from a cough that had lingered since spring. He dared not think what that might mean. Worse, the marriage with Sprague was a disaster; husband and wife had quarrelled furiously in his presence at Narragansett. Chase blamed himself for everything. But what good would that do? "Bates favors Bates," he added.

Sumner was not listening. "Yes! Accept!" he exclaimed. "Complete your great reformation by purifying the Constitution, and upholding those measures by which the republic will be saved!"

"Mr. Sumner, I have not been asked to accept anything yet. I have twice seen the President since I got back, and never alone. He is kind. But he says nothing. I feel that I do not know him."

"I do," said Sumner, with Olympian simplicity. "I shall manage this."

But Sumner took the precaution of calling on Mrs. Lincoln first. He found her in the Blue Room, shortly before her afternoon levee. She was talking with great concentration to a dour, bearded man.

Mary was startled to see the man who, three weeks earlier, had asked the President to withdraw from the election. But Mr. Sumner was Mr. Sumner. Partisan as she was to the point, she knew, of monomania, Mr. Sumner must be humored. Although he was brilliant and cosmopolitan, he was also unworldly. In any case, he had befriended her during that first terrible year in what she sometimes referred to as Secession City.

"Mr. Sumner, sir. This is an honor, sir. Allow me to present Mr. Wakeman, the new Surveyor of the Port of New York."

582

Single-handed, Mary had got Wakeman appointed in September; he had now come to express his gratitude. Between the wealthy Wakeman's good offices and the now reassured reelection of her husband, Mary's mood was considerably lightened; also, her mailbag. After the fall of Atlanta, the stores had stopped dunning her. Recently, she had even gone to Lothrop's, and in the pleasant, panelled private room ordered a hundred pairs of French kid gloves, despite Keckley's muttered warnings. They were safe for four years. She need not look beyond that.

Sumner was his usual courtly, attentive self. When she teased him about the events of August, he said, naïvely, "But we were losing the war. We had no choice but to try someone new. Then Mr. Lincoln surprised us. He started to win the war. Our prayers were answered. So now there will be no opposition to him from within our party—even the unspeakable Butler accepts that."

Mary enjoyed victory; and this was victory indeed for her husband. As the Blue Room filled up with guests—twice the pre-Atlanta number—she did the honors.

When the President looked into the crowded room, Sumner was ready for him. Lincoln was as affable as if the mid-August scene had not occurred. But when Sumner started to extol Chase, Lincoln stopped him. "Sumner, I have the greatest admiration for Mr. Chase. As you know, I also admire Mr. Blair. In fact, symmetry might require that Blair, as the lawyer who was counsel for the slave Dred Scott, should succeed the Chief Justice who decided against Scott, and brought me here—and brought us all this big trouble."

Sumner became eloquent on the subject of Chase. But when he threatened to become interminable, Lincoln stopped him with a gesture. "I must say hello to the folks now. As for Mr. Chase, I have one fear. He is somewhat insane on the subject of the presidency. How do I know if I make him chief justice that he won't spend all his time on the bench conniving to be president?"

"I am shocked, sir . . ." Sumner began.

"I would be shocked, too, if this were to happen. Since the chief justiceship is an end in itself, you can't put someone there who hasn't got his mind on the shop."

"If I were to guarantee that Mr. Chase—"

"We can never guarantee anyone else and, sometimes, in politics, we can't even guarantee ourselves. Tell Mr. Chase my mind is open." Mrs. Gideon Welles approached with two ladies to present to the President. "Tell him," said Lincoln, almost as an afterthought, "that I'd appreciate it if he'd make a few speeches for us, in Ohio—and, maybe, Indiana, too. Mrs. Welles," the President beamed, "what have you brought me?"

To the extent that such a monument to statesmanship as Sumner could be said to slip away, he slipped away; and went to Sixth and E, where despair now not only reigned but deepened; Sumner, however, was optimistic; he was also adamant. Chase must pack his carpetbag and go to Ohio. There were things, he told the wretched Chase, higher than mere personal convenience.

But Sumner did not spell them out. He did not want to. In any case, he was just another of the voices that tormented Chase, who consoled himself with St. Paul's curious words to the Corinthians: "There are, it may be, so many different kinds of voices in the world, and none of them is without signification."

On Tuesday, November 8, 1864, there was rain at Washington City. The President's Park was a sea of yellow mud. Only Welles and Bates had shown up that morning for a brief Cabinet meeting. Fessenden was in New York City, negotiating loans. Usher and Dennison were in their home states, voting. Seward was in New York, where he had been campaigning, while Stanton was in bed, seriously ill with the bilious fever. Mary had also taken to her bed with a headache that was midway between her usual nervous headache and The Headache. Tad, in the uniform of a colonel, had been sent off to Georgetown to the house of friends, whose sons were a part of his private regiment. Keckley hovered about the living quarters of the Mansion, ministering to Madam. The waiting room was empty. Edward was gone. Nicolay was in Illinois, getting out the vote. General Dix had helped him find a Negro to take his place in the army; there had been no newspaper scandal.

Only the Tycoon and Hay were stirring in the gloomy house on Election Day. There had been no visitors, save a Californian journalist that the Ancient had taken to; and Hay had taken against. What had to be done had been done, thought Hay, listing the states in a notebook. Later, as the returns came in, he would record the vote, district by district. He had put the states in alphabetical order, leaving out, he suddenly noticed, the eight-day-old state of Nevada.

Hay had already noted in his book the results of a preliminary election in October, involving Pennsylvania, Indiana and Ohio. The most doubtful of the three, Indiana, had been the most pro-Lincoln. Thanks to the confused efforts of Cameron and Stevens, Pennsylvania was a nearer thing. Fortunately, the Ohio and Pennsylvania soldiers in Washington's hospitals had been allowed to vote. The Ohians were ten to one for the Union. The Pennsylvanians less than three to one. The worst vote of all was from Carver Hospital, which Lincoln and Stanton passed each day.

When the returns from Carver were read out, Stanton had fumed, and Lincoln had laughed. "That's pretty hard on us, Mars. They know us better than the others." Lincoln's own military guard voted for him, 63 to 11.

It was plain to everyone that the soldier vote would be the key to the election. In an extraordinary effort to secure every possible military vote, Stanton had so worn himself out that he was now seriously ill. Those states that allowed their men to vote in the field presented no difficulty. But Illinois—all-important to Lincoln—made no such allowance. Consequently, Grant's army was being stripped of every Illinois soldier; and the trains were crowded with furloughed soldiers, going home to vote for Lincoln.

Hay could not make up his mind why it was that these men were all so dedicated to Lincoln and to the Union. If he were a private in the field, he would be tempted to vote for McClellan and peace. In a curious way, Lincoln, privately, held the same view. He was certain that Illinois was lost, and he did not trust in the soldier vote, despite the evidence of October.

Just before seven in the evening, Hay had found Lincoln at his writing table. He, too, had made a list of the states in alphabetical order. He, too, had forgotten Nevada, which Hay pointed out to him. "It is only three electoral votes, but even so."

"Even so, I will need them," Lincoln agreed, writing in "Nevada." Then he showed Hay his prediction.

Hay whistled. "You think it is as close as that?"

Lincoln nodded. "In the electoral college the most I can get is 120 votes to 114 for McClellan."

Hay saw that, of the important states, Lincoln had given McClellan New York, Pennsylvania and Illinois. He gave himself New England and the West. "Then the military vote will make all the difference," said Hay, handing back the paper.

"As they make the war," said the Ancient. "Well, let's go to the Telegraph Room, and learn our fate."

Together, with only Lamon in attendance, they crossed the dark empty street to the War Department. The steamy rain had let up for a moment and in the glare of gaslight the wet sidewalk shone like onyx, thought Hay, whose recent poems had been studded with precious and semiprecious stones. A guard in a rubber cloak saluted as the President bypassed the awkward turnstile which was supposed to control the traffic to and from Stanton's empire; and went instead to a side door, where a soaked and steaming sentinel saluted him; and opened the door.

A half-dozen orderlies came to brief attention. The Tycoon waved at them; and they went about their business. The business of one of them was to give the President the returns from Indianapolis—a majority of 8000 for Lincoln; since this was higher than that of the October vote, the Tycoon brightened. But he did not believe the next message from Forney. "You will carry Philadelphia by ten thousand votes." Lincoln shook his head. "I think he's a little on the excitable side."

They went upstairs to the Telegraph Room, where Lincoln made himself comfortable on a lounge. Originally, this large room had been a library, connected by a door to the office of the secretary of war. One of Stanton's first acts had been to move the army's telegraph headquarters from General McClellan's command to the War Department. Just off the Telegraph Room was a small office, where the military codes were kept. The man at the machine greeted the President, who asked for Major Eckert.

"Here he is," said the army's chief telegrapher. In the doorway stood the young major, covered with mud.

"Thank God Mr. Stanton can't see you, Eckert." The Tycoon shook his head with mock horror. "These things are progressive, you know. The first wallow in the mud is carefree, and joyous. But the next is less so. Finally, you cannot stop. Wherever there is mud, there you will be, Major, rolling and twisting and rooting like a hog!"

"I fell, sir. In the street. I was watching somebody up ahead who was slipping and sliding so comically that I started to laugh, and fell on my face." An orderly brought Eckert a towel. As he mopped up, the Tycoon told of the evening of the day that had decided the contest for Senate between him and Douglas. "It was a night like this. I'd read the returns, and knew I'd lost. So I started to go home, along a path worn hog-back and slippery. Then one of my feet slipped and kicked the other and I fell, but I landed on my feet anyway, and said to myself, 'Well, that was just a slip not a fall.'"

The next return was an estimate. Lincoln would carry the state of Maryland by 5000 votes; the city of Baltimore by 15,000. "That is a pleasant surprise, if true," he said.

Hay kept his notes. The California journalist Noah Brooks joined them. Previously, he had worked in Illinois, where the Tycoon had first known him. He flattered the President outrageously; and treated the President's secretaries with disdain. Nicolay was not only positive that Brooks was angling for the job of secretary in the second term, but "He is welcome to it," Nicolay had said.

The suspicious Lamon had reluctantly allowed a half-dozen highly partisan officers to keep the President company. Gideon Welles had also joined the long watch.

At nine o'clock the serious returns began. Although storms in the midwest interrupted and delayed the Illinois returns, by midnight it was clear that Lincoln had carried his home state. He immediately sent an orderly to the White House. "Tell Mrs. Lincoln. She's even more anxious than I am."

As Hay recorded the satisfactory returns from Massachusetts, Lincoln was telling Brooks, "I'm enough of a politician to know when things are pretty certain, like the Baltimore convention. But about this thing I'm far from certain."

"You should feel pretty confident now," said Brooks. The air of sycophancy was too much for Hay. He hoped it would be too much for the Tycoon during the second term, which seemed now to be at hand.

As New Jersey began to slip toward McClellan, the Tycoon grew philosophical. "It's strange about these elections I'm involved in. I don't think of myself as a particularly vindictive or partisan man but every contest I've ever been involved in—except the first for Congress—has been marked by the greatest sort of bitterness and rancor. Can it be me, I wonder, that provokes all this, without knowing it?"

"I should think it was the times, not you, sir," said Brooks. "And lucky for us, you are there to mediate."

Hay decided that, for once, the Tycoon showed alarming bad taste in his companions. Was the second term to be one of vague complacencies and intrigue? Was the simple good Ancient that Hay knew to be corrupted by youthful flatterers? Perhaps he himself should stay on. But then he thought of the Hellcat; and realized that he could not stay at the White House four more months, much less years. In fact, he had made up his mind that after the first of the year he would move to Willard's and then some time after the inaugural in March, he would go—as would Nicolay.

Seward arrived at midnight, in time for the supper that Major Eckert had had prepared in the War Department kitchen. The premier was in an exultant mood. He had returned on the so-called Owl Train from the North. "We shall take New York State by forty thousand votes," he announced.

"While McClellan sweeps the city. Have some fried oysters." Lincoln and an unknown general were helping fill up everyone's plate with food.

Eckert himself was now manning the telegraph machine. "Here comes New York," he said.

But Seward preferred to give his version of what was happening in that most imperial of all the states. "Governor Seymour threatened to call out the national guard, to scare away our people. So Butler promptly called out the army to scare off the national guard.

587

He's been arresting Democratic agents all day." Seward poured himself champagne; and toasted Ben Butler.

Eckert reported: "McClellan has carried New York City by thirty-five thousand votes."

"That was pretty much my estimate," said the Tycoon, nibbling at a fried oyster.

"McClellan has also carried the state by four thousand votes," said Eckert.

"Not possible!" Seward nearly dropped his glass. "There is fraud here."

"That was *not* my estimate," said Lincoln, abandoning the rest of the oyster. "But I was certain that I would lose the state."

"Well, you have won the election," said Brooks.

"Not quite..."

Eckert announced that Kentucky seemed secure for McClellan. Hay began to add; and subtract. He was obliged to do on paper what the Tycoon could do in his head. Each state's electoral vote was on file in that swift, subtle but distinctly odd brain. Hay could not see how Lincoln could lose. Nevertheless, if New York's electoral votes were to go to McClellan, the margin of victory might resemble, more and more, the Ancient's original gloomy estimate.

Then Eckert, with a grin, announced: "Correction from New York. Lincoln not McClellan carried the state by four thousand votes, and Governor Horatio Seymour is defeated."

There was cheering in the room, and when Seward insisted that the Tycoon drink a glass of champagne, he did so. "Remember your hopes and dreams for Seymour this very night?" Seward teased Lincoln. "Just think, it might have been President Seymour, with you as his midwest manager."

"Fate has spared us," said Lincoln, demurely.

Eckert announced, "Steubenville, Ohio, the hometown of Mr. Stanton, has gone Republican."

"We are safe!" Lincoln exclaimed. Then, in wheezing imitation of Stanton, he said, "Let's give three cheers for Steubenville!"

When the cheering ceased, Seward observed, at large, "We owe Mr. Stanton a lot tonight. He got out the soldier vote, and they are the ones who have made all the difference."

Lincoln nodded, suddenly somber. "It is true," he said. "But I myself cannot see why they voted as they did—grateful as I am."

"They are loyal to you." Again Seward raised high his glass. "They are also loyal to the army, to the Union, to themselves and to what they have done these last four years, and to all their dead."

"I will drink to that," said Lincoln; and finished the glass of champagne. "Certainly, I am honored that they have voted for me. Honored and surprised, with all the dead thus far." The voice trailed off.

"*They* would favor you, too, if they could vote," said Seward, expansively.

"The dead?" Lincoln sounded startled. Then he shook his head. "No, Governor. The dead would not vote for me, ever, in this— or any other—world."

8

THREE DAYS LATER, LINCOLN MET WITH THE ENTIRE CABINET, except for Stanton, whose illness was beginning to cause alarm.

Lincoln had carried all but three states: New Jersey, Delaware and Kentucky. He had a popular majority of a half-million votes; and so he was, just barely, a majority president.

Seward was euphoric. He could not stop talking; he wished that he could stop but the fit was upon him. "Even if we carried New York State by four thousand votes instead of the forty thousand we first thought, it is an extraordinary achievement, given the forces against us, from press to governor to Copperheads."

Hay entered. "Sir, a report from Nicolay, in Illinois. You have carried Illinois by twenty-five thousand votes." The Cabinet applauded. Lincoln looked at the report a moment; then he laughed. "I see that I have lost my home county of Sangamon to McClellan. I also lost the state of my birth, Kentucky, to McClellan. It would appear that where I am best known, I am least popular."

"Doubtless, that explains your triumph in Nevada," said Seward.

Hay gave the President the latest news from the War Department. The Tycoon announced: "General McClellan has resigned his commission as major-general, and departs, immediately, for a holiday in Europe."

There was, again, applause from the Cabinet. Meanwhile, Lincoln had given Hay a sealed sheet of paper. "Gentlemen, do you remember last summer when I asked you all to sign your names to the back of a sheet of paper whose inside I did not show you? Well, this is it." Lincoln held up the paper; then he gave it to Hay. "Now, Mr. Hay, see if you can get this open without tearing it." Hay took a paper knife and, like a surgeon, made a series of complex insertions. The Tycoon had glued the paper shut at the oddest of angles.

When the document was open, Lincoln read it aloud to the Cabinet. "'This morning, August 23, 1864, as for some days past, it seems exceedingly probable that this Administration will *not* be reelected.'" Lincoln glanced at Seward, who was obliged to nod his agreement. "'Then it will be my duty to so cooperate with the President-elect, as to save the Union between the election and the inauguration; as he will have secured his election on such ground that he cannot possibly save it after.'" Lincoln put down the note. "This was written about a week before McClellan was nominated. Since I was fairly sure that he would win, I had made up my mind that when he did, I'd ask him here and say, 'Look, we've got nearly five months before you take office. I still have the executive power, while you have the confidence of the country. So let us together raise all the troops that we can and end this war together.'"

The Cabinet looked appropriately grave, except for Seward, who said, "And the general would answer you, 'Yes, yes'; and the next day when you saw him again and pressed your views on him, he'd say, 'Yes, yes'; and nothing would ever have got done."

"At least," said the Tycoon, "I should have done my duty and my conscience would be clear."

"We need not grieve for Little Mac," said Fessenden, newly returned from New York City. "I am told he has been offered the presidency of the Illinois Central Railroad, at ten thousand dollars a year."

"He will answer 'yes' to that quick enough," Seward conceded.

"So," said Lincoln, "would I. In his place, that is—where I thought I would be last August."

Gideon Welles then spoke with some delight of the imminent departure from Washington of the now former Senator Hale, a man of corruption, who had caused the Navy Department much grief. Perhaps he should be punished further; perhaps he should be investigated by the Attorney-General. But Lincoln raised a large hand, and said, "In politics the statute of limitations must be short."

Since Seward had never known a good politician who was not vengeful, Lincoln was either not a good politician or an anomaly. Seward inclined to the last.

After the Cabinet meeting, Lincoln met with Francis P. Blair. "You will think, sir," began the Old Gentleman, now very old indeed but still retaining his Jacksonian fire, not to mention impersonation, "that I am here on behalf of Monty, who deserves to be the next chief justice."

590

"I had a suspicion that that might be in your mind," said the President, looking at the pale, truncated obelisk to Washington. "Certainly, it is in my mind."

"Well, as long as it is there, I will say no more. You have done enough for the Blairs to entitle you to their gratitude and that of their posterity forever." This sentiment brought forth a degree of saliva which the old man reflexively mopped up, eyes on the portrait of his friend, Jackson. "Actually, I'm here on other business. As you know, I was once on good terms with Jefferson Davis."

"I know," said Lincoln.

"I want to go to Richmond." The Old Gentleman was abrupt; Jacksonian. "I want to talk to him. I want to end this war."

"How?"

"I want to persuade him to make peace, to return to the Union, and to join with us in driving the French-Hapsburg forces out of Mexico."

Lincoln was noncommittal. "That is Governor Seward's dream, too. But is it Mr. Davis's?"

"Let me find out. I have a perfect excuse to go to Richmond. Those bastards who looted my house took all my papers, and now I want them back. Davis will understand that. He'll let me come to Richmond. Then I shall tell him my plan."

Lincoln nodded, as if in deep thought; then he said, "Wait until Savannah falls. Then come to me, and I'll give you a safe passage to City Point, or wherever Grant happens to be."

"Not until then?" The Old Gentleman looked somewhat disappointed.

"I think we must tighten the noose a bit more. Also, the slavery question should be solved by then. I have a hunch that this Congress is going to ask for an amendment to the Constitution to abolish slavery once and for all. When that is done, Mr. Davis, for better or worse, will know just where he stands."

David knew exactly where *he* stood with Mr. Thompson: he had been fired, as the wild boys would call it; let go; dismissed. "I have for some time, David, felt that you were not entirely present when you were present, and often when I needed your assistance, you were not present at all." Mr. Thompson stood, sadly, in front of his long, gleaming row of Latin-inscribed ceramic jugs. The curling gold Gothic letters shone in the bright morning light. "I did my best to overlook your absences, out of friendship to your mother. I, also, I shall tell you now, detected in you, from the beginning, the makings of a first-class druggist. Anyone who can saw wood can be a doctor of medicine but to be a fine druggist is to be an artist born not made. We are the true scientists, and deep in our powders and our elixirs and in our subtle mixings of

591

same, there is health, and there is God. I pray that you will take counsel with yourself before it is too late." Mr. Thompson opened his wallet. "Your wages, which ceased the day before the election, which was a holiday—though our work is never done despite the day."

"But I worked all day yesterday . . ." David argued another five dollars out of Mr. Thompson. In a sense, he was glad to be gone. A lifetime in the back room of a drugstore was even worse than a lifetime in the front room, getting to meet everybody, as Mr. Thompson did. In the last year he had told Mr. Thompson that he had been sick so often that he had now run out of illnesses. The year before, David had worked part-time for Walsh's, a druggist at the Navy Yard, not far from his mother's house. Mr. Thompson had an understanding with Mr. Walsh, and during one of David's many "convalescences," it was agreed that he work close to home. But that had come to an end when the two druggists compared notes one day and found that much of the time David had been working for neither. Now the curtain was falling forever, thought David, dramatically, on his career as a prescription clerk. Fortunately, there was plenty of work at the theaters; and, best of all, his friend Wilkes was back in town.

For the last time, David shut the door of Thompson's behind him; and heard, for the last time, the small bell attached to the inner handle clatter. Then he stepped out into Fifteenth Street, a free man. The rain had ceased and the sky was clear. A brisk wind smelled of winter. The mud had turned to hard earth, while the hogs in the alleys seemed more than usually alert. In a good mood, David made his way along New York Avenue to the Surratt house in H Street.

The city was filled to bursting with shiftless ex-slaves and equally, to David's hardened eye, shiftless white men from the South, who had taken the oath and now had no place to go and no work to do. They sat in open places, making fires out of trash and drinking corn liquor. They were not supposed to be armed but all had knives; and, at the slightest provocation, used them. There were now parts of the city where not even David dared go at night.

A regiment of cavalry swept down the avenue, stopping all traffic. But David no longer even noticed the Yankee troops. Like all true Washingtonians, he knew he was living in a city that had been occupied by the enemy and there was nothing to be done about it except mind his own business, which was to kidnap President Lincoln and hold him for a ransom of one hundred thousand captured Confederate soldiers.

Just before the election, the entire Surratt family had moved into the H Street house. Mrs. Surratt had rented the place at

Surrattsville for five hundred dollars a year to a man called Lloyd. Since John was no longer postmaster, there was no reason for them to stay in the country when they could live in the city, where he might find proper work, and Mrs. Surratt could make money by turning 541 into a boardinghouse. John had been reluctant to give up his night-rides. But Mrs. Surratt had convinced him that their future was in the city, not at a country crossroads in Maryland. Of them all, Annie was best pleased.

David entered the front parlor—the back parlor where old Mr. Surratt had died now contained the very lively Mrs. Surratt, who greeted David warmly but hurriedly. "Annie's out, giving lessons..."

"Is John—?"

"Here I am." John entered the parlor in his shirt-sleeves. He had finally grown a small chin-beard in imitation of Jefferson Davis. "I'm the handyman," he complained.

"You find any work?"

John sighed. "Labor, yes. Proper work, no. There's an opening at the Adams Express Company. I've applied." He threw himself on the sofa. "I wish I were back home, where I could be useful."

"There's a lot you can do here," said David, significantly. But nothing that he ever said could be made to *sound* significant, the way that Wilkes could do with a simple drop in his voice. In any case, since no one took David E. Herold seriously, nothing that he said was ever listened to with any respect or attention, except by Wilkes, late at night when they made their plans. Booth's blond girl had come to Thompson's the day after the election. "He's at the National," she whispered. Then she fled; presumably back to Ohio Avenue, where her sister kept a fancy house. From Sal, David had learned that Ella Turner was in love with Booth, who paid a certain amount to her sister to keep her relatively pure for him. It was Ella's dream that he would one day marry her.

David had found Booth shattered by the election. "What is the point to killing the tyrant now, when he will be succeeded by yet another tyrant in the loathsome form of the traitor Johnson?" In the back room of Scipione Grillo's restaurant, Booth would often sound as if he was acting in a tragical play. David always found such moments entirely thrilling, particularly when he was included in the drama.

"We had our last chance on August 13, when you were to pass him the fatal cup, and I memorialized the deed with a diamond, cutting into the glass of a window in a hovel at Meadville where I was stopping, jubilant at the thought of this glorious tyrannicide which, alas, failed." David had apologized, at length. There had indeed been a plan for him to try, once again, to poison the

593

President, and for once, the exact day that the poison would be taken was known in advance.

The President had not slept in a week. Late in the afternoon of August 12, the President's doctor had asked Thompson for a sleeping potion to be delivered the next morning—to be tried out that night. This was the moment, Sullivan declared. David agreed; with Booth behind him—at Meadville; with the whole Confederate government at Richmond, presumably behind Booth; with history back of them all...

But David had lost his nerve. On the morning of the 13th, plain laudanum had gone over to the Mansion; and that night Old Abe had enjoyed a sound night's sleep. Nevertheless, David was hailed by Sullivan as a brave if unlucky soldier whose gun had misfired a second time.

For the moment, the President was safe from murder. The Tennessee turncoat Andrew Johnson was considered even more dangerous than Lincoln. But the Confederacy was now reeling from the effects of Grant's grinding-down strategy. There were almost no men left to fight.

Enter John Wilkes Booth, at the eleventh hour.

Enter a couple named Holohan into the front parlor. "Where is your mother, Johnny?" asked the lady.

"She's upstairs, fixing your rooms, Mrs. Holohan. She said for you to go on up." The couple vanished up the stairs. "Boarders," said John sadly. "We also have a girlfriend of Annie's staying here. And a chap I was at the seminary with sleeps with me. Thirty-five dollars a month, room and board. That's all. Why don't you join us? Three to a bed."

David shook his head. "I'm living at home now. Like they say, I was just now fired. So I don't know how I'll live, except doing odd jobs at the theaters."

"That makes two of us with nothing to live for."

"Don't speak so soon." David then proceeded to tell John about a friend of his—he was careful to mention no names—who had a plan to save the Confederacy. At first, John was skeptical. "This whole city's nothing but a garrison. So how are you going to kidnap the chief of the whole thing in the middle of his army and navy? I could see shooting him. That wouldn't be hard. But to kidnap him..." John shook his head.

"You tell my friend that. He's well connected. He's rich. All he needs is somebody who knows the Maryland roads. That's when I thought of you. I wanted you to meet him last month but he had to go to Mountroyal."

"Where?" John showed a sudden interest.

"It's a place up in Canada somewhere. Anyway, when he was in Mountroyal..."

"Montreal." John corrected him. He got up. "That's where our secret service keeps its eye on the Yanks. Where's this friend of yours stopping?"

In the lobby of the National Hotel, Wilkes Booth sat on a horsehair sofa next to Bessie Hale, who was weeping quietly into a handkerchief. Booth appeared to be soothing her. Then, while she was blowing her nose, David caught his eye. Booth made a gesture for him and John to wait by the windows. As they crossed to the large palm tree where Booth and David had plotted before, Booth led Miss Hale to the main stairs. Slowly, she ascended. Quickly, Booth crossed the crowded lobby to the palm tree. Cleverly, David introduced John Surratt to Booth, without ever mentioning Booth's name.

They pulled three chairs close together in front of one of the windows that looked onto crowded Sixth Street. Propriety obliged Booth to explain Miss Hale's presence in the lobby of his hotel. "Her father was not re-elected to the Senate, so they have given up their house and moved in here. Poor girl. She cannot bear the thought of returning to Rochester, New Hampshire. I was consoling her." He turned to John. "You, sir, are a Surratt of Surrattsville?"

"That's right. Only now we are all of nearby H Street."

"You have served our country well," said Booth. "I have heard you spoken of in many interesting places. I am looking for a farm to buy."

"I know them all, in that area, anyway."

"I should like to be on a road—out of the way but good enough—to Richmond."

"I know all the roads, sir, that lead to Richmond."

Booth fixed his dark, honey-colored eyes on Surratt; then he seemed to come to a conclusion. "Let us go to my room and partake of the house specialty, milk-punch and cigars."

On the morning of December 6, 1864, William Sprague entered the long, half-empty bar of the National Hotel. He was eager not for milk-punch but for gin. He was less eager for his meeting with a man who had identified himself in an unsigned note as "a friend of Harris Hoyt, with urgent news."

Sprague seated himself in the darkest corner of the bar and ordered gin; then he glanced at the day's business of the Senate. The Attorney-General, Mr. Bates, had resigned at the end of November. Lincoln had then appointed James Speed of Kentucky to take his place. Since James Speed was the brother of Joshua, a Springfield crony of the President, thee Senate Judiciary Committee decided that it might have a salutary effect on the newly reelected President if he were obliged to wait a few days while they did their best to find out just who Mr. Speed was. Also, the Radicals were not happy that such an important post had gone to a man from a border-state which had voted for McClellan. Sprague was taking no part in this game. Sprague was not interested in attorneys-general. Sprague was interested in cotton.

A swarthy Southerner, dressed like a Baptist minister on circuit, sat himself down beside Sprague. "Senator, I'm pleased to meet you at last. Mr. Hoyt speaks so highly of you. As does Mr. Prescott. As does Mr. Reynolds. As does your cousin Byron."

"That's natural," said Sprague, "that Byron should."

The Southerner ordered straight rum. He sat in almost sacerdotal silence until the rum had gone, in one single swallow, from glass to stomach. Then he said, "You know that the *Sybil* was caught by the navy, two weeks ago."

"Yes," said Sprague, "I know." The *Sybil* was a British ship, en route from Matamoros to New York. The ship's hold was full of cotton for Sprague and his colleagues. As always, there were no records of any kind aboard the ship to show where the cotton was destined other than the Custom's House at New York, presided over by the amiable Hiram Barney. In the past, once a shipment had arrived, Byron or Reynolds or Prescott would pay a call on Barney; and the cotton would be released. But, lately, there had been problems. In response to accusations of improper bonding and bribery, a congressional committee was now holding hearings into Custom's House affairs. Since the war was apt to be over long before the hearings ended, Sprague was not much concerned. Besides, the Custom's House was a Republican spoil; and the Congress was securely Republican, as was the President. There was no cause for alarm. He ordered his second gin.

"Then I suppose you also know that our friend Mr. Charles L. Prescott has been arrested by the military authorities at New York."

Sprague gasped. The pince-nez fell from his nose onto the table; a lens cracked. "You broke your glasses," said the messenger of ill tidings.

"How...?" was the only word that Sprague could get out.

"We don't know. Maybe the army traced the cargo through the ship's London owner. Or, maybe somebody at the Custom's House tipped them off. Anyway, I was able to get to Prescott. He's scared to death. He thinks Hoyt double-crossed him. He's fixing to give a complete confession today."

596

"Complete?" Sprague's nearsighted eyes squinted as if his life depended on making out the shape of the approaching danger.

"He will tell the commanding general of the Department of the East the whole story."

"Dix."

"What was that, Senator?"

"General John A. Dix. I know him. I don't run the firm. Byron does. I'm a senator. I'm not in business. Haven't been since 'sixty-one. I was the first volunteer of the war. I don't know anything about cotton. Don't care."

"You may not care, Senator, but others care—for their own hides. Prescott's naming you."

"Can't." Sprague was now panicky. He put on the cracked pince-nez. "I'll go to Dix. Where's Hoyt?"

"New York City, I think."

"Find him," said Sprague, throwing coins on the table. "I don't know a thing. What was done in Texas was to help the Union people there. That's all." Sprague shook the messenger's hand; and left.

There was a crowd in front of Sixth and E. Two policemen came toward Sprague, who nearly bolted. But the two men both saluted, and smiled; and one said, "Congratulations, Senator."

Sprague entered the first parlor. Kate, who had not been speaking to him lately, threw her arms around him. "The next best thing!" she exclaimed. "For now, anyway."

"What?"

"Father's chief justice. The President sent the message to the Senate this morning." Suddenly, she smelled the gin on his breath. "Why weren't you at the Senate?"

"I had a business meeting." Sprague approached his radiant father-in-law. "Congratulations, sir."

"My dear boy!" Carried away, Chase actually embraced Sprague. Sumner and Wade applauded. Kate joined them. She teased Sumner. "You are responsible for this, for putting Father on the shelf. But we shall have the last word."

"Now, Kate," said Chase, "if you can't get cream, you settle for milk."

"He's worth more to us on the bench for a lifetime," said Wade, "than in the White House for four years, where all you do is think of the next election like someone I cannot name..."

"Who has seen the light, however," said Sumner. "He is also no fool. Lincoln realizes that the two great issues that you will have to deal with are the Constitutional abolition of slavery, which is now at hand, and a defense of our wartime monetary policies, which you invented."

"In a somewhat *ad hoc* fashion," said Chase, beginning to wonder whether or not he, as chief justice, could annul what he, as secretary of the treasury, had done. In any case, this was a time of perfect joy for him. Kate might think that he had been put on the shelf, but there was no law that said a chief justice could not become the president. Four years was not a long time. Once he had made all of his positions plain on the Olympian bench, he could, if he chose, step down into the battlefield; and seize the ultimate prize.

On Friday morning, the Senate unanimously confirmed Chase as chief justice. In the afternoon, Chase and his family went up to the Capitol for the swearing-in ceremony. Chase wore a new judge's robe of black silk, a present from Sprague but chosen by Kate. Just before they got to the Supreme Court chamber, where all of fashionable Washington was gathered, they were stopped in the rotunda by Mr. Forney. Beneath the newly painted white-and-lilac dome, Forney said, "I'm afraid, Mr. Chase, we still don't have an attorney-general, and without him to sign the letters patent, you can't be sworn in. Not until the Judiciary Committee passes on Mr. Speed can you take your oath."

"When will that be?" asked Kate.

"Tomorrow, I should think. Yes, definitely tomorrow, by noon."

"Ah, well," said Chase, catching a glimpse of his reflection in the glass that covered a large painting of Pocahontas. The black robe was certainly majestic in its effect. Chief Justice of the United States, he whispered to himself; then he hummed, off-key, a hymn to that aged rock which had so miraculously cleft for him.

Although there was no attorney-general the next day, the crowd had again assembled. But this time Chase had been warned not to come to the Capitol. The installation was postponed to Monday the 12th.

There was now a constant procession of callers to Sixth and E, until recently a house to be avoided by the ambitious. Every lawyer of consequence in the United States thought it necessary to come in person to congratulate the heir of Jay and Marshall and Taney.

Since the country's beginning, there had been only five chief justices—as opposed to sixteen presidents. Of the three co-equal branches of government—executive, legislative and judicial—only the judiciary, at whose apex was the Supreme Court, served for life; and only the Supreme Court could determine the mysteriously elastic Constitution's meaning. This was the ultimate power in a republic, thought Chase. Nevertheless...

On Saturday morning, Sprague received a telegram from a friend in New York City. By order of General John A. Dix, the

598

Provost Marshal had arrested Byron Sprague and William H. Reynolds "for furnishing aid and comfort to the enemy." The two men had been stopping at the same hotel in New York City. Now they were at Fortress Lafayette, with Prescott.

A second telegram, half an hour later, reported the arrest of Harris Hoyt. Could a senator be arrested? This was the Constitutional issue of most poignant interest to Sprague. When he casually mentioned the subject to his father-in-law, who was answering letters and telegrams, Chase had replied absently, "Oh, never! Unless, of course, you've committed murder or—" Chase held up a letter. "An autograph from Mr. Whittier! At last! Where was I? Oh, murder—or treason. Katie!" Chase called out.

Sprague hurried to his own study at the other end of Sixth and E, where he wrote a dozen different versions of a telegram to be sent to General Dix. The burden: do nothing until I write a letter of explanation. Plainly, he would be the next to be arrested.

That afternoon, the telegram dispatched, Sprague sat at his desk, writing a letter to General Dix which would reveal that his only interest in the matter was political and, of course, familial. He had had no connection with the cotton business since the beginning of the war, whose first volunteer he had been. The firm was in the charge of his cousin Byron, which was why he was now writing. He felt that an interview between himself and General Dix would clear up an admittedly confused matter. He was certain that his cousin had broken no law. As for Byron's associates, he could not vouch. Needless to say, the political ramifications were such that everyone must proceed with a degree of caution in order not to embarrass the President or the new Chief Justice. Sprague was careful to omit from the letter any reference to Harris Hoyt.

At five o'clock, the letter was finished. He had already arranged for a friend to take it the next morning on the cars to New York. He had also given the friend verbal instructions for Hoyt, who posed the only real danger to him. If Hoyt were to say that Sprague's interest in the matter was simply to be useful to the Union, Hoyt would be freed. Sprague did not say how. Sprague did not know how. But Hoyt must not tell what he knew; at least not until after Monday. Chase must first be sworn in.

Kate entered the study, a folded newspaper in either hand. "What have you done? These papers—they all but name you by name."

"Nothing. It's a mix-up. Byron's been arrested. So has Reynolds. Prescott. Some nonsense about getting cotton illegally from Texas. I don't know." Sprague sealed the letter; his hands were shaking.

Kate saw the hands. "You do know."

"I don't. I will, though. I've written General Dix, asking for an explanation."

Kate read from the *Providence Press*: "'. . . our streets have been full of rumors to the implication of certain prominent citizens engaged in contraband traffic with the rebels.' That is treason."

"Well, that's not me. Can't be. I run the *Providence Press*."

"Do you run the *New York Times*, which says. . ."

"Since when are you such a believer in newspapers? Look what they write about your father. . ."

"Byron's in prison. Your own cousin. The man you picked to manage the business, *your* business. Oh, you are deep in this."

Sprague stood up. "If I am deep in this, then so are you, Mrs. Sprague."

"What does that mean?" Kate's face was now scarlet with anger.

Sprague was icy. "Just that you are my wife. For better or for worse. Well, this is worse. Yes, I have been getting cotton from Texas. How do you think I keep my mills running? Your father wouldn't give me a permit. So I get the cotton, illegally, through the Custom's House in New York, with the help of your father's friend and appointee Mr. Hiram Barney."

"You are. . ." Kate was breathing hard, as if from some huge physical exertion. "You are a traitor!"

"That's the legal word. But I'm not going to be hanged if I can help it."

Kate stared at him, as if he had suddenly ceased to exist for her as husband or even acquaintance. Then she said, deliberately, "But you deserve to be hanged."

"I don't like that, Kate." Sprague wrote his own name on the envelope, thus franking it. "It is ungrateful. I've done a lot for you. For your father. . ."

"For yourself!"

"Well, why not? Can't I be as selfish as the pair of you? Forever conniving, with my money!"

"Money!" Kate hurled the word at him as if it were the ultimate curse. "Damn your money!"

In the parlor at the other side of Sixth and E, Chase heard the astonishing phrase shouted by his daughter. Fortunately, no one else was within earshot. He had been sitting, alone, reading the oath that he would be called upon to recite next Monday.

Chase now moved, quickly, toward his son-in-law's study, not wanting to hear more but unable *not* to hear more.

"It's a little late to damn what you've spent so much of. I paid for Chase for president. I pay for both of you to live. I pay for
600

everything. Well, when I pay, I expect some return. That's business."

"You want us to protect you, is that it? You want the Chief Justice to protect you..."

"He ain't chief justice yet, and if word gets around before Monday, he won't ever be chief justice..."

Chase stood, unobserved, at the study door. What on earth were they quarrelling about this time? It sounded even worse than the explosion at Narragansett Pier the previous summer. And what had *he* to do with *what* word getting around?

"You have been our ruin," said Kate, as if with wonder that someone so insignificant as Sprague should have brought *them* down.

"Maybe. Maybe not." Sprague rang for the butler.

Chase selected that moment to enter the study. "I thought I heard angry words," he said mildly. "At such a happy time."

"It is nothing, Father." Chase's eyes were drawn, from force of habit, to the newspapers in Kate's hands. What new horrors had the press decided to launch? But Kate threw the newspapers onto the fire as if that had been the only reason for visiting her husband's study.

The butler appeared. Sprague gave him the letter; and told him where he was to take it. Then Sprague poured himself a tumbler full of brandy. "We were talking about money," said Sprague to Chase. "It is a dull subject." He drained the glass without flinching.

"I know. I know." Chase was, suddenly, uneasy. Something had gone wrong. Something very serious had gone wrong. He excused himself; and retreated to his own study, expecting Kate to follow. But when she did not, Chase was obliged to send for her. He then went, carefully, through the *New York Times*, one of the newspapers that she had been holding; and he read the latest dispatch from Providence. Chase was less shocked than surprised that Sprague had been so clumsy. In their common dangerous jungle, the first rule was to cover one's tracks.

Kate had been ill, off and on, since the spring. She had lost weight; grown pallid; coughed in a way that suggested some sort of asthma rather than consumption. But since Tuesday, she had been her old luminous self. Now she had retrogressed. "What is it, Father?"

"You tell me, Katie." He pushed the newspaper on his desk toward her. "I think that I have worked it out."

Kate nodded. "I wish you had not, especially now."

"I'm glad that I have, especially now. Does he say that he is guilty?"

"'Aid and comfort to the enemy' is the phrase that describes what he has done."

Chase's head began, slightly, to ache. "Treason," he said, lisp and all.

"Yes." As Kate told her father the story, his headache became more like a breaking open of the skull. When she had finished, he was in such pain that he could hardly speak. "I shall not take the oath on Monday."

"You must!"

"I cannot. I have already been accused of corruption, wrongly, by Blair. I have been accused, wrongly, of selling cotton permits..."

"You neither sold nor gave one to my husband..."

"Who will believe that? I clung, mistakenly, I see, to Hiram Barney at the Custom's House, though he is more Mr. Lincoln's friend than mine." Chase rose. "I must go to the President. I must refuse this office."

"No! We have worked too hard to get this far."

"This far? My child, we shall go right over the cliff if I'm sworn in at the same time my son-in-law is indicted for treason."

"You did not know it at the time of the swearing in..."

"But I do know. It is all over, Kate."

"No!" This time the voice was a scream. "If you withdraw now, I will never speak to you again! I mean it. We are one thing, you and I. He is nothing. Forget him. Let him hang. He has nothing to do with us. He never has. From the beginning, I hated him..." Then, to Kate's plain astonishment and her father's horror, she vomited. They stood, facing each other, while she tried to hold back the sudden torrent with both hands.

"My God, Katie! What is wrong?"

But the retching ceased as suddenly as it had begun. She dried her face with a handkerchief. "No, I am not ill, Father. But I am three months pregnant. I should have told you."

"Oh, God!" This time Chase did not, he hoped, use the Lord's name in vain. Rather, he was praying aloud for three immortal souls. Then, in the end, he agreed to go through with the swearing in.

Sprague seemed in control of events. He expected, he said, "good news" from New York City. As for Chase, he was close to breakdown. He had spent his life in the service of moral principle. Now he was to pretend to the world and, worse, to himself, that he knew nothing of his son-in-law's crimes. Fortunately, justice is blind, he thought grimly. Three lives in one scale; honor in the other.

At noon on Monday, just as they were to set out for the Capitol, where a large crowd had assembled, Mr. Forney sent word that there was still no attorney-general; but, tomorrow, definitely the installation would take place. Now all that Chase could do was read the newspapers carefully for "interesting dispatches from Providence, Rhode Island."

By Thursday morning, the tension at Sixth and E had increased to near-hysteria. Five times a large crowd had assembled at the Capitol for the installation of the first chief justice since Taney took office in 1836; and five times the crowd was sent home. People talked of nothing else. As yet, thought Chase, they did not speak of Sprague. Each morning, after his prayers, he vowed that he would send the President his withdrawal. Each noon, after he had been with Kate, he forgot his vow. All that mattered was Kate's happiness; and that of his grandchild. But he lived in hourly terror of the press; and of Sprague, who was showing uncharacteristic tact. He was never in Chase's part of the house; and seldom in his own. Apparently, Sprague was bringing every sort of pressure to bear on General Dix.

On Thursday morning Hay happened to be in Stanton's office on an errand for the President. Hay discussed the business at hand; then started to go. Stanton stopped him. "Sit down, Major. There's something I'd like to... share with you."

Mystified, Hay sat beside Stanton's fortress of a desk. The thought of the secretive Mars sharing anything with anyone was unusual. Stanton opened a folder; stared at it with watery eyes. "General Dix has arrested four men who have been accused of trading in cotton, illegally, with the South. One of them is Byron Sprague."

Hay nodded; he, too, had read the veiled newspaper accounts. "I've met Byron Sprague. When I was at Brown. He runs Senator Sprague's business for him."

Stanton stared, thoughtfully, at Hay. "This is a delicate matter, as I've told General Dix. The first conspirator to be arrested has made a confession implicating Senator Sprague, as well as the other three. Now a second conspirator, as of Monday, says that Senator Sprague was *not*, knowingly, involved. General Dix wants to know whether charges should be brought against Senator Sprague."

Hay was now very nervous indeed. Stanton was deliberately involving him, rather than the President, in this matter. Hay pulled out his watch. "In one hour Mr. Chase becomes chief justice."

"Yes," said Stanton; and waited.

"Obviously, he could not be chief justice if all of this were public knowledge."

"No," said Stanton; and waited.

"But once he is sworn in, should his son-in-law be indicted for treason, he might, perhaps, be obliged—or feel obliged—to resign."

"Yes," said Stanton; and waited.

Hay was one of the few people in Washington who knew that it had been Stanton's dream to be himself the chief justice; he had even gone so far as to have mutual friends intercede with the Tycoon. But Lincoln wanted Stanton to stay where he was; even more to the point, Grant wanted him at the War Department. Once Stanton realized that he himself had no chance, he had worked hard for the appointment of Chase; and it was hard work. If the Tycoon could be said to dislike anyone on earth, it was Salmon P. Chase. In fact, at one point, he had said, with deep feeling, "I'd rather swallow this buckthorn chair than appoint Chase." But the Tycoon had bowed to radical pressure; and to Stanton.

"On balance," said Hay, thinking as rapidly as possible, "the Administration needs Mr. Chase on the bench. There is the Constitutional amendment on abolition to be considered, not to mention . . ." Hay stopped; and stared at Stanton; who stared right back at him.

"As I understand it," Hay proceeded carefully, "the immediate issue is whether we decide to believe the first man's confession or the second man's confession." Stanton's nod was just perceptible. "Since there is a clear-cut choice for General Dix, I suspect that he should incline to the second confession until he has actually got to the truth of the matter, which may take some time. Meanwhile, to charge with treason a United States senator—a *Republican* senator—in the midst of war is not"—Hay was pleased at his own sublime piety—"in the public interest, particularly if it will also compromise the Chief Justice *and* the President who appointed him."

Stanton nodded; and shut the folder. "I shall instruct General Dix to leave Senator Sprague out of all this until we know more than we know now. Will you tell the President?"

Hay matched Stanton's own imperious tone. "Will you?"

"No. I see no need," said Stanton. "He has enough to concern him now."

"Then I will say nothing, and for exactly the same reason."

With difficulty, Hay was able to squeeze into the small but elegant Supreme Court chamber where, in earlier times, the Senate had met. The domed chamber with its gallery was crowded not only with the local fashionables but with the entire congressional Jacobin contingent. The high court conducted its affairs on a basis in an apse opposite the audience, who sat in a semicircle between slender marble columns. Hay stationed himself next to one of the marble columns where stood Charles Sumner in a state of high excitement. "This is the greatest day in the history of the Court," said Sumner.

"It is a great day," said Hay, noncommittally, looking about until he found Kate, pale but majestic in a purple gown, her young sister, Nettie, on one side of her and Sprague on the other. Sprague's pale face was somewhat flushed. Gin or brandy? Hay wondered. Or fear of an arrest during the ceremony?

An usher appeared on the dais and said in a low churchly voice, "The honorable justices of the Supreme Court of the United States." A side door opened, and the senior justice entered, his arm through Chase's. They were followed by the other eight justices, among them Lincoln's enormously fat old crony Judge Davis of Springfield, who had been responsible for the disastrous commitment to make Cameron secretary of war. Yet the Tycoon had forgiven Davis, thought Hay; and raised him on high.

Each justice took a position in front of his own chair; bowed to left and right. Then Chase stepped to the center of the dais where stood the senior justice, who gave him a piece of paper, which he took with a trembling hand.

Hay stared at Chase closely, as he read, "'I, Salmon P. Chase, do solemnly swear that I will, as Chief Justice of the United States, administer equal and exact justice to the poor and to the rich . . .'"

Hay looked at Sprague; at Kate; at Chase. All three were aware of their common danger. This was indeed courage, Hay decided; or a fit of collective madness. Whose will, Hay wondered, had prevailed?

"'. . . in accordance with the Constitution and laws of the United States, to the best of my ability.'" Chase gave the sheet of paper back to the senior justice; then took a deep breath and raised his eyes to Heaven and proclaimed, "So help me God!"

And Abraham Lincoln, Hay added to himself while Ben Wade, sitting close by, said, in a voice that all could hear, "'Lord, now lettest thou thy servant depart in peace . . . for nine eyes have been thy salvation.'"

At Hay's side, Charles Sumner said, "Amen."

605

9

IT WAS DARK WHEN THE PRESIDENT, ACCOMPANIED ONLY BY A servant, came aboard the steamer *River Queen*, anchored in the Hampton Roads. The ship's master saluted the President, as Seward and Major Eckert came forward to greet him. "You made good time, sir," said Eckert, checking his watch.

"We made an early start," said Lincoln. "We also left in total secrecy, which means that no one on earth except probably the *New York Herald* knows that I am here."

"Let's hope that they don't," said Seward. "Come on inside, or whatever you're supposed to say in a boat."

The ship's low-ceilinged salon was large and comfortably finished. Seward had arrived the day before; and he did the honors as host. The President requested coffee; and settled into an armchair that had been screwed to the deck. Through portholes the lights of Fortress Monroe glowed.

Major Eckert sat very straight on a stool, while President and Premier lounged in their chairs. Eckert had been acting as messenger between the Administration and the three Southern commissioners who were now aboard a nearby steamer, the *Mary Martin*. "They will join us here tomorrow at any time you propose," said Eckert.

"Well, the sooner the better. So let's say first thing after breakfast. Now"—Lincoln turned to Seward—"I'm only here because of General Grant's urging. Since these fellows won't accept our pre-conditions, I can't see that we have much to say to each other. But Grant says their intentions are good, whatever that may mean."

"I told General Grant that he was *not* to join in the preliminary discussions with the commissioners," said Eckert. "Those were my instructions from Mr. Stanton. I think the general was angry with me, even when I pointed out to him that if *he* were to make an error, the repercussions would be terrible, while if *I* blunder, no one cares."

"I assume," said Lincoln, with a smile, "that he is still very angry with you?"

"Yes, sir." Eckert smiled, too. "Fortunately, when the war is over, I go back to business—beyond his reach."

Seward ran his hand through his Lear-wild hair. "It seems,"

he said, "that Jefferson Davis is willing to give these men a free hand, up to a point, but I'm not sure just what that point is."

"They must accept the laws of the Union, and the abolition of slavery." Lincoln was very much to his own point. "If they do this, the war is over, and I will try to recompense the slave-owners."

"Old Mr. Blair thinks that they will agree," said Seward. "I don't."

Lincoln shook his head. "The Old Gentleman is like a young man, riding back and forth through the lines to Richmond. He also dreams a lot, like a young man. What's your impression, Governor, of the three gentlemen?"

"I don't think they'll give way on the subject of slavery. But reimbursement is certainly a temptation. Also, they are just about flat broke—and they've run out of men. I would say the end is at hand. But . . ."

"But they will not relax what they regard as their principles," said Eckert. "I've talked to them at length."

"*He's* a curious little man, isn't he?" Lincoln took a mug of coffee from Mr. Seward. "Alexander Stephens was a great figure in the House when I was in Congress. Great, that is, in intellect. He is about the size of a large doll . . ."

"He is very brilliant," said Eckert, disapprovingly.

"I'm afraid," said Seward, "that the Old Gentleman has been misrepresenting us to the rebels."

"The Mexican scheme?"

Seward nodded. "Sound as it is, it is *not*, alas, your policy."

Lincoln sighed. "We shall be talking at cross-purposes. Particularly, if they persist in Mr. Davis's myth that we are two countries at war when the sole purpose of our war is to demonstrate that we are one."

The next morning Alexander H. Stephens of Georgia, vice-president of the Confederate States of America, accompanied by John A. Campbell, a former justice of the United States Supreme Court, and R. M. T. Hunter, a former United States senator, entered the salon where Lincoln and Seward were waiting for them. Bright-eyed and red-cheeked from the cold, Stephens was wrapped in yards of rough woollen cloth, which he proceeded to unravel. When he finally stepped forth from his cocoon, and crossed to Lincoln, hand outstretched, the President said, "Was there ever such a small nubbin after so much shucking?"

Stephens laughed, as they shook hands. "I'm glad to see you are just the same, Mr. Lincoln. I had feared that you might have grown even taller with all this greatness."

"The only greatness that I have is in the way of trouble."

"Then we have," said Stephens, "something to share."

Seward did his best to keep the conversation to the point. But, as usual with Lincoln, there were stories to be told, as well as what seemed to be idle meanderings which, Seward now understood, were highly meaningful evasions and delicate avoidances.

The first jarring note had to do with the abolition of slavery. At first, Lincoln had been most sympathetic; had even put himself in Stephens's place and speculated on what he would do if he were, like Stephens, a Georgia politician. He would, he reckoned, suggest a gradual emancipation—over five years, say—so that the two races could have time to work out a way of living together under such altered circumstances.

"But, perhaps, my fellow Georgians would say that they would prefer to keep their slaves." Stephens warmed his tiny hands on a mug of coffee.

"That is not possible," said Lincoln.

"But if I understand you correctly, you freed *our* slaves as a *military necessity*, and not because you favored abolition in principle."

Lincoln nodded. "That is true."

"So if we make peace, there is no longer a military necessity, and then we shall be as we were, won't we?"

Seward intervened. "The Thirteenth Amendment to the Constitution, if ratified, will change all that."

"What," asked Campbell, "is the Thirteenth Amendment? There were only twelve when I was on the Court."

"Congress passed the amendment to abolish slavery in all the United States on January 31, three days ago," said Seward. "Naturally, two thirds of the states must ratify it. Should you be within the Union by then, you will be able to vote 'no.' If not..."

"This changes everything," said Stephens. He put down the mug. "Mr. Blair gave us to believe that there was a—a continental alternative."

Lincoln shook his head. "That is Mr. Blair's solution. It is not mine. It is possible that one day we may be obliged to go to war with the French in Mexico but before that happens we must make the Union whole again."

"The price of wholeness," said Stephens, wanly, "must be paid, it seems, by us."

"No, that is not quite true. I believe that I can raise four hundred million dollars to recompense the slave-owners. I have considerable *unofficial* support for this, from persons whose names would astonish you."

"If this were to happen," said Hunter, "if the slaves were all paid for and set free, how would they live? They have always been accustomed to an overseer. They are used to working only under

608

compulsion. Now you take away this direction, and no work at all would be done. Nothing would be cultivated, and both blacks and whites would starve."

"Well, you know better than I what it is like to live in a slave society. But the point you make kind of reminds me of this farmer back in Illinois..."

Seward prayed that the story would be relevant. They were now at the heart of the negotiations; and he had become somewhat hopeful.

Lincoln was now describing a mythical Mr. Case who had got himself a large herd of hogs, and then wondered how he was going to feed them. Finally he was inspired to plant an immense field of potatoes, so that when the hogs were sufficiently grown he would be able to turn the whole herd into the field, thus saving himself the double labor of feeding the hogs and digging up the potatoes. But then a neighbor came along and reminded him that the frost comes early in Illinois, while butchering time isn't till winter, so the ground would be frozen a foot deep for quite a time. So how were his hogs going to get to their potatoes? This took Mr. Case by surprise. But, finally, he stammered, 'Well, it may be hard on their snouts but I reckon they will just have to root, hog, or die'!" Lincoln laughed loudly; and quite alone.

Seward thought the story peculiarly tasteless and even harsh. He started to change the subject when Lincoln, aware that he had misfired, said, "What I mean to say is that even if things prove to be as hard as you think they will be, I have a notion that you will be surprised at how well both whites and blacks survive."

They talked for four hours; and to no end. At one point, Lincoln took the line that although anyone and everyone who chose to take the oath to the Union was welcome to, there were certain individuals who might merit punishment for having incited others to rebellion.

Hunter addressed this. "Mr. President," he began. It was the first time, Seward noted, that the Southerners had referred to Lincoln by his title. Since Lincoln never referred to Stephens as Vice-President, much less to Davis as President, the commissioners had been careful to return the compliment of omission. "If we understand you correctly, you think that we of the Confederacy have committed treason, that we are traitors to your government, that we have forfeited our rights, and are proper subjects for the hangman. Is not that, really, what you are saying?"

"Yes," said Lincoln, without any emphasis. "That is what I have been saying from the beginning of this great trouble."

Stephens stared at the deck. No one spoke for a long time.

Seward tried to think of something to say that would ameliorate the impasse; but could not.

Finally, Hunter observed, with an attempt at lightness, "So while you are the President, we are safe from hanging—just as long as we behave ourselves."

"If there were . . . or if there had been . . . some easy way out of all this," said Lincoln, slowly, "I would long since have taken it."

"We had hoped," said Stephens, "for the Mexican solution."

"As a courtesy to you, I will reconsider it. But I am not apt to change my mind."

The conference was over. Seward had ordered champagne, which was now served. "At least," said Seward, "we shall celebrate, if not the reunion of the states, our personal re-union on the high seas!"

Lincoln and Stephens gossiped about old times, while the former associate justice of the Supreme Court, Mr. Campbell, told Seward, "I cannot think of a worse choice for chief justice than Mr. Chase."

"You sound like Monty Blair," said Seward, much amused.

"Oh, I'm not objecting on political grounds. Of course, I'm opposed to him there. But Chase doesn't know the first thing about the law."

"Oh, he'll pick it up, the way the rest of us have done."

"He won't," said Campbell, who, Confederate or not, still knew his Washington. "He'll be too busy running for president. I know that old faker."

"Personally—and privately—I think you are right," said Seward. Then he added, mischievously, "Why don't you tell the President what you think?"

"It's too late. Besides, I don't want to be hanged for lèse-majesté as well as treason."

On the deck, the President said farewell to the Southerners. A cold wind blew out of the west, and the sky was dark at midday. On the rough sea below, a launch waited to take the commissioners back to their ship. "Well, Stephens," said Lincoln, leaning down to peer into the small man's face, much as he had done, thought Seward, when he had met Tom Thumb, "as there's been nothing we could do for our country, is there anything I can do for you personally?"

"No." Stephens paused; then said, "Well, I wouldn't mind having back a nephew you've been holding prisoner on Johnson's Island."

"You shall have him." Lincoln wrote the name in his notebook. Farewells were said. The commissioners got into their launch.

Lincoln and Seward watched as the Southerners were rowed across to the *Mary Martin*.

"Well, Governor, it looks as if we are in this now to the end."

Seward nodded. "I had no real hopes. They cannot give way after all that... has happened."

The commissioners were now at the railing of their ship. The launch from the *River Queen* was still alongside the *Mary Martin*, and a Negro oarsman was handing one of the ship's crew a crate of champagne. Seward turned to the boatswain, "May I use your horn, sir?"

The boatswain handed over the horn. Seward bellowed through it, "We've sent you a present!"

The commissioners smiled and waved their thanks. "Keep the champagne," Seward boomed across the wintry sea, "but return the Negro!"

"Well, Governor, that was almost worth the trip," said Lincoln, waving a last good-bye to his one-time friend, Alexander Stephens. As he turned to go inside, he blew on his fingers, which were now always cold. Then he said, "They are just about at an end."

"That is my impression. How much longer, do you think?"

"A hundred days," said Lincoln. "Naturally, I do not dare reckon the number of lives yet to be lost."

Three days later, Lincoln proposed to the Cabinet his scheme for reimbursing the slave-owners. To a man, the Cabinet opposed him. He started to argue with them; then gave it up. Hay wondered if the Tycoon had been serious or not. There were times when he seemed to be playing a complex game that required all sorts of feints and parries. Lincoln wrote his state papers in much the same crablike way. First, he would scribble sentences onto squares of pasteboard instead of ordinary paper which did not shuffle quite so easily—and he did a lot of shuffling in the course of a major address, particularly the one that he was now writing for his second inaugural. When Lincoln had finally prepared a draft, Hay would take the cards in what he prayed was their final order to a printer, who would then put the whole maze of words and ideas into type so that Lincoln could start all over again the elaborate process of revision.

Hay had never seen the Ancient quite so concerned with a speech as he was with this one. He wanted to justify the war; he also wanted to describe, without being too specific, how he would reconstruct the Union when the war ended. "This thing had better wear pretty well," he said to Hay, as he began to mark up the first printer's copy. "This is going to have to be my political testament."

* * *

That was much the view in the parlor of Mrs. Surratt's boarding-house on the morning of March 4, Inauguration Day. While Annie taught a young girl to play piano at one end of the parlor, John Surratt and David sat at the other end, discussing in low voices the latest change in plans. During the winter, Booth had assembled a more or less devoted band of men, mostly Southern, mostly young. Ned Spangler was the oldest, while the youngest, Lewis Payne, had been one of Mosby's raiders. Payne had first met Booth at Richmond in 1861, when he had formed a deep attachment to the actor. Four years later, quite by accident, Booth saw the half-starved Payne in the streets of Baltimore. Payne had been wounded at Gettysburg; had taken the oath; had no life at all to live until Booth swept him into the conspiracy. In addition, there were two other former Confederate soldiers, both from Baltimore; one had been at school with Booth. Finally, there was George Atzerodt, a German-born boatman who specialized in smuggling from one side of the Potomac River to the other.

As David had suspected, John Surratt had taken to Booth. Certainly, they were as one in their passion for the Confederacy. During the winter, David had even grown somewhat jealous of their intimacy. Often the two would vanish upstairs together in the National Hotel while David would be sent off on an errand. But then, whenever he was beginning to feel disaffected, Wilkes would say or do something that would delight him, and remind him once again that this was the perfect older brother that he had never had, a necessary reminder as he was now living at home with all seven sisters—even the attached ones had somehow, simultaneously, come home, temporarily unattached; and Mrs. Herold never ceased to weep and cook, scold and pray.

When it was announced that the President would attend Ford's Theater on January 18, to see Edwin Forrest in *Jack Cade*, a suitably revolutionary figure, Booth had gone into action. Two horses were stabled back of the theater. Atzerodt's boat was at the river bank. The two Baltimoreans and Booth were at the President's box while Lewis Payne and David were backstage. At a signal from Booth, a friendly actor would switch off all the gaslights in the theater. The President would then be seized, tied up and lowered to the stage, where the powerful Payne would carry him to the waiting horses. For two days, the plan was carefully re-hearsed. But then, on the night of January 18, the President did not go to the theater.

There had been a good deal of grumbling among the conspir-ators; and Booth saw fit to stay away from Washington for most of February. But the Baltimoreans and Payne were still in the city, living at Booth's expense, while John Surratt, when denied a leave of absence from Adams Express, took "French leave." David continued to help out Spangler at Ford's.

Now Booth had reappeared, more than ever fervent, as the Confederacy disintegrated beneath the grinding of Grant to the north of Richmond and the fire of Sherman to the south. "I only fear it's not too late," said John Surratt.

"Then it will be the last thing that we can do for our tragical country," said David, who had taken to using Booth's grander phrases.

"I don't know why he's so bent on seizing him at the theater, where it's hard enough to get anybody down from a box to the stage and then to backstage, much less a man who's guarded." John was not as taken with Booth's theatricality as David. John inclined to practical, secret measures, as befitted a night-rider.

"There's only the one Pinkerton man," said David, who had heard all the arguments. "And then nobody will know what's happening when the lights are all turned off."

"But we'll be in the dark, too." At the other end of the parlor, Annie was now playing "Dixie," to her young student's amusement. "Our best chance was always Seventh Street Road, when he'd go to the Soldiers' Home."

"But there were all those soldiers all last summer with him. I thought our best chance was the other day at the hospital—"

"Where he didn't go," said John.

"Well, we almost got—who was it?—by mistake, in the carriage?"

"Mr. Chase. The wrong chase for us," said John, laughing at his own simple joke. "He said something odd last night."

"Mr. Chase?"

"No. Mr. Booth. We went over to the Capitol together, to watch Congress adjourn..."

"That's when I had to see to Spangler and the horses." As usual, David had not been included. He wondered why it was that Booth seemed to prefer John's company to his own. Could education make such a difference? Yet, when it came to theater, David knew far more than John Surratt; and when it came to the actor Wilkes Booth, David knew almost more than anyone. On the other hand, John knew the Maryland roads better than he did and it had already been decided that John would guide Booth and the captive President through all the back roads to Richmond.

"Well, as we were about to push through the crowd in front of the door to the gallery of the House of Representatives, there was this statue of Lincoln against the wall. And Booth said, 'Who's that?' The likeness is poor but I recognized it, and told Booth, who said, 'What's he doing here before his time?'"

"Well, what is he?" asked David, who thought the question sensible.

"It was the way he said it. Then, later, at Skippy's, where we got drunk, he kept quoting from Shakespeare, about the death of tyrants..."

"*Julius Caesar*," said David, knowledgeably. "Only this time, like he says, he's going to play Brutus which his brother Edwin always gets to play like they did in New York last fall, the three brothers, with Wilkes as Mark Anthony and Junius Brutus as..."

"I think he's going to try to kill him today, at the Capitol," said John, abruptly.

"Kill him?" David turned to Surratt, who was playing with the hilt of the Bowie knife that he had taken to wearing in his boot. David had also tried to keep a knife in his boot but the boot was tight, and he had rubbed raw the skin of his ankle. He now kept the knife in his belt. "What's the point? Alive, he's worth a half-million Confederate soldiers. Dead, he ain't worth a thing."

"That's what I said at Skippy's. But he took no notice of me. He just said would I come to the Inaugural and stand by, and if need be get him across the river. I said what if I wouldn't? He said, then you would."

"But I don't know the roads that well." David told John Surratt what John knew anyway.

"Well, he thinks you do. I said I'm *in* this for a kidnapping but *out* of it for a murder."

"Why has he changed?"

Surratt shrugged. "I don't know. But I think—I could be wrong—that he got word from Richmond to stop. I also know there's another plot afoot to kill old Abe..."

"Who?"

"I got a theory. But I'm not saying." Surratt grinned, maddeningly. "Anyway I guess he now figures that if Richmond don't want his help, he might just as well do what he wants to do on his own and in his own way before anybody else does."

"So he'll get his chance to go play Brutus and stick Lincoln with a knife?"

"He's got a pistol."

Lewis Payne entered the parlor; and seemed to fill it. Annie and her pupil tried not to stare at him; and stared at him, making discordant chords in the process. Payne's face was like that of one of the Greek or Roman statues at the Capitol, while his smooth muscular neck was almost as big around as David's chest. He walked like some sort of lion in a zoo, ready to leap over the fence and kill everyone in sight, except for Wilkes, whom he worshipped. Late at night at Skippy's or wherever they might all go,
614

Payne would sit as if he were alone, except for Wilkes, in the middle of a dangerous jungle, the gray-blue eyes watchful, while the huge muscles of his legs and arms were visible through the cloth of a brand-new dark-blue jacket with many buttons. Even when he sat quite still, the muscles would loosen and contract, just like a cat's. He was a genuine bona-fide killer, thought David, with awe. But then Payne had been famous as a Mosby raider, under his real name Lewis Powell, which he had changed when he took the oath for fear that he might be wanted for special treatment by the army that he had so harassed in the days when Mosby was lord of the Shenandoah Valley, and Lewis Powell was known as "the terrible Lewis."

Lewis's voice was surprisingly soft, with a deep-South Florida accent. "Captain wants you boys to the Capitol," he said. "We'll take up our position at the foot of this platform they built where Old Abe will stand. Captain's going to be up in the stand, on the Capitol steps, just back of Old Abe."

John was sharp. "Why does he want us there?"

David wondered if John might be as jealous of Payne's closeness to Wilkes as he himself was of John's to Wilkes.

"Spangler got this one horse ready," said Payne. "That's all. Just one horse. So if Captain suddenly wants to make a run for it, why, we help him to this horse."

"He means to shoot him?" John whispered, though there was no way that Annie and her student could hear them through the loud strains of "Maryland, My Maryland."

"What the Captain fixes to do he fixes to do. We follow orders. Come on."

Meekly, David and John Surratt followed orders; followed the young giant from the parlor.

In the lobby of the National Hotel, Booth stared out the window at the rain that had been falling since dawn. Pennsylvania Avenue was slick with yellow mud in which pigs and sodden chickens rushed wildly about, as horses and people, in even greater numbers, moved onto the Capitol, hidden now by a miasmic fog that had drifted in from the river.

The lobby of the National was crowded. Umbrellas did much damage as they opened and shut; or refused to open and shut. In the upstairs halls, beds had been lined up to accommodate the out-of-towners.

Bessie Hale, finally, appeared. "I'm sorry, Mr. Booth! I'm late..."

"I care not," he murmured, "You are here."

"Oh, you sound just like you did when you were Romeo last winter. What was Avonia Jones really like?"

"Just another actress, too old to play Juliet."

"I didn't like her at all, particularly when she was on the balcony. She let you down. But I haven't. I did have all sorts of trouble with the tickets. I finally had to go to Major French yesterday; he's in charge of the ceremony." Bessie was rummaging through her reticule until she found a card, which she gave Booth. "This ticket will get you into the Capitol and onto the steps of the east portico but not onto the platform where the President will be, and Father and I. You know," Bessie's voice lowered somewhat, "we're going to Spain!"

"Oh?" Booth was staring thoughtfully at the card. "A long holiday?"

"No, no. Father is to be minister to Spain. We're all so thrilled! I mean not to have to go back to New Hampshire . . . Will you come to see us?"

Booth, with a spacious gesture, bowed low and kissed her hand. "You have but to send me a single line, a single word—'Come!'—and I shall be at your side wherever you are on earth!"

"That means Madrid. If you will, really, come," said Bessie. Then they were joined by Booth's friend, the night clerk of the National Hotel: "Always befriend the night clerk," was Booth's distilled actors' wisdom. Bessie went to join her parents.

At ten o'clock, the rain was still falling, but a north wind had risen and the river fog was gone. Bejewelled and splendidly gowned, Mary entered Hay's office. "Where is Mr. Lincoln?"

Hay took mild pleasure in telling Madam that the Tycoon and Nicolay had gone earlier and unheralded to the Capitol, where the President still had bills to sign. "My God!" she exclaimed. "This is not possible! We have the parade together along the avenue."

"Marshal Lamon thought that the President should not expose himself to the crowd. So he will meet you inside the Capitol, when the Vice-President is sworn in." To Hay's surprise, Madam was reasonable; and approved Lamon's plan. Then Hay told her that she would go to the Capitol in the company of Captain Robert Lincoln, a valued member of General Grant's personal staff: Robert had finally won the battle with his mother but only on condition that he never be out of Grant's sight.

Shortly before noon, the rain stopped and the small crowd at the east portico of the Capitol now became a large one. A platform of raw planks covered the steps. At the center of the platform, near the edge, there was a round table with a glass of water at its

616

center. The President would make his speech just back of the table, while, behind him, a long row of chairs would contain the Cabinet and the justices of the Supreme Court. Higher up the steps, the Congress, the diplomats and the ladies would have a fine view of several thousand umbrellas, all crowded together in the muddy plaza, where the only bright color was provided by strips of sodden bunting attached to window ledges.

David remembered the small crowd of four years ago; and the soldiers in every window, ready to shoot. Today there were even more soldiers than then, but the crowd was no longer secesh. In fact, there were surprisingly few natives of the city on hand, as opposed to people from all over the Union, including far-off California.

David stood next to old Spangler, a bit to the left of where the President would be sworn in above their heads. Thanks to Payne, they were crowded so close to the platform that they could see nothing except the planks and the Yankee soldiers, who seemed to have no particular instructions. One of them—a monkey-faced Irish boy—kept stepping on David's foot.

Spangler muttered, "I pray to God that Johnny's not going to do anything crazy."

"If he does," said David, "it'll be the last thing he ever does. They got ten thousand soldiers here."

"And nothing to save him but a horse tethered across the way." Spangler shook his head. "He'll never get off that platform alive."

"That's if he ever gets onto it." Ordinarily, Wilkes made excellent sense, even if he often sounded as if he were acting in a play that he hadn't yet learned. But, in the last few days, Wilkes's speeches had begun to alarm David. It was plain that Wilkes was perfectly capable of killing Old Abe in front of the whole world, and then getting himself shot with a last testament to be published by his sister to whom he had given, he had told David, a sealed envelope to be opened only at his death. David was dazzled by the splendor of it all. This was history. This was life lived to the full, and to a thunderous climax. But he was not entirely certain that he wanted to be a part of what, after all, was not David Herold's apotheosis so much as the unique death scene of the world's youngest star.

Booth's quarry was now seated in the gallery of the Senate, chin resting on his hand, and face expressionless. Below him, in front of the Vice-President's chair, the Vice-President-elect of the United States, Governor Andrew Johnson of Tennessee, stood, blind drunk.

A one-time tailor, Johnson was a cleanshaven, square-jawed, severe-looking man. Seward had served with him in the Senate before the war and always found him affable if somewhat dim. But neither the face—scarlet—nor the manner—wild—was dim today. Behind Johnson sat the outgoing Vice-President, Mr. Hamlin, who did not seem to know which way to look. Just before the ceremony, Hamlin had whispered to Seward that Johnson had been drunk ever since he got to Washington. As Johnson was only just recovered from typhoid fever, the combination of whiskey and physical disability had proven lethal. The members of the Supreme Court, to Johnson's left and right, all looked stunned, save Chase, who sat as one graven in marble and thus indifferent to the backwoods oratory that now flowed from Johnson's lips.

The distinguished audience, glittering with gold and silver braid, with full-dress swords and epaulets and feathered hats, with bright stars and chains, was now drawn into Johnson's confidence. He was, he pointed out four times, plebian. At the fourth use of the word, Seward whispered to Welles, who was at his side, "Surely, he protests too much."

"Disgusting," said Welles. This seemed the general view. A low murmur began in the chamber as the speech went on, and on. Although Lincoln did not change expression, Seward noticed that the President had begun to contract in his chair, as if he were willing himself elsewhere. Meanwhile, Hamlin was now visibly and sharply tugging at Johnson's coattail.

Undaunted, Johnson shrieked, "Tennessee has bent the tyrant's rod! She has broken the yoke of slavery!" The secretary of the Senate, Forney, now moved, tactfully, toward Johnson, a humble smile set on his lips. "No state can go out of this Union!" proclaimed Johnson.

"*That* is true orthodoxy," said Seward, enjoying Welles's horror, not to mention Stanton's constant refrain: "The man is crazed."

"And, moreover, Congress cannot eject a state from the Union!" The loud bray went on until, in a sudden concerted movement, Vice-President, Chief Justice and Senate secretary managed to swing Johnson around, so that his broad back was to the distinguished assembly, thus making it possible for the chalk-faced Chase to administer the oath of office. But unwilling to let go forever a moment so marvelous, Johnson turned once more to the Chamber and, holding up the Bible, he roared, "I kiss this book in the face of my nation of the United States!"

By then, the President was halfway up the aisle. As he passed Seward, the premier said, "I believe that Mr. Johnson is overcome with emotion on his return, in so dramatic a manner, to the Senate."

Both Lincoln's eyebrows were, for an instant, raised; then he turned to Major French, who was to lead him onto the portico.

"Do not let Johnson speak outside," he said. Then the President left the chamber, and Seward and Cabinet followed.

In the rotunda, they all paused; and waited to be joined by the Supreme Court—and Andrew Johnson, assisted by Forney. "Your hat, Mr. Vice-President," said Forney, giving the statesman his tall silk hat. Johnson took the hat and with a beatific smile put it not on his head but over his face.

"Disgusting," said Stanton.

"But not unwise, considering," said Seward, as they marched between the lines of policemen onto the portico; where a cold wind now blew and the sky was mottled with leaden clouds.

Since Booth had been unable to find a seat, he stood in a crowd at the foot of a statuary group, some thirty feet above the government of the United States. Booth's hand was in the right-hand pocket of his overcoat, fingers wrapped about the stock of a pistol.

As Lincoln rose to speak, he presented a perfect, unmissable target. But Booth was distracted, as was everyone, by the sudden emergence of the sun. The President now stood in a circle of dazzling unexpected light.

"Fellow countrymen!" The familiar high voice echoed and reverberated in the open plaza. From where David stood, he could just make out Lincoln's right hand, in which he held a half-sheet of foolscap on which his speech had been printed in two columns. "At this second appearing to take the oath of the presidential office, there is less occasion for an extended address than there was at the first."

A short speech, thought Seward, comfortably looking out across the plaza at the dark umbrellas, tall silk hats, low military hats, bright bayonets. It was hard to believe that four years had passed since last they were on this platform. Of course, with age, time appears to go more swiftly than it does in youth. Even so, Seward half expected to see baleful old Winfield Scott in his carriage on the hill opposite, as well as young—what was his name?—the Zouave who was killed at the start of the war. He had been such a hero. But since then there had been so many killed that Seward could no longer take seriously the idea of anyone's death. Doubtless, men must have responded in such a numbed fashion to the Great Plague of Europe. As for political survival, only two members of the original Cabinet were still in office, himself and Welles. Even the newcomer Fessenden would soon be gone: he had been reelected to the Senate, and his place taken by Hugh McCulloch, who . . .

Seward had now begun to listen to—as opposed to hear—Lincoln's speech. "While the inaugural address was being delivered from this place, devoted altogether to *saving* the Union without war, insurgent agents were in the city seeking to *destroy* it without war—seeking to dissolve the Union and divide effects by negotiation." How seriously, thought Seward with wonder, they had taken those arrogant, foolish Virginians. "Both parties deprecated war, but one of them would *make* war rather than let the nation survive, and the other would *accept* war rather than let it perish."

Suddenly, there was a slow but gathering wave of applause across the plaza. Lincoln stopped, as if unprepared for this response. He looked out over the audience until there was again silence. Then, in the silence, he continued to wait until Seward feared that he had lost his place. But Lincoln had not lost but found the place to say the four words that brought tears even to Seward's eye. "And the war came."

At the back, Hay blew his nose. He had not seen the final speech, nor had Nicolay. They had studied the scraps of pasteboard that had come their way, but it had all been a puzzle, rather like the war itself.

"Neither party expected for the war the magnitude or the duration which it has already attained. Neither anticipated that the *cause* of the conflict might cease with or even before the conflict itself should cease. Each looked for an easier triumph, and a result less fundamental and astounding."

Mary sat, with Robert at her side; and listened, carefully, as she rarely did to speeches since most speakers were, as her Kentucky father had always said, mere bags of wind. "Both read the same Bible and pray to the same God; and each invokes his aid against the other." Mary liked the way that the President constantly linked North and South as both or as each. "It may seem strange that any men should dare to ask a just God's assistance in wringing their bread from the sweat of other men's faces, but let us judge not, that we be not judged." Mary began to weep. Had not Ben said the same thing to her at Mrs. Laury's last séance? "The prayers of both could not be answered. That of neither has been answered fully."

"The Almighty has His own purposes. 'Woe unto the world because of offenses.'" In his black silk robe, Chase murmured along with the President the Biblical text. He had always taken the President for an infidel, but now, on this solemn occasion, Lincoln seemed ready to revert to the true religion of their fathers. Yet it was odd that although the President now spoke freely of God and the Almighty, he never once mentioned His Son, who was crucified and born again. Chase wondered if, perhaps, Lincoln saw himself as that Son; but then, quickly, he dismissed the
620

thought. Lincoln's essential simplicity and humility combined with a total absence of the historical—much less religious—imagination made such an ambition beyond him. Lincoln was cunning mediocrity at its most, to Chase, dispiriting.

Booth's forefinger was now on the trigger to his pistol. It was nothing to die upon a stage. In fact, it was slightly ludicrous, as his father had once notoriously demonstrated. But to actually kill and be killed in such a place as this and at such a time...

The voice rang out, louder and clearer than its slight echo from across the plaza. "With malice toward none, with charity for all, with firmness in the right, as God gives us to see the right, let us strive on to finish the war we are in, to bind up the nation's wounds, to care for him who shall have borne the battle and for his widow and his orphan—to do all which may achieve and cherish a just and a lasting peace among ourselves and with all nations."

The President put down the speech. The applause roared all about him. Booth aimed the pistol in his pocket at this most visible of targets; and pressed the trigger.

The President turned to Chase, who had risen, open Bible in his hand. In a loud voice, Chase administered the oath. He had practised the short speech so many times that he did not once lisp. Then, for the second time, hand on the Bible, Lincoln declared with a new resonance, darkened by all the blood that had been shed, thought Chase, the famous oath writ in Heaven: "I do solemnly swear that I will faithfully execute the office of the President of the United States, and will, to the best of my ability, preserve, protect, and defend..." This time, Hay noted, the key word "defend" was not so strident as the first time. "...the Constitution of the United States, so help me God."

As the cannon boomed a twenty-one gun salute, Booth's fingers inside his pocket examined the pistol: he had forgotten to release the safety catch.

10

ON THE EVENING OF MARCH 24, 1865, THE *RIVER QUEEN* CAST anchor in the James River off City Point. On the deck stood the President, Mrs. Lincoln and Tad, who held a pistol in one hand and an American flag in the other. All around them ships of every size rode at anchor while the river bank was massed with arms and provisions. On a bluff, an improvised city of tents and huts and sheds was visible in the light of fires and kerosene lamps. From the main deck, Captain Robert Lincoln waved to his parents; then he hurried off.

"I expect he's going to fetch General Grant." Lincoln pointed to the bluff above the river port. "Grant's headquarters are up there."

"Is Robert a *real* captain?" asked Tad, aiming his revolver at the Commander-in-Chief.

"Of course, he is, Taddie," said Lincoln. "And don't aim guns at people like that."

In due course, General and Mrs. Grant and Robert were rowed alongside the *River Queen*. "How common she looks," murmured Mary.

"Now, Mother." Mary did not like the way that Lincoln had used exactly the same tone with her that he had used with Tad.

Mary embraced Robert while Tad climbed onto his shoulders. Grant shook hands with the President first; then with Mary. She noted that he did not look either of them in the eye. On the other hand, Julia Grant was not able to look anyone in the eye since one eye was permanently turned toward her aquiline nose while the other looked as if it would like to escape the wild gaze of its neighbor.

Lincoln led the Grants into the salon, where all the lamps had been lit. "We were poisoned by the ship's water on the way down," said Lincoln. "But we got us some decent water at Fortress Monroe."

"The water's foul here," said Grant. "We boil it." Mary wondered if Grant ever actually drank a substance so insipid. In the full light of the salon she studied him carefully. He *appeared* to be clear-eyed and sober. Of course, the presence of Mrs. Grant was known to be a guarantee of sobriety.

"Welcome to City Point, Mrs. Lincoln." Julia Grant was gracious in a way that Mary did not entirely like. It was as if City Point—and the army—were hers.

Mary smiled and bowed; and did not answer. Lincoln wanted to go ashore right then and there, and though Grant told him there was little to see at night, the President insisted.

Mary was then left alone with Mrs. Grant, who proceeded to make herself at home by sitting down on the only sofa in the salon. Mary said nothing; but she was certain that her glare was sufficient to convey to Mrs. Grant the enormity of her breach of etiquette. No one could sit, unbidden, in the presence of the First Lady. Slowly, and silently, Mary lowered herself onto the sofa. The two ladies were now so close to each other that their skirts overlapped.

Mary sat erect, looking straight ahead. After a moment's uneasy silence, Mrs. Grant moved from the sofa to a small chair opposite. "Did you have a pleasant journey?" asked Mrs. Grant.

"Yes," said Mary.

There was another, somewhat longer, silence; then Mrs. Grant said, "I believe General Sherman arrives tomorrow. He comes by sea from North Carolina. It will be the first that we have seen of him since he took Atlanta and Savannah."

"That will be nice for you," said Mary. But then she could not resist adding, "I hope he will explain why three months after he occupied Atlanta, he then burned the city down."

"He thought it was necessary, to protect his rear as he moved north."

"Obviously, he must have thought it necessary. But he has made negotiating a peace much more difficult for my husband."

"I do not think, Mrs. Lincoln, that there will be a negotiated peace now. The war will not end until my husband has taken Richmond."

"How often have we heard that!" Mary gave Julia Grant a wide smile; and blinked her eyes, to show what a good humor she was in. She was pleased to see Mrs. Grant grow somewhat red in the face. A highly satisfactory silence settled in the salon; and remained settled until Tad came rushing in to say that he had been ashore. "But I came right back. We were stopped, Mr. Crook and me, by soldiers who said, 'Who goes there?' and 'What's the password?' and things like that. When I said, 'It's me,' they didn't know me. So I told Mr. Crook we better come back here before they shoot us."

"Such a . . . charming boy," said Mrs. Grant.

"Yes," said Mary, aware of the calculated hesitation before the adjective. "We have met *your* oldest boy," she added; and characterized that supremely plain child not at all.

Three days later Lincoln, Grant, Sherman and Admiral Porter met in the ship's salon while Mary took to her bed with certain preliminary signs of The Headache.

"I cannot tell you gentlemen what a pleasure it is to get away from Washington," said Lincoln.

"That's why I asked you, sir," said Grant. "I had a feeling you might want to take a trip, and get some rest."

"And what more restful place to be than at the front?" Lincoln smiled.

"We expect Sheridan any time now." Grant had placed a map of Virginia on a table. "He is making an arc from the valley here to Harrison's Landing there. At the moment he is crossing the James River just below us. Once he and his cavalry arrive, we should be able to take Petersburg—at last."

"At last," Lincoln repeated. He turned to Sherman. "Certainly, when your army joins that of General Grant, it will be all over."

"Yes, sir." Sherman was a slight wiry man, with uncombed wiry red hair and the pale eyes of, suitably, a bird of prey. "There's nothing left of the rebellion, except Johnston in North Carolina and Lee up here, and Lee can't have more than fifty thousand men."

"So we outnumber him three to one right now." Lincoln looked at Grant, who nodded. "Then there will be one more battle, at least."

Grant nodded, again.

"It would be good to avoid it, if we can. There's been so much bloodshed." Lincoln turned to Grant, "When Richmond falls, or even before, what is to prevent Lee and his army from getting on the cars and going south to North Carolina, and joining up with Johnston? They could live off the country down there and go on fighting us for years."

"For one thing, sir, they won't be able to take the cars." Sherman's voice was light but emphatic.

"What's to prevent them? They still control at least two railroad lines to the south and to the west."

"They don't control them where we have been, and we've been everywhere now except this last stretch from North Carolina to here."

"Yes," said Lincoln. "You have been there but you are now *not* there. You are here, or you soon will be. Well, the railroads are still where they were."

"Oh, the roads are still there," said Sherman, "but the rails are gone. We have torn them up. They can't be used."

624

"It's not hard to put the rails and the ties back down again. We did that at Annapolis when the war was new."

Sherman chuckled. "I don't think you understand my boys. What was wood they burned, and what was metal they put in the fire and made corkscrews of. There's not a railroad out of Virginia that Lee could ever use."

Lincoln whistled, comically. "You don't do things by halves, do you?"

"No, sir," said Sherman. "You remember when we first met four years ago?"

"Of course I do." Lincoln spoke somewhat too quickly. "With your brother Senator Sherman, wasn't it?"

Sherman ignored Lincoln's hesitancy. "I said to you then that this would be a long and terrible war, and you said you didn't think it would be all that long and, anyway, you supposed that even if it was, you'd manage somehow to keep house."

"Did I say that?" Lincoln shook his head with wonder. "Well, I am only a politician, you know, and we tend to say stupid things. What's worse, of course, is we do them, too. Well, you were the better prophet. So tell me, what do you prophesy next for us?"

"This time, sir, *you* are what the prophet must contemplate. Because once the fighting stops, the future is going to be what you make of it."

Grant stared hard at Lincoln. "Sherman's right. You'll have to decide everything. Like what do we do with the rebel armies? With the generals? With the politicians? What shall we do with Jefferson Davis?"

"Mr. Davis..." Lincoln's face lightened. "That reminds me of this man who took the temperance pledge. Then he went to the house of a drinking friend who tried to tempt him, but he would not be tempted. He asked for lemonade. So the lemonade was brought to him. Then the friend pointed to a bottle of brandy and said, 'Wouldn't it taste better with some of that in it?' and the temperance man said, 'Well, if it is added unbeknown to me, I wouldn't object.'"

The three men laughed. Admiral Porter said, "In other words, if Mr. Davis were to escape to another country you wouldn't mind?"

Lincoln merely smiled; then he said, "I am for getting the Union back to what it was as quickly and as painlessly as possible."

"You will have your problems with Congress," said Sherman, a senator's brother.

"Well, that is my job. I must say, Sherman, I'd feel safer if you were back in North Carolina with your army."

625

Sherman laughed. "I promise you it will not disintegrate that quickly."

Lincoln stretched his arms until there was a creaking sound from the vicinity of the shoulder blades. Then he said, suddenly, "Sherman, do you know why I took a shine to you and Grant?"

"I don't know, sir. I do know you have been kinder to me than I ever deserved."

"Well, it's because, unlike all the other generals, you never found fault with me." Lincoln rose. "At least not so that I ever heard."

Lincoln then took a long fire-ax from its bracket on the bulkhead. "Let's see if you fellows can do this." Lincoln grabbed the ax at the end of its haft and held it away from his body, arm outstretched and parallel to the deck. One by one, the others tried to do the same but, in each case, the weight was too great. "It is a sort of trick of balance," said Lincoln.

"And muscle," said Sherman.

The next day President and generals rode out to the main encampment of the Army of the James to witness a grand review. Mrs. Lincoln and Mrs. Grant followed in an ambulance, which kept to a corduroy road that had been set across a sea of red Virginia mud and swampland. Mary had never in her life known such discomfort, not to mention pain; a headache had now installed itself just back of her eyes and would not go away.

At the back of the swaying and lurching ambulance Mary and Julia Grant sat on a bench, side by side, when they were not thrown together. One of General Grant's aides sat opposite them, apologizing for the state of the road.

"It's never comfortable," said Mrs. Grant, clutching the wagon's side.

"We can endure the discomfort," said Mary regally. "But, surely," she addressed the officer, "we are going to be late for the review?"

"I think not," said the man. "Of course, the driver is deliberately slow."

"Then tell him we should like to go faster."

"But I don't think that's wise," said Julia Grant and the eye closest to Mary turned, impudently, away.

"But we *must* go faster!" Mary exclaimed. The officer gave the order to the driver, and the horses sprang forward just as flat marsh gave way to a section of corduroy road made up of trees of different sizes. The ambulance sprang into the air. The two ladies, as one, left their seat and would have departed the ambulance entirely had the back section not been roofed in. As it was, two large, splendidly decorated hats prevented the heads beneath from breaking open but at the cost of two miraculous examples of the milliner's craft, now crushed. As Mary fell back into the seat, she screamed, "Stop! Let me out! I shall walk!"

The ambulance stopped. The ornamental pheasant that had been the central decoration of Mrs. Grant's hat had slipped forward onto her forehead, and one glossy wing now pathetically caressed her round cheek. "Mrs. Lincoln, no! Please."

Mary was halfway out of the carriage, when the officer pulled her back in. "Madam," he said, soothingly, "the mud is three feet deep here. No one can walk."

"Oh, God!" shouted Mary, directly to the Deity, who did not answer her. As she sat back in the bench, head throbbing and eyes shut, she felt, one by one, the wax cherries that had made beautiful her hat come loose and fall to the ambulance floor exactly as the originals would have done when ripe.

But Mary had predicted correctly. They were late for the review. On a great muddy field, an army division was going through its paces. Mrs. Grant, helpfully, identified the commanding general in the distance, James Ord. Meanwhile, the ambulance approached the review stand, a slender woman on a great horse cantered past them. "Who is that?" asked Mary. "I thought women were forbidden at the front."

"They are," said Julia Grant, "but that is General Griffin's wife. She has a special permit."

"From the President himself," said the aide, with a smile which was, for Mary, lasciviousness writ scarlet in the air. She responded with a scream; and was pleased to see some of the redness go from those hideous, mocking lips.

"*She* has had an interview with the President? Is that what you are hinting at? A *private* interview?" Mary could hear a mocking snigger from Mrs. Grant at her side. They were all in it together. "Yes, that is what you want people to believe. But no woman is ever alone with the President. So tell as many lies as you please . . ."

General Meade was now at the ambulance. Mary turned to him for alliance. As he helped her down, she said, most craftily, she thought, "General Meade, it has been suggested to me that that woman on the horse has received *special* permission to be at the front, given her by the President himself."

Meade said, "No, Mrs. Lincoln. Not by the President. Such permissions are given, and very rarely, by Mr. Stanton."

"See?" Mary wheeled on her tormentors. She addressed the corrupt officer. "General Meade is a gentleman, sir. It was not the President but the Secretary of War who gave permission to this slut." Mary savored her triumph. Fortunately, General Meade was very much a gentleman, from one of Philadelphia's finest old

627

families; and so he acted as if nothing had happened as he escorted her to the reviewing stand. But Mary was conscious that her two mortal enemies were just behind her, heads together, whispering obscenities to each other. Well, she would bide her time.

As Mary took her seat facing an entire division drawn up at present arms, she saw the President, flanked by Generals Grant and Ord, begin his ride down the long dark-blue line of troops. As the President came to each regiment, the men would cheer him and he would remove his hat. Back of the three men, there were a dozen high-ranking officers, and a good-looking young woman on a horse.

"Who is that?" asked Mary.

Mrs. Grant said, "It is Mrs. Ord, the general's wife."

"She is riding next to my husband."

"She is actually," said Mrs. Grant, gently, "riding next to *her* husband, General Ord."

Mary turned to General Meade for assistance but he had moved away to the telegraph hut at the end of the reviewing stand. In his place, there was a solicitous colonel. "Sir, has that woman been riding with the President all during the review?" Mary watched his face very carefully; she knew that she could tell in an instant if he was lying; it was as if her eyes could see with perfect clarity straight past his dull face and deep into his brain.

"Why, yes," said the colonel.

"Actually, she is with *her* husband, Mrs. Lincoln..." began Julia Grant.

"I am quite capable of calculating the distance—look now!" Mrs. Ord was indeed alongside the President. "My God!" Mary exclaimed. "*She is pretending to be me!* They will think that that vile woman is me! Does she suppose that *he* wants *her* at his side like that?"

A young major rode up. The colonel said, quickly, "Here is Major Seward, the nephew of the Secretary of State..."

"Mrs. Lincoln." The Major saluted Mary.

"I know all about Mr. Seward," Mary began, noticing the young man's parrot's beak of a nose, so like that of his uncle, her enemy.

Major Seward was aware that they had been watching the President and Mrs. Ord, who were not riding side by side. "The President's horse is very gallant," said Major Seward, with all the corrupt insolence of his uncle. "He insists on riding by the side of Mrs. Ord's horse."

"What," Mary cried, pushed now to the very edge of public humiliation, "do you mean by that?"

Major Seward's response was an abrupt retreat. Meanwhile,

President and generals had moved off the field toward the Petersburg front while Mrs. Ord rode toward the reviewing stand. Mary could not believe her eyes. The woman's insolence was beyond anything that she had ever had to endure in her life. The woman dismounted; and walked over to the reviewing stand. "Welcome, Mrs. Lincoln," she said.

Mary rose in her place. She left exalted. At last, she could strike at her enemies a mortal blow. "You whore!" said Mary, delighted that she was able to control so well her voice. Then, word by word, sentence by sentence, effortlessly, she told the slut what she thought of her and of her behavior. Mary felt as if she were floating over the landscape like a cloud, a thundercloud, true, but a serene one. All that needed to be said to this now scarlet-faced woman was said. From high up, the cloudlike Mary saw the tears flow down the vicious face; saw the Colonel as he tried to divert her from her necessary task; saw Julia Grant as she dared to interrupt her.

In a way, Julia Grant was the worst, of course. Whores were whores everywhere and the good wife could always manage to shame them or, if they were truly shameless, to drive them away. But Mrs. Grant was a threat. Mrs. Grant was the wife of a hero—a butcher-hero, of course, but still a hero to the stupid public. Mrs. Grant was also insolent. She had sat unbidden in the presence of the First Lady. But then it was no secret that she was already scheming to be herself First Lady one day. "I suppose," said Mary, with incredible cunning and the kindliest of smiles, "that you think you'll get to the White House yourself, don't you?"

Mrs. Grant—whose eyes were as crossed and flawed as her character—dared to answer, "We are quite happy where we are, Mrs. Lincoln."

"Well, you had better take it if you can get it." Mary was delighted with her own subtlety. She was, however, somewhat taken aback by the sound of a woman screaming. Could it be Mrs. Ord? No, *she* was weeping silently. Mary wondered where the screaming was coming from as she said, coolly, "It's very nice, the White House." Then Mary saw the fiery nimbus around Julia Grant's head; and then Mary realized that the screaming that she heard was herself. Then Mary ceased to be conscious of where she was.

But it was not The Headache, because that same evening, aboard the *River Queen*, Mary was almost herself again. Naturally, she had been humiliated by Mrs. Ord in public view; and insulted by Mrs. Grant in private. But Mary presided at the dinner table with, she thought, admirable poise. She did find it disturbing that she could not recall how she had got from the reviewing stand back to the ship. In fact, as they sat at dinner with six staff officers—and Mrs. Grant to the President's right and General Grant to Mary's right, she was not entirely certain how the dinner had begun. But now that everything was going so smoothly, she felt that she could murmur to Grant, "I hope that you will, in future, control Mrs. Ord, whose exhibition today, in pursuit of my husband, caused so much unfavorable comment."

General Grant's response was not clear. But the President said, "Now, Mother, I hardly knew the lady was present."

"For no want of trying," Mary was regal. "Anyway, why should she, or any woman, be here?"

"Ord needs her," said Grant.

"The way General Grant needs me at times," said Mrs. Grant.

"Oh, we know all about *those* times," Mary began. But the President cut her off. "Mother, the army band is coming aboard after dinner. There will be dancing."

"We thought it might be gay," said Mrs. Grant. "In all this horror. To forget for a moment."

"I am glad if it makes you glad." Mary was consummately gracious. She turned to Lincoln. "Everyone seems agreed that General Ord is the principal reason why the Army of the James has been stopped here for so many, many months now." Mary felt that she had now outflanked the Grants. "If he were to be replaced might we not be able to win the war more quickly?"

"Now, Mother..." Lincoln seemed very distant from her at his end of the table. She had some difficulty in hearing his voice but she had no difficulty hearing General Grant, who said, "Ord is a fine officer. I cannot do without him."

As Mary explained to General Grant the urgent need to replace Ord, she felt a sudden swimming ecstasy that suffused her entire body and mind. Simultaneously, again like a cloud or, perhaps, the moon, she was floating far, far above the table. She was a little girl in Lexington again; and there were her dolls, far below, at a tea party.

On April 1, Mrs. Lincoln returned to Washington for a brief visit. Both she and the President had been alarmed by a vivid dream that he had had: the White House was afire. This was the pretext for her return. But she would be back, she said, with a small group of friends, and Keckley.

For several days, Lincoln had installed himself in the telegraph office next to Grant's log-cabin headquarters. He took delight in personally sending news to Stanton at the War Department; and there was a good deal of news. From all directions, Union troops were now moving against Richmond. The arrival of Sheridan had, in effect, sealed off the city.

"It is a good thing," said Grant, as he prepared to go to the front, "that Sherman will take no part in the last battle."

Lincoln gazed down at the small general with some surprise. "Surely," he said, "there is glory enough for all."

"There isn't," said Grant. "That's the problem. The army we have here is the Eastern army. More important, it is the *Northern* army. And the war is of special importance to the North. But this army has always failed. If Sherman were to join us, the country will say that the east starts wars that westerners have to finish."

"You know, General," said Lincoln thoughtfully, "you have the makings of a very superior politician."

Grant nearly smiled. "Just as you, sir, have the makings of a very superior military tactician."

"I am not at all sure just how I am supposed to take that," said Lincoln, as they walked from telegraph office to headquarters.

"Tell me something." Grant stopped at the cabin door. He looked very young in the sharp spring sunlight, the brown beard glossy as fox fur and the blue eyes glowing. "Did you at any time in the last four years doubt the final success of the cause?"

"Never," said Lincoln, "for one moment."

Grant nodded. "That's what I told Sherman."

A kitten appeared at the cabin door. Absently, Lincoln scooped it up and scratched its ears as they went into the busy war-room, where orderlies came and went and all the lines on the map of Virginia now converged on Richmond.

On April 2, General Grant occupied Petersburg: Lee had pulled back to Richmond. It was now urgent that Lee not be allowed to break out of the area.

"It is our fear," said Admiral Porter to the President, as they rode in the cars to Petersburg, "that he will retreat into North Carolina, and join up with Johnston's army. If he does, they could hold that state for a long time."

Lincoln nodded. "It must end now, once and for all." He stared out the window at the trees in new green-yellow leaf; and at the signs of war—abandoned earthworks, dead horses, skulls, the casings of shells.

At the Petersburg depot Captain Robert Lincoln greeted his father. "Welcome to Petersburg, sir," he said, saluting the President.

Lincoln returned the salute; and said: "We have taken our time getting here, but we got here, finally." Lincoln mounted the horse that Robert had brought him. Then, surrounded by a cavalry contingent, they rode through the streets of the town, deserted save for timid blacks.

Grant met them on the porch of the house which he had secured for himself as a headquarters.

Lincoln shook Grant's hand. "I've had a sneaking suspicion for some days now," he said, "that you were going to wind this thing up at last. Now you're doing it."

Grant took his time lighting a large cigar. Then he said, "Mr. President, at eight-fifteen this morning, General Weitzel accepted the surrender of Richmond. Last night, Mr. Davis and his so-called government moved on to Danville. General Lee is now trying to escape to the south. But we won't let him. At last, we have him where we want him."

Lincoln stood in the hard, dried mud of the street, frowning at the ground. As he continued mysteriously to lose weight, he had grown more stooped; he was now, he liked to say, a close student of the earth. But then he looked up, and said, "It looks, General, as if our work is just about done."

"We took too long, sir. But we started in perfect ignorance, both sides."

"We are not ignorant now," said Lincoln. "If anything, we know too much of war, and all its costs . . . I shall myself telegraph the news to the nation. I, who have brought so much bad news to so many people, can now at least proclaim the end of this vast trouble."

The next day, aboard Admiral Porter's flagship, the *Malvern*, Lincoln and his party steamed upriver and into Richmond harbor, where the ship promptly went aground. But Admiral Porter was ready with a twelve-man ceremonial barge to transport the President to the enemy capital.

On the wharf there was a large crowd of Negroes, who kept asking, "Who is it?" When told that the man was President Lincoln, they could not believe it. But then when Lincoln stood up and, Tad's hand in his, stepped ashore, they began to cheer and some of them, shyly, asked to shake his hand, while others wanted only to touch him.

With Admiral Porter at his side, Lincoln moved up the street, guarded by twelve edgy sailors, armed with carbines.

As they moved down the center of the trafficless street, crowds began to form; there were now whites as well as blacks. Every telegraph pole had men clinging to it, eager to glimpse the incarnation of Yankee evil, Old Abe—or Old Nick—himself. Tad's guard, Mr. Crook, kept murmuring into Lincoln's ear, "I don't like the look of this crowd." But although there was no sign of greeting, there was no notable expression of hostility. Nevertheless,
632

at one point the nervous Admiral Porter said, "Sir, why don't we stop here at this hotel, and wait for General Weitzel's men."

"Oh, I find this more interesting, Admiral," Lincoln pointed to a section of the main street where a public building had been so shelled that only its highly ornamental facade still stood. "We have done a lot of damage to this city," said Lincoln, with a certain wonder.

As they passed through the ruins, a light wind started up and, suddenly, down the street, like thousands and thousands of large square leaves, government documents swirled. "What begins in paper," said Lincoln wryly, as his ankles were wrapped round with government records, "ends in paper."

Then they turned a corner and the undamaged Greek temple of the state capitol was now visible on its hill. As the Union flag went up the flagpole, the sailor-escort cheered—and Crook leapt in front of Lincoln, arms spread wide so that his entire large body could shield the President's narrow one.

Lincoln looked up at the window where Crook had seen danger. "There's no one there," he said.

"There was, sir. A man with a gun, sir."

"I have *my* pistol," said Tad, delighted.

"You won't need it today, Taddie," said Lincoln, continuing his walk.

Closer to the capitol, they stopped in front of the notorious Libby Prison. When someone shouted, "Tear it down," Lincoln said, "No. We will leave it as a monument." Then, to Admiral Porter's relief, a cavalry escort appeared, making it possible for the President to ride the rest of the way to an austere gray stucco house with a pillared doorway.

Here the cavalry commander stopped. "It is the Confederate Executive mansion, Mr. President. It is now yours."

Lincoln dismounted. For a moment, he paused to dry his face with a handkerchief; then he and Tad and Admiral Porter entered Jefferson Davis's house.

They were met by an elderly black man, who said, "I worked for Mr. Davis, who told me to keep the house nice for the Yankees."

"I am sure that you have." Lincoln opened a door into a room with a long table surrounded by chairs. From habit, Lincoln seated himself at the head of the table.

"That was Mr. Davis's chair," said the old man.

"It is now Mr. Lincoln's," said Admiral Porter.

"Could you bring me some water, please?" was Lincoln's only request. As the old man hurried from the room, General Weitzel, sweating heavily, entered and saluted the Commander-in-Chief.

"Richmond is yours, sir. I'm sorry we were not at the dock to meet you but you arrived ahead of schedule."

"That's all right. What news from the front?" As Tad and Crook explored the house, Weitzel reported to Lincoln the day's activities. Lee was still in the vicinity, and Grant was preparing for a final military confrontation.

The old man returned with water for the President and whiskey for the general and the admiral. As they toasted victory, Weitzel reported that seven hundred buildings had been destroyed in the city; and that many whites as well as blacks had been left homeless. "What are your instructions to me, sir, on how I am to treat the local population?"

"Well, I am not ready to give you my final views on the subject but if I were you I'd let 'em up easy." Lincoln nodded; and repeated, "Let 'em up easy."

Suddenly, Lincoln looked about the room, as if aware for the first time of the magnitude of what had happened. "It is so much like a dream," he said at last, "but then I dream so much these days that it is hard for me to tell sometimes what is real and what is not."

"This is real, sir," said Admiral Porter. "You are seated in the chair of Jefferson Davis, and he is all but a fugitive from your justice."

Lincoln smiled. "If that is all he has to fear, he would be safe enough. I have no justice, or anything else now. It is fate that guides us all—and necessity. You see, I must be here, just as he must be in flight; just as the war must end." Lincoln ran one hand across the smooth table top. "And the Union be so restored that no one will ever be able to see the slightest scar from all this great trouble, that will pass now the way a dream does when you wake at last, from a long night's sleep."

11

ELIHU B. WASHBURNE HAD NEVER SEEN THE PRESIDENT SO curiously passive. He lolled on the lounge in his office, tie loosened and collar open. He had lost, Washburne reckoned, thirty to forty pounds. The Indian-black hair of beard and head were now marked with gray, while the face had been burned to a coppery Indian shade by the Virginia sun. For once, Lincoln complained of his health: "My hands and feet feel like they've been kept in the icehouse all summer long."

"You're not ill, are you?"

"I don't think so. But if I am, I am a happy sick man." Lincoln smiled, absently.

"Speaking of sick men, will Seward resign?" Some days earlier the Secretary of State had been thrown from his carriage. He had dislocated a shoulder; broken both jaws and both arms; lay now in a metal brace, delirious and incoherent much of the time.

"Oh, I don't think so. I hope not. Broken bones mend, after all. To think he and Welles are all that's left of my famous—and infamous—Combination Cabinet." Lincoln chuckled. "That seems such a long time ago. Now we have a whole new set of problems."

Washburne nodded. "The Jacobins are getting set to punish the rebels."

"Well, we shall have to crack the whip a bit over Mr. Wade and his friends..." Lincoln paused; then he did something that he had not done for a long time. He simply drifted away in midsentence from the immediate subject. "What is the debt of the state of Illinois now?"

Startled, Washburne shook his head. "I don't know for sure. I *do* know that it is considerable, thanks to your Internal Improvements Act."

"Now that was more Judge Douglas's invention than mine."

"*If* we are to believe your campaign biography." In 1860, Washburne had been astonished at Lincoln's refusal to take public responsibility for any of their state's debt. Yet, as a leader in the legislature, Lincoln had voted for roads and bridges and canals with such a wild abandon that the state soon had a debt of fifteen million dollars, while the state's bonds were selling for fifteen cents to the dollar. Interest on the bonds regularly exceeded by far the state's total revenues.

"I note," said Lincoln, slyly, picking up a Springfield newspaper, "that the state is now beginning to pay interest on those bonds and that by 1882 they will all be paid off. Meanwhile, we were able to internally improve Illinois in the most spectacular way."

Washburne grunted. "Bridges without rivers under them, roads that go nowhere..."

"Mere details." Lincoln sat back in his chair. "I am looking ahead again."

"More realistically than before, I hope. Our state was damn near wrecked by what you legislators did."

"I know. That's why I've been studying the matter. None of us who favored such expenditures can take much pride in what happened. Only we may have to do something like it once again. You see, if I am to reimburse the slave-owners—"

"You *still* want to do that?" Washburne was amazed. Since the rebels had held on to the very end, he saw no reason to do anything at all for them.

"Yes. I think it only just. It will also be a quick way of getting money into the South for reconstruction." Lincoln sighed. "Then we'll need money to colonize as many Negroes as we can in Central America."

Washburne shook his head with wonder. "When you get hold of an idea you don't ever let it go, do you?"

"Not until I find a better one. Can you imagine what life in the South will be like if the Negroes stay?"

"It will be hard," said Washburne. "But most of the Negroes don't seem to want to go. But if they do go, where will you find four million white people in the South who can do the work that the slaves did?"

"All the more reason," said Lincoln, reasonably, "to reimburse the slave-owners."

Hay appeared in the doorway. "Mr. Stanton is here, sir. He has a message for you."

Lincoln pulled himself into a sitting position. Washburne noticed the languor of his movements; he was like a man to whom the air itself has become resistant. "It is unusual for Mars to bring me a message when Major Eckert is our official Mercury."

Stanton was now in the room. He did not greet either man. Instead he held a yellow flimsy close to his red eyes, and said, "At four-thirty P.M., this arrived. From General Grant. I shall now read. 'General Lee surrendered the Army of Northern Virginia this afternoon on terms proposed by myself. The accompanying additional correspondence will show the conditions fully.'" Stanton gave Lincoln the telegram. For a moment they were all silent. Then Lincoln got to his feet, and said, with what sounded to Washburne like wonder, "Our work is done."

"You have seen us through," said Stanton; and he shook the President's hand. Much moved, Washburne did the same. It was as if his old friend had ceased entirely to exist as a human being and in his place there was now, suddenly incarnate, an entire and undivided nation.

All through the day and early evening, crowds filled the White House grounds and the avenue beyond. Every public building had been illuminated, and the misty night glowed with huge transparencies. Some proclaimed: "U.S. Army, U.S. Navy, U.S. Grant". The post office displayed a young express rider with the legend "Behold, I bring you good tidings of great joy," while Jay

Cooke and Company, in an excess of self-congratulation, announced, in colored lights: "The busy bees—Bullets, Balls, Bonds," as well as "Glory to God, who hath US Grant'd the Victory."

As the crowd waited for the appearance of the President, Tad kept them amused by waving a captured Confederate flag. But then he, too, was captured by Mr. Crook, who lifted him out of the window by the seat of his pants.

In an upstairs bedroom, Lincoln stood with Hay and Noah Brooks, reading over his speech. He had been working on it all day. The text had given him a great deal of trouble. He wanted to strike the expected note of triumph but, more important, he wanted to spell out the way that the Union was now to be reconstructed. He also wanted to outmaneuver as rapidly as possible the vindictive Jacobins of the Congress. Although Noah Brooks still wrote for a Sacramento newspaper, it was more or less common knowledge that he would take the place of Nicolay, who was to go to Paris as consul-general as soon as the transfer from one secretary to the other had been made. Hay had almost decided to go home to Warsaw, Illinois, when Seward had sent for him and said, "I believe that every young man should live for as long as possible in Paris, in order to perfect his French and strengthen his morals, which is more easily done in a capital where vice is not only everywhere but so repellent that no temptation is possible. Therefore, I have elevated Mr. Bigelow to be our minister—James Gordon Bennett having refused the honor—and I have given you Mr. Bigelow's one-time post as secretary to the Legation. I also did not think it fair to separate you from Nicolay."

Hay had accepted the post with delight. The thought of Paris made the coming separation from the Tycoon more bearable. After all, most of his grown-up life had been spent with Lincoln. Hay had arrived at the White House a green twenty-two-year old; now he was twenty-six and there was nothing of the American political world that he did not know. Although he would miss the Tycoon, he would not in the least miss the miasmic mansion, as he had taken to calling the hideous ramshackle old house, infested with rats and termites over which gold leaf and damask had been spread in an attempt to disguise the progressive rot. Also, neither Hay nor Nicolay thought much of Noah Brooks and the new young men who would soon replace them. At one point, Hay had considered staying on as Brooks's aide. After all, Brooks was ten years his senior and an old Illinois friend of Lincoln's. But then the thought of four more years in the same house as the Hellcat caused him to say no. Life had become intolerable in the miasmic mansion; and it was time to move on. Hay pitied the

637

Ancient, trapped in a haunted house with a wife gone mad; and no one save the sycophantish Noah Brooks to talk to.

Brooks looked out the window at the crowd. "I think it's time," he said.

Lincoln nodded. Then, candle in his left hand, speech in his right hand, glasses on his nose, Lincoln stepped out onto the ledge. The crowd cheered. As the tall, thin figure stood silhouetted against the glow of the transparencies across the park, Hay suddenly saw Lincoln as a sort of human lightning conductor, absorbing all the fire from Heaven for all of them.

To Hay's amazement, the cheering did not die down, as it usually did before a speech. Instead it became more and more intense, even violent. Hay had another image. This was not so much a crowd as a stormy sea, whose huge waves were crashing over the house. Tad, seated at his father's feet, clapped his hands over his ears. During all this, the Tycoon remained very still in the open window, unsmiling face illuminated from beneath by the candle in his hand.

At last, as suddenly as a storm stops, the cheering stopped; and Lincoln began to speak. Hay knew that this was the wrong speech for such an exuberant gathering. But Lincoln had insisted that he must declare himself as soon as possible on the issue of the returned states.

Lincoln read the first page, which was filled with all the expected references to victory. Then he had difficulty with the candle; and Brooks stepped forward and held the candle for him. As Lincoln finished the first page, he dropped it. Tad caught it, and said, "Gimme another."

The President proceeded to lay before the crowd—and the country beyond—his own case for acceptance of Louisiana into the Union, even though there might be objections to this or that aspect of the way in which the state's government was being organized. "Concede that the new government of Louisiana is only to what it should be as the egg is to the fowl; we shall sooner have the fowl by hatching the egg than smashing it." Thus he answered the radicals in Congress. He also emphasized that Louisiana would vote in favor of the Thirteenth Amendment, abolishing slavery. On the vexing question of giving the Negro the vote, Lincoln conceded, "It is also unsatisfactory to some that the elective franchise is not given to the colored man. I would myself prefer that it were now conferred on the very intelligent and those who serve our cause as soldiers."

John Wilkes Booth and Lewis Payne were standing beneath a street lamp at the edge of the Presidential Park. "My God! He will let the niggers vote!" Booth was horrified. Then he whispered in Payne's ear. "Shoot him now."

Payne shook his head. "Not now, Captain. It's too risky. And he's too far away. Later..."

The President finished his speech. There was less applause than at the beginning. The band played, until rain started to fall, and the crowd dispersed.

"Well," said Booth, as he and Payne hurried down Pennsylvania Avenue to Sullivan's Saloon, "that is the last speech that he will ever give. Because now I shall put him through."

Over the Capitol, in fiery letters, was the legend "This is the Lord's doing; it is marvelous in our eyes." When Booth read these words aloud, he laughed. "The Lord has more marvels yet to work, and other instruments as yet undreamed of."

At the very back of Sullivan's Bar, David Herold and Atzerodt were waiting. David had never before seen Wilkes quite so worked up, as he related to them the President's speech. "It is what we all feared from the beginning, that the nigger would be put over us."

"Where is John Surratt?" asked Atzerodt.

"He's gone to Canada," said David. "He's run out on us."

"We don't need him," said Booth. "We are enough—just us—to redeem our cause."

As the various attempts to kidnap Lincoln failed, Surratt had grown more critical of Booth. Finally, when Richmond fell, he told David that he now saw no point to a kidnapping. When Booth began to speak of murder, Surratt said that he saw no point to that at all and so, to avoid any further involvement with the conspiracy, he had left for Canada. This at least was the story that John had wanted David to believe. Wilkes himself was silent on the subject.

As Booth drank brandy and the others drank Sullivan's best beer—Sullivan himself had gone to Richmond to see old friends—the last battle of the Confederacy was designed at the low pinewood table in the back of the smoky saloon.

Booth had two playbills. One for Ford's Theater; the other for Grover's. "The secret service is expecting the President and General Grant to go to the theater together at the end of this week. I assume if they go Friday, it will be either to Grover's patriotic rally or to Ford's Laura Keene comedy. Whichever it is, we shall be ready." Booth fixed David with his dark honey-colored eyes. "I will take care of the President and General Grant. Lewis will kill, at exactly the same time, Mr. Seward, while Atzerodt will kill the Vice-President at the Kirkwood House Hotel. With one swift stroke, we shall behead the government. Then we make our way to North Carolina and join up with Johnston's men, who are still fighting in the hills."

"If we get away," said Atzerodt, the least enthusiastic of the lot.

"If we don't, we don't. But I think we will. Particularly if they go to Ford's Theater, where I've already got two horses that Ned Spangler's seeing to. With David here, we'll cross over into Maryland, and with his knowledge of the roads, we'll soon be with our friends in Richmond, Yankees or no Yankees."

David had, by now, convinced himself that he knew every road that there was to Richmond. Actually, in the last six months, he had spent a good deal of time in Maryland with John Surratt, and he was reasonably certain that he could get Wilkes safely through to Richmond. He was surprised at how little fear he felt. But then had he not twice tried to poison Old Abe? Or at least that was what the people who most mattered to him thought that he had done, which was almost as good as actually having done it.

Then Lewis Payne, in his soft voice, proposed that they drink the captain's health for "He is the last of the heroes of our cause—and the most immortal." They all drank to Booth.

As they drank to Booth and immortality, Abraham Lincoln was dreaming of death. As usual, he was sleeping lightly, alone in a small room off the large bedroom where Mary slept in the huge carved wooden bed.

Suddenly, Lincoln was awakened by an unnatural stillness in the old house, where planks never ceased creaking or rats moving about in the walls. He opened his eyes in the dark. For an instant, he wondered if he might not be dead and in the grave. Then he heard the sound of sobbing. He got out of bed, and went into Mary's room. The lights were on; but she was not there. Still in his nightshirt, he went out into the upstairs hall. But neither Lamon nor Crook was on duty. The hall was empty. He looked into the secretary's room; the bed was empty.

Then he went downstairs to find that the main hall was empty as well; and there were no doorkeepers or ushers or messengers in sight. Finally, he entered the East Room, which was crowded with people. At the room's center, on a catafalque covered with black velvet, a body lay wrapped in a sheet, the face covered by a cloth.

Grim-faced people were filing past the body. Some were sobbing; others simply stared, horrified. Lincoln crossed to one of the soldiers who stood guard at the room's entrance. "Who is dead in the White House?" he asked.

"The President," said the soldier, seeming to look through him, as if he were not visible. "He was killed by an assassin." Then a
640

woman at the catafalque suddenly shrieked; and Lincoln awakened in his own bed, face covered with sweat. What does *that* mean? he wondered. Is it I or another? Are dreams the opposite of the future, or the same? He lay for a long time in the dark; and wondered.

On Friday morning, April 14, 1865, at eleven o'clock, the Cabinet met; General Grant was in attendance; and Fred Seward sat in for his father.

In the secretary's room, Captain Lincoln sat at Hay's desk and Hay sat at Nicolay's desk, now vacant while the consul-general-to-be made a tour of the South on behalf of the Tycoon. Robert Lincoln had placed a handsome portrait of Robert E. Lee over the mantepiece. "I showed it to Father at breakfast."

"Was he pleased?"

"He said Lee looked most handsome, and he was glad the war was over."

"Now we have a new war with the radicals—and Ben Butler."

Since Lincoln's speech on the return of Louisiana to the Union, the radicals had been at work. They wanted, very simply, to overthrow the Executive and then dictate through Congress a harsh peace to the South. The endlessly ambitious and brilliantly dishonest Ben Butler had now allied himself with the other Ben, Wade, as well as with Chandler and Stevens and Sumner and the whole canting crew. Hay was convinced that they would try to make some sort of coup against the Administration. But when he told the Tycoon his fears, Lincoln had only laughed. "I have General Grant and General Sherman and General Sheridan with me. I can't see what Congress is going to do against them."

But Lamon was worried. He spoke, darkly, of plots to kill or remove the President. But even Hay thought it unlikely that Ben Butler would go so far as to attempt a military coup. On the other hand, Congress was capable of all sorts of legislative tricks, which would be upheld by Chief Justice Chase, who had, according to Lamon, every characteristic of a dog save loyalty.

"Where is Lamon?" asked Robert.

"Gone on an errand to Richmond."

Edward entered the office. "It's been confirmed for tonight," he said. "Tad and his friends—"

"—who are legion," said Robert.

"—will go to Grover's and the President and General Grant and their wives will go to Ford's. Will you wish to go, Captain?"

"Laura Keene?"

"In *Our American Cousin*," said Hay.

"No, thank you." Edward left the room. Robert turned to Hay. "We might explore the city's marble alleys together."

"Why not?" said Hay.

The President was now discussing dreams with the Cabinet. "It is amazing how often dreams are mentioned in the Old and New Testaments . . ."

"And in Shakespeare," said Welles, more at home with that author.

Lincoln nodded, absently. Then he turned to General Grant, who sat opposite him at the green-baize-covered table. "I just asked you for news of Sherman in North Carolina because I think we are about to hear of an important victory. You see, before every great event in the war, I have had the same exact most peculiar dream. I am on a singular—an indescribable—vessel, moving rapidly toward an indefinite shore—and I am oarless, and drifting. I had that dream before Sumter, Bull Run, Antietam, Gettysburg, Stone River, Vicksburg and Wilmington."

"Well," said Grant, dryly, "Stone River was certainly no victory, thanks to Rosecrans, and nothing very great ever came of it. In fact, a few more such fights would have ruined us."

"We must differ on that," said Lincoln. "In any case, my dream preceded it."

"At least," said Welles, "this time the dream can't presage a victory or a defeat because the war is over."

"There are still a few rebels loose," said Lincoln, unwilling to give up the idea of military news.

"Perhaps, sir," said Fred Seward, "the dream comes before some great change or disorder, and you feel an uncertainty that enters your dreams."

"It is a possibility," said Lincoln.

Stanton then proceeded to demonstrate his usual impatience with dreams, or anything not tangible. He presented the President with a copy of his own plan for the reconstruction of the Union. He had also prepared copies for the other members of the Cabinet. Lincoln took the document; glanced at it; then said, at large, "This is, of course, the single great problem facing us, and we must attend to it as soon as possible. In fact, before Congress comes back in December. We have . . . nine months." He smiled. "In which to give birth to a new Union."

"Something we could hardly do if Ben Wade and the Senate were in session," said Welles.

"That is why I have made my proposals," said Stanton. "The organization of Virginia is the key. Once matters are settled satisfactorily there, we shall have the pattern for the rest of the rebel states."

642

Welles did not agree. "Virginia is an anomaly. We have controlled a number of the border counties for some time, and we have a pro-Union governor. Although he has not been elected by the rest of the state, I think we should act as if he had been."

Lincoln agreed. "The problems, of course, will begin in December. If Congress doesn't like the way we have organized these states, Congress can refuse to seat their delegations. I can't control what Congress does. But I have the power to maintain order within these states, and I can support their governors, which I will do."

"And when you do that, Congress will come around," added Stanton, ominously.

"I hope so." Lincoln was tentative. "Certainly, I want no bloody work now the war is over. No one need expect me to take part in hanging or killing more men, even the worst of them."

"Including Jefferson Davis?" asked Fred Seward.

"Well . . ." Lincoln looked out the window, as if he might get a glimpse of his one-time rival in flight down the river.

The Postmaster-General suggested that the President would probably not be sorry if the rebel leaders were to leave the country.

Lincoln nodded. "I shouldn't be at all sorry to have them out of the country, but I'm all for making sure that they do go."

The Cabinet adjourned at one o'clock. Fred Seward reminded the President that Lord Lyons's replacement had arrived from London, and would like to present his letters of credential.

"Let's do it tomorrow," said Lincoln. "At two o'clock. In the Blue Room. But I'll want to read the speech you've written for me before I give it. We don't want me to make a bad impression, stumbling over your big words."

Then Lincoln motioned for General Grant to follow him into his office. "I am sorry," he said, "about tonight. The press has made a big to-do about us all being together, and everyone will be there to see you."

"I know they will. I mean, sir," Grant stammered, "I know they will be there for both of us, but Mrs. Grant is firm. We must take the cars for Philadelphia this afternoon. The children . . ." Grant trailed off.

"I understand. Well, it cannot be helped. I only said that I'd go because of you and Mrs. Grant, and to please the crowd."

"The crowd!" Grant suddenly exclaimed. "I am heartily sick of this show business! I have never been so pawed over in my life."

"You had better get used to it, General."

"Do you think so?"

"Yes, I think so." Lincoln held out his hand. "Good-bye, General."

"Good-bye, Mr. President." Grant left. Lincoln entered the closet just off his office; and proceeded to wash his face at the washstand, where Hay found him. "I asked the Speaker of the House for tonight. But he has another engagement."

"Well, rustle up somebody. And order the carriage for five o'clock."

"Yes, sir. Mr. Johnson is here."

"Who?" Lincoln dried his face.

"The Vice-President, sir. Should I ask *him* for tonight?"

Lincoln shook his head; and Hay left the room.

As Andrew Johnson entered the office, Lincoln was studying Stanton's memorandum. In private, Johnson was more given to silence than in public, where the sight of an audience tended to overstimulate him. The fact that he and Lincoln barely knew each other made their relations awkward despite Lincoln's calculated attempts at openness. "I should have asked *you* to come to the Cabinet meeting today," said the President, putting down the memorandum. "We are discussing the reconstruction of the Southern states, a subject on which you are an authority. But I confess"—Lincoln made a comical gesture—"I am so used to a Vice-President who seldom ever paid me a call that I have to be reminded that there is such a personage."

"Whatever I can do, I will do, Mr. President. I am no friend of slave-owners."

"As the world knows." Johnson's desire to hang them all was notorious. "But I wish no harm to our ordinary citizens," he said, carefully.

Lincoln nodded. "Then you will disapprove, as I do—this is between us—Mr. Stanton's plan, which is that the people at the South must take orders from us as long as we feel like treating them as conquered. I want them back in the Union, preferably before December, as free citizens, able to govern themselves. General Grant agrees with me in this." Lincoln stared hard at Johnson.

"I certainly agree... in this. After all, we are speaking of the people from whom I come."

"You are not the *only* man of the people, Andy." Lincoln selected an apple from a bowl, and gave it to Johnson; then he took one for himself. "I am glad we understand each other. Because there is going to be a lot of honking of geese on Capitol Hill before we're through."

At five o'clock, the President and Mrs. Lincoln got into their carriage. "Are you sure," asked Mary, "you don't want me to ask Mr. Johnson or someone to drive with us?"

"No, Mother, just us today."

The afternoon was clear and bright; and the spring flowers were already beginning to blossom, helter-skelter, where the military encampments had been at the foot of Washington's monument and in the grounds of the Smithsonian Institution, recently razed by fire. A cavalry detachment accompanied the carriage. Earlier that day, Lincoln and Stanton had argued, yet again, about protection. Lincoln thought that now, with the war over, he was of less interest to the assassin. Stanton said that now, more than ever, he was in danger. Lamon would have agreed; but he was in Richmond. Nevertheless, just before Lamon had gone South, he warned the President to stay away from the theater or any public place where his presence had been advertised in advance.

"Perhaps," Lincoln said, as the carriage swung down the less-peopled side of Pennsylvania Avenue, "we might stay at home tonight."

"But it's Laura Keene's last night; and she is counting on us." Mary frowned. "I cannot get over General Grant's rudeness. Yesterday he was coming with us, and today he is not."

"I suppose it is Mrs. Grant, wanting to get home to her children." The carriage paused as a line of ambulances passed in front of them. When Lincoln was recognized, the wounded cheered him. He removed his hat and held it in his hand until the last ambulance had passed.

Mary was concerned with Mrs. Grant. "I suspect that she does not dare to face me after the scene that she made at City Point. I have never seen anyone so out of control. She is an ambitious little thing. So is he, for that matter. I was watching from the window when he walked back to Willard's this morning. There was an enormous crowd all around him, as if he were you."

"Well, he isn't me but he *is* General Grant, Mother, and that's something very special."

The carriage proceeded down a side street toward the Navy Yard. "He is running for president. I can tell. I can always tell."

"So you can. So you can. And he's welcome to it. We've had our crack at it. So if he wants to take over, let him."

"Four years," said Mary. "When I was young that sounded like forever. Now it is nothing. Four weeks. Four days. Time rushes past us like the snowflake on the river."

"When it's all over," said Lincoln, "I want to go west. I want to see California and the Pacific Ocean."

"Well, *I* want to go to Europe. I must see Paris . . ."

"Certainly, a lot of Paris has already come your way, Molly. Fact, Paris clings to your person from shoes to hats."

"Oh, Father! I buy so little now. Keckley makes everything, anyway. Where will we live?"

"Springfield. Where else? I'll practise some law with Herndon..."

"If you do, I will divorce you." Mary was indignant. "Father, how could you live in Springfield now? Much less practise law with Billy."

"What else am I to do? I'll be sixty-one years old. I'll have to do something to make a living. So that means the law..."

"In Chicago then." Mary had already envisaged a fine new house on the lake-front, where palaces were now beginning to rise.

"If we can afford it. Well, today I refuse to be worried about anything." Although gaunt, Lincoln's face was like that of a man who had just been let out of prison. "I have not been so happy in many years."

"Don't say that!" Mary was suddenly alarmed. She had heard him say these exact words once before; with ominous result.

"Why not? It is true."

"Because... the last time you said those same words was just before Eddie died."

Lincoln looked at her a moment; then he looked at the Capitol on its hill to their left. "I feel so personally—complete," he said, "now that the new lid is on. And I also feel so relieved that Congress has left town, and the place is empty."

After dinner that evening, Mary went to change her clothes for the theater while Lincoln sat in the upstairs oval parlor and gossiped with the new governor and the new senator from Illinois; he also treated them to a reading from Petroleum V. Nasby. Then Noah Brooks announced the Speaker of the House, Mr. Colfax, a man who never ceased smiling no matter what the occasion. "Sir, I must know"—he smiled radiantly, teeth yellow as maize— "if you intend to call a special session of the Congress in order to consider Mr. Stanton's proposals for reconstruction."

If Lincoln was taken aback by the reference to Stanton's supposedly private memorandum, he made no sign. "No, I shall not call a special session. After the superhuman labors of the last session, I believe Congress deserves its rest."

Colfax beamed his disappointment. "In that case, I shall make my long-deferred trip to the west."

Lincoln spoke with some interest of Colfax's proposed tour of the mountain states. Then Lincoln was reminded that when Senator Sumner was recently in Richmond, he had purloined the gavel of the speaker of the Confederate Congress. "Sumner is threatening to give it to Stanton. But I want you to have it, as proper custodian for this particular spoil of war."

Colfax's delight was hyenaish. "I should like nothing better."

"Well, you tell Sumner I said you're to have it."

Mary swept into the room; splendidly turned out for the theater. She was unanimously complimented.

"I think," said Brooks, looking at his watch, "that it is time to go."

"All in all," said Lincoln, collecting Mary's arm, "I would rather not go. But as the widow said to the preacher..."

"Oh, Father, not that one!" Bickering amiably, they proceeded downstairs to the waiting carriage, which contained the daughter of Senator Harris of New York and her fiancé, Major Rathbone, the best company that Hay could find at such short notice.

As Lincoln got into the carriage, he said to Crook, "Goodbye." Then an old friend from Chicago appeared in the driveway, waving his hat. "I'm sorry, Isaac, we're going to the theater. Come see me tomorrow morning." Accompanied by one officer from the Metropolitan Police, the carriage pulled out into the avenue.

A long row of carriages blocked the entire east side of Tenth Street, except for the main entrance to the brightly illuminated theater where Mr. Ford's young brother was waiting. The play had already begun.

As young Mr. Ford led the presidential party up the stairs to the dress circle, where a box had been prepared for them at stage-left, the sharp-eyed actors onstage recognized the President and they began to interpolate lines of dialogue. A heavy play on the word "draught" was being made, which allowed the irrepressible Laura Keene to look up at the Presidential box and exclaim, "The draft has been suspended!" Then she shook her head vigorously until her much-admired ringlets threatened to detach themselves from her cap.

Thus cued, the audience began to cheer the President and General Grant. But it was only the President who showed himself, for a moment, in the box. Then Lincoln sat back in a large rocking chair; and a curtain screened him from the audience.

At ten o'clock, mounted and armed, Booth, Herold and Payne were in the street. At a gesture from Booth, David and Payne set out for Seward's house, while Booth rode up the back alley to Ford's Theater, where a stagehand helped him tie up his bay mare. Booth then walked around to the front of the theater, and entered the lobby. He waved at the doorkeeper. "I hope you don't want me to buy a ticket?"

The man said, no; and continued to count ticket receipts, while several cronies stared at Booth until the doorkeeper introduced them to the youngest star, who asked for a chew of tobacco. Then, as Booth made his way up the stairs to the dress circle, he saw that there was an empty chair to the presidential box. The policeman was not at his post. This was an unexpected bit of good luck.

In the half-light from the proscenium arch, Booth opened the door and stepped inside the vestibule to the box. The President was only a few feet in front of him, silhouetted by calcium light. To the President's right sat Mrs. Lincoln and to their right a young couple occupied a sofa.

As the audience laughed, Booth removed from his right-hand pocket a brass derringer; and from his left-hand pocket a long, highly sharpened dagger.

Mary had been resting her elbow, casually, on Lincoln's forearm; but then, aware that this was a most unladylike thing to do, she sat up straight and whispered into Lincoln's ear, "What will Miss Harris think of my lolling up against you like this?"

Lincoln murmured, "Why, Mother, she won't think anything about it."

At that moment, from a distance of five feet, Booth fired a single shot into the back of the President's head. Without a sound, Lincoln leaned back in the chair; and his head slumped to the left until it was stopped by the wooden partition. Mary turned not to Booth but to her husband, while in the wings, an actor stared, wide-eyed, at the box. He had seen everything.

Major Rathbone threw himself upon Booth, who promptly drove his dagger straight at the young man's heart. But Rathbone's arm deflected the blade. Miss Harris shrieked, as Booth shoved past her and jumped onto the railing of the box. Then, with the sort of athletic gesture that had so delighted his admirers in this same theater, he leapt the twelve feet from box to stage. But, as on several other occasions when Booth's effects proved to be more athletic and improvised than dramatic and calculated, he had not taken into account the silken bunting that decorated the front of the box. The spur of one boot got entangled in the silk, causing him to fall, off-balance, to the stage, where a bone in his ankle snapped.

Rathbone shouted from the box, "Stop that man!" Booth shouted something unintelligible at the audience; and hurried off stage.

In the box, Mary now stood, screaming. Miss Harris tried to comfort her. Laura Keene herself came; and she held the unconscious President's head in her lap until a doctor arrived to examine the wound. The bullet had gone into the back of Lincoln's head above the left ear and then downward and to the right, stopping just below the right eye.

At the White House, Hay and Robert Lincoln were sitting comfortably in the upstairs parlor, drinking whiskey, when the new doorkeeper, Tom Pendel, broke in on them. "The President's been shot!"

As Hay hurried after Robert to the waiting carriage, he had a dreamlike sense that he had already lived through this moment before. Pendel was hysterical. "Mr. Seward's been murdered, too. The whole Cabinet's been murdered!"

"Who?" asked the stunned Robert as they drove through the crowd that had begun to fill up Tenth Street. "Who has done this?"

"Rebels?" Hay could not think.

In the small bedroom of a cabbage-scented boardinghouse, the Ancient lay at an angle on a bed that was, needless to say, too short for him. This is the last time, Hay thought inanely, that he will be so inconvenienced.

Lincoln lay on his back, breathing heavily, as a doctor tried with cotton to staunch the ooze of blood from the shattered skull. Lincoln's right eye was swollen shut; and the skin of the right cheek was turning black. Hay noted that the long bare arms on the coverlet were surprisingly muscular. Lately, he had tended to think of the Ancient as mere skin and bone. In the next room, he could hear the sobbing of Mrs. Lincoln. In the bedroom itself, he could hear, as well as witness, the sobbing of Senator Sumner, posed like a widow at the head of the bed. Where was his bodyguard? wondered Hay, who had never despised Sumner more than now. In a corner sat Welles, old and frowzy beneath his wig.

Members of the Cabinet came and went. Only Stanton remained; in total charge. When Robert asked, "Is there any hope at all?" Stanton had answered for the doctor, "There is none. He will simply sink. The brain is destroyed. The wound is mortal." Then Stanton turned to an aide. "Telegraph the news to General Grant in Philadelphia. He is to return immediately. But with a full complement of guards." To another, he said, "Go to the Chief Justice. Tell him what has happened. We will need him to swear in the new president."

An official from the State Department arrived to report: "A man broke into the Old Club House. The servant says he sounded like a dyed-in-the-wool rebel. He went upstairs and stabbed Mr. Seward, but that iron contraption on his jaw saved him. He's not hurt at all. But Fred Seward's head is broken; he is unconscious."

"I was with both of them less than an hour ago," said Stanton, bemused. "The man escaped?"

"Yes, sir."

Mary Lincoln entered the room. "Oh, Robert!" she cried. "What is to happen to us?" She looked down at her husband. "Father, speak to us! You can't die like this, not now. It is unthinkable.

Robert, fetch Taddie! He'll speak to Taddie. He won't let himself die if Taddie's here."

Robert looked at Stanton, who shook his head. Then Mary gave a great shriek and threw herself on Lincoln's body. "Don't leave us!"

"Get that woman out of here," said Stanton, suddenly brutal to a lady whom he had for so long done his best to charm. He need never charm her again, thought Hay. "Don't let her back in."

Sumner and the man from the State Department led Mary out of the room, just as the Vice-President made his awkward entrance.

"Sir," said Stanton, suddenly deferential. "I wish you to remain under constant guard—the soliders that I just assigned to you are at the Kirkwood House—until we know who the enemy is. I am sure that they meant to kill you, too."

"He . . . will die?" Johnson stared with wonder at the figure on the bed.

"Yes, sir. I have already made the necessary preparations. Mr. Chase has been notified. When the time arrives, he will come to your hotel, and administer the oath of office."

"We have been struck," said Johnson, with no great emphasis or—for him—grandiloquent flourish, "a mighty blow."

"Yes, sir. But *he* is lucky. He will belong to the ages, while we are obliged to live on in the wreckage."

As night became morning, Stanton sat next to Robert, beside the bed. Stanton's right hand, in which he still held his hat, supported his left elbow.

Shortly after seven o'clock Abraham Lincoln took a deep breath; exhaled it slowly; and died. Like an automaton, Stanton raised his right arm high in the air; then, precisely, he set his hat squarely on his head and then, as precisely, he removed it. He got to his feet. "The Cabinet will now meet," he said, "to discuss the notification and the swearing-in of President Johnson, and the orderly continuance of this government."

Mary was led into the room. Moaning softly, she lay across the still body; then, finally, of her own accord, she stood up, dry-eyed from so much weeping and said, to no one in particular, "Oh, my God! And I have given my husband to die." Robert led her from the room.

Hay stared at the Ancient, who seemed to be smiling, as the doctor tied a cloth under the chin to keep the mouth from falling ajar. He looked exactly as if his own death had just reminded him of a story. But then Hay realized that never again would the

Ancient be reminded of a story. He had become what others would be reminded of.

David Herold had waited outside Seward's house as long as he dared. From the screams, it sounded as if Payne was killing everyone in the house. Finally, David could bear it no longer. He mounted his horse and rode into Pennsylvania Avenue, where, as luck would have it, a man from the stables shouted, "You're late! You've had that horse too long. Turn him in."

David's response was to spur the horse into Fourteenth Street until he came to F Street, where he turned east. He had only one thought now. He must find Wilkes.

At the Navy Yard bridge, a sentry stopped David, and asked him his name. David answered, "Smith." When asked his business, he said that he lived on the other side of Anacostia Creek at White Plains. The sentry let him pass; but told him that, henceforth, the bridge would be shut to everyone at nine o'clock. David thanked him; and rode on. Finally, on the Bryantown Road, David caught up with Wilkes, who had been riding hard; and all alone.

"Success?" asked Booth.

"Yes," said David.

"I, too," said Booth. That was all that they said to each other until they got to Surrattsville. Here David dismounted; and went into what had been the Surratt tavern but was now John Lloyd's. As prearranged, Lloyd brought them a pair of carbines and a bottle of whiskey. David gave Wilkes the whiskey, which he drank, still seated on the horse. Wilkes refused the carbines. "I have broken my ankle," he said, coolly.

"Anything else you need?" asked Lloyd.

Booth said, "Nothing more. But I will tell you some news, if you want to hear it."

"I'm not particular," said Lloyd.

"I am pretty certain," said Booth, spurring his horse, "that we have assassinated the President and the Secretary of State."

With that, Booth and David were gone. This was what David had dreamed of for as long as he could remember. To do some heroic deed, and then ride all through the night, his true brother at his side. Wilkes's words to Lloyd kept reverberating in his head: "We have assassinated the President..." What greater work could a Confederate hero do?

At four-thirty in the morning they arrived at the house of a doctor friend, who attended to Wilkes's ankle, which was broken in such a way that the bones were at a right angle to one another. Then Wilkes asked for a razor; and shaved off his moustache.

Later, when it was daylight, the nervous doctor said that they would have to move on. Word was beginning to spread through the area, not to mention the world, that John Wilkes Booth had murdered the President. There was no news, David was sorry to hear, of Mr. Seward. Anyway, all that mattered was that Wilkes thought that he, David Herold, had done as he was told, and that they were now, the two of them, friends and true brothers, immortal.

12

ALTHOUGH EUGÉNIE, EMPRESS OF THE FRENCH, MUST HAVE been about forty years of age, John Hay never ceased to find her as attractive as he found her husband, the Emperor Napoleon III, repellent. At the reception for the diplomatic corps on January 1, 1867, in the palace of the Tuileries, Hay kept to the splendid drawing room where Eugénie held court and avoided the statelier room where the emperor and his ministers stood, next to an elaborate, gilded throne in which the emperor never sat.

Eugénie's hair had been naturally dark red, and was still red; while her complexion had always been pale, and was still pale. The sad eyes were gray. She wore a ruby-red dress of velvet, cut low to reveal an explosion of diamond necklaces. Hay did his best not to stare, and could not take his eyes off her. But then he had spent four years in Washington, watching women imitate Eugénie; now he was able to look with awe upon the original herself. As the Spanish-born empress stood beneath a life-size portrait of her predecessor Marie-Louise, the wife of the real Napoleon, she used an ivory fan subtly to communicate with others. Hay regarded her with all the pleasure that he might have found in watching a splendid sunrise or, perhaps, considering the chronic fragility of the French political system, sunset.

All around the gold-encrusted room, gold-encrusted diplomats stood while members of the palace staff in violet uniforms tried, without success, to make themselves useful. At regular intervals, members of the emperor's personal guard were placed, at attention, like so many statues in blue and gold. Although it was still light outside, the chandeliers were ablaze; and wood fires burned in every marble fireplace. Hay was pleased to be conspicuous in the plain blue uniform of an American lieutenant colonel; but then he was more than ever a dedicated republican, not to mention implacable foe of despots, even a despot whose wife was a perfect sunset.

The outgoing American minister, John Bigelow, came toward Hay. Bigelow was accompanied by a stout, pink-cheeked old man and a beautiful young girl, definitely more sunrise than sunset. "Mr. Hay is my first secretary," said Bigelow to the old man and young girl, who turned out to be the American historian Charles Schermerhorn Schuyler and his daughter Emma, the Princesse d'Agrigente, a lady celebrated for her salon at which one never found her husband, the heir to the great Napoleon's marshal. Although Hay had never before met the splendid princess, he knew all about her unhappy marriage; and knew that absolutely no one was sorry for her in a city where unhappy marriages were the rule. The prince lived elsewhere with his mistress. The princess lived with her children, as if she were a wealthy widow; lived untouched by any scandal, which was not the rule in Paris.

But then Emma herself was rare, decided Hay, when she turned her dark eyes on him and said in softly accented English, "I am a true American, yet I have never set foot in the United States."

"It is my fault," said the amiable Mr. Schuyler. "I left New York in 'thirty-six, to be, like you, a diplomat. Only I went to Italy where I was married, and . . ."

". . . and you never went home," said Emma. "Well, I cannot wait to go."

"Nor can I," said Bigelow. "How I miss New York!"

"You will be missed here," said Mr. Schuyler. "After all, if it hadn't been for you, Mr. Seward would have had us at war with France by now."

"Oh, now you exaggerate." Bigelow was appropriately modest. But Hay knew that if Bigelow had not exactly averted a war with France over Mexico, he had certainly contained a crisis.

In November, Hay had personally decoded Seward's ultimatum to Napoleon, calling upon him to withdraw his troops from Mexico, as previously agreed, even though it could mean the death of that unfortunate French puppet the Emperor Maximilian. Bigelow had decided to substitute for Seward's harangue a polite note, highly acceptable to the French, who were duly appreciative. Mr. Schuyler himself had written of Bigelow's diplomatic coup in the *Atlantic Monthly*. Now Bigelow was going home, his place to be taken not by His Satanic Majesty James Gordon Bennett, who had decided that he preferred to reign in New York's hell than serve in diplomacy's heaven, but by General John A. Dix, the same general who, at Stanton's insistence, had dropped all charges against Senator Sprague and his fellow traitors.

The fact that Dix was quite aware that Hay knew all about the

Sprague affair had cast a certain pall over their first meeting. At a second meeting, when Hay had offered his resignation, he had been disappointed when it was promptly accepted. But Seward had come to the rescue; and Hay was to return to Washington as a special assistant to the Secretary of State. Nico remained relatively secure at the consulate, despite constant rumors that President Johnson wanted his own man to fill the magnificent rooms at number 47, Avenue des Champs-Elysées.

Bigelow moved away, leaving Hay with the splendid princess and her father. "You look so young," she said, "to have been the President's secretary."

"I am ... or I was at the time." Hay was still quite used to being called young. On first being presented to the emperor, Napoleon had said to him in English, "Are you not young to be colonel?" Hay's brevet-rank. Then the empress had gazed at him with eyes almost as beautiful as those of the princess and said, "Are you not young to be *a* colonel?" The imperial court was not noted for its wit, though the emperor could, when he chose, drop the devastating brick. Lately, he had taken an almost personal dislike to the buildings that were being constructed for the great world exhibition. Of the main hall he had said, "It looks like a gasometer!"

Both father and daughter questioned Hay at length about Lincoln. What sort of man had he been? They seemed surprised when Hay said, "He was always very sure of himself." As Hay spoke, he thought of the highly unsure little emperor in the next room. "From the beginning, he knew that he was the first man in the country, and that he was bound to get his way, *if* he lived."

"You surprise me," said Schuyler. "One always thinks of him as being so ... humble."

"Humble men never rise so high nor do so much."

"Who killed him?" asked the princess, with entirely American directness.

"The actor Booth," said Hay, smoothly. "With the help of a group of fools that he had gathered around him. Then Booth was killed in a Virginia barn, and the fools were all hanged, including a lady called Mrs. Surratt, who was probably innocent. But at the time, Mr. Stanton was hanging everybody in sight. Anyway, Booth had already made a sort of confession in a letter to his brother-in-law."

"I cannot believe," said the princess, with entirely Parisian suspiciousness, "that it was just one mad actor—and some fools. Surely, the Southerners were behind the plot?"

"They deny it, and I believe them. They had nothing to gain by the President's death, and everything to lose. After all, only
654

Lincoln could have controlled the radicals in Congress. Mr. Johnson has—" Hay remembered that he was a diplomat. "Mr. Johnson has his problems with the radicals."

"What has happened to Mrs. Lincoln?" asked the princess, changing the subject in order to show Hay that she was not taken in by his highly diplomatic response.

"She lives in Chicago. The President left an estate of nearly a hundred thousand dollars. Of course, she spends a good deal of money."

To Hay's surprise it was the father not the daughter who returned to the subject of the plot. "I hear so many intriguing rumors from old friends," he said. "For instance, I have heard it suggested that there was indeed a plot in which the actor, Booth, was simply used by certain radical elements in Congress."

Hay smiled. "If that could be proved, don't you think that Mr. Stanton would be the first to want to hang Senator Wade or Senator Chandler or General Butler, the three likeliest conspirators?"

"But I had heard," said Mr. Schuyler, almost apologetically, "that Mr. Stanton was involved, too. Hence, the speed—and secrecy—with which Booth's allies were tried in Mr. Stanton's own military court; and then hanged."

Hay thought that he had heard every possible Lincoln rumor; but this was new. Certainly, Stanton was the most compulsively devious man that Hay had ever dealt with. He was, also, very close to the radicals in Congress. As a result, there was great tension, currently, between him and President Johnson, who was pursuing Lincoln's moderate policy toward the South, with his Secretary of War undercutting him at every turn. Politically, Stanton and Lincoln would have fallen out, if the President had lived. But since all that Stanton was in the world he owed to Lincoln, Hay thought it most unlikely that he would conspire to kill the President.

Certainly Hay could never forget the scene in the East Room, when the President lay in state. All day mourners filed past the casket on its black catafalque. Hay was standing near the door, Tad's hand in his, when Stanton entered; and Tad said—very clearly for him—"Mr. Stanton, who killed my father?" Stanton had given a sort of cry; and hurried from the room. In fact, Stanton was so enraged and demoralized by the murder that he had ordered Ford's Theater to be forever shut, an eccentric gesture in the eyes of many but typical of the bereaved odd man who was now being mentioned as party to the murder of, perhaps, the only man that he ever liked.

Hay tried to explain Stanton to Mr. Schuyler; but it was never easy to explain Stanton to anyone.

Fortunately, Hay was able to fuel somewhat the European love of intrigue. "One interesting thing, which might relate to what you have heard. We do know now that there was a *second* plot afoot. We also know that Booth got wind of it, and he was afraid that others might strike before he did."

"Now that," said Mr. Schuyler, "might be the solution. Do you think that the radical element in Congress would be capable of such a plot?"

"Oh, yes!" Hay was delighted at the prospect of a future trial of Wade and Chandler and Butler—and Sumner, too. Why not? Hang every last one of them. "After all, the daughter of one of the radical senators was a close friend of Booth's; and actually got him a ticket to attend the Second Inaugural."

"Oh, you must write about all this, Mr. Hay!" The princess was now properly stimulated.

"I think I probably shall, with Mr. Nicolay, the President's other secretary."

"Where," asked Mr. Schuyler, "would you place Mr. Lincoln amongst the presidents of our country?"

"Oh, I would place him first."

"*Above* Washington?" Mr. Schuyler looked startled.

"Yes," said Hay, who had thought a good deal about the Tycoon's place in history. "Mr. Lincoln had a far greater and more difficult task than Washington's. You see, the Southern states had every Constitutional right to go out of the Union. But Lincoln said no. Lincoln said this Union can never be broken. Now, that was a terrible responsibility for one man to take. But he took it, knowing he would be obliged to fight the greatest war in human history, which he did, and which he won. So he not only put the Union back together again, but he made an entirely new country, and all of it in his own image."

"You astonish me," said Mr. Schuyler.

"Mr. Lincoln astonished us all."

"I rather think," said Charles Schermerhorn Schuyler to his daughter, "that we should take a look at this new country, which plainly bears no resemblance to the one I left, in the quiet days of Martin Van Buren."

"Well, come soon," said Hay. "Because who knows what may happen next?"

"I have been writing, lately, about the German first minister." Mr. Schuyler was thoughtful. "In fact, I met him at Biarritz last summer when he came to see the emperor. Curiously enough, he has now done the same thing to Germany that you tell us Mr.

Lincoln did to our country. Bismarck has made a single, centralized nation out of all the other German states."

Hay nodded; he, too, had noted the resemblance. "Bismarck would also give the vote to people who have never had it before."

"I think," said Mr. Schuyler to the princess, "we have here a subject—Lincoln and Bismarck, and new countries for old."

"It will be interesting to see how Herr Bismarck ends *his* career," said Hay, who was now more than ever convinced that Lincoln, in some mysterious fashion, had willed his own murder as a form of atonement for the great and terrible thing that he had done by giving so bloody and absolute a rebirth to his nation.

AFTERWORD

How much of *Lincoln* is generally thought to be true? How much made up? This is an urgent question for any reader; and deserves as straight an answer as the writer can give. I have introduced fewer invented figures in *Lincoln* than I did in *Burr* and *1876*. All of the principal characters really existed, and they said and did pretty much what I have them saying and doing, with the exception of the Surratts and David Herold (who really lived and worked at Thompson's, which was actually closer to New York Avenue than to Pennsylvania Avenue.) As David's life is largely unknown until Booth's conspiracy, I have invented a low-life for him.

Readers of the other novels in these chronicle will recognize Charlie Schuyler (*Burr* and *1876*), Emma (*1876*) and the vile ubiquitous William de la Touche Clancey—they are fictional. As for Lincoln and the other historical figures, I have reconstructed them from letters, journals, newspapers, diaries, etc. Occasionally, I have done some moving around. At the time of Kate Chase's Boxing Day reception, McClellan had been sick in bed for almost a week; but I needed him at the Chases'. I have not done this sort of thing often. I have not done it at all with the President.

For those who may be alarmed at my version of the Gettysburg Address, I used not Lincoln's final tinkered-with draft but what someone who was there (Charles Hale of the Boston *Daily Advertiser*) wrote down. Finally, I must thank Professor David Herbert Donald of Harvard's History Department not only for his books on Lincoln and Herndon and on Charles Sumner, but for his patient reading—and correction—of the manuscript. Any further errors, if they exist, are mine, not his.

G.V.

January 25, 1984

Gore Vidal wrote his first novel, *Williwaw* (1946), at the age of nineteen while overseas in World War II.

During four decades as a writer, Vidal has written novels, plays, short stories and essays. He has also been a political activist. As a Democratic candidate for Congress from upstate New York, he received the most votes of any Democrat in a half century. From 1970 to 1972 he was co-chairman of the People's Party. In California's 1982 Democratic primary for U.S. Senate, he polled a half million votes, and came in second in a field of nine.

In 1948 Vidal wrote the highly praised international best seller *The City and the Pillar*. This was followed by *The Judgment of Paris* and the prophetic *Messiah*. In the fifties Vidal wrote plays for live television and films for Metro-Goldwyn-Mayer. One of the television plays became the successful Broadway play *Visit to a Small Planet* (1957). Directly for the theater he wrote the prize-winning hit *The Best Man* (1960).

In 1964 Vidal returned to the novel. In succession, he created three remarkable works: *Julian, Washington, D.C., Myra Breckinridge*. Each was a number-one best seller in the United States and England. In 1973 Vidal published his most popular novel, *Burr*, as well as a volume of collected essays, *Homage to Daniel Shays*. In 1976 he published yet another number-one best seller, *1876*, a part of his on-going American chronicle, which now consists of—in chronological order—*Burr, Lincoln, 1876, Emprie, Hollywood*, and *Washington, D.C.*

In 1981 Vidal published *Creation*, "his best novel," according to the New York *Times*. In 1982 Vidal won the America Book Critics Circle Award for criticism for his collection of essays, *The Second American Revolution*. A propos *Duluth* (1983), Italo Calvino wrote (*La Repubblica*, Rome): "Vidal's development...along that line from *Myra Breckinridge* to *Duluth* is crowned with great success, not only for the density of comic effects, each one filled with meaning, not only for the craftsmanship in construction, put together like a clockwork which fears no word processor, but because this latest book holds its own built-in theory, that which the author calls his "après-poststructuralism.' I consider Vidal to be a master of that new form which is taking shape in world literature and which we may call the hyper-novel or the novel elevated to the square or to the cube."

**37 WEEKS ON THE *NEW YORK TIMES*
BESTSELLER LIST!
250,000 HARDCOVERS IN PRINT!
LINCOLN
THE YEAR'S MOST ACCLAIMED NOVEL
A MONUMENTAL PORTRAIT OF A MAN AND
A NATION BY OUR GREATEST LIVING
HISTORICAL NOVELIST, GORE VIDAL**

In this profoundly moving work of epic
proportion and intense human sympathy,
Abraham Lincoln is observed by his loved ones,
his rivals, and his future assassins. Seen
by his wife, Mary, who adores him even as she
is going mad... by the Machiavellian Secretary of
State, Seward, who begins by scorning
Lincoln and ends by worshipping him... by
Lincoln's rival, Salmon P. Chase, and
his beautiful daughter, Kate... by David Herold,
the druggist's clerk at the center of the
plot that will eventually take Lincoln's life...
and by the twenty-three-year-old presidential
secretary, John Hay, who comes to know
Lincoln intimately during his four years in the
White House, Lincoln emerges as a complex and
towering figure who presided over some of
the most divisive and dangerous years in
American history. In a brilliantly realized, vividly
imagined work of fiction, Gore Vidal gives us a
portrait of America's great president that is at
once intimate and public, stark and complex,
and that will become for future generations the
living Lincoln, the definitive Lincoln.

U.S. **$6.99**/Canada $7.99

ISBN 0-345-31221-X

Cover printed in USA